ALEXANDRE DUMAS

(père) lived a life as romantic as that depicted in his famous novels. He was born on July 24, 1802, at Villers-Cotterêts, France, the son of Napoleon's famous mulatto general Dumas. His early education was scanty, but his beautiful handwriting secured him a position in Paris in 1822 with the duc d'Orléans, where he read voraciously and began to write. His first play, *Henri III et sa cour* (1829), scored a resounding success for its author and for the romantic movement. Numerous dramatic successes followed (including the melodrama *Kean*, later adapted by Jean-Paul Sartre), and so did numerous mistresses and adventures. He took part in the revolution of 1830, caught cholera during the epidemic of 1832, fathered two illegitimate children (the first, Alexandre Dumas [fils], became a famous author also) by two different mistresses and then married still another mistress. His lavish spending and flamboyant habits led to the construction of his fabulous Château de Monte-Cristo, and in 1851 he fled to Belgium to escape creditors. He died on December 5, 1870, bankrupt, but still cheerful, saying of death, "I shall tell her a story, and she will be kind to me."

Dumas's overall literary output reached over 277 volumes, but his brilliant historical novels made him the most universally read of all French novelists. With collaborators, mainly Auguste Maquet, Dumas wrote such works as *The Three Musketeers* (1843–44); its sequels, *Twenty Years After* (1845) and the great mystery *The Man in the Iron Mask* (1848–50); and *The Count of Monte Cristo* (1844). "L'action and l'amour" were the two essential things in his life and in his fiction. He declared he "elevated history to the dignity of the novel" by means of love affairs, intrigues, imprisonments, hairbreadth escapes and duels. His work ignored historical accuracy, psychology and analysis, but its thrilling adventure and exuberant inventiveness continues to delight readers, and Dumas remains one of the prodigies of nineteenth-century French literature.

Bantam Classics
Ask your bookseller for these other World Classics

GREEK DRAMA, edited by Moses Hadas

THE COMPLETE PLAYS OF SOPHOCLES

TEN PLAYS, Euripides

THE COMPLETE PLAYS OF ARISTOPHANES

PLAUTUS: THREE COMEDIES (translated by Erich Segal)

THE AENEID, Virgil (translated by Allen Mandelbaum)

INFERNO, Dante (translated by Allen Mandelbaum)
PURGATORIO, Dante (translated by Allen Mandelbaum)
PARADISO, Dante (translated by Allen Mandelbaum)

THE PRINCE, Machiavelli

CANDIDE, Voltaire

FAUST, Johann Wolfgang von Goethe

THE COUNT OF MONTE CRISTO, Alexandre Dumas
THE THREE MUSKETEERS, Alexandre Dumas

THE HUNCHBACK OF NOTRE DAME, Victor Hugo

MADAME BOVARY, Gustave Flaubert

FATHERS AND SONS, Ivan Turgenev

ANNA KARENINA, Leo Tolstoy
THE DEATH OF IVAN ILYICH, Leo Tolstoy

THE BROTHERS KARAMAZOV, Fyodor Dostoevsky
CRIME AND PUNISHMENT, Fyodor Dostoevsky
THE IDIOT, Fyodor Dostoevsky
NOTES FROM UNDERGROUND, Fyodor Dostoevsky

CYRANO DE BERGERAC, Edmond Rostand

20,000 LEAGUES UNDER THE SEA, Jules Verne
AROUND THE WORLD IN EIGHTY DAYS, Jules Verne

FOUR GREAT PLAYS, Henrik Ibsen

FIVE MAJOR PLAYS, Anton Chekhov

THE METAMORPHOSIS, Franz Kafka

The Count of Monte Cristo
by Alexandre Dumas

Translated and abridged
by Lowell Bair

BANTAM BOOKS

TORONTO · NEW YORK · LONDON · SYDNEY · AUCKLAND

RL 6, IL age 14 and up

THE COUNT OF MONTE CRISTO

A Bantam Book

PRINTING HISTORY
The Count of Monte Cristo *was first published in 1844.*
First Bantam publication / October 1956.
Bantam Classic edition / March 1981
2nd printing . . . July 1981
3rd printing . . . September 1982

Library of Congress Catalog Card Number: 56-10489

Cover painting, Portrait of the Sculptor, Paul Lemoyne *(1819)
by Jean Auguste Dominique Ingres (1780-1867). Oil on canvas,
18-¾" x 14-½". Courtesy of the Nelson Gallery-Atkins Museum,
Kansas City, Missouri, and the Nelson Fund.*

ISBN 0-553-21112-9

Published simultaneously in the United States and Canada

---

*Bantam Books are published by Bantam Books, Inc. Its trademark,
consisting of the words "Bantam Books" and the portrayal of a
rooster, is Registered in U.S. Patent and Trademark Office and in
other countries. Marca Registrada. Bantam Books, Inc., 666 Fifth
Avenue, New York, New York 10103.*

PRINTED IN THE UNITED STATES OF AMERICA

O   12 11 10 9 8

THE COUNT OF MONTE CRISTO

Chapter 1

On February 24, 1815, the watchtower at Marseilles signaled the arrival of the three-master *Pharaon,* coming from Smyrna, Trieste and Naples.

The quay was soon covered with the usual crowd of curious onlookers, for the arrival of a ship is always a great event in Marseilles, especially when, like the *Pharaon,* it has been built, rigged and laden in the city and belongs to a local shipowner.

Meanwhile the vessel was approaching the harbor under topsails, jib and foresail, but so slowly and with such an air of melancholy that the onlookers, instinctively sensing misfortune, began to wonder what accident could have happened on board. However, the experienced seamen among them saw that if there had been an accident, it could not have happened to the ship herself, for she had every appearance of being under perfect control. Standing beside the pilot, who was preparing to steer the *Pharaon* through the narrow entrance of the harbor, was a young man who, with vigilant eyes and rapid gestures, watched every movement of the ship and repeated each of the pilot's orders.

The vague anxiety hovering over the crowd affected one man so much that he could not wait until the ship entered the harbor: he leaped into a small boat and ordered the boatman to row him out to meet the *Pharaon.*

When he saw this man coming toward him, the young sailor left his post beside the pilot and walked over to the side of the ship, holding his hat in his hand. He was a tall, slender young man, no more than twenty years old, with dark eyes and hair as black as ebony. His whole manner gave evidence of that calmness and resolution peculiar to those who have been accustomed to facing danger ever since their childhood.

"Ah, it's you, Dantès!" cried the man in the boat. "What's happened? Why does everything look so gloomy on board?"

"A great misfortune, Monsieur Morrel!" replied the young man. "We lost our brave Captain Leclère off Civitavecchia."

"What about the cargo?" asked the shipowner eagerly.

"It arrived safely, Monsieur Morrel, and I think you'll be satisfied on that score, but poor Captain Leclère——"

"What happened to him?" asked the shipowner, visibly relieved.

"He died of brain fever, in horrible agony. He's now at rest off the Isle of Il Giglio, sewed up in his hammock with one cannon ball at his head and another at his feet." The young man smiled sadly and added, "How ironic—he waged war against the English for ten long years and then died in his bed like anyone else."

"Well, we're all mortal," said the shipowner, "and the old must make way for the young, otherwise there would be no promotion."

As they were passing the Round Tower, the young sailor called out, "Make ready to lower topsails, foresail and jib!" The order was executed as smartly as on board a man-of-war. "Lower away and brail all!" At this last order all the sails were lowered and the ship's speed became almost imperceptible.

"And now, if you'd like to come aboard, Monsieur Morrel," said Dantès, seeing the shipowner's impatience, "you can talk to your purser, Monsieur Danglars, who's just coming out of his cabin. He can give you all the information you want. As for myself, I must look after the anchoring and dress the ship in mourning."

The shipowner did not wait to be invited twice. He grasped the line which Dantès threw to him and, with an agility that would have done credit to a sailor, climbed up the ladder attached to the ship's side. Dantès returned to his duties, while Danglars came out to meet Monsieur Morrel. The purser was a man of twenty-five or twenty-six with a rather melancholy face, obsequious to his superiors and arrogant to his subordinates. He was as much disliked by the crew as Edmond Dantès was liked by them.

"Well, Monsieur Morrel," said Danglars, "I suppose you've heard about our misfortune."

"Yes, I have. Poor Captain Leclère! He was a brave and honorable man."

"And an excellent seaman, too, grown old between the sky and the water, as a man should be when he's entrusted with the interests of such an important firm as Morrel and Son."

"But," said the shipowner, watching Dantès preparing to drop anchor, "it seems to me a man doesn't have to be old to do his work well, Danglars. Our friend Edmond there doesn't look as though he needs advice from anyone."

"Yes," said Danglars, casting Dantès a glance full of hatred, "he's young and he has no doubts about anything. As soon as the captain was dead he took command without consulting anyone, and he made us lose a day and a half at the Isle of Elba instead of coming straight back to Marseilles."

"As for taking command," said the shipowner, "it was his duty as first mate, but he was wrong to waste a day and a half at the Isle of Elba, unless the ship needed some sort of repairs."

"The ship was as sound as I am and as I hope you are, Monsieur Morrel. Wasting that day and a half was nothing but a whim of his; he just wanted to go ashore for a while, that's all."

"Dantès," said Morrel, turning toward the young man, "come here, please."

"Excuse me, sir, I'll be with you in a moment," said Dantès. Then, turning to the crew, he called out, "Let go!" The anchor dropped immediately and the chain rattled noisily. Dantès walked over to Morrel.

"I wanted to ask you why you stopped at the Isle of Elba."

"It was to carry out an order from Captain Leclère. As he was dying he gave me a package to deliver to Marshal Bertrand there."

"Did you see him, Edmond?"

"Yes."

Morrel looked around and drew Dantès off to one side. "How is the emperor?" he asked eagerly.

"He's well, as far as I could tell. He came into the marshal's room while I was there."

"Did you talk to him?"

"No, he talked to me," said Dantès, smiling.

"What did he say?"

"He asked me about the ship, when it had left for Marseilles, what route it had taken and what cargo it was carrying. I think that if the ship had been empty and I had been its owner he would have tried to buy it from me, but I told him I was only the first mate and that it belonged to the firm of Morrel and Son. 'I know that firm,' he said. 'The Morrels have been shipowners for generations and there was a Morrel in my regiment when I was garrisoned at Valence.'"

"That's true!" exclaimed Morrel, delighted. "It was Policar Morrel, my uncle. He later became a captain." Then, giving Dantès a friendly tap on the shoulder, he said, "You were quite right to follow Captain Leclère's instructions and stop at the Isle of Elba, although you might get into trouble if it became known that you gave the marshal a package and spoke to the emperor."

"How could it get me into trouble?" asked Dantès. "I don't even know what was in the package, and the emperor only asked me the same questions he would have asked any other newcomer. But excuse me for a moment, sir; I see the health and customs officers coming on board."

Danglars stepped up as the young man walked away. "Well," he said, "he seems to have given you some good reasons for his stopover."

"He gave me excellent reasons, Monsieur Danglars."

"That's good; it's always painful to see a friend fail to do his duty."

"Dantès did his duty well," replied the shipowner. "It was Captain Leclère, who ordered the stopover."

"Speaking of Captain Leclère, didn't Dantès give you a letter from him?"

"No. Was there one?"

"I thought Captain Leclère gave him a letter along with the package."

"What package, Danglars?"

"Why, the one Dantès delivered to the Isle of Elba."

"How do you know he delivered a package there?"

Danglars flushed. "The captain's door was ajar when I was passing by," he said, "and I saw him give Dantès a package and a letter."

"He didn't say anything to me about it, but if he has the letter I'm sure he'll give it to me."

Danglars was silent for a moment, then he said, "Monsieur Morrel, please don't mention it to Dantès; I must have been mistaken."

Just then Dantès returned and Danglars walked away.

"Well, Dantès, have you finished now?"

"Yes, sir."

"Then will you come to dinner with us?"

"Please excuse me, Monsieur Morrel, but I think I owe my first visit to my father. Just the same, I'm grateful for the honor of your invitation."

"You're right, Dantès. You're a good son. But we'll be expecting you after you've visited your father."

"Excuse me again, Monsieur Morrel, but after that first visit there's another one that's equally important to me."

"Oh, yes; I was forgetting that there's someone who must be waiting for you as impatiently as your father—the beautiful Mercédès. You're a lucky man, Edmond, and you have a very pretty mistress."

"She's not my mistress, sir," said the young sailor gravely. "She's my fiancée."

"That's sometimes the same thing," said Morrel, laughing.

"Not with us, sir," replied Dantès.

"Well, I won't keep you any longer; you've taken care of

my affairs so well that I want to give you as much time as possible to take care of your own. Do you have anything else to tell me?"

"No."

"Didn't Captain Leclère give you a letter for me before he died?"

"He was unable to write, sir. But that reminds me that I must ask you for two weeks' leave." ·

"To get married?"

"First of all; and then to go to Paris."

"Very well, take as long as you like, Dantès. It will take at least six weeks to unload the cargo, and we won't be ready to put to sea again before another three months or so. But in three months you'll have to be here. The *Pharaon*," continued the shipowner, patting the young sailor on the shoulder, "can't leave without her captain."

"Without her captain!" cried Dantès, his eyes flashing with joy. "Do you really intend to make me captain of the *Pharaon*?"

"If I were alone, my dear Dantès, I'd shake your hand and say, 'It's done.' But I have a partner, and you know the Italian proverb, 'He who has a partner has a master.' The thing is at least half done, though, since you already have one vote out of two. Leave it to me to get you the other one; I'll do my best."

"Oh, Monsieur Morrel!" cried Dantès, grasping the shipowner's hand with tears in his eyes. "I thank you in the name of my father and of Mercédès."

"That's all right, Edmond. Go see your father, go see Mercédès, then come back to see me."

"Don't you want me to take you ashore?"

"No, thanks; I'll stay on board and look over the accounts with Danglars. Were you satisfied with him during the trip?"

"That depends on how you mean the question, sir. If you're asking me if I was satisfied with him as a comrade, the answer is no; I think he's disliked me ever since the day we had a little quarrel and I was foolish enough to suggest that we stop for ten minutes at the Isle of Monte Cristo to settle it, a suggestion which I was wrong to make and which he was right to refuse. But if you're speaking of him as a purser, I think there's nothing to be said against him and that you'll be quite satisfied with the way he's done his work."

"If you were captain of the *Pharaon*, would you be glad to keep him?"

"Whether I'm captain or first mate, Monsieur Morrel," replied Dantès, "I'll always have great respect for those who have the confidence of my shipowners."

"Good, good, Dantès! I see you're a fine young man in every way. But don't let me hold you back any longer—I can see how anxious you are to leave."

"May I take your skiff?"

"Certainly."

"Good-bye, Monsieur Morrel, and thank you from the bottom of my heart."

The young sailor leaped into the skiff and sat down in the stern, giving orders to be rowed to the Canebière. Smiling, the shipowner watched him until he saw him jump ashore, after which he was immediately swallowed up in the crowd. When he turned around, Morrel saw Danglars standing behind him, also following the young sailor's movements. But there was a great difference in the expression of the two men as they both watched Edmond Dantès.

Chapter 2

Let us leave Danglars, possessed by the demon of hatred and trying to breathe some evil insinuation against his comrade into the shipowner's ear, and follow Dantès, who, after having walked the entire length of the Canebière, turned into the Rue de Noailles, entered a small house on the left side of the Allées de Meilhan, ran up four flights of dark stairs and stopped before a half-open door which revealed the interior of a little room. It was the room in which his father lived.

"Father! My dear father!"

The old man uttered a cry and turned around, then fell into his son's arms, trembling and pale.

"What's the matter, father?" exclaimed the young man anxiously. "Are you ill?"

"No, no, Edmond, my son, my child, no; but I wasn't expecting you, and the joy of suddenly seeing you like this——"

"They say joy never harms anyone, so I came straight here as soon as I landed. I've come back safely and we're going to be happy together."

"That's wonderful, my boy!" said the old man. "But how are we going to be happy? Do you mean you're not going to leave me any more? Tell me about your good fortune."

"May God forgive me for rejoicing in a good fortune brought about by another man's death, but it's happened and I don't have the strength to regret it. Captain Leclère is dead and it looks as though I'm going to take his place. Can you imagine that, father? A captain at the age of twenty! With a salary of a hundred louis, plus a share in the profits! Isn't that really more than a poor sailor like me could ever hope for?"

"Yes, my son, you're very lucky."

"And with the first money I earn I want to buy you a little house, with a garden . . . What's the matter, father? You don't look well."

"It's nothing; it will pass," said the old man; but his strength failed and he fell backward.

"You need a glass of wine," said Edmond. "That will make you feel better. Where do you keep your wine?"

"I don't need any," said the old man, trying to hold back his son.

"Yes, you do," said Edmond. "Just tell me where it is." He opened two or three cupboards.

"Don't bother looking. There's no more wine."

"No more wine!" exclaimed Edmond, turning pale and looking alternately at his father's hollow cheeks and the empty cupboards. "Have you been short of money, father?"

"I don't need anything, now that you're here."

"But—but I gave you two hundred francs when I left three months ago," stammered Edmond.

"Yes, that's true, Edmond, but you forgot a little debt you owed to our neighbor Caderousse. He reminded me of it and told me that if I didn't pay it for you he'd go to see Monsieur Morrel about it. I was afraid that might do you harm, so I paid him."

"But I owed Caderousse a hundred and forty francs! Did you give it to him out of the two hundred francs I left you?"

The old man nodded.

"And you lived for three months on sixty francs!" exclaimed Edmond. "May God forgive me!"

"It doesn't matter, now that you're here."

"Yes, I'm here now, with a good future before me and a little money already. Here, father, take this and send for some things right away." He emptied the contents of his pockets onto the table: a dozen pieces of gold, five or six five-franc coins and some small change.

The old man's face brightened. "Whose is that?" he asked.

"It's mine—yours—ours! Take it and buy provisions. And don't worry: tomorrow there will be more. Also, I have some contraband coffee and some excellent tobacco for you on the ship. You'll have it tomorrow. . . . Listen, I hear someone coming."

"It's probably Caderousse coming to welcome you back from your trip."

"More lips that say one thing while the heart thinks another," muttered Edmond. "Just the same, though, he's a neighbor who once did us a favor, so he's welcome here."

A moment later Caderousse entered. He was a man of about twenty-five, with black hair and beard. He was holding a piece of cloth which, being a tailor, he intended to turn into the lining of a coat. "So you're back, Edmond!" he said in a heavy Marseilles accent and with a broad grin which revealed his white teeth.

"Yes, I'm back, and ready to be of service to you in any way I can," replied Edmond, scarcely concealing his coldness beneath these polite words.

"Thank you, but fortunately I don't need anything. In fact, other people sometimes need me." Edmond started. "Oh, I'm not talking about you," continued Caderousse. "I lent you some money and you paid it back, so now we're quits."

"We're never quits with those who have done us a favor," said Edmond. "Even when we no longer owe them money, we still owe them gratitude."

"Why talk about that? What's past is past. Let's talk about your return, my boy. I ran across our friend Danglars down at the harbor and he told me about it. He also told me you have a high place in Monsieur Morrel's favor now. But you shouldn't have refused his invitation to dinner. If a man wants to become a captain, it's always a good idea to flatter his shipowner a little."

"I hope to become a captain without that."

"So much the better! All your old friends will be glad to see you succeed, and I know someone else who won't be at all sorry to hear about it."

"Do you mean Mercédès?" asked the old man.

"Yes, father," said Edmond, "and now that I've seen you, now that I know you're well and have everything you need, with your permission I'll go see Mercédès." He embraced his father, nodded to Caderousse and went out.

Caderousse remained for a moment, then took his leave of Edmond's father, went downstairs and met Danglars, who was waiting for him.

"Well," said Danglars, "did he talk to you about his hope of becoming captain?"

"He talked as though it had already happened, and it's already made him arrogant. He offered his services to me as though he were a great man."

"Is he still in love with Mercédès?"

"Head over heels! He's on his way to see her now, but unless I'm mistaken he's in for an unpleasant surprise."

"What do you mean?"

"I don't know much for sure, but I do know that every time Mercédès comes into town she's accompanied by a husky young Catalan with an ardent expression on his face."

"You say Dantès is on his way to see her now?" asked Danglars.

"Yes, he left just before I did."

"Then let's go in the same direction. We'll stop at La Réserve and wait for the news over a bottle of wine."

"Who's going to tell us any news?"

"We'll be beside the road and we can tell what's happened from the expression on Dantès' face."

"Let's go, then," said Caderousse. "But you'll pay for the wine, won't you?"

"Certainly," replied Danglars.

The two friends walked rapidly away.

Chapter 3

A hundred paces or so from the spot where Danglars and Caderousse sat sipping their wine was the village of the Catalans.

One day a mysterious group of people set out from Spain and settled on the narrow strip of land which they still inhabit today. Their leader, who could speak a little Provençal, asked the commune of Marseilles to give them the barren promontory on which they had run their boats ashore. The request was granted and three months later those seagoing gypsies had built a small village. Today, three or four centuries later, they still remain faithful to their little promontory and do not mix with the population of Marseilles. They marry only among themselves and preserve the customs and language of their original homeland.

In one of the houses on the only street of this little village, a beautiful young girl, with jet-black hair and eyes as soft as those of a gazelle, was standing leaning against the wall. Before her sat a young man of about twenty, tilting his chair nervously and looking at her with a mixture of uneasiness and anger. His eyes were questioning her, but her firm, steadfast gaze dominated him.

"Listen, Mercédès," said the young man, "it's almost Easter again—a good time for a wedding. Give me an answer!"

"I've already answered you a hundred times, Fernand; you must be your own enemy to keep on asking me. I've never encouraged your hopes. I've always said to you, 'I love you like a brother, but never ask anything more of me because my heart belongs to someone else.' Haven't I always told you that, Fernand?"

"Yes, you've always been cruelly frank with me."

"Besides, why should you want to marry me, a poor orphan girl whose only fortune is a cabin that's falling into ruin?"

"I don't care how poor you are, Mercédès! I'd rather have you than the daughter of the proudest shipowner or the richest banker in Marseilles! All a man needs is an honorable wife and a good housekeeper. Where could I find anyone better than you in both respects?"

"Fernand," replied Mercédès, shaking her head, "a woman becomes a bad housekeeper and can't even guarantee to remain an honorable wife if she loves someone other than her husband. Be satisfied with my friendship: it's all I can promise you, and I never promise anything I'm not sure of being able to give."

Fernand stood up, paced back and forth for a few moments, then stopped in front of her, clenching his fists and scowling. "Tell me once more, Mercédès," he said, "is this your final answer?"

"I love Edmond Dantès," replied the girl coldly, "and no other man will ever be my husband."

"And will you always love him?"

"As long as I live."

Fernand bowed his head in despair and heaved a sigh which sounded like a groan. Then, suddenly looking up, he hissed between his teeth, "What if he dies?"

"If he dies, so will I."

"What if he forgets you?"

"Mercédès!" shouted a joyful voice outside the house.

"Ah!" cried the girl, blushing with happiness and love. "You see, he hasn't forgotten me! There he is now!" She ran to the door, opened it and called out, "Here I am, Edmond!" Fernand recoiled as though he had seen a snake, and sank down again into his chair.

Edmond and Mercédès fell into each other's arms. The fierce Marseilles sun shining in through the door covered them with a flood of light. At first they saw nothing around them; their overwhelming happiness isolated them from the rest of the world. Then Edmond suddenly became aware of a somber face glaring at him out of the shadows. Fernand had unconsciously put his hand to the handle of the knife in his belt.

"Excuse me," said Dantès, "I didn't realize there were three of us." Turning to Mercédès, he asked, "Who is this gentleman?"

"He'll be your friend, Edmond, because he's my friend. He's my cousin Fernand, the man I love most in the world after you. Don't you recognize him?"

"Ah, yes!" said Edmond. Keeping Mercédès' hand clasped in his, he held out his other hand to Fernand. But Fernand remained as motionless and silent as a statue. Edmond looked inquiringly at Mercédès, who was trembling and upset, then at Fernand, who scowled threateningly. He saw everything at a glance. His face darkened with anger. "I didn't expect to find an enemy in your house when I hurried here to see you," he said.

"An enemy!" cried Mercédès, with an indignant look at her cousin. "You have no enemy here! Fernand is like a brother to me. He's going to shake hands with you in friendship." She looked imperiously at Fernand, who, as though hypnotized, slowly held out his hand to Edmond. Like a furious yet powerless wave, his hatred had broken against the command which the girl exercised over him.

But as soon as he touched Edmond's hand he knew he had done everything that was within his power. He turned abruptly and rushed out of the house. "Oh!" he cried, running like a madman and clutching his head between his hands. "How can I get rid of him? What can I do? What can I do?"

"Where are you going in such a hurry, Fernand?" called out a voice. He stopped short, looked around and saw Danglars sitting at a table with Caderousse in the arbor of a tavern.

"Well," said Caderousse, "why don't you come on over? Are you in such a hurry that you don't have time to talk to your friends?"

"Especially when they have a full bottle of wine in front of them," added Danglars.

Fernand looked at the two men with a dazed expression on his face and said nothing.

"He seems dejected," remarked Danglars, nudging Caderousse with his knee. "Could we be wrong? Could it be that Dantès has won out over him after all?"

"Maybe so," replied Caderousse. "We'll see." Turning to Fernand, he said, "Well, come on! Make up your mind!"

Fernand wiped away the sweat streaming down his forehead and walked slowly into the arbor. "Hello," he said. "You called me, didn't you?" He sat down, slumped forward on the table and let out a groan that was almost a sob.

"You know what, Fernand?" said Caderousse. "You look like a rejected lover!" He accompanied this little jest with a coarse laugh.

"What are you talking about?" said Danglars. "A handsome young man like Fernand is never unlucky in love. You must be joking, Caderousse."

"No, I'm not. Just listen to the way he's sighing. Come on,

Fernand, look up and talk to us. It's impolite not to answer your friends when they ask about your health."

"My health is fine," said Fernand, clenching his fists but still not raising his head.

"Ah, you see, Danglars," said Caderousse, winking at his friend, "this is how things are: Fernand here, who's a brave Catalan and one of the best fishermen in Marseilles, is in love with a pretty girl named Mercédès, but unfortunately she's in love with the first mate of the *Pharaon*. Now, since the *Pharaon* put into port today . . . well, you understand."

"No, I don't understand," said Danglars.

"Poor Fernand has been dismissed," continued Caderousse.

"And what if I have?" said Fernand, raising his head and looking at Caderousse like a man searching for someone on whom to vent his anger. "Mercédès is free to love anyone she wants to, isn't she?"

"Ah, if you take it like that," said Caderousse, "that's another story! I thought you were a Catalan. I've always heard that a Catalan was not a man to let himself be pushed aside by a rival. And I've always heard that Fernand Mondego, especially, was terrible in his vengeance."

"Poor fellow!" exclaimed Danglars, pretending to pity the young man from the bottom of his heart. "He didn't expect Dantès to come back like this without warning. He thought he might be dead, or unfaithful. A thing like that is always more painful when it happens suddenly."

"Well, in any case," said Caderousse, who kept drinking as he spoke and on whom the wine was beginning to have an effect, "Fernand isn't the only one to be annoyed by Dantès' happy return, is he, Danglars?"

"No, that's true, and I might almost say that it will bring him bad luck."

"It doesn't matter, though; in the meantime, at least, he'll marry the beautiful Mercédès."

Danglars looked scrutinizingly at Fernand, on whom Caderousse's words fell like drops of molten lead. "When will the wedding be?" he asked.

"Oh, it hasn't taken place yet!" muttered Fernand.

"No, but it will," said Caderousse, "just as surely as Dantès will be made captain of the *Pharaon*. Isn't that right, Danglars?"

Danglars started at this unexpected thrust and turned to look at Caderousse in order to see if it had been premeditated. But he saw nothing but envy in his drunken face. "All right, then," he said, filling up the glasses, "let's drink to Captain Edmond Dantès, husband of the beautiful Mercédès!"

Caderousse raised his glass with a heavy hand and emptied it at one gulp. Fernand took his and dashed it to the ground.

"Well, well!" exclaimed Caderousse. "What do I see there at the top of the hill? Take a look, Fernand; you can see better than I can. I think my eyes are starting to blur; you know how treacherous wine is. It seems to me I see two lovers walking along, hand in hand . . . God forgive me! They don't know we can see them and they're kissing!"

None of the anguish visible in Fernand's face escaped Danglars. "Do you know them, Fernand?" he asked.

"Yes," replied Fernand dully, "it's Dantès and Mercédès."

"Ah!" cried Caderousse. "You see! I didn't even recognize them! Hey, Dantès! Hey!, young lady! Come over here a minute and tell us when the wedding's going to be. Fernand's so stubborn he won't tell us."

"Be quiet!" said Danglars, pretending to restrain Caderousse, who, with the tenacity of the drunk, was leaning outside the arbor. "Try to stand up and leave the lovebirds to their lovemaking. Look at Fernand—*he's* acting sensibly."

Danglars looked at the two men and thought, "These fools are useless to me: one of them's a drunkard and the other's a coward. I'm afraid Dantès' good luck is going to hold out. He'll marry the girl, become captain of the *Pharaon* and have the laugh on all of us, unless"—a smile passed over his lips —"unless I take a hand in things."

"Hey there!" Caderousse continued to shout, half erect and leaning on the table. "Edmond! Don't you see your friends, or are you too proud to talk to them?"

"Not at all, Caderousse," replied Dantès. "I'm not proud, but I'm happy, and I think happiness makes a man even blinder than pride."

"That's a very good excuse," said Caderousse. "Hello there, Madame Dantès!"

"That's not my name yet," replied Mercédès gravely, "and they say it brings bad luck to call a girl by the name of her fiancé before she's married, so please call me Mercédès."

"I suppose the wedding will take place very soon, won't it, Monsieur Dantès?" said Danglars, bowing to the young couple.

"As soon as possible, Monsieur Danglars. Today all the preliminaries will be arranged at my father's house, and tomorrow, or day after tomorrow at the latest, we'll have the betrothal feast here at the tavern. All our friends will be there, which means you're invited, Monsieur Danglars, and you too, Caderousse."

"And what about Fernand?" asked Caderousse with a dull laugh. "Is he invited too?"

"My wife's friend is my friend," answered Dantès, "and we'd deeply regret it if he were absent from such an occasion."

Fernand opened his mouth to reply, but his voice died in his throat and he was unable to utter a single word.

"The preliminaries today and the betrothal feast tomorrow or the next day!" exclaimed Danglars. "You're certainly in a hurry, captain!"

"Monsieur Danglars," said Dantès, smiling, "let me tell you the same thing Mercédès told Caderousse just now: don't give me a title that doesn't belong to me yet. It might bring me bad luck."

"Excuse me," replied Danglars; "I only meant to say that you seem to be in quite a hurry. Yet there's plenty of time: it will be a good three months before the *Pharaon* puts to sea again."

"A man is always in a hurry to be happy. But in this case it's not only because of selfishness: I must go to Paris."

"Oh, really? Do you have business there?"

"Not on my own account. Our poor Captain Leclère asked me to do something for him there. As you can understand, it's a sacred duty. But don't worry, I'll come straight back."

"Yes, I understand," said Danglars. Then he thought to himself, "He's probably going to Paris to deliver the letter the marshal gave him. . . . By God! That letter gives me an idea, an excellent idea! Ah, Dantès, my friend, you're not yet entered in the *Pharaon's* log as number one!" Then, as Dantès began to walk away, he called out, *"Bon voyage!"*

"Thank you," replied Dantès, turning around and giving him a friendly nod. The two lovers went on their way, as blissful as two souls rising up to heaven.

Chapter 4

The weather was splendid the next day. The sun rose clear and bright, tinging the foamy crests of the waves with a reddish purple. Preparations for the betrothal feast had been made in a large room on the second floor of La Réserve, with whose arbor we are already acquainted. The feast was scheduled to begin at noon, but by eleven o'clock the tavern was filled with impatient guests. They were the favored sailors of the *Pharaon* and several soldiers, friends of Dantès.

It was rumored that Monsieur Morrel himself was coming to the feast, but this was such a great honor for Dantès that hardly anyone dared believe it. When the shipowner actually did arrive, he was greeted by hearty cheers from the sailors of the *Pharaon*. His presence was taken as confirmation of the report that Dantès was to be their captain, and since he was well liked by the crew, they were thankful that for once the shipowner's choice was in harmony with their own desires.

Danglars and Caderousse were sent out to notify Dantès of Monsieur Morrel's arrival and tell him to hurry, but they had taken scarcely a hundred steps when they saw the small bridal party approaching. Edmond and Mercédès were accompanied by four bridesmaids and Edmond's father. Behind them walked Fernand, wearing an evil smile. But Edmond and Mercédès did not notice this; they were so happy that they saw nothing but themselves and the beautiful blue sky which seemed to be blessing them.

As soon as they were within sight of La Réserve, Monsieur Morrel went downstairs and came out to meet them, followed by the other guests. Then they all climbed back up the wooden staircase, which creaked for five minutes under their heavy footsteps. The hors d'oeuvres were served as soon as they sat down.

"What a silent party!" exclaimed Edmond's father as he inhaled the fragrance of a glass of yellow wine which had just been placed before Mercédès. "It certainly doesn't sound as though there were thirty lighthearted people here!"

"Husbands aren't always lighthearted," remarked Caderousse.

"The fact is," said Dantès, "that right now I'm too happy to be gay. If that's what you mean, you're right. Joy sometimes has a strange effect: it can oppress us almost as much as sorrow."

"You're not worried about anything, are you?" said Danglars. "It seems to me everything's going perfectly for you."

"That's exactly what worries me," replied Dantès. "I don't think man was meant to attain happiness so easily. Happiness is like those palaces in fairy tales whose gates are guarded by dragons: we must fight in order to conquer it. I don't know what I've done to deserve the good fortune of being Mercédès' husband."

"Husband!" exclaimed Caderousse, laughing. "Not yet, captain. Just try to act like her husband now and see how you're received!"

Mercédès blushed. Fernand twisted in his chair and wiped away the large beads of sweat which gathered on his forehead like the first raindrops of a storm.

Just then confused sounds were heard on the staircase. Heavy footsteps, a hubbub of voices and the clanking of swords rose above the sounds of merrymaking within the tavern. Everyone became silent. There were three loud knocks on the door.

"Open in the name of the law!" cried a resounding voice. No one answered. The door opened and a police commissary entered, followed by four armed soldiers led by a corporal.

"What's the matter?" asked Monsieur Morrel, stepping up to the commissary, whom he knew. "There must be some mistake."

"If there's a mistake, Monsieur Morrel," replied the commissary, "it will soon be corrected. In the meantime, I have a warrant for arrest, and I must do my duty. Which one of you gentlemen is Edmond Dantès?"

All eyes turned to the young man who, strongly agitated but nevertheless maintaining his dignity, stepped forward and said, "I'm Edmond Dantès, sir. What do you want with me?"

"Edmond Dantès, you are under arrest."

"Under arrest!" cried Dantès, turning pale. "But why?"

"I don't know, but you'll be told the reason at your first examination."

Monsieur Morrel realized that further discussion was useless. A commissary with a warrant for arrest is no longer a man, but a statue of the law, cold, deaf and mute. Dantès' father, however, rushed toward the commissary; there are some things which the heart of a father or a mother will never understand. He begged and supplicated. Tears and prayers accomplished nothing, but his despair was so great that the commissary was touched by it. "Calm yourself, sir," he said. "Your son may only have neglected some customs formality, and it's quite possible he'll be released as soon as he's given the information desired."

Meanwhile Dantès had shaken hands with his friends and told them: "Don't worry; the mistake will soon be cleared up, probably even before I reach the prison." He walked down the stairs, preceded by the commissary and surrounded by the soldiers. A carriage was waiting for him at the door. He climbed into it. The commissary and two soldiers climbed in after him, the door closed and the carriage set out for Marseilles.

Chapter 5

In one of the houses of aristocratic architecture on the Rue du Grand-Cours, another betrothal feast was being celebrated on the same day and at the same hour. But, instead of humble workers, sailors and soldiers, the guests of this feast were members of the highest stratum of Marseilles society. They were former magistrates who had resigned their offices during the usurper's reign, old officers who had deserted their posts to join Condé's army, and young men who had been raised by their families in bitter hatred of the emperor. Napoleon, who was then king of the Isle of Elba, ruling over a population of five or six thousand after having heard shouts of "Long live Napoleon!" from a hundred and twenty million subjects in ten different languages, was regarded by these people as a man whose downfall was complete and final. To these joyful and triumphant royalists it seemed that life was beginning anew, that they were awakening from a terrible nightmare.

The Marquis of Saint-Méran, an old man wearing the cross of Saint Louis, stood up and proposed a toast to King Louis XVIII. The response was enthusiastic: glasses were raised instantly and the ladies took off their bouquets and strewed the table with flowers.

"Ah," said the Marquise of Saint-Méran, a woman with forbidding eyes, thin lips and an aristocratic and elegant figure despite her fifty years, "if all those revolutionists who persecuted us during the Terror were here now, they would have to agree that ours was the true devotion, for we remained faithful to a crumbling monarchy while they attached themselves to the rising sun and made their fortunes while we were losing everything we owned. They would have to admit that our king was truly Louis the Beloved, while their usurper was never anything except Napoleon the Cursed. Isn't that right, Monsieur de Villefort?"

"Excuse me, madame, I wasn't following the conversation."

"Leave the young people alone," said the marquis. "They're going to be married soon, and they naturally have other things than politics to talk about."

"Forgive me, mother," said a lovely young girl with blond hair and soft eyes. "I was monopolizing Monsieur de Villefort's attention."

"You're forgiven, Renée," said the marquise with a tender smile which was surprising to see on such a stern countenance. "I was saying, Monsieur de Villefort, that the Bonapartists had neither our conviction, our enthusiasm nor our devotion."

"Yes, madame, but they have something which replaces all that: fanaticism. Napoleon is the Mohammed of the West for all those vulgar but highly ambitious people. For them he's not only a legislator and a master, he's a symbol, the personification of equality. Robespierre represented a 'lowering' equality: he brought kings to the guillotine, while Napoleon represented an 'elevating' equality: he raised the people to the level of the throne."

"I suppose you know, Monsieur de Villefort," said the marquise, "that what you're saying has a strong odor of revolution about it. But I forgive you; one can't expect the son of a Girondin to be entirely free from a spice of the old leaven."

Villefort flushed crimson. "It's true that my father was a Girondin, madame," he said, "but I've separated myself not only from his opinions but even from his name. My father was, and perhaps still is, a Bonapartist and his name is Noirtier; I am a royalist and my name is Villefort. Let the revolutionary sap dry up and die in the old trunk, madame, and consider the young shoot which has grown apart from it without having the power, or even the desire, to detach itself from it entirely."

"Bravo, Villefort!" said the marquis. "Well spoken! I've always tried to persuade my wife to forget the past, but without success; perhaps you'll be more fortunate than I."

"Very well," said the marquise, "let's forget the past, I'm quite willing. I only ask that you be inflexible in the future, Monsieur de Villefort. If a conspirator should fall into your hands, remember that you'll be closely watched because you're from a family which may be in league with the conspirators."

"Alas, madame," said Villefort, "my profession, and especially the times in which we live, require me to be severe. I've already had several political accusations to deal with and they've given me an opportunity to prove my severity. And unfortunately we haven't yet finished with these matters."

"Really?" asked the marquise.

"I'm afraid not. Napoleon is on the Isle of Elba, almost within sight of our shores. His presence there keeps the hopes of his partisans alive."

"Yes," said the marquise, "but either the king rules or he does not. If he rules, his government must be strong and its officials inflexible; it's the only way to prevent evil."

"Unfortunately, madame," said Villefort, smiling, "a deputy public prosecutor always arrives after the evil has been done."

"Then it's up to you to repair it."

"Allow me to say once again, madame, that we don't repair evil, we only avenge it."

Just then a servant entered and whispered something into Villefort's ear. He excused himself, left the table and returned a few moments later. "My time is never my own," he said to his fiancée. "They've come to disturb me even here with you, at my own betrothal feast."

"What's the matter?" asked the girl anxiously.

"I've just been told about a very serious matter. It seems a small Bonapartist plot has been discovered."

"Really?" exclaimed the marquise.

"Here's the letter of denunciation." He read aloud:

"The public prosecutor is hereby informed, by a friend of the throne and of religion, that Edmond Dantès, first mate of the ship *Pharaon*, which arrived this morning from Smyrna, after having stopped at Naples and the Isle of Elba, has been entrusted by Murat with a letter to the usurper, and by the usurper with a letter to the Bonapartist party of Paris. Confirmation of his crime can be obtained by arresting him, for the letter will be found either on his person, in his father's house, or in his cabin on board the *Pharaon*."

"But," said Renée, "that letter is anonymous, and it's addressed to the public prosecutor, not to you."

"Yes, but the public prosecutor is absent. His secretary was instructed to open all his correspondence. He opened this one, sent for me and, being unable to find me, gave orders to have the man arrested."

"Where is he now?" asked Renée.

"At my house."

"Then go, my boy," said the marquis. "Don't neglect your duty in order to stay with us. Go where the service of the king calls you."

Villefort had scarcely left the room when he abandoned his joyous expression and took on the grave air of a man called upon to decide on the life or death of his fellow man. Actually, however, aside from the thought of his father's political opinions, which might prove disastrous for his future if he did not separate himself completely from them, Gérard de Villefort was at that moment as happy as it is given to a man to be. Although only twenty-seven years old, he was already rich and held a high position in the magistracy; he was about to marry a pretty girl whom he loved, not passionately, but reasonably, as befits a deputy public prosecutor. And in addition to her beauty, which was remarkable, Mademoiselle de Saint-Méran belonged to a family which stood in high favor at court. Furthermore, she had a dowry of a hundred and fifty thousand francs and could expect to inherit another half-million some day. The combination of all these things composed for Villefort a happiness which was nothing short of dazzling.

He found a police commissary waiting for him at the door. The sight of this man immediately brought him down to earth again. Putting on an even more serious expression, he said to him, "I've read the letter. You did well to arrest that man. Now give me all the information you have about him and the conspiracy."

"We don't know anything about the conspiracy yet, sir. All the papers found on the man have been placed on your desk under seal. As you read in the letter, the prisoner's name is Edmond Dantès and he's first mate of the three-master *Pharaon*, which trades in cotton with Alexandria and Smyrna and belongs to the firm of Morrel and Son."

Just then Villefort was approached by a man who seemed to have been waiting for him to pass. It was Monsieur Morrel. "Monsieur de Villefort!" he called out. "I'm glad I was able to find you. A fantastic, ridiculous mistake has been made: the first mate of my ship, Edmond Dantès, has been arrested."

"I know that, sir," replied Villefort. "I'm on my way to question him."

"Oh!" cried Morrel, carried away by his friendship for the young man, "you don't know him! He's the gentlest, most trustworthy man in the world!"

Villefort, as we have seen, belonged to the aristocratic segment of the city and Morrel to the plebeian; the first was a zealous royalist, while the second was suspected of having hidden Bonapartist leanings. Villefort looked disdainfully at Morrel and replied coldly, "You may be sure, sir, that you have not appealed to me in vain if the accused is innocent. But we live in a difficult time, sir, and if he is guilty I shall be forced to do my duty." Having arrived before his house as he spoke these words, he entered majestically, after having taken his leave of the shipowner with icy politeness.

The antechamber was full of soldiers and policemen guarding the prisoner. Villefort cast a swift glance at Dantès, took the bundle of papers which a policeman handed him and walked out of the room. His first impression of Dantès was good, but he had often heard it said as a profound political maxim that we must distrust our first impulses, and he applied the maxim to his impressions as well as his impulses. He therefore stifled his kindly feelings, assumed the expression he reserved for grave occasions and sat down at his desk with a menacing frown.

Dantès entered a moment later. He was still pale, but calm

and smiling. He greeted his judge with easy politeness and looked around for a seat.

"What is your name and occupation?" asked Villefort, fingering the notes the policeman had given him when he entered.

"My name is Edmond Dantès, and I'm first mate of the ship *Pharaon*, which belongs to Morrel and Son."

"How old are you?"

"Nineteen."

"What were you doing when you were arrested?"

"I was attending my own betrothal feast," replied Dantès, his voice trembling slightly. "I'm about to marry a woman with whom I've been in love for three years."

Villefort started in spite of himself. The coincidence shook his usual impassivity and struck a chord of sympathy in the depths of his soul. He, too, was about to be married; and he had now been called upon to destroy the joy of a man who, like himself, was on the point of attaining his supreme happiness. "The philosophical comparison will make a good impression in Monsieur de Saint-Méran's salon," he thought, and he proceeded to compose in advance the little speech he would make. This done, he turned his attention back to Dantès and asked:

"Have you ever served under the usurper?"

"I was about to be drafted into the navy when he fell from power."

"I've been told that you have radical political opinions," said Villefort, who had been told nothing of the sort, but who had no qualms about posing the question in the form of an accusation.

"My political opinions, sir? I'm almost ashamed to say so, but I've never had anything that might be called an opinion. I'm only nineteen, as I've already told you, and I know very little. I wasn't destined to play any important role in life. Anything I am and anything I may be in the future, if I receive the position I hope for, I owe to Monsieur Morrel. All my opinions are limited to these feelings: I love my father, I respect Monsieur Morrel, and I adore Mercédès. That's all the information I can give you, sir. As you can see, it's not very interesting."

Villefort watched Dantès closely. The young man was so candid and open, so full of affection for his fellow man, including even his stern judge, that it seemed to Villefort that each word he spoke was a proof of his innocence.

"Do you have any enemies?" asked Villefort.

"Enemies? No, I'm not important enough to have made any.

As for my character, I may be a little too quick-tempered, but I've always tried to control myself with my subordinates. I have twelve sailors under my orders; question them, sir, and they'll all tell you they love and respect me."

"If you've made no enemies, you may at least have aroused some jealousy. After all, you're about to become a captain at the age of nineteen and you're about to marry a beautiful woman who loves you, which is a rare stroke of good luck on this earth. Either of these two things may have made certain people envious of you."

"Yes, you may be right; I'm sure you know human nature better than I do. But if these envious people are among my friends, I'd rather not know who they are, because then I'd be forced to hate them."

"You're wrong to think that way: we must always try to see things around us as clearly as possible. And you seem to be such a worthy young man that I'm going to help you throw some light on your situation by showing you the written denunciation which has brought you before me. Here it is—do you recognize the handwriting?"

Dantès read the letter. A dark cloud passed over his face and he said, "No, sir, I don't recognize this handwriting. It's disguised, but it's quite plain. I'm lucky," he added, giving Villefort a look of gratitude, "to be dealing with a man like you, because this is the work of a real enemy." The way the young man's eyes flashed as he spoke these words revealed to Villefort all the violent energy that was hidden under the gentleness which had impressed him so deeply at first.

"Now," said Villefort, "answer me frankly, not as a prisoner before a judge, but as a man in a false position speaking to another man who has his interest at heart: what truth is there in this anonymous accusation?" He dropped the letter on his desk with an expression of disgust.

"I'll tell you the whole truth, sir, and I swear to it on my honor as a sailor, by my love for Mercédès, and by my father's life. After we left Naples, Captain Leclère fell ill with brain fever. Feeling that he was about to die, he called me to him and said, 'My dear Dantès, swear to me on your honor that you will do what I'm about to ask you; it's a matter of great importance.'

"'I swear it, captain,' I said.

"'After my death,' he said, 'you'll take command of the ship, since you're first mate. Head for the Isle of Elba, go ashore at Porto Ferraio, ask for the marshal and give him this letter. You may be given another letter or entrusted with a mission. That mission was to have been for me, but you'll carry it out in my place and all the honor will be yours.'

" 'I'll do it, captain,' I said, 'but it may not be as easy to see the marshal as you think.'

" 'Here's a ring which will remove all obstacles,' he said, and he gave me a ring. Two hours later he became delirious; the next day he was dead."

"Then what did you do?"

"What anyone else would have done in my place, sir. The request of a dying man is always sacred, but for a sailor the request of a superior officer is an order which must be carried out. I arrived at the Isle of Elba the next day and went ashore alone. As I had predicted, I had some difficulty in seeing the marshal at first, but I sent him the ring and all doors were opened to me. The marshal gave me a letter addressed to Paris and asked me to deliver it in person. I promised him I would do so, for it was in accordance with the last wishes of my captain. I landed at Marseilles, quickly took care of all the formalities on board, then went to see my fiancée, whom I found more beautiful and loving than ever. Finally, sir, I was attending my own betrothal feast,. I was going to be married the same day and I intended to leave for Paris tomorrow, when I was arrested on the basis of this denunciation which you now seem to despise as much as I do."

"You seem to be telling the truth," said Villefort. "If you're guilty, it's only through imprudence, and even your imprudence is justified by your captain's orders. Give me the letter you received on the Isle of Elba, give me your word of honor to appear whenever you may be summoned, and go back to your friends."

"Do you mean I'm free, sir?" cried Dantès, overcome with joy.

"Yes, but first give me the letter."

"You must have it already, sir; they took it along with my other papers."

"Just a moment," said Villefort to Dantès, who was taking his gloves and hat. "To whom is the letter addressed?"

"To Monsieur Noirtier, Rue Coq-Héron, in Paris."

A thunderbolt could not have struck Villefort more suddenly or unexpectedly. He sank back into his chair, from which he had risen to pick up the bundle of papers that had been taken from Dantès, drew out the fateful letter and glanced at it with indescribable terror. "Monsieur Noirtier, 13 Rue Coq-Héron," he murmured, turning still paler.

"Yes ,sir," replied Dantès, surprised. "Do you know him?"

"No!" said Villefort emphatically. "A loyal servant of the king does not know conspirators."

"Is the letter about a conspiracy?" asked Dantès, who, after believing himself to be free, now began to be more alarmed than at first. "In any case, sir, as I've already told you, I know nothing about the contents of the letter."

"Yes," murmured Villefort, "but you know the name of the man to whom it's addressed."

"I had to know that in order to deliver it, sir."

"Have you shown this to anyone else?" asked Villefort, reading the letter.

"To no one, sir. I swear it."

"No one else knows that you were to deliver a letter from the Isle of Elba to Monsieur Noirtier?"

"No one except the man who gave it to me, sir."

"This is too much! Too much!" muttered Villefort as he read the letter. His tightly compressed lips, his trembling hands and his flashing eyes awakened painful apprehensions in Dantès.

"If he knows what's in this letter," thought Villefort, "and if he ever learns that Noirtier is Villefort's father, I'm ruined, ruined forever!"

He made a violent effort to control himself, then said to Dantès, as calmly as possible, "I see now that there are very serious charges against you. I no longer have the power, as I thought at first, to set you free immediately. You know how I've tried to help you, but I must continue to hold you prisoner for a while, as short a time as possible. The main evidence against you is this letter, and, as you see . . ." He stepped over to the fireplace, threw the letter into the flames and stood watching it until it had been reduced to ashes. "As you see," he continued, "I've destroyed it."

"Oh!" cried Dantès, "you're more than just, sir; you're kindness itself!"

"I think you now realize that you can have confidence in me, so listen to my advice. I'll keep you here until tonight. Someone else may come to question you. If so, tell him about everything you've told me except the letter. Not one word about that."

"I promise, sir," said Dantès.

"If anyone asks you about it, deny it. Deny it firmly and you'll be saved."

"I'll deny it, sir, don't worry."

"Good!" said Villefort. He pulled a bell cord and a moment later the police commissary entered.

"Follow this gentleman," said Villefort to Dantès. The latter bowed, gave him one last look of gratitude and went out.

As soon as the door had closed behind him, Villefort's strength failed him and he sank into his chair, half fainting. "Oh, my God!" he murmured. "If the public prosecutor had been in Marseilles he'd have seen the letter and I'd have been lost! Oh, father, will you always be an obstacle to my happiness? Must I struggle eternally against your past?"

Then suddenly an unexpected light seemed to dawn in his mind. A smile appeared on his lips and his haggard eyes became fixed and seemed to be staring at a thought. "Yes!" he said. "That letter, which could have ruined me, may make my fortune instead. Come on, Villefort: to work!"

After making sure that the prisoner was no longer in the antechamber, the deputy public prosecutor hurried to his fiancée's house.

Chapter 6

As he passed through the antechamber, the police commissary motioned to two gendarmes, who placed themselves on either side of Dantès. A door leading to the Palace of Justice was opened and they passed through one of those long dark corridors which bring an involuntary shudder to all those who enter them.

Just as Villefort's apartment communicated with the Palace of Justice, so the Palace of Justice communicated with the prison. After turning down a number of different corridors, Dantès and his escort came to an iron door. It opened and clanged shut behind him. He now breathed a different air, foul and heavy; he was in prison.

He was led to a rather clean cell whose appearance aroused no fear in him; besides, Villefort's reassuring words still echoed in his ear. Night soon fell and the cell was plunged in darkness. With the loss of his sight, his hearing became more acute. At the slightest sound he would stand up and walk to the door of his cell, convinced that he was about to be set free, but soon the sound would die away in another direction and he would sink back onto his stool.

Finally, toward ten o'clock, just as he was beginning to lose hope, he heard footsteps outside in the corridor. They stopped before his cell, a key turned in the lock and the massive door opened, revealing the dazzling light of two torches. Dantès saw four gendarmes

"Have you come for me?" he asked.

"Yes."

"Were you sent by the deputy public prosecutor?"

"Of course."

The knowledge that they had been sent by Villefort relieved the unfortunate young man of all anxiety. He placed himself calmly in the middle of his escort. A police van was waiting for him in the street. The door was opened and he felt himself being pushed inside before he had time to say anything, although he had no intention of resisting. A moment later he was sitting between two gendarmes, with the other two seated opposite him. The heavy van set out for its unknown destination.

When it finally stopped, Dantès found himself in the port. Two of the gendarmes got out first, then Dantès was followed by the other two. The four of them led him to a boat which a customs officer was holding alongside the quay by a chain. He was soon seated in the stern of the boat, still surrounded by the four gendarmes, while a police officer placed himself in the bow. The boat was shoved off, four oarsmen began to row vigorously and before long Dantès found himself outside the harbor. "Where are you taking me?" he asked one of the gendarmes.

"You'll know soon enough."

"But——"

"We're forbidden to give you any information."

Dantès said no more. He waited silently and thoughtfully, trying to pierce the shadows of the night with the practiced eye of a sailor accustomed to space and darkness. Meanwhile the oarsmen had stopped rowing and hoisted a sail. Finally, despite his reluctance to question the gendarme a second time, Dantès said to him:

"Comrade, in the name of your conscience I beg you to take pity on me and answer me. I've been falsely accused of some sort of treason, but I'm a good and loyal Frenchman. Where are you taking me? Tell me and, on my honor as a sailor, I'll do nothing except resign myself to my fate."

"Unless you're blindfolded or have never been outside the harbor of Marseilles," replied the gendarme, "you must be able to guess where you're going by now. Look around you."

Dantès stood up and looked in the direction the boat was moving. Several hundred yards ahead rose the steep black rock on which stood the somber Château d'If.

The unexpected appearance of this dreaded prison, with its centuries-old tradition of terror, produced the same effect on Dantès as the sight of the gallows on a man condemned to death.

"Oh, my God!" he cried out. "The Château d'If: What are we going there for?" The gendarme smiled. "You can't be taking me there to be imprisoned!" went on Dantès. "The Château d'If is a state prison, used only for important political prisoners. I've committed no crime. Am I really going to be imprisoned there?"

"Probably."

"But Monsieur de Villefort promised——"

"I don't know what Monsieur de Villefort promised you," said the gendarme. "All I know is that we're going to the Château d'If—— Wait! Quick, men, come here!" Dantès had tried to throw himself into the sea, but four vigorous arms pulled him back as soon as his feet left the bottom of the boat. He fell back howling with rage.

"All right, my friend," said a gendarme, pinning him down with his knee, "if you make one more movement, just one, I'll put a bullet through your head!" And Dantès felt the muzzle of a carbine pressed against his temple.

A short time later he felt the boat strike something and realized they had landed. His guards pulled him to his feet, made him climb out of the boat and dragged him toward the steps which led up to the citadel. He made no useless resistance; his slowness came from inertia rather than opposition. He felt numb, and he staggered as though he were drunk. He was aware of steps which forced him to raise his feet, he noticed that he had gone through a door which had closed behind him, but he did everything mechanically and he seemed to be surrounded by a thick fog. He finally came to a halt. Certain that he could no longer flee, the guards released him.

After a wait of ten minutes or so a voice said, "Have the prisoner follow me; I'll take him to his cell."

"Go on," said one of the gendarmes, pushing him.

Dantès followed his guide into a room which was almost entirely underground, whose bare, oozing walls seemed to be impregnated with tears. A sort of lamp standing on a stool, its wick swimming in fetid oil, illuminated this frightful lodging and allowed Dantès to see his guide, a subaltern jailer with dirty clothes and a stupid face.

"This is your room for tonight," he said. "It's late and the governor is asleep. Tomorrow, when he's read his instructions concerning you, he may have you put into another cell. In the meanwhile, here's some bread, there's water in that jug and there's some straw on the floor over there in the corner. You have everything a prisoner could wish for. Good night." Before Dantès could say anything in reply, the jailer picked up the lamp, walked out and locked the door behind him, leaving the cell in utter darkness.

When the first rays of dawn were beginning to bring back a little light to the cell, the jailer reappeared, having received orders to leave the prisoner where he was. Dantès had not moved. He seemed to have been nailed to the same spot where he had stopped when he entered the night before. He had spent the whole night standing up, without sleeping for a single instant. The jailer walked up to him but Dantès did not seem to see him. He tapped him on the shoulder. Dantès started and shook his head.

"Haven't you slept?" asked the jailer.

"I don't know."

"Aren't you hungry?"

"I don't know."

"Do you want anything?"

"I want to see the governor."

"That's impossible."

"Why?"

"Because the regulations of the prison don't allow prisoners to request it."

"What *is* allowed here?"

"Better food, if you pay for it, walks outside, and sometimes books."

"I don't need books, I don't feel like taking a walk and the food is good enough for me. I want only one thing: I want to see the governor."

"Listen," said the jailer, "don't start brooding over something impossible like that or you'll go mad within two weeks."

"Do you think so?"

"Of course. That's how madness always begins. For example, there was a priest who used to have this same cell. It was constantly offering to give the governor a million francs if he would set him free that finally twisted his brain."

"What happened to him?"

"They put him into a dungeon."

"Listen," said Dantès, "I'm not a priest and I'm not mad. I can't offer you a million francs, but I can offer you three hundred francs if you'll deliver a letter to a girl named Mercédès the next time you go to Marseilles . . . not even a letter, just two or three lines."

"If I took those two or three lines and got caught with them, I'd be discharged. I make a thousand francs a year here, not counting the food, so I'd be an idiot to risk losing a thousand francs on the chance of earning three hundred."

"Listen, then: if you refuse to deliver a letter to Mercédès, or at least let her know I'm here, some day I'll be hiding behind the door when you come in and I'll break open your head with this stool."

"Threats!" cried the jailer, stepping back and putting himself on the defensive. "The priest began like that. Within three days you'll be raving mad, just as he is. It's a good thing there are dungeons in the Château d'If."

Dantès picked up the stool.

"All right! All right!" said the jailer. "Since you're so set on it, I'll go tell the governor."

"Good!" said Dantès. He set the stool on the floor and sat down on it with bowed head and haggard eyes, as though he actually were mad.

The jailer went out and returned an instant later with four soldiers and a corporal. "By order of the governor," he said, "take the prisoner to the floor below this one."

"To the dungeon?" asked the corporal.

"That's right. We have to put madmen with madmen."

The four soldiers took hold of Dantès, who fell into a kind of apathy and followed them without resistance. He descended fifteen steps, the door of a cell was opened and he entered, mumbling to himself, "He's right: they have to put madmen with madmen."

Chapter 7

In his small study at the Tuileries in Paris, seated at a walnut table which he had brought back from his exile in Hartwell and to which he was greatly attached, King Louis XVIII listened rather absent-mindedly to a gray-haired, aristocratic-looking gentleman of about fifty. His Majesty continued to make notes in the margin of his edition of Horace as this gentleman spoke to him.

"What were you saying?" said the king.

"That I'm extremely worried, sire. I have good reason to believe that a storm is brewing in the South."

"I'm afraid you've been misinformed, duke. I know for certain that the weather is fine down there." Intelligent as he was, Louis XVIII was given to facile jesting.

"Your Majesty may be quite right in counting on the good sense of the French people, but I don't think I'm entirely wrong in fearing the possibility of some desperate attempt."

"By whom?"

"By Bonaparte, or at least by his partisans."

"My dear Blacas," said the king, "your alarm is keeping me from working."

"And your feeling of security keeps me from sleeping, sire. My alarm doesn't come from vague, unfounded rumors, but from an intelligent, trustworthy man who has just arrived from Marseilles to tell me, 'A great danger threatens the king.' I therefore came to you immediately, sire. I think it extremely important that you see Monsieur de Villefort."

"Monsieur de Villefort!" exclaimed the king. "Is he the man who just arrived from Marseilles? Why didn't you tell me his name immediately?"

"I thought the name was unknown to Your Majesty."

"Not at all. He's a serious-minded young man, honorable, intelligent and, above all, ambitious. Furthermore, you know his father by name."

"His father?"

"Yes; his name is Noirtier."

"Noirtier the Girondin?"

"Precisely."

"And Your Majesty has employed the son of such a man?"

"Blacas, my friend, you don't understand these things. I told you Villefort was ambitious. He would sacrifice anything to his ambition, even his own father."

"Shall I bring him to you, sire?"

"Yes, immediately."

The duke hurried out of the room with the alacrity of a young man and returned a short time later with Villefort. As the door opened, the latter found himself face to face with the king. He stopped short.

"Come in, Monsieur de Villefort, come in," said the king.

Villefort bowed and took a few steps forward, waiting for the king to question him.

"Monsieur de Villefort," said Louis XVIII, "the duke here informs me you have something important to tell us."

"The duke is right, sire. I have come to Paris as rapidly as possible to inform Your Majesty that, in the exercise of my duties, I have discovered a conspiracy of dire importance, a veritable tempest which directly threatens Your Majesty's throne. Sire, the usurper has manned three vessels and has by now almost certainly left the Isle of Elba. His destination is unknown, but he will surely attempt a landing either at Naples, or on the Tuscany coast, or in France itself. Your Majesty is no doubt aware that the usurper has maintained partisans in both Italy and France."

"Yes, I know that," said the king, strongly agitated. "But please continue. How did you learn these facts?"

"I learned them in Marseilles from a man whom I had been watching for a long time and whom I had arrested the day I left for Paris. This man, a turbulent sailor whom I had previously suspected of Bonapartism, had made a secret trip to the Isle of Elba. The marshal there entrusted him with a verbal message for a certain Bonapartist in Paris, whose name I was unable to make him tell me. But I did learn that he was to instruct this Bonapartist in Paris to prepare his adherents for a return of the usurper within a short time."

"And where is this man now?" asked the king.

"In prison, sire."

"Ah, here's Monsieur Dandré!" cried the duke. The Minister of Police had just appeared on the threshold. He was pale, trembling and almost wild-eyed with terror.

The king violently pushed back the table at which he was sitting and cried out, "What's the matter, baron? You look panic-stricken! Does your alarm have anything to do with what Monsieur de Villefort was just telling me?"

"Sire—sire——" stammered the baron.

"Speak!"

The Minister of Police threw himself at the king's feet in despair and cried out, "A terrible disaster, sire! The usurper left the Isle of Elba on the twenty-eighth of February and on the first of March he landed in France, at a little port near Antibes."

"The usurper landed in France near Antibes, only two hundred and fifty leagues from Paris, on the first of March, and you learned of it only today, the third of March? Impossible! Either you've been misinformed or you're mad!"

"Alas, sire, it's only too true!"

Louis XVIII made a gesture of unspeakable anger and alarm and leaped to his feet. "In France!" he cried. "The usurper is in France! Wasn't he being watched? But who knows, perhaps certain persons were in league with him!"

"Oh, sire!" exclaimed the duke. "A man like Monsieur Dandré cannot be accused of treason. We were all blind; he merely shared the common blindness."

"But——" began Villefort. Then, stopping short, he said, "Forgive me, sire, forgive me! I was carried away by my zeal."

"Go on, speak boldly," said the king. "You were the only one to warn us of the disaster. Help us now to remedy it."

"Sire," said Villefort, "the usurper is detested in the South. It will not be difficult to make Provence and Languedoc rise up against him."

"No doubt," said the minister, "but he's advancing by way of Gap and Sisteron."

"He's advancing!" exclaimed the king. "Do you mean he's marching on Paris?"

The Minister of Police kept a silence which was equivalent to the most complete avowal.

"In that case," said the king, "I have no further need of you and you may withdraw. What remains to be done now concerns the Minister of War. . . . Monsieur de Villefort, you are no doubt quite tired from your long journey; go get some rest. You'll stay at your father's house, won't you?"

Villefort felt as though he were about to faint. "No, sire," he said. "I'll stay at the Hôtel de Madrid, in the Rue de Tournon."

"Oh, yes," said the king, smiling, "I was forgetting that you're not on good terms with Monsieur Noirtier, which is another sacrifice to the royal cause for which I must reward you."

"Sire, the kindness you have already shown me is a reward which so far surpasses all my ambitions that I have nothing more to ask."

"Be that as it may, we shall not forget you. In the meantime, take this." The king took off the cross of the Legion of Honor, which he customarily wore next to the cross of Saint Louis, and handed it to Villefort.

Villefort's eyes filled with tears of pride and joy. He took the cross and kissed it.

"Go now," said the king. "And if I should happen to forget you—a king's memory is short—don't be afraid to bring yourself to my attention."

As Villefort was leaving the Tuileries with the Minister of Police, the latter said to him, "You've made a magnificent beginning, Monsieur de Villefort. Your fortune is assured now."

"I wonder how long it will take," thought Villefort.

Chapter 8

Events followed one another swiftly. The story of Napoleon's strange, miraculous return from Elba is well known. Unexampled in the past, it will probably remain unimitated in the future.

Louis XVIII made only feeble efforts to parry the blow. The monarchy which he had scarcely finished reconstructing trembled on its insecure foundations, and a single gesture from Napoleon was enough to bring down the whole edifice, which had been nothing more than a formless mixture of ancient prejudices and new ideas. Villefort therefore gained nothing from the king except a gratitude which was not only useless but even dangerous. Napoleon would no doubt have dismissed him had it not been for the protection of his father, Monsieur Noirtier, who had great power at the Court of the Hundred Days.

Villefort kept his post, but his marriage, while not abandoned, was postponed until happier times. If Napoleon remained in power, Villefort would require a different wife, and his father undertook to find one for him; if, on the other hand, a second Restoration were to bring Louis XVIII back to the throne, Monsieur de Saint-Méran's influence would be twice as great as before and a marriage with his daughter would become more advantageous to Villefort than ever.

As for Dantès, he remained a prisoner. Lost in the depths of his dungeon, he heard nothing about either the fall of Louis XVIII or the collapse of the empire.

Three times during this brief revival of the empire known as the Hundred Days, Monsieur Morrel came to see Villefort and insist that Dantès be set free, and each time Villefort calmed him with promises and hopes. Then came Waterloo. Morrel no longer came to see Villefort. He had done everything he could for his young friend; to make new efforts to procure his liberty under that second Restoration would have been simply to compromise himself uselessly.

When Louis XVIII returned to the throne, Villefort asked for and obtained the post of public prosecutor which was vacant at Toulouse. Two weeks later he married Mademoiselle de Saint-Méran, whose father stood in higher favor at the court than ever.

During Napoleon's short return to power, Danglars was afraid. He expected to see Dantès reappear at any moment, threatening, strong, and eager for vengeance. He therefore handed Monsieur Morrel his resignation and entered the service of a Spanish merchant. He left for Madrid and nothing more was heard of him.

Fernand showed less concern. Dantès was absent; that was all he needed to know, and he did not seek to learn what had become of him. Meanwhile the empire made one last appeal to its soldiers, and every man capable of bearing arms rushed to obey the voice of the emperor. Fernand left along with the others, leaving Mercédès behind and tormented by the dark, terrible thought that his rival might return during his absence and marry the woman he loved.

His devotion to Mercédès, the compassion he seemed to have for her sorrow, the zeal with which he anticipated her slightest desire—all these things produced the effect which signs of devotion always produce in a noble heart. Mercédès had always been fond of Fernand as a friend; her affection was now deepened by a new feeling: gratitude. He went off to the army with the hope that, if Dantès did not return, Mercédès might some day belong to him.

Mercédès was left alone. Bathed in tears, she was seen ceaselessly wandering around the little village of the Catalans, sometimes standing motionless in the blazing heat of the southern sun, sometimes sitting on the beach, listening to the eternal moaning of the sea and asking herself whether it would not be better to let herself sink into the depths rather than undergo the cruel suffering of a wait without hope. She did not lack the courage to do the deed; it was her religion which came to her aid and saved her from suicide.

Dantès' father lost all hope when the empire fell. Five months after he had been separated from his son he breathed his last in Mercédès' arms. Monsieur Morrel paid for his funeral and discharged the small debts which the old man had incurred during his illness. It took more than benevolence to do this: it took courage. The South was aflame, and to help the father of a Bonapartist as dangerous as Dantès, even on his deathbed, was a crime.

Chapter 9

Dantès passed through all the stages of misery endured by prisoners forgotten in a dungeon. He began with pride, which is the result of hope and a consciousness of innocence; then he began to doubt even his innocence; finally his pride collapsed and he began to pray, not yet to God, but to men. He begged to be taken from his cell and put into another one, even if it should be darker and deeper. A change, even disadvantageous, would afford him a distraction of several days. He begged to be given books and to be allowed to take walks outside. None of these things was granted to him, but he continued to ask for them.

Finally, having exhausted all his human resources, Dantès turned to God. He remembered the prayers his mother had taught him and found meanings in them of which he had formerly been unaware. For the happy man prayer is only a jumble of words, until the day when sorrow comes to explain to him the sublime language by means of which he speaks to God.

Despite his fervent prayers, however, he remained a prisoner. His soul became dark and a cloud seemed to pass before his eyes. His mind was filled with a single thought: that of his happiness destroyed for no apparent reason.

Then his despondency gave way to wrath. He roared blasphemies which made his jailer recoil in horror, and dashed himself furiously against the walls of his prison. The informer's letter which Villefort had shown him, which he himself had touched, came back to his mind. He seemed to see each line of it blazing forth in letters of fire. He told himself that it was the hatred of men, not the vengeance of God, which had plunged him into the abyss where he now found himself. He doomed these unknown men to all the tortures his fiery imagination could contrive, but even the cruelest ones seemed too mild and too short for them, for after the torment would come death, which would bring them, if not rest, at least the insensibility which resembles it.

The thought that death brings release from suffering led him to the idea of suicide. Once he had given himself up to it he found consolation in it. All his pain and sorrow seemed to flee from his cell at the silent approach of the angel of death. His life seemed more bearable when he reflected that he could cast it aside like a tattered garment whenever he chose.

There were two ways to die: the first was to tie his handkerchief to a bar of the window and hang himself; the second was to starve himself. The first was repugnant to him. He had been raised to have a horror of pirates, men who were hanged from the yardarms of ships. Hanging was therefore something dishonorable which he could not bring himself to undergo. He chose the second alternative and swore to carry it through. "I'll throw my food out the window," he thought, "and it will look as though I've eaten it."

From that day onward, twice a day, he threw his food out the small barred window through which he could see nothing but the sky; at first gaily, then thoughtfully, then regretfully. He had formerly found his food repulsive, but now hunger made it appear appetizing to the eye and exquisite to the smell; sometimes he would stand for over an hour staring at a piece of rotten meat or a crust of black, moldy bread. But then he would remember the oath he had sworn to himself, and the fear of despising himself kept him from violating it. Finally the day came when he no longer had the strength to stand up in order to throw away his supper.

The next day he could no longer see and could scarcely hear. The jailer believed him to be seriously ill; Dantès expected death within a short time. A numbness, which was not without a certain feeling of well-being, took possession of him. The pangs in his stomach ceased. When he closed his eyes he saw bright flashes of light.

Suddenly, toward nine o'clock at night, he heard a faint noise coming from the wall next to which he was lying. So many loathsome animals had made their noises in his cell that he had gradually become accustomed to them and did not let his sleep be disturbed by them. But this time, whether because his senses had been intensified by abstinence, because the noise was actually louder than usual or because at that supreme moment everything took on greater importance, Dantès raised his head to listen. He heard a regular scratching sound which

might be coming from either a large claw, a powerful tooth
or some sort of instrument. The sound continued for about
three hours, then he heard what seemed to be something
crumbling and there was silence.

The next morning it began again, so distinctly that he could
hear it without effort. "There's no doubt now," he said to himself. "Since the sound goes on even in the daytime it must
be some prisoner working to escape. Oh, if I were only with
him, how I'd help him." Then a dark cloud suddenly passed
over the hope that had dawned in his mind: what if the sound
were caused only by workmen repairing some nearby cell?
It would be easy to find out by asking the jailer, but such a
question might be dangerous. Unfortunately Dantès was so
weak and giddy that he was unable to think consecutively.
He could think of only one way to restore his lucidity: he
took the broth which the jailer had left for him and drank it.
He soon felt order returning to his scattered thoughts.

After a time he said to himself, "There's one way I can find
out without risk. I'll knock on the wall; if it's a workman he'll
stop for a moment and try to guess the cause of the sound,
but then he'll go back to work. But if it's a prisoner the sound
will frighten him; he'll stop working and won't begin again
until night, when he'll assume that everyone else is asleep."

He stood up. This time his legs were steady and his eyes
saw clearly. He went over to a corner of his cell, pulled out
a stone which had been loosened by the dampness and struck
the wall three times at the spot where the noise could be heard
most distinctly.

The noise stopped as if by magic. Dantès listened intently.
The entire day passed without a renewal of the noise. "It's a
prisoner!" said Dantès to himself with unspeakable joy. Life
came surging back to him. He did not sleep that night but
he still heard no sound from the wall.

The next morning he devoured the food which the jailer
brought him. He continued to listen for the noise to begin
again, exasperated by the prudence of that prisoner who had
not guessed that he had been distracted from his work of
escape by another prisoner who was as eager to be free as
he was. Three days went by, seventy-two hours counted minute by minute! Then one evening, after the jailer had made
his last visit, Dantès pressed his ear to the wall for the
hundredth time and seemed to feel an almost imperceptible
vibration. He walked around his cell several times to calm
himself, then returned to the same spot and put his ear to the
wall again. He was no longer in doubt: something was taking
place on the other side of the wall. The prisoner had recognized the danger of his first maneuver and had adopted an-

other; in order to continue his work in greater safety, he had probably substituted the crowbar for the chisel.

Encouraged by this discovery, Dantès resolved to come to the aid of the tireless worker. He pushed back his bed, behind which the work seemed to be going on, and looked around for an object which he could use as a tool. He saw nothing. He had no knife or any other sort of metal instrument. He had so often assured himself that the iron bars in the windows were solidly attached that he knew it was useless to try them again. He had only one resource: to break his earthenware pitcher and use one of the jagged fragments. He picked it up and dropped it to the floor. It flew into pieces.

He chose two or three sharp fragments, hid them under his mattress and left the others scattered on the floor. Breaking the pitcher was such a natural accident that the jailer would show no concern over it.

Dantès had the whole night before him, but it was difficult to work in the darkness and he soon felt his shapeless tool being blunted against the hard stone. He therefore pushed his bed back in place and waited for daylight. All night long he listened to the unknown prisoner carrying on his underground work.

When the jailer came the next morning, Dantès told him the pitcher had slipped out of his hands and fallen to the floor. The jailer grumbled and went off to get a new pitcher without taking the trouble to remove the pieces of the old one. He returned a while later, told the prisoner to be more careful in the future and went out. As soon as he was gone, Dantès pushed back his bed and saw that his work of the night before had been useless, for he had attacked the stone directly, rather than the mortar around it. His heart pounded with joy when he discovered that he could scrape away bits of this mortar. They were extremely small bits, to be sure, but within half an hour he had scraped off a handful of them.

Three days later he had succeeded in removing all the mortar from around the stone. He now had to dislodge it. He tried to do so with his fingernails, but they were insufficient for the task. The fragments of the pitcher broke when he tried to use them as levers. After an hour of vain efforts, he stood up, full of anguish. Was he to be stopped right at the beginning? Would he have to wait, inert and useless, while the other prisoner did everything?

Suddenly an idea occurred to him and he smiled. Every day the jailer brought him his soup in a saucepan which had a metal handle. Dantès would have given ten years of his life for that metal handle. That day, as usual, the jailer filled his bowl from the saucepan. After he had left, Dantès placed the bowl on the floor between the door and the table. The next time the jailer entered, he stepped on the bowl and broke it to pieces. This time Dantès was not to blame; he was wrong to leave his bowl on the floor, to be sure, but the jailer ought to have looked where he was going, so he contented himself with grumbling. Then he looked around to find something else into which he could pour the soup, but there was nothing.

"Leave the saucepan," said Dantès. "You can pick it up again tomorrow."

This suggestion appealed to the jailer's laziness: he would have no need to go upstairs, come back down and then go up again. He left the saucepan. Dantès shivered with joy. After waiting an hour to make sure the jailer would not change his mind, he pushed back his bed and began to prey out the loosened stone, using the handle of the saucepan as a lever. An hour later he had pulled the stone from the wall, making an excavation of more than a foot and a half in diameter. Then, eager to take advantage of that night in which chance, or rather his own ingenuity, had placed such a precious instrument in his hands, he continued to work furiously.

The next morning the jailer placed a piece of bread on his table. "Didn't you bring me another bowl?" asked Dantès.

"No. You break everything: first your pitcher, then your bowl. I'll leave you the saucepan and pour your soup into it."

Dantès raised his eyes to heaven and clasped his hands under his blanket. That piece of metal aroused deeper gratitude in his heart than the greatest stroke of good fortune he had ever known in his former life.

However, he had noticed that his work had caused the other prisoner to stop. But this was no reason to stop working; if his neighbor would not come to him, he would go to his neighbor. He worked all day without stopping. By evening he had, thanks to his new tool, taken at least ten handfuls of mortar and small stones from the wall. He interrupted his work when the time came for the jailer's evening visit and straightened out the twisted handle of the saucepan as best he could.

He resumed his efforts after the jailer had left, but after two or three hours of labor he encountered an obstacle. He felt it with his hands and realized that he had reached a beam which ran directly across the passage he had begun.

"Oh, my God! My God!" he cried out. "I prayed to you so long and I thought you had listened to me at last. Dear God, have pity on me. Don't let me die in despair."

"Who speaks of God and despair in the same breath?" said a muffled voice which seemed to come from under the earth.

Dantès felt his hair stand on end but he called out: "In the name of God, speak to me again, whoever you are!"

"Who are you?" asked the voice.

"A wretched prisoner," answered Dantès.

"How long have you been here?"

"Since February 28, 1815."

"What was your crime?"

"I'm innocent."

"Then what are you accused of?"

"Of conspiring for the return of Napoleon."

"What! Do you mean that Napoleon is no longer in power?"

"He abdicated at Fontainebleau in 1814 and was exiled to the Isle of Elba. But how long have you been here, not to know all that?"

"Since 1811."

Dantès shuddered; that man had been in prison four years longer than he had.

"Very well, stop digging," said the voice, speaking rapidly. "At what depth is the excavation you've made?"

"It's on a level with the ground."

"How is it hidden?"

"Behind my bed."

"Has anyone ever moved your bed since you've been in prison?"

"Never."

"What's outside your cell?"

"A corridor."

"Where does the corridor lead to?"

"To a courtyard."

"Alas!" murmured the voice.

"What's the matter?" cried Dantès.

"I was mistaken—the imperfection of my drawings misled me. One inaccurate line on my plan was equivalent to fifteen feet in reality, and I took the wall in which you're digging for the wall of the citadel."

"But you would only have reached the sea."

"That's what I wanted. I intended to jump into the sea and swim to the Isle of Daume or the Isle of Tiboulen, or even to the mainland."

"Would you have been able to swim that far?"

"God would have given me the strength. But now all is lost. Seal up your passage carefully, don't work any more and wait till you hear from me."

"At least tell me who you are."

"I'm—I'm prisoner number twenty-seven."

"Don't you trust me?" asked Dantès. He heard a bitter laugh.

"How old are you? Your voice seems to be that of a young man."

"I don't know my age because I haven't measured the time since I came here. All I know is that I was nineteen when I was arrested in 1815."

"Not quite twenty-six," murmured the voice. "Well, a man isn't yet a traitor at that age."

"Oh, no!" cried Dantès. "I'd let them cut me to pieces before I'd betray you!"

"Your age reassures me. I'll come to you. Wait for me."

"When will you come?"

"Let me calculate the risks; I'll give you a signal."

"But you won't abandon me, will you? We'll escape together; or if we can't escape, we'll talk together. If you're young, I'll be your comrade; if you're old, I'll be your son."

"Very well," said the voice. "Until tomorrow, then."

Dantès stood up, placed the stone back in the wall and pushed his bed in front of it. From that moment on he gave himself up completely to his new happiness. He was no longer going to be alone, and he might even be free.

That night he thought the other prisoner would take advantage of the silence and the darkness to renew his conversation with him, but he was mistaken. He heard nothing all night long. The next morning, however, after the jailer's visit, he heard three knocks on the wall. "Is it you?" he asked. "Here I am!"

"Has your jailer gone?" asked the voice.

"Yes. He won't come back until this evening. We have twelve hours of freedom."

A moment later Dantès heard the sound of a mass of stones and earth falling and a hole appeared in the bottom of the passage he had begun to dig. Then he saw a head emerge through this hole, and soon a man had climbed up out of it and into his cell.

Chapter 10

Dantès threw his arms around his new friend, for whom he had waited so long and impatiently, and drew him over to the window, so that he could see him as clearly as possible in the dim light which entered the cell.

He was a rather short man whose hair had turned white, more from suffering than from age. His piercing eyes were almost hidden under thick gray eyebrows; his beard, which was still black, hung down to his chest. His thin face, furrowed with deep lines, was that of a man more accustomed to exercising his mental faculties than his physical strength. As for his clothes, it was impossible to distinguish their original form, for they were in tatters.

He appeared to be at least sixty-five years old, but a certain vigor in his movements suggested that part of his apparent age might be due to his long captivity. He received Dantès' exuberant outbursts with pleasure; for a moment his icy soul seemed to melt in the presence of this ardent young man. He responded to him with a certain warmth, despite his bitter disappointment at finding himself in another cell when he had expected to find freedom instead.

"First of all," he said, "let's see if it's possible to conceal the opening from your jailer." He pushed the stone back into its hole. "This stone was removed quite carelessly," he remarked. "Didn't you have any tools?"

"Do you?" asked Dantès in amazement.

"I made some for myself. Except for a file, I have everything I need: a chisel, pincers and a crowbar." And he showed him a strong sharp blade with a wooden handle.

"How did you make that?"

"From one of the clamps of by bed. It was with this tool that I dug the whole passage from my cell to yours, a distance of about fifty feet."

"Fifty feet!" cried Dantès with a sort of terror.

"Yes, but all my work was in vain: the corridor in front of your cell leads to a courtyard full of guards. From here there is no way to escape. But God's will be done." The old man's face took on an expression of profound resignation. With a mixture of amazement and admiration, Dantès looked at this man who could thus renounce so philosophically a hope which had sustained him for so long.

"Now will you tell me who you are?" asked Dantès.

"Yes, if that still interests you now that I'm unable to be of any use to you. I'm the Abbé Faria. I've been in the Château d'If since 1811, but before that I was imprisoned in the fortress of Fenestrella for three years. In 1811 I was transferred from Piedmont to France."

"But why were you imprisoned?"

"Because in 1807 I dreamed of the project which Napoleon tried to carry out in 1811; because, like Machiavelli, instead of all the principalities which made Italy a nest of weak, tyrannical little kingdoms, I wanted to see a single great empire; because I thought I had found my Caesar Borgia in a crowned fool who pretended to understand my views in order to betray me."

Dantès did not understand how a man could risk his life

for such things. "Aren't you," he asked, beginning to share his jailer's opinion, "the priest that everyone believes to be —ill?"

"You mean mad, don't you?"

"I didn't dare to say it," said Dantès, smiling.

"Yes, yes," said Faria with a bitter laugh, "I'm the one they think is mad."

Dantès stood silent for a moment, then said, "Have you given up the idea of escape?"

"I now see that escape is impossible; it would be rebelling against God to attempt something which is against His wishes."

"Why lose hope? Wouldn't it be asking too much of Providence to expect to succeed the first time? Why not dig another passage in another direction?"

"Another passage! Do you know what I've already done? Do you know that it took me four years to make my tools? Do you know that for two years I scratched and scraped earth as hard as granite? Do you know that I had to dislodge stones which I would never have thought myself capable of even moving? Do you know that in order to find a place to deposit all those stones and all that earth I had to pierce the wall of a staircase, and that that staircase is now so full that I have no place to put even a handful of dust? Finally, do you know that I thought myself to be almost at the end of my labor and felt that I had just enough strength left to finish it when I suddenly learned that it had all been in vain? Oh, no, I'll do nothing more to reconquer my freedom, since it's God's will that it be lost forever."

Dantès bowed his head in order not to let the priest see that his joy at having found a companion prevented him from sympathizing fully with his sorrow.

"In my twelve years in prison," continued Faria, "I've carefully thought over all the famous escapes in history. Successful escapes are extremely rare and most of them have been thought out in great detail and patiently prepared. Still, some of them have been due to chance, and those are the best. From now on we'll wait for an opportunity and, if it comes, we'll take advantage of it."

"You were able to wait," said Dantès, sighing. "Your long labor gave you a constant occupation, and when you didn't have your work to distract you, you had your hopes to console you."

"That hasn't been my only occupation," said the priest.

"What else do you do?"

"I write and study."

"Do they give you paper, pens and ink?"

"No, but I make my own."

"You make your own paper, pens and ink?" cried Dantès.
"Yes."

Dantès looked at him in admiration, but it was difficult to believe what he said. Faria sensed his doubt and said, "When you come to my cell I'll show you an entire book, the result of all the thoughts, research and study of my whole life. It's *A Treatise on the Possibility of a General Monarchy in Italy*."

"And you wrote it here?"

"Yes, on two shirts. I've invented a preparation which makes cloth as smooth and solid as parchment. And I make excellent pens from the cartilage of the heads of those enormous hake they sometimes serve us."

"What about ink?" asked Dantès. "How do you make that?"

"There was once a fireplace in my cell," said Faria. "It was closed up some time before I arrived, but it was apparently used for many years, because the inside of it is covered with a thick layer of soot. I dissolve some of that soot in some of the wine they give me every Sunday and it makes good ink. When I wish to call especial attention to a certain passage, I prick one of my fingers and write with my own blood."

"And when can I see all that?" asked Dantès.

"Whenever you like," replied Faria.

"Oh, right away!"

"Follow me, then," said the priest. He turned and disappeared into the underground passage. Dantès followed him.

After passing through the underground corridor, bending down but without difficulty, Dantès arrived at the opposite end, which opened into the priest's cell. The floor of the cell was paved; it was by lifting one the flagstones in the darkest corner of it that the priest had begun the laborious undertaking of which Dantès had seen the end.

As soon as he entered the cell, the young man examined it carefully, but at first sight its appearance presented nothing extraordinary. "I'm very anxious to see your treasures," he said to the priest.

Faria went over to the fireplace and removed the stone which had formerly been the hearthstone, revealing a rather deep cavity. Here were hidden the objects of which he had spoken to Dantès. "What would you like to see first?" he asked.

"Show me your work on the monarchy in Italy."

Faria pulled out three or four rolls of cloth composed of strips about four inches wide and eighteen inches long, all numbered and covered with writing. The writing was in Italian, which Dantès, being a Provençal, understood perfectly.

"It's all here," said Faria. "It was only a week ago that I wrote *finis* at the bottom of the seventy-eighth strip. Two of my shirts and all my handkerchiefs went into it. If I ever regain my freedom and if there's a publisher in Italy with the courage to print it, my reputation is made."

He showed Dantès the pens he had made. The young man looked around for the instrument with which he had been able to cut them so precisely. "You're wondering where the knife is, aren't you?" said Faria. "Here it is. It's my masterpiece, made from an old iron candlestick." It was as sharp as a razor. "And I've made myself a lamp so that I can carry on my work at night," continued Faria.

"How did you make it?"

"I separate the fat from the meat they bring me, I melt it and it gives me a sort of thick oil." He showed Dantès his lamp.

"But what do you do for matches?" asked Dantès.

"I pretended to have a skin disease, I asked for some sulphur and they gave it to me."

Dantès set the objects down on the table and bowed his head, overwhelmed by the power and perseverance of the priest's mind.

"That's not all," said Faria. "It wouldn't be wise to keep all my treasures in one hiding-place. Let's close this one." They put the stone back in place. The priest sprinkled dust over it and smoothed it out with his foot, then went over to his bed and pulled it back. Behind it, covered by a perfectly fitting stone, was a hole in which there was a rope ladder twenty-five to thirty feet long. Dantès examined it and found it to be amazingly strong. "How did you get the rope for this wonderful piece of work?" he asked.

"First from several shirts that I had, then from unraveling my sheets during the three years I was imprisoned in Fenestrella. I managed to take the thread with me when I was transferred to the Château d'If and I continued working on the ladder here."

"But didn't your jailers notice that your sheets had no hems?"

"I sewed them up again with this needle." He showed Dantès a fish bone, long, sharp and still threaded. "At first I thought of removing the bars and escaping through the window," he went on. "As you can see, this window is a little wider than the one in your cell, and I would have widened it a little more when I was ready to escape. But this window opens onto an inside courtyard, so I finally abandoned the plan as too risky. But I've kept the rope ladder in case some unexpected opportunity should present itself."

As he seemed to be examining the ladder, Dantès was thinking of something else. An idea had just entered his mind: this man, so intelligent, so ingenious, so profound, might be able to see clearly into the dark mystery of his own misfortune, which he himself had never been able to fathom.

"What are you thinking about?" asked Faria, smiling.

"I was thinking that you've told me about your life but that you know nothing about mine."

"Your life, young man, has been too short to contain anything of great importance."

"It contains an immense misfortune, at least," said Dantès, "a misfortune which I didn't deserve, and I wish I could blame men for it instead of blaspheming against God as I've sometimes done."

"Tell me your story, then," said the priest, closing his hiding-place and pushing his bed back in place.

Dantès told him what he called the story of his life, which was limited to a voyage to India and two or three voyages to the Near East. Finally he came to his last voyage and told of the death of Captain Leclère, the package the latter gave him to deliver to the Isle of Elba, the letter which the marshal there gave him to deliver to Monsieur Noirtier in Paris, then his arrival in Marseilles, his visit to his father, his love for Mercédès, the betrothal feast, his arrest, his questioning, his temporary imprisonment in the Palace of Justice, and finally his transfer to the Château d'If. From then on Dantès knew nothing more, not even how long he had been a prisoner.

When he had finished, Faria remained silent, lost in thought. After a time he said, "There is a maxim of jurisprudence which says, 'If you wish to discover the guilty person, first find out to whom the crime might be useful.' To whom might your disappearance be useful?"

"To no one!" cried Dantès. "I wasn't important enough."

"Don't say that; everything is relative. You were about to be made captain of the *Pharaon*, weren't you?"

"Yes."

"And you were about to marry a beautiful young girl?"

"Yes."

"Now, first of all, was it to anyone's interest that you should not become captain of the *Pharaon?*"

"No, the crew all liked me. In fact, if they'd been able to elect their own captain I'm sure they'd have elected me. There was only one man on board who had any reason to dislike me: I once had a quarrel with him and proposed to settle it by a duel, which he refused to do."

"Aha! What was that man's name?"

"Danglars. He was the purser."

"If you had become captain, would you have kept him on the ship?"

"Not if I'd had the choice; I thought I'd noticed some inaccuracies in his accounts."

"Good. Now, was anyone present during your last conversation with Captain Leclère?"

"No, we were alone."

"Could anyone have overheard you?"

"I suppose so; the door was open. In fact . . . Wait a minute . . . Yes! Danglars passed by just as Captain Leclère gave me the package."

"Good," said the priest. "We're on the right track. Did you take anyone ashore with you when you landed at the Isle of Elba?"

"No one."

"What did you do with the letter you received there?"

"I put it into my portfolio."

"Did you have your portfolio with you?"

"No, it was on the ship. I didn't put the letter into the portfolio until I was back on board."

"What did you do with it between the time you left the island and the time you put it into the portfolio?"

"I carried it in my hand."

"Therefore, when you came back on board, everyone could see that you were carrying a letter, is that right?"

"Yes."

"Including Danglars?"

"Yes."

"Now," said Faria, "listen to me and try to remember as clearly as you can. Can you tell me how the denunciation was worded?"

"Oh, yes! I read it three times, and every word is engraved in my memory." And he repeated the anonymous letter word for word.

The priest shrugged his shoulders. "It's as clear as daylight," he said. "You must have a very innocent heart not to have guessed it immediately. What kind of handwriting did Danglars have?"

"He wrote a good, round hand."

"How was the anonymous letter written?"

"With a backward slant."

Faria smiled and said, "The handwriting was disguised, wasn't it?"

"It was too bold for that."

"Wait," said Faria. He took one of his pens and wrote a few lines with his left hand on a piece of his specially prepared cloth. Dantès shrank back and looked at him almost in terror. "It's amazing," he exclaimed, "how much that other writing looked like this."

"That means the denunciation was written with the left hand. I've observed that almost all handwritings done with the left hand are similar. Now let's proceed to the second question: was it to anyone's interest that you should not marry Mercédès?"

"Yes! There was a young man who loved her, a Catalan named Fernand."

"Do you think he was capable of writing the letter?"

"No, although he was quite capable of stabbing me. Besides, he didn't know any of the things that were in the letter. I didn't tell anyone about it, not even Mercédès."

"Did Fernand know Danglars?"

"No . . . Yes! I remember now: I saw them sitting together in the arbor of a tavern two days before my marriage was to take place. Danglars was friendly and mocking, Fernand was pale and agitated. They were with a tailor named Caderousse whom I knew very well, but he was dead drunk."

"What we've deduced about your two friends so far has been child's play," said Faria, "but now I want you to give me some very precise details."

"Question me, then, for you seem to see my life more clearly than I do myself."

"Who examined you after your arrest?"

"The deputy public prosecutor."

"How did he treat you?"

"Very kindly."

"Did you tell him everything?"

"Yes."

"Did his attitude change at any time during the examination?"

"Yes: when he read the letter I received on the Isle of Elba he seemed to be greatly upset by my misfortune."

"Are you sure it was your misfortune that upset him?"

"Well, he gave me one great proof of his sympathy: he burned the letter before my eyes and said, 'That was the only evidence against you and, as you see, I've destroyed it.'"

"That action was too sublime to be natural."

"Do you think so?"

"I'm sure of it. To whom was the letter addressed."

"To Monsieur Noirtier, 13 Rue Coq-Héron, Paris."

"Do you think it's possible that the deputy may have had some reason for wanting that letter to disappear?"

"Perhaps; he made me promise two or three times, in my own interest, he said, not to speak about the letter to anyone, and he made me swear never to utter the name of the man to whom it was addressed."

"Noirtier . . . Noirtier . . ." repeated Faria thoughtfully.

"I once knew a Noirtier at the court of the Queen of Etruria, a Noirtier who had been a Girondin during the revolution. . . . What was the name of the deputy who questioned you?"

"Villefort."

Faria burst out laughing. "Poor young man!" he exclaimed. "That deputy was kind to you?"

"Yes."

"He burned the letter before your eyes and made you swear never to utter the name of Noirtier?"

"Yes."

"Do you know who Monsieur Noirtier was? He was the deputy's father."

"His father! His father!" cried Dantès, standing up and clutching his head between his hands as though to prevent it from bursting.

"Yes, his father, whose name is Noirtier de Villefort."

A dazzling light seemed to flash through Dantès brain and things which had until then remained dark and obscure now became crystal-clear to him. Villefort's change of attitude during the examination, the letter he had destroyed, the oath he had demanded, his almost supplicating voice, which, instead of threatening, seemed to be imploring—all this came back to Dantès' memory at once. He uttered a cry and reeled like a drunken man for a moment, then he rushed into the passage leading back to his own cell, crying out as he left, "Oh! I must be alone to think over all this!"

Back in his cell, he fell onto his bed, where the jailer found him that evening, his eyes staring into space, his features drawn, motionless and mute as a statue.

During those hours of meditation, which flowed by like seconds, he formed a terrible resolution and swore a fearful oath.

At length a voice roused him from his reverie. It was Faria inviting him to have supper with him. Dantès followed him. The stiff, determined expression of his face indicated that he had taken a resolution. Faria looked at him steadfastly and said, "I regret having helped you clarify your past and having told you what I did."

"Why?"

"Because I've instilled in your heart a feeling that wasn't there before: vengeance."

Dantès smiled. "Let's talk about something else," he said. The priest looked at him for a moment longer and shook his head sadly; then, as Dantès had requested, he began to talk about something else.

The old prisoner was one of those men whose conversation

contains a vast amount of information and continuously holds the listener's interest, but it was not at all self-centered; the unfortunate man never spoke of his own misfortune. Dantès listened to each word with admiration. "You must teach me a little of what you know," he said after a time, "even if only in order not to be bored with me. It seems to me now that you must prefer solitude to the company of a man as uneducated and limited as I am."

"Alas, my boy," said Faria, smiling, "human knowledge is quite limited. When you've learned mathematics, physics, history and the three or four living languages I speak, you'll know everything I do. It won't take more than two years to teach you all that."

"Two years!" exclaimed Dantès. "Do you think I can learn all those things in two years?"

"You won't learn to use all of them in that time, but you will learn their principles."

That same evening the two prisoners drew up a plan for Dantès' education and began to carry it out the next day. Dantès had a prodigious memory and a quick, keen intelligence. His mathematical turn of mind gave him a facility for all kinds of calculation, while the poetic strain which is in every sailor breathed life into demonstrations reduced to numbers and lines. He already knew Italian and a little modern Greek, which he had picked up on his voyages to the East. With the aid of these two languages, he soon understood the structure of all the others. Within six months he was beginning to speak Spanish, English and German. The days passed swiftly, but each one was so instructive that at the end of a year he was a different man.

As for Faria, Dantès noticed that, despite the distraction which his presence afforded him, he grew gloomier day by day. His mind seemed to be occupied with a single, constant thought. He would fall into a deep reverie, sigh involuntarily, stand up suddenly and begin pacing up and down his cell. One day he stopped short in the midst of his pacing and cried out, "Oh, if only there were no sentry!"

"Have you found a way to escape?" asked Dantès eagerly.

"Yes, if the sentry were blind and deaf."

"He'll be blind and deaf," said the young man in a tone of resolution which frightened the priest.

"No!" cried Faria. "I'll have no bloodshed!"

Dantès wanted to discuss the subject further, but Faria shook his head and refused to say anything more.

Three more months went by.

"Are you strong?" asked Faria one day.

Without answering, Dantès picked up the chisel, bent it double and then straightened it out again.

"Will you agree not to kill the sentry except as a last resource?"

"Yes, I swear."

"Then we can carry out our plan."

"How long will it take?"

"At least a year. Here's my plan." Faria showed Dantès a drawing he had made. It was a plan of their two cells and the passage joining them. From the middle of this passage they would excavate a tunnel which would lead them under the gallery where the sentry paced back and forth. There they would loosen one of the flagstones with which the floor of the gallery was paved. This stone would give way under the weight of the soldier, who would fall into the excavation below. Dantès would seize him, bind and gag him, and then the two prisoners would go through one of the windows of the gallery, climb down the wall with the aid of their rope ladder and escape.

Dantès clapped his hands and his eyes sparkled with joy. The plan was so simple that it was bound to succeed. He and Faria went to work that very day.

For over a year they worked, during which time Faria continued to educate Dantès as the work went on. After fifteen months the excavation was finished and they could hear the sentry walking back and forth above them. Now all they had to do was to wait for a dark, moonless night. They prevented the flagstone from giving way prematurely by propping it up with a small wooden beam which they had found in the foundations. Dantès had just finished putting it in place when he suddenly heard Faria, who had remained behind in Dantès' cell, cry out in pain. He hurried back and found the priest in the middle of the floor. He was pale, his fists were clenched and his forehead was streaming with perspiration.

"Oh, my God!" cried Dantès. "What's the matter?"

"I'm lost," said Faria. "Listen to me: a terrible illness, perhaps fatal, is about to seize me; I can feel it coming on. I had an attack of it the year before I was imprisoned. There's only one remedy for this illness. Run to my cell and lift up the foot of the bed, which is hollow. Inside it you'll find a small bottle half full of a red liquid. Bring it to me—— No, no, the jailer might see me here. Help me get back to my cell while I still have the strength."

Without losing his head, Dantès carefully led Faria through the underground passage and, when they had reached Faria's cell, laid him down on his bed.

"Thank you," said the priest, shivering in every limb as

though he had just come out of ice-cold water. "The attack is coming. I'm going to have a cataleptic fit. I may not make a movement or utter a sound, but on the other hand I may foam at the mouth, stiffen convulsively and shriek. If I do, try not to let them hear me, because they'd put me into another cell and we'd be separated forever. When you see me motionless, cold and apparently dead, then, and only then, pry apart my teeth with the knife and pour eight to ten drops of this liquid into my mouth. Perhaps it will revive me."

"Perhaps?" exclaimed Dantès in anguish.

"Help! Help!" cried Faria. "I'm— I'm dy——"

The attack was so sudden and so violent that he was unable to finish the word. His eyes dilated, his mouth became twisted, his cheeks turned purple and he writhed, foamed and shrieked. As Faria himself had instructed him to do, Dantès smothered his cries under the blanket. This phase of the attack lasted for two hours, then he stiffened in one last convulsion and turned as cold, as pale and as inert as marble. Dantès took the knife, carefully pried Faria's clenched teeth apart with it, counted out ten drops of the red liquid and waited.

An hour went by and still Faria did not make the slightest movement. Dantès stared at him, clutching his head between his hands. Finally a faint touch of color appeared in his cheeks, his eyes, which had remained open and staring, took on an expression of life, a weak sigh escaped from his lips and he made a movement.

"Saved! Saved!" cried Dantès.

Faria could not yet speak, but he stretched out his hand toward the door with visible anxiety. Dantès listened and heard the jailer's footsteps approaching. He jumped up, rushed over to the entrance of the passage, plunged into it, replaced the stone above his head and returned to his own cell. The door opened a moment later and the jailer found the prisoner sitting on his bed as usual. As soon as his footsteps had died away in the corridor, Dantès, without thinking of eating, hurried back to Faria's cell.

The priest had regained consciousness, but he was still lying on his bed, helpless and inert. "I didn't think I'd see you again," he said.

"Why not?" asked Dantès. "Did you think you were going to die?"

"No, but everything is ready for your escape and I expected you to leave."

Dantès flushed with indignation. "Without you!" he cried. "Did you think I was capable of that?"

"I see now that I was mistaken. Oh, I'm so weak, so help-less!"

"Your strength will come back," said Dantès, sitting down on the bed beside Faria and taking his hands.

Faria shook his head. "The last time," he said, "the attack lasted for half an hour, after which I was hungry and got up unaided. This time, I'm unable to move either my right leg or right arm. The third attack will either kill me or leave me completely paralyzed."

"No, no, don't worry, you won't die. If you have a third attack, you'll be free by then, and we'll save you the same way we saved you this time, better than this time, in fact, because you'll have the best medical care obtainable."

"My friend," said the old man, "don't deceive yourself. The attack I've just undergone has condemned me to lifetime im-prisonment. I'll never be able to swim again. This arm is para-lyzed, not just for the moment, but forever. Believe me, I've been reflecting on this illness ever since I had my first attack of it. I was expecting it, for it runs in my family. My father died from the third attack of it, and so did my grandfather. The physician who gave me this medicine, and he was none other than the famous Cabanis, predicted the same fate for me."

"He was mistaken!" cried Dantès. "And as for your paraly-sis, that doesn't bother me at all. I'll swim with you on my shoulders."

"My boy," said Faria, "you're a sailor and a good swimmer, so I'm sure you know that a man weighted down with such a burden would be unable to swim more than fifty strokes. No, I'll stay here until the hour of my deliverance, which can now be nothing except the hour of my death. As for you, leave, escape! You're young, lithe and strong. Don't worry about me."

"Very well, then," said Dantès, "I'll stay too." He stood up, solemnly stretched out his hand over the old man and said, "I swear by the blood of Christ that I will never leave you while you are still alive!"

Faria looked at the noble-hearted, straightforward young man and read the sincerity of his oath in his face, which was animated by an expression of the purest devotion.

"So be it," said the old man. "I accept. Thank you." Then, taking his hand, he said, "Perhaps you'll be rewarded some day for your disinterested devotion, but now, since I cannot and you will not leave, we must fill in the tunnel under the gallery. The sentry may notice a hollow sound when he walks over it, which would lead to our discovery and separation. Go do it now. Take all night if necessary, and don't come back here until tomorrow morning, after the jailer's visit. I'll have something important to tell you then."

Dantès took Faria's hand, then left his friend with obedience and respect.

Chapter 11

When Dantès entered Faria's cell the next morning he found him sitting calmly with a piece of paper in his left hand, the only hand which he could now use. He showed Dantès the paper without a word.

"What's that?"

"Look at it closely," said the priest, smiling.

"I'm looking at it as closely as I can, and I see nothing except a half-burned piece of paper with Gothic letters written on it in some sort of strange ink."

"This piece of paper, my friend," said Faria, "is my treasure, half of which belongs to you from this day on."

Dantès broke into a cold sweat. In all the time he had known Faria, he had avoided speaking of the famous treasure which caused him to be considered mad by everyone else in the prison.

Faria smiled and said, "I know what you're thinking from the way you shudder. But don't worry, I'm not mad. This treasure really exists, and if Fate allows me to possess it, you will possess it too. No one has ever been willing to listen to me because they all thought I was mad. But you know I'm not, so listen to me and then decide whether or not to believe me."

"My friend," said Dantès, "your attack has tired you. Wouldn't you like to rest a little now? I'll listen to your story tomorrow, but today all I want to do is take care of you. Besides," he added, smiling, "a treasure isn't a very pressing matter for us right now, is it?"

"Very pressing!" exclaimed the old man. "How do we know I won't be seized with the third attack tomorrow? I see you don't believe me. Since you need proof, read this paper, which I've never shown to anyone else."

"Tomorrow, my friend," said Dantès, reluctant to encourage the old man's madness.

"We'll wait till tomorrow to talk about it, but read this paper now."

"Quiet!" exclaimed Dantès. "Footsteps! Someone's coming —I must leave. Good-bye." Then, happy to escape listening to a story which would only have convinced him more firmly

of his friend's derangement, he slipped into the underground
passage with the speed and agility of a serpent.

He remained in his own cell the rest of the day, trying in
this way to postpone the terrible moment when he would be
forced to admit to himself that Faria was mad. But after the
jailer's visit, Faria, seeing that Dantès had still not returned,
tried to come to him instead. Dantès shuddered as he heard
the old man painfully dragging himself through the passage
with his paralyzed arm and leg. He had to help him, for he
would never have been able to crawl up through the narrow
opening alone.

"Here I am, obstinately and mercilessly pursuing you," said
Faria with a benevolent smile. "You thought you could escape
from my generosity, but you can't. Listen to me."

Dantès realized that he had no choice. He invited Faria
to sit down on his bed, then placed himself before him on
the stool.

"As you know," began Faria, "I was once the secretary
and close friend of Cardinal Spada, the last prince of that
name. It is to that worthy lord that I owe all the happiness I
have known in this world. He was not rich, although the
wealth of his family was proverbial; I have often heard the
expression, 'rich as a Spada.' His palace was my paradise. I
educated his nephews, who eventually died, and when he was
alone in the world I tried to repay him for all he had done
for me by absolute devotion to his every wish.

"The cardinal's house soon held no secrets for me. I often
saw him carefully examining old books and eagerly searching through dusty family manuscripts. One day I protested
to him about the whole nights he spent occupied with this
useless work, and the exhaustion and dejection which always
followed them. He smiled bitterly and opened a book on the
history of the city of Rome. There, in the twentieth chapter
of the life of Pope Alexander VI, I saw the following lines,
which I have never forgotten:

" 'The great wars of Romagna were ended. After finishing
his conquest, Caesar Borgia needed enough money to buy all
of Italy. The pope also needed money to rid himself of Louis
XII of France, who was still formidable despite his recent
reverses. It was therefore necessary to make some profitable
speculation, which was becoming more and more difficult in
the exhausted and impoverished Italy of those days.

" 'His Holiness had an idea: he decided to create two new
cardinals. By choosing two of the greatest and richest men
in Rome, he could make the undertaking extremely profitable.
First, he could sell the positions and titles which these two
cardinals already held; second, he could count on the two new

cardinals to pay him a high price for the honor he
bestow on them. There was a third part to the speculat
which will appear later.

" 'The pope and Caesar Borgia found the future cardinals in
Giovanni Rospigliosi, who alone held four of the highest offices
in the Holy See, and Caesar Spada, one of the richest and
noblest men in Rome. Caesar Borgia soon found purchasers
for the offices they were about to leave vacant. The result
was that Rospigliosi and Spada paid to become cardinals, while
eight other men paid to become what these two had been before. Eight hundred thousand crowns passed into the coffers
of the speculators.

" 'Let us now consider the third part of the speculation.
When the pope had made Rospigliosi and Spada into cardinals
and was sure that they had gathered their fortunes together in
order to pay their very real debt of gratitude and establish
themselves in Rome, he and Caesar Borgia invited them to
dinner. This gave rise to a dispute between the Holy Father
and his son. Caesar was of the opinion that they ought to use
one of the devices which were always at the disposal of his
intimate friends. First there was the famous key with which
certain persons were asked to open a certain cupboard. This
key had a small iron point, due to the negligence of its maker.
The lock of the cupboard was difficult to open, and when the
person put pressure on the key, he would prick himself with
the point and die the next day. Then there was the ring with
the lion's head, which Caesar put on his finger when he shook
hands with certain persons. The lion bit into the skin of the
chosen hand, and the bite was fatal within twenty-four hours.

" 'Caesar therefore proposed to his father either that he
send the two cardinals to open the cupboard or that he give
them each a cordial handshake, but Alexander VI replied,
"Let's not begrudge these worthy cardinals the cost of a
dinner; something tells me we'll get our money back. Besides,
you're forgetting that indigestion makes itself felt immediately,
while the results of a prick or a bite don't occur until a day
or two later."

" 'Caesar gave in to this reasoning and the two cardinals
were invited to dinner. The table was prepared in a vineyard
which the pope owned near San Pietro in Vincoli, a charming
residence of which the cardinals had often heard.

" 'Rospigliosi, still overwhelmed by his new office, prepared
his stomach and his most pleasing smile. Spada, a prudent
man who loved no one but his nephew, a young captain with a
promising career, took pen and paper and made out his will.
Next he sent word to his nephew to wait for him near the
vineyard, but his messenger was unable to find the young man.

ited with these papal invitations. Since
ought its civilizing influence to Rome, it
enturion sent by some tyrant to tell you,
u to die"; rather, it was a legate with a
ent by the pope to tell you, "His Holiness
with him."

" 'The pope was waiting for Spada when he arrived at the vineyard. The first face which struck his eyes was that of his nephew, who was the object of much friendly attention from Caesar Borgia. Spada turned pale; Caesar shot him a glance full of irony, indicating that he had foreseen everything, that the trap had been well prepared.

" 'The dinner began. Spada was able only to ask his nephew, "Did you receive my message?" The nephew answered that he had not and understood the meaning of the question perfectly, but it was too late, for he had just drunk a glass of excellent wine which the pope's butler had set aside for him. Spada was liberally supplied from another bottle. An hour later, a physician declared them both dead from eating poison mushrooms. Spada died on the threshold of the vineyard; his nephew expired before his own door while making a sign which his wife did not understand.

" 'Caesar and the pope hastened to seize Spada's will on the pretext of searching through his papers. But the will consisted only of a piece of paper on which Spada had written these words: "To my beloved nephew I bequeath my coffers and my books, including my gold-cornered breviary, desiring that he keep this in memory of his affectionate uncle." The heirs searched everywhere, admired the breviary, carried off the furniture and were amazed that a man as rich as Spada should turn out to be such a worthless uncle: there was no treasure anywhere. Caesar and his father searched, rummaged and investigated, but they found nothing. Spada had left only two palaces and a vineyard, which remained in the family, being unworthy of the rapacity of the pope and his son.

" 'The months and the years went by. After the death of the pope and his son, the Spada family was generally expected to resume the princely mode of life they had enjoyed before, but this was not the case. They continued to live in doubtful comfort and the whole somber affair remained shrouded in mystery. The public rumor was that Caesar, shrewder than his father, had taken both fortunes away from the pope. I say "both" because Cardinal Rospigliosi, having taken no precautions, was completely despoiled.'

"So far," said Faria, smiling, "the story doesn't seem too senseless, does it?"

"Not at all!" said Dantès. "In fact, I find it full of interest. Please go on."

"I continue: 'The Spada family gradually accustomed themselves to this obscurity. Some of the descendants were soldiers, others were diplomats, churchmen or bankers; some grew rich, others lost what little fortune remained to them.'

"Now," said Faria, "I come to the last of the family, the Count Spada whose secretary I was. The famous breviary had remained in the family and it was Count Spada who possessed it. It had been handed down from father to son, for the strange clause in the only will that was ever found had made it a veritable relic, which the family kept with almost superstitious veneration.

"I was almost sure that the treasure had profited neither the Borgias nor the Spadas, that it still remained without an owner, like those treasures in Arabian tales which sleep in the bowels of the earth guarded by some genie. I searched everywhere, and countless times I·added up the income and the expenditures of the family for the past three hundred years, but all in vain: I remained ignorant and Count Spada remained poor.

"When my patron died, he bequeathed me his library of five thousand volumes, including the famous breviary, and a thousand crowns, on condition that I have annual masses said for him and write a history of his family, which I did.

"One day in 1807, a month before my arrest and two weeks after the death of Count Spada, I was reading for the thousandth time the papers I was putting in order, for the palace had been sold to a stranger and I was about to leave Rome and settle in Florence. Tired by my assiduous study and made drowsy by a rather heavy lunch, I let my head drop between my hands and went to sleep. It was three o'clock in the afternoon.

"I awoke as the clock was striking six. I raised my head and found myself in darkness. I rang for someone to bring me a light, but no one came. I took a candle and began to search for a piece of paper, which I intended to light from the embers that were still flickering in the fireplace. I hesitated, however, fearing that in the darkness I might mistake some valuable document for a worthless piece of paper. Then I remembered that in the famous breviary, which was lying on the table beside me, I had seen an old piece of paper, yellowed with age, which had apparently been put there as a bookmark and which had come down through the centuries, maintained in its place by the family's veneration. I groped for it in the darkness, found it, twisted it and lit one end of it.

"But as the flames rose I saw yellow letters appear on the

paper, as if by magic. I was seized with a sort of terror; I
crumpled the paper in my hand, smothered the flames. Then
I lit the candle directly from the embers and, with indescribable emotion, smoothed out the crumpled paper. I soon real-
izèd that the letters had been written in invisible ink which
became apparent only when placed in contact with heat. A
little more than a third of the paper had been consumed by
the flames. It was the same paper I showed you this morning.
Read it now; when you've finished, I'll supply the missing
words for you."

Faria handed the paper to Dantès, who, this time, eagerly
read the following words:

        This 25th day of April, 1498, ha
    to dinner by His Holiness Alexander
    not content with having made me pay f
    hat, he may wish to have my inheri
    therefore reserve for me the
    and Bentivoglio, who were poisoned, I de
    Guido Spada, my sole heir, that I have bu
    which he has visited with me, na
    little island of Monte Cristo, ev
    ingots, gold, money and
    existence of this treasure, an
    lifting the twentieth rock in a st
    small creek to the east. Two ope
    these caves; the treasure is in the fu
    second one. I bequeath this enti
    as my sole heir.
            April 25, 1498   CA

"Now," said Faria, "read this." He handed Dantès a second
sheet of paper on which more fragments of lines were written.
Dantès took it and read:

                                    ving been invited
                                VI, and fearing that,
                                or my cardinal's
                                tance as well and
                            fate of Cardinals Crapara
                                clare to my nephew,
                                    ried in a place
                            mely, in the caves of the
                                erything I possess in
                    jewels, that I alone know of the
                            d that he will find it by

raight line from the
nings have been made in
rthest corner of the
re treasure to my nephew,
ESAR † SPADA

"Now put the two fragments together and judge for yourself," said Faria when Dantès had finished reading. Dantès
obeyed; the two joined fragments produced the following:

This 25th day of April, 1498, having been invited
to dinner by His Holiness Alexander VI, and fearing that,
not content with having made me pay for my cardinal's
hat, he may wish to have my inheritance as well and
therefore reserve for me the fate of Cardinals Crapara
and Bentivoglio, who were poisoned, I declare to my nephew,
Guido Spada, my sole heir, that I have buried in a place
which he has visited with me, namely, in the caves of the
little island of Monte Cristo, everything I possess in
ingots, gold, money and jewels, that I alone know of the
existence of this treasure, and that he will find it by
lifting the twentieth rock in a straight line from the
small creek to the east. Two openings have been made in
these caves; the treasure is in the furthest corner of the
second one. I bequeath this entire treasure to my nephew,
as my sole heir.
April 25, 1498   CAESAR † SPADA

"Well, now do you understand?" asked Faria.
"This is the cardinal's declaration, and his real will?" said
Dantès, still incredulous.
"Yes! Yes!"
"Who reconstructed it this way?"
"I did. With the aid of the unburned half, I worked out the
rest by measuring the length of the lines by that of the paper,
then fathoming the meaning of the missing words by the
meaning of those I had before my eyes."
"And what did you do when you had solved the mystery?"
"I left Rome immediately, taking with me the beginning of
my great work on the unity of the Kingdom of Italy. But the
imperial police, which, in those days, was strongly opposed to
the unification of Italy, had been watching me for a long time.
My sudden departure aroused their suspicion and I was arrested just as I was about to embark at Piombino.
"Now, my friend," continued Faria, looking at Dantès with
an almost paterial expression, "you know as much about it

as I do. If we should escape together, half the treasure is
yours; if I die here and you escape alone, it all belongs to
you."

"But," asked Dantès hesitantly, "doesn't the treasure have
a more legitimate owner than you somewhere in the world?"

"No, you can put your mind at ease on that score. The
family has died out completely. Besides, the last Count Spada
made me his heir: in bequeathing me that symbolic breviary,
he bequeathed me everything it contained. No, if we ever get
our hands on that fortune we can use it without remorse."

Dantès thought he must be dreaming; he alternated between
incredulity and joy.

"I kept the secret from you for such a long time," went on
Faria, "first because I wanted to make sure of you, and then
because I wanted to surprise you."

"That treasure belongs to you, my friend," said Dantès,
"and I have no right to it: I'm not even related to you."

"You're my son!" cried the old man. "You're the child of
my captivity. My profession condemned me to celibacy, but
God sent you to me to console both the man who could not
be a father and the prisoner who could not be free."

Faria held out his hand to the young man, who threw his
arms around his neck and wept.

Chapter 12

Now that the treasure, which had for so long been the
object of Faria's meditations, could assure the future happiness
of the young man he truly loved as a son, its value had
doubled in his eyes. Every day he spoke of the immensity of
the treasure, explaining to Dantès all the good a man could
do for his friends in our modern times with such a fortune.
At those moments Dantès' face would darken, for he remembered the oath of vengeance he had sworn, and he thought
of how much harm a man could do to his enemies in our
modern times with such a fortune.

Faria did not know the Isle of Monte Cristo, but Dantès
did. He had often passed by that small island, located twenty-
five miles from Pianosa, between Corsica and the Isle of Elba,
and once he had landed there. It was, and still is, completely
deserted; it is a rock of almost conical form which seems to
have been thrust up from the bottom of the sea by some
volcanic cataclysm.

As Faria had predicted, his arm and leg remained paralyzed

and he lost almost all hope of ever reaching the treasure himself, but he continued to dream of an escape for his young companion. For fear the letter might be lost, he made Dantès learn it by heart, word for word.

Then one night Dantès awoke suddenly with the impression that someone had called him. He opened his eyes and tried to penetrate the darkness. His name, or rather a plaintive voice trying to articulate his name, reached his ears. He leaped out of bed and listened. No doubt of it, the voice was coming from Faria's cell.

"Good God!" murmured Dantès. "Could it be that . . . ?" He shoved back his bed, rushed into the underground passage and was soon at the opposite end of it; the flagstone was raised. By the flickering light of the lamp we have already described, he saw the old man, his face deathly white and contracted by the horrible symptoms which Dantès already knew and which had filled him with such terror the first time he saw them.

"Well, my friend," said Faria resignedly, "you understand, don't you? There's no need for me to explain anything to you. Think only of yourself from now on, of making your captivity bearable and your escape possible. You'll no longer have a half-dead body tied to you, paralyzing all your movements. God is doing something good for you at last, and it's high time for me to die."

Dantès could do nothing except clasp his hands and cry out, "Oh, my friend! My friend!" Then, regaining a little of his courage, he said, "I saved you once and I'll save you again!" He lifted the foot of the bed and took out the small bottle, which was still one-third full of the red liquid.

"There's no hope," said Faria, shaking his head, "but you may try if you wish. I'm growing cold, I feel the blood rushing to my brain, and that horrible trembling is beginning to shake my whole body. In five minutes the attack will begin in earnest; in a quarter of an hour there will be nothing left of me but a corpse."

"Oh!" cried Dantès, his heart breaking.

"Do as you did before, only this time don't wait so long. After you've poured twelve drops down my throat, if you see that I'm not regaining consciousness, pour the rest. Now carry me to my bed, I can't stand up any longer."

Dantès picked up the old man and laid him on his bed.

"And now, my friend," said Faria, "sole consolation of my wretched life, you whom heaven gave me a little late, but gave me nonetheless, at this moment when I am about to be separated from you forever, I wish you all the happiness and all the prosperity that you deserve. My son, I bless you."

Dantès dropped to his knees, leaning his head against the bed.

A violent shock interrupted the old man. "Farewell! Farewell!" he murmured, pressing Dantès' hand convulsively.

The attack was terrible. Twisted limbs, swollen eyelids, bloody foam, a motionless body—this was all that remained of the intelligent being who had been there only a moment before. When he believed it to be the right time, Dantès pried Faria's teeth apart with the knife and poured twelve drops of the liquid into his mouth. He waited for ten minutes, a quarter of an hour, half an hour; there was no sign of a movement. Trembling, his forehead streaming with cold sweat, he decided the time had come to try his last resource. He poured the rest of the liquid into Faria's mouth.

The medicine produced a galvanic effect. The old man shook violently in every limb, his eyes opened, frightening to behold, and he heaved a sign which sounded like a shriek. Then his trembling body gradually became rigid again. Finally the last murmur of his heart ceased, his face grew livid and the light faded entirely from his eyes, which remained open.

It was six o'clock in the morning. The first feeble rays of dawn invaded the cell, casting weird reflections over the face of the corpse and giving it an appearance of life from time to time. As long as the struggle between day and night lasted, Dantès was still able to doubt, but as soon as day won out he realized fully that he was alone with a corpse. An overwhelming terror seized him; he no longer dared press that hand hanging over the edge of the bed, nor look at those vacant, staring eyes which he had vainly tried several times to close, but which had always opened again. He blew out the lamp, hid it carefully and fled from the cell, replacing the stone behind him as well as he could.

He left none too soon, for the jailer was coming. This time he began his visit with Dantès' cell. Nothing indicated that he was aware of what had happened. He went out. Burning with impatience to know what would happen in the cell of his unfortunate friend, Dantès crawled back into the underground passage in time to hear the jailer calling for aid. Other jailers soon arrived, then came the heavy, measured footsteps of soldiers. Behind them came the governor.

Dantès heard the bed creaking as they tried to rouse the dead man. The governor ordered them to throw water in his face, then, seeing that this had no effect, he sent for the doctor. The governor left the cell and several words of compassion, mingled with crude jokes and laughter, reached Dantès' ears.

"Well," said one voice, "the old lunatic's gone off to find his treasure. *Bon voyage!*"

"With all his millions he still didn't have enough to pay for his shroud," said another.

"Oh, the shrouds of the Château d'If don't cost much."

"Since he's a priest, maybe they'll go to a little extra expense for him."

"That's right: he'll have the honor of the sack."

Dantès listened without losing a word, but he did not understand much of what was being said. Soon the voices died away and it seemed to him that everyone had left the cell. He was nevertheless afraid to go back in: a jailer might have been left behind to guard the dead man.

After an hour or so the silence was broken by a faint noise which gradually grew louder. It was the governor coming back, followed by the doctor and several officials.

There was a moment of silence; the doctor was evidently examining the body. He declared the prisoner dead and diagnosed the cause of death.

"Not that I doubt your competence, doctor," said the governor, "but we can't be satisfied with a mere examination in such cases. I just ask you to carry out the formalities prescribed by law."

"Very well, then," said the doctor, "heat up the irons."

This order made Dantès shudder. He heard hurried footsteps and the sound of a door being opened. Several moments later a jailer came back into the cell. Then the thick, nauseating odor of burning flesh penetrated the wall behind which Dantès was listening in horror. Beads of sweat burst out on his forehead and for a moment he thought he was going to faint.

"You see: he's really dead," said the doctor. "That burn on the heel is decisive. The poor madman is cured of his madness and delivered from his captivity."

Dantès heard a sound like the rustling of cloth. The bed creaked, there were heavy footsteps like those of a man lifting a burden and the bed creaked once again under the weight which had been placed back on it.

"Will there be a mass?" asked one of the officials.

"Impossible," replied the governor. "The chaplain asked me for a week's leave yesterday and he's already gone. If the poor priest hadn't been in such a hurry he'd have had his requiem."

"That's all right," remarked the doctor, with the impiety common to those of his profession; "God won't give the devil the pleasure of receiving a priest."

There was a burst of laughter. Meanwhile the body had been laid out.

"Tonight," said the governor.

"What time?" asked one of the jailers.

"At around ten or eleven o'clock, as usual."

"Shall we watch over the body?"

"What for? Just lock the door as though he were still alive."

The footsteps went away and the voices died down. Then a silence more mournful than that of solitude—the silence of death—invaded everything and chilled the depths of Dantès' heart. He slowly raised the stone with his head and cast a swift glance around the cell. It was empty. He entered.

Stretched out on the bed, faintly illuminated by the pale ray of daylight coming in through the window, he saw a sack of coarse cloth under whose ample folds he could discern the outlines of a long, stiff form. It was Faria's shroud, that shroud which, according to the jailers, cost so little. It was all over; Dantès was separted forever from his old friend. Faria, his helpful, kind companion, now existed only in his memory. He sat down on the edge of the frightful bed, plunged in deep and bitter melancholy.

Alone! He was alone again! The idea of suicide, which his friend's presence had driven away, now rose up again like a phantom beside his corpse. "If only I could die," he said, "I'd go where he's gone and I'd be with him again. But how can I die?" He thought for a moment, then said, smiling, "It's very easy: I'll stay here and attack the first man who comes in. I'll strangle him and they'll guillotine me."

But then he recoiled from the idea of such an infamous death and swiftly passed from despair to a burning thirst for life and freedom. "Die? Oh, no!" he cried out. "What would be the point of having lived and suffered so much if I were going to die now? No, I want to live, to fight on to the end. I want to win back the happiness that was taken away from me. I must punish my enemies before I die, and I may also have some friends to reward. But they'll forget me here, and the only way I'll ever leave this dungeon is like Faria."

As he spoke these words he sat stock-still, staring into space like a man suddenly struck by a terrifying idea. Then he stood up, put his hand to his forehead as though he were dizzy and murmured, "Who sent me this thought? Was it you, O God? Since only the dead leave here, I'll take the place of a corpse!"

Without giving himself time to reconsider his desperate resolution, he leaned over the hideous sack, slit it open with the knife which Faria had made, took out the corpse, carried it into his own cell, put it on his bed, wrapped around its head the rag which he himself always wore, pulled his blanket over it, kissed the cold forehead one last time, tried once again to close the rebellious eyes, which persisted in remaining open, and turned the head to the wall so that when the jailer brought in his evening meal he would think he was already asleep, as he often was. Then he went back into Faria's cell, took out the needle and thread, threw off his clothes so that the jailers would feel bare flesh under the sackcloth, slipped into the sack, placed himself in the same position as the corpse and sewed up the sack again from the inside. If the jailers had happened to come in at that moment they would have heard the beating of his heart.

His plan was all worked out: if the gravediggers discovered that they were carrying a living man instead of a corpse, he would quickly rip open the sack with his knife and take advantage of their terror to escape; if they tried to stop him, he would use the knife on them. If they carried him all the way to the cemetery and laid him in a grave, he would let himself be covered over, then, since it would be night, as soon as the gravediggers had turned their backs, he would force his way up through the soft earth and escape. He hoped the weight would not be too heavy for him to raise, otherwise he would be smothered to death. But even this possibility did not dismay him: at least everything would be finished.

Toward seven o'clock in the evening his anxiety began in earnest. He trembled in every limb and his heart felt as though it were being gripped in an icy vise. The hours passed without bringing the slightest movement in the prison; so far his ruse had not been discovered. Finally he heard footsteps on the stairs. The time had come. He summoned up all his courage, held his breath and tried to repress the pounding of his heart.

The door opened and a dim light reached his eyes. Through the cloth covering him he saw two shadows approach the bed. A third one stood in the doorway holding a lantern. The first two men took hold of the sack from both ends. Dantès made his body rigid.

"He's very heavy for such a skinny old man," said one.

"They say every year adds half a pound to the weight of a man's bones," said the other.

They carried him out on a stretcher and the funeral procession, led by the man with the lantern, went up the stairs. Suddenly Dantès felt the cold, fresh night air and the sharp wind from the sea. The sensation filled him with both joy and anxiety.

They carried him some twenty yards further, then stopped and laid the stretcher on the ground. Dantès heard one of the men walking away. "Where am I?" he wondered.

His first impulse was to try to escape, but fortunately he controlled himself. A few moments later he heard one of the men walk up to him and drop a heavy object on the ground. At the same time he felt a rope tied around his feet with painful tightness.

"Have you made the knot?" asked the man who had remained idle.

"Yes, and it's well made, I'll answer for that."

"All right, then, let's go."

The stretcher was raised again and the procession continued on its way. The sound of the waves breaking against the rocks on which the Château d'If is built reached Dantès more distinctly with every step.

"What miserable weather!" said one of the men. "I wouldn't like to be at sea tonight."

"Yes," said the other, "there's a good chance the priest may get his feet wet!" They both burst out laughing.

Dantès did not understand the joke, but his hair stood on end nevertheless.

"Here we are," said the first man after a while.

"No, further on, further on! You know the last one got smashed on the rocks and the next day the governor called us a couple of lazy rascals."

They went on a few more steps, then Dantès felt them pick him up by the head and feet and swing him back and forth.

"One! Two! Three!"

With the last word he felt himself flung into space. Fear clutched at his heart as he fell like a wounded bird, down, down, down. Finally, after what seemed an eternity, there was a tremendous splash and he plunged like an arrow into the icy sea. He uttered a scream which was immediately choked off as the water closed over his head. He was being swiftly dragged to the bottom by a cannon ball tied to his feet.

The sea is the cemetery of the Château d'If.

Chapter 13

Although he was stunned and almost suffocated, Dantès nevertheless had the presence of mind to hold his breath and rip open the sack with the knife which he still held in his right hand. But he was still being dragged downward by the cannon ball tied to his feet. He bent double and cut the rope just as he was about to suffocate. Then he kicked vigorously and rose to the surface of the sea. He paused only long enough to take a deep breath, then dived again to avoid being seen.

When he came up the second time, he was already fifty yards away from the spot where he had plunged into the sea.

Above his head he saw a black, stormy sky; before him lay the dark plain of the sea, whose waves were beginning to churn as though before the approach of a storm, while behind him, blacker than either the sky or the sea, the granite giant rose up like a threatening phantom. He decided to head for the Isle of Tiboulen, the nearest uninhabited island, about one league away. But how was he to find it in the thick darkness which surrounded him? Suddenly he saw the Planier lighthouse shining like a star. If he headed straight for this lighthouse, he would pass the Isle of Tiboulen on his left; by heading a little to the left, therefore, he ought to place the island in his path. He noticed with joy that his years of forced inaction had taken away none of his strength and agility and that he was still master of the element in which he had played so often as a boy.

An hour passed, during which Dantès continued to swim in the direction he had chosen. "Unless I'm mistaken," he thought, "I shouldn't be far from the Isle of Tiboulen now. But what if I'm mistaken?" He shuddered and tried to float for a while in order to rest himself, but the sea had become so rough that it was impossible. "Well, then," he said, "I'll go on to the end, till my arms are exhausted, till I'm seized with cramps, and then I'll sink to the bottom." He began to swim with the strength and drive of despair.

Suddenly it seemed to him that the sky, which was already dark, became still darker, and that a thick, heavy cloud was descending on him. At the same time he felt a sharp pain in his knee. His imagination instantly told him that he had been struck by a bullet and that he would soon hear the sound of the shot. But he heard no shot. He put out his hand and felt something solid; he drew up his other leg and felt land. He then saw what it was that he had taken to be a cloud: twenty yards ahead of him rose a mass of strangely shaped rocks which looked like an immense, petrified fire. It was the Isle of Tiboulen.

Dantès stood up, took a few steps forward, then murmured, "Thank God!" and lay down on the jagged rocks, which seemed softer to him than any bed he had ever known. In spite of the wind, the storm, and the rain which was beginning to fall, he went to sleep.

An hour later he was awakened by the roar of a tremendous clap of thunder. He took refuge beneath an overhanging rock just before the storm burst in all its fury. A flash of lightning which seemed to open the heavens to the very throne of God illuminated the space around him and, a quarter of a league away, he saw a small fishing boat appear, carried along by the wind and the waves. It vanished between two waves, then reappeared an instant later on the crest of another wave, approaching with frightful rapidity. Dantès cried out and looked around for something to wave to them and warn them they were approaching their doom, but they were well aware of it themselves. By the light of another flash of lightning he saw four men clinging to the masts and rigging, while a fifth clutched the tiller of the broken rudder. Then he heard a terrible crash, followed by agonized cries. A third flash of lightning showed him the little boat smashed against the rocks and, among the wreckage, heads with desperate faces and arms stretched up toward heaven. Then all was dark again. Dantès quickly climbed down the slippery rocks, at the risk of falling into the sea himself. He looked and listened, but he neither saw nor heard anything more: no more cries, no more human efforts; there was nothing left except the storm with its roaring winds and foaming waves.

Little by little, the wind died down. The big gray clouds rolled off westward and soon a long reddish streak appeared on the eastern horizon. Light suddenly touched the waves and turned their foamy crests into golden plumes. Daylight had come.

"In two or three hours," thought Dantès, "the jailer will enter my cell, find the corpse of my poor friend and give the alarm. They'll question the two men who threw me into the sea and who must have heard the cry I uttered. Boats filled with armed soldiers will begin searching the sea for me and the cannon will alert the coast not to give shelter to a naked, hungry fugitive. I'll be at the mercy of the first peasant who wants to earn twenty francs by turning me in. Oh, my God! My God! You know how much I've suffered! Help me now that I can no longer help myself!"

Just as he finished this fervent prayer, he saw on the horizon the lateen sail of a ship which his experienced eye recognized as a Genoese tartan coming from Marseilles. "Oh!" he cried, "to think that I could swim out to that ship in half an hour if I weren't afraid of being recognized as a fugitive and taken back to Marseilles! Those men are all smugglers and semi-pirates; they'd rather sell me than perform an unprofitable good deed. What story could I invent to deceive them? I have it: I'll say I'm one of the sailors from the boat that was smashed on the rocks last night! There won't be anyone to contradict me, because the crew all drowned." So saying, he looked toward the spot where the little vessel had perished. A few planks were still floating there and he saw with a start that the cap of one of the sailors had come to rest on the point of a rock.

Dantès dived into the sea, swam over to the cap, put it on his head, took hold of one of the planks and began kicking toward the spot where he estimated that the ship would pass.

When he was close enough, he made a supreme effort, lunged almost entirely out of the sea, waved his cap and uttered a loud cry. The ship turned toward him and he saw the crew make ready to lower a boat. Thinking he no longer needed the plank, he let go of it and began to swim vigorously toward the boat. But he was counting on a strength which he no longer had. His legs and arms began to stiffen, his movements became heavy and irregular, and his chest began to heave. The two rowers in the boat redoubled their efforts and one of them called out to him in Italian, "Courage!" Dantès thrashed desperately for a while, then sank below the surface. He felt himself being pulled up by the hair, then he fainted.

When he opened his eyes again he found himself lying on the deck of the tartan. One sailor was rubbing his limbs with a woolen blanket; another, the one who had called out "Courage!" to him, was holding a gourd to his mouth; while a third, the captain of the ship, was looking at him with that selfish pity which most men feel in the presence of a misfortune which they have escaped yesterday and which may strike them tomorrow.

"Who are you?" asked the captain in bad French.

"I'm a Maltese sailor," replied Dantès in equally bad Italian. "We were coming from Syracuse. A storm caught us off Cape Morgiou last night and smashed our ship against those rocks over there. I'm the only one who survived. When I saw you coming I held on to a piece of the wreckage and swam out to meet you, but I'd have drowned if one of your sailors hadn't grabbed me by the hair."

"That was me," said a sailor with a frank, open face. "It was time, too, because you were sinking."

"Yes, I was," said Dantès, holding out his hand to him. "Thank you, my friend."

"I almost hesitated to pull you out, though," said the sailor. "With your six-inch beard and your hair a foot long, you looked more like a bandit than an honest man."

Dantès abruptly recalled that he had cut neither his hair nor his beard the whole time he had been in prison. "Once when I was in danger," he said, "I made a vow to Our Lady of Piedigrotta not to cut my hair or my beard for ten years. The ten years are up today and I almost celebrated it by drowning."

"Now, what are we going to do with you?" asked the captain.

"Whatever you like. I'm a good sailor, so you can leave me at the first port you touch and I'm sure to find work on some merchant ship."

"Do you know the Mediterranean?"

"I've been sailing on it since I was a child. There are few harbors, even the most difficult, that I couldn't take a ship into and out of with my eyes closed."

"Well, then, captain," said Jacopo, the sailor who had saved Dantès' life, "why can't he stay with us?"

"Very well," said the captain to Dantès, "I'll take you on if you're not too unreasonable."

"Just pay me what you pay the others."

"All right," said the captain. "Now, Jacopo, do you have any extra clothes you can lend this man?"

"I have a pair of trousers and a shirt."

"That's all I need," said Dantès. Jacopo slid down a hatchway and came up an instant later with the two garments.

"Do you need anything else?" asked the captain.

"I'd like a piece of bread and another drink of that fine rum I tasted just now." Jacopo handed him the gourd and another sailor brought him a piece of bread.

Dantès asked if he could take over the helm. The helmsman, delighted to be relieved of his duties, looked at the captain, who motioned him to give up his place to his new shipmate. Dantès took over, keeping his eyes fixed on the coast of Marseilles.

"What day of the month is it?" he asked Jacopo, who had sat down beside him.

"The twenty-eighth of February."

"What year?"

"What do you mean? Don't you know what year it is?"

"I was so frightened last night," replied Dantès, laughing, "that I almost lost my mind, and my memory is still confused, so I'll ask you again, what year is it?"

"It's 1829," said Jacopo.

It had been fourteen years, to the day, since Dantès had been arrested. He was nineteen when he entered the Château d'If; he was now thirty-three. A sad smile passed over his lips as he wondered what had become of Mercédès during all that time when she must have believed him to be dead. Then his eyes flashed with hatred as he thought of the three men to whom he owed his long and cruel captivity, and he renewed the oath of vengeance against Danglars, Fernand and Villefort which he had already sworn in prison. And this oath was no longer a vain threat, for at that moment the fastest ship in the Mediterranean could not have overtaken the little tartan as she scudded along under full sail toward Leghorn.

Dantès had been on the *Jeune-Amélie,* the Genoese tartan, for less than a day when he realized that he was dealing with smugglers. He therefore had the advantage of knowing what the captain was without the captain's knowing what he was. He adhered rigidly to his original story, filling it out with all sorts of accurate details about Naples and Malta, which he knew as well as he did Marseilles, and even the shrewd Genoese captain accepted his story completely.

When they reached Leghorn, Dantès was eager to see whether he would recognize himself, for he had not seen his own face for fourteen years. As soon as they landed, he went to a barber to have his hair and beard cut. When the barber had finished, Dantès asked for a mirror and looked at himself.

He was now thirty-three years old, as we have said, and his fourteen years of prison had greatly altered his face. He had entered the Château d'If with the round, smiling face of a happy young man who has made a good beginning in life and who counts on the future to unfold itself as a natural deduction from the past. All that was now changed. His oval face had lengthened; his smiling lips had taken on the firm lines of resolution; his eyebrows had become arched beneath a single thoughtful wrinkle; his eyes wore a look of deep sadness, with occasional flashes of dark hatred; his skin, which had been away from the sunlight for so long, had grown pale; the deep learning he had acquired was reflected in his face by an expression of intelligent self-confidence. Furthermore, although he was naturally rather tall, he had acquired that stocky vigor of a body which constantly concentrates its strength within itself. Furthermore, his eyes, which had been so long in darkness and semi-darkness, had developed the faculty of distinguishing objects in the dark, like those of the hyena and the wolf.

Dantès smiled as he looked at himself. It was impossible that his best friend, if he still had any friends, would recognize him; he did not even recognize himself.

When he returned to the *Jeune-Amélie,* the captain renewed his offer to take him on as permanent member of the crew, but Dantès, who had other plans, would agree only to an engagement of three months.

Within a week after her arrival at Leghorn, the ship was filled with muslin, cotton, English gunpowder and tobacco on which the excise authorities had neglected to affix their seal. It was now a question of getting all this out of Leghorn free of duty and landing on the shore of Corsica, where certain speculators would take over the task of smuggling the goods into France.

They set sail, and Dantès once again found himself moving across that blue sea which he had seen so often in his dreams during his imprisonment.

When the captain came up on deck the next morning, he found Dantès leaning over the bulwarks and gazing, with a strange expression on his face, at a pile of granite rocks which shone pink in the rising sun: it was the Isle of Monte Cristo. The *Jeune-Amélie* passed it about three-quarters of a league to starboard. Fortunately, Dantès had learned to wait. He had waited fourteen years for his freedom; he could certainly wait six months or a year for his wealth. He repeated the cardinal's letter word for word in his mind.

Two and a half months went by, during which Dantès became as skillful a smuggler as he was a sailor. He had become acquainted with all the smugglers along the coast and learned all the masonic signs by which these semi-pirates recognized one another. He had passed his Isle of Monte Cristo at least twenty times, but without a single opportunity to land there.

He therefore decided that as soon as his engagement with the captain of the *Jeune-Amélie* was ended he would rent a small bark and go to the Isle of Monte Cristo on some pretext or other. He would be able to search for his treasure at leisure, but he would no doubt be spied upon by the men who took him there; this was simply a risk he would have to take. Try as he might, he could think of no way to get to the island without being taken there by someone else.

He was still grappling with this problem when one evening the captain, who had great confidence in him and was anxious to keep him in his service, took him to a tavern in the Via del Oglio which was a favorite meeting-place for the smugglers of Leghorn. On this particular evening an undertaking of great importance was being discussed. It concerned a ship laden with Turkish carpets, cashmere and cloth from the Levant. It was necessary to find some neutral ground where the exchange could be made, and then attempt to land the goods on the coast of France. The profit would be enormous if the undertaking succeeded: fifty to sixty piasters per man.

The captain of the *Jeune-Amélie* suggested that the Isle of Monte Cristo, being completely deserted and free of soldiers and customs agents, would be a good place to unload the cargo. When he heard the name of Monte Cristo, Dantès trembled with joy. He stood up to hide his emotion and walked around the smoky tavern. When he returned it had been decided that they would land on Monte Cristo and that they would leave the following night.

Chapter 14

At seven o'clock the next evening everything was ready; they rounded the lighthouse at ten minutes past seven, just as the beacon was being lit. The sea was calm and there was a fresh wind blowing from the southeast.

By five o'clock the next evening the Isle of Monte Cristo was clearly visible. They landed at ten o'clock. The *Jeune-Amélie* was the first to arrive at the rendezvous. Despite his usual self-control, Dantès could not restrain himself. He rushed ashore before any of the others and would have kissed the earth if he had dared. But it would have been useless to begin his search at night, so he regretfully put it off until the next day. Besides, a signal from half a league out to sea, which the *Jeune-Amélie* answered by a similar signal, had just indicated that it was time to go to work. The late-comer, reassured by the signal, soon appeared, white and silent as a ghost, and dropped anchor a short distance off shore. Then the work of unloading the cargo began. As he worked, Dantès thought of the shouts of joy he would draw from all those men if he were to tell them of the thought with which his mind was constantly filled.

No one suspected anything, however, and when he took a gun the next morning and announced his intention of going off to shoot one of the wild goats which could be seen leaping from rock to rock, his excursion was attributed only to either a love of hunting or a desire for solitude. Jacopo was the only one who insisted on going with him and Dantès was afraid to oppose him, lest he arouse some suspicion. But he managed to kill a goat before they had gone a quarter of a league and sent Jacopo to carry it back to his companions, inviting them to cook it and signal him when it was done by firing a shot into the air.

Dantès continued on his way, looking back from time to time, until he finally reached the spot where he supposed the caves to be. Examining everything with meticulous attention, he noticed that on several rocks there were notches which had apparently been made by the hand of man. They seemed to have been cut with a certain regularity, probably to indicate a tráil. These signs gave Dantès hope. Why could they not have been carved by the cardinal in order to guide his nephew? He followed them until they stopped, but they had taken him to no cave. A large round rock perched on a solid

base seemed to be the only goal to which they led. It occurred to him that, instead of being at the end of the trail,
he was at the beginning. He turned and retraced his steps.

Meanwhile his companions had finished cooking the goat.
Just as they were taking it off the improvised spit they saw
Dantès leaping from rock to rock. They fired a shot to signal
to him. He changed direction and came running toward them.
But as they were all watching him, his foot slipped and they
saw him stagger on the edge of a rock and disappear. They
all rushed forward at once, for they all loved Dantès despite
his superiority.

They found him bleeding and almost unconscious. He had
apparently fallen from a height of twelve to fifteen feet. They
poured some rum down his throat and he soon opened his
eyes, complaining of a sharp pain in his knee, a feeling of
heaviness in his head and unbearable twinges of pain in his
back. They tried to carry him to the shore, but as soon as
they touched him he groaned and said he did not feel strong
enough to continue. The captain, who was obliged to leave
that same morning, insisted that they try to get him on board
the ship, but Dantès declared that he would rather die where
he was than suffer the attrocious pain which so much movement would inflict on him. "Just leave me a supply of bis-
cuits, a gun to hunt with and a pickaxe to build some sort of
shelter with in case you should be delayed in coming back
for me," he said.

"But you'll starve!" said the captain. "We'll be gone at
least a week."

"Listen, captain," said Jacopo, "here's the answer to the
problem: I'll stay here with him and take care of him."

"Do you mean you'd give up your share of the profit in
order to stay with me?" asked Dantès.

"Yes," replied Jacopo, "and without regret."

"You're a good friend, Jacopo," said Dantés, "and God
will reward you for your good will, but I don't need anyone.
A day or two of rest will put me back on my feet." He shook
Jacopo's hand affectionately, but his resolution to stay, and
stay alone, remained unshakable. The smugglers finally gave
him the things he had requested and left him.

An hour later the little ship was almost out of sight. Then
Dantès stood up, as agile and light on his feet as one of the
wild goats of the island, took his gun in one hand and his
pickaxe in the other, and ran toward the rock at which the
trail of notches ended.

"Now," he exclaimed, thinking of the story of the Arabian
fisherman which Faria had told him, "open sesame!"

After following the trail of notches in the opposite direction, Dantès found that it led to a little creek which was wide enough at the mouth and deep enough at the center to enable a boat to enter it and remain hidden. He deduced that the cardinal, not wishing to be seen, had landed at that creek, hidden his boat in it, then followed the line marked out by the notches and, at the end of that line, buried his treasure. It was this supposition that led him back to the large circular rock.

But there was one thing which upset his whole theory: The rock must weigh at least two or three tons; how could the cardinal have hoisted it up to the base on which it rested?

Suddenly an idea occurred to him: perhaps, instead of being raised, it had been lowered. He climbed above the rock to search for its original resting place. He soon discovered that a slope had been made; the rock had slid down it to its present position, where it had been fixed in place by another rock about the size of an ordinary building stone, which had been used as a wedge.

Dantès chopped down an olive tree, cut off its branches and tried to pry up the rock with the trunk. But the rock was so heavy and was held so firmly in place by the rock wedge beneath it that no human strength could have budged it. He reflected for a moment and decided that he would have to direct his efforts against the wedge. He looked around him; his eyes fell on the powder horn his friend Jacopo had left him.

With his pickaxe he carved out a long hole between the large rock and the wedge and filled it with gunpowder. He then made a fuse by tearing a strip of cloth from his handkerchief and rolling it up with powder inside it.

He lighted the fuse and ran back. The explosion was not long in coming: the upper rock was lifted from its base for an instant by the tremendous force and the rock wedge beneath it was shattered into a thousand pieces.

Dantès came back to the spot. The upper rock, now almost without support, was hanging over the cliff. He walked around it, chose the loosest spot, placed his tree trunk in a crevice and began to pry with all his might. The rock tottered, then finally gave way completely and tumbled headlong into the sea. In doing so it revealed a square stone with an iron ring set in the middle of it.

Dantès uttered a cry of surprise and joy. His legs trembled so violently and his heart beat so wildly that he was obliged to stop for a moment. Then he put his lever through the iron ring and lifted vigorously, displacing the square stone. Beneath it he saw a steep staircase leading down into the dark depths of a cave.

Anyone else would have rushed forward with a shout of joy; Dantès stopped doubtfully and turned pale. "I mustn't let myself be shattered by disappointment," he said to himself, "or else all my suffering will have been in vain." He then began to climb down into the cave with a smile of doubt on his lips, murmuring that ultimate word of human wisdom: "Perhaps!"

After he had been in the cave for a few seconds, his eyes, accustomed as they were to seeing in the dark, were able to penetrate into every corner. The walls of the cave were of granite. He recalled the words of the cardinal's letter: "In the furthest corner of the second opening." He had found only the first cave; now he must search for the second one. He sounded the wall with his pickaxe. At length he found a spot where the granite gave forth a hollower and deeper sound. He struck it again, more vigorously. This time he noticed something strange: his blow had chipped a sort of plaster off the wall, revealing a softer, grayish stone beneath it. The opening in the granite wall had been sealed up with another kind of stone and then covered over with this plaster, on the surface of which the appearance of granite had been imitated. He struck the stone with the sharp end of his pickaxe: it penetrated to a depth of about one inch.

Dantès went to work. After some time he noticed that the stones had not been cemented together, but simply piled on top of one another and covered with a layer of plaster. He shoved the point of his pickaxe into one of the interstices, pushed down on the handle and, to his great joy, one of the stones fell at his feet. From then on he had only to pull each stone toward him with his pickaxe. Finally, after hesitating once again for several seconds, he entered the second cave.

It was as empty as the first. The treasure, if it existed, was buried in the furthest corner. The hour of anguish had arrived: two feet of earth was all that lay between Dantès and supreme joy or supreme despair. He walked over to the corner and, as though seized by a sudden resolution, energetically attacked the ground. At the fifth or sixth blow his pickaxe struck metal. He struck a little to one side of the spot; he still encountered resistance, but not the same sound. "It's a wooden chest bound with iron," he said to himself.

Just then a passing shadow cut off the daylight for an instant. Dantès dropped his pickaxe, picked up his rifle and rushed out of the cave. A wild goat had leaped over the entrance to the first cave and was grazing a few feet away. Dantès thought for a moment, cut down a small pine tree, lit it from the remaining flames of the fire over which the smugglers had cooked their goat and came back to the cave with this torch. He did not want to lose a single detail of what he was going to see.

He held his torch up to the small excavation he had made and saw that he was not mistaken: his blows had struck wood and metal. He planted the torch in the ground and went on with his work. A short time later he had cleared away a space about three feet long and two feet wide and could clearly see an oaken chest bound with wrought iron. In the middle of the lid on a silver plaque were the arms of the Spada family, which Dantès easily recognized, for Faria had drawn them for him countless times. It was impossible to doubt it now: the treasure was there. No one would have taken such precautions in order to put an empty chest back in place.

Dantès rapidly cleared away the earth around the chest. Soon the center lock appeared, then the handles at each end, all delicately wrought in the manner of that period when art made precious even the basest of metals. He took the chest by the two handles and tried to lift it, but it was impossible. He tried to open it; it was locked. He inserted the sharp end of his pickaxe between the chest and the lid and pushed down on the handle. The lid creaked, then flew open.

Dantès was seized with a sort of giddy fever. He cocked his gun and placed it beside him. Then he closed his eyes like a child, opened them and stood dumbfounded.

The chest was divided into three compartments. In the first were shining gold coins. In the second, unpolished gold ingots packed in orderly stacks. From the third compartment, which was half full, Dantès picked up handfuls of diamonds, pearls and rubies. As they fell through his fingers in a glittering cascade, they gave forth the sound of hail beating against the windowpanes.

After he had touched them, fingered them, and buried his trembling hands in the gold and precious stones, Dantès ran out of the cave with the wild exaltation of a man who has come to the brink of madness. He climbed up on a rock from which he could see the surrounding sea. He was alone, all alone with those incalculable, unheard-of, fabulous riches which belonged to him! But was he dreaming or waking? He needed to see his gold again, yet he felt that, for the moment, he did not have the strength to look at it. He pressed his head between his hands for an instant, as though to prevent his reason from escaping, then he began to run frenziedly around the island, frightening the wild goats and seagulls with his shouts and gesticulations. Then he returned, still doubting

his senses, rushed into the cave and found himself once again
in the presence of his mine of gold and jewels. This time he
fell to his knees, convulsively pressed his hands over his
pounding heart and uttered a prayer that was intelligible to
God alone.

Chapter 15

The next day, Dantès filled his pockets with precious stones,
carefully buried the chest again and disguised the entrance to
the cave until no trace of it was visible. Then he began to wait
impatiently for his companions to return. He had no desire
to stay on the island looking at his gold and diamonds, like a
dragon guarding a useless treasure. It was time for him to go
back among men and take up the rank, influence and power
which great wealth gives in this world.

The smugglers returned on the sixth day. Dantès recognized
the *Jeune-Amélie* from a distance and dragged himself down
to the shore. When his companions landed he told them that,
although he was still in pain, he was considerably better. Then
he listened to the account of their adventures. Their trip had
been successful and all of them, especially Jacopo, regretted
that Dantès had been unable to take part in it in order to have
his share of the profits, which would have been fifty piasters.
Dantès managed not to smile at this. Since the *Jeune-Amélie*
had come to Monte Cristo only for him, he boarded her that
evening and went on to Leghorn.

In Leghorn he sold four of his smallest diamonds for five
thousand francs each. The next day he bought a small ship
for Jacopo, adding a hundred piasters to the gift to enable him
to hire a crew, on condition that Jacopo go to Marseilles and
ask for news of an old man named Louis Dantès and a young
woman called Mercédès. Jacopo thought he must be dreaming.
Dantès told him that he had become a sailor only on a youth-
ful impulse and that upon arriving in Leghorn he had received
an inheritance from his uncle. Dantès' superior education
made this story plausible and Jacopo did not doubt its truth
for an instant. The next day Jacopo set sail for Marseilles.
He was to meet Dantès later at Monte Cristo.

That same day, Dantès took leave of the crew of the *Jeune-
Amélie,* giving each of them a handsome present and promising to let the captain hear from him.

Dantès went to Genoa. The day of his arrival, he bought a
small yacht which had been ordered by an Englishman who
had heard that the Genoese were the best shipbuilders of the

Mediterranean. The Englishman had agreed to a price of forty thousand francs; Dantès offered sixty thousand on condition that the yacht be turned over to him immediately. The shipbuilder offered to help Dantès engage a crew, but Dantès replied that he was in the habit of sailing alone and that the only thing he desired was that a secret compartment be built in the cabin. The compartment was finished the next day, and two hours later Dantès sailed out of the harbor of Genoa, headed for the Isle of Monte Cristo.

He arrived toward the end of the second day. His yacht was an excellent sailer and had covered the distance in thirty-five hours. The island was deserted. He went to his treasure and found it exactly as he had left it. By the next day his immense fortune had been transferred to his yacht and locked up in the secret compartment.

Dantès waited for eight days, during which he maneuvered his yacht around the island, studying it as a horseman studies his mount. By the end of that time he had recognized all its good qualities and all its defects; he promised himself to augment the former and remedy the latter.

Jacopo arrived on the eighth day and tied up his small ship alongside Dantès' yacht. He had a sad answer to each of the two questions Dantès had asked: old Louis Dantès was dead and Mercédès had disappeared. Dantès' expression remained calm when he heard this news, but he immediately went ashore and refused to have anyone go with him. He returned two hours later. Two sailors from Jacopo's crew came on board his yacht to help him sail it. He gave orders to head for Marseilles.

The news of his father's death was not unexpected; but what had become of Mercédès? There were also other things he wanted to know which he could trust no one else to find out for him. In Leghorn his mirror had shown him that he ran no risk of being recognized. Furthermore, he had every means of disguise at his disposal. One morning, therefore, the yacht, followed by Jacopo's ship, boldly sailed into the harbor of Marseilles and stopped opposite the very spot where Dantès had set out for the Château d'If.

It was not without a certain anxiety that Dantès saw a gendarme coming out to meet him in the quarantine boat, but, with the perfect self-assurance which he had acquired, he presented an English passport he had bought in Leghorn and went ashore without difficulty.

Chapter 16

Those who have journeyed through the South of France on foot may have noticed halfway between Bellegarde and Beaucaire a small inn, in front of which hangs a sheet of iron bearing a grotesque representation of the Pont du Garde. For the past seven or eight years this inn had been kept by a man and his wife whose only servants were a chambermaid and a stable boy, a staff which was more than sufficient now that the canal between Beaucaire and Aiguemortes had taken almost all the traffic off the road on which the inn was situated.

The unfortunate innkeeper was none other than Dantès' old friend Gaspard Caderousse. His pale, thin, sickly wife was almost constantly in the grip of a fever which kept her in her bedroom on the second floor while her husband went about his daily tasks. To her never-ending complaints against their fate, he usually answered only, "Be quiet! It's God's will."

One morning as Caderousse was standing in the doorway of the inn, looking up and down the deserted road with a melancholy air, a horseman appeared in the distance, coming from the direction of Bellegarde. The rider was a priest, dressed in black and wearing a three-cornered hat despite the fierce heat of the sun. He dismounted before the inn, wiping the perspiration from his forehead with a red cotton handkerchief. Caderousse eagerly came out to meet him. The priest stared at him with peculiar attention for two or three seconds, then said, in a pronounced Italian accent, "You're Monsieur Caderousse, aren't you?"

"Yes, sir," said the innkeeper, surpirsed, "I'm Gaspard Caderousse, at your service."

"Weren't you once a tailor?"

"Yes, but that turned out badly. The weather is so hot in Marseilles that I wouldn't be surprised if people finally stopped wearing any clothes at all. . . . Speaking of heat, wouldn't you like something to drink?"

"Yes, bring me a bottle of your best wine and we'll go on with our conversation."

When Caderousse returned a few minutes later he found the priest sitting on a stool with his elbows on a table. "Are you alone?" asked the priest as his host set a glass and a bottle of wine in front of him.

"Practically alone. My poor wife is always sick, so she can't be of much help to me."

"Oh, you're married?" said the priest with a certain interest. He cast around him a glance which seemed to estimate the true value of the dilapidated furnishings of the inn.

"You can see I'm not rich," said Caderousse, sighing. "But what can you expect? Being an honest man isn't enough to bring prosperity in this world.'" The priest looked at him piercingly. "Yes, an honest man!" repeated Caderousse, returning the priest's steadfast gaze. "That's one thing I can boast of, and not everyone nowadays can say the same thing."

"You're fortunate if your boast is true," said the priest, "because I am firmly convinced that, sooner or later, the good are rewarded and the wicked are punished."

"Your profession requires you to say that," said Caderousse bitterly, "but everyone is free not to believe what you say."

"You're wrong to speak that way," said the priest, "for I myself may soon give you proof of what I say."

"What do you mean?" asked Caderousse with surprise.

"First of all I must make sure you're really the man I'm looking for. . . . In 1814 or 1815 did you know a sailor named Dantès?"

"Dantès? Yes, I knew him, poor Edmond! In fact, he was one of my best friends. Do you know him? Is he still alive? Is he free? Is he happy?"

"He died in prison, wretched and hopeless."

Caderousse turned pale. He turned away and the priest saw him wipe a tear from his eye with a corner of the red handkerchief which he wore around his head. "Poor boy!" he murmured. "There's another proof of what I was telling you, that God is good only to the wicked. Ah, the world is going from bad to worse!"

"You seem to have been quite fond of him," said the priest.

"Yes, I was very fond of him," said Caderousse, "although I must admit I envied his happiness for a short while. But since then I can assure you I've felt great pity for his misfortune." There was a silence during which the priest searchingly scrutinized the innkeeper's face. "Did you know him?" went on Caderousse.

"I was called to his deathbed to give him the last consolation of religion. And there, on his deathbed, he swore to me by Jesus Christ that he did not know the cause of his imprisonment."

"That's true, he couldn't know it," said Caderousse. "No, he wasn't lying, poor boy."

"He therefore begged me to bring to light the cause of the misfortune which he himself never understood," continued the priest, "and to clear away the stain from his memory. A rich

Englishman who was in prison with him, but who was released at the second Restoration, owned a diamond of great value. When he left prison, he gave it to Dantès, who had once taken care of him like a brother during a long illness he had suffered. Instead of using it to bribe his jailers, who might well have taken it and then betrayed him, Dantès always kept the diamond in case he should get out of prison, for it would have assured his fortune."

"It must have been a diamond of great value, as you say," said Caderousse, his eyes shining.

"Everything is relative," said the priest. "It was of great value for Dantès. It has been appraised at fifty thousand francs."

"Fifty thousand francs!" exclaimed Caderousse.

"I have it in my possession now. Dantès made me the executor of his will. 'I had three good friends and a fiancée,' he told me, 'and I'm sure all four of them still miss me. One of my good friends was named Caderousse.'" Caderousse shuddered. "'Another was named Danglars,'" continued the priest without appearing to notice Caderousse's emotion, "'and the third was my rival, but he also loved me; his name was Fernand. As for my fiancée, her name is Mercédès. Go to Marseilles, sell this diamond, divide the money into five parts and give it to the only people on earth who love me.'"

"Why did he say five parts?" asked Caderousse. "You've mentioned only four persons."

"The fifth one is dead: he was Dantès' father. I was told about it in Marseilles," went on the priest, making an effort to appear indifferent, "but he died so long ago that I was unable to learn any of the details. Would you happen to know anything about it?"

"No one knows better than I do," replied Caderousse. "I lived next door to him. . . . Oh, yes, he died less than a year after his son disappeared, poor old man!"

"How did he die?"

"I think the doctors called his illness gastric enteritis; those who knew him said he died of sorrow. But I almost saw him die, and I say he died of——" Caderousse stopped short.

"Died of what?" asked the priest anxiously.

"Of hunger!"

"Of hunger!" cried the priest, leaping from his stool. "Why, even the lowest animals don't die of hunger! A dog wandering through the streets will always find someone to throw him a crust of bread! And you tell me a man died of hunger in the midst of other men who call themselves Christians? Impossible! Oh, it's impossible!"

"I've told you the truth," said Caderousse.

"And you're wrong to tell it!" said a voice from the staircase.

The two men turned around and saw the sickly face of Caderousse's wife, who had dragged herself to the head of the stairs to listen to their conversation. She was sitting on the top step with her head on her knees.

"It's no business of yours," said Caderousse. "This gentleman asked me for some information. It wouldn't be polite to refuse."

"No, but it's not prudent to tell him, either. How do you know why he wants to make you talk, idiot?"

"Your husband has nothing to fear, madame," said the priest, "as long as he speaks frankly. I can assure you that no harm will come to you because of me."

Caderousse's wife mumbled a few unintelligible words, let her head drop back to her knees and continued to tremble with fever, leaving her husband free to resume his conversation, but placed in such a way that not a word of it would escape her.

"But the poor old man must have been forsaken by everyone if he died such a death," said the priest.

"No, Mercédès and Monsieur Morrel didn't forsake him," said Caderousse, "but the old man took a profound dislike for Fernand, the same Fernand," added Caderousse with an ironic smile, "that Dantès named as one of his friends."

"Wasn't he really his friend?" asked the priest.

"Gaspard!" said the voice from the top of the stairs. "Be careful of what you say!"

Caderousse's only reply to the interruption was a gesture of impatience. "Is it possible to be the friend of a man whose wife you covet?" he said. "Dantès had a heart of gold, he called all those people his friends. . . . Poor Edmond! I suppose it's better he never found out; it would have been too hard for him to forgive them as he was dying. And no matter what they say, I'm more afraid of the curse of a dead man than the hatred of a living one."

"Do you know how Fernand wronged Dantès?"

"I certainly do."

"Then tell me about it."

"Gaspard, you can do as you like," said Madame Caderousse, "but if you listen to me you won't say anything."

"This time I think you're right," said Caderousse.

"You don't want to tell me anything about it?" asked the priest.

"What good would it do? If Edmond were alive and came to me to find out once and for all which people were his real friends and which were his enemies, I'd tell him. But he's

dead and buried, according to what you've told me, so he can
no longer hate anyone or take revenge on anyone. Let's leave
all that in the past."

"Do you want me to give these people, whom you consider
false friends, a gift intended to reward them for their faith-
fulness?"

"No, you're right," said Caderousse. "Besides, what would
poor Edmond's gift mean to those people? A drop of water
falling into the ocean!"

"Yes, but don't forget that those people could crush you
with their little finger if they wanted to," said his wife.

"Do you mean to say they've become rich and powerful?"
asked the priest.

"Don't you know their story?"

"No, tell it to me."

Caderousse reflected for a moment. "No," he said, "it
would take too long."

"You're free to remain silent if you wish, my friend," said
the priest in a tone of utter indifference, "and I respect your
scruples. We'll say no more about it and I'll sell the diamond."
He took the diamond from his pocket and let it glitter before
Caderousse's dazzled eyes.

"Come look at this!" Caderousse called out hoarsely to his
wife.

"A diamond!" said Madame Caderousse, standing up and
walking down the stairs. "Where did it come from?"

"Didn't you hear? It's a diamond that Dantès left to his
father, his fiancée and his three friends, Fernand, Danglars
and me."

"A man who betrays you is not your friend," muttered
Madame Caderousse.

"Yes, that's what I was saying," said Caderousse. "It would
be almost a profanation, a sacrilege, to give a reward to treason, perhaps even crime."

"It will be your own fault," said the priest calmly, putting
the diamond back into the pocket of his cassock. "Now tell
me where I can find Dantès' friends, so that I can carry out
his last wish."

Large beads of perspiration broke out on Caderousse's forehead. He saw the priest stand up, walk over to the door as if
to look at his horse, and then turn back. Caderousse and his
wife looked at each other with an indescribable expression.

"The whole diamond would be for us," said Caderousse.

"Do you really think so?"

"A priest wouldn't lie to us."

"Do whatever you think best," said his wife. "I leave it to
you." She climbed slowly up the stairs. At the last step she

turned around for a moment and said, "Think it over carefully, Gaspard!"

"I've already made up my mind," said Caderousse.

"What have you decided?" asked the priest.

"To tell you everything."

"I think that's the best thing to do; not that I'm anxious to hear about things you'd prefer not to tell me, but it will be better if I can distribute Dantès' legacy according to his true wishes."

"I hope so," said Caderousse, his cheeks flushed with hope and cupidity.

"I'm listening."

"First of all," began Caderousse, "I must ask you to promise me something."

"What?"

"I want you to promise me that if you make use of the information I'm about to give you, you will never tell anyone you heard it from me, because the people I'm going to talk about are rich and powerful, and they could destroy me as easily as breaking a glass."

"Don't worry, my friend; I'm a priest and I never reveal confessions made to me. Remember that our only purpose is to carry out the last wishes of our friend, so speak frankly and without hatred. I'll probably never know the persons you're going to mention; besides, I'm Italian, not French, and I'll soon be going back to my monastery, which I left only to comply with the request of a dying man."

Caderousse seemed reassured. "In that case," he said, "I'll tell you the real truth about the men poor Edmond thought were such sincere and devoted friends. It's a sad story. You probably know the beginning, don't you?"

"Yes, Edmond told me everything that happened up to the time he was arrested at his own betrothal feast."

"Well, after Edmond was arrested, Monsieur Morrel left to get some information on his arrest. The news he brought back was very sad. Edmond's father went home alone and spent the whole day in his room. He didn't sleep at all that night; I lived on the floor underneath and I could hear him pacing up and down all night long. I didn't sleep either, for that matter: I was terribly upset by the old man's grief and each step he took hurt my heart as much as if he were actually stepping on my chest.

"The next day, Mercédès came to Marseilles to ask for Monsieur de Villefort's help, but she accomplished nothing. Then she visited the old man. When she saw how grief-stricken he was and found out that he hadn't slept or eaten since the day before, she wanted to take him with her and take care of him, but he refused. 'No,' he said, 'I won't leave this house. My poor son loves me more than anything else in the world, and if he gets out of prison this is the first place he'll come. What would he say if I weren't here to meet him?'

"He began to isolate himself more and more every day. Monsieur Morrel and Mercédès often came to see him, but his door was locked and, although I was sure he was at home, he wouldn't answer. On one of the rare days when he received Mercédès, he said to her, 'Believe me, my daughter, he's dead, and instead of our waiting for him, he's waiting for us. I'm lucky because I'm the oldest: I'll be the first one to see him again.'

"However good you may be, you soon stop seeing people who make you sad; after a while the old man was completely alone. The only people I saw coming to see him were strangers who would leave his room carrying some sort of package. I realized later what was in those packages: he was selling the little he owned in order to live. Finally he'd sold everything he had. He owed three months' rent. The landlord threatened to put him out, then agreed to give him one more week. I found out about this because the landlord stopped by to see me on his way down.

"For the first three days I heard him pacing up and down as usual, but on the fourth day I heard nothing. I went up to see him. His door was locked, but I looked in through the keyhole. He looked so pale and haggard that I thought he must be seriously ill. I sent word to Monsieur Morrel and Mercédès; they both came immediately. Monsieur Morrel brought a doctor, who gave a diagnosis of gastric enteritis and prescribed a fast. I was there, and I'll never forget the old man's smile when he heard that prescription.

"From then on he left his door unlocked; he had an excuse for not eating: the doctor had ordered him to fast. The next time Mercédès saw him he looked so bad that she wanted to take him into her home and take care of him, as she had asked to do at first. Monsieur Morrel agreed with her, but the old man refused again. Monsieur Morrel left a purse with money in it on the mantelpiece, but the old man still wouldn't eat anything. Finally, after nine days of despair and fasting, he passed away. As he died he cursed those who were responsible for his misfortune and said to Mercédès, 'If you see my Edmond, tell him I died blessing him.' "

The priest stood up and paced the floor for a few moments. After a time he said hoarsely, "What a terrible misfortune!"

"And all the more terrible because it didn't come from God, but from men alone."

"Now tell me about those men," said the priest. "But remember," he added almost threateningly, "you agreed to tell me everything. Who were those men who made the son die of despair and the father of hunger?"

"They were two men who were jealous of him, one because of love and the other because of ambition: Fernand and Danglars."

"How did their jealously manifest itself?"

"They denounced him as a Bonapartist agent."

"But which of the two denounced him? Which one is really guilty?"

"Both of them. One wrote the letter and the other mailed it."

"Where was the letter written?"

"In the tavern, the day before the betrothal feast."

"But you were there!" cried the priest suddenly.

"Who told you I was there?" asked Caderousse, astonished.

The priest realized he had anticipated the story. "No one," he said, "but you know the details so well that you must have been a witness."

"It's true," said Caderousse in a choked voice. "I was there."

"And yet you didn't oppose their infamous deed," said the priest. "That makes you their accomplice."

"They'd given me so much to drink that I hardly knew what I was doing. I protested as much as I was able to in that state, but they told me the whole thing was only a joke."

"But the next day you could see it wasn't a joke. You were there when he was arrested."

"Yes, and I wanted to tell what I knew, but Danglars persuaded me not to. 'If he should happen to be really guilty,' he told me, 'anyone who upholds him will be taken for his accomplice.' I was afraid of politics the way it was carried on in those days, so I kept quiet. It was cowardly of me, I admit it, but it wasn't a crime."

"I see: you only let things take their course."

"Yes," replied Caderousse, "and I still regret it night and day. I've often asked God to forgive me for it. It's the only thing I ever did in my whole life that I could seriously reproach myself for, and I'm sure it's the cause of all my bad luck: I'm still expiating a moment of selfishness. Whenever my wife complains I always tell her, 'Be quiet, it's God's will.'" He bowed his head with every appearance of sincere repentance.

"You've spoken very frankly," said the priest. "A man who can accuse himself like that deserves to be forgiven."

"Unfortunately," said Caderousse, "Edmond is dead and he never forgave me."

"He didn't know."

"Well, perhaps he knows now," said Caderousse. "They say the dead know everything."

There was a silence. The priest stood up and walked thoughtfully back and forth for a time. Then he came back and sat down again. "You mentioned a certain Monsieur Morrel several times," he said. "Who was he?"

"He was the owner of the *Pharaon*."

"What part did he play in this sad story?"

"The part of an honest, courageous and loyal man. He interceded for Dantès at least twenty times. When the emperor returned, he wrote, begged and threatened so strongly that after the second Restoration he was persecuted as a Bonapartist. He often came to see Dantès' father, as I've already told you, and offered to take him into his home. The day before the old man died, as I've also told you, he left a purse on the mantelpiece. The money it contained paid for his funeral and paid off his debts, so that the poor old man at least died as he had lived: without doing wrong to anyone. I still have the purse."

"Is Monsieur Morrel still alive?"

"Yes."

"Then he must be a man blessed by God, he must be rich and happy."

Caderousse smiled bitterly and said, "Yes, he's happy, as I am."

"Monsieur Morrel is unhappy?"

"He's on the brink of poverty and, worse still, of dishonor. After twenty-five years of hard work, after having acquired the most honorable place in the business world of Marseilles, Monsieur Morrel is completely ruined. He's lost five ships in two years, and three other firms have gone bankrupt on him. His only hope now is the same *Pharaon* that poor Dantès sailed on. She's on her way from India with a cargo of cochineal and indigo. If she goes down like the others, he's lost."

"Does the unfortunate man have a wife and children?"

"Yes, he has a wife who's borne up under everything like a saint. He has a daughter who was about to marry a man she loves, but now his family won't let him marry the daughter of a ruined man. Finally, he has a son who's a lieutenant in the army. But that only doubles the poor man's sorrow. If he were alone, he'd blow his brains out and that would be the end of it."

"It's terrible!" exclaimed the priest. "And what became of Danglars? He was the guiltiest, wasn't he, the instigator?"

"He left Marseilles and went to work for a Spanish banker. During the war with Spain he contracted to furnish some of the French army's supplies and made a fortune. He speculated with his money and quadrupled it. After the death of his first wife, who was the daughter of the banker he worked for, he married a widow, Madamme de Nargonne, whose father is a chamberlain and in high favor at court. He'd already made himself a millionaire; he was now made a baron. Today he's Baron Danglars, he has a mansion in the Rue du Mont-Blanc, ten horses in his stable, six lackeys in his antechamber, and I don't know how many millions in his coffers."

"And what about Fernand?" asked the priest. "How could a poor Catalan fisherman, without education or resources, make a fortune? I confess I don't understand it."

"No one else understands it, either. There must be some strange secret in his life that no one knows about."

"But by what visible steps did he reach his wealth and position?"

"Well, Fernand was drafted into the army a few days before the second Restoration. He was put into a regiment that was about to leave for the frontier. He took part in the battle of Ligny. The night of the battle he was on sentry duty outside the door of a general who was in secret contact with the enemy. That same night the general went over to the English. He proposed to Fernand that he go with him; Fernand deserted his post and followed him.

"This would have meant a court-martial for Fernand if Napoleon had stayed in power, but it was a recommendation to the Bourbons when they took over the throne. He was made a lieutenant when he came back to France, and he was a captain by the time the war with Spain began, which was when Danglars was making his first speculations. Since Fernand was a Spaniard, he was sent to Madrid to sound out the feelings of his compatriots. There he met Danglars, became very friendly with him, promised his general support from the royalists in the capital and in the provinces, guided his regiment along routes known to him alone and guarded by royalists and, in general, rendered such services during that short campaign that he was finally promoted to colonel, received the cross of an Officer of the Legion of Honor and was made a count."

"Fate! Fate!" murmured the priest.

"Yes, but that's not all. When the war with Spain was over, Fernand's career was threatened by the long peace which seemed likely to reign over Europe. Greece had risen up against Turkey and had just begun her war of independence. All eyes turned toward Athens; it was fashionable to pity and uphold the Greeks. Fernand asked for and obtained permission to serve in Greece without losing his rank in the French

army. Some time later it was learned that the Count of Morcerf—this was the name he now bore—had entered the service of Ali Pasha with the rank of instructor-general. Ali Pasha
was killed, as you know, but before he died he rewarded
Fernand by leaving him a large sum of money. Fernand returned to France and was promoted to lieutenant general. Today he lives in a magnificent mansion in Paris, at 27 Rue du
Helder."

The priest opened his mouth to speak, hesitated an instant,
then said with an effort, "And what about Mercédès? I was
told she'd disappeared."

"Disappeared? Yes, she disappeared, but as the sun dis-
appears at night to rise brighter than ever the next day."

"Did she make her fortune too?" asked the priest with an
ironic smile.

"Mercédès is now one of the greatest ladies of Paris," said
Caderousse. "At first she was completely overcome with grief
at losing Edmond; I've already told you how she begged Monsieur de Villefort for help and how devoted she was to Edmond's father. In the midst of her despair she was struck by
another misfortune: Fernand left to go into the army. She
knew nothing of what he had done to Edmond and she loved
him like a brother. When he left, she was all alone. Three
months went by without word from either Edmond or Fernand. All she had before her eyes was an old man slowly dying of despair.

"One night Fernand walked in wearing his lieutenant's uniform. His absence hadn't been the main cause of her grief, but
at least he was a part of her past life which had now returned
to her. She received him with a joy which he mistook for love,
but which was actually only happiness at no longer being
alone in the world.

"Then Edmond's father died, as I've told you. If he'd lived,
Mercédès might never have married another man, for he'd
have been there to reproach her with her unfaithfulness. Fernand knew that. When he learned of the old man's death, he
came back. The first time he hadn't said a word about love to
Mercédès; this time he reminded her that he loved her. She
asked him for six more months to mourn and wait for Edmond."

"Well, that made eighteen months in all," said the priest
with a bitter smile. "What more could any lover ask?" Then
he murmured the words of the English poet: "Frailty, thy
name is woman!"

"Six months later," went on Caderousse, "the wedding took
place in the Eglise des Accoules."

"The same church in which she was to have married Edmond," muttered the priest. "The only difference was in the bridegroom."

"Although Mercédès seemed calm after her marriage," continued Caderousse, "it's still true that she fainted once when she passed by the tavern where she'd celebrated her betrothal feast eighteen months before with the man she'd have realized she still loved if she'd dared look into the depths of her heart.

"I saw Fernand at that time. He was happier, but he was still worried because he was afraid Edmond might reappear at any moment. Almost immediately after their marriage, he and his wife moved away; the Catalan village held too many dangers and too many memories."

"Did you ever see Mercédès again?" asked the priest.

"Yes, at the time of the war with Spain I saw her at Perpignan, where Fernand had left her. She was then educating her son."

The priest started. "Her son!" he exclaimed.

"Yes, her son Albert."

"But how could she educate her son?" asked the priest. "It seems to me Edmond said she was a simple fisherman's daughter, beautiful but uneducated."

"Oh!" said Caderousse, "did he know his own fiancée so little? If crowns were only for the most beautiful and intelligent heads, Mercédès would be a queen now. As her fortune grew, she grew with it. She learned drawing, she learned music, she learned everything. Between you and me, though, I think she learned all that only to distract herself; I think she put all those things in her head in order to forget what was in her heart. She's rich, she's a countess, and yet——"

"Yet what?"

"Yet I'm sure she's not happy."

"What makes you think so?"

"Well, when my own misfortune began to be too unbearable, I thought perhaps my old friends might help me in some way. I went to see Danglars, but he wouldn't even receive me. Fernand had one of his servants give me a hundred francs."

"So you didn't see either one of them?"

"No, but Madame de Morcerf saw me. As I was leaving, a purse fell at my feet. It contained twenty-five louis. I looked up quickly and saw Mercédès closing the shutters."

"And what about Monsieur de Villefort?" asked the priest.

"Oh, he wasn't my friend. I didn't even know him, so I didn't ask him for anything."

"But don't you know what became of him and what part he played in Edmond's misfortune?"

"No. I only know that, some time after he had Edmond

arrested, he married Mademoiselle de Saint-Méran and left Marseilles. No doubt fortune has smiled on him like the others, no doubt he's rich like Danglars and covered with honors like Fernand. I alone have remained poor, miserable and forgotten by God."

"You're mistaken, my friend," said the priest. "God may seem to forget sometimes, when His justice is inactive, but He always remembers sooner or later, and here's the proof." So saying, he took the diamond from his pocket and handed it to Caderousse. "Take this, my friend," he said, "it's yours."

"What! For me alone?" cried Caderousse. "You're not mocking me, are you?"

"This diamond was to be divided among Edmond's friends, but he had only one friend. Take it and sell it. It's worth fifty thousand francs, as I've told you, and I hope that will be enough to put an end to your poverty. Take it, but in exchange——" Caderousse, who was already touching the diamond, drew back his hand. The priest smiled. "In exchange," he continued, "give me the red silk purse that Monsieur Morrel left on old Dantès' mantelpiece. You told me you still had it, didn't you?"

Caderousse, more and more astonished, went over to a large oaken cupboard, opened it and took out a faded red silk purse. The priest took it and gave Caderousse the diamond. Then, amid Caderousse's effusive declarations of gratitude, he walked out, mounted his horse, bade Caderousse farewell and rode off in the same direction from which he had come.

When Caderousse turned around he saw his wife standing behind him, paler than ever. "Well," she said, "is what I heard true?"

"What? That he gave us the whole diamond?" said Caderousse, almost mad with joy.

"Yes."

"There's nothing truer! Here it is!"

His wife looked at it for a moment, then said in a dull voice, "What if it were only an imitation diamond?"

Caderousse reeled. "Imitation?" he murmured. "Why should he have given me an imitation diamond?"

"To learn your secret without paying you for it, idiot!"

Caderousse was dazed by the weight of this supposition. "Oh!" he said after a silence, taking his hat and placing it over the red handkerchief he wore around his head. "We'll find out about that."

"How?"

"There's a fair at Beaucaire and there are jewelers from Paris there: I'm going to show the diamond to them. Take care of the inn; I'll be back in two hours." He rushed out the door and began to run down the road.

"Fifty thousand francs!" said Madame Caderousse to herself. "It's a lot of money . . . but it's not a fortune."

Chapter 17

The day following the scene at Caderousse's inn, a man in his early thirties, with both the appearance and the accent of an Englishman, presented himself before the Mayor of Marseilles.

"Monsieur," he said, "I am the head clerk of the firm of Thomson and French, of Rome. For the past ten years we have been dealing with the firm of Morrel and Son here in Marseilles. Our dealings with them now involve approximately one hundred thousand francs, and we are somewhat uneasy about this money, for we have heard reports that the firm is threatened with bankruptcy. I have come from Rome expressly to ask you for information on the matter."

"Monsieur," replied the mayor, "I know that Monsieur Morrel has been dogged by misfortune for the last four or five years, but, although I myself am his creditor to the extent of ten thousand francs, I am not in a position to give you any information on the state of his finances. If you ask me my personal opinion of Monsieur Morrel, I will tell you that he is an extremely honest man who has so far met all his obligations with scrupulous exactitude, but that's all I can tell you. If you wish to know more, I suggest that you see Monsieur de Boville, the Inspector of Prisons. I believe he has two hundred thousand francs invested in the firm. Since his investment is much greater than mine, if there is really anything to fear you will no doubt find him better informed than I am."

The Englishman took leave of the mayor and, with that gait peculiar to the sons of Great Britain, went off to see the Inspector of Prisons.

Monsieur de Boville was in his office. The Englishman asked him the same question he had just asked the mayor.

"Oh!" cried Monsieur de Boville. "Your fears are unfortunately very well grounded, and you see a desperate man before you. I have two hundred thousand francs invested in Monsieur Morrel's firm. That money was to be my daughter's dowry, and we intended to have the wedding two weeks from now. I was to receive a hundred thousand francs on the fifteenth of this month and another hundred thousand on the fifteenth of next month. Then, less than half an hour ago,

Monsieur Morrel came here to see me and told me that if his ship, the *Pharaon*, hasn't arrived by the fifteenth, it will be impossible for him to make his payment to me. I'm afraid it looks like bankruptcy."

"You're quite worried about your investment, then?"

"I consider it as good as lost."

"Very well, I'll buy it from you."

"At an enormous discount, I suppose?"

"No, for two hundred thousand francs. Our firm doesn't do business that way."

"And how would you pay?"

"Cash." The Englishman took out a roll of banknotes which contained at least twice as much as the amount of Monsieur de Boville's investment. A flash of joy passed over the latter's face, but he made an effort to control himself and said, "I must warn you that, in all probability, you'll receive less than six per cent of that sum."

"That doesn't concern me," replied the Englishman, "it concerns the firm of Thomson and French, in whose name I am acting. It may be that they wish to hasten the ruin of a rival firm. All I know is that I am prepared to pay you the sum if you will sign a deed of assignment. But I must ask you for a commission."

"Why, that's only fair!" cried Monsieur de Boville. "The commission is usually one and a half—do you want two—three—five—more than that?"

"Monsieur," said the Englishman, laughing, "I am like my firm: I don't do business like that. No, my commission is quite different."

"Tell me, then."

"You're the Inspector of Prisons, aren't you?"

"Yes."

"And you keep a register with notes concerning each prisoner?"

"Yes, there's a record of each prisoner."

"Good. I was raised in Rome by a poor priest who suddenly disappeared one day. I later learned he had been imprisoned in the Château d'If, and I'd like to learn the details of his death."

"What was his name?"

"The Abbé Faria."

"Oh, I remember him quite well!" said Monsieur de Boville. "He was mad; he claimed to know the location of an immense fortune and offered fantastic sums to the government in exchange for his freedom. He died five or six months ago, last February. I remember the date because the poor fellow's death was accompanied by a very peculiar circumstance."

"Might I know what the circumstance was?" asked the Englishman.

"Well, Faria's cell was about fifty feet away from that of a former Bonapartist agent, one of those who contributed most to the usurper's return in 1815, a very dangerous man. I saw him in his cell in 1816 or 1817 and he made a deep impression on me; I'll never forget his face."

The Englishman smiled almost imperceptibly.

"It seems that Dantès——"

"Was that the dangerous Bonapartist's name?" asked the Englishman.

"Yes, Edmond Dantès. It seems that Dantès had either procured some tools or made them, for an underground passage was found between the cells of the two prisoners."

"I suppose the passage was made for the purpose of escaping?"

"Precisely. But unfortunately Faria was seized with a cataleptic fit and died. Dantès, however, still saw a way to escape. Thinking, no doubt, that prisoners who died in the Château d'If were buried in an ordinary cemetery, he carried Faria's body into his own cell, placed himself in the sack in which the body had been sewn up and waited for the burial. But the Château d'If has no cemetery: the bodies of dead prisoners are simply thrown into the sea with a cannon ball tied to their feet. You can imagine Dantès' surprise when he felt himself thrown from the top of the cliff. I wish I could have seen his face."

"That would have been difficult," remarked the Englishman.

"No matter!" said Monsieur de Boville, who was in a very good humor now that he was assured of recovering his two hundred thousand francs. "I can imagine what it looked like." He burst out laughing.

"So can I," said the Englishman, who also began to laugh, but in the reserved manner peculiar to the English. Then he said, "So the fugitive was drowned, was he?"

"He certainly was."

"Very well. Now let's come back to the registers."

"Oh, yes, excuse me; my story led me away from the subject. Come into my office and I'll show you the records."

They both went into Monsieur de Boville's office. Everything was in perfect order. The Englishman sat down in an armchair and the inspector brought him the register and the folder concerning the Château d'If, inviting him to look through them as long as he liked; while he himself sat down in a corner and read a newspaper.

The Englishman quickly found the records relating to Abbé Faria, but the story told to him by Monsieur de Boville had apparently interested him greatly, for, after perusing these documents, he continued to leaf through the records until he came to those concerning Edmond Dantès. Everything was there: the letter of denunciation, the examination, Morrel's petition and Villefort's recommendations. He quietly folded the letter of denunciation and put it in his pocket. Then he read the examination, noted that the name of Noirtier was mentioned nowhere in it and looked over Morrel's petition dated April 10, 1815, in which, since Napoleon was in power at that time, he exaggerated the services Dantès had rendered to the imperial cause. He now understood everything: during the second Restoration that petition had become a terrible weapon in Villefort's hands. He was therefore not surprised when he saw the following words beside Dantès' name in the register:

EDMOND DANTES.   Ardent Bonapartist. Took active part in return from Elba.
To be kept in solitary confinement and under careful watch.

He compared these notes with the certificate attached to Morrel's petition and saw that the handwriting was the same: they had both been written by Villefort.

"Thank you," said the Englishman, closing the register. "I have everything I need. And now it's my turn to keep my promise. Make out a deed of assignment and I'll give you the money."

Monsieur de Boville hurriedly drew up the document while the Englishman counted out the banknotes.

Chapter 18

Anyone who had left Marseilles a few years before, knowing the firm of Morrel and Son, and then returned at the period of our story, would have found it greatly changed. Instead of that atmosphere of animation and well-being which radiates from a prosperous house, instead of the busy clerks hurrying through the corridors, instead of the courtyard filled with bales of merchandise and ringing with the shouts and laughter of the porters, what would have struck him immediately would have been the feeling of sadness and inertia.

Of the numerous employees who had formerly peopled the offices, only two now remained: one was a young man of twenty-three or twenty-four named Emmanuel Herbaut, who was in love with Monsieur Morrel's daughter and had stayed on with the firm despite all his family's efforts to make him resign; the other was an old one-eyed cashier named Coclès, a good, patient and devoted man, but absolutely inflexible when it came to arithmetic, the one point on which he would have stood his ground against the whole world, even against Monsieur Morrel if necessary. He had been with the firm for twenty years and he saw no reason to alter his faith in it now. The payments due at the end of the previous month had been made promptly and in full.

But since that victorious end of the month, Monsieur Morrel had spent many cruel hours. He had had to unite all his resources in order to make those payments; fearing that word of his distress might leak out in Marseilles if he were seen taking such extreme measures, he took a trip to the fair at Beaucaire to sell some of his wife's jewelry and part of their silverware. Thanks to this sacrifice, he had saved the honor of his firm, but his funds were now exhausted. The return of the *Pharaon* was his only hope of being able to meet a payment of one hundred thousand francs due to Monsieur de Boville on the fifteenth of that month and other payments totaling three hundred thousand francs due on the fifteenth of the following month. But another ship which had left Calcutta at the same time as the *Pharaon* had arrived in Marseilles two weeks ago and there was still no news of the *Pharaon*.

Such was the state of affairs when the representative of the firm of Thomson and French called on Monsieur Morrel. He was received by Emmanuel, who instructed Coclès to take him to Monsieur Morrel's office. On the staircase they met a beautiful young girl of sixteen or seventeen, who looked at the stranger with anxiety.

"Monsieur Morrel is in his office, isn't he, Mademoiselle Julie?" asked the cashier.

"Yes, I think so," said the girl hesitantly. "See if my father is in first, Coclès, then announce this gentleman."

"It would be useless to announce me, mademoiselle," said the Englishman. "Monsieur Morrel doesn't know my name. I'm the head clerk of Thomson and French, a firm which does business with your father's."

The girl turned pale and continued on her way down the stairs, while Coclès and the stranger continued to go up. She entered Emmanuel's office as Coclès, using a key which he alone possessed, opened a door on the third floor, led the

stranger into an antechamber, went through a second door
and closed it behind him, then came back an instant later
to tell the stranger he could enter.

Monsieur Morrel stood up and offered the stranger a seat.
The worthy shipowner had changed greatly in fourteen years.
He was now fifty; his hair had turned white, his forehead
had become wrinkled with care and his eyes, formerly so
firm and decisive, had grown vague and irresolute.

The Englishman looked at him with a curiosity that was
obviously mingled with genuine interest. "You know whom
I represent, don't you?" he asked.

"My cashier tells me you're the head clerk of Thomson
and French."

"That's correct. My firm has a number of payments to make
in France this month and next. Knowing your rigorous exactitude, they have obtained as many bills with your signature
on them as possible and have instructed me to collect the
money from you as they fall due."

Morrel heaved a sigh and passed his hand over his forehead. "You have bills signed by me, then?" he asked.

"Yes," said the Englishman, taking out a bundle of papers.
"First of all, here's a deed of assignment for two hundred
thousand francs made out to our firm by Monsieur de Boville. Do you acknowledge this debt to Monsieur de Boville?"

"Yes, it's an investment he made in my firm at four and
a half per cent nearly five years ago. Half of it is due on
the fifteenth of this month and half on the fifteenth of next
month."

"That's right. Then here are various bills due at the end
of this month and totaling thirty-two thousand five hundred
francs."

"I acknowledge them," said Morrel, flushing with shame
at the thought that he was perhaps about to be unable to
honor his own signature for the first time in his life. "Is
that all?"

"No, we also hold these bills due at the end of next month.
Their total is fifty-five thousand francs. In all, we hold bills
for two hundred and eighty-seven thousand five hundred
francs."

It would be impossible to describe Monsieur Morrel's suffering during this enumeration. "Two hundred and eighty-
seven thousand five hundred francs," he repeated mechanically.

"That's right," replied the Englishman. "Now," he continued, after a moment of silence, "I will not conceal from
you, Monsieur Morrel, that, despite your reputation of perfect
integrity, there is a persistent rumor in Marseilles that you
are not in a position to meet your obligations."

Morrel paled markedly at this almost brutal frankness. "I took over this firm from my father," he said, "after he himself had managed it for thirty-five years. In all that time not a single bill signed by Morrel and Son has ever been present for payment without being honored."

"Yes, I know that," replied the Englishman. "But as one man of honor to another, tell me frankly, will you pay these bills with the same exactitude?"

"Such a frank question deserves a frank answer," said Morrel. "Yes, I'll pay them if, as I hope, my ship arrives safely, for its arrival will restore the credit which my successive misfortunes have destroyed. But should the *Pharaon*, my last resource, fail to arrive—it's cruel to say, but I'm afraid I'll be forced to suspend my payments."

"As I was coming here," said the Englishman, "I saw a ship entering the harbor."

"I know; it was coming from India also, but it's not mine," said Morrel. Then he added softly, "This delay isn't natural. The *Pharaon* left Calcutta on the fifth of February; it ought to have been here a month ago."

"What's that?" asked the Englishman, listening intently. "What's that noise?"

"Oh, my God!" exclaimed Morrel. "What can have happened now?"

There was a great bustle of footsteps on the stairs. The two men also heard a cry of distress. Morrel stood up to go over and open the door, but his strength failed him and he sank back into his chair. Then the noise stopped, but Morrel still seemed to be expecting something.

There was the sound of a key being turned in the lock of the outer door.

"There are only two people who have a key to that door: Coclès and Julie," murmured Morrel. Just then the second door opened and his daughter appeared, her cheeks bathed in tears. She threw herself in his arms and said, "Oh, father, father! Courage!"

"The *Pharaon* has been lost, hasn't it?" asked Morrel in a choked voice.

The girl said nothing, but she nodded, pressing her head against her father's chest.

"And the crew?"

"They were all saved by the ship that just came into port."

Morrel looked up with an expression of sublime resignation and gratitude. "Thank you, dear God," he said. "At least you've struck no one but me."

At this moment Madame Morrel came in sobbing, followed by Emmanuel. Behind them, in the antechamber, were seven

or eight half-naked sailors. The Englishman started when he
saw these men and took a step toward them, but then he
restrained himself and withdrew to the furthest corner of
the room.

"How did it happen?" asked Morrel.

"Come in, Penelon," said Emmanuel, "and tell us about it."

An old sun-tanned sailor stepped forward holding a battered hat in his hands. "Hello, Monsieur Morrel," he said,
as though he had left Marseilles only the day before.

"Hello, my friend," said the shipowner, who could not help
smiling despite his tears. "Where's the captain?"

"He's sick, Monsieur Morrel, and he stayed at Palma, but,
God willing, he'll be here in a few days as healthy as I am."

"That's good. . . . Now, Penelon, tell me about it."

Penelon rolled his quid of tobacco from his right cheek
to his left, wiped his lips, turned around and shot a long
jet of blackish saliva into the antechamber. Then he took a
step forward and began:

"Well, sir, we were somewhere between Cape Blanc and
Cape Boyador, sailing along with a good south-southwesterly
breeze, when Captain Gaumard came up to me—I forgot to
tell you I was at the helm—and said, 'Penelon, what do you
think of those clouds coming up on the horizon over there?'
I just happened to be looking at them myself right then.

" 'I'll tell you what I think of them, captain,' I said. 'I
think they're coming up a little faster than they have a right
to, and I think they're too dark for clouds that aren't up to
something they shouldn't be.'

" 'I think you're right,' said the captain. 'We're in for a
gale.'

" 'A gale!' I said. 'Anyone who buys what's happening over
there for a gale will make a nice profit on his money. It's
an out-and-out hurricane or I've never seen one.' You could
see the wind coming up the way you can see the dust at
Montredon.

"Well, after we'd been tossed around for twelve hours
straight, the ship sprang a leak. 'Penelon,' said the captain,
'I think we're sinking. I'll take the helm; you go below and
take a look at the hold.'

"When I got below I saw there was already three feet of
water in the hold. I ran back up topside yelling. 'Man the
pumps! Man the pumps!' It was already too late! We went
to work, but it seemed as if the more we pumped out, the
more there was. After four hours of work I said, 'Since she's
going to sink anyway, we might as well just let her sink. You
can only die once!'

" 'Is that how you set an example, Penelon?' said the captain. 'Just wait a minute.' He went to get a pair of pistols from his cabin. 'I'll blow out the brains of the first man who leaves the pumps!' he said. Well, nothing makes a man braver than a good reason like that. Then, too, the wind had died down a little by then. But the water was still coming in, not much, about two inches an hour. Two inches an hour seems like nothing, but in twelve hours it makes twenty-four inches, which is two feet. Two feet plus the three we already had made five feet. Now when a ship has five feet of water in her belly, she's no good to anyone.

" 'All right, men,' said the captain, 'that's enough. We've done everything we could to save the ship, now let's save ourselves. To the boat, men, as fast as you can!'

"We loved the *Pharaon*, Monsieur Morrel, but no matter how much a sailor loves his ship, he loves his own hide even more. We didn't argue with the captain when he told us to get into the boat, especially since the ship seemed to be groaning and saying to us, 'Hurry up! Leave! Leave!' And she wasn't lying, poor *Pharaon*, because we could actually feel her sinking under us. We had the boat in the sea in less time than it takes to tell, with all eight of us inside it. We weren't any too soon, either. Right after I jumped into the boat the deck burst with a noise like the broadside of a man-of-war. Ten minutes later her bow plunged downward, then her stern, then she began to turn around like a dog chasing his tail, and then—no more *Pharaon!*

"As for us, we went for three days without eating or drinking and we were already talking about drawing straws to see which one of us would feed the others when the *Gironde* picked us up and took us back to Marseilles. And that's exactly how it happened, Monsieur Morrel, on my word of honor as a sailor. Isn't that right, men?" There was a general murmur of assent.

"You did well, my friends," said Monsieur Morrel. "You're all fine men and I knew in advance that I'd have nothing to blame but my own bad luck. It's the will of God, not the fault of men. Now, how much pay do I owe you?"

"Oh, let's not talk about that, Monsieur Morrel."

"I insist on talking about it," said the shipowner with a sad smile.

"Well, we've got three months' pay coming," said Penelon.

"Coclès, give two hundred francs to each one of these brave men. In other times I'd have added, 'And give each man two hundred francs extra,' but these are unfortunate times for me, my friends, and the little money I have left no longer belongs to me, so please excuse me and don't think any less of me because of it. Now take your money and if you find another ship, sign on board; you're free now."

The last part of his sentence produced a strong effect on the worthy sailors. They looked at one another in bewilderment. Penelon almost swallowed his quid of tobacco, but fortunately he put his hand to his throat in time. "What!" he exclaimed, choking. "Are you discharging us, Monsieur Morrel? Are you dissatisfied with us?"

"No, no, my friends," said Morrel, "I'm not at all dissatisfied with you, quite the contrary. But what else can I do? I have no more ships, so I no longer need sailors. And I have no more money to build other ships with."

"Well, if you don't have any more money, don't pay us! We'll get along all right without it."

"Enough, enough, my friends," said Morrel, choked with emotion. "We'll see each other again some day, in happier times. Emmanuel, go with them and see that my wishes are carried out." He made a sign to Coclès, who walked out of the office. The sailors followed him, and were in turn followed by Emmanuel.

"And now," said Morrel to his wife and daughter, "leave me for a moment; I must speak with this gentleman." He glanced toward the representative of Thomson and French, who had stood silently in his corner throughout the entire scene. The two women withdrew, leaving the two men alone.

"Well," said Morrel, sinking into his chair, "you saw and heard everything; there's nothing more I can tell you."

"I saw," said the Englishman, "that you have just been the victim of a new disaster which was as undeserved as the others, and this has confirmed me in my desire to be helpful to you. I'm one of your principal creditors, am I not?"

"You at least hold the bills which fall due within the shortest time."

"Would you like me to postpone the date of payment?"

"A postponement would save my honor and therefore my life."

"How long would you like?"

Morrel hesitated. "Two months," he said.

"Very well, then, I'll give you three."

"But do you think your firm will——"

"Don't worry, I take full responsibility. Today is the fifth of June; renew these bills for the fifth of September. I'll be here at eleven o'clock in the morning"—the clock had just struck eleven—"on the fifth of September."

The new bills were made out, the old ones torn up and the

poor shipowner at least had three more months in which to assemble his last resources.

The Englishman received Morrel's thanks with his usual reserve, then bade him good-bye. On the stairs he met Julie. She pretended to be going down, but in reality she had been waiting for him.

"Oh, monsieur——" she began, clasping her hands.

"Mademoiselle," said the stranger, "you will receive a letter signed 'Sinbad the Sailor.' Do exactly what that letter tells you to do, no matter how strange it may appear to you."

"Very well."

"Do you promise to do what the letter says?"

"I swear it."

"Good. Farewell, mademoiselle. Continue to be the good and upright girl you are now and I'm sure God will reward you by giving you Emmanuel as your husband."

Julie uttered a little cry and turned as red as a cherry. The stranger continued on his way. In the courtyard he met Penelon, who had a roll of banknotes in each hand and seemed unable to decide whether to keep them. "Come with me, my friend," said the Englishman, "I want to talk to you."

Chapter 19

The postponement so unexpectedly granted by the representative of Thomson and French seemed to Monsieur Morrel like one of those returns of good fortune which announce to a man that fate has at last grown weary of attacking him. The only way in which Monsieur Morrel could explain the conduct of Thomson and French to himself was on the supposition that they had adopted this line of reasoning: "It is better to uphold a man who owes us nearly three hundred thousand francs and receive the money three months late, rather than to hasten his bankruptcy and recover only six or eight per cent of our debt."

Unfortunately, however, Morrel's other creditors did not follow this reasoning; some of them, in fact, reached the opposite conclusion. Their bills were therefore presented for payment with scrupulous punctuality. It was only thanks to the postponement which the Englishman had granted him that Morrel was able to pay them.

Nothing more had been seen of the representative of Thomson and French; he had disappeared one or two days after his visit to Morrel. As for the crew of the *Pharaon*, they had apparently all found a place on some other ship, for they had also disappeared.

Monsieur Morrel spent more than two months in unsuccessful efforts to renew his credit. On the twentieth of August it was learned that he had taken a seat in a coach leaving Marseilles. This immediately gave rise to the supposition that his declaration of bankruptcy had been set for the end of the month and that he had left in advance in order not to be present on that painful occasion. But when the thirty-first of August arrived, Coclès paid every bill presented to him. This came as a great surprise to those who had been predicting Morrel's ruin, but, with the tenacity peculiar to prophets of disaster, they merely postponed the expected bankruptcy to the end of September.

Monsieur Morrel returned to Marseilles on the first of September. His family had been waiting for him with great anxiety, for his trip to Paris was his last chance of salvation. He had thoughts of Danglars, who was now a millionaire and who still owed him a debt of gratitude, for it was due to Morrel's recommendation that he had obtained the position with the Spanish banker in whose service he had begun to amass his immense fortune. Danglars had unlimited credit and could therefore save Morrel without taking a single franc from his pocket: all he had to do was to guarantee a loan and Morrel was saved. Morrel had been thinking of him for a long time, but there are certain instinctive repugnances which are beyond one's control and Morrell had put off approaching him as late as possible. And he was right, for he returned to Marseilles overcome by the humiliation of a refusal.

He uttered no complaints or recriminations on his return, however. He kissed his wife and daughter, shook hands warmly with Emmanuel, shut himself in his office and sent for Coclès.

"This time we're lost," said the two women to Emmanuel. Then, after a short discussion, they decided that Julie would write to her brother, who was in garrison at Nîmes, asking him to come at once.

Although he was only twenty-two years old, Maximilien Morrel already had great influence over his father. He was a firm, upright young man who, when the time had come for him to choose his life's work, had decided on a military career. He studied at the École Polytechnique and graduated with a brilliant record. For the past year he had been a lieutenant and he now had good prospects of being promoted at an early date.

Julie and her mother were not mistaken about the gravity

of the situation. A short time after Morrel went into his office with Coclès, Julie saw the latter come out pale and trembling, with an expression of utter despair on his face. She tried to question him, but he continued to descend the stairs and would say nothing except, "Oh, mademoiselle! What a terrible disaster! I would never have thought it possible!"

Emmanuel tried to reassure the two women, but he was not very convincing; he knew too much about the state of the firm's finances not to be keenly aware of the great catastrophe which threatened the Morrel family.

The next day Monsieur Morrel appeared quite calm and went to his office as usual. That evening after dinner, however, he took his daughter in his arms and pressed her to his breast for a long time. Julie later remarked to her mother that, although he was outwardly calm, she had noticed that his heart was pounding violently.

The two following days went by in almost the same manner. On the evening of the fourth of September, Monsieur Morrel asked his daughter to give him back the key to his office. She was startled by this request, which struck her as sinister. Why should her father ask her for that key which she had always had, and which had been taken away from her in her childhood only as a punishment?

"What have I done wrong to make you take the key back?" she asked.

This simple question brought tears to Morrel's eyes. "Nothing, my child," he replied. "I need it, that's all."

Julie pretended to look for the key. "I must have left it in my room," she said. She went out, but instead of going to her room she went to consult Emmanuel.

"Don't give your father that key," said the young man. "And, if possible, stay with him every moment tomorrow morning." She tried to make him explain himself, but he would say nothing more.

The next morning Monsieur Morrel was kinder to his wife and more affectionate to his daughter than he had ever been before. He looked lovingly at Julie and kissed her repeatedly. She remembered Emmanuel's instructions and tried to follow him when he left to go to his office, but he gently pushed her back and said, "Stay with your mother," in such a way that she dared not disobey him.

She remained standing in the same place after he had gone, motionless and silent. Then the door opened and she looked up with an exclamation of joy. "Maximilien!" she cried.

At this cry Madame Morrel ran forward and threw herself into the arms of her son. "What's happened?" asked the

young man, looking first at his mother, then at his sister.
"Your letter frightened me and I came as fast as I could."

"Julie," said Madame Morrel, making a sign to her son,
"go tell your father Maximilien has arrived."

Julie rushed out of the room, but at the bottom of the
staircase she found a man holding a letter in his hand. "You're
Mademoiselle Julie Morrel, aren't you?" he said with a pronounced Italian accent.

"Yes, I am," stammered Julie, "but what do you want with
me? I don't know you."

"Read this," said the man, holding out the letter to her.
Julie hesitated. "Your father's salvation depends on it," said
the messenger. She snatched the letter from his hands, tore
it open and read the following:

> Go immediately to 15 Allées de Meilhan, ask the
> porter for the key to the room on the sixth floor, enter
> that room, take the red silk purse which you will find
> on the mantelpiece and bring this purse to your father.
> It is essential that he have it before eleven o'clock. You
> promised to obey me blindly; I now remind you of your
> promise.
>
> ### SINBAD THE SAILOR

Julie raised her eyes from the letter with a cry of joy. She
looked for the man who had brought it to her, but he had
disappeared.

Meanwhile, Madame Morrel had told her son everything.
The young man knew of the successive disasters which had
struck his father, but he had not known how serious his
situation really was. He stood dumbfounded for a moment,
then suddenly turned and rushed up the stairs to his father's
office. As he stood knocking vainly on the door, he saw his
father coming from his bedroom, pressing to his side an object
which he was trying to conceal beneath his coat. He cried
out in surprise when he saw Maximilien, for he had not known
of his arrival.

Maximilien ran down the stairs and threw his arms around
his father's neck. But then he stepped back abruptly and
turned as pale as death. "Father," he said, "why are you
carrying a pair of pistols under your coat?"

"Maximilien," replied Morrel, looking steadfastly at his
son, "you're a man now, and a man of honor. Come with me,
I'll tell you about it."

The two men went up to the office. Morrel laid the pistols
on one end of his desk and pointed to an open ledger. This

ledger contained a precise summary of his situation. "Read," he said.

Maximilien read and remained silent for a moment, overcome with emotion. "Have you exhausted all your resources?" he said finally.

"All."

"In half an hour then," said Maximilien grimly, "our name will be dishonored."

"Blood washes away dishonor."

"You're right, father, and I understand you," said Maximilien. He threw his arms around his father and for an instant those two noble hearts beat against each other.

"Now go to your mother and your sister," said Morrel.

"Give me your blessing, father," said the young man, dropping to his knees.

Morrel took his son's head between his hands and said, "Yes, I bless you in the name of three generations if irreproachable men. Listen to what they say to you through my voice: Providence can rebuild the edifice which misfortune has destroyed. On seeing that I have died such a death, the most implacable men will take pity on you. Work, young man, struggle zealously and courageously, spend only what is necessary to keep yourself, your mother and your sister alive, in order that you may repay my debts, in order that one day, in this same office, you will be able to say, 'My father died because he was unable to do what I am doing today; but he died calmly and peacefully because he knew I would do it.'"

"Oh, father, father!" cried the young man. "If only you could live!"

"If I live, everything changes; I become only a man who did not honor his own word, who failed to meet his obligations. But if I die, my body will be that of an unfortunate but honorable man. If I live, you'll be ashamed to bear my name; if I die, you'll hold your head high and say, 'I am the son of a man who killed himself because he was unable to keep his word for the first time in his life.'"

The young man groaned, but he appeared to be resigned. For the second time conviction entered, not his heart, but his mind.

"And now, farewell," said Morrel. "I need to be alone. You'll find my will in my bedroom."

Maximilien stood hesitantly for a moment, then pressed his father convulsively in his arms and rushed out of the room.

After his son had gone, Morrel put out his hand and pulled the bell cord. Coclès appeared a moment later.

"My dear Coclès," said Morrel in a tone which would be impossible to describe, "stay in the antechamber. When the representative of Thomson and French arrives, announce him to me." Coclès did not answer; he nodded, withdrew to the antechamber, sat down and waited.

Morrel sank back into his chair and looked at the clock. He had only seven more minutes. His pistols were loaded. He picked up one of them, murmuring his daughter's name. Then he put it down again, took his pen and wrote a few words of farewell to his daughter. He looked up at the clock again when he had finished; he now counted not by minutes, but by seconds. He picked up the pistol with his eyes fixed on the hands of the clock. He started at the noise he made when he cocked the weapon.

Just then he heard the door of his office open. He did not turn around when he heard Coclès announce, "The representative of the firm of Thomson and French." Morrel moved the pistol toward his mouth.

Suddenly he heard a cry: it was his daughter's voice. He turned around and saw her. The pistol dropped from his hand.

"Father! Father!" she cried, out of breath and wild with joy. "Saved! You're saved!" She held up a red silk purse. "Look! Look!" she said.

Morrel took the purse, troubled by a vague feeling that he had seen it before. In one compartment of the purse was the bill for two hundred and eighty-seven thousand five hundred francs. It was marked paid. In the other compartment was a diamond the size of a walnut: with these words written on a small piece of parchment: "Julie's dowry." Morrel passed his hand over his forehead. He thought he must be dreaming. Just then the clock struck eleven.

"Tell me, my child," said Morrel, "where did you get this purse?"

"In a house in the Allées de Meilhan."

"But it doesn't belong to you!"

Julie showed him the letter she had received that same morning.

"Monsieur Morrel!" cried a voice from the staircase. Then Emmanuel came in, his face beaming with joy and excitement. "The *Pharaon!*" he cried; "the *Pharaon!*"

"What about the *Pharaon?* Are you mad, Emmanuel? You know she sank!"

"The *Pharaon!* She's coming into port!"

Morrel's strength failed him and he fell back into his chair. His mind was completely unable to assimilate this series of unbelievable, unheard-of, fabulous events.

Maximilien rushed into the room. "Father!" he cried. "Why did you tell me the *Pharaon* was lost? She's coming into port now!"

"My friends," said Morrel, "if this is true, we must believe in a miracle. Let's go down to the port, and God have mercy on us if the news is false."

They found Madame Morrel waiting on the stairs; the poor woman had not dared come up to the office.

A large crowd of people had gathered at the port. They all made way for Morrel and every voice called out, "The *Pharaon!* The *Pharaon!*"

And, true enough, opposite the Tower of Saint-Jean was a ship with the words, "Pharaon. Morrel and Son, Marseilles" painted on her stern in white letters. She was an exact duplicate of the other *Pharaon* and was laden, like the other one, with a cargo of cochineal and indigo. As she prepared to drop anchor, Captain Gaumard stood on deck shouting orders and Penelon waved to Monsieur Morrel.

As Morrel and his son embraced each other amid the cheers of the entire crowd, a man whose face was half covered by a black beard stood watching the scene hidden behind a sentry-box. "Be happy, noble heart," he murmured. "God bless you for all you have done and all you will do."

With a smile of satisfaction and happiness on his face, he left his hiding-place, walked unnoticed to the water's edge and called out, "Jacopo! Jacopo!"

A boat came alongside, received him and took him out to a beautifully rigged yacht. He leaped on board with the agility of a sailor. From there he took one last look at Monsieur Morrel, who, weeping with joy, was shaking hands with everyone around him and looking vaguely for his unknown benefactor, whom he seemed to be searching for in the sky.

"And now," said the man on the yacht, "farewell to kindness, humanity and gratitude. Farewell to all sentiments that gladden the heart. I have substituted myself for Providence in rewarding the good; may the God of vengeance now yield me His place to punish the wicked!"

With these words he made a signal and the yacht put out to sea.

Chapter 20

Baron Franz d'Epinay and Viscount Albert de Morcerf, two young French gentlemen, had decided to go to Rome for the carnival, and had therefore reserved a suite in the Hôtel de Londres.

They found on their arrival that the suite consisted of two small bedrooms and a living room. The bedrooms overlooked the street, a fact which Signor Pastrini, the hotel-keeper, stressed as though it added an incalculable value to the suite. All the other rooms on the floor were rented to a very rich personage who, according to Signor Pastrini, was either Sicilian or Maltese.

"The rooms are satisfactory, Signor Pastrini," said Franz, "but now we'd like some supper. And we'll need a carriage for tomorrow and the days following."

"You'll have the supper immediately," replied the hotel-keeper, "but the carriage is another matter."

"What do you mean, another matter!" cried Albert. "Let's be serious, Signor Pastrini; we need a carriage."

"We'll do everything we can to get you one, sir. That's all I can say."

"And when will we have the answer?" asked Franz.

"Tomorrow morning."

"Look," said Albert, "we'll pay a little more, that's all. I know how it is in Paris: twenty-five francs for ordinary days, thirty or thirty-five francs for Sundays and holidays."

"I'm afraid you won't be able to find a carriage in Rome even for double that sum."

"Then we'll put horses on my carriage; it's slightly battered from the journey, but that doesn't matter."

"There are no horses available."

Albert looked at Franz with the expression of a man who has been given an incomprehensible answer. "Do you understand that, Franz? No horses! Well, then, we can have post horses, can't we?"

"They were all rented over two weeks ago. The only ones left now are those which are absolutely necessary for the continuation of the service."

"What do you say to that?" asked Franz.

"I say that when a thing is beyond my comprehension, I stop thinking about it and pass on to something else. Is our supper ready, Signor Pastrini?"

"Yes, Excellency."

"Very well, let's have it."

"But what about the carriage and the horses?" said Franz.

"Don't worry about them, my friend, they'll come all by themselves. It's only a question of price."

And Albert de Morcerf, with that admirable philosophy which believes that nothing is impossible for a man whose purse is full, ate his supper, went to bed, slept soundly and dreamed that he was racing through the carnival in a carriage and six.

Franz rang as soon as he awoke the next morning. Signor Pastrini answered his call in person.

"Well," said the hotel-keeper triumphantly without even waiting for Franz to question him, "I was right not to promise you anything yesterday, Excellency. You're too late: there's not a single carriage available in Rome for the last three days of the carnival."

"Which, of course, are just the days when a carriage is absolutely necessary," remarked Franz.

"Well, I don't think much of your Eternal City," said Albert.

"There are no carriages available from Sunday morning till Tuesday night, Excellency, but from now till Sunday you can have fifty if you like," said Pastrini, desirous of maintaining the dignity of the capital of the Christian world in the eyes of his guests.

"Ah, that's something at least," said Albert. "Today is Thursday; who knows what may happen between now and Sunday?"

"Do you still wish to have a carriage till Sunday?"

"Of course!" exclaimed Albert. "Do you think we want to run around Rome on foot, like lawyers' clerks?"

"When would you like the carriage?"

"In an hour."

"It will be waiting for you at the door in an hour."

Franz had several letters to write to France, so he let Albert have the carriage all day.

At five o'clock Albert returned. He had delivered his letters of recommendation, procured invitations for all his evenings and seen the city of Rome. One day had been sufficient for him to do all that. "I have a surprise for you," he said to Franz.

"What is it?"

"It's impossible to get a carriage and horses for the carnival, isn't it?"

"It certainly is."

"But we could get a cart, couldn't we?"

"Perhaps."

"And a pair of oxen?"

"Probably."

"Well, then, there you are! I'm going to have the cart decorated and we'll dress as Neapolitan harvesters."

"By God!" exclaimed Franz. "For once you've had a good idea! Have you told anyone else about it?"

"Yes, the hotel-keeper. He assured me that nothing could be easier. I wanted to have the oxen's horns gilded, but he told me that would take three days, so we'll have to do without that little luxury."

Just then the door opened and Signor Pastrini put in his head.

"Well," said Albert, "have you found the cart and oxen?"

"I've found something better than that," replied Pastrini with an extremely self-satisfied air.

"What is it?" asked Franz.

"I suppose you know that the Count of Monte Cristo lives on the same floor as you. Well, he has learned of your difficulty and would like to offer you two seats in his carriage and two seats before his window in the Palazzo Rospoli."

Franz and Albert looked at each other. "Should we accept such an offer from a stranger?" asked Albert.

"What kind of a man is this Count of Monte Cristo?" asked Franz.

"He's a very great lord, either Sicilian or Maltese, I don't know which; but in any case he's as noble as a Borghese and as rich as a gold mine."

"It seems to me," said Franz to Albert, "that if this man is as well-mannered as our host says he is, he ought to have conveyed his invitation in some other way, either by writing to us or——"

At this moment there was a knock on the door.

"Come in," said Franz.

A servant wearing an extremely elegant livery appeared in the doorway. "From the Count of Monte Cristo, for Monsieur Franz d'Epinay and Monsieur Albert de Morcerf," he said, handing two cards to the hotel-keeper, who in turn handed them to the two young men. "The Count of Monte Cristo," continued the servant, "requests the honor of calling on these gentlemen tomorrow morning and would like to know what hour is convenient for them."

"Tell the count," said Franz, "that, on the contrary, it is we who shall have the honor of calling on him tomorrow morning."

The servant withdrew.

"Now that's what I call overwhelming us with politeness," said Albert. "You're right, Signor Pastrini, your Count of Monte Cristo is a very noble gentleman."

"I take it you accept his offer?" said Pastrini.

"Yes, of course," replied Albert. "However, I admit I regret the loss of our cart and harvesters, and if it weren't for the windows in the Palazzo Rospoli, I think I'd go back to my original idea. What do you say, Franz?"

"I say it's the windows in the Palazzo Rospoli that decide me too."

The next morning Franz sent for Signor Pastrini, who presented himself with his usual obsequiousness. It was nine o'clock.

"Do you think we can call on the Count of Monte Cristo at this hour?" asked Franz.

"Certainly!" replied Pastrini. "The count is a very early riser. I'm sure he's been up for over two hours."

"In that case, Albert, if you're ready, let's go thank our neighbor for his courtesy."

"Let's go!"

Franz and Albert did not have far to go. Pastrini preceded them and rang the doorbell for them; a servant opened the door.

"*I Signori Francesi,*" said Pastrini. The servant bowed and motioned them to enter.

They walked through two rooms furnished with an elegance they would not have thought possible in Signor Pastrini's hotel, then they came into a drawing room of extraordinary elegance. An oriental rug covered the floor; on the walls hung magnificent paintings, interspersed with splendid weapons and trophies; large tapestried curtains hung before each door.

"If Your Excellencies will take a seat," said the servant, "I will inform the count that you are here." He disappeared through one of the doors.

Franz and Albert exchanged a glance, then looked again at the furniture, the paintings and the weapons. It all seemed even more magnificent the second time they looked at it than the first.

"Well, what do you think of this?" said Franz.

"I think our neighbor must be either a stockbroker who made a very successful speculation or some prince traveling incognito."

"Ssh! We'll soon find out, because here he is."

A door opened and a curtain was pushed aside to make way for the owner of all those riches.

"Gentlemen," said the Count of Monte Cristo as he entered, "please accept my excuses for making you call for me, but I was afraid I might disturb you if I visited you at an earlier hour. Besides, you told me you were coming and I kept myself at your disposal."

"Franz and I are very grateful to you, count," said Albert. "You've solved a great problem for us. We were inventing all sorts of fantastic vehicles when your gracious invitation arrived."

"It's that idiot Pastrini's fault that I didn't come to your aid sooner," said the count, motioning the two young men to sit down on a sofa. "He told me nothing about your problem. As soon as I learned I could be of use to you, I was glad of the opportunity to pay you my respects." The two young men bowed. "Also," continued the count, "there's to be an execution at the Piazza del Popolo today. I told my steward yesterday to find me a window overlooking the scene, so perhaps I can also render you that service." He reached out his hand and pulled a bell cord.

A moment later a man of forty-five or fifty entered the room. "Monsieur Bertuccio," said the count, "have you obtained a window overlooking the Piazza del Popolo, as I instructed you to do yesterday?"

"Yes, Excellency," replied the steward, "but it was quite late."

"What?" said the count, frowning. "Didn't I tell you to get me a window?"

"Yes, and Your Excellency has one, but it had already been rented to Prince Lobanieff and I was obliged to pay a hundred——"

"That will do, Monsieur Bertuccio, spare these gentlemen the details of your arrangement; you got the window, that's all we need to know. Give the address of the house to the coachman." The steward bowed and prepared to withdraw. "Just a moment," said the count, "ask Pastrini if he has received the program of the execution."

"That won't be necessary," said Franz, taking a notebook from his pocket. "I saw the program and copied it down. Here it is."

"Very well, then, Monsieur Bertuccio, you may withdraw. Notify us when lunch is ready. Will you gentlemen do me the honor of having lunch with me?"

"We don't want to abuse your hospitality, count," said Albert.

"Not at all! It will give me great pleasure. You'll be able to return the favor some day in Paris. Monsieur Bertuccio, have the table set for three."

The count took Franz's notebook and read aloud: "'The following men will be executed today, February 22: Andrea Rondolo, guilty of the murder of the honored and venterated Don Cesare Terlini, and Peppino, alias Rocca Priori, convicted of complicity with the detestable bandit Luigi Vampa and the men of his band. The first will be *mazzolato,* the second will be decapitated.' That was the original program, but I was in the home of Cardinal Rospigliosi last night and I was told that one of the prisoners has been reprieved."

"Which one?" asked Franz.

"The second one," replied the count. "That will deprive you of a decapitation, but there's still the *mazzolato,* which is quite a curious form of execution the first time you see it, or even the second. But decapitation is too simple; nothing unexpected ever happens. Europeans know nothing when it comes to executions and tortures," added the count contemptuously. "They're in the childhood, or rather the old age, of cruelty."

"You sound as though you'd made a comparative study of methods of execution all over the world, count," remarked Franz.

"There are few of them I haven't seen," replied the count coldly.

"And you found pleasure in watching such horrible sights?"

"My first feeling was repugnance, then indifference, then curiosity."

"Curiosity! That's a terrible word to use."

"Why? Death is the only really serious preoccupation in life. Isn't it worth while, therefore, to study the different ways in which the soul can take leave of the body, and how, according to their character, their temperament and even the customs of their country, different individuals undergo this passage from from being to nothingness? As for myself, I can tell you one thing: the more one sees others die, the easier it becomes to face death oneself. Thus, in my opinion, death is perhaps an ordeal, but it is not an expiation."

"I don't understand you very well," said Franz. "Please explain yourself; you've no idea how strongly you've aroused my curiosity."

"Listen," said the count, his face taking on an expression of hatred, "if a man has tortured and killed your father, your mother, your sweetheart, in short, one of those beings who leave an eternal emptiness and a perpetually bleeding wound when they are torn from your heart, do you think society has given you sufficient reparation because the blade of the guillotine has passed between the murderer's trapezius and his occipital bone, because the man who made you undergo long years of mental and emotional suffering has undergone a few seconds of physical pain?"

"Yes, I know," said Franz, "human justice is sadly lacking in consolation; it can only shed blood in exchange for blood. But we mustn't ask it to do more than it can."

"And I've mentioned only a very simple case," went on the count, "the case in which society avenges the death of one individual by the death of another. But aren't there all sorts of suffering which a man can undergo without being provided by society with any means of vengeance whatsoever? Aren't there crimes for which the impalement of the Turks, the troughs of the Persians or the rolled tendons of the Iroquois would be too gentle, and which are nevertheless left unpunished by our indifferent society? Answer, aren't there such crimes?"

"Yes," said Franz, "and it's in order to punish them that dueling is tolerated."

"Ah, dueling!" cried the count. "A fine method of vengeance! A man has taken your sweetheart from you, seduced your wife or dishonored your daughter; from a life which had a right to expect from God the share of happiness which He promised every human being in creating him, he has made an existence of pain, misery or infamy; and you believe his crime avenged because you have thrust a sword into his chest or lodged a bullet in his head? Come, come! And of course he may even emerge victorious, with his sin washed away in the eyes of the world. No, no; if I ever wanted to take vengeance on someone, that's not how I'd do it."

"You disapprove of dueling, then? You would refuse to fight a duel?" asked Albert, astonished to hear such a strange theory.

"No, not at all," said the count. "Let me make myself clear: I would fight a duel for an insult, a blow or a lie, and I'd do it with hardly a thought because, thanks to the skill I've acquired in all bodily exercises and the gradual way in which I've accustomed myself to danger, I'd be almost certain of killing my opponent. Oh, yes, I'd fight a duel for something of that sort; but for slow, profound, infinite and eternal suffering I'd try to avenge myself by inflicting similar suffering. 'An eye for an eye, and a tooth for a tooth.' "

"But," said Franz, "with that theory, which makes you your own judge and executioner, it would be difficult to stay clear of the power of the law. Hatred is blind, anger is foolhardy, and he who pours out vengeance risks having to drink a bitter draft."

"If he's poor and inept, yes; but not if he's rich and clever. Besides, the worst that can happen to him is a public execution, and what does he care about that, as long as he has had his vengeance? I'm almost sorry that wretched Peppino won't be decapitated as the program says; you'd see how long it lasts and whether it's really worth speaking of. . . . But this is a strange conversation to be having during the carnival. How did we begin talking about such things? Oh, yes, I remember: I mentioned that I could offer you a place at my window. And you'll have it, too, but for now let's go to lunch. Here comes someone to announce that it's ready." The two young men stood up and walked into the dining room.

During the meal, which was excellent and admirably served, Franz tried to catch Albert's eye in order to read there what impression their host's words had made on him, but Albert was apparently unconcerned with everything except his own hearty appetite. As for the count, he hardly touched the food set before him; he seemed as though he might have sat down at table with his guests only in order to be polite, and that he was awaiting their departure in order to be served some strange dish of his own.

At the end of the meal Franz took out his watch and said, "Excuse us, count, but we still have a thousand things to do."

"May I ask what they are?"

"Some sort of costume is absolutely necessary for the carnival and we don't have any yet."

"Don't worry about that. We have a private room at the Piazza del Popolo; I'll have costumes brought to us and we can change into them right there, after the execution. It's half-past twelve now, gentlemen; we have no time to lose."

As Franz, Albert and the Count of Monte Cristo approached the Piazza del Popolo, the crowd grew denser and they could see two things rising above the heads of the people: the obelisk, surmounted by a cross, which marks the center of the square, and the two tall wooden uprights of the guillotine, with the metal blade glittering between them.

The window, which had been rented at such an exorbitant price, was on the third floor of a large mansion situated betwen the Vai del Babuino and the Monte Pincio. It was in a sort of dressing room adjoining a bedroom; by closing the door between the two rooms, the occupants of the dressing room could enjoy the spectacle in privacy.

Outside, the entire square seemed to have been transformed into a vast amphitheater. Every window and balcony was packed with spectators, and every projection on the front of a building which could support a man had its living statue. The count was right: the most interesting sight in life is death.

Suddenly the noise of the crowd died down as if by magic. The door of the church had opened. A group of penitents appeared first, each holding a lighted candle in his hand and wearing over his head a gray sack with eyeholes cut into it. Behind the penitents came a tall man who was bare from the waist up. At his left side hung a large knife in a sheath; over his shoulder he carried a large iron mace. This man was the exeuctioner. Behind him walked, in the order in which they were to be executed, first Peppino and then Andrea, each accompanied by two priests. Andrea was being held up under each arm by a priest. From time to time both men kissed a crucifix which was held out to them by the confessor.

At this sight alone Franz felt his legs go weak. He looked at Albert; he was as pale as his shirt. Only the count appeared impassive.

Meanwhile the two condemned men had come close enough for their features to be distinguished. Peppino was a handsome young man with suntanned skin and a wild, proud look in his eyes. Andrea was short and fat, and his face had a look of base cruelty.

"I thougfit you said there was to be only one execution," said Franz to the count.

"I told you the truth," replied Monte Cristo coldly.

"But there are two prisoners."

"Yes, but one of them is about to die and the other still has long years of life ahead of him."

"It seems to me that if his reprieve is going to come, there's no time to be lost."

"Here it comes now. Look," said the count.

True enough, just as Peppino arrived at the foot of the guillotine, a penitent burst through the ranks of the soldiers, who made no effort to stop him, ran up to the leader of the penitents and handed him a piece of paper. The leader of the penitents read the paper, raised his hand and cried out, "Praises be to God and to His Holiness the Pope! Peppino, alias Rocca Priori, has been pardoned!" Loud cheers arose from the crowd.

"Peppino pardoned!" shouted Andrea, completely awakened from the torpor into which he seemed to have fallen. "Why pardon for him and not for me? We were to die together! They promised me he'd die before I did! They don't have the right to make me die alone! I won't die alone! I won't die alone!" He tore himself away from the two priests, writhing, shrieking and making frenzied efforts to break the cords which bound his hands together. The executioner motioned to two of his assistants, who leaped down from the platform of the guillotine and seized the condemned man.

"What's happening?" asked Franz, for, since the entire scene had taken place in Roman dialect, he had not understood very clearly.

"What's happening?" said the count. "Don't you understand? That human being who's going to die down there is furious because his fellow man isn't going to die with him. If he had his choice, he'd tear the other man to pieces with his teeth and nails rather than let him go on enjoying life while he himself is about to be deprived of it. Oh, mankind, race of crocodiles! How well I recognize you down there, and how worthy you are of yourselves!"

As Andrea struggled with the two executioner's assistants he cried out, "He must die! I want him to die! They don't have the right to kill me alone!" The struggle was frightful to see, but the two assistants finally carried Andrea to the top of the platform. The entire crowd had turned against him by now and twenty thousand voices were shrieking, "Kill him! Kill him!"

Franz stepped back, but the count seized his arm and held him in place. "What's the matter?" said the count. "If you're feeling pity, it's very badly placed. If you saw a mad dog in the street you'd shoot it without pity, even though the poor animal's only crime was to have been bitten by another dog. Yet here you are taking pity on a man who was bitten by no other man, but who nevertheless killed his benefactor and who now, no longer able to kill because his hands are tied, wants to bring on the death of his companion in captivity, his comrade in misfortune! No, no; look, look."

The recommendation had become needless, for Franz was fascinated by the horrible spectacle. The two assistants had carried the condemned man to the top of the platform and there, despite his struggling, biting and shrieking, had forced him to kneel. The executioner raised his mace and the two assistants stepped back. The condemned man tried to stand up, but the mace crashed down on his left temple, making a dull, heavy sound. The man fell face downward like an ox, then rolled over on his back. The executioner dropped his mace, drew his knife and slit open the man's throat. Then he stood up on the man's stomach and began to knead it with his feet. Each time he pressed down with his foot, a jet of blood spurted from the man's throat.

Franz started backward and sank half-fainting into a chair. Albert remained standing, but his eyes were closed and he clung tightly to the window curtain. The count was as erect and triumphant as the avenging angel.

Chapter 21

When Franz came back to his senses, he found Albert drinking a glass of water which his pallor indicated he needed greatly, while the count was already changing into the costume of a court jester. He looked down into the square. Everything had disappeared: guillotine, executioners and victims; nothing was left except the noisy, joyous crowd. "What happened?" he asked.

"Nothing," replied the count, "absolutely nothing, as you can see, except that the carnival has begun; let's change into our costumes quickly. Look, Monsieur de Morcerf is setting you an example."

Albert was indeed absent-mindedly putting on his taffeta

trousers over his black trousers and his patent leather boots.

It would have been ridiculous of Franz to be so squeamish as not to follow his companions' example. He therefore put on his costume and his mask, which was certainly no paler than his face.

The count's carriage was waiting for them downstairs, full of confetti and bouquets. It would be difficult to imagine a more complete transformation than that which had come over the Piazza del Popolo. Instead of the somber and silent spectacle of death, the square now presented the aspect of a wild, tumultuous orgy. A crowd of masks poured in from all sides, issuing from doors and descending from windows; vehicles rolled in from every street, laden with harlequins, dominoes, noblemen, grotesques, knights and peasants, all shouting, gesticulating, throwing confetti, bouquets and eggs filled with flour at friends and strangers alike, without anyone taking offense or doing anything about it except to laugh. Imagine the wide and beautiful Via del Corso lined from one end to the other with mansions of four or five stories, each with all its balconies hung with tapestries and all its windows draped; at these balconies and windows, three hundred thousand spectators, Romans, Italians, foreigners from the four corners of the earth; in the street, a wild, untiring, joyful crowd dressed in fantastic costumes: gigantic cabbages walking along, heads of buffaloes bellowing on the bodies of men, dogs walking on their hind legs; in the midst of all this a mask raised to reveal a beautiful face which one would like to follow, but from which one is separated by demons like those one sees in one's dreams—imagine all that and you will have a faint idea of the carnival at Rome.

After they had gone around the square twice, the count had his carriage stopped in front of the Palazzo Respoli and asked his companions for permission to leave them. "Gentlemen," he said as he alighted, "when you grow tired of being actors and wish to become spectators again, you know that you have a place at my windows. In the meantime, my coachman and my carriage are at your disposal."

Franz thanked the count for his generous offer. After they had gone on their way again, Albert turned to him and said, "Did you see it?"

"What?"

"Look, there it goes: that carriage full of women dressed as Roman peasants! I'm sure they're charming ladies."

"What a shame you were masked! You might have been able to make up for your lack of amorous success so far in Italy."

"Oh," said Albert, half joking and half serious, "I don't

think the carnival will go by without bringing me some compensation."

Despite Albert's hopes, however, the day passed without any adventure other than meeting the carriage with the Roman peasants two or three more times. At one of these meetings, whether by accident or by design, Albert's mask came loose. He also threw a bouquet into the carriage. One of the ladies was apparently touched by this gallant gesture, for when the young men's carriage passed the next time, she threw a bouquet of violets into it. Albert snatched it up and, since Franz had no reason to believe it had been meant for him, he let Albert keep it. Albert put it victoriously in his buttonhole and the carriage continued its triumphant course.

"Well!" said Franz. "That looks like the beginning of an adventure."

"Laugh if you like," replied Albert, "but I really think it is."

His opinion was reinforced some time later when they passed the carriage again: the lady who had thrown the bouquet to Albert clapped her hands when she saw it in his buttonhole.

The next morning the Count of Monte Cristo called on them in person and said, "Gentlemen, I've come to tell you that I leave my carriage at your disposal from now until the end of the carnival. I have two others with me, so you won't be depriving me of anything. If we have anything to say to each other, we can meet at the Palazzo Rospoli."

The two young men made a few feeble protests, but they actually had no good reason for refusing his offer, especially since it was so agreeable to them, so they finally accepted it. The count stayed with them for a quarter of an hour or so, speaking on all subjects with great facility. He was very well acquainted with the literature of all countries. A glance at his walls had proved to Franz and Albert that he was a connoisseur of painting. Several words he spoke in passing during their conversation proved to them that the sciences were not unknown to him; he seemed to have made an especially thorough study of chemistry.

Some time later Franz and Albert went downstairs to the waiting carriage. Albert had sentimentally placed his bouquet of faded violets in his buttonhole.

Not long after they entered the Via del Corso, a bouquet of fresh violets was thrown into their carriage. Albert put it in his buttonhole in place of the other one, but he kept the faded bouquet in his hand and raised it to his lips the next time they passed the ladies' carriage, an action which seemed to please not only the lady who had thrown it to him but also her gay companions. Needless to say, the flirtation between Albert and the lady with the violets continued all day.

When they came back to the hotel that evening, Franz found a letter from the embassy informing him that he would have the honor of being received the following day by the pope.

He spent the day at the Vatican and came straight back to the hotel. At ten minutes past five, Albert entered. He was bubbling over with joy. The lady with the violets had raised her mask as she passed his carriage. She was lovely.

Franz gave Albert his sincere compliments, and Albert accepted them as his due. He had decided to write to her the next day. It will be easily understood that Franz was not selfish enough to stand in Albert's way in such a promising adventure. He therefore promised his friend that he would leave the carriage to him alone the next day and content himself with watching the carnival from the windows of the Palazzo Rospoli.

The next day he saw Albert pass up and down the Via del Corso several times. He had an enormous bouquet whose purpose was probably to convey his amorous epistle.

That evening Albert was not joyful: he was ecstatic. He was absolutely convinced that his lovely lady would answer his letter. Franz anticipated his desires by telling him that all the noise of the carnival had tired him and that he intended to spend the next day reading and writing in his room.

Albert's expectations were not disappointed. The next evening Franz saw him come rushing into his room waving a piece of paper.

"Did she answer?" cried Franz.

"Read." This word was uttered with an expression impossible to describe. Franz took the letter and read:

Tuesday night at seven o'clock, leave your carriage opposite the Via dei Pontefici. A girl dressed as a Roman peasant will snatch your *moccoletto* from your hand. Follow her. When you arrive at the bottom step of the San Giacomo Church, be sure you have a pink ribbon tied to the shoulder of your costume so that she can recognize you.

From now until then, you will not see me.

Constancy and discretion.

"Well, what do you think of that, my friend?" asked Albert when Franz had finished reading it.

"I think it looks as if you're in for an extremely pleasant adventure."

"I think so too, and I'm afraid you may have to go to the Duke of Bracciano's ball alone." Franz and Albert had both received an invitation from the famous Roman banker that very morning.

Tuesday, the last and most animated day of the carnival, finally arrived. The theaters open at ten o'clock in the morning on that day, for Lent begins at eight o'clock that night. On Tuesday all those who, from lack of time, money or enthusiasm, have so far taken no part in the festivities now mingle in the orgy and contribute their share to the general noise and excitement.

Toward the end of the afternoon the *moccoletti* vendors appear on the scene. The *moccoletti*, or *moccoli*, are candles of varying size which give rise to two preoccupations among the participants of the Roman carnival: first, how to keep one's own *moccoletto* burning; second, how to extinguish the *moccoletti* of others.

Franz and Albert hastened to buy their *moccoletti* along with everyone else. As night drew on, two or three stars began to shine above the crowd. This was like a signal: ten minutes later thousands of lights were flickering and dancing in the streets, accompanied by an uproar the like of which no human ear has ever heard anywhere else on earth.

Albert kept looking at his watch every five minutes until finally it was seven o'clock. The two friends had just reached the corner of the Via dei Pontefici. Albert leaped out of the carriage with his *moccoletto* in his hand. Two or three revelers tried to extinguish it or snatch it away from him, but Albert, a skillful boxer, sent them sprawling on the pavement and continued moving toward the San Giacomo Church.

Franz looked after Albert and saw him reach the bottom step of the church. Then a woman, masked and wearing the costume of a Roman peasant, put out her arm and took his *moccoletto;* this time Albert made no resistance. Franz was too far away to hear the words they exchanged, but they were evidently not hostile, for he saw them go off together arm in arm.

Sudenly the bell which signals the end of the carnival rang out and at the same instant all the *moccoletti* were extinguished as if by magic. It was as though a single immense gust of wind had blown them all out. Franz found himself in utter darkness.

All the tumult died away at the same moment, as if the same mighty wind which had blown out the lights had also blown away the noise. Nothing was heard except the rumbling of carriages taking the revelers home; nothing was seen except a few rare lights flickering in windows.

The carnival was over.

Franz had never experienced such a sharp transition from gaiety to sadness; it was as though the magic breath of some demon had changed Rome into one vast tomb.

He went back to the hotel and found dinner waiting for him. Since Albert had informed him that he did not expect to return until quite late, he sat down to table alone.

At eleven o 'clock Albert still had not returned, so Franz ordered the carriage and set out for the Duke of Bracciano's house. Since Franz and Albert had both arrived in Rome with letters of recommendation addressed to the duke, his first question was to ask Franz where his companion was. Franz answered that he had lost him from sight just as the *moccoletti* were being extinguished.

"And he hasn't returned yet?" asked the duke.

"I waited for him till eleven."

"Do you know where he went?"

"No, not exactly; but I think he had some sort of rendezvous."

"It's a bad night to be out late," said the duke. "You know Rome better than he does; you shouldn't have let him go."

"I might as well have tried to stop a runaway horse. But I left word at the hotel that I'd be here tonight and told them to let me know when he comes back."

"Here comes one of my servants now," said the duke; "I think he's looking for you."

The duke was not mistaken. When the servant saw Franz he came up to him and said, "Your Excellency, Signor Pastrini would like to inform you that a man is waiting for you at the hotel with a letter from Monsieur de Morcerf."

"Why didn't the man bring me the letter here?"

"The messenger gave me no explanation."

"And where is the messenger?"

"He left as soon as he saw me enter the ballroom to deliver his message to you."

Franz took his hat and left immediately. As he approached the hotel he saw a man standing in the middle of the street. He was sure it was the man who had brought the letter from Albert. He went toward him, but, to his surprise, it was the man who spoke first:

"What do you want with me?" he asked, stepping back like a man who wishes to stay on his guard.

"Are you the man who has a letter for me from Monsieur de Morcerf?" asked Franz.

"What's your name?"

"Baron Franz d'Epinay."

"The letter is addressed to you."

"Is there an answer?" asked Franz, taking the letter.

"Yes—at least your friend hopes there will be."

"Come in with me and I'll give you the answer."

"I prefer to wait here," said the messenger, laughing.

"Why?"

"You'll understand when you read the letter."

Franz went inside, lit a candle and read the following:

Dear Franz,

As soon as you read this, please take my letter of credit from my portfolio, which is in a drawer of my desk. Take your own letter of credit also if mine is insufficient, hurry to Torlonia's, draw four thousand piasters and give it to the man who brings you this letter. It is urgent that I have this money without delay.

I will say no more; I count on you as you could count on me.

Your friend,
ALBERT DE MORCERF

P.S.—I now believe in Italian bandits.

Below these words appeared the following, written in a different handwriting:

Se alle sei della mattina le quattro mile piastre non sono nelle mie mani, alle sette il conte Alberto avrà cessato di vivere.[1]

LUIGI VAMPA

This second signature explained everything, and he understood why the messenger had been so reluctant to enter the hotel. Albert had fallen into the hands of the famous bandit leader whose existence he had treated as a fable.

There was no time to lose. Franz ran over to Albert's desk, found the portfolio and took out the letter of credit: it was for six thousand piasters, but Albert had already spent half of this amount. As for Franz, he had no letter of credit. Since he lived in Florence, and had come to Rome for seven or eight days only, he had taken only a hundred louis with him, of which no more than fifty remained. He therefore lacked seven or eight hundred piasters to make up the sum demanded. Suddenly he thought of the Count of Monte Cristo. He was

[1] "If the four thousand piasters are not in my hands by six o'clock in the morning, at seven o'clock Count Albert will have ceased living."

about to call for Signor Pastrini when he saw him appear in person in the doorway.

"Signor Pastrini," asked Franz eagerly, "do you know if the count is at home?"

"Yes, Excellency, he just came in."

"Then please go ask him if I may be allowed to see him."

Pastrini hurried off to carry out his instructions and returned a few minutes later. "The count is awaiting you, Excellency," he said.

Franz found the count in a small room which he had not seen before and which was encircled by divans.

"What good wind blows you here at this hour?" said the count. "Have you perhaps come to ask me to have supper with you? That would be very kind of you."

"No, I've come to talk to you about an extremely serious matter. Are we alone?"

The count stepped over to the door and came back. "Quite alone," he said.

Franz handed him Albert's letter and said, "Read this." Then, after the count had read it, he asked, "What do you think of it?"

The count frowned and was silent for a moment. "Where's the man who brought you this letter?" he asked.

"In the street."

"I'll call him."

"That would be useless; he refused to come into the hotel."

"He may have refused to come to your rooms," said the count, "but he won't make any difficulties about coming to mine." He went over to the window, which overlooked the street, and whistled in a certain way. The man stepped out from against a wall and walked to the middle of the street.

"*Salite!*" said the count in a tone in which he would have given an order to a servant. The messenger obeyed without hesitation or delay. A few seconds later he was at the count's door.

"Ah, it's you, Peppino!" said the count.

Instead of answering, Peppino fell to his knees, seized the count's hand and pressed his lips to it several times.

"I see you haven't yet forgotten that I saved your life," said the count. "That's strange, for it was over a week ago."

"No, Excellency, and I will never forget it," replied Peppino in a tone of profound gratitude

"Never? That's a long time! But at least I'm impressed that you believe it. Stand up and answer my questions." Peppino cast an uneasy glance at Franz. "Oh, you can speak before this gentleman," said the count. "He's a friend of mine."

"All right," said Peppino, "ask me questions and I'll answer."

"How did Viscount Albert fall into Luigi's hands?"

"Excellency, several times the Frenchman's carriage passed the one in which Teresa was riding."

"Luigi's mistress?"

"Yes. The Frenchman made eyes at her and, just to amuse herself, Teresa answered him; the Frenchman threw bouquets to her and she threw one to him. All this was with the chief's permission, of course; he was in the same carriage with her."

"What!" exclaimed Franz. "Luigi Vampa was in that carriage?"

"He was driving, disguised as a coachman," replied Peppino. "The Frenchman took off his mask and Teresa, still with the chief's permission, took off hers; the Frenchman asked for a rendezvous and Teresa gave it to him, but, instead of Teresa it was Beppo who was waiting for him on the steps of San Giacomo Church."

"What!" exclaimed Franz once again. "That peasant girl who snatched his *moccoletto*———"

"Was a boy of fifteen," said Peppino. "But your friend needn't be ashamed of falling into the trap. Beppo has caught many others besides him!"

"And Beppo took him outside the city?" asked the count.

"That's right. A carriage was waiting at the end of the Via Macello. The Frenchman gallantly gave Beppo his arm and climbed in with him. Beppo told him he was going to take him to a villa one league outside of Rome, and the Frenchman assured him he would go with him to the end of the world. But the Frenchman began to get too familiar on the way, so Beppo put a pair of pistols to his head. The driver stopped the horses, turned around and also drew his pistols. At the same time, four of our men, who had been hiding on the banks of the Almo, came running up to the carriage. The Frenchman tried to defend himself—in fact, I hear he almost strangled Beppo—but there was really nothing he could do against five armed men. He stopped struggling and they took him to Luigi and Teresa, who were waiting for him in the Catacombs of Saint Sebastian."

"Well," said the count, turning to Franz, "that's quite a story, isn't it?"

"It would strike me as very funny," said Franz, "if it had happened to anyone except poor Albert."

"The fact is," said the count, "that if you hadn't come to me your friend's amorous adventure would have cost him dearly. As it is, though, a bad fright is the worst thing that will happen to him. He's in a very picturesque spot, too. Have you ever been in the Catacombs of Saint Sebastian?"

"No."

"Well, then, here's a good opportunity to go and see them!" The count rang and a servant appeared. "Have the carriage brought out," said the count. "It won't be necessary to wake the coachman; Ali will drive."

A few moments later the carriage was heard driving up in front of the door. The count looked at his watch and said, "Half-past midnight. We could have left at five o'clock in the morning and still arrived in time, but I'm afraid the delay would have made our friend spend a bad night, so it's better to go rescue him from the hands of the infidels at once."

Franz and the count went out, followed by Peppino.

The route the carriage followed was the ancient Appian Way, with its border of tombs. It seemed to Franz that from time to time he saw a sentinel emerge from behind a ruin, then disappear at a signal from Peppino.

A short distance before the Circus of Caracalla the carriage stopped, Peppino opened the door and Franz and the count stepped out. "We'll be there in ten minutes," said the count to Franz. Then he took Peppino off to one side and gave him an order in a low voice. Peppino took a torch from the carriage and left. Five minutes passed, then Franz and the count walked along the downward path which Peppino had taken until they arrived at the bottom of a small valley. There they could distinguish two men talking together in the darkness.

"Shall we go on, or should we wait here?" asked Franz.

"Let's go on," said the count. "Peppino must have notified the sentinel of our approach."

One of the men, in fact, was Peppino himself; the other was a bandit on sentry duty. "Please follow me, Excellency," said Peppino to the count; "the entrance to the catacombs is only a few yards from here."

"Very well," said the count. "Lead the way."

Behind a clump of bushes and in the midst of a number of rocks, they saw an opening scarcely large enough for a man to pass through. Peppino slipped into it first. After he had taken a few steps, the underground passage widened. He stopped, lit his torch and turned around to see if the others were following him. Franz and the count had to walk bent over and would have had difficulty walking side by side. They had gone some fifty paces when they were stopped by a cry of "Who goes there?" At the same time they saw the light of their torch reflected from the barrel of a carbine in the darkness.

"Friend!" said Peppino. He stepped forward and said a few words in an undertone to this second sentry, who, like the first one, bowed and motioned the visitors to continue on their way.

Behind the sentry was a flight of about twenty steps. Franz and the count walked down them and found themselves at a sort of crossroads: five passages diverged like the rays of a star. The walls, hollowed out into niches in the shape of coffins, indicated that they had finally come to the catacombs. In one of these cavities, whose size was impossible to distinguish, they could see several rays of light.

The count placed his hand on Franz's shoulder and said, "Would you like to see a bandit camp at rest?"

"Certainly," replied Franz.

"All right, then, come with me. Peppino, put out the torch."

Peppino obeyed; Franz and the count found themselves in total darkness, although fifty yards or so ahead of them they could see the flickering red glow, which became still more visible when Peppino put out his torch. They went on in silence, the count guiding Franz as though he had the peculiar faculty of being able to see in the dark. They came to three arches, the center one of which served as a door. On the other side was a large square room entirely surrounded by niches like those already described. In the middle of this room stood four stones which had once been used as altars, as was indicated by the crosses that still surmounted them. A single lamp placed on the base of a pillar illuminated with a pale, flickering light the strange scene which offered itself to the eyes of the two visitors hidden in the shadows.

A man was sitting before the lamp, reading with his back toward the arch through which the newcomers were looking at him. This man was the chief of the band, Luigi Vampa. Around him, grouped according to their fancy, were about twenty bandits, each with his carbine within reach of his hand. At the opposite end of the room a sentry was silently walking up and down before another opening, which was distinguishable only because the shadows seemed thicker at that spot.

When the count thought Franz had gazed long enough on this picturesque tableau, he put his finger to his lips as a signal for silence, climbed the three steps leading up to the room, entered it through the center arch and began to walk toward Vampa, who was so deeply absorbed in his reading that he did not hear the sound of the count's footsteps.

"Who goes there?" cried the sentry, who was less preoccupied and who saw a sort of shadow approaching his chief from behind. At this cry Vampa leaped to his feet and pulled a pistol from his belt. In an instant all the bandits were standing, and the barrels of twenty carbines were pointing at the count.

"Well, my dear Vampa," said the count in a perfectly calm voice, "this seems like a great deal of ceremony to greet a friend!"

"Ground arms!" cried the chief, making an imperious gesture with one hand while he respectfully took off his hat with the other. Then, turning to the singular personage who dominated this entire scene, he said, "Excuse me, count, but I was so far from expecting the honor of a visit from you that I didn't recognize you."

"It seems your memory is equally short in all things, Vampa," said the count, "and that not only do you forget people's faces, but also the agreements you make with them."

"What agreement have I forgotten, count?" asked the bandit in the tone of a man who, if he has committed an error, is anxious to correct it.

"Wasn't it agreed that you would respect not only me but all my friends as well?"

"And how have I broken that agreement?"

"You have seized Viscount Albert de Morcerf and taken him here. That young man is a friend of mine, he is staying in the same hotel as I am, for the past week he has been riding in my carriage, and yet, I repeat, you have seized him, taken him here and held him for ransom."

"Why wasn't I told about this?" asked the chief, turning toward his men, who drew back before his look. "Why did you make me break my word to the count? If I thought one of you knew about this I'd blow his brains out!"

"I told you there had been an error," said the count, turning toward Franz.

"You're not alone?" asked Vampa anxiously.

"I came with the man to whom the ransom letter was addressed. I wanted to prove to him that Luigi Vampa is a man of his word."

Franz entered the room. The chief stepped forward to meet him and said, "Welcome, Excellency. You heard what the count said to me and what I replied. I will add only that I would not have had such a thing happen even for the four thousand piasters at which your friend's ransom was set."

"But where is he?" asked Franz, looking anxiously around. "I don't see him."

"I trust nothing has happened to him," said the count, frowning.

"He's in there," said Vampa, pointing to the opening before which the sentry was pacing. "I'll go myself to tell him he's free." He went toward the place which had been serving as Albert's prison. Franz and the count followed him. Vampa drew back a bolt and pushed open a door. By the light of a lamp similar to the one which illuminated the other room, they saw Albert, wrapped in a cloak one of the bandits had lent him, lying in a corner sound asleep.

"Well, well!" said the count, smiling. "Not bad for a man who was to be shot at seven o'clock in the morning!"

Vampa looked at Albert with considerable admiration for his courage. "You're right, count," he said, "this man must be one of your friends." Then, going over to Albert and touching him on the shoulder, he said, "Please wake up, Excellency."

Albert stretched and rubbed his eyes. "Ah, it's you, captain!" he said. "You should have let me sleep: I was dreaming I was dancing with a charming lady at the duke's ball." He looked at his watch. "Why the devil did you wake me up at this hour?" he exclaimed.

"To tell you that you're free, Excellency."

"Has my ransom been paid?"

"No, Excellency. But a man to whom I can refuse nothing has come for you."

"That man is very kind!" Albert looked around and saw Franz. "What!" he said to him, "are you the one who——"

"No, not I," replied Franz, "but our neighbor, the Count of Monte Cristo."

"Well, then, count," said Albert gaily, straightening his cravat, "I hope you'll regard me as eternally obliged to you, first for the carriage, and now for this!" He held out his hand to the count. The latter shuddered as he took it, but he took it nevertheless.

Vampa watched this scene with amazement. He was apparently accustomed to seeing his prisoners tremble before him, yet here was a prisoner whose high spirits had never faltered. As for Franz, he was delighted at the way Albert had upheld the honor of their country.

"If you'll hurry," said Franz to Albert, "we'll still have time to go to the duke's ball, and you can take up your dance where we interrupted it, so that you'll have nothing to hold against Signor Vampa, who has behaved like a gallant gentleman throughout this whole affair."

"You're right; we can be there by two o'clock. Signor Vampa, are there any other formalities to fulfill before we take leave of you?"

"None, Excellency," replied the bandit. "You're as free as the air."

"In that case, I bid you farewell and wish you a long and

happy life. Come, gentlemen." And Albert, followed by Franz and the count, descended the stairs and walked across the large square room. All the bandits were standing with their hats in their hands.

"Peppino," said the chief, "give me the torch."

"What are you going to do?" asked the count.

"I'm going to lead the way for you myself, Excellency. It's the smallest honor I can do you." Taking the torch from Peppino, Vampa walked before his guests, not like a servant performing a servile duty, but like a king preceding a delegation of ambassadors. At the entrance to the catacombs he bowed and said, "And now, count, allow me to repeat my apologies. I hope you won't harbor any resentment against me for what has happened."

"Not at all, my dear Vampa," said the count. "Besides, you make up for your mistakes in such a gallant way that one is almost tempted to be grateful to you for having committed them."

"Gentlemen," said Vampa, turning to the two young men, "the offer may not be very attractive to you, but if you should ever wish to pay me a second visit, you will always be welcome, no matter where I am." Franz and Albert bowed. "Have you something to ask me?" said Vampa, smiling.

"Yes," replied Franz, "I admit I'm curious to know what book you were reading so attentively when we arrived."

"Caesar's *Commentaries,*" said the bandit. "It's my favorite book."

"Well, are you coming?" said Albert.

"Yes, I'm coming," said Franz as he stepped out into the open air.

"And now, count," said Albert, "let's go back as quickly as possible; I'm looking forward to finishing my evening at the duke's ball!"

When he awoke the next morning, Albert's first thought was to ask Franz to go with him to pay the count a visit. He had already thanked him the night before, but he felt that he ought to thank him more than once for such a service. Franz, who was both terrified and fascinated by the Count of Monte Cristo, did not wish to let Albert go to see him alone, so he went with him. They were shown into the drawing room, where the count appeared five minutes later.

"Count," said Albert, "allow me to repeat this morning what I expressed rather badly last night: that I will never forget how you came to my aid and that I will always remember that I owe my life to you."

"My dear neighbor," replied the count, laughing, "you exaggerate your obligation to me. You're indebted to me for nothing except a small saving of twenty thousand francs on your travel budget, which is hardly worth mentioning."

"No, count, my obligation to you is great," said Albert, "and I've come to ask you if I, or my friends, or my acquaintances could be of any service to you."

"Well, Monsieur de Morcerf," said the count, "I admit I was expecting your offer and that I accept it gladly. I've already made up my mind to ask you for a great favor."

"What is it?"

"I've never been to Paris and——"

"What!" cried Albert. "You've lived all this time without ever seeing Paris? That's incredible!"

"Incredible but true. However, for some time I've been feeling, like you, that it's impossible for me to go on being ignorant of the capital of the intelligent world. Furthermore, I might have made this indispenable journey long ago if I'd known someone who could introduce me into Paris society. Now your offer has decided me. Will you undertake, my dear Monsieur de Morcerf,"—the count accompanied these words with a strange smile—"to introduce me into that world which will be so foreign to me when I arrive in France?"

"Oh, gladly! I and all my friends are at your disposal."

"I accept your offer, then," said the count. "I've been making my plans for quite some time and this is the opportunity I needed in order to carry them out."

"When will you arrive in Paris?"

"When will you arrive yourself?"

"Oh, in two or three weeks."

"Very well, then," said the count, "I'll give you three months to return; as you can see, I'm allowing you a wide margin."

"And three months from now you'll knock on my door?" asked Albert joyfully.

"Would you like to make an appointment to the day and to the hour? Let me warn you that I'm exasperatingly punctual."

"To the day and to the hour," said Albert. "I'd like nothing better."

"All right, so be it. Today is the twenty-first of February and it's half-past ten in the morning. Will you expect me on the twenty-first of May at half-past ten in the morning?"

"I certainly will, and lunch will be ready."

"What's your address?"

"27 Rue du Helder."

The count wrote the address in his notebook.

"Will I see you before I leave?" asked Albert.

"That depends—when do you leave?"

"At five o'clock tomorrow afternoon."

"In that case, I'll tell you good-bye now. I have a matter to take care of in Naples and I won't be back here until Saturday night or Sunday morning. And you, baron," said the count to Franz, "are you leaving also?"

"Yes."

"For France?"

"No, for Venice. I'm going to stay in Italy for another year or two."

"Very well, then, gentlemen, I wish you *bon voyage*," said the count, shaking hands with each of the two friends. It was the first time Franz had touched the count's hand; he started, for it was as cold as the hand of a corpse.

"One last time," said Albert, "it's agreed, isn't it: the twenty-first day of May at half-past ten in the morning?"

"The twenty-first of May, at half-past ten in the morning," repeated the count.

At this the two young men bowed to the count and went out.

"What's the matter?" said Albert to Franz as they were returning to their rooms. "You look worried."

"Yes, I admit it," said Franz. "The count is a very strange man and I'm a little uneasy about the appointment he made with you in Paris."

"What! Are you mad, Franz?"

"Mad or not, I'm still uneasy."

Chapter 22

In the house at 27 Rue du Helder in Paris to which Albert de Morcerf had invited the Count of Monte Cristo, preparations were being made on the morning of May 21 to receive the guest.

Albert de Morcerf lived in a house situated at one corner of a large courtyard. Only two of its windows overlooked the street; three others faced the courtyard and two others the back of the garden. Between the courtyard and the garden stood the spacious and fashionable residence of the Count and Countess of Morçerf, built in the unsightly Imperial style. In this choice of a house for Albert it was easy to discern the tactful foresight of a mother who, not wishing to be separated from her son, had nevertheless realized that a young man of his age needs to be completely free.

On the morning of the appointment, Albert was sitting in

his small drawing room on the ground floor. At a quarter to ten his valet entered with several newspapers, which he laid on a table, and a bundle of letters, which he handed to Albert.

"What time would you like lunch, sir?" asked the valet.

"At exactly half-past ten. I don't have much confidence in the count's promise, but at least I want to be sure of fulfilling my end of the bargain."

The valet withdrew. Albert threw himself on the divan, took up the newspapers, looked at the theater page, made a grimace of distaste on learning that an opera, not a ballet, was to be given that night, and finally cast aside, one after the other, the three most widely read newspapers of Paris. "These newspapers become more boring every day," he muttered, in the middle of a prolonged yawn.

Just then a light carriage stopped before the door and an instant later Albert's valet returned to announce Monsieur Lucien Debray. A tall, pale, fair-haired young man with self-confident gray eyes and thin, cold lips walked into the room without speaking or smiling.

"Good morning, Lucien!" said Albert. "Your punctuality is almost frightening. I expected you to be the last to arrive, but you're the first one and you're even ahead of time. It's miraculous! Has the ministry been overthrown, by any chance?"

"No, don't worry; we're always tottering, but we never fall."

"Monsieur Beauchamp!" announced the valet.

"Come in, come in, mighty pen!" said Albert, standing up and stepping forward to meet the young man. "Look, here's Debray, who detests you without reading what you write, or at least so he says."

"He's quite right," said Beauchamp. "He's like me: I criticize him without knowing what he's doing. Good morning." The minister's secretary and the journalist exchanged a handshake and a smile.

"We're waiting for only two more people now," said Albert, "and we'll sit down to table as soon as they arrive."

"What sort of people are they?" asked Beauchamp.

"A gentleman and a diplomat."

"That means waiting about two hours for the gentleman and a little longer for the diplomat."

"Not at all," said Albert. "We'll have lunch at exactly half-past ten, come what may."

"Monsieur de Château-Renaud and Monsieur Maximilien Morrel!" announced the valet.

"Ah, now we're all here," said Beauchamp. "Those are the two people you were waiting for, aren't they, Albert?"

"Morrel . . ." murmured Albert, surprised. "Morrel? Who's that?"

But before he had finished speaking, Monsieur de Château-Renaud, a handsome young man of thirty and a gentleman to his fingertips, took Albert's hand and said to him, "Allow me to introduce Captain Maximilien Morrel, my friend and, what's more, my saviour. Salute my hero, viscount." He stepped aside to allow Albert to see the tall, noble young man with the wide forehead, piercing eyes and black mustache whom the reader will remember having seen in Marseilles in circumstances dramatic enough to prevent him from being forgotten. A handsome uniform, half French and half Oriental, set off his broad chest decorated with the cross of the Legion of Honor. The young officer bowed with easy politeness; he was graceful in every movement because he was strong.

"Monsieur de Château-Renaud knew in advance what pleasure it would give me to make your acquaintance," said Albert with friendly courtesy. "You're his friend already, now become mine."

"Very good," said Château-Renaud, "and I hope, viscount, that if the occasion should arise, he'll do the same thing for you as he did for me."

"What did he do?" asked Albert.

"Oh," said Maximilien, "it's hardly worth mentioning; the baron is exaggerating."

"What!" exclaimed the Baron of Château-Renaud. "It's not worth mentioning? In that case, life isn't worth mentioning!"

"It seems clear to me, baron, that Captain Morrel once saved your life."

"That's absolutely correct."

"How did it happen?" asked Beauchamp.

"Well, as you all know, I once took it into my head to make a trip to Africa," began Château-Renaud, "and since it seemed a shame to let my talents go to waste, I decided to try out my two new pistols on the Arabs, so I set sail for Oran. From there I went to Constantinople and arrived just in time to see the siege abandoned. I began to retreat along with the others. For forty-eight hours I endured the rain during the day and the snow at night, but on the third morning my poor horse died of cold and I had to continue the retreat on foot. Suddenly I saw six Arabs galloping toward me to cut off my head. I shot two of them with my rifles and two with my pistols, but there were still two more of them and none of my guns were loaded. One of them seized me by the hair—that's why I wear it short now; you never know what may happen

—and the other put his sword to my throat. I could already feel the cold steel when the gentleman you see here came charging down on them, shot the one holding me by the hair and split the other one's head with his saber. Captain Morrel had set himself the task of saving a man's life on that particular day and, as chance would have it, I was the man."

"Yes," said Maximilien, "it was the fifth of September, which is the anniversary of a day when my father was miraculously saved. As far as it's within my power, I try to celebrate that day every year by performing some——"

"Some heroic action, isn't that right?" interrupted Château-Renaud. "The story to which Captain Morrel is alluding is an extremely interesting one which he'll tell you some day when you know him better. But for now let's fill our stomachs and not our memories. What time are we having lunch, Albert?"

"At half-past ten."

"Exactly?" asked Debray, taking out his watch.

"Oh, you'll allow me five minutes' grace," said Albert, "because I'm expecting a saviour too."

"Whose saviour?"

"Mine, of course! Did you think I couldn't be saved like anyone else, and that the Arabs were the only ones who cut off heads? I was in Rome for the carnival this year and——"

"We know that," said Beauchamp.

"Yes, but what you don't know is that I was seized by bandits."

"There are no bandits," said Debray. "Why don't you admit that your cook is late and that, like Madame de Maintenon, you're about to give us a story instead of food? We're all amiable enough to forgive you and listen to your story, fantastic though it promises to be."

"I'll tell you the story, but, fantastic though it may be, I swear it's true from beginning to end. The bandits seized me and took me off to a very gloomy place known as the Catacombs of Saint Sebastian. They announced to me that I was being held for a ransom of four thousand piasters. Unfortunately, though, I had only fifteen hundred with me; it was toward the end of my stay in Italy and my letter of credit was almost exhausted. I wrote a note to Franz—Oh, yes! Franz was there, so, if you like, you can write to him and ask him whether I'm lying or not—I wrote to Franz that if the four thousand piasters hadn't arrived by six o'clock in the morning I would soon go to join the glorious martyrs in whose company I had the honor to find myself. And I can assure you that Monsieur Luigi Vampa—that's the name of the chief of the bandits—would have scrupulously kept his word."

"And so Franz arrived with the four thousand piasters?" asked Château-Renaud.

"No, he simply came accompanied by the gentleman I'm expecting soon and whom I hope to introduce to you. He spoke a few words to the bandit chief and I was set free."

"And I suppose they even apologized for having seized you," remarked Beauchamp.

"Yes, they did just that," said Albert.

"Why, it must have been Ariosto himself!"

"No, he's simply the Count of Monte Cristo."

"There is no Count of Monte Cristo," said Debray.

"I don't think there is," added Château-Renaud with the conviction of a man who has the whole of European nobility at his fingertips. "Has anyone ever heard of a Count of Monte Cristo anywhere?"

"Perhaps he comes from the Holy Land," said Beauchamp. "One of his ancestors may have owned Calvary, as the Mortemarts once owned the Dead Sea."

"Excuse me," said Maximilien, "perhaps I can clear up the matter for you. Monte Cristo is the name of a little island which I've often heard my father's sailors speak of. It's a grain of sand in the middle of the Mediterranean."

"That's right," said Albert, "and the man I'm telling you about is the king and master of that grain of sand. He probably bought his title of count somewhere in Tuscany. But that doesn't change the fact that my Count of Monte Cristo exists."

"Everybody exists, there's nothing astonishing about that!"

"Everybody exists, it's true, but not the way he does. That man has often made me shudder; one day, for example, we were watching an execution together and I thought I was about to faint, but it was more from seeing him and listening to him talk coldly about all the tortures on earth than it was from watching the executioner carry out his duties and listening to the cries of the condemned man."

"After he saved your life, did he make you sign a contract, written on flame-colored parchment, in which you surrendered your soul to him?"

"Go on, laugh!" said Albert, somewhat nettled. "Laugh as much as you like, gentlemen. When I look at you dapper Parisians, accustomed to the Boulevard de Gand and your promenades in the Bois de Boulogne, and then when I think of that man, it seems to me we're not of the same species!"

"Thank you, I'm flattered!" said Beauchamp.

"Nevertheless," added Château-Renaud, "your Count of

Monte Cristo is no doubt a gallant man, except for his little arrangements with Italian bandits."

"There are no Italian bandits!" said Debray.

"And no Count of Monte Cristo, either." added Beauchamp. "Listen, the clock just struck half-past ten."

"Admit it was all nothing but a nightmare and let's have lunch," said Beauchamp.

But the vibrations of the clock had scarcely died away when the door opened and the valet announced, "His Excellency the Count of Monte Cristo!" No one had heard the sound of a carriage in the street or of footsteps in the antechamber; even the door had opened noiselessly.

The count appeared in the doorway, dressed with the greatest simplicity, but the most exacting dandy could have found no fault with his apparel. He smiled and walked toward Albert, who eagerly came forward and shook his hand.

"Count," said Albert, "I was just announcing your visit to some of my friends whom I've invited here for this occasion and whom I would now like to introduce to you. This is the Count of Château-Renaud, whose nobility goes back to the Twelve Peers and whose ancestors had seats at the Round Table; Monsieur Lucien Debray, Secretary to the Minister of the Interior; Monsieur Beauchamp, a formidable journalist and the terror of the French government; and finally, Monsieur Maximilien Morrel, Captain of Spahis."

At this last name the count, who had until then had bowed courteously but coldly and impassively, involuntarily took a step forward and his pale cheeks flushed slightly. "You wear the uniform of the new French conquerors," he said. "It's a handsome uniform."

"Yes," said Albert, "and beneath that uniform beats one of the bravest hearts in the French army."

"Oh, Monsieur de Morcerf!" interrupted Maximilien.

"Let me speak, captain. We've just learned," continued Albert, "that Monsieur Morrel has performed such a heroic deed that, although I saw him for the first time only today, I would like to ask him the favor of allowing me to present him to you as one of my friends."

"Ah, Captain Morrel has a noble heart!" said the count. "So much the better!"

This exclamation, which was prompted by the count's own thoughts rather than by what Albert had just said, surprised everyone, especially Maximilien himself, who looked at Monte Cristo in amazement.

"Gentlemen," said Albert, "my valet tells me that lunch is ready. Allow me to show you the way, count."

They all passed into the dining room and each man took his place.

The count was, as we have already noted, a very moderate eater. Albert noticed this and said, "I'm afraid, count, that our French food may not please you. I ought to have asked you about your tastes and prepared something more to your liking."

"If you knew me better," replied the count, smiling, "you wouldn't trouble yourself about a matter which has so little importance for a traveler who, like myself, has lived on macaroni in Naples, *polenta* in Milan, *olla podrida* in Valencia, *karrick* in India, *pilau* in Constantinople and swallows' nests in China. I eat everything and everywhere, but I eat little; and today, when you reproach me for my moderation, I happen to have a good appetite, for I haven't eaten since yesterday morning."

"What! Since yesterday morning?" exclaimed the guests. "You haven't eaten for twenty-four hours?"

"No," replied Monte Cristo. "I was a little behind schedule on my journey here, so I didn't want to stop."

"Didn't you eat in your carriage?" asked Albert.

"No, I slept, as I usually do when I'm bored and don't have the energy to amuse myself or when I'm hungry and have no desire to eat."

"Can you go to sleep at will?" asked Albert.

"More or less."

"Do you have a recipe for that?"

"Yes, an infallible one."

"Might we know what it is?" asked Debray.

"Certainly," said Monte Cristo, "I make no secret of it. It's a mixture of some excellent opium for which I made a special trip to Canton in order to get the purest quality, and of the best hasheesh grown in the Orient. You mix these two ingredients in equal proportions and make them into pills, which you swallow when you need them. The effect is produced within ten minutes."

"But," said Beauchamp, who, as a journalist, was extremely incredulous, "do you carry this drug with you at all times?"

"At all times," replied Monte Cristo.

"Would it be indiscreet to ask to see those precious pills?" continued Beauchamp, hoping to trip him up.

"Not at all," said the count. And he drew from his pocket a marvelous case formed from a single hollowed-out emerald. Inside it were five or six greenish little balls about the size of a pea. They gave off an acrid, penetrating odor.

The case was passed around the table, but the guests were much more interested in the amazing emerald from which it was made than in the pills it contained.

"That's a magnificent emerald," said Château-Renaud, "and the largest one I ever saw."

"I had three like it," said Monte Cristo. "I gave one of them to the Grand Seigneur, who had it mounted on his sword, and the other to His Holiness the Pope, who had it set in his tiara opposite another emerald, similar but not so beautiful, which was given to his predecessor, Pius VII, by the Emperor Napoleon. I kept the third one for myself and had it hollowed out, which took away half its value but made it more adapted to the use I wanted to make of it."

Everyone looked at Monte Cristo in amazement. He spoke so simply that it was obvious that he was either mad or was telling the truth. The emerald which they had all held in their own hands made them inclined to believe he was telling the truth.

"And what did those two sovereigns give you in exchange for your magnificent gift?" asked Debray.

"The Grand Seigneur gave me a woman's freedom," replied the count, "and His Holiness gave me a man's life."

"Peppino was the man whose life you saved, wasn't he?" cried Albert.

"Perhaps," said Monte Cristo, smiling.

"You have no idea how delighted I am to hear you speak this way, count!" said Albert. "I've described you to my friends as a fabulous man, a wizard out of the *Arabian Nights,* a sorcerer out of the Middle Ages; but Parisians are so subtle in paradoxes that they take the most incontestable truths for caprices of the imagination when these truths don't fit into their everyday lives. Please tell these gentlemen yourself, count, that I was seized by Italian bandits and that without your generous intervention I'd probably be awaiting the Last Judgment in the Catacombs of Saint Sebastian today, instead of entertaining them in my humble little house. And please tell me also, for my own information, how you managed to inspire such respect in the bandits of Rome, who respect so few things. Franz and I were overcome with admiration."

"I've known the famous Luigi Vampa for over ten years," said the count. "One day when he was a young boy and still a simple shepherd, I gave him a gold coin for showing me my way and, in order not to be under any obligation to me, he gave me a dagger which he had carved himself and which you must have seen in my collection of weapons. Years later, whether because he had forgotten that exchange of gifts which ought to have made us friends or because he didn't recognize me, he tried to capture me, but it was I who captured him, along with a dozen or so of his men. I could have turned him over to Roman justice, which is quite expeditious and would have acted still more promptly in his case, but I did not. I released him and all his men."

"On condition that they sin no more," said the journalist, laughing. "I'm glad to see they've scrupulously kept their word."

"No," replied the count, "only on condition that they always respect me and my friends, which is why I was able to deliver our host from their hands. Futhermore, Monsieur de Morcerf, as I've already told you, I had an ulterior motive in saving you: I wanted to call on you to introduce me into Paris society when I visited France. You may have considered that a passing fancy at the time, but today it's a reality to which you must submit under pain of breaking your word."

"I'll keep my word," said Albert, "but I'm afraid you may be quite disappointed. You're accustomed to splendid scenery, picturesque events and fantastic horizons, while France is such a prosaic country and Paris is such a civilized city that there's only one service I can render you and for which I'm entirely at your disposal: to introduce you everywhere or have you introduced by my friends. I don't dare suggest that you share my lodgings, as I shared yours in Rome, for there isn't room for a shadow here, unless it's the shadow of a woman."

"Ah, yes," said the count, "in Rome you mentioned something about the possibility of a marriage when you returned to Paris. Are congratulations in order?"

"Nothing is definite yet, but I hope before long to be able to introduce you to, if not my wife, at least my fiancée: Mademoiselle Eugénie Danglars."

"Eugénie Danglars!" said the count. "Let's see now, isn't her father Baron Danglars?"

"Yes; do you know him?"

"I don't know him," said the count indifferently, "but I probably won't be long in making his acquaintance because I have an account opened with him through the firms of Richard and Blount of London, Arstein and Eskeles of Vienna, and Thomson and French of Rome."

As he spoke these last words, Monte Cristo looked at Maximilien Morrel out of the corner of his eye. The young man started as though he had received an electric shock. "Thomson and French!" he exclaimed. "Do you know that firm?"

"They're my bankers in Rome," said the count calmly. "Could I be of service to you with them?"

"Perhaps you might help us learn something we've never been able to learn. That firm once rendered a great service to ours, but, for some reason, they've always denied doing so."

"I'll be glad to help you in any way I can, captain," said the count.

"Just a moment," said Albert, "we've strayed pretty far from our subject. We were about to discuss finding a suitable house for the Count of Monte Cristo. Come, gentlemen, let's put our heads together: where shall we lodge this new guest of the city of Paris?"

"In the Faubourg Saint-Germain," said Château-Renaud. "He'll find a charming little house with a courtyard and garden there."

"You don't know anything but your gloomy Faubourg Saint-Germain," said Debray. "Don't listen to him, count. Take a house on the Chaussée-d'Antin; it's the real center of Paris."

"No, on the Boulevard de l'Opéra," said Beauchamp. "You'll see the whole city of Paris parade before your eyes there."

"What about you, Morrel," said Château-Renaud, "don't you have any ideas on the subject?"

"Yes, I do," said the young man, smiling, "but I was expecting the count to be tempted by one of the brilliant prospects which have just been described to him. Since he's given no answer, however, I think I can allow myself to offer him a suite in a charming little house my sister has been renting for the past year in the Rue Meslay."

"You have a sister?" asked Monte Cristo.

"Yes, and an excellent one."

"Married?"

"She's been married for nine years."

"Is she happy?"

"As happy as a human creature is allowed to be; she married the man she loved, the man who remained faithful to us in our misfortune: Emmanuel Herbaut. I'm staying with them during my leave. My brother-in-law and I are at your disposal, count."

"Thank you, captain. I'll content myself with being introduced to your sister and your brother-in-law, if you'll be so kind as to do me that honor, but the reason I didn't accept the suggestion of any of these gentlemen is that I already have a house. I sent my valet on ahead of me and he should have bought me a house and had it furnished by now."

"I presume your valet knows Paris, then," said Beauchamp.

"This is the first time he's ever been in France and he can't speak."

"Is it Ali?" asked Albert in the midst of the general surprise.

"That's right: Ali, my mute Nubian. You saw him in Rome, I believe."

"Yes," relied Albert, "I remember him perfectly. But how could you have sent a Nubian to buy you a house in Paris, and a mute to furnish it for you? He's sure to have done everything all wrong, poor fellow."

"On the contrary, I'm sure he's chosen everything according to my taste; as you know, my tastes aren't like those of everyone else. He arrived here a week ago and he no doubt went over the entire city with the instinct of a good hunting dog. He knows all my whims, preferences and needs, and I'm sure he's arranged everything to my liking. He knew I'd arrive today at ten o'clock and he was waiting for me at the Barrière de Fontainebleau to give me this piece of paper: it's my new address. Here, read it." Monte Cristo handed the piece of paper to Albert.

"30 Champs Elysées," read Albert.

"Now that's really original!" exclaimed Beauchamp.

"And very princely," added Château-Renaud.

"Do you mean to say you don't know anything about your own house yet?" asked Debray.

"No," said Monte Cristo. "I didn't want to be late for my appointment here, so I changed clothes in my carriage and came directly to Monsieur de Morcerf's door."

The young men looked at one another. They were not sure whether Monte Cristo was joking or not, but he spoke in such a simple and direct manner that it was impossible to suppose that he was lying. Besides, why should he be lying?

"I see we'll have to be content with rendering the count the little services that are within our power," said Beauchamp. "As a journalist, I can open all the theaters in Paris to him."

"Thank you," said Monte Cristo, smiling, "but I've already ordered my steward to reserve me a box in each one of them."

"Is your steward also a mute Nubian?" asked Debray.

"No, he's not. I believe you know him, Monsieur Morcerf."

"Is he by any chance that worthy Signor Bertuccio who is such an expert at renting windows?"

"Precisely. He's a fine man who was once a soldier, and and also a smuggler; in fact, he's been just about everything a man can be. I wouldn't even swear that he wasn't once mixed up with the police over some stabbing."

"Well, then," said Château-Renaud, "you have a complete household: you have a house on the Champs Elysées, servants and a steward. All you need now is a mistress."

"I have something better than that," said Monte Cristo. "I have a slave. You rent your mistresses at the opera house or the theater; I bought mine in Constantinople. I had to pay more, but I now have nothing to worry about on that score."

"But you're forgetting," said Debray, laughing, "that your slave became free the moment she set foot on French soil."

"Who will tell her that?" asked Monte Cristo.

"Why, the first person she sees!"

"She speaks nothing but modern Greek."

"Ah, that's different."

"Will we see her, at least?" asked Beauchamp. "Or, since you have a mute, do you also have eunuchs?"

"No. I don't carry Orientalism that far!" said Monte Cristo. "Everyone around me is free to leave me and, on leaving me, will have no further need of me or anyone else. Perhaps that's why no one leaves me."

They had long since passed to dessert and cigars.

"It's half-past two," said Debray, standing up. "Your guest is charming, Albert, but sooner or later one must leave even the best of company. It's time for me to return to the ministry."

As Beauchamp was about to leave he said to Albert, "Well, I won't go to the Chamber today; I have something better for my readers than a speech by Monsieur Danglars."

"Please, Beauchamp," said Albert, "not a word, I beg you! Don't deprive me of the distinction of presenting the count and explaining him. Isn't he a strange man?"

"He's more than that," said Château-Renaud, "he's one of the most extraordinary men I've ever seen. Are you coming, Morrel?"

"As soon as I give the count my card. He's promised to pay me a visit."

"And you may be sure I will," said the count.

Maximilien Morrel went out with Château-Renaud, leaving Monte Cristo alone with Albert de Morcerf.

Chapter 23

When the other guest had gone, Albert said to Monte Cristo, "Allow me to begin my duties as your cicerone by showing you a typical Paris bachelor's apartment."

Albert led the count to his study, which was his favorite room. Monte Cristo was a worthy appreciator of all th : objects Albert had collected here: old chests, Japanese porcelain, Oriental cloth, Venetian glassware and weapons from every country in the world. Everything was familiar to him and, at first glance, he recognized the century and the country of origin. Albert had expected to explain things, but instead the count gave him a little course in archeology, minerology and natural history.

Albert took his guest into the salon, whose walls were covered with the works of modern painters. He expected to have something new to show the strange traveler this time, but, to his great surprise the count, without having to look at the signatures, was able to name the painter of each work, and in such a way that it was easy to see that not only were the names of these artists familiar to him, but he had carefully studied and evaluated the talent of each of them.

From the salon they went into the bedroom, which was a model of both elegance and simple good taste. The only painting there was a portrait signed by Leopold Robert. This picture attracted the count's attention immediately. It was a portrait of a young woman about twenty-six years old with a dark complexion, fiery eyes and languishing eyelids. She was dressed like a Catalan fisherwoman, with a black and red bodice and gold pins in her hair. She was looking at the sea; her lovely profile stood out against a background of waves and sky. Monte Cristo stood staring at this portrait in silence for a time, then he said, in a perfectly calm voice, "You have a beautiful mistress, viscount, and her costume, which is no doubt a masquerade costume, is exquisitely becoming to her."

"That's a mistake for which I wouldn't forgive you if there were another portrait beside this one," said Albert. "That's a portrait of my mother. It was painted six or eight years ago. As far as I know, the costume is a product of her own imagination, and the resemblance is so good that it seems to me I can still see her as she was in 1830. She had the portrait painted during my father's absence, thinking, no doubt, that it would be a pleasant surprise for him on his return, but strangely enough, it displeased him. Not wishing to part with such a work of art altogether, my mother gave it to me. Excuse me for discussing family affairs but since you are soon going to have the honor of meeting my father, I thought it would be best to tell you before him. I wrote to him from Rome, telling him about the service you rendered me there, and both he and my mother are eager to have the opportunity to thank you for it."

Albert called his valet and ordered him to inform the Count and Countess of Morcerf that the Count of Monte Cristo would call on them shortly. Albert and Monte Cristo followed the valet as he left.

In the salon of the Morcerf residence they came face to face with the Count of Morcerf himself. He was a man in his early forties, but he appeared to be at least fifty, and his black mustache and eyebrows contrasted strangely with his almost white hair, which was cut short in the military manner.

"Father," said Albert, "allow me to introduce the Count of Monte Cristo, the generous friend whom I was fortunate enough to meet in the difficult circumstances I've already described to you."

"You are welcome here," said the Count of Morcerf, bowing to Monte Cristo with a smile. "In saving the life of our son you have rendered us a service which commands our eternal gratitude. The countess was in her dressing room when your visit was anounced; she will be down within ten minutes."

"It's a great honor for me," said Monte Cristo, "to make the acquaintance, on my first day in Paris, of a man whose worth equals his reputation and who has been justly rewarded by fortune. But h̶a̶s̶n̶'̶t̶ ̶ to offer you?"

d now I'm grateful to
you as I have blessed you, that
rt."

ain, more deeply than the first
Mercédès.

the count for being obliged to
he session began an hour ago

tess. "I'll try to make up to the
n, turning to Monte Cristo, she
onor of spending the rest of the

ou for your offer, madame, but I
y and I came straight here.

pleasure of seeing you another

out answering, but his gesture
e of assent.

onte Cristo to the door, he re-
had gone to her boudoir. "Are
her?" he asked as he entered.
on you were very pale."

he countess asked, "What is this
a family name, the name of an

itle, mother. Monte Cristo is the
h the count has bought. In any
bility, although the general opin-
ery great lord."

y he is?" asked Mercédès, ap-
ortance to this question.

ble!"

gilded doorpost. She had been there for several seconds, long enough to overhear the visitor's last words.

Monte Cristo stood up and bowed deeply to the countess, who responded with a silent and ceremonious bow.

"What's the matter?" asked Morcerf. "Is the heat of the salon too much for you?"

"Are you ill, mother?" cried Albert, rushing toward Mercédès.

She thanked both of them with a smile. "No," she said, "but I was slightly overcome with emotion at seeing for the first time the man without whom our house would now be in mourning. Count," she continued, walking toward Monte Cristo with the majesty of a queen, "I owe my son's life to you, for which I bless you. And ____ ____ to you for giving me the chance to thank ____ ____ ____ is, from the bottom of my hea____

Monte Cristo bowed once ag____ time; he was even paler than ____

"I've already apologized to ____ leave him," said Morcerf. "T____ and I'm to make a speech."

"Go on, then," said the coun____ count for your absence." Then ____ said, "Would you do us the ho____ day with us?"

"I'm extremely grateful to y____ I arrived in Paris only toda____ haven't even seen my house ye____

"Then can we count on the ____ time?" ____ked Mercédès.

Mont____ Cristo bowed with ____ could ____ ____ave been taken for o____

Af____ ____ Albert had shown M____ turned ____ to find that his mothe____ you ____ sure you're not ill, mo____ "W____ ____en you came into the sa____ ____ There was a silence, then ____ ____ me of Monte Cristo? Is it ____ state or simply a title?"

"I think it's nothing but a ____ name of a small island whic____ case, he makes no claim to n____ ion in Rome is that he's a v____

"How old would you sa____ parently attaching great imp____

"Thirty-five or thirty-six."

"So young? That's impossi____

"Father," said Albert, "allow me to introduce the Count of Monte Cristo, the generous friend whom I was fortunate enough to meet in the difficult circumstances I've already described to you."

"You are welcome here," said the Count of Morcerf, bowing to Monte Cristo with a smile. "In saving the life of our son you have rendered us a service which commands our eternal gratitude. The countess was in her dressing room when your visit was anounced; she will be down within ten minutes."

"It's a great honor for me," said Monte Cristo, "to make the acquaintance, on my first day in Paris, of a man whose worth equals his reputation and who has been justly rewarded by fortune. But hasn't fortune still a marshal's baton to offer you?"

"Oh, I've left the service," said Morcerf, blushing slightly. "The July revolution was apparently glorious enough to allow itself to be ungrateful for any service which did not date from the imperial period, so I tendered my resignation. I entered politics and I now devote myself to industry and the study of the useful arts, something for which I had a desire during my twenty years in the army, but for which I had no time."

"That's the kind of thing that makes your country superior to all others," said Monte Cristo. "You were a gentleman of high birth and you had a large fortune, yet you were willing to earn your promotions as an obscure soldier. Then, after you had become a general, a peer of France and a commander of the Legion of Honor, you were willing to begin a second apprenticeship, with the hope of no other reward than that of some day being useful to your fellow men. That, Monsieur de Morcerf, was a magnificent, I will even say sublime gesture!"

Albert looked at Monte Cristo in astonishment; he was not accustomed to hear him speak with such enthusiasm.

"If I weren't afraid of tiring you, count," said the general, obviously charmed by what Monte Cristo had said, "I'd take you to the Chamber with me. Today's debate will be rather interesting for someone who isn't acquainted with our modern senators."

"I'd be very grateful to you if you would renew that invitation another time," replied Monte Cristo, "but today I've been given the hope of meeting the countess and I'd like to wait for her."

"Here's my mother now!" said Albert.

Monte Cristo turned around quickly and saw Madame de Morcerf standing in the doorway of the salon. She was pale and when Monte Cristo turned to look at her she let drop her arm, which, for some reason, she had been leaning against the gilded doorpost. She had been there for several seconds, long enough to overhear the visitor's last words.

Monte Cristo stood up and bowed deeply to the countess, who responded with a silent and ceremonious bow.

"What's the matter?" asked Morcerf. "Is the heat of the salon too much for you?"

"Are you ill, mother?" cried Albert, rushing toward Mercédès.

She thanked both of them with a smile. "No," she said, "but I was slightly overcome with emotion at seeing for the first time the man without whom our house would now be in mourning. Count," she continued, walking toward Monte Cristo with the majesty of a queen, "I owe my son's life to you, for which I bless you. And now I'm grateful to you for giving me the chance to thank you as I have blessed you, that is, from the bottom of my heart."

Monte Cristo bowed once again, more deeply than the first time; he was even paler than Mercédès.

"I've already apologized to the count for being obliged to leave him," said Morcerf. "The session began an hour ago and I'm to make a speech."

"Go on, then," said the countess. "I'll try to make up to the count for your absence." Then, turning to Monte Cristo, she said, "Would you do us the honor of spending the rest of the day with us?"

"I'm extremely grateful to you for your offer, madame, but I arrived in Paris only today and I came straight here. I haven't even seen my house yet."

"Then can we count on the pleasure of seeing you another time?" asked Mercédès.

Monte Cristo bowed without answering, but his gesture could have been taken for one of assent.

After Albert had shown Monte Cristo to the door, he returned to find that his mother had gone to her boudoir. "Are you sure you're not ill, mother?" he asked as he entered. "When you came into the salon you were very pale."

There was a silence, then the countess asked, "What is this name of Monte Cristo? Is it a family name, the name of an estate or simply a title?"

"I think it's nothing but a title, mother. Monte Cristo is the name of a small island which the count has bought. In any case, he makes no claim to nobility, although the general opinion in Rome is that he's a very great lord."

"How old would you say he is?" asked Mercédès, apparently attaching great importance to this question.

"Thirty-five or thirty-six."

"So young? That's impossible!"

"But it's true nevertheless. He told me so on several different occasions when he had no reason not to tell the truth."

Mercédès bowed her head as though weighed down by a flood of bitter thoughts. "Does he like you, Albert?" she asked, with a nervous shudder.

"I think so."

"And are you—fond of him?"

"Yes, I like him, despite what Franz d'Epinay says about him—Franz claimed the count was a man who had come back from the next world."

The countess made a movement of terror. "Albert," she said in a strange voice, "I've always put you on your guard against new acquaintances. You're a man now, and as capable of giving advice as of taking it, but let me tell you once again: Be careful, Albert."

"If I'm to take advantage of your advice, mother, I'll have to know what to guard against. The count doesn't gamble, he drinks nothing but water mixed with a little Spanish wine, and he's so rich that he certainly won't ask to borrow money from me. What have I to fear from him?"

"You're right," said Mercédès, "my fears are foolish, especially in regard to a man who saved your life. . . . By the way, did your father receive him well? He's so busy and he's sometimes so worried about his affairs that he might, unintentionally——"

"Father was perfect," interrupted Albert, "and furthermore he seemed highly flattered by several compliments the count slipped into the conversation with such ease that it seemed as though he'd known him for thirty years. They parted the best of friends; in fact, father even wanted to take him to the Chamber with him."

Mercédès said nothing. She was so deeply absorbed in her own thoughts that her eyes had gradually closed. Albert stood looking at her with that filial affection which is all the more tender and loving in children whose mothers are still young and beautiful. Then, thinking she had dozed off, he tiptoed out of the room and carefully closed the door behind him.

Chapter 24

Meanwhile the count had reached his new residence on the Avenue des Champs Elysées. Two men came out to meet his carriage when it drew up before the door. One was Ali, who smiled at his master with an incredible outburst of joy and who felt himself amply repaid by a look from Monte Cristo.

The other bowed humbly and presented his arm to help the count alight from his carriage.

"Thank you, Monsieur Bertuccio," said the count. "Is the notary here?"

"He is in the small salon, Excellency."

The count passed into the small salon, led by Bertuccio, who showed him the way. The notary was waiting for him.

"Are you the notary empowered to sell the country house I wish to buy?" asked Monte Cristo.

"Yes, sir."

"Have you brought the deed of sale?"

"Here it is, sir."

"Now, where is this house I'm buying?" asked Monte Cristo nonchalantly.

The notary looked at him in astonishment and said, "Do you mean to say, sir, that you haven't even seen it?"

"How the devil could I have seen it? I arrived in Paris for the first time in my life only this morning; in fact, this is the first time I've ever set foot in France."

"I understand, sir. The house you're buying is situated in Auteuil."

At these words Bertuccio paled visibly.

"And where is Auteuil?" asked the count.

"It's only a short distance from here, sir," replied the notary. "It's a little beyond Passy, in a charming location in the middle of the Bois de Boulogne."

"So near? But that's not in the country! Why have you chosen me a house at the gates of Paris, Monsieur Bertuccio?"

"But Excellency," cried Bertuccio, "I had nothing to do with choosing that house! Please be so kind as to think back, to remember——"

"Ah, yes, now I remember," said the count. "I read an advertisement in the newspaper and let myself be misled by the lying title, 'Country House.' "

"There's still time, Excellency," said Bertuccio eagerly. "If you wish me to search elsewhere I'll find a house in a better location."

"No, never mind," said the count indifferently. "Since I have this one I might as well keep it."

"And you're quite right, sir!" said the notary earnestly. "It's a charming residence."

"Very well, then," said the count, "hand me the contract."

He signed rapidly, then said, "Bertuccio, give this gentleman fifty-five thousand francs." The steward walked out of the room and returned with a stack of banknotes, which the notary carefully counted.

"Are there any other formalities?" asked the count.

"No, sir."

The count nodded in a way which said clearly, "I don't need you any longer; you may go." The notary bowed deeply and withdrew.

"Monsieur Bertuccio," said the count, "didn't you once tell me you'd traveled in France?"

"In certain parts of France, yes, Excellency."

"Then you no doubt know the suburbs of Paris."

"No, Excellency, no," replied the steward with a sort of shudder which the count, a keen judge of emotions, rightly attributed to deep anxiety.

"That's unfortunate," said the count, "because I want to go to see my new house this evening and you could have given me some useful information on the way to Auteuil."

"To Auteuil?" cried Bertuccio, whose copper-colored complexion became almost livid. "Do you want me to go to Auteuil?"

"What's so astonishing about that? You're a member of my household, aren't you?"

Bertuccio bowed his head before the count's imperious gaze and stood motionless without answering.

"What's the matter with you?" said Monte Cristo. "Are you going to make me ring twice for my carriage?"

Bertuccio rushed into the antechamber and cried out in a hoarse voice, "His Excellency's carriage!"

The count sat down and wrote two or three letters. As he was sealing the last one his steward reappeared and said, "The carriage is at the door, Excellency."

"Very well; take your hat and gloves."

"Am I going with you, sir?"

"Of course; I intend to live in that house, so I'll have to give you my orders."

Bertuccio followed his master without any further objection, but Monte Cristo noticed that he crossed himself as he walked out of the house and that he mumbled a prayer when he had taken his seat in the carriage.

Twenty minutes later they were in Auteuil. "We shall stop at 28 Rue de la Fontaine," said Monte Cristo, looking steadfastly at Bertuccio.

Beads of sweat broke out on Bertuccio's forehead, but he obeyed the count's order: he leaned out the window of the carriage and called to the coachman, "Stop at 28 Rue de la Fontaine."

Night had fallen during the trip, or rather a black cloud, charged with electricity, had given a solemn and dramatic appearance to the premature shadows. The carriage stopped and the footman leapt down to open the door. Monte Cristo and Bertuccio alighted.

"Knock on the door and announce me," said the count.

Bertuccio knocked. The door opened and the porter appeared.

"This is your new master," said the footman, handing the porter the notary's order.

"The house has been sold, then?" asked the porter.

"Yes," replied Monte Cristo, "and I'll try to see to it that you have no cause to regret losing your former master."

"Oh, I won't miss him much, sir, because we almost never saw him. He hasn't come here in over five years."

"What was the name of your former master?"

"The Marquis of Saint-Méran."

"That name sounds familiar to me," said the count. "Let's see, now, the Marquis of Saint-Méran . . ." He appeared to be searching his memory.

"An old gentleman," continued the porter, "a loyal supporter of the Bourbons; he had a daughter who married Monsieur de Villefort, who was public prosecutor at Nîmes and then at Versailles."

Monte Cristo glanced at Bertuccio and saw that he was as white as the wall against which he was leaning to keep from falling.

"And didn't that daughter die?" asked the count. "It seems to me I heard that somewhere."

"Yes, sir, she died twenty-one years ago; and since that time the poor marquis hasn't been back here more than three times."

"Thank you," said the count, accompanying his words with the gift of two gold coins which brought forth an explosion of blessings and sighs.

"Take one of the lanterns from the carriage and show me around the house, Bertuccio," said the count. Bertuccio obeyed without objection, but the trembling of his hand showed how much it cost him to do so.

After inspecting the first floor, they went up to the second. In one of the bedrooms there the count noticed the entrance of a spiral staircase. "Here's a private staircase," he said. "Light my way, Monsieur Bertuccio, and we'll see where it leads to."

"It leads to the garden, sir," said Bertuccio.

"How do you know that, may I ask?"

"I mean it probably leads there, sir."

"Well, then, let's find out for sure."

Bertuccio heaved a sigh and led the way. The staircase did,

in fact, lead to the garden. When he came to the outside door, Bertuccio stopped, panic-stricken and almost fainting.

"Well?" said the count.

"No! No!" cried Bertuccio. "No, sir, I can't go any further! It's impossible!"

"What do you mean?" asked the count coldly.

"It's not natural, sir! Of all the suburbs of Paris, you bought a house in Auteuil, and of all the houses in Auteuil, you bought the one at 28 Rue de la Fontaine! As if there were no other house in Auteuil except the one in which the murder was committed!"

"You're a true Corsican, Bertuccio: always mysteries and superstitions! Come, take your lantern and let's have a look at the garden."

Bertuccio picked up the lantern and obeyed. The count stopped before a clump of trees. Bertuccio could contain himself no longer. "Get away, sir, I beg you!" he cried. "You're standing right on the same spot!"

"What spot?"

"The spot where he fell."

"I'm afraid you've gone mad, Monsieur Bertuccio," said the count. "Try to pull yourself together and explain to me what you're talking about."

"I've told about it only once in my life," replied Bertuccio, "and that was to the Abbé Busoni. Such things should be told only under the seal of confession."

"In that case, Monsieur Bertuccio, I'll be forced to send you back to your confessor. I don't like members of my household to be afraid to go into my garden at night. Also, I admit that I wouldn't be at all happy to receive a visit from the police on your account. I knew you were once a smuggler, but I didn't know you had other strings to your bow. You are no longer in my service, Monsieur Bertuccio."

"Oh, Excellency!" cried the steward. "If it's a question of remaining in your service, I'll speak, I'll tell you everything!"

"That's different, then," said Monte Cristo. "But if you're about to lie, reconsider: it would be better for you not to speak at all."

"No, sir, I swear by the salvation of my eternal soul that I'll tell you everything! Where shall I begin?"

"Wherever you like, since I know nothing of your story."

"But I thought the Abbé Busoni told you——"

"Yes, he told me a few details, but that was seven or eight years ago and I've forgotten almost everything he said."

"Well, then, it all begins in 1815, but I can remember it all as clearly as though it were yesterday. I had a brother, an older brother, who was in the service of the emperor. He was a lieutenant in a regiment composed entirely of Corsicans. That brother was my only friend; we became orphans when I was five and he was eighteen, and he raised me as though I were his son. He was married in 1814, under the Bourbons. When Napoleon came back from the Isle of Elba, my brother rejoined his army.

"One day we received a letter from him. (I forgot to tell you we were living in the little village of Rogliano, in Corsica.) The letter told us the army had been disbanded and that he was returning by way of Châteauroux, Clermont-Ferrand, Le Puy and Nîmes. He asked me to send some money to Nîmes, where he would pick it up from a certain hotel-keeper with whom I had dealings."

"Did your dealings with him involve smuggling?" asked Monte Cristo.

"A man has to make a living, sir."

"Yes, of course. Go on."

"I loved my brother deeply, as I've already told you, Excellency, so I decided to take him the money myself, instead of sending it to him. I had a thousand francs; I left half of it with my sister-in-law, Assunta, and set out for Nîmes with the other half.

"Now it was just the time when the famous massacres were taking place in the South of France. Organized bands of assassins were killing everyone suspected of being a Bonapartist. I was almost wading in blood when I entered Nîmes. There were corpses everywhere and the assassins were killing, pillaging and burning. When I saw that I shuddered, not for myself: I was a simple Corsican fisherman and had nothing to fear, but my brother was still wearing the uniform of one of the emperor's soldiers and therefore had everything to fear.

"I ran to see our hotel-keeper. My fears had been justified: my brother had arrived in Nîmes the night before and had been killed at the very door of the hotel. I did everything I could to find out who his murderers were, but they were so dreaded that no one dared to tell me their names. Then I went to see the public prosecutor, whose name was Villefort. He was from Marseilles and had only recently been promoted. They say he was one of the first to report Napoleon's return from Elba.

" 'My brother was murdered yesterday,' I told him. 'I don't know who did it, but it's your duty to find out.'

" 'Who was your brother?' asked Villefort.

" 'A lieutenant in a Corsican regiment.'

" 'A soldier in the army of the usurper, then?'

" 'A soldier in the French army.'

" 'Every revolution has its catastrophes,' said Villefort, 'and your brother was a victim of this one, which is unfortunate. But if we had to prosecute every case of vengeance taken against the partisans of the king by the partisans of the usurper while they were in power, your brother would perhaps have been sentenced to death. What's happening now is only natural: it's the law of reprisals.'

" 'What!' I said. 'How can you talk like that, you, a magistrate?'

" 'You Corsicans are all mad,' said Villefort. 'You think your compatriot is still emperor. You should have come here two months ago; it's a little late now. Leave my office; and if you won't leave, I'll have you thrown out.'

" 'All right,' I said to him, 'since you know Corsicans so well, you must know how they keep their word. You think my brother deserved to be killed because you're a royalist and he was a Bonapartist. I'm a Bonapartist too, and I have only one thing to say to you: I'm going to kill you. From this moment I declare a vendetta against you. The next time we meet, it will mean that your last hour has come.' Then, before he could recover from his surprise, I opened the door and ran out."

"What!" said Monte Cristo. "With your honest face, Monsieur Bertuccio, you did such a thing to a public prosecutor? Did he at least know the meaning of the word 'vendetta'?"

"He knew it so well that from then on he never went out alone, and he had the police look everywhere for me. Fortunately I was so well hidden that they never found me. Then he became afraid to stay in Nîmes any longer. He asked permission to change his residence and, since he was a man with influence, he was named public prosecutor at Versailles. But, as you know, there's no such thing as distance for a Corsican who has sworn to avenge himself on his enemy, and I was never more than half an hour behind his carriage all the way to Versailles.

"The important thing was not simply to kill him—I'd had dozens of chances to do that—but to kill him without being discovered or arrested; my life no longer belonged to me, for I had my sister-in-law to protect and provide for. I watched Villefort constantly for three months. Finally I discovered that he made mysterious trips to Auteuil, to this very house. But instead of coming in through the front door, he would leave his horse or his carriage at the inn and enter through the little door you see here.

"I left Versailles and moved to Auteuil, for it seemed to me I'd have a better chance of catching him there. I found out that the house belonged to the Marquis of Saint-Méran, as the porter has already told you, Excellency, and that the marquis was Villefort's father-in-law. Since the marquis lived in Marseilles, the house was useless to him and he had just rented it to a young widow who was known only as 'the baroness.'

"One night as I was looking over the wall, I saw a beautiful young woman walking in this garden. I saw immediately that she was pregnant and that her pregnancy was rather far advanced. A few moments later the little door opened and a man entered. The young woman rushed to meet him, they threw themselves in each other's arms, embraced tenderly and went into the house together. The man was Monsieur de Villefort. I realized that when he came out he would probably cross the whole garden alone."

"And did you ever learn the woman's name?" asked the count.

"No, Excellency," replied Bertuccio, "as you'll see, I didn't have time to learn it."

"Go on."

"I might have been able to kill him that night, but I wasn't familiar with the garden and I was afraid that might prevent me from escaping if he should have time to cry out for help.

"Three days later, at about seven o'clock at night, I saw a servant leave the house and gallop away on horseback. He came back three hours later, covered with dust; his message had been delivered. Ten minutes after that, another man opened the door of the garden and went in. I hadn't seen Villefort's face, but I recognized him by the pounding of my heart. I took out my knife and climbed over the wall. I hid in the clump of trees nearest to where I believed Villefort would pass on his way out.

"Two hours later the door opened and Villefort came out. As he came toward me, I saw that he was carrying what at first I thought was a weapon of some kind, but then I saw it was only a spade. He stopped opposite the clump of trees where I was hidden and began to dig in the ground. It was only then that I noticed he was carrying something under his coat, which he had taken off to give himself more freedom of movement. My hatred became mixed with curiosity and I decided to wait and see what Villefort was doing. After a while I saw him take out a box about two feet long and eight inches wide from underneath his coat, put this box into the hole he had dug and cover it over with earth. Then I rushed at him, sank my knife into his chest and said, 'I'm Giovanni Bertuccio! Your death for my brother and your treasure for his wife! My vengeance is more complete than I expected.' I don't know if he heard these words; I don't think he did, because he fell without uttering a sound. I dug up the box, took it and ran out of the garden through the little door in the wall."

"Was there a handsome sum in the box?" asked Monte Cristo.

"It wasn't money, Excellency. I ran as far as the river, sat down on the bank and opened the box. Inside it I saw a new-born baby whose purple face showed that it must have been smothered to death. Then it seemed to me I felt a slight heartbeat; I began to breathe air into its lungs and after a quarter of an hour I heard it utter a cry. I uttered a cry also, but a cry of joy. 'God hasn't cursed me,' I said to myself, 'because He's allowed me to give life to one human being in exchange for the life I took away from another.'

"The fine swaddling clothes in which the child was wrapped showed that its parents were wealthy. I took the precaution of cutting them in half, so that one of the two letters with which they were marked was on the half I took and the other was on the remaining half. Then I left the child in front of an orphanage, rang the doorbell and ran away as fast as I could. Two weeks later I was back in Rogliano and I said to Assunta, 'Console yourself, my sister: Israël is dead, but I've avenged his death.' Then I told her everything that had happened.

" 'Giovanni,' said Assunta, 'you should have brought back that child. We'd have taken the place of the parents he's lost and we'd have called him Benedetto in honor of the blessing God bestowed on us.'

"My only answer was to give her the half of the swaddling clothes I had kept in order to claim the child if we should some day become richer."

"What were the letters on the swaddling clothes?" asked Monte Cristo.

"An H and an N, surmounted by a baron's crown."

"I'm curious to learn two things," said the count.

"What are they, Excellency?"

"What became of the little boy—you did say it was a little boy, didn't you, Monsieur Bertuccio?"

"No, Excellency, I don't think I did, but in any case it *was* a little boy. What was the other thing you wished to know?"

"I'd like to know what crime you were accused of when you asked for a confessor and the Abbé Busoni came to see you for that reason in the prison at Nîmes."

"It's a rather long story, Excellency."

"That doesn't matter. It's only ten o'clock; as you know,

I sleep very little, and I don't suppose you feel much like sleeping right now."

Bertuccio bowed and resumed his story.

"Partly in order to drive away the memories that haunted me and partly in order to provide for my poor brother's widow, I went back to the trade of smuggling with greater energy than ever before. Since my brother had been murdered in the streets of Nîmes, I refused to go back to that town. The result of this was that the innkeeper with whom we had formerly carried on our smuggling affairs, seeing that we were no longer coming to him, came to us and opened another inn, called the Pont du Gard Inn, on the road between Bellegarde and Beaucaire. We had a dozen or so places like that, where we could deposit our merchandise and where we could hide from the customs agents and the police if necessary.

"One day as I was about to leave on a smuggling expedition, Assunta said to me, 'I'll have a surprise for you when you come back.' I questioned her about it but she would tell me nothing. When I came back six weeks later, the first thing I saw was a cradle with a baby in it. Assunta had gone to Paris during my absence and claimed the child. Ah, Excellency, I confess that when I saw that helpless little creature sleeping in his cradle my chest swelled and tears came to my eyes. 'You're a good woman, Assunta, and Providence will bless you,' I said.

"Alas, though, that child was the very means God had chosen to punish me. A more perverse character was never manifested at an earlier age, and yet no one can say it was because of his upbringing, for my sister-in-law treated him like the son of a prince. By the time he was eleven his closest friends were a group of young men between eighteen and twenty years old who had already been in a number of escapades which deserved a more serious name and about whom the police gave us several warnings.

"I was about to leave on an important expedition. Assunta always defended Benedetto in our discussions of him, but she admitted that several times she had noticed the disappearance of rather large sums of money, so I told her of a place where she could safely hide our little treasure. Then I left for France.

"We were to land our cargo in the Gulf of Lyons. It was in 1829 and smuggling operations were becoming more and more difficult. Order had been completely established by then and the coasts were therefore patrolled more carefully than ever.

"Our operations went off smoothly in the beginning. We tied up our ship, which had a double bottom in which we hid

our smuggled goods, among all the other ships that lined both
banks of the Rhone. From there we began to unload our
cargo and pass it into the city by means of certain people who
were in contact with us. Either because our success had made
us careless or because we were betrayed, one night as we were
about to sit down to supper, our cabin boy came running in
to tell us that a squad of customs police were headed in our
direction. We leaped to our feet but it was already too late:
our ship was surrounded. I went down into the hold, slid out
through a port and swam under water until I reached a small
canal that connects the Rhone with the canal that runs from
Beaucaire to Aigues-Mortes. Once I arrived there I was safe,
for I could follow the canal without being seen. It wasn't by
accident that I chose this route; I believe I've already told
you, Excellency, about an innkeeper from Nîmes who had
opened an inn on the road between Bellegarde and Beaucaire."

"What was his name?" asked the count, who was apparently
beginning to take a certain interest in Bertuccio's story.

"His name was Gaspard Caderousse, Excellency. He was a
husky man of about forty who had more than once proved
his courage and presence of mind in difficult situations."

"You say this was in 1829," said the count. "What month
was it?"

"June; the third of June."

"I see; June third, 1829," said the count. "Go on."

"As I said, I decided to take refuge in Caderousse's inn.
Even under ordinary circumstances we didn't go in through
his front door, so I certainly didn't do it this time, for he
might have had some traveler staying at his inn. I slipped
through the garden hedge and was soon in a sort of loft in
which I had more than once spent the night when I had no
better bed. This loft was separated from the main room of
the inn only by a wooden partition in which peepholes had
been made to enable us to watch for the opportune moment
to make our presence known. Just as I slipped into the loft
this time I saw Caderousse come in with a stranger. I kept
quiet and waited.

"The man with Caderousse was one of those traveling
merchants who come to sell jewelry at the Beaucaire fair. 'The
priest didn't deceive us,' said Caderousse to his wife. 'The
diamond is genuine and this gentleman, one of the most important jewelers of Paris, is ready to give us fifty thousand
francs for it. But in order to be sure the diamond really
belongs to us, he'd like you to tell him, as I've already done,
the miraculous way it fell into our hands. In the meantime,
sir, sit down and I'll bring you something to cool you off.'

" 'Tell me about it, madame,' said the jeweler, no doubt anxious to take advantage of Caderousse's absence to see if his wife's story would be the same in all details.

" 'Well,' said Madame Caderousse, 'it was a completely unexpected blessing from heaven. Fourteen years ago my husband knew a sailor named Edmond Dantès, who went to prison. In prison he met a rich Englishman who gave him a diamond when he was set free. Dantès wasn't so lucky, for he died in prison. Just before he died he left us the diamond and told the priest who came this morning to deliver it to us.'

" 'That's the same story your husband told me,' said the jeweler, 'and I suppose it may very well be true, unlikely though it seems at first. Now all we have to do is to agree on the price.'

" 'What!' said Caderousse. 'I thought we'd already agreed on the price I asked for!'

" 'I offered you forty thousand,' said the jeweler.

" 'Forty thousand!' cried Madame Caderousse. 'We certainly won't let it go for that price! The priest told us it was worth fifty thousand.'

" 'I'll go as high as forty-five thousand, but not another sou,' said the jeweler.

" 'All right, then,' said Caderousse, 'we'll sell it to someone else.'

" 'As you like, my friend,' said the jeweler, 'but I brought the money with me, as you can see.' He took out a roll of banknotes and a handful of gold, which sparkled before Caderousse's eyes. Caderousse was torn by indecision. He turned to his wife and whispered, 'What do you think?'

" 'Give him the diamond,' she replied. 'If he goes back to Beaucaire without it he'll denounce us, and we'll never be able to find the Abbé Busoni again to support our story.'

" 'So be it, then,' said Caderousse to the jeweler, 'take the diamond for forty-five thousand francs.'

"The jeweler counted out fifteen thousand francs in gold and thirty thousand francs in banknotes.

" 'Wait a minute, I'll light a lamp,' said Madame Caderousse. 'It's getting dark in here and we might make a mistake.' Night had fallen during their discussion, and with it came the storm which had been threatening to burst for half an hour, although none of the three of them seemed to have taken notice of it.

" 'Would you like to stay for supper?' asked Caderousse.

" 'Thank you,' answered the jeweler, 'but I must get back to Beaucaire; my wife will be worried.' Just then there was a clap of thunder and a flash of lightning lit up the room.

" 'Are you going to leave in weather like that?' asked Caderousse.

" 'Oh, I'm not afraid of thunder.'

" 'And what about robbers? The road is never very safe during the fair.'

" 'As for robbers,' said the jeweler, 'these are for them.' And he pulled out two loaded pistols.

" 'All right, then, *bon voyage*,' said Caderousse.

" 'Thank you,' said the jeweler. He took his cane and opened the door to go out. As he did so there was a terrific gust of wind which almost blew out the lamp.

" 'And to think that I have to walk two leagues in weather like that!' said the jeweler.

" 'Stay,' said Caderousse, 'you can sleep here tonight.'

" 'Yes, stay,' said his wife in a trembling voice, 'we'll take good care of you.'

" 'No, I must get back to Beaucaire tonight. Good-bye.'

" 'Why did you invite him to sleep here tonight?' asked Madame Caderousse when the jeweler had gone.

" 'Why, so he wouldn't have to go back to Beaucaire tonight,' said Caderousse, starting.

" 'Oh,' said the wife, 'I thought it was for something else.'

" 'Why do you have such ideas!' cried Caderousse. 'And if you have them, why don't you keep them to yourself? Listen! You've offended God!' As he said these words there was a tremendous clap of thunder and a bluish flash of lightning. Then the thunder died slowly away, as though regretful at having to leave the accursed house. Madame Caderousse crossed herself. At the same time, in the midst of that terrified silence which usually follows a clap of thunder, they heard someone knock on the door. They both started and looked at each other in alarm. 'Who is it?' cried Caderousse, putting his hands over the money lying on the table.

" 'It's Monsieur Joannes, the jeweler.'

" 'You see!' said Madame Caderousse. 'You said I'd offended God, but God has just sent him back to us!' Caderousse turned pale and sank into his chair, but she walked decisively over to the door, opened it and said, 'Come in, Monsieur Joannes.'

" 'It looks as if the devil doesn't want me to go back to Beaucaire tonight,' said the jeweler, who was soaked to the skin. 'You've offered me your hospitality, Monsieur Caderousse, and I've come back to sleep here tonight.'

"Caderousse mumbled a few words and wiped away the sweat that was streaming down his forehead. His wife locked the door behind the jeweler.

" 'Are there any other guests staying in your inn tonight?' asked Monsieur Joannes.

" 'No.'

" 'I'm not inconveniencing you?'

" 'Inconveniencing us? Not at all, Monsieur Joannes!' said Madame Caderousse graciously.

"Caderousse looked at his wife in surprise. While the jeweler stood warming himself before the fire, she laid out the leftovers from their dinner, to which she added two or three fresh eggs. 'There,' she said, putting a bottle of wine on the table, 'you can eat supper whenever you're ready.' The jeweler sat down to supper and Madame Caderousse served him with all the care of an attentive hostess. When he had finished she said to him, 'You must be tired. I've put clean sheets on the bed; go upstairs now and sleep well.' The jeweler stayed for another quarter of an hour to see if the storm might die down, then, seeing that it was growing even worse, he said good night to his host and hostess and went upstairs to bed. Madame Caderousse looked after him eagerly, but Caderousse turned his back to him.

"I recalled all these details later, but they made little impression on me as I watched them taking place. Aside from the story of the diamond, which struck me as somewhat unlikely, it all seemed perfectly natural. Since I was extremely tired, I decided to sleep for a few hours and then leave in the middle of the night.

"I was sound asleep when I was awakened by a pistol shot, followed by a terrible shriek. Then I heard groans and stifled cries as though some sort of struggle were taking place. One particularly loud cry, which faded away to a groan, roused me from my lethargy completely. Everything was quiet now. Then I heard a man's footsteps coming down the stairs. He entered the downstairs room, walked over to the fireplace and lit a candle. It was Caderousse. His face was pale and his shirt was covered with blood. He went upstairs again with the lighted candle and came back down a moment later with the diamond in his hand. He rolled it up in his red handkerchief, which he tied around his neck. Then he went over to the cupboard, took out the banknotes and the gold, rushed out the door and disappeared into the darkness.

"Everything became clear to me then and I reproached myself as though it were I who was guilty. I seemed to hear a groan: perhaps the poor jeweler was still alive. I pressed my shoulder against one of the planks that separated my loft from the rest of the house. It gave way. I picked up the candle and began to run up the stairs, but I found them blocked by a body: it was the corpse of Madame Caderousse.

The pistol shot I heard had been aimed at her. I stepped over her body and went into the bedroom. It was in terrible disorder. The unfortunate jeweler was lying on the floor in a pool of blood which flowed from three large wounds in his chest; in a fourth wound was a kitchen knife with only its handle showing. I tripped over the second pistol, which was not cocked; its powder had probably gotten wet. I went over to the jeweler. He was not yet dead. At the sound of my footsteps, he opened his eyes, moved his lips as though trying to speak, then died.

"The horrible scene had almost made me lose my reason. Now that I could no longer be of help to anyone, I had only one desire: to flee. I ran down the stairs, holding my head in my hands and roaring in terror.

"Downstairs there were five or six customs agents and two or three gendarmes. They seized me. I was in such a state of shock that I didn't even try to resist. I tried to speak, but I could only utter inarticulate cries. Then I realized that they took me for the murderer. I pulled away from the two men who were holding me and began to shout, 'I didn't do it! I didn't do it!' Two gendarmes pointed their carbines at me and said, 'If you make one movement, you're dead. You can tell your little story to the judge in Nîmes.' They handcuffed me, attached me to the tail of a horse and took me to Nîmes.

"I had been followed by a customs agent who had lost me in the vicinity of the inn. Suspecting that I would spend the night there, he had gone back for reinforcements. They had arrived just in time to hear the pistol shot and arrest me in the middle of such evidence of guilt that I realized immediately how hard it would be for me to prove my innocence. My only hope was to ask the judge to order a search for a certain Abbé Busoni. If Caderousse had invented his story, if that priest did not exist, I was clearly lost, unless Caderousse himself were caught and confessed everything.

"Two months went by, during which, I must say it to my judge's credit, every effort was made to find the priest. Then, on the eighth of September, five days before the date set for my trial, the Abbé Busoni came to my prison and said he had heard that a prisoner there wanted to speak to him. You can easily understand how overjoyed I was to see him. I told him everything I had witnessed in the inn and, contrary to my expectations, he supported Caderousse's story about the diamond. It was then that, impressed by his understanding charity and hoping that he might pardon me for the only crime I had ever committed, I told him, under the seal of confession, all the details of the adventure at Auteuil. My spontaneous confession of this first murder, which nothing forced me to reveal, convinced him that I had not committed the second one. He promised to do everything he could to persuade my judges that I was innocent.

"I had proof of his efforts when my trial was postponed to the following session of court. In the meantime, Caderousse was arrested in a foreign country and brought back to France. He admitted everything, but attributed the premeditation and instigation to his wife. He was sentenced to hard labor for life and I was set free."

"Was it then that you came to me with a letter from the Abbé Busoni?" asked Monte Cristo.

"Yes, Excellency; he seemed to take considerable interest in me. 'Smuggling will be your downfall,' he told me. 'Abandon it if you get out of prison.'

"'But how can I make a living and provide for my poor sister-in-law?' I asked.

"'One of my penitents, who has great respect for me, has asked me to find him a trustworthy steward. If you like, I'll recommend you to him, but I want you to swear I'll never have any cause to regret it.'

"I raised my hand to swear, but he said, 'It won't be necessary; I know Corsicans and I like them. Here's my letter of recommendation.' And he wrote me the letter I gave to you, Excellency. Now let me ask you with pride, Excellency: have you ever had reason to complain of me?"

"No," replied the count, "I admit with pleasure that you're a loyal servant, Monsieur Bertuccio, although you lack confidence in me."

"I, Excellency?"

"Yes, you. Why is it that you have a sister-in-law and an adopted son, and yet you've never said a word to me about either of them?"

"Alas, Excellency, I still haven't told you the saddest part of my life. I went back to Corsica, but when I arrived in Rogliano I found the house in mourning. There had been a horrible scene which my neighbors still remember vividly. My poor sister-in-law, following my instructions, had refused the demands of Benedetto, who wanted her to give him all the money in the house. One morning he threatened her and disappeared for the rest of the day. Assunta wept, for she had a true mother's heart for the wretched boy. He came back at eleven o'clock that night with two of his friends. They seized her and one of them, I tremble at the thought that it may have been Benedetto himself, said, 'Let's torture her, then she'll tell us where the money is!'

"My neighbor Wasilio was in Bastia at the time; his wife was in the house alone. She was the only one who saw and heard what was happening in my sister-in-law's house. Two of the young men held Assunta while the other one locked the doors and windows. Then, smothering her shrieks of terror, they began to hold her feet over the fire to make her tell them where her treasure was hidden. But her clothes caught fire in the struggle and they let go of her in order not to be burned themselves. She was found the next morning, half burned but still breathing. The cupboard had been broken open and the money was gone. As for Benedetto, he left Rogliano and never came back; I haven't seen or heard of him since then. It was after learning this tragic news that I came to you, Excellency. I didn't mention either Benedetto or Assunta to you because Benedetto had disappeared and Assunta was dead."

"The Abbé Busoni did well to send you to me," said Monte Cristo, "and you did well to tell me your story, for I'll have no more bad thoughts about you. And now, to end this discussion of your adventures, which will be our last, remember these words, which I have often heard spoken by the Abbé Busoni himself: For every evil there are two remedies: time and silence."

The count, after taking one last walk around the garden, went back to his carriage. Bertuccio, seeing how pensive he was, silently climbed up and sat down beside the coachman. The carriage set out for Paris.

Chapter 25

The next day, toward two o'clock in the afternoon, a carriage drawn by two magnificent English horses stopped before the Count of Monte Cristo's door. In it was a man wearing a blue coat with silk buttons of the same color, brown trousers and a white vest crossed by an enormous gold chain. His hair was so black and hung down so far over his forehead that it hardly seemed natural, for it was completely out of keeping with the deep wrinkles it failed to conceal; he was, in short, a man of fifty or fifty-five who tried to appear forty. Putting his head through the window of his carriage, he sent his groom to ask whether the Count of Monte Cristo was at home.

The groom knocked on the porter's window and asked, "Is this the Count of Monte Cristo's residence?"

"His Excellency lives here, but he's engaged now," replied the porter.

"In that case, here's the card of my master, Baron Danglars. Please take it to the Count of Monte Cristo and tell him that the baron stopped on his way to the Chamber in order to have the honor of seeing him."

"I don't speak to His Excellency, but his valet will deliver the message."

The groom returned to the carriage and reported the answer he had been given.

"He must be a prince, then, this man they call His Excellency and to whom no one but his valet has the right to speak!" said Danglars. "But that's all right: since he has a credit opened with me, he'll have to see me when he needs money." He sat back in his carriage and called out to the coachmen, so loudly that he could be heard on the other side of the street, "To the Chamber of Deputies!"

Monte Cristo, who had been notified of the baron's visit in time to see him, had been studying him from behind a window-blind with the aid of a pair of powerful binoculars.

"Ali!" he called out, striking a copper gong. Ali appeared. "Call Bertuccio," said Monte Cristo.

Bertuccio entered at almost the same moment. "Did Your Excellency wish to see me?" he asked.

"Yes. Did you see the horses that stopped in front of my door just now?"

"Certainly, Your Excellency. They're extremely handsome horses."

"Why is it," said Monte Cristo, frowning, "that when I've asked you to get me the two finest horses in Paris, there are two horses in Paris as handsome as mine and yet they're not in my stable?"

On seeing the count's frown and hearing the stern intonation of his voice, Ali bowed his head.

"It's not your fault, Ali," said the count in Arabic, with a gentleness which one would not have expected to find either in his voice or on his face. "You know nothing about English horses." Ali's features took on their look of serenity once again.

"Your Excellency," said Bertuccio, "the horses you mention weren't for sale."

Monte Cristo shrugged and said, "Don't you know that anything is for sale to a man who's willing to pay the price?"

"Monsieur Danglars paid sixteen thousand francs for them, sir."

"Well, then, you should have offered him thirty-two thousand. He's a banker, and a banker would never miss a chance to double his capital."

"Are you speaking seriously, sir?" asked Bertuccio.

Monte Cristo looked at him as though astonished that he should ask such a question. "I have a call to make at five o'clock this afternoon," he said. "I wish to have those horses harnessed to my carriage and waiting for me then."

"May I point out to Your Excellency that it's now two o'clock?" said Bertuccio timidly.

"I know," was Monte Cristo's only reply.

At five o'clock the count struck his gong three times. (One stroke was for Ali, two for Baptistin and three for Bertuccio.) The steward entered.

"My horses!" said Monte Cristo.

"They're harnessed to your carriage, sir."

The count went outside and saw the horses he had admired in front of Danglars' carriage three hours earlier. "They're really handsome horses," he said. "You were right to buy them, although you were a little late."

"I had great difficulty getting them, sir," said Bertuccio, "and I had to pay a very high price for them."

"Are they any less handsome because of that?" asked the count, shrugging his shoulders.

Bertuccio turned to go away. "Wait," said Monte Cristo, stopping him. "I need an estate on the seacoast—in Normandy, for example, between Le Havre and Boulogné. It must have a small harbor which my corvette can enter; she draws only fifteen feet of water. The ship must always be ready to put to sea, no matter what hour of the day or night I give the order. Make inquiries about such an estate and, when you hear of one, go to see it. If you're satisfied with it, buy it in your own name. The corvette is on her way to Fécamp now, isn't she?"

"I saw her put to sea the same evening we left Marseilles."

"And the yacht?"

"She's at Martigues."

"Very well. Correspond with the two captains from time to time to make sure they don't go to sleep."

The count climbed into his carriage and ordered his coachman to drive him to the residence of Baron Danglars.

The baron's white and gold salon was well known on the Rue de la Chaussée-d'Antin. It was there that he had his visitor shown on his arrival, in order to dazzle him right from the start.

"Have I the honor of addressing Monsieur de Monte Cristo?" asked the baron when he entered.

"And have I the honor of addressing Baron Danglars,

Chevalier of the Legion of Honor and Member of the Chamber of Deputies?" The count was repeating the titles he had read on the baron's card. Danglars felt the thrust and bit his lip.

"I've received a letter from the firm of Thomson and French," said Danglars, "but I must admit that it's meaning isn't very clear to me. In fact, I came by your house today to ask you to explain it to me."

"I'm listening, and I'll be glad to help you."

"I have the letter right here," said Danglars, drawing it from his pocket. "It opens an unlimited credit for you with my firm."

"Well, baron, what's obscure about that?"

"Nothing; but the word 'unlimited'——"

"Do you think the firm of Thomson and French isn't perfectly reliable?" asked Monte Cristo as naïvely as he could.

"Oh, perfectly reliable!" replied Danglars with an almost mocking smile. "But in financial matters the word 'unlimited' is so vague. . . . Vagueness is doubtfulness, and the wise man will stay away from doubtful things. Let me try to make myself clear by asking you to name the sum you expect to draw on me."

"The reason I opened an unlimited credit with you is precisely that I don't know how much money I'll need."

The banker leaned back in his chair with a heavy, arrogant smile and said, "Oh, don't be afraid to ask; you may be sure that my funds, limited though they may be, are sufficient to meet the highest demands, and even if you were to ask for a million——"

"Pardon?"

"I said a million," repeated Danglars, with all the self-assurance of stupidity.

"But what good would a million do me?" said the count. "If I needed only a million I wouldn't have bothered opening a credit for such a trifling sum! Why, I always carry at least that much with me." So saying, he drew from his card-case two treasury bonds for five hundred thousand francs each.

A man like Danglars must be bludgeoned, not merely pricked, and this blow had its effect. He stared at Monte Cristo in a daze.

"Come now, admit that you mistrust the firm of Thomson and French," continued the count. "I allowed for that possibility and, although I don't know much about business, I took my precautions. Here are two other letters like the one that was sent to you. One is from the firm of Arstein and Eskeles, of Vienna, opening an unlimited credit for me with

Baron de Rothschild; the other is from Baring, of London, and is addressed to Monsieur Lafitte."

This was the *coup de grâce:* Danglars was vanquished. He opened the two letters with trembling hands and verified the signatures with a scrupulousness which would have been insulting to Monte Cristo if he had not been aware of the banker's bewilderment.

"Here are three signatures which are worth many millions!" said Danglars, standing up as though to pay tribute to the power of gold personified in the man sitting before him. "Three unlimited credits! Excuse me, count, but, while I'm no longer mistrustful, I'm still astonished."

"Well, then," said Monte Cristo, "now that we understand each other, now that there's no longer any mistrust between us, shall we fix an approximate sum for the first year; say, six million, for example?"

"Very well, six million," said Danglars hoarsely.

The count stood up.

"I must confess one thing to you, count," said Danglars. "I thought I was rather well acquainted with all the large fortunes of Europe, yet yours was completely unknown to me. Is it of recent date?"

"No, on the contrary, it's very old. It's a sort of family treasure which it was forbidden to touch and which was tripled by the accumulation of interest. The period fixed by the testator expired only a few years ago, so your ignorance was quite natural. You'll learn more about it in a short time." He accompanied these words with one of those pale smiles which had so frightened Franz d'Epinay.

"Yes, that will be for later, when we know each other better," said Danglars. "For today I'll content myself with presenting you to Madame Danglars; excuse my eagerness, count, but a client like you is almost part of the family."

Monte Cristo bowed as a sign that he accepted the honor. Danglars rang and a servant appeared. "Is the baroness at home?" asked Danglars.

"Yes, sir."

"Is she alone?"

"No, madame has company."

"And who is madame's company? Monsieur Debray?" asked Danglars with a joviality that made Monte Cristo smile inwardly, for he was already acquainted with the banker's transparent family secrets.

"Yes, sir, it's Monsieur Debray," replied the servant.

Danglars nodded. Turning to Monte Cristo he said, "Monsieur Debray is an old friend of ours and is Secretary to the

Minister of the Interior. As for my wife, she lowered herself by marrying me, for she comes from an ancient family: she was Mademoiselle de Servières, and later a widow of the Marquis of Nargonne."

"I haven't had the honor of meeting Madame Danglars, but I've already met Monsieur Lucien Debray."

"Where was that?"

"At Monsieur Albert de Morcerf's house."

"Ah, you know the young viscount?"

"We were in Rome together during the carnival."

"Oh, yes, I think I heard about some strange adventure of his with bandits, some sort of miraculous escape. I believe he told my wife and daughter about it when he returned from Italy."

"The baroness awaits you, gentlemen," said the servant, entering the room once again.

"Allow me to show you the way," said Danglars to the Count of Monte Cristo.

Madame Danglars, whose beauty was still outstanding despite her thirty-six years, was at her piano, while Lucien Debray sat looking through an album. Debray had already had time to tell the baroness quite a number of things about the count. Her curiosity, aroused by both Albert's stories and the new details brought to her by Lucien, was now at its height. She therefore received her husband with a smile, which was contrary to her custom, and gave the count a ceremonious yet gracious bow. Debray exchanged a semi-familiar greeting with the count and an intimate one with Danglars.

"Allow me to introduce the Count of Monte Cristo," said Danglars. "I will say only one thing about him which will make him a great favorite of our fair ladies: he has come to Paris with the intention of staying here for a year and spending six million francs during that time, which means that we may expect a series of balls, dinners and supper parties."

"You've chosen a very bad time to come here," said Madame Danglars. "Paris is detestable in summer. There are no balls, receptions or banquets, the Italian opera is in London and the French opera is everywhere except in Paris. Our only entertainment consists of a few wretched horse races at the Champ de Mars and Satory. Do you like horses, count?"

"I've spent a good part of my life in the Orient, madame, and, as you know, the Orientals appreciate only two things in this world: the nobility of horses and the beauty of women."

Just then Madame Danglars' confidential maid entered and whispered a few words into her mistress's ear. The baroness turned pale and said, "Impossible!" Then, turning to her husband, she said, "Is what my maid tells me true?"

"What has she told you?" asked Danglars, visibly agitated.

"She says that when my coachman went to harness my horses to my carriage he found that they weren't in the stable. May I ask what that means?"

"Listen to me——" said Danglars.

"Oh, I'll listen to you, because I'm very curious to hear what you're going to tell me. I'll ask these gentlemen to be our judges and I'll begin by telling them the facts. Gentlemen, Baron Danglars has ten horses in his stable. Two of them are mine; they're magnificent horses, the finest in Paris. You know them, Monsieur Debray—my dappled grays. Now, just when I'm about to lend my carriage to Madame de Villefort to go to the Bois de Boulogne tomorrow, these two horses are nowhere to be found! Monsieur Danglars has no doubt managed to make a few thousand francs on them and sold them. Oh, what an abominable breed these speculators are!"

"My dear, those horses were too spirited," said Danglars. "They were only four years old and they made me terribly frightened for your sake. I'll find you other horses like them, even finer, if there are any; but they'll be calm, gentle horses which won't inspire me with such terror."

The baroness shrugged her shoulders with an air of profound contempt.

"My God!" exclaimed Debray. "Unless I'm mistaken, I see your horses harnessed to the count's carriage!"

"My dappled grays!" cried Madame Danglars. She rushed over to the window. "Yes, they're mine!"

Danglars was dumbfounded.

"Can it be possible?" said the count, affecting astonishment.

Danglars said nothing; he foresaw a disastrous scene in the very near future. Debray, who also felt the storm approaching, left on some invented pretext. Monte Cristo, who did not wish to spoil his advantage by remaining too long on this occasion, bowed to Madame Danglars and withdrew, abandoning the baron to his wife's anger.

"Very good!" thought the count as he left. "I've accomplished my aim: the Danglars' domestic peace is now in my hands and I'm about to win the gratitude of both the baron and the baroness at one stroke. I would have liked to be introduced to Mademoiselle Eugénie Danglars, but we have ample time ahead of us and that can wait till later." With this reflection he climbed into his carriage and returned home.

Two hours later, Madame Danglars received a charming letter from the Count of Monte Cristo in which he stated that, not wishing to make his entrance into Paris society by distressing a pretty woman, he would be grateful to her if she would take back her horses, which he had sent to her along with the letter. They were wearing the same harness she had seen on them that morning, except that the count had had a diamond inserted in each of the rosettes they wore on their ears.

Danglars also received a letter in which the count asked his permission to satisfy a millionaire's whim and begged him to excuse the Oriental manner in which he had sent back the horses.

That evening Monte Cristo went to his country house at Auteuil, accompanied by Ali.

The next afternoon, Ali, summoned by the gong, entered the count's study.

"Ali," said Monte Cristo, "I understand you're very skillful in throwing the lasso. Is that right?"

Ali nodded and drew himself up proudly.

"Good. Could you stop an ox with a lasso?"

Ali nodded.

"A tiger?"

Another nod.

"A lion?"

Ali pretended to throw a lasso and imitated a choked roar.

"I understand. Have you hunted lions?"

Ali nodded proudly.

"But could you stop two runaway horses?"

Ali smiled.

"Very well, then, listen: A short time from now a carriage will pass by drawn by two runaway dappled gray horses, the same ones I had yesterday. Even at the risk of being trampled, you must stop them in front of my door."

Ali went out into the street and traced a line on the pavement in front of the door; then he came back inside and pointed out the line to the count, who had been watching him. The count tapped Ali gently on the shoulder; it was his way of thanking him. The Nubian went outside, sat down in front of the house and began to smoke his chibouk.

Suddenly a distant but rapidly approaching rumble was heard; then a carriage appeared. The coachman was vainly trying to stop the horses, which were running wildly at tremendous speed. Inside the carriage, a young woman and an eight-year-old boy were clinging to each other, so terror-stricken that they were unable even to utter a cry. A stone under a wheel or a low-hanging tree would have been enough to cause the carriage to be smashed.

Ali suddenly set down his chibouk, drew a lasso from his

pocket, threw it, caught the front legs of the left-hand horse and let himself be dragged along for three or four steps. But at the end of those three or four steps, the horse fell, preventing the other horse from continuing its wild race. The coachman leaped down from his seat, but Ali had already seized the second horse by the nostrils in an iron grip and, neighing in pain, it sank down beside its companion.

All this was done in the time it takes for a bullet to hit its mark. It was nevertheless long enough for a man to dart out of the house in front of which the accident occurred, followed by several of his servants. As soon as the coachman opened the door of the carriage, this man lifted out the lady, who was clutching a pillow with one hand and pressing her fainting son to her bosom with the other. Monte Cristo carried them both into his house and set them down on a divan. "You're safe now, madame," he said.

The woman pointed to her son with a look that was more eloquent than any entreaty. The child was still unconscious.

"Yes, madame, I understand," said the count, examining the boy, "but there's no cause for alarm. He hasn't been injured in any way; he only fainted from fear."

"Oh, don't tell me that just to reassure me! Look how pale he is! Oh, my son, my child, my Edouard! Speak to your mother! Please, sir, send for a doctor! I'll give my entire fortune to anyone who can bring back my son to me!"

Monte Cristo opened a small chest, drew out a flask containing a blood-red liquid and allowed a single drop of it to fall between the child's lips. Although still pale, the boy opened his eyes almost immediately.

On seeing this, his mother became almost delirious with joy. "Where am I?" she cried. "And to whom do I owe so much happiness after such a cruel ordeal?"

"Madame," said Monte Cristo, "you're in the house of a man who considers himself lucky to have the opportunity of sparing you pain."

"It was all because of my cursed curiosity!" said the lady. "Everyone in Paris was speaking of Madame Danglars' magnificent horses, and I was foolish enough to want to try them."

"What!" exclaimed the count in admirably feigned surprise. "Do those horses belong to the baroness?"

"Yes, do you know her?"

"I've had the honor of meeting her, and I'm doubly glad to have saved you from the danger in which those horses placed you because you might have attributed it to me: I bought those horses from the baron yesterday, but the baroness seemed so grieved at having lost them that I sent them back to her the same day."

"Then you must be the Count of Monte Cristo whom Hermine spoke to me about yesterday."

"Yes, I am, madame."

"And I'm Madame Héloïse de Villefort."

The count bowed as though he had just heard a name that
was completely unknown to him.

"Oh, how grateful Monsieur de Villefort will be!" said
Héloïse. "You've saved his son and his wife at the same time.
If it hadn't been for your courageous servant, this dear child
and I would both have been killed. I do hope you'll allow me
to give that man a reward worthy of his devotion."

"Please don't spoil Ali for me, madame," said Monte Cristo.
"Ali is my slave; in saving your life, he served me, and it's
his duty to serve me."

"But he risked his life," said Madame de Villefort.

"I once saved that life, madame; it therefore belongs to me."

Madame de Villefort was silent; perhaps she was thinking
about this man who made such a deep impression on everyone
who saw him. During this moment of silence, Monte Cristo
examined the child whose mother was covering him with
kisses. He was small and thin, and had the pallor which usually goes with red-haired children, yet his rounded forehead
was covered with a forest of rebellious black hair which, falling down to his shoulders and framing his face, doubled the
vivacity of his eyes, which were full of sly malice and childish
wickedness. His first movement was to shake himself free of
his mother's embrace and open the small chest from which
the count had taken the flask containing the red liquid. With
the air of a child who is accustomed to satisfying all his whims,
he began to uncork the different bottles without asking anyone's
permission.

"Don't touch that, my boy!" said the count sharply. "Some
of those liquids are dangerous, not only to taste, but even to
inhale."

Madame de Villefort turned pale and pulled her son back
to her. When her fear had passed she cast a short but expres-
sive glance at the chest.

"Is this your usual residence, count?" she asked, standing up.

"No, madame, it's only a sort of *pied-à-terre* in the country.
I live at 30 Avenue des Champs Elysées. . . . But I see you're
completely recovered and ready to go. I'll have those same
horses harnessed to my carriage and Ali will have the honor
of driving you home while your coachman remains here to
repair your carriage. When he's finished, I'll have it taken directly to Madame Danglars by a team of my horses."

"But I'd be afraid to go with those horses again."

"Oh, you'll see, madame," said Monte Cristo. "In Ali's hands they'll be as gentle as lambs."

Indeed, Ali had just approached the horses holding a sponge soaked in aromatic vinegar, with which he rubbed their nostrils and wiped away the foam and sweat that covered their foreheads. Then he harnessed them to the count's carriage and climbed up on the seat. To the great astonishment of the onlookers, who had seen the horses running as though carried along by a whirlwind, he was obliged to use the whip on them to get them to start, and even then they went along at such a slow trot that it took nearly two hours to reach Madame de Villefort's home in the Faubourg Saint-Honoré.

Chapter 26

That same evening, Monsieur de Villefort put on a black coat and white gloves, got into his carriage and alighted at 30 Avenue des Champs Elysées.

If the Count of Monte Cristo had lived in Paris society longer, he would have appreciated Monsieur de Villefort's visit at its full worth. Monsieur de Villefort was not only a magistrate, he was almost a diplomat, and he paid very few visits. He gave a ball once a year and appeared at it for only fifteen minutes. He never went to the theater, the concert hall or any other public place. Sometimes, but rarely, he would play a game of whist, being careful to choose partners worthy of him: an ambassador, perhaps, a prince or an archbishop.

Such was the man whose carriage drew up before Monte Cristo's door. The valet announced Monsieur de Villefort just as the count, leaning over a large map, was tracing out an itinerary from Saint Petersburg to China. The public prosecutor entered with the same stately, measured tread with which he entered the courtroom.

"Count," he said, "the outstanding service you rendered my wife and my son today has made it my duty to thank you. I have therefore come to carry out that duty and express my deepest gratitude to you." As he spoke these words, the magistrate's face lost none of its usual arrogance and his neck and shoulders retained the inflexible stiffness which made his flatterers describe him as a living statue of the law.

"I'm very happy to have been able to save a mother's son for her," replied Monte Cristo with icy coldness, "for maternal love is said to be the most sacred of all sentiments, and this happiness on my part dispensed you from a duty whose performance honors me, to be sure, for I know that Monsieur de Villefort is not prodigal with the honor he does me, but, however precious it may be, it is worth less to me than my inner satisfaction."

Villefort, astonished at this unexpected reply, started like a soldier who feels himself pierced beneath his armor and a slight movement of his disdainful lip indicated that he did not consider the Count of Monte Cristo to be a very civil gentleman. He looked around for something which might serve as a pretext for changing the subject of conversation. Seeing the map which Monte Cristo had been examining, he said, "Are you interested in geography, count? It's a rewarding study, especially for a man who, like you, according to what I've been told, at least, has seen every country represented on that map."

"Yes," replied the count, "I've made a psychological study of every human species, on the assumption that it would then be easier to go from the whole to the part, rather than beginning with the part and going to the whole."

"Ah, so you're a philosopher!" said Villefort after a moment of silence during which, like an athlete meeting a formidable adversary, he had gathered his strength. "Well, count, if I were like you and had nothing to do, I can assure you I'd find a less gloomy occupation."

"It's true," said Monte Cristo, "that man is a very ugly creature when one examines him closely. But you just remarked that I had nothing to do. Do you think *you* have something to do, Monsieur de Villefort? Or, to speak more clearly, do you think that what you do is worth being called something?"

Villefort's astonishment doubled at this second thrust delivered so vigorously by his strange adversary.

"Your eyes are fixed only on the social organization of humanity," continued Monte Cristo. "You see nothing but the springs of the machine and not the sublime workman who makes it function. You recognize around you only those whose positions have been assigned to them by some minister or king; you are unable to see those men whom God has placed above kings and ministers by giving them a mission to fulfill, rather than a position to occupy."

"And do you regard yourself as one of those extraordinary beings?" asked Villefort, more and more astonished and unable to decide whether the man to whom he was speaking was inspired or mad.

"Yes, I'm one of them," said Monte Cristo coldly, "and I don't believe any other man has ever found himself in a position like mine. The domains of kings are limited by natural barriers or changes of customs or language. My kingdom is as large as the world, for I am neither Italian, French, Hindu, American or Spanish: I am a cosmopolite. I adopt all customs and I speak all languages. You think I'm French because I speak French with the same ease and correctness as you. But Ali, my Nubian, thinks I'm an Arab; Bertuccio, my steward, thinks I'm a Roman; Haydée, my slave, thinks I'm a Greek. Therefore, since I am from no country, since I ask no government for protection, and since I regard no man as my brother, I am not deterred by any of the scruples or obstacles that paralyze the efforts of the weak. I have only three adversaries. The first two are distance and time, but with persistence I am able to overcome them. The third one is the most terrible: the fact that I am mortal. Only that can stop me before I reach my goal. Unless I die, I will always be what I am. That is why I tell you things you have never heard before, even from the lips of a king, for kings have need of you and other men are afraid of you. Who has not said to himself, in a society as ridiculously organized as ours, 'Some day I may have to go before the public prosecutor'?"

"But even you can say that to yourself, count, for as long as you live in France you must naturally submit yourself to French law."

"I know that, Monsieur de Villefort, but when I enter a country I study, by my own methods, all the men who may be either advantageous or disadvantageous to me and I come to know them as well as they know themselves, or perhaps better. The result of this is that any public prosecutor with whom I might have to deal would find himself in a much more difficult situation than I."

"In other words," said Villefort hesitantly, "human nature is weak and all men, according to you, have committed—errors?"

"Yes, either errors or crimes."

"And you alone are perfect?"

"No, not perfect," replied the count, "only impenetrable. I maintain my pride in the face of men, but I abandon it before God, who drew me out of nothingness to make me what I am."

"I admire you, count," said Villefort, "and if you are really strong, really superior and really either perfect or impenetrable, which, as you rightly say, comes to almost the same thing, then I can only say to you: Be proud and masterful, that's the law of domination. But you must at least have some ambition or other."

"Yes, I have one."

"What is it?"

"As it happens to every man at least once in his life, I was once raised by Satan to the top of the highest mountain on earth. From there he showed me the whole world and said to me, as he said to Christ, 'Son of man, what wouldst thou have in order to worship me?' I thought for a long time, for a terrible ambition had been devouring my heart, then I replied, 'I have always heard of Providence, yet I have never seen it or anything resembling it, which makes me think it does not exist. I want to be Providence, for the greatest, the most beautiful and the most sublime thing I know of in this world is to reward and punish.' But Satan bowed his head and sighed. 'You are mistaken,' he said, 'Providence does exist, but it is invisible; you have never seen anything resembling it because it works by secret springs and moves in hidden ways. All I can do for you is to make you one of the agents of Providence.' I made the bargain with him; I may lose my soul because of it, but if I had it to do over again I would do the same thing."

Villefort looked at the count in rapt amazement. "You say you fear nothing but death?" he asked.

"I didn't say I feared it; I said that it alone could stop me."

"What about old age?"

"My mission will be accomplished before I'm old."

"And madness?"

"I almost went mad once, and you know the axiom, *'Non bis in idem';* it's an axiom of jurisprudence and therefore falls within your range of knowledge."

"There are other things to fear besides death, old age and madness," said Villefort. "There is, for example, apoplexy, that thunder bolt that strikes you without destroying you, but after which everything is finished. Come to my house some day, count, and I'll show you my father, Monsieur Noirtier de Villefort, one of the fieriest Jacobins of the French Revolution, a man who has not perhaps, like you, seen all the kingdoms of the earth, but who did help to overthrow one of the mightiest of them. Yet the rupture of a blood vessel in his brain changed all that, not in a day, not in an hour, but in a second. Monsieur Noirtier, the former Jacobin, the former senator, a man who laughed at the guillotine, the cannon and the dagger, a man for whom France was only a vast chessboard, this formidable Monsieur Noirtier became 'that poor Monsieur Noirtier,' a paralyzed old man, a mute, frozen corpse awaiting its final decomposition."

"What do you conclude from this, Monsieur de Villefort?"

"I conclude that my father, led astray by his passions, has

committed one or more of those wrongs which escape human justice but not divine justice, and that God has struck him down because of this."

Monte Cristo, with a smile on his lips, pushed down into the depths of his heart a roar which would have made Villefort flee in terror if he had been able to hear it.

"I must leave you now, count," said Villefort, who had stood up some time before, "but I leave filled with an esteem which I hope will be agreeable to you when you know me better, for I am not an ordinary man, not at all. And you have already made Madame de Villefort your eternal friend."

When the public prosecutor had gone, Monte Cristo said to himself, "Now that my heart is full of poison, let's go seek the antidote." He struck the gong once. "I'm going up to see madame," he said to Ali. "Have the carriage ready in half an hour."

Chapter 27

It was noon; the count had set aside an hour to be spent with Haydée. The young Greek occupied an apartment completely separate from the count's and furnished in the Oriental manner: the floors were covered with thick Turkish carpets, the walls were hung with brocades and in each room there was a wide divan with piles of cushions to be placed according to the will of those who used them.

Haydée was lying on the floor on blue satin cushions, leaning back against the divan while her softly rounded arm encircled her head. Her pose, quite natural for a woman of the Orient, would have been somewhat affected for a French woman. Her face represented Grecian beauty in all the perfection of its type, with its large, soft black eyes, its straight nose, coral lips and pearly teeth. And over all this was the bloom and freshness of youth: Haydée was no more than nineteen or twenty years old.

Monte Cristo called for the Greek attendant and sent her to ask Haydée if he might visit her. Haydée raised herself up on one elbow when he entered and held out her hand to him with a smile.

"Why did you ask permission to come here?" she asked in the sonorous language of the daughters of Athens and Sparta. "Are you no longer my master? Am I no longer your slave?"

"Haydée," replied the count, "we're in France now and you're therefore free."

"Free to do what?"

"Free to leave me."

"Leave you! Why should I leave you?"

"We're going to see many people, and if, among the handsome young men you meet, you were to find one who pleased you, I wouldn't be so unjust as to——"

"I've never seen a man handsomer than you and I've never loved anyone except my father and you."

"Do you remember your father, Haydée?"

Haydée smiled. "He's here and here," she said, placing her hand over her eyes and over her heart.

"And where am I?" asked Monte Cristo, smiling.

"You're everywhere."

Monte Cristo took her hand to kiss it, but she withdrew it and offered her forehead.

"Now, Haydée," he said, "you know that you're free, that you're the mistress here, that you're a queen. You may go on wearing your national costume or discard it, as you like; you may stay here when you like and go out when you like; there will always be a harnessed carriage waiting for you; Ali and Myrto will accompany you and will be at your orders. But there is one thing I must ask of you."

"Tell me."

"Keep the secret of your birth and say nothing about your past; never utter the name of your illustrious father or of your poor mother."

"I've already told you, my lord, that I'll see no one."

"That Oriental seclusion may be impossible in Paris, Haydée. Continue to learn about the life here, in northern countries, as you did in Rome, Florence, Milan and Madrid; the knowledge may always be useful to you, whether you return to the Orient or go on living here."

Haydée raised her large moist eyes to the count and said, "You mean whether *we* return to the Orient, don't you, my lord?"

"Yes; you know I'll never leave you. It's not the tree that leaves the blossom, but the blossom that leaves the tree."

"I'll never leave you, my lord," said Haydée, "for I'm sure I couldn't live without you."

"Poor child! In ten years I'll be old and you'll still be young. You love me as you loved your father."

"You're mistaken, my lord, I didn't love my father as I love you; my love for you is quite different. When my father died, I went on living; but if you were to die, I'd die too."

The count held out his hand to her with a smile of deep tenderness; she pressed her lips to it as usual. Then he went out, murmuring to himself these lines by Pindar: "Youth is a blossom whose fruit is love; happy is he who plucks it after watching it slowly ripen."

The carriage was ready according to his orders. He climbed into it and set off at a gallop.

Chapter 28

A few minutes later Monte Cristo arrived at 7 Rue Meslay. In the porter who opened the door of the courtyard, the count recognized old Coclès, but Coclès did not recognize the count. Baptistin leaped down from his seat to ask if Monsieur and Madame Herbault and Monsieur Maximilien Morrel were at home to the Count of Monte Cristo.

"To the Count of Monte Cristo!" cried Maximilien, throwing away his cigar and hurrying out to meet the visitor. "Thank you very much, count, for not forgetting your promise!" And the young officer shook the count's hand so warmly that there could be no doubt about his sincerity.

"Come with me," said Maximilien, "I want to introduce you myself. A man like you shouldn't be announced by a servant. My sister is in the garden cutting off the dead roses and her husband is reading the newspapers there. Wherever Madame Herbault is, you may be sure that Monsieur Herbault is within a radius of four yards and reciprocally, as they say at the École Polytechnique."

At the sound of their footsteps, a young woman of about twenty-five, wearing a silken morning gown, raised her head. It was our little Julie, who had become, as the representative of Thomson and French had predicted, Madame Emmanuel Herbault. She uttered a little cry on seeing a stranger. Maximilien began to laugh.

"It was treacherous of my brother to bring you here, sir," she said to the count. "He never considers his sister's vanity. . . . Penelon! Penelon!"

An old man digging in a bed of Bengal roses stuck his spade into the ground and walked over, holding his cap in his hand and doing his best to hide a quid of tobacco by pushing it toward the back of his mouth. His bronzed face and his bold, keen eyes made it easy to recognize him as an old sailor, tanned by the tropical sun and weathered by countless gales. "I believe you hailed me, Mademoiselle Julie," he said. "Here I am." He had kept the habit of calling his employer's daughter "Mademoiselle Julie" and had never been able to accustom himself to calling her Madame Herbault.

"Penelon," said Julie, "go tell Monsieur Emmanuel about

this gentleman's visit." Then, turning to the count, she said, "Will you allow me to leave you for a moment?" Without waiting for a reply, she disappeared behind a clump of trees and slipped into the house by a side entrance.

A short time later Emmanuel appeared and greeted his visitor with great courtesy. Then, after having shown the count around the garden, he led him into the house. The salon was impregnated with the scent of the flowers which filled an enormous Japanese vase. Julie, now properly dressed and impeccably groomed (she had accomplished this feat in ten minutes), was waiting to receive the count.

Birds could be heard chirping in a nearby aviary; laburnum and acacia trees spread their leaves against the blue velvet curtains; everything in this charming little retreat breathed serenity, from the songs of the birds to the smiles of its owners. The count had been keenly aware of this air of happiness from the moment he entered. He stood silent and thoughtful, forgetting that the others were waiting for him to continue the conversation after the first exchange of greetings. He finally became conscious of this almost embarrassing silence and made an effort to pull himself out of his reverie.

"Madame," he said, "forgive me for an emotion which must be surprising to you, accustomed as you are to the peace and happiness I find here; but for me it's such a rare experience to see satisfaction in a human face that it's hard for me to take my eyes off you and your husband."

"It's true that we're happy," replied Julie, "but we had to suffer for a long time and few people have paid as high a price for their happiness as we have."

The count's face took on an expression of curiosity. "And did God send you consolation in your suffering, as he does to everyone?" he asked.

"Yes, count," said Julie, "we can truly say that He did, for He did for us what He does only for His elect: He sent us one of His angels."

The count's cheeks turned red and he coughed in order to be able to hide his emotion by putting his handkerchief before his face. Then he began to pace around the room.

"Our magnificence must make you smile, count," said Maximilien.

"No, not at all," replied Monte Cristo. He pointed to a hollow crystal globe inside which was a silk purse carefully placed on a black velvet cushion. "I was just wondering about this purse with a piece of paper in one compartment and a rather handsome diamond in the other," he said.

"That's the most precious of all our family treasures, count," said Maximilien gravely.

"The objects inside that purse are relics of the angel I mentioned just now," said Julie.

"Count," said Maximilien, lifting the crystal globe and reverently kissing the silk purse, "this once touched the hand of a man who saved my father from death, us from ruin and our name from dishonor. This letter was written by him on a day when my father had made an extremely desperate resolution, and the same unknown benefactor gave this diamond to my sister for her dowry."

Monte Cristo opened the letter and read it with indescribable happiness. It was the letter addressed to Julie and signed "Sinbad the Sailor."

"Did you say 'unknown'?" asked the count. "Has the man who rendered you this service always remained unknown to you?"

"Yes, we've never had the joy of shaking his hand," replied Maximilien, "although it's certainly not because we haven't begged God to grant us that favor. He was an Englishman who presented himself to my father as a representative of the firm of Thomson and French of Rome. That's why you saw me start the other day when you mentioned that Thomson and French were your bankers. It happened in 1829; tell me, in the name of God, did you know that man?"

"Let's see," said Monte Cristo, "was he a man about my size, slightly taller and thinner, prehaps, who always wore a high collar and always had a pencil in his hand?"

"Oh, then you know him!" cried Julie, her eyes sparkling with joy.

"No, I'm only guessing. I once knew a Lord Wilmore who used to perform generous actions like that without revealing his identity. He was a strange man who didn't believe in the existence of true gratitude. Since then, however, he may have had proof that he was mistaken."

"Oh, if you know him, take us to him!" cried Julie. "If we could only see him, he'd have to believe in our gratitude!"

"Alas," said Monte Cristo, trying to stifle the emotion in his voice, "if Lord Wilmore was your benefactor, I'm afraid you'll never find him. When I left him two or three years ago in Palermo he was preparing to leave for all sorts of faraway countries and I doubt that he'll ever return. Besides, you shouldn't build any hopes on my remarks: Lord Wilmore is probably not the man you're searching for. He and I were close friends; I knew all his secrets, but he never said a word about this matter."

"Yet you thought of him immediately," said Julie.

"I was only guessing."

"Besides, Julie," said Maximilien, coming to the count's aid, "don't forget what our father said to us so often: 'It wasn't an Englishman who gave us our happiness.' "

Monte Cristo started. "Your father said——" he began.

"Yes, count," said Maximilien, "my father saw a miracle in that action. He believed in a benefactor who had come back from the tomb to help us. It was a touching superstition, and while I didn't believe in it myself, I had no wish to destroy my father's belief in it. And when he was about to die, that thought became a conviction: his last words were, 'Maximilien, it was Edmond Dantès!' "

The count's pallor became almost frightening; all his blood rushed to his heart and he was unable to speak for a moment. He looked at his watch as though he had forgotten the hour, took his hat, paid his compliments to Madame Herbault in an abrupt and embarrassed manner, shook hands with Emmanuel and Maximilien and said, "Madame, allow me to repeat my visit another day. I like your house, and I'm grateful to you for your reception, for this is the first time I've forgotten myself in many years." He then strode swiftly out of the room.

"He's a strange man, the Count of Monte Cristo," said Emmanuel.

"Yes," said Maximilien, "but I believe he has a good heart and I'm sure he likes us."

"As for me," said Julie, "his voice went straight to my heart, and two or three times it seemed to me that it wasn't the first time I had heard it."

Chapter 29

When the Count of Monte Cristo arrived at the Villefort residence with the intention of repaying Monsieur de Villefort's visit, the mention of his name set the whole household into a commotion. Madame de Villefort was in the salon when he was announced. She immediately sent for her son, so that he might renew his thanks to the count.

After the first exchange of formalities, the count asked about Monsieur de Villefort.

"My husband is dining with the chancellor," replied the young woman. "He left just a moment ago, and I'm sure he'll be sorry to have missed seeing you. . . . By the way, Edouard, where's your sister Valentine? Go have her sent here so that I can introduce her to the count."

"Do you have a daughter, madame?" asked Monte Cristo.

"She's Monsieur de Villefort's daughter by his first marriage."

A few moments later Valentine entered the salon. She was a tall, slender young lady of nineteen with chestnut hair, dark blue eyes and long white hands. When she saw her mother with the stranger about whom she had already heard so much, she bowed without any of the affected shyness common to young girls and with such grace that the count's attention redoubled.

"Tell me, madame," said the count, looking back and forth between Madame de Villefort and Valentine, "haven't I already had the honor of meeting you and this young lady somewhere else? I've thought about it before, and when Mademoiselle de Villefort entered just now it was like another ray of light on my obscure memory."

"It's improbable, count. We rarely go out," said Madame de Villefort.

"No, it wasn't in Paris. . . . Excuse me while I try to remember—the memory seems to involve bright sunshine and some sort of religious festival——"

"Perhaps the count saw us in Italy," said Valentine.

"That's right, mademoiselle!" cried Monte Cristo. "It was in Perugia during the festival of Corpus Christi in the garden of the hotel."

"I remember being in Perugia," said Madame de Villefort, "but I don't remember having had the honor of seeing you."

"Let me help your memory, madame. It was a scorching hot day. You were waiting for your carriage, which had been delayed because of the festival. Mademoiselle de Villefort took a walk in the garden and your son ran off chasing a bird. Don't you remember sitting there on a stone bench and talking with someone?"

"Oh, yes," said the young woman, blushing, "I talked with a man wearing a long cape—a doctor, I believe."

"I was that man, madame. I'd been living in that hotel for two weeks. I'd just cured my valet of the fever and the hotelkeeper of jaundice, so that I was regarded as a great doctor there."

"But you cured illness, so you really were a doctor, weren't you?"

"No, madame, although I have made a thorough study of chemistry and the natural sciences."

At this moment the clock struck six. "It's six o'clock, Valentine," said Madame de Villefort, visibly agitated. "Aren't you going to see if your grandfather is ready for dinner?"

Valentine stood up, bowed to the count without saying a word, and left.

"Was it because of me that you sent Mademoiselle de Ville-fort away?" asked the count when Valentine had gone.

"Not at all!" replied Madame de Villefort. "It's just that this is the hour when we usually serve Monsieur Noirtier his dinner. I suppose you know about the deplorable condition of my husband's father?"

"Yes, madame, Monsieur de Villefort has spoken to me about it."

"Excuse me for mentioning our domestic misfortunes to you, count. I interrupted you just as you were telling me you were a skillful chemist."

"Oh, I didn't say that, madame," replied Monte Cristo with a smile. "I simply studied chemistry because, intending to live in the Orient, I decided to follow the example of King Mithridates."

"*Mithridates, rex Ponticus,*" said Edouard, cutting out pictures from a magnificent album, "he's the one who used to have a cup of poison with cream every morning for breakfast."

"Edouard, you wicked child!" cried Madame de Villefort, snatching the mutilated album from the hands of her son. "You're unbearable! Leave us alone and go see your sister in your grandfather's room."

"I won't go unless you give me the album," said the child, seating himself firmly in a large armchair.

"All right, then, take it and leave us alone," said Madame de Villefort. She gave him the album and led him out of the room.

"Let's see if she closes the door behind him," said the count to himself.

Madame de Villefort carefully closed the door behind the child; the count did not appear to notice.

"Your son was quoting Cornelius Nepos when he mentioned King Mithridates," said Monte Cristo, "which shows that he's quite advanced for his age."

"Yes, he learns easily," replied the flattered mother. "His only fault is that he's extremely willful. . . . With regard to what he was saying, do you believe that King Mithridates really took those precautions and that they were efficacious?"

"I certainly do, madame. I myself took the same precautions to avoid being poisoned in Naples, Palermo and Smyrna, and they saved my life in all three places."

"Oh, yes; I remember your telling me something of that sort in Perugia."

"Really?" said the count in admirably feigned surprise. "I don't recall mentioning it."

"And how did you go about accustoming yourself to poison?"

"It's quite simple. Suppose you know in advance what poison will be used against you; suppose it's brucine, for example." ·

"Brucine comes from the *brucea ferruginea,* doesn't it?" asked Madame de Villefort.

"Precisely, madame," replied Monte Cristo. "I see I have little to teach you; such knowledge is rare in women. . . . Well, then, suppose the poison is brucine. The first day you take one milligram of it, the second day two milligrams, and so on until you're taking ten milligrams on the tenth day. Then you begin to add two milligrams each day until on the twentieth day you're taking thirty milligrams, a dose which does you no harm but which would be extremely dangerous to someone who hasn't taken the same precautions."

"I've often read the story of King Mithridates," said Madame de Villefort thoughtfully, "but I always took it for a fable."

"No, madame, it's quite true. Furthermore, not only do the Orientals use poison to make themselves a suit of armor, but they also use it as a dagger. And they use it so skillfully that human justice is left without a clue. Go outside France, to Cairo, or even to Naples or Rome, and you'll see men who appear to be in perfect health, but about whom some demon could whisper in your ear, 'That man has been poisoned for three weeks; in another month he'll be dead.' The poison attacks some specific organ of the body, brings on an illness which is quite well known to science but fatal nevertheless, and there you have a murder that will remain forever unknown to justice."

"It's frightening, but it's admirable!" said Madame de Villefort, who had been listening with motionless attention. "It's fortunate such poisons can be prepared only by chemists; otherwise one half of the world would poison the other."

"Either by chemists or people who have studied chemistry," remarked Monte Cristo.

"You yourself must be a great chemist, count, for that medicine you gave my son, which brought him back to life so quickly——"

"Don't form any false ideas about that, madame: one drop of that liquid brought your son back to consciousness, but three drops would have forced blood to his lungs in such a way as to give him palpitations of the heart and ten would have killed him. You may recall how quickly I snatched the bottles away from him."

"It's a terrible poison, then?"

"Oh, no. First of all, let's recognize that the word 'poison' has no meaning, since, in medicine, the most violent poisons become health-giving remedies when they are used properly."

"What is it, then?"

"It's a preparation made for me by a very learned friend of mine, who also taught me to use it."

"I see; it must be an excellent antispasmodic."

"A perfect one, madame, as you saw for yourself. I often use it myself—with all possible caution, of course," added Monte Cristo, smiling.

"I'm sure you do," said Madame de Villefort in the same tone. "As for myself, I'm extremely nervous and inclined to fainting, but I have no learned friend like yours, so I'm obliged to go on using Monsieur Planché's antispasmodic."

"I prefer my own."

"Certainly; so would I, especially after having seen for myself what it can do. But I suppose it's a secret, and I'm not indiscreet enough to ask you for it."

"But I'm gallant enough to offer it to you, madame," said Monte Cristo, standing up.

"Oh, count!"

"Remember one thing, however: it's a remedy in small doses, but a poison in large doses. One drop of it restores life, as you've seen; five or six drops would kill infallibly. And it's all the more dangerous because if those five or six drops were mixed in with a glass of wine they wouldn't change the taste of it at all."

The clock had just struck half-past six. A servant entered to announce the arrival of a friend who had come to dine with Madame de Villefort.

"If this were our third or fourth meeting instead of our second," said Madame de Villefort, "and if I had the honor of being your friend instead of simply being indebted to you, I'd insist on keeping you here for dinner, and I wouldn't let myself be daunted by a first refusal."

"Thank you very much, madame," replied Monte Cristo, "but I also have another engagement which I must keep."

"Very well, then, count; but please don't forget my remedy."

"Certainly not, madame! To forget that, I'd have to forget the hour of conversation I've just had with you, which is completely impossible."

The count bowed and withdrew. His results had surpassed his expectations. "I'm sure the seed I've sown hasn't fallen on barren ground," he said to himself as he went out.

And the next day, true to his promise, he sent Madame de Villefort the remedy she had requested.

Chapter 30

Several days later, Albert de Morcerf came to call on the Count of Monte Cristo in his house on the Champs Elysées, which had already taken on that palatial air which the count, thanks to his immense fortune, always gave to even his temporary residences.

Albert was accompanied by Lucien Debray. It seemed to the count that Debray's visit was prompted by a twofold curiosity, half of which emanated from the Rue de la Chaussée-d'Antin: that Madame Danglars, in other words, unable to examine with her own eyes the house of a man who gave away horses worth thirty thousand francs and went to the opera with a Greek slave girl wearing a million francs' worth of diamonds, had instructed Debray, through whose eyes she was accustomed to seeing, to bring her back what information he could. Outwardly, however, the count appeared to be aware of no connection between Debray's visit and the baroness's curiosity.

"You see Baron Danglars quite often, don't you?" he asked Albert.

"Of course; you know what I told you."

"It still holds good, then?"

"Oh, yes; it's a settled matter."

"Is she pretty?"

"Very pretty, even beautiful; but she has a kind of beauty I don't appreciate. I'm unworthy of her!"

"You talk about her as though you were already her husband!" said Monte Cristo. "You don't seem very enthusiastic about this marriage."

"Mademoiselle Danglars is too rich for me," said Albert. "That frightens me."

"I admit," said Monte Cristo, "that it's difficult for me to understand your repugnance for a young lady who's both rich and beautiful."

"Oh, I'm not the only one who objects to the marriage. My mother is also against it; I think she has something against the Danglars family. . . . You're so lucky to be free, count!"

"Well, then, be free yourself! Who's to prevent you?"

"It would be too great a disappointment to my father if I didn't marry Mademoiselle Danglars."

"Marry her, then," said the count with a strange shrug of his shoulders.

"On the other hand," said Albert, "it would cause my mother more than disappointment: it would cause her pain."

"Then don't marry her."

"I'll see; I'll try to decide what I should do. You'll advise me, won't you? Perhaps you can help me to get out of this embarrassing situation. . . . But if worse comes to worst, I'll quarrel with my father to avoid causing my mother pain."

Monte Cristo turned away; he seemed to be agitated. "Well," he said to Debray, who was sitting on the other side of the room with a pencil in one hand and a notebook in the other, "what are you doing, sketching?"

"No, I'm calculating how much Danglars made on the last rise in Haitian bonds. They went from two hundred and six to four hundred and nine in three days, and the wise banker bought large amounts at two hundred and six. He must have made three hundred thousand francs. Yet today the bonds fell to two hundred and five."

"If Monsieur Danglars gambles to win or lose three hundred thousand francs in one day, he must be enormously rich," said the count.

"He's not the one who gambles!" exclaimed Debray. "It's Madame Danglars. She's very daring."

"If I were you," said Albert, "I'd cure her of that; it would be a service to her future son-in-law."

"What do you mean?"

"I'd teach her a lesson. Your position as the minister's secretary makes you an authority on the news: each time you open your mouth all the stockbrokers in Paris take down every word you say. Make her lose a hundred thousand francs a few times and she'll soon become more cautious."

"I don't understand," stammered Debray.

"It's quite simple," continued Albert. "One day you tell her some sensational piece of news, some telegraphic dispatch that only you could know about: that Henry the Fourth was seen yesterday at Gabrielle's, for example. That will cause the market to rise, she'll speculate and then she'll be sure to lose when Beauchamp writes in his newspaper the next day, 'The rumor, emanating from otherwise well-informed quarters, that King Henry the Fourth was seen at Gabrielle's day before yesterday is absolutely groundless; King Henry the Fourth has not left the Pont Neuf.' "

Debray gave a forced laugh. Monte Cristo, though outwardly indifferent, had not missed a word of this conversation, and he had deduced a certain secret from his keen observation of Debray's embarrassment.

This embarrassment, which Albert had completely failed to

notice, caused Debray to cut short his visit; it was quite obvious that he felt uneasy.

"Tell me," said Monte Cristo to Albert after he had shown Debray to the door, "is your mother really as opposèd to your marriage as you say?"

"So much so that Madame Danglars almost never comes to our house, and I don't think my mother has been in her house twice in her whole life."

"Well, then," said the count, "I feel free to speak openly to you. Monsieur Danglars is my banker, and Monsieur de Villefort has overwhelmed me with politeness in thanking me for a service which chance placed me in a position to render him. From all this I foresee an avalanche of dinner parties and receptions. Now, in order not to appear to be trying to outdo everyone later, I'm planning to invite Monsieur and Madame Danglars and Monsieur and Madame de Villefort to dinner in my country house in Auteuil. If I were to invite you and your parents, it would seem to be a sort of matrimonial rendezvous, or at least it would strike your mother that way, especially if Monsieur Danglars brings his daughter. I would therefore incur your mother's displeasure, and I wish to avoid that at all cost."

"Thank you for speaking so frankly to me, count," said Albert. "I'll be glad to forego your invitation. I'll tell my mother about your thoughtfulness, too, and I'm sure she'll be extremely grateful to you, although my father, of course, would be furious if he knew."

The count laughed. "Your father won't be the only one who's furious," he said. "Monsieur and Madame Danglars will wonder why I didn't invite you and will consider me a very ill-mannered man. Be sure to provide yourself with some plausible previous engagement and write me a note about it. As you know, bankers trust nothing unless it's in writing."

"I'll do better than that, count. My mother's been wanting to go to the seaside. What day is your dinner party?"

"Saturday."

"And today is Tuesday. Very well, we'll leave tomorrow evening and the next day we'll be in Tréport. I'll go to see Monsieur Danglars right now and tell him my mother and I are leaving Paris tomorrow. I haven't seen you and I know nothing about your dinner party."

"And what about Monsieur Debray, who just saw you here with me?"

"Yes, that's true."

"No, I invited you informally here and you told me you couldn't come because you were leaving for Tréport."

"Good; that's settled, then. And now, let me invite you to come to see my mother and me some time before tomorrow."

"I'm very grateful to you for the invitation," replied the count, "but I'm afraid I can't accept it. I have an important appointment with Major Bartolomeo Cavalcanti, a man from one of the oldest and noblest families of Italy, and his son Andrea, a young man of about your age who's going to make his entrance into Paris society with the help of his father's millions. I'll give the major a good dinner and he'll leave his son in my keeping. I'll promise to keep watch over him and then my duty will be done."

"If by any chance your Major Cavalcanti should want to find a wife for his son," said Albert, "I'd be glad to help him meet a certain young lady who's rich, of noble birth on her mother's side and can claim the title of baroness from her father."

"Have you really come to that?"

"Oh, count, you have no idea how grateful to you I'd be if you could help me to remain a bachelor!"

"All things are possible," replied Monte Cristo gravely.

Chapter 31

The count had not lied to Albert when he refused his invitation to dinner on the grounds that he was expecting a visit from an Italian major.

The clock had just struck seven. Bertuccio, following his orders, had left for the count's house in Auteuil two hours earlier. A carriage stopped in front of the count's Paris residence and deposited a man of about fifty-two years of age. This man's small, angular head, white hair and thick gray mustache made him easily recognizable to Baptistin, who had received a precise description of the visitor in advance and was waiting for him in the vestibule.

The stranger was introduced into the most modest salon. The count was waiting for him there and stepped forward to meet him with an affable air. "Welcome, sir," he said. "I was expecting you."

"Really? Are you sure I'm the one you were expecting, Excellency?"

"Of course. But we can make sure if you like."

"Oh, as long as you're sure I'm the one you were expecting, that's good enough for me." The stranger seemed to be slightly uneasy.

"Just the same, let's make sure," said Monte Cristo. "Let's

see now: you're Marquis Bartolomeo Cavalcanti, aren't you?"

"Bartolomeo Cavalcanti," repeated the stranger joyfully. "Yes, that's right."

"Ex-major in the Austrian service?"

"Was I a major?" asked the old soldier timidly.

"Yes, a major. That's the name we give in France to the rank you held in Italy."

"That's fine with me; you know——"

"Besides, you were sent to me by someone."

"Yes."

"By that excellent Abbé Busoni?"

"That's right!" cried the major happily.

"And you have a letter?"

"Here it is."

Monte Cristo took the letter and read it. "Yes, that's right," he said: ". . . 'Major Cavalcanti, a worthy nobleman of Lucca, descendant of the Cavalcanti of Florence, possessing an income of half a million'——"

"Did you say half a million?" asked the major.

"Yes, it's written here in black and white; and it must be true because no one knows more about the great fortunes of Europe than the Abbé Busoni."

"Then it must be half a million; but I had no idea it was so much."

Monte Cristo continued reading: "**He lacks** only one thing for his happiness: to find his beloved son, who was carried off in his childhood, either by enemies of his noble family or by gypsies. I have given him the **hope**, count, that you can help him find this son for whom he has been vainly searching for fifteen years.' "

The major looked at Monte Cristo with an indefinable expression of anxiety.

"I can help you find him," said the count.

"Then the letter is true?"

"Did you doubt it, major?"

"No, not for a single instant! A serious man like the Abbé Busoni would never say such things jokingly. . . . But you haven't finished reading the letter, Excellency."

"Oh, yes; there's a postscript: 'In order to save Major Cavalcanti the trouble of transferring his funds, I am sending him two thousand francs for his traveling expenses and a credit on you for the forty-eight thousand francs you owe me.' "

The major followed the reading of this postscript with visible anxiety.

"Very well," was the count's only comment.

"Then the postscript——"

"What about it?"

"Do you receive it as favorably as the rest of the letter?"

"Certainly. The Abbé Busoni and I maintain an account between us. I'm not sure whether it's precisely forty-eight thousand francs I owe him now, but we don't quibble over a few thousand francs one way or the other."

"Then you'll advance me the forty-eight thousand francs?"

"Whenever you like."

The major's eyes opened wide in astonishment.

"Please have a seat, major," said Monte Cristo. "I don't know what's the matter with me: I've kept you standing here for a quarter of an hour."

The major drew up an armchair and sat down.

"So, major," said the count, "you live in Lucca, you're rich, you're of noble birth, you enjoy the respect and admiration of your fellow men and only one thing is lacking to make you completely happy?"

"Only one thing, Excellency."

"And that one thing is to find your son again?"

"Yes, but that's very important to me," said the worthy major, raising his eyes and making an effort to sigh.

"Now, Monsieur Cavalcanti, tell me about this beloved son; I've heard it said that you had remained a bachelor."

"People thought so, and I——"

"And you yourself supported the belief; there was a sin of your youth that you wanted to keep hidden, not for your own sake—a man is above such things—but for the sake of your son's poor mother."

"Yes, for the sake of his poor mother!"

"She belonged to one of the noblest families of Italy, didn't she?"

"A patrician of Fiesole, count! A patrician of Fiesole."

"And what was her name?"

"You want to know her name?"

"Oh, it's useless for you to tell me," said the count. "I know it already."

"You know everything, count," said the major, bowing.

"Her name was Oliva Corsinari, wasn't it?"

"That's right; Oliva Corsinari."

"And you finally married her despite family opposition, didn't you?"

"Yes, I finally did."

"Have you brought your documents?"

"What documents?" asked the major.

"The certificate of your marriage to Oliva Corsinari and your son's birth certificate. His name is Andrea, isn't it?"

"I think so."

"You think so?"

"I'm afraid to say for sure—it's been so long since I saw him last."

"That's true," said Monte Cristo. "But, do you have the documents?"

"I'm sorry, but no one told me I'd need them and I neglected to take them with me. Are they necessary?"

"Indispensable. Not having them might make him miss some magnificent marriage. In France it's not sufficient, as it is in Italy, to go to a priest and say, 'We love each other; unite us.' In France there is also a civil ceremony, for which one must furnish proof of one's identity. Fortunately, however, I have the documents I mentioned."

"You have them?"

"Yes."

"Wonderful!" exclaimed the major, who was beginning to fear that the absence of the documents might raise some difficulty with regard to the forty-eight thousand francs. "I would never have thought you had them!"

"One can't think of everything. Fortunately the Abbé Busoni thought of it for you."

"What an admirable man! He sent them to you?"

"Here they are. Give them to your son and tell him to take great care of them. I'm sure you realize the value of these documents."

"I regard them as priceless."

"Now, about the young man's mother——"

"My God!" exclaimed the major. "Do we need her too?"

"No, major," replied Monte Cristo. "Besides, isn't she——"

"Yes, of course. She——"

"Paid her tribute to Nature?"

"Yes, alas!"

"So I was told. She died ten years ago."

"And I still mourn her loss, count," said the major, drawing a handkerchief from his pocket and wiping his eyes.

"Console yourself, major; we're all mortal. But now that we've refreshed your memory, you must have guessed by now that I've been saving a surprise for you."

"A pleasant surprise?"

"Ah, I see it's impossible to deceive the eye and the heart of a father. You've already sensed that he's here."

"Who's here?"

"Your child, your son, your Andrea."

"Very good, very good!"

"I understand your emotion," said Monte Cristo, "and I realize that I must give you time to compose yourself. Also,

I want to prepare the young man for this much desired interview, for I assume he's as impatient as you are."

"I'm sure he is."

"Well, then, in less than a quarter of an hour he'll walk in through that door."

"By the way," said the major, "as you know, I took only two thousand francs with me, and——"

"And you need money, don't you? Of course you do. Here's eight thousand francs; I still owe you forty thousand."

The major's eyes gleamed. "Would you like a receipt, Excellency?" he asked.

"You can give me a receipt for everything later when I've given you the whole amount. Such precautions are useless between honest men."

"Yes, of course; between honest men."

"And now would you allow me to make a suggestion?"

"I'd be grateful to you."

"It would do no harm if you were to stop wearing that coat."

"Really?" said the major, looking at the garment with a certain affection.

"Yes. It's still fashionable in Italy, but, elegant though it may be, it's been out of style in Paris for quite some time."

"That's a shame," said the major. "But what shall I wear?"

"You'll find a coat in your trunks."

"In my trunks? I brought only a suitcase!"

"That's all you took with you, but you sent your trunks on ahead. They're now in the Hôtel des Princes, in the Rue Richelieu, which is where you reserved your lodgings. I assume you had the foresight to instruct your valet to pack your trunks with everything you'll need. You'll wear your uniform for important occasions; that makes a good impression. And don't forget your medals."

"Very good! Very good!" said the major, passing from one dazzling surprise to another.

"And now, Monsieur Cavalcanti," said the count, "prepare to see your son Andrea again." Bowing graciously to the enraptured major, Monte Cristo walked out of the room.

In the neighboring salon was a rather elegantly dressed young man who had arrived half an hour earlier. Baptistin had had no difficulty in recognizing him: he was clearly the tall young man whose blond hair, red beard and black eyes had been described by Monte Cristo.

When the count entered the salon the young man was sprawled out on a sofa, absent-mindedly tapping his boot with a gold-headed cane. On seeing the count he leaped to his feet and asked, "Are you the Count of Monte Cristo?"

"Yes; and have I the honor of speaking to Viscount Andrea Cavalcanti?"

"Viscount Andrea Cavalcanti," repeated the young man nonchalantly.

"I believe you have a letter of introduction for me."

"I didn't mention it because the signature seemed so strange to me."

" 'Sinbad the Sailor,' isn't it?"

"Yes."

"He's a friend of mine, an Englishman; he's very rich, and eccentric almost to the the point of madness. His real name is Lord Wilmore."

"Ah, then he's the same Englishman who—— Very well. I'm at your service, count."

"If what you tell me is true," said the count, smiling, "I hope you'll be kind enough to give me a few details about yourself and your family."

"I'd be glad to, count," said the young man with a volubility that proved the soundness of his memory. "I am, as you've said, Viscount Andrea Cavalcanti, son of Major Bartolomeo Cavalcanti, a descendant of the Cavalcanti family whose name is inscribed in the Golden Book of Florence. At the age of five I was carried off by a treacherous tutor, so that I haven't seen my father for fifteen years. I've been trying to find him ever since I reached the age of reason, but in vain. Finally this letter from your friend Sinbad informed me that he was in Paris and authorized me to address myself to you to obtain news of him."

"That's all very interesting," said the count, "and you were right to come to me because your father is here at this very moment."

Since his entrance into the salon the count had not taken his eyes off the young man; he had admired the self-assurance of his gaze and the firmness of his voice. But on hearing the words, "your father is here at this very moment," young Andrea started and cried out, "My father! My father is here?"

"Yes," replied the count. "Your father, Major Bartolomeo Cavalcanti."

The young man's terrified expression vanished instantly. "Yes, of course," he said. "Major Bartolomeo Cavalcanti—you say my dear father is here now, count?"

"Yes; you'll see him in a moment. He's a little stiff and pompous, perhaps, but that's because he's been a soldier for so long. Besides, a great fortune makes it easy to overlook many things."

"My father is rich, then?"

"A millionaire—an income of half a million francs."

"In that case," said the young man anxiously, "will I find myself in a—pleasant situation?"

"Extremely pleasant. He's going to give you an allowance of fifty thousand francs a year for as long as you stay in Paris."

"Does he plan to stay in Paris for long?"

"His duties won't allow him to stay for more than a few days."

"Oh, dear father!" said Andrea, clearly delighted by this prompt departure.

"Well," said Monte Cristo, pretending to have misinterpreted the tone in which these words were spoken, "I won't keep you waiting any longer: step into the next room and you'll find your father."

Andrea bowed deeply to the count and entered the adjoining salon. When he had gone, the count touched a hidden spring and a painting on the wall slid aside to reveal an opening enabling him to see into the next room.

Andrea closed the door behind him and walked toward the major, who stood up as soon as he heard his footsteps.

"Father!" said Andrea loudly enough for the count to hear him behind the closed door. "Is it really you?"

"Yes, my son," said the major gravely.

"What good fortune to see each other again after so many years of separation!" continued Andrea, still looking toward the door.

"Yes, it was a long separation."

"And we'll never part again?"

"I'm afraid so, my son. You've come to regard France as your second home, haven't you?"

"To tell the truth," said the young man, "I'd be heartbroken if I had to leave Paris."

"And I couldn't live anywhere except in Lucca; I'll go back to Italy as soon as possible."

"But before you go, father, I'm sure you'll give me the documents that will enable me to prove my ancestry."

"Yes, I came here expressly to give them to you. Here they are."

Andrea seized the documents avidly and examined them with a rapidity and an assurance which indicated a practiced eye. Looking at the major with a strange smile, he said in excellent Italian, "Aren't there any prisons in Italy?"

"What do you mean?"

"In France a forgery like this, dear father, would cost you at least five years in Toulon."

"I beg your pardon?" said the major, endeavoring to assume an air of majesty.

"How much are you getting for being my father?" asked Andrea, pressing the major's arm. The major started to speak. "Ssh!" said Andrea, lowering his voice. "Here, I'll set you an example of confidence: I'm getting fifty thousand francs a year to be your son."

The major looked around anxiously.

"Oh, don't worry—we're alone," said Andrea. "Besides, we're speaking Italian."

"All right, then," said the major. "I'm getting fifty thousand francs in a lump sum."

"Monsieur Cavalcanti, do you believe in fairy tales?"

"I didn't before, but now I'm forced to."

"You think I can believe in the count's promises, then?"

"Yes, but we'll have to play our parts well, since they insist on my being your father."

"Who are 'they'?"

"I have no idea—whoever it was who wrote to us."

"You got a letter?"

"Yes."

"From whom?"

"From a certain Abbé Busoni."

"Do you know him?"

"I never laid eyes on him."

"What was in the letter?"

"You won't tell anyone?"

"Of course not; our interests are the same."

"Read it, then."

The major handed a letter to Andrea, who read aloud:

You are poor and a wretched old age awaits you. Would you like to become, if not rich, at least independent? If so, leave for Paris immediately, go to see the Count of Monte Cristo at 30 Avenue des Champs Elysées and ask him to introduce you to the son whom you had by the Marquise de Corsinari and who was taken away from you at the age of five. Your son's name is Andrea Cavalcanti.

In case you should have any doubt about my intention to be of service to you, you will find enclosed a check for two thousand francs and a letter of introduction to the Count of Monte Cristo, with whom I have opened a credit of forty-eight thousand francs for you.

Be at the count's house on May 26 at seven o'clock in the evening.

ABBÉ BUSONI

"I received a letter almost like this one," said Andrea.
"From the Abbé Busoni?"

"No; from Lord Wilmore, an Englishman who goes by
the name of Sinbad the Sailor. Here's the letter."

The major read:

You are poor and you have only a wretched future
ahead of you. Would you like to be free and rich and
have an illustrious name? If so, go to see the Count of
Monte Cristo, 30 Avenue des Champs Elysées in Paris,
on May 26 at seven o'clock in the evening, and ask him
for your father. You are the son of Major Bartolomeo
Cavalcanti and Marquise Oliva Corsinari, as you will
see from the documents which the major will give to
you and which will enable you to present yourself under
that name to Paris society.

As for your rank, an allowance of fifty thousand
francs a year will enable you to maintain it properly.

Enclosed is a check for five thousand francs and a
letter of introduction to the Count of Monte Cristo,
whom I have instructed to take care of all your needs.

SINBAD THE SAILOR

"That's wonderful!" said the major. "Have you seen the
count?"

"I just left him."

"Did he agree to everything?"

"Everything."

"Do you understand anything about all this?"

"Nothing at all. But in any case, let's play the game to
the end."

"So be it; you'll see that I'm worthy to be your partner."

"I haven't doubted that for an instant, my dear father."

"You honor me, my dear son."

The count chose this moment to enter the salon. On hearing the sound of his footsteps, the two men threw themselves
into each other's arms.

"You seem to find your son according to your liking,
major," said the count.

"I'm overwhelmed with joy, count."

"And you, young man?"

"Oh, count, I'm bursting with happiness."

"Excellent!" said the count. "And now you may go, gentlemen."

"When shall we have the honor of seeing you again,
count?" asked the major.

"Oh, yes, when shall we have that honor?" asked Andrea.

"This Saturday if you like. I'm having several people to dinner in my house in Auteuil, 28 Rue de la Fontaine."

"At what time shall we come?" asked Andrea.

"Toward half-past six," replied the count.

"We'll be there," said the major, touching his hat.

The two Cavalcanti bowed to the count and left. The count went over to the window and watched them cross the courtyard arm in arm. "There go a pair of scoundrels!" he thought. "What a shame they aren't really father and son!"

Chapter 32

The reader must now allow us to take him to the wall surrounding Monsieur de Villefort's house, where we shall meet some people with whom we are already acquainted.

Maximilien Morrel was the first to arrive at the grilled iron gate, where he stood looking for a shadow among the trees of the garden and listening for the sound of a silken slipper on the sand of the path.

He finally heard the awaited footsteps, but he saw two shadows approaching instead of one. Valentine had been delayed by a visit from Madame Danglars and Eugénie which had lasted longer than she expected. In order not to miss her rendezvous, Valentine had decided to invite Eugénie to take a stroll in the garden, which would enable Maximilien to see for himself that the delay was unavoidable.

The young man understood everything with the rapid intuition of a lover and felt greatly relieved. After half an hour of strolling, the two young ladies walked back toward the house, leading Maximilien to suppose that Eugénie's visit was about to come to an end.

Several moments later Valentine reappeared alone. However, for fear that indiscreet eyes might be following her return, she walked slowly and, instead of going directly to the grill, she sat down on a bench and after inconspicuously examining every clump of trees in the garden and glancing down every pathway. Then, when she had taken all these precautions, she ran over to the grill.

"Hello, Valentine," said a voice.

"Hello, Maximilien; I kept you waiting, but you saw the reason, didn't you?"

"Yes, I recognized Mademoiselle Danglars. I didn't know you two were such close friends."

"Who told you we were close friends?"

"No one, but the way you were walking and talking together

made me think so. You looked like two schoolgirls exchanging secrets."

"We *were* exchanging secrets, as a matter of fact," said Valentine. "She was telling me how she detested the idea of marrying Albert de Morcerf and I was telling her how unhappy I was at the thought of marrying Franz d'Epinay. As I talked to her about the man I can never love, I was thinking of the man I'll always love."

"Does Mademoiselle Danglars also love someone else?" asked Maximilien.

"She says she doesn't, but that she has a horror of getting married. She says she'd give anything to be able to lead a free and independent life and that she almost wishes her father would lose his fortune so she could become an artist like her friend Louise d'Armilly. But let's not waste our time talking about her; we have only ten more minutes together."

"What's wrong, Valentine? Why do you have to leave me so soon?"

"Madame de Villefort has asked me to come to see her; she says she has something to tell me which may affect part of my fortune. But as far as I'm concerned, they can take my fortune; I'm too rich. Then maybe they'll leave me alone. You'd love me just as much if I were poor, wouldn't you, Maximilien?"

"You know I'll always love you! What would I care about wealth or poverty as long as my Valentine was by my side and I was sure no one could ever take her away from me! But aren't you afraid your stepmother's message may be about your marriage?"

"I don't think so."

"In any case, don't be afraid, Valentine: I'll never belong to another woman as long as I live."

"Do you think it makes me happy to hear that, Maximilien?"

"Forgive me, it was thoughtless of me. What I started to tell you is that I saw Albert de Morcerf the other day and he told me Franz has written to him saying he'll be back in Paris soon."

Valentine turned pale and leaned against the gate for support. "Can that be what Madame de Villefort wants to tell me?" she cried. "But no, she wouldn't be the one to tell me."

"Why not?"

"Because—I'm not sure, but, even though she's never opposed my marriage openly, I still think she's not in favor of it."

"Really? In that case, I'm very fond of Madame de Villefort! If she's against your marrying Franz, then maybe you can break off the engagement and she'll be willing to listen to another proposal."

"Don't pin your hopes on that, Maximilien. It's not the husband my stepmother objects to, but marriage itself."

"What do you mean? If she's so opposed to marriage, why did she get married herself?"

"You don't understand, Maximilien. As I told you, I'm too rich. I have an income of nearly fifty thousand francs from my mother. My grandparents, the Marquis and Marquise of Saint-Méran, will leave me the same amount, and my other grandfather, Monsieur Noirtier, has made it clear that he intends to leave everything he has to me. The result of all this is that my brother Edouard, who has nothing to inherit from Madame de Villefort, is poor. Madame de Villefort worships her son. Now, if, instead of marrying, I were to enter a convent, my whole fortune would go to my father, who would pass it on to Edouard."

"It's strange to see such avarice in a young and beautiful woman!"

"Don't forget that it's not for herself but for her son. The avarice with which you reproach her is, from the standpoint of maternal love, almost a virtue."

"But why don't you simply give part of your fortune to her son?"

"How could I make such a suggestion to a woman who's constantly talking about her disinterestedness? . . . Listen: someone's calling me."

"Oh, Valentine," said Maximilien, "put your little finger through the grill and let me kiss it!"

"Would that make you happy?"

"Oh, yes!"

Valentine stood up on a bench and put, not her little finger, but her whole hand through the opening. Maximilien seized the beloved hand and ardently pressed his lips to it, but it slipped away from him almost instantly and he heard Valentine running toward the house, frightened, perhaps, by her own sensations.

Chapter 33

After the departure of Madame Danglars and her daughter, while Valentine was in the garden speaking with Maximilien, Monsieur de Villefort and his wife went to the room of Monsieur de Villefort's father. After dismissing Barrois, an old servant who had been in Monsieur Noirtier's service for more than twenty-five years, they sat down on either side of him.

Monsieur Noirtier was seated in his wheelchair, in which he was placed in the morning and from which he was lifted at night. Sight and hearing were the only senses which, like two sparks, still animated that physical body already so close to the grave. As often happens when one organ is used to the exclusion of others, in his eyes were concentrated all the energy, strength and intelligence which had formerly been distributed throughout his body and mind. He commanded with his eyes, he thanked with his eyes; and it was almost frightening to see them flashing with anger or sparkling with joy in that otherwise stony face. Only three persons were able to understand his language: Villefort, Valentine and his old servant, Barrois. But since Villefort saw his father only when absolutely necessary, all the old man's happiness lay in his granddaughter; and through devotion, patience and love, Valentine had come to be able to read all his thoughts in his eyes.

"Father," said Villefort, "the reason we dismissed Barrois and didn't bring Valentine with us is that Madame de Villefort and I have something to tell you which can't be discussed before a young girl or a servant. We're sure that what we have to tell you will please you."

The old man's eyes remained expressionless.

"Father, Valentine is to be married three months from now."

"We were sure you'd be interested in the news," said Madame de Villefort, "since Valentine has always seemed to have a special place in your heart. The young man we've chosen for her has a sizable fortune and an honorable name, and his conduct and tastes are such as to guarantee her happiness. Furthermore, his name is probably not unknown to you: he's Monsieur Franz de Quesnal, Baron of Epinay."

When Madame de Villefort pronounced this name, Noirtier's eyelids fluttered like lips trying to speak and released a flash of lightning. Villefort, who knew of the political enmity which had once existed between his father and Franz's father, understood this agitation quite well, but he pretended not to notice it and said, "We haven't forgotten you in the arrangements, father: we've made sure that, since Valentine returns your deep affection for her, her new husband will agree to have you come and live with them, so that you will have two children to look after you instead of one."

Something frightful was taking place in the old man's soul: a cry of pain and rage must have risen in his throat and, unable to burst forth, choked him, for his face had turned almost purple.

"Monsieur d'Epinay and his family are also pleased with the marriage," said Madame de Villefort. "His family, by the way, consists of only an uncle and an aunt; his mother died in giving birth to him and his father was assassinated in 1815."

"A mysterious assassination," added Villefort, "whose authors have never been discovered, although suspicion has hung over a number of people. The real criminals would be lucky to be in our place, to have a daughter to offer to Monsieur Franz d'Epinay in order to allay the last shadow of suspicion."

Noirtier had mastered his feelings with a strength whose existence one would not have suspected in that shattered frame. "Yes, I understand," his eyes said to Villefort, and his look expressed both profound scorn and intelligent anger. Villefort clearly understood this look and answered it with a slight shrug. Then he motioned his wife to stand up.

"We must go now," said Madame de Villefort. "Shall I send Edouard to pay his respects to you?"

It had been arranged that the old man would express assent by closing his eyes, refusal by blinking them several times, and a desire for something by looking up at the ceiling. If he wanted to see Valentine, he would close his right eye only; if he wanted Barrois he would close his left eye.

At Madame de Villefort's suggestion he blinked his eyes energetically. She bit her lips in the face of this obvious refusal and asked, "Shall I send Valentine, then?"

"Yes!" said the old man by closing his eyes instantly.

Monsieur and Madame de Villefort bowed and left the room.

Valentine entered a few moments later. Her first glance at her grandfather told her how much he was suffering and how much he had to tell her.

"Oh, grandfather!" she cried. "What's happened? You're angry about something, aren't you?"

"Yes," he said by closing his eyes.

"With whom are you angry? Is it my father? No. My stepmother? No. Are you angry with me?"

Noirtier closed his eyes.

"You're angry with me?" cried Valentine, astonished. "I haven't seen you all day. Did someone tell you something about me?"

"Yes."

"Let's see now; let me think. . . . Monsieur and Madame de Villefort just left here, so it must have been they who told you something that made you angry. Do you want me to go ask them what it was so that I can apologize to you?"

"No."

"What could they have told you? . . . I have it!" she said, lowering her voice and coming closer. "Did they talk to you about my marriage?"

"Yes!" replied the old man's eyes angrily.

"Are you afraid I'll abandon you, grandfather, that my marriage will make me forget you?"

"No."

"Then they told you Monsieur d'Epinay has agreed to have you live with us?"

"Yes."

"Then why are you angry?"

The old man's eyes took on an expression of infinite tenderness.

"I understand," said Valentine, "it's because you love me, and you're afraid I'll be unhappy, isn't that right?"

"Yes."

"You don't like Monsieur d'Epinay?"

"No! No! No!" repeated Noirtier's eyes.

"Listen," said Valentine, kneeling before him and putting her arm around his neck, "I don't like Monsieur d'Epinay either." A sparkle of joy appeared in his eye. "Oh, if only you could help me break off the marriage!" continued Valentine. "You would have been such a powerful protector for me before your misfortune, but now you can do nothing except understand me and share my happiness and sorrow."

As she said this, there was such a deep look of cunning in Noirtier's eyes that she seemed to read these words in them: "You're wrong; I can still do much for you."

Noirtier looked up at the ceiling, a sign that he wanted something.

"What do you want, grandfather?" asked Valentine. She began to recite the letters of the alphabet, stopping to watch his eyes at each letter. At N he signaled, "Yes."

"Ah, it begins with an N," said Valentine. "All right, is it Na? Ne? Ni? No?"

"Yes."

"It begins with No?" said Valentine. "Good." She went over and took out a dictionary, opened it before Noirtier and began to run her finger up and down the columns. At the word "notary" he signaled her to stop.

"Is it a notary you want, grandfather?"

"Yes."

"Do you want me to send for one right away?"

"Yes."

"Is that all you want?"

"Yes."

Valentine rang and told a servant to go ask Monsieur and Madame de Villefort to come to Monsieur Noirtier's room.

Monsieur de Villefort entered, led by Barrois. "My grandfather wants to see a notary," said Valentine.

"But why do you need a notary?" asked Villefort.

"If Monsieur Noirtier asked for a notary, it's obviously because he needs one," said Barrois, who acknowledged no other master than Noirtier, "and I'll therefore go and bring one."

"You shall have a notary if you insist," said Villefort to Noirtier, "but I'll apologize to him for both you and myself, because it will make an extremely ridiculous scene."

"Just the same," said Barrois, "I'm going to bring one." And the old servant walked triumphantly out of the room.

Villefort sat down and waited. Noirtier watched him with complete indifference, but, out of the corner of his eye, he had ordered Valentine to remain also.

Three-quarters of an hour later, Barrois returned with a notary.

"You have been sent for by Monsieur Noirtier de Villefort here," said Villefort after the first exchange of greetings with the notary. "His paralysis has deprived him of the use of his limbs and his voice. It's hard even for us to grasp a few scraps of his thoughts."

Noirtier appealed to Valentine with his eyes, an appeal so serious and imperative that she immediately said to the notary, "I understand everything my grandfather wishes to say."

"It's true, sir," added Barrois, "everything, absolutely everything, as I told you on the way here."

"Monsieur Noirtier closes his eyes when he wishes to say 'yes' and blinks them several times when he wishes to say 'no,'" said Valentine. "And however difficult it may seem to you to discover his thoughts, I'll demonstrate it to you in such a way that you'll have no doubts on the subject."

"Very well, then," said the notary, "let's try it. Do you accept this young lady as your interpreter, Monsieur Noirtier?"

"Yes," signaled the old man.

"Good. Now, why did you send for me?"

Valentine named all the letters of the alphabet until she came to W, where Noirtier's eloquent eyes stopped her. Then she began to ask him, "Wa—We—Wi—" He stopped her at the third syllable. She opened the dictionary under the notary's attentive eyes. "Will," said her finger, stopped by Noirtier's eyes.

"Will!" exclaimed the notary. "Monsieur Noirtier wants to make his will! It's quite clear."

"Yes," signaled Noirtier several times.

"This is marvelous!" said the notary to the amazed Ville-fort.

"Yes, but I think the will would be still more marvelous," said Villefort. "The words won't put themselves on paper without by daughter's inspiration, and I'm afraid she's too interested a party to be a suitable interpreter of Monsieur Noirtier's obscure wishes."

"No! No!" signaled the old man.

"What!" exclaimed Villefort. "Valentine is not an interested party in your will?"

"No."

"Monsieur de Villefort," said the notary, who was looking forward to relating this picturesque episode to his friends, "nothing now seems easier to me than what I regarded as impossible only a few minutes ago. This will be a valid will if, according to the law, it is read in the presence of seven witnesses approved by the testator and sealed by a notary in their presence. Furthermore, in order to make it completely incontestable, one of my colleagues will assist me and, contrary to custom, be present at the dictation of the will. Is that satisfactory to you, Monsieur Noirtier?"

"Yes," replied Noirtier, delighted at having been understood.

Barrois, who had heard everything and anticipated his master's wishes, was already on his way to bring the second notary. Villefort sent for his wife. A quarter of an hour later everyone was gathered in Noirtier's room and the second notary had arrived. The first notary said to Noirtier, "Have you some idea of the amount of your fortune?"

"Yes."

"I am now going to name several figures in ascending order. You will stop me when I reach the figure which you believe to represent the amount of your fortune. It's more than three hundred thousand francs, isn't it?"

"Yes," signaled Noirtier.

"Do you possess four hundred thousand francs?"

Noirtier's eyes remained motionless.

"Five hundred thousand? Six? Seven? Eight? Nine?"

Noirtier closed his eyes.

"You possess nine hundred thousand francs?"

"Yes."

"And to whom do you wish to leave this fortune? To Mademoiselle Valentine de Villefort?"

Noirtier blinked his eyes in the most meaningful manner.

"Are you sure you're not mistaken?" asked the notary, surprised.

"No!" repeated Noirtier. "No!"

Valentine was overwhelmed, not at having been excluded from his will, but at having provoked the sentiments which usually dictate such an act. But Noirtier looked at her with such a profound expression of tenderness that she cried out, "Oh, I see, grandfather: it's only your fortune you've taken away from me, but you still leave me your love!"

"Yes, yes, certainly!" said Noirtier's eyes with an expression that left do doubt in Valentine's mind.

Meanwhile this refusal had brought unexpected hope to Madame de Villefort. She approached the old man and asked, "Is it to your grandson Edouard that you leave your fortune, then?"

His eyes blinked in a terrible way; they almost expressed hatred.

"Is it to your son, Monsieur de Villefort?" asked the notary.

"No."

The two notaries looked at each other in bewilderment. Villefort and his wife flushed, one from shame, the other from anger.

"But what have we all done to you, grandfather?" asked Valentine.

Noirtier fixed his gaze on her hand.

"My hand?" she asked.

"Yes."

"Ah, you see how useless it is, gentlemen," said Villefort. "My poor father is mad."

"Oh!" cried Valentine suddenly. "I understand! It's my marriage, isn't it, grandfather?"

"Yes! Yes! Yes!"

"You're angry at us for the marriage, aren't you?"

"Yes."

"You don't want me to marry Monsieur Franz d'Epinay, do you?"

"No."

"Are you disinheriting your granddaughter because she's about to marry against your wishes?" asked the notary.

"Yes."

"And what do you intend to do with your fortune if Mademoiselle de Villefort marries Monsieur d'Epinay? Will you leave it to some other member of your family?"

"No."

"Will you leave it to the poor, then?"

"Yes."

"What is your decision in view of this, Monsieur de Villefort?" asked the notary.

"Nothing. I know that my father never changes his mind, so I'll simply resign myself. His nine hundred thousand francs will leave the family, but I will not yield to an old man's whim and I will continue to act according to my conscience." Villefort withdrew with his wife, leaving his father to make out his will as he saw fit.

Chapter 34

When Monsieur and Madame de Villefort returned from Noirtier's room, they learned that the Count of Monte Cristo had come to pay them a visit and was waiting for them in the salon.

After the first compliments, the count said, "I've come to remind you of your promise for Saturday."

"How could we possibly forget it?" said Madame de Villefort.

"Are you entertaining in your house on the Champs Elysées?" asked Villefort.

"No, it's going to be in my country house at Auteuil."

"Auteuil!" exclaimed Villefort. "Oh, yes, I remember now: my wife told me you had a house in Auteuil because that's where she was taken after her accident. What part of Auteuil is it?"

"Rue de la Fontaine."

"Rue de la Fontaine!" cried Villefort in a choked voice. "What number?"

"Twenty-eight."

"Then it's you who bought Monsieur de Saint-Méran's house!"

"Monsieur de Saint-Méran?" asked Monte Cristo. "Did that house belong to him?"

"Yes," said Madame de Villefort, "and I'll tell you a curious thing about it. You find it to be a pleasant house, don't you?"

"Charming."

"Well, my husband was always unwilling to live in it."

"I don't like Auteuil, count," said Villefort, making an effort to control himself.

"I hope your antipathy won't deprive me of the pleasure of receiving you Saturday," said the count.

"No—I hope to—believe me, I'll do my best to———" stammered Villefort.

"Oh, no excuses!" said Monte Cristo. "I'll expect you Saturday at six o'clock. If you don't come, I'll be forced to believe there's some sort of gloomy legend attached to that old house, which remained uninhabited for twenty years."

"I'll be there, count, I'll be there!" said Villefort quickly.

"Thank you," said Monte Cristo. "And now, please allow me to take leave of you. I'm about to go see something which has often made me thoughtful for hours on end."

"What is it?"

"A telegraph. I was almost ashamed to say it, but now you know."

"A telegraph?" repeated Madame de Villefort.

"Yes, that's right. I've often seen those black, shining arms rising from the top of a hill or at the end of a road, and it has never been without emotion for me, for I've always thought of those strange signs cleaving the air for three hundred leagues to carry the thoughts of one man sitting at his desk to another man sitting at his desk at the other end of the line. It has always made me think of genii, sylphs or gnomes; in short, of occult powers, and that amuses me. Then one day I learned that the operator of each telegraph is only some poor devil employed for twelve hundred francs a year, constantly occupied in watching another telegraph four or five leagues away. I then became curious to see that living chrysalis at close quarters and watch the comedy he plays for the other chrysalis by pulling on his strings."

"What telegraph are you going to visit?" asked Villefort.

"Which line would you advise me to study?"

"Why, the one that's the busiest now, I suppose."

"That would be the line from Spain, wouldn't it?"

"Yes. But you'd better hurry; it will be dark in two hours and you won't be able to see anything."

"Thank you," said Monte Cristo. "I'll tell you about my impressions when I see you Saturday."

The next day Debray left his office and hurried to the Danglars residence.

"Does your husband have any Spanish bonds?" he asked Madame Danglars.

"He certainly does! He has six million francs' worth."

"He must sell them at any price."

"Why?"

"Because Don Carlos has escaped from Bourges and returned to Spain."

"How do you know that?"

"Why, the way I always know the news," said Debray, shrugging.

The baroness did not wait to be told twice. She ran to her husband, who ran to his stockbroker and ordered him to sell at any price. When it was seen that Baron Danglars was selling, Spanish bonds immediately fell. Danglars lost five hundred thousand francs, but he got rid of all his bonds.

That evening the following story appeared in *Le Messager*:

Telegraphic dispatch—King Don Carlos has escaped the vigilance exercised over him in Bourges and has returned to Spain across the Catalonian frontier. Barcelona has risen up in his favor.

All evening no one talked of anything except Danglars' foresight in selling his bonds and of his good fortune in losing only five hundred thousand francs in such a disaster. Those who had kept their bonds or bought Danglars' regarded themselves as ruined and spent a very bad night. The next day they read the following in *Le Moniteur*:

The report published in yesterday's issue of *Le Messager* concerning Don Carlos' flight and the revolt of Barcelona is absolutely untrue. King Don Carlos has not left Bourges and peace reigns all over Spain.

The misinterpretation of a telegraphic sign due to fog was the cause of the error.

Spanish bonds rose to double the price to which they had fallen. The total of what Danglars had lost and what he had failed to gain was one million francs.

Chapter 35

Seen from the outside, Monte Cristo's house in Auteuil had nothing splendid about it, nothing of what one might expect of a residence chosen by the magnificent Count of Monte Cristo. But this simplicity was in accord with the count's wishes; he had given explicit orders to leave the exterior of the house completely unchanged. As soon as the door was opened, however, the scene changed. Monsieur Bertuccio had surpassed himself in the good taste he showed in the furnishings and in the rapidity with which he had the work carried out. He would have been especially glad to have the garden transformed, but the count had expressly forbidden him to alter it in any way.

The best proof of Bertuccio's skill and the count's profound science was that the old house, which had been deserted and somber for twenty years, had been awakened from its long slumber in a single day and was now alive, singing and flourishing, like those houses which we have cherished for a long time and in which, when we have the misfortune to leave them, we involuntarily leave part of our soul.

Only one room in the house had been left untouched: a bedroom on the second floor from which one could leave by a private staircase. The servants passed in front of this room with curiosity; Bertuccio passed it in terror.

At exactly six o'clock Captain Maximilien Morrel arrived on his horse Médéah. Monte Cristo met him on the front steps with a smile on his lips.

"I'm sure I'm the first to arrive," said Maximilien. "I wanted to be able to talk to you alone for a while before the others came."

At that very moment, however, two riders on winded horses and a carriage drawn by a sweating team drew up in front of the house. Lucien Debray quickly dismounted, went to the door of the carriage, opened it and gave his hand to Madame Danglars as she alighted. In doing so she gave him a little sign which would have been imperceptible to anyone except Monte Cristo. But nothing escaped the count's eye and he saw a small white note pass from Madame Danglars' hand into Debray's with an ease which indicated long practice in this maneuver.

Baron Danglars alighted after his wife, looking as pale as if he were coming from the grave instead of from his carriage. He began absent-mindedly pulling off the blossoms of a magnificent orange tree; then he addressed himself to a cactus, but the cactus, less good-natured than the orange tree, pricked him outrageously. The baron rubbed his eyes as though he were awakening from a dream.

"Major Bartolomeo Cavalcanti and Viscount Andrea Cavalcanti!" announced Baptistin.

A black satin collar fresh from the manufacturer's hands, a well-trimmed beard, a gray mustache, self-assured eyes, a major's uniform decorated with five crosses—such was the appearance of Major Bartolomeo Cavalcanti. Beside him, wearing brand-new clothes and a broad smile, was his devoted son, Viscount Andrea Cavalcanti.

As Maximilien, Debray and Château-Renaud stood talking together, their eyes traveled from the father to the son, naturally lingering longer on the latter.

"Cavalcanti!" said Debray.

"That's a fine name," said Maximilien.

"Yes," said Château-Renaud, "the Italians name themselves well, although they dress themselves badly."

"You're hard to please," said Debray. "His clothes are from an excellent tailor and they're brand-new."

"That's precisely what I don't like," replied Château-Renaud. "The young man looks as though he were dressed well for the first time in his life."

"Who are those two gentlemen?" said Danglars to Monte Cristo.

"Major Cavalcanti and his son."

"That tells me their name, but nothing else."

"Oh, yes, it's true you're not acquainted with the Italian nobility. The Cavalcanti are a race of princes."

"A large fortune?" asked the banker.

"Enormous."

"What do they do?"

"They try unsuccessfully to spend their whole fortune. They have a credit open with you, by the way, or at least so they told me when they came to see me day before yesterday. In fact, I invited them especially on your account. I'll introduce you to them."

"It seems to me they speak excellent French."

"The son was educated in France. You'll find him full of enthusiasm for French women; he has his heart set on finding a wife in Paris."

"Now that's a fine idea!" said Danglars sarcastically.

Madame Danglars looked at her husband with an expression which would ordinarily have presaged a storm, but on this occasion she remained silent.

"Monsieur and Madame de Villefort!" announced Baptistin.

Despite all his self-control, Villefort was visibly agitated. Monte Cristo felt his hand tremble when he greeted him.

"Only women know how to dissimulate their emotions," thought the count as he watched Madame Danglars smile at Villefort and embrace his wife.

Monte Cristo looked up and saw Bertuccio standing in the small salon next to the one in which he was receiving his guests. He went over to him and asked, "Did you want something, Monsieur Bertuccio?"

"You haven't told me how many places to set for dinner, Excellency."

"Ah, yes, that's true. Well, you can count them for yourself."

"Has everyone arrived, Excellency?"

"Yes."

The steward looked through the half-open door. Monte Cristo's eyes were riveted on him.

"Oh, my God!" cried Bertuccio.

"What's the matter?" asked the count.

"That woman!"

"Which one?"

"The one wearing the white dress and so many diamonds —the blonde one!"

"Madame Danglars?"

"I don't know what her name is, but she's the one, Excellency! She's the woman in the garden, the one who was pregnant! The one who was waiting for——"

"For whom?"

Bertuccio, without answering, pointed to Villefort in much the same way Macbeth pointed to Banquo. "Oh! Oh!" he murmured finally. "Do you see?"

"What? Whom?"

"Him!"

"Monsieur de Villefort, the public prosecutor? Certainly I see him!"

"But didn't I kill him? Isn't he dead?"

"Of course he's not dead! You can see that for yourself. Instead of stabbing him between the sixth and seventh rib on the left side, as is customary with Corsicans, you no doubt stabbed him a little above or below. Come now, control yourself and count: Monsieur and Madame de Villefort, two; Monsieur and Madame Danglars, four; Monsieur de Château-Renaud, Monsier Debray and Monsieur Morrel, seven; Major Bartolomeo Cavalcanti, eight."

"Eight," repeated Bertuccio.

"Just a moment, Monsieur Bertuccio, don't be in such a hurry to leave: you're overlooking one of my guests. Look a little to the left there, that's Monsieur Andrea Cavalcanti, the young man who's just turning this way."

This time the steward almost uttered a cry, but Monte Cristo's glance made it die away on his lips.

"Benedetto!" murmured Bertuccio.

"It's half-past six, Monsieur Bertuccio," said the count severely. "That's the hour at which I ordered dinner to be served. You know I don't like to wait."

Monte Cristo returned to the salon where his guests awaited him while Bertuccio staggered back to the dining room, stopping to support himself against the wall from time to time.

Five minutes later the double doors of the salon opened and Bertuccio, making one last heroic effort, announced: "Dinner is served."

Monte Cristo offered his arm to Madame de Villefort. "Monsieur de Villefort," he said, "please escort Madame Danglars." Villefort obeyed and the guests passed into the dining room.

The meal was magnificent. Monte Cristo's efforts were directed more toward satisfying his guests' curiosity than their appetite. It was an Oriental feast which he offered them, but Oriental in the manner of Arabian fairy tales. All the different kinds of fruit which the four corners of the world can send to fill Europe's horn of plenty were piled high in Chinese vases and Japanese bowls. Rare birds with the brilliant part of their plumage, monstrous fish lying on silver platters, every wine from the Archipelago, Asia Minor and the Cape, contained in decanters whose exotic shapes seemed to add flavor to their contents—all this passed in review before the astonished eyes of the count's guests.

"This is all extremely delightful," said Châteu-Renaud, "but what I admire most about you, count, is the promptness with which your orders are carried out. You bought this house only five or six days ago, yet it has already been completely transformed. It was uninhabited for at least ten years and it was sad to see it with its shutters and doors closed and grass growing in the courtyard. In fact, if it hadn't belonged to the father-in-law of a public prosecutor, one might have taken it for one of those accursed houses in which some horrible crime has been committed."

Villefort, who, until then, had not touched any of the three or four glasses of extraordinary wine placed before him, quickly picked up one of them and drank it down in one gulp.

Monte Cristo waited for a moment, then, in the midst of the silence which followed Château-Renaud's words, he said, "It's strange, but the same thought occurred to me the first time I entered this house. There was one room in particular, an ordinary bedroom hung with red damask, which for some reason struck me as extraordinarily dramatic. Now that we've finished dinner, perhaps you'd like to see it. We can have coffee later in the garden." He looked questioningly at his guests. Madame de Villefort stood up and all the others followed suit.

Villefort and Madame Danglars remained in place for an instant, looking at each other. "We must go there," said Villefort, standing up and offering her his arm.

There was nothing particularly strange about the bedroom, except that, although night was falling, it was not lighted and that it had kept all the marks of age and long neglect, while the other rooms had been completely rejuvenated. These two things, however, were enough to give it a gloomy aspect.

The guests made a number of remarks to the effect that the bedroom did indeed present a sinister appearance.

"Yes," said Monte Cristo, "notice how strangely the bed is placed, look at those somber, blood-colored hangings; and those two faded portraits, with their livid lips and their frightened eyes, don't they seem to be saying, 'I saw!' But that's not all." He went over and opened a door concealed behind the hangings on the wall. "Look at this little staircase and tell me what you think of it. Can't you see someone descending it step by step in the darkness, bearing some sinister

made the young man's anger die down: the
...aint had just blown upon it. He started up his
...Is it my fault," he said, "that I'm having good
...u're still having bad luck?"
... is really good then? This isn't a rented tilbury
...en't rented clothes? That's wonderful! I know
...good heart. If you have two overcoats, I'm sure
...he one of them; I used to give you my share of
...ans when you were hungry."
...ue," said Andrea.
... appetite you had!" said Caderousse. "Is it still as
...sed to be?"
...inly is," said Andrea, laughing.
... good dinner you must have had with that prince
...se you just left!"
...nly a count, not a prince."
...nt? He's rich, isn't he?"
...ut don't count on anything from him: I don't think
...d him an easy man to deal with."
...don't worry: I have no designs on your count and
... him all for you. But," added Caderousse with an
...nt smile, "that will cost you something, you know."
...right, how much do you need?"
...nk I could live on a hundred francs a month, but——"
...what?"
... I wouldn't be living very well. With a hundred and
...ancs a month I'd be very happy."
...re's two hundred," said Andrea, handing Caderousse ten
...uis.
...od," said Caderousse.
...e to see me on the first of every month and, as long
... my allowance, you'll get yours."
... I wasn't mistaken," said Caderousse. "You're a fine
...it's a blessing when good fortune comes to people
...Now ...ell me about your good luck."
...o y...need to know that?"
...ill ...trust me, don't you?"
...und my father."
...ther?"
...are, as long as he pays?"
...father's name?"
...anti."
...sfied with you?"
...e satisfied so far."
...you to this father?"
...Monte Cristo."

burden which he's eager to hide from the eyes of men, if not those of God?"

Madame Danglars hung, half fainting, on Villefort's arm and he himself was obliged to lean against the wall.

"What's the matter, madame?" cried Debray. "You're so pale!"

"It's quite simple," said Madame de Villefort. "The count is telling us horrible stories with the intention of making us all die of fear."

"Is your terror real, madame?" asked Monte Cristo.

"No," replied Madame Danglars, "but you have a way of supposing things which gives them an illusion of reality."

"It's only the work of my imagination," said Monte Cristo, smiling. "One can just as easily imagine this room as the honest bedroom of a mother, this bed as one which has just witnessed a birth, and this staircase as the passage by means of which, in order not to disturb the mother's regenerating sleep, the doctor, the nurse, or perhaps the father himself carries out the newborn child."

This time Madame Danglars, instead of being reassured by the touching picture the count had painted, uttered a groan and fainted completely.

"Madame Danglars is ill," stammered Villefort. "Perhaps she ought to be taken to her carriage."

She was carried instead to the adjoining bedroom. Monte Cristo let one drop of a red liquid fall on her lips and she regained consciousness. He looked around for Monsieur Danglars, but the banker, being in no mood for poetic impressions, had gone down into the garden and was talking with Major Cavalcanti about a project to build a railroad between Leghorn and Florence. Monte Cristo took Madame Danglars' arm and led her into the garden, where they found Monsieur Danglars taking his coffee between Major Cavalcanti and his son.

"Tell me, madame," said the count, "did I really frighten you terribly?"

"No, count; as you know, things impress us according to the frame of mind we happen to be in."

"And then," said Villefort with a forced laugh, "a mere supposition is enough to——"

"You may believe me or not, as you like," said the count, "but I'm convinced that a crime was once committed in this house."

"Be careful," said Madame de Villefort, "we have the public prosecutor with us tonight."

"So we have," said Monte Cristo, "and I may as well take

advantage of it to make my declaration in the presence of witnesses."

"This is all extremely interesting," said Debray. "If there's really been a crime here it will help our digestion admirably."

"There has been a crime," said Monte Cristo. "Come this way, gentlemen, and especially you, Monsieur de Villefort: in order for the declaration to be valid it must be made to the proper authorities." He took Villefort and Madame Danglars by the arm and drew them with him to a dark corner of the garden. The other guests followed.

"Here, in this very spot," said the count, tapping the ground with his foot, "in order to rejuvenate these old trees I had some compost put into the soil. As my workmen were digging they uncovered a wooden box, or rather the iron bands which had once bound a wooden box, in the midst of which was the skeleton of a newborn baby. I hope you'll admit that this is no fantasy or mine." He felt Madame Danglars' arm stiffen and Villefort's wrist tremble.

"A newborn baby!" repeated Debray. "That's a serious matter!"

"What do they do to infanticides in this country?" asked Major Cavalcanti naïvely.

"Why, they cut off their heads," replied Danglars.

"Yes, that's correct, isn't it, Monsieur de Villefort?" asked Monte Cristo.

"Yes, count," replied Villefort in a voice that was scarcely human.

Monte Cristo saw that the two persons for whom he had prepared the scene had reached the limit of their strength and he did not wish to push them too far. "But we're forgetting our coffee," he said, leading his guests back to the table which had been placed in the middle of the lawn.

Villefort leaned close to Madame Danglars' ear, and whispered, "I must see you tomorrow."

"Where?"

"In my office; it's the safest place."

"I'll be there."

Chapter 36

As the evening wore on, Madame de Villefort manifested a desire to return to Paris, which Madame Danglars had not dared to do, despite her obvious agitation. At his wife's re-

---

quest, therefore, Monsi... for departure.

Just as Andrea Caval... tilbury, he felt a hand o... thinking that Danglars or... him something, but instead... strange, sun-tanned bearded... ironic smile which revealed... those of a wolf or a jackal.... this face or because he was s... pearance, Andrea started and... want?" he asked.

"I want you to save me the... Paris. I'm very tired and, since... did this evening, I can hardly sta... climb into your handsome carriag... to town."

Andrea turned pale, but he said...

"It's just a whim of mine," conti... hands into his pockets and looking... "You can understand that, can't you, ...

On hearing this name, Andrea walke... said, "This man has just come back fro... on and I want him to tell me about it... to the outskirts of town and hire a cab f...

The groom walked off in surprise.

"All right, get in," said Andrea to hi... drove past the last house of the village wit... word while his companion sat beside h... keeping silent. When they were outsi... looked around to make sure no one... then he stopped his horse, turned to... "Why have you come here to bo...

"And you, my boy—why do...

"What makes you think I mi...

"Because when we left eac... told me you were going to P... you went to Paris."

"What's wrong with t...

"Nothing at all; in f...

"Aha!" said Andrea...

"You put it so cr...

"That would be... ing you."

"Don't be angry with... to make me demanding."

"The man you had dinner with tonight?"

"Yes."

"Listen, why don't you try to get him to hire me as a grandfather, since he seems to be in the market for relatives?"

"I'll talk to him about you. In the meantime, what are you going to do?"

"It's very kind of you to ask about that," replied Cade-rousse.

"Since you're taking such an interest in me," said Andrea, "it seems to me I have a right to ask for a little information about you."

"That's true. Well, I'm going to rent a room in an honest house, put on some decent clothes, have myself shaved every day and go read the newspapers in some café; at night I'll go to the theater. I'll seem like a retired baker, which is my dream."

"Good. If you carry out that plan and behave yourself, everything will go very well. And now that you have what you want, hop out of my tilbury and disappear."

"Oh, no, my friend!"

"Why not?"

"Because I'm dressed in rags, I have no papers at all and I have two hundred francs in gold in my pocket: I'd be sure to be arrested at the barrier. In order to justify myself, I'd be forced to say it was you who gave me the money. That would lead to an investigation and they'd find out I left the prison of Toulon without asking permission. Then they'd take me back there and that would be the end of my dream of living like a retired baker. No, my boy, I prefer to remain honorably in Paris."

Andrea frowned and stopped his horse. As he glanced searchingly around him, his hand moved innocently into his pocket, where it touched the trigger guard of a small pistol. In the meantime Caderousse, who had not taken his eyes off his companion, had put his hands behind his back and gently opened a long Spanish knife which he always carried in case of emergency. The two friends were clearly well suited to understand each other, which they did: Andrea's hand slipped harmlessly from his pocket and rose to his red mustache, which he caressed silently for some time.

"All right," he said finally, "we'll go into Paris together. But how will you get past the barrier without arousing suspicion? It seems to me that with those clothes you'll be running a greater risk in my tilbury than you would on foot."

"Wait," said Caderousse; "you'll see." He took Andrea's hat and put it on, along with the overcoat which the groom had left behind.

"What about me?" asked Andrea. "Am I going to be bareheaded?"

"It's windy tonight—the wind could easily have blown off your hat."

"Let's get it over with, then," said Andrea.

They passed the barrier without incident. Andrea stopped his horse at the first side street and Caderousse leaped out of the tilbury.

"What about my hat and my servant's overcoat?" said Andrea.

"You wouldn't want me to risk catching a cold, would you?" replied Caderousse. "Good-bye, Benedetto!" And he vanished down the side street.

Andrea sighed and said to himself, "I suppose it's impossible to be perfectly happy in this world!"

Chapter 37

On his way back from Monte Cristo's house in Auteuil, Debray arrived at the door of the Danglars residence just as Madame Danglars was returning home. With the air of a man familiar with the house, he entered the courtyard first, threw the reins of his horse to a footman and offered his arm to Madame Danglars to accompany her to her apartment.

At the door of her bedroom they met Mademoiselle Cornélie, her confidential maid. "What is my daughter doing?" asked Madame Danglars.

"She studied all evening and then went to bed," replied Mademoiselle Cornélie.

"But it seems to me I hear her piano now."

"That's Mademoiselle d'Armilly—she plays for Mademoiselle Eugénie while she's in bed."

"I see," said Madame Danglars. "Come and undress me."

They entered the bedroom. Debray stretched out on a large sofa while Madame Danglars passed into her dressing room with Mademoiselle Cornélie.

"Monsieur Lucien," said Madame Danglars to Debray through the door of her dressing room, "haven't you always complained that Eugénie never speaks to you?"

"I'm not the only one to make such a complaint," replied

Debray, playing with Madame Danglars' small dog, which, recognizing his status as a friend of the family, was extremely friendly to him.

"That's true," said Madame Danglars, "but I think that will change one of these mornings and that you'll see Eugénie walk into your office."

"Why?"

"To ask you for an engagement at the opera! I've never seen such an obsession with music: it's ridiculous for a fashionable young lady like her!"

Debray smiled and said, "Let her come with her parents' consent and we'll give her an engagement, although we're rather poor to pay for such an extraordinary talent as hers."

"You may go now, Cornélie," said Madame Danglars. "I don't need you any longer."

Cornélie went out. A moment later, Madame Danglars came out of her dressing room in a charming negligee and sat down beside Debray. Then she began to caress her little dog absent-mindedly. Debray looked at for a few moments in silence. "Answer me frankly, Hermine," he said. "Something's bothering you, isn't it?"

"No, nothing's bothering me." Madame Danglars stood up, breathed deeply and looked at herself in a mirror. "I look terrible tonight," she said.

Debray was about to stand up also and reassure her on this point when suddenly the door opened and Baron Danglars appeared. Madame Danglars turned around and looked at her husband with an astonishment which she took no pains to conceal.

"Good evening, madame," said the banker. "Good evening, Monsieur Debray."

Madame Danglars assumed that this unexpected visit signified something like a desire to make amends for the bitter words which had escaped from him during the day. Arming herself with a dignified air, she turned to Debray without answering her husband and said, "Please read me something, Monsieur Debray."

Debray, who had been made slightly uneasy by this visit at first, regained his composure when he saw Madame Danglars' calm. He reached out his hand for a book.

"Excuse me, madame," said Danglars, "but you'll tire yourself by staying up so late and Monsieur Debray lives far from here."

Debray was thunderstruck, not because of the baron's tone, which was perfectly calm and polite, but because, beneath this calm and politeness, he detected a certain unwonted

determination on the baron's part to do something other than
follow his wife's wishes.

Madame Danglars was also surprised and manifested her
astonishment by a look which would no doubt have given
her husband pause if his eyes had not been fixed on the
financial page of a newspaper. Her haughty glance was therefore completely wasted.

"Monsieur Debray," said Madame Danglars, "I assure you
I'm not at all sleepy and that I have hundreds of things to
tell you this evening; you'll have to stay and listen to them
even if you go to sleep on your feet."

"At your service, madame," replied Debray phlegmatically.

"My dear Monsieur Debray," said Danglars, "please don't
force yourself to stay up and listen to my wife's foolishness
tonight: you can listen to it just as well tomorrow. Tonight
I'm going to reserve her company for myself because I have
some very important things to discuss with her."

This time the blow was so direct that both Debray and
Madame Danglars were stunned; they looked at each other
as though each hoped to draw help from the other in the
face of this aggression. But the irresistible power of the
master of the house prevailed and the husband was victorious.

"Don't think I'm turning you out of my house, Monsieur
Debray," continued Danglars. "It's just that certain unexpected circumstances make me wish to have a conversation
with my wife this evening; it happens so seldom that I'm
sure you won't hold it against me."

Debray stammered a few words, bowed and left. "It's
unbelievable," he said to himself, "how these husbands, who
seem so ridiculous to us, still manage to gain the upper hand
over us so easily!"

When Debray had gone, Danglers took his place on the
sofa, closed the book which had remained open and, striking
a terribly pretentious pose, began to play with the dog. But
the dog did not have the same affection for him as for Debray
and tried to bite him; Danglars picked it up by the skin of
the neck and threw it across the room onto a chair. The
animal uttered a cry as it flew through space; but, arrived at
its destination, it crouched silently and motionlessly behind
a cushion, overcome with surprise at such unaccustomed
treatment.

"You're making progress," said Madame Danglars. "Usually
you're only crude; tonight you're brutal."

"That's because I'm in a worse humor than usual."

Madame Danglars looked at her husband with uttter disdain. Ordinarily these scornful glances exasperated the proud
Danglars, but this time he seemed to pay no attention.

"What do I care about your bad humor?" asked Madame Danglars, irritated by her husband's impassiveness. "Keep it in your own bedroom or in your office; and since you have clerks who work for you, take it out on them."

"That's bad advice and I won't follow it," replied Danglars. "My clerks are honest men who make my fortune for me and whom I pay much less than they deserve, if I reckon their worth according to what they bring in. No, I won't take out my anger on them; I'll take it out on those who eat my dinners, wear out my horses and ruin my fortune."

"And who are these people who ruin your fortune? Explain yourself more clearly."

"You understand me very well, but if you persist in denying it, let me inform you that I just lost seven hundred thousand francs on the Spanish bonds."

"Is it my fault you lost seven hundred thousand francs?"

"In any case it wasn't mine."

"Once and for all," said Madame Danglars sharply, "let me tell you not to talk money to me; it's a language I learned neither from my parents nor in the house of my first husband."

"I'm sure you didn't: none of them had a sou. Nevertheless, I thought you took a keen interest in my financial operations."

"Whatever made you believe such a ridiculous thing?"

"Oh, it's not hard to explain," said Danglars. "For example, last February you spoke to me about the Haitian bonds; you had dreamed that a ship sailed into Le Harve with the news that a payment which everyone considered to have been postponed indefinitely was about to be made in full. I know the lucidity of your dreams, so I secretly bought up all the Haitian bonds I could find and I made four hundred thousand francs on them, of which you received one hundred thousand. What you did with that money is not my concern.

"In March a railroad franchise was about to be granted. Three companies presented themselves as candidates for it, all three of them offering equal guarantees. You told me your instinct led you to believe the franchise would be given to the company known as the Société du Midi and, although you claim to have no interest in business, I believe your instinct to be highly developed in certain matters. I therefore bought two-thirds of the shares of that company. The franchise was granted to it as you predicted, its shares tripled in value and I made a million francs, of which I gave you two hundred and fifty thousand as pin money. How did you spend it?"

"Come to the point!" cried Madame Danglars, trembling with anger and impatience.

"Be patient; I'm almost finished. In April you had dinner at the minister's house, where you overheard a secret conversation about the expulsion of Don Carlos. I bought up Spanish bonds; the expulsion took place and I made six hundred thousand francs. You received one hundred and fifty thousand francs, which you disposed of according to your fancy. I don't ask you to account for your money to me, but the fact remains that you received half a million francs this year.

"But now things begin to go less smoothly: three days ago you were discussing politics with Monsieur Debray and you gathered from what he said that Don Carlos had returned to Spain. I began to sell my bonds; the news spread, there was a panic and soon I wasn't selling my bonds, but giving them away. The next day it turned out the news was false, and it had caused me a loss of seven hundred thousand francs."

"Well?"

"Since I give you a quarter of my winnings, you owe me a quarter of my losses; a quarter of seven hundred francs is one hundred and seventy-five thousand."

"You're talking nonsense, and I don't see what Monsieur Debray has to do with any of this."

"If by any chance you don't have the hundred and seventy-five thousand francs I'm demanding, you'll have to borrow it from your friends, and Monsieur Debray is one of your friends."

"This is an outrage!" cried Madame Danglars.

"Let's not have any histrionics, or you'll force me to say that I can see Monsieur Debray gloating over the half a million francs you counted out to him this year and telling himself that at last he's found something the most skillful gamblers have never been able to discover: a game in which you win without putting up any money and lose nothing when you lose."

"Do you dare to tell me you knew nothing about these things till now?" cried Madame Danglars furiously.

"I won't say I knew and I won't say I didn't; I'll say only this: observe my conduct in the four years since we stopped being husband and wife and you'll see that it's always been consistent. Some time after our rupture you decided to study music with that famous baritone who made such a successful début at the Théâtre-Italien; as for myself, I decided to study dancing with that dancer who made such a reputation for herself in London. It cost me a hundred thousand francs for both of us, but I said nothing because harmony is necessary in a household and a hundred thousand francs isn't too much to pay so that a husband and wife can learn dancing and singing thoroughly. Soon you grew tired of singing and decided to take lessons in diplomacy from a secretary of the minister. I let you study: what did it matter to me as long as you paid for your lessons out of your own funds? But now I see that you've begun to dip into mine and that your apprenticeship may cost me seven hundred thousand francs a month. It's time to call a halt: either the diplomat gives free lessons, and I'll go on tolerating him; or else he never sets foot in this house again. Do you understand me?"

"This is too much!" cried Madame Danglars, choking with anger. "You've gone beyond all limits of common decency!"

Danglars shrugged his shoulders. "What silly creatures they are," he said, "these women who consider themselves geniuses because they carry on their love affairs without getting themselves talked about all over Paris! But even if you'd managed to hide your peccadilloes from your husband—which is the ABC of the art, since most of the time the husband doesn't want to see anything—you'd still be only a pale imitation of half your friends. Not one of your actions has escaped me for the past sixteen years while you were applauding your own skill and remaining firmly convinced that you were deceiving me. The result of my pretended ignorance is that there hasn't been one of your lovers, from Monsieur de Villefort down to Monsieur Debray, who hasn't trembled before me. I allow you to make me hateful, but I will prevent you from making me ridiculous; and above all I forbid you to ruin my fortune."

Up to the moment when her husband pronounced the name of Monsieur de Villefort, Madame Danglars had retained a large measure of self-assurance, but on hearing that name she turned pale, leaped to her feet and stepped toward her husband as though to tear from him the rest of the secret, which perhaps he did not know, but which he might know and not wish to reveal. "Monsieur de Villefort!" she cried. "What do you mean by that?"

"I mean that your first husband, seeing perhaps that there was no advantage to be gained from a public prosecutor, died of grief and anger when he returned from an absence of nine months to find you'd been pregnant for six months. Why did he die instead of killing? Because he had no fortune to save. But I do have a fortune to think of. Monsieur Debray, my partner, has made me lose seven hundred thousand francs; let him bear his share of the loss and we'll go on as before. Otherwise, let him go bankrupt for the hundred and seventy-five thousand francs and do what all bankrupts do: disappear. I won't deny he's a charming young man when his information is correct; but when it isn't, there are at least fifty others in the world who are worth more than he is."

Madame Danglars was overwhelmed. She sank into a chair, thinking of Villefort, the scene at Monte Cristo's house and the strange series of disasters which had befallen her one after another in the past few days.

Danglars did not even look at her, although she was doing her best to faint. He walked out of the room without saying another word, so that Madame Danglars, as she came out of her state of semi-consciousness, was able to convince herself with some success that she had only had a bad dream.

Chapter 38

The next day, at the hour when Debray usually stopped by to pay a short visit to Madame Danglars on the way to his office, his carriage did not appear in the courtyard. Soon afterward Madame Danglars ordered her own carriage and left. Danglars, hidden behind a window curtain, watched her departure, which he had been expecting. He gave orders to be notified as soon as she came back, but at two o'clock she still had not returned.

At two o'clock the baron went to the Chamber. When he came out he instructed his coachman to drive him to 30 Avenue des Champs Elysées, where he found the Count of Monte Cristo at home.

"What's the matter, baron?" asked Monte Cristo when he saw him. "You look disturbed, and that frightens me; a worried capitalist is like a comet: he always presages some disaster for the world."

"I've been pursued by bad luck for several days," said Danglars, "and I hear nothing but bad news. My latest misfortune was a bankruptcy in Trieste."

"Are you speaking of Jacopo Manfredi, by any chance?"

"Precisely! Just think of it: a man with whom I'd been dealing for I don't know how long, and never a mistake, never a delay, a man who paid like a prince. I advance him a million francs and all of a sudden Jacopo Manfredi suspends his payments! Along with the Spanish affair, that makes a fine end of the month for me!"

"Was it really a loss for you, the Spanish affair?"

"It certainly was! It cost me seven hundred thousand francs. . . . But, as long as we're talking about business," added Danglars, delighted to find a way of changing the subject, "Suppose you tell me what I'm to do for Monsieur Cavalcanti."

"Why, give him money, if his credit seems good to you."

"It seems excellent to me. He came to see me this morning and I gave him forty thousand francs. He also opened a credit of five thousand francs a month for his son."

"Sixty thousand francs a year!" said Monte Cristo. "What does he expect a young man to do with five thousand francs a month?"

"Of course, if the young man should need a few thousand francs extra——"

"Don't advance it to him: his father wouldn't make it good. You don't know these Italian millionaires; they're real misers."

"Do you mean to say you don't trust this Cavalcanti?"

"Of course I trust him!" said Monte Cristo. "I'd gladly give him ten million francs on his signature alone. His fortune is beyond doubt."

"All these wealthy Italians usually marry among themselves, don't they?" asked Danglars nonchalantly. "I suppose they like to combine their fortunes."

"That's true, they usually do. But Cavalcanti is an eccentric man who never does anything like other people. I'm convinced he's brought his son to France so that he'll find a wife here."

"Do you really think so?"

"I'm sure of it."

"Do you know anything about his fortune?"

"I hardly know him; all I know about him is what he's told me himself and what the Abbé Busoni has told me. Just this morning the Abbé Busoni was telling me that Cavalcanti was tired of seeing his fortune lie dormant in Italy, which is a dead country, and that he wanted to find some way of investing it in either France or England. When his son marries he'll probably give him two or three million francs. If he marries a banker's daughter, for example, his father may invest in the firm of his son's father-in-law."

"Yes, but he'll no doubt find some princess to marry, won't he?"

"Not necessarily; these great Italian lords frequently marry ordinary mortals. But why are you asking me these questions? Do you have someone in mind for Andrea to marry?"

"To tell you the truth," said Danglars, "it doesn't seem like a bad speculation to me, and I'm a speculator."

"You're not thinking of your daughter, are you? Isn't she already engaged to Albert de Morcerf?"

"Monsieur de Morcerf and I have discussed the marriage

on several occasions, it's true, but Madame de Morcerf and
Albert——"

"Do you mean to say it's not a good match? Albert may
not be as rich as your daughter, but you can't deny that he
bears an honorable name."

"No doubt, but I prefer my own name," said Danglars. "I
wasn't born a baron, but at least Danglars is my real name."

"Do you mean to say that the Count of Morcerf's real
name isn't Morcerf?"

"It certainly isn't! I was made a baron, so I really am a
baron, but he made himself a count, so he isn't really a
count."

"Impossible!"

"Listen, count," continued Danglars, "I've known Monsieur
de Morcerf for thirty years. As you know, I make no secret
of my origins. Well, when I was a humble clerk, Morcerf
was a humble fisherman."

"What was he called then?"

"Fernand Mondego."

"Are you sure?"

"He sold me enough fish for me to know him!"

"Then why are you marrying your daughter to his son?"

"Because Fernand and Danglars are both of humble birth,
they both acquired a title and they both became rich; one is,
therefore, essentially as good as the other—except for certain things that have been said about him which have never
been said about me."

"What do you mean?"

"Nothing."

"Just a minute; I understand. What you've just said has
refreshed my memory: I heard the name of Fernand Mondego
mentioned in Greece."

"In connection with the Ali Pasha affair?"

"Precisely."

"That's the big mystery," said Danglars, "and I admit I'd
have given a lot to find out about it."

"That wouldn't have been difficult if you'd really wanted
to. You have correspondents in Greece, haven't you?"

"Of course."

"In Yanina?"

"I have correspondents everywhere."

"All right, then, write to your correspondent in Yanina
and ask him what part a Frenchman named Fernand Mondego played in the Ali Pasha affair."

"You're right!" exclaimed Danglars, standing up. "I'll
write today!"

"And if you should learn some scandalous piece of news . . ."

"I'll tell you about it."

Danglars hurried out of the count's house and into his carriage.

Chapter 39

Let us leave the banker rushing back to his office and follow Madame Danglars, who, as we have said, left her house at half-past twelve.

The antechamber of Monsieur de Villefort's office in the Palace of Justice was crowded, but Madame Danglars was not obliged even to give her name: as soon as she entered, a clerk came up to her, asked her if she was the lady to whom the public prosecutor had given an appointment and led her to Monsieur de Villefort's office through a private corridor.

The magistrate was writing with his back toward the door. He did not look around when Madame Danglars entered, but as soon as the clerk's footsteps had died away in the corridor, he stood up, bolted the door and drew the curtains. When he had made sure he could be neither seen nor heard, he turned to Madame Danglars and said, "It's been a long time since I had the pleasure of talking with you and I regret that on this occasion we've met to discuss an extremely painful matter."

"I think you can understand my emotion," said Madame Danglars. "In this room in which so many criminals have trembled and felt ashamed and in which I now sit trembling and ashamed, I can't help feeling that I'm also a criminal and that you're a threatening judge. But I think you'll agree that if I've sinned I was severly punished for it last night."

"Almost too severely for your strength, poor woman," said Villefort, taking her hand. "And yet I must tell you that we haven't yet come to the end of this affair. How was that terrible past revived? How did it rise up like a phantom from the grave and from the depths of our hearts?"

"By chance, no doubt."

"Chance! No, no, it wasn't by chance."

"Wasn't it by chance that the Count of Monte Cristo bought that house? Wasn't it by chance that his workmen discovered the child buried beneath the trees, poor innocent little creature!"

"His workmen discovered nothing," said Villefort dully, "and instead of weeping, we ought to tremble."

"What do you mean?" cried Madame Danglars.

"I mean that the Count of Monte Cristo did not unearth the skeleton of a child in his garden because no child was buried there."

"Then where was it that you buried our child? What reason did you have to deceive me?"

"Listen to me," said Villefort, "and you'll pity me for bearing a burden of grief for twenty years without ever imposing any of it on you. You remember how the child was handed to me immediately after its birth and how we believed it to be dead."

Madame Danglars made a movement as though she were about to leap to her feet, but Villefort stopped her with a gesture imploring her attention. "We believed it to be dead," he repeated. "I put it into a box, dug a grave in the garden and buried it. I had hardly finished covering it with earth when the Corsican rushed at me. I felt a sharp pain, I tried to cry out but was unable to, and then I fell, thinking I was about to die. I'll never forget your sublime courage when I dragged myself to the bottom of the stairs and found that, despite your own suffering, you had come down to help me. I struggled against death for three months and then my doctor ordered me to go south for my convalescence, which lasted for six months. When I returned to Paris I learned that you had married Monsieur Danglars. I also learned that the house in Auteuil had been uninhabited since we left it. I went there at five o'clock in the afternoon, went up to the bedroom and waited for nightfall.

"All the thoughts which had haunted me during my convalescence now seemed more threatening than ever to me. The Corsican who stabbed me had seen me bury the child. If he learned who you were, might he not make you pay dearly for his silence? Wouldn't the secret give him another means of vengeance when he found out he hadn't really killed me? It was urgent that I eliminate all trace of that terrible secret. I waited until it was completely dark before I decided to go down into the garden. I think I'm as brave as any man, but when I opened the door and saw a long streak of pale moonlight shining on the spiral staircase like a specter, I almost cried aloud and it seemed to me I was about to go mad. I finally managed to control myself and started down the stairs. The only thing I was unable to control was a strange trembling in my knees. I clutched the railing at every step; if I had let go of it I would have fallen.

"In the garden I picked up the spade and the shaded lantern I had left there that afternoon. I began to dig. Yet even after I had dug a hole twice as big as the first one I still found nothing. I thought perhaps I was digging in the wrong place. I oriented myself again, remembering all the details, then I made the hole even larger. Nothing! The wooden box wasn't there!"

"It wasn't there?" said Madame Danglars in a choked voice.

"Don't think I stopped there," continued Villefort. "I thought the Corsican might have dug up the box, thinking it contained a treasure, and then, when he saw his error, dug another hole and buried it again. I searched the entire garden but I found nothing, absolutely nothing. I tried to think reasonably. 'Why did that man carry away the corpse?' I asked myself."

"Why, you've already said it," said Madame Danglars, "it was in order to have proof of our secret."

"No, it wasn't that. He wouldn't have kept the corpse for a year: he would have showed it to a magistrate and made a declaration. But he hadn't done that. No, there was an even more terrible possibility: the child may still have been alive and the Corsican may have saved it."

Madame Danglars uttered a cry and gripped Villefort's hands. "My child was alive!" she screamed. "You buried my child alive! You weren't sure he was dead, and yet you buried him!" She stood up before him, almost threatening.

Villefort realized that in order to turn away this storm of maternal feeling he would have to communicate some of his own terror to Madame Danglars. "If that child is alive and someone knows it, we're lost," he said in a low voice. "And since the Count of Monte Cristo told us about finding the skeleton of a child where no child was buried, he knows our secret! That's why I asked you to come here: I wanted to warn you. Tell me," he continued, looking at her even more steadfastly than before, "you've never spoken to anyone about our affair, have you?"

"Never!"

"Do you keep a diary?"

"No."

"Do you ever talk in your sleep?"

"No, I sleep like a child; don't you remember?"

Madame Danglars blushed; Villefort turned pale. "I remember," he said, "I could hardly hear your breathing."

"What now?" asked Madame Danglars.

"I know what I have to do now," said Villefort. "Within a

week I'll know who Monsieur de Monte Cristo is, where he comes from, where he's going and why he speaks to us of children buried in his garden."

He shook Madame Danglars' hand, which she gave him with reluctance, and respectfully showed her to the door.

Chapter 40

That same day Albert de Morcerf paid a visit to the Count of Monte Cristo. The count received him with his customary smile.

"I got back from Tréport less than an hour ago," said Albert, "and my first visit is for you."

"That's very kind of you."

"Do you have any news to tell me?"

"Yes, Monsieur Danglars came to dinner at my country house."

"I'm well aware of that already, since it was in order to avoid his presence that my mother and I went to Tréport."

"But he also had dinner with Monsieur Andrea Cavalcanti."

"Your Italian prince?"

"Let's not exaggerate: he claims only the title of viscount. He was there with his father, Monsieur and Madame Danglars, Monsieur and Madame de Villefort, Monsieur Debray, Maximilien Morrel and—let's see—oh, yes, Monsieur de Château-Renaud."

"Did they talk about me?"

"Not a word."

"That's too bad."

"Why? It seems to me you'd prefer them to forget you."

"Yes, but if they didn't talk about me it means they were thinking about me a good part of the time, and that makes me unhappy."

"What do you care, as long as Mademoiselle Danglars wasn't with them to think about you? It's true, though, that she may have been thinking about you at home."

"I'm sure she wasn't; or at least if she was, I'm sure she was thinking about me in the same way I think of her."

"What touching affection! Do you really hate each other?"

"Listen," said Albert, "Mademoiselle Danglars would make a charming mistress, but as a wife——"

"So that's how you think of your future wife!" said Monte Cristo, laughing.

"It's a crude way of putting it, perhaps, but it's still true. It's too bad she'll have to become my wife before I can get what I want from her. I'm horrified at the thought of living with her, talking to her, listening to her sing and having her compose her music and her poetry in my presence for the rest of my life. You can always leave a mistress, but with a wife it's another story! You have to live with her forever! And it gives me nightmares to think of living with Mademoiselle Danglars forever."

"Don't be too worried about having to marry Mademoiselle Danglars," said the count. "Just let things take their course; you may not be the first one to take back your word. Do you seriously want to break off the engagement?"

"I'd give a hundred thousand francs to have it broken off!"

"In that case, you can be happy: Monsieur Danglars is ready to give twice that much for the same purpose."

"If that's true, it's a wonderful stroke of luck!" said Albert, who was nevertheless unable to keep himself from frowning slightly. "But what are Monsieur Danglars' reasons?"

"Ah, that's human nature! Here's a man ready to chop another man's self-esteem to pieces with an axe, yet he cries out in pain when his own is pricked with a needle."

"Even so, it seems to me that Monsieur Danglars——"

"Ought to be delighted with you, isn't that right? But he's a man of such bad taste that he's even more delighted with someone else."

"Who is it?"

"I don't know; but keep your eyes and ears open and you may be able to find out for yourself."

Chapter 41

Madame and Mademoiselle de Villefort had gone to a ball together, having failed to persuade Monsieur de Villefort to accompany them. After their departure, the public prosecutor shut himself up in his study, as was his custom in the evening. He sat down before a pile of papers which would have frightened any other man, but which, in ordinary times, would hardly have been sufficient for his robust appetite for work.

This time, however, the papers were only a pretext. Villefort had not gone into his study to work, but to reflect. After he had locked his door and given orders not to be disturbed for anything except a matter of great importance, he sat down in his armchair and began to think over once again the events of the last few days which had filled him with such somber anxiety and bitter memories.

As he sat there trying to reassure himself, he heard the

rumble of a carriage in the courtyard. Then he heard footsteps coming up the stairs, accompanied by sobs and lamentations. He unbolted the door of his study and a few moments later an old lady entered unannounced, her eyes swollen from weeping. "Oh, what a terrible thing!" she said. "I'll die too! Oh, yes, I'll certainly die!" She sank into the chair nearest the door and burst out sobbing. Villefort stood up and ran over to his mother-in-law, for the old lady was Madame de Saint-Méran, his first wife's mother.

"What has happened, madame?" he said. "What has upset you like this? Isn't Monsieur de Saint-Méran with you?"

"Monsieur de Saint-Méran is dead," said the old marquise dully.

"Dead? Dead so—suddenly?" stammered Villefort.

"Yes—carried away by a stroke of apoplexy that was fatal almost instantly. I can no longer weep, I suppose that at my age one has no more tears left, yet it seems to me that if one suffers one ought to be able to weep. . . . Where's Valentine? I want to see her."

Villefort thought it would be terrible to tell her that her granddaughter was at a ball; he said simply that Valentine had gone out with her stepmother and that he would send someone after her immediately.

"Hurry, I beg you, as quickly as possible!" said the old lady.

Villefort took her arm and led her to her chamber. "You must rest now," he said. Then, while Madame de Saint-Méran knelt, praying from the depths of her heart, he himself went to bring his wife and daughter back from the ball.

Valentine found her grandmother in bed. Silent caresses, painful swellings of the heart, choked sighs, hot tears—such were the only recountable details of her visit. Madame de Saint-Méran, overwhelmed by her grief, finally succumbed to her fatigue and fell into feverish sleep. A glass and a pitcher of orangeade, her customary beverage, were placed on a small table beside her bed.

She was still in bed when Valentine entered her room the next day. Her fever had not diminished; on the contrary, she seemed to be in the grip of a violent nervous irritation.

"Oh, grandmother, are you suffering still more?" asked Valentine.

"No, my daughter, but I was waiting impatiently for you to come before I sent for your father. I want to talk to him."

Valentine did not dare oppose her grandmother's wishes. Villefort entered a few moments later.

"You're planning to marry Valentine to Monsieur Franz d'Epinay, aren't you?" said Madame de Saint-Méran to him without any preamble, as though she were afraid her time might run short.

"Yes, madame," replied Villefort.

"He's the son of the General d'Epinay who was assassinated a few days before the usurper returned from Elba, isn't he?"

"Yes."

"And he isn't reluctant to marry the granddaughter of a Jacobin?"

"Our civil dissensions are fortunately extinguished now, madame. Monsieur d'Epinay was only a child when his father died; he hardly knows Monsieur Noirtier and will see him, if not with pleasure, at least with indifference."

"It it a good match?"

"In every way. Monsieur d'Epinay is one of the most distinguished young men I know."

Valentine had remained silent throughout this conversation.

"Well, then," said Madame de Saint-Méran, after several moments of reflection, "you must hurry because I don't have much longer to live."

"Oh, grandmother!" cried Valentine.

"I know what I'm saying," continued the marquise. "You must hurry so that, since Valentine no longer has a mother, she will at least have her grandmother to bless her marriage."

"It will be done according to your wishes," said Villefort, "especially since your wishes coincide with my own. As soon as Monsieur d'Epinay returns to Paris——"

"But grandmother," interrupted Valentine, "we're in mourning now—would you like to have a marriage in such sad circumstances?"

"Let's hear none of those commonplace reasons that prevent the weak from building a solid future for themselves!" answered the marquise energetically. "I was married right after my mother's death, and I was never unhappy because of that."

"You're still obsessed with the idea of death," said Villefort.

"I tell you I'm going to die, do you understand me? However impossible it may seem to you, last night, right where you're standing now, coming from the corner of the room where there's a door leading into Madame de Villefort's dressing room, I saw a white, silent form approach me."

Valentine uttered a cry.

"You were only agitated by your fever, madame," said Villefort.

"Doubt if you like," said the marquise, "but I'm sure of what I say. I saw that white form approaching and, as though

God didn't wish me to have to rely on the evidence of only one of my senses, I heard it move my glass, the same one you see there on the table now. It was the soul of my husband coming to call me to him."

"Don't let such mournful ideas take possession of you, madame," said Villefort. "You'll live a long time yet, happy, loved and respected, and we'll make you forget."

"Never! Never! Never!" said the marquise. "And now I want to see a notary in order to make sure all our property will go to Valentine after my death."

"Oh, grandmother!" cried Valentine, pressing her lips to the old lady's forehead. "Do you want to make me die also? Oh, you have a high fever. It's not a notary we must send for, but a doctor."

"A doctor?" said the marquise, shrugging her shoulders. "I'm not in pain; I'm thirsty, that's all."

"What would you like to drink?"

"I always drink orangeade, you know that. My glass is on the table there, please hand it to me."

Valentine picked up the glass with a certain uneasiness, for it was the same glass which, according to her grandmother, had been moved by the phantom the night before.

The marquise emptied it at one draught. Then she turned over on her pillow and repeated, "The notary! The notary!"

Villefort left the room and Valentine sat down beside her grandmother's bed. Two hours passed, during which the marquise sank into agitated sleep. Then a servant entered to announce that the doctor was waiting in the salon.

Valentine went rapidly downstairs. The doctor, Monsieur d'Avrigny, was a friend of the family and one of the ablest physicians in Paris. He was especially fond of Valentine, whom he had brought into the world.

"Oh, Monsieur d'Avrigny!" said Valentine. "We've been waiting for you so impatiently! It's my poor grandmother. . . . Do you know about our misfortune?"

"No."

"Alas," said Valentine, forcing back a sob, "my grandfather is dead."

"Monsieur de Saint-Méran?"

"Yes. He died of a sudden attack of apoplexy. My poor grandmother is obsessed by the idea that he's calling to her to join him."

"What are her symptoms?"

"She has a strange nervous excitation and she's very restless in her sleep; she claims that last night she saw a phantom enter her room and that she was even able to hear the sound it made when it moved her glass."

"Your grandmother isn't the type of woman who would ordinarily have hallucinations," said Monsieur d'Avrigny. "It all seems very strange to me."

"Go up to see her now, please, doctor."

"Are you coming with me?"

"I'm afraid to," said Valentine, "because she forbade me to send for you. I'm terribly upset, too; I'll take a walk in the garden and try to calm myself."

It is not difficult to imagine which part of the garden Valentine chose for her promenade. After picking a rose to put in her hair, she turned into the shady lane which led to the grilled gate. As she walked along she seemed to hear a voice calling her name. She stopped in surprise. It was Maximilien's voice.

With the intuition peculiar to lovers and mothers, Maximilien had guessed that something was happening in the Villefort residence which concerned his love for Valentine. It was not the hour when he usually came to the grill, so it was only chance, or, if you prefer, a lucky presentiment in Valentine which led her into the garden.

"You, at this hour!" exclaimed Valentine.

"Yes," said Maximilien; "I've come to bring you bad news and to ask if you have any to tell me."

"Speak, then, Maximilien, but my grief is already deep enough as it is."

"Dear Valentine," said Maximilien, trying to control his emotion enough to be able to speak coherently, "please listen to me carefully, because what I'm about to say to you is very serious. Have they set the date for your marriage yet?"

"I won't hide anything from you, Maximilien. This morning my grandmother, whom I had counted on for support, announced that she wants the marriage contract to be signed the day after Monsieur d'Epinay returns to Paris."

A painful sigh burst from the young man's chest. "That will be tomorrow, then," he said, "because Monsieur d'Epinay arrived in Paris this morning. The time has come for you to give me an answer that will mean either life or death to me: What do you intend to do?"

Valentine bowed her head, overwhelmed with emotion.

"This is no time to abandon ourselves to sterile regret," continued Maximilien. "There are people who are willing to suffer and swallow their tears at leisure, and God will no doubt reward them in heaven for their resignation; but those who have the will to struggle strike back at fate in retaliation for the blows they receive. Do you intend to fight back at fate, Valentine? That's what I came here to ask you."

Valentine started and looked at him with fear in her eyes.

The idea of resisting her father and her grandmother had not even occurred to her.

"What are you saying to me, Maximilien?" she exclaimed. "Are you asking me to fight against my father's orders, against the wishes of my dying grandmother? That's impossible! Your heart is too noble not to understand me, dear Maximilien. No, I won't struggle against fate; I'll save my strength to struggle against myself, to swallow my tears, as you put it."

"You're right," said Maximilien phlegmatically. "I understand you. You don't wish to irritate your father or disobey your grandmother, and tomorrow you'll sign the marriage contract."

"But what else could I do?"

"Are you seriously asking me for advice?"

"Of course! You know how devoted I am to you."

"Then here's what I propose to you: First let me take you to my sister's house, then we'll leave for Algeria, England or America, unless you'd prefer to go to some obscure province, wait till our friends have overcome your family's resistance and then return to Paris."

Valentine shook her head and said, "That's the advice of a madman, Maximilien, and I'd be even more mad than you if I didn't stop you immediately with the word: Impossible!"

"You're right, Valentine, I'll say it once again. I'm a madman, as you say, and you've proved to me that passion can blind even those who are ordinarily the most clear-headed. Thank you for reasoning without passion. All I can do now is to wish you a life so calm, happy and full that there will be no place in your memory for me. Good-bye, Valentine."

"Where are you going?" cried Valentine, reaching through the grill and clutching Maximilien's sleeve, quite sure that his apparent calm was not real. "Before you leave me, tell me what you're going to do!"

Maximilien smiled sadly but said nothing.

"Oh, tell me! Tell me, I beg you!"

"Don't worry," said Maximilien, "I have no intention of making Monsieur d'Epinay responsible for my fate. Another man in my position might threaten to provoke him to a duel, but that would be senseless. He didn't even know I existed when he agreed to the marriage. I have no quarrel with him and I swear to you I'll leave him alone. I've never taken myself for the melancholy hero of a novel, but, without making any speeches or swearing any oaths, I've placed my whole life in your hands. You're about to leave me and, as I've already told you, you're right to act as you do, but the fact remains that when you're gone my life will be lost. This is what I'm going to do: I'll wait until the last second before you're married, for I don't want to risk losing any unexpected stroke of good fortune, and for a man condemned to death even miracles enter into the category of ordinary possibilities. I'll wait, therefore, until my misery is certain and without remedy, and then I'll kill myself as surely as I am the son of the most honorable man who ever lived in France."

Valentine was seized by a convulsive trembling; her arms fell to her sides and two large tears rolled down her cheeks. "Oh!" she cried. "Have pity on me, Maximilien! You will live, won't you?"

"No, on my word of honor. But what will it matter to you? You'll have done your duty and your conscience will be clear."

Valentine fell to her knees, clutching her heart.

"Good-bye, Valentine," repeated Maximilien.

"Dear God," said Valentine, raising her eyes to the sky, "you can see that I've done everything within my power to be an obedient daughter. But I'd rather die of shame than of remorse. You'll live, Maximilien, and I won't belong to anyone but you. Give me your orders, I'm ready to obey. But listen to me, Maximilien, if I can in some way delay the marriage, will you wait for me?"

"I swear I will. And I want you to swear to me that you will never allow that wedding to take place, that even if they drag you before the priest by force you'll say no."

"I swear it."

"I trust you, Valentine. But if your family won't listen to you, if Monsieur d'Epinay is called in tomorrow to sign the contract, then——"

"Then I'll join you and we'll flee together. I'll send you a note to tell you what happens."

"Thank you, my beloved Valentine. As soon as I know the hour, I'll come here; you'll climb over the wall and into my arms. I'll have a carriage waiting to take you to my sister's house."

"Go now," said Valentine. "Good-bye."

Maximilien listened until the sound of her footsteps had died away, looking up and thanking God for allowing him to be loved so strongly. Then he hurried home.

He waited all the rest of that day and the following day without any word from Valentine. Then on the morning of the third day he received this note:

Tears, supplications and prayers have done nothing. The signing of the marriage contract is set for nine o'clock tonight.

I have given you my word, Maximilien, and my heart
belongs to you. I will meet you at the grill tonight at a
quarter to nine.

VALENTINE

Maximilien reread the note at least twenty times during
the day, thinking with inexpressible emotion of the moment
when Valentine would say to him, "Here I am, Maximilien,
take me."

He had prepared everything for their flight: he had hidden
two ladders near the outside of the wall and a carriage was
waiting to take him there at any moment.

At eight o'clock that night he had already arrived before the
wall and concealed his horses and carriage behind a ruined
building. He spent his time pacing up and down and going up
to the grill at ever shortening intervals to peer into the dark
garden, vainly seeking the sight of a white dress and the sound
of footsteps. Finally he heard the clock of Saint-Philippe du
Roule strike half-past nine. It was a terrible moment for Maximilien. The slightest rustling of leaves in the garden, the faint-
est whisper of the wind brought beads of sweat to his forehead
and made him place his foot on the bottom rung of the ladder.
In the midst of these oscillations between fear and anxiety he
heard the clock strike ten. It occurred to him that Valentine's
strength might have failed her as she fled through the garden
on her way to him and that she was now lying unconscious in
some pathway. The demon who suggested this thought to him
continued to whisper in his ear until the hypothesis became a
certainty. When he heard the clock strike half-past ten he
could wait no longer. He climbed to the top of the wall and
jumped down on the other side.

A few seconds later he could see the house clearly. The
sight verified something he had suspected from the glimpses
he was able to obtain through the grill: the house was almost
dark, instead of being brightly illuminated as would be natural
for such an important ceremony as the signing of a marriage
contract. Maximilien was almost as frightened by its darkness
and silence as he was by Valentine's absence. Frantic, wild
with anxiety, determined to see Valentine again at any cost,
he advanced to the edge of the garden and was preparing to
run across the open space between him and the house as
swiftly as possible when he heard the sound of voices carried
to him by the wind. He stepped back into a clump of trees.
The moon came out from behind a cloud and he saw Monsieur de Villefort coming toward him accompanied by a man
dressed in black, whom he recognized as Doctor d'Avrigny.
He withdrew to the center of the clump of trees.

The footsteps of the two men soon stopped and Maximilien heard Villefort say, "Ah, doctor, God has turned against my house! Don't try to console me, my wound is too deep. She's dead! Dead!"

A cold sweat broke out on Maximilien's forehead and made his teeth chatter. Who was it who had died?

"I didn't bring you out here to console you, Monsieur de Villefort," said the doctor, "quite the contrary."

"What do you mean?" asked Villefort anxiously.

"I mean that behind the disaster which has just struck you there may be an even greater one. I have a terrible revelation to make to you."

Villefort sank weakly down on a bench while the doctor remained standing before him. Maximilien listened, frozen in terror.

"Speak doctor," said Villefort. "I'm prepared for anything."

"Madame de Saint-Méran was an aged woman, it's true," said the doctor, "but she was in excellent health."

Maximilien began to breathe again.

"She died of sorrow, doctor," said Villefort. "After living with her husband for forty years——"

"It wasn't sorrow," said the doctor. "Sorrow may kill in certain rare cases, but it doesn't kill in a day, in an hour, in ten minutes! Now that we're alone, there's something I must tell you."

"My God, what is it?"

"That the symptoms of tetanus and those of poisoning by vegetable matter are absolutely identical."

Villefort leaped to his his feet, then, after standing silent for a moment, sank back down on the bench. "In the name of God, doctor," he said, "do you realize what you're saying to me?"

"I'm well aware of the seriousness of my statement and the character of the man to whom I'm making it."

"Are you speaking to me as friend or as a magistrate?" asked Villefort.

"As a friend, for the moment at least. The two symptoms are so identical that I'd hesitate to make a signed declaration of what I'm telling you. Nevertheless I observed Madame de Saint-Méran's death agony for three-quarters of an hour and it is my conviction not only that she was poisoned but that I can name the poison which killed her. Madame de Saint-Méran died from a large dose of brucine or strychnine."

Villefort clutched the doctor's hand and cried out, "Oh, it's impossible! I must be dreaming! How horrible to hear such things from a man like you! In the name of God, doctor, tell me you may be mistaken!"

"I may be mistaken, but——"

"But what?"

"But I don't think so. Did anyone have an interest in Madame de Saint-Méran's death?"

"No, of course not! My daughter is her sole heiress. Only Valentine—— Oh, my God! If such an idea ever occurred to me I'd stab my heart to punish it for harboring a thought like that!"

"I'm not accusing anyone," said Doctor d'Avrigny; "don't misunderstand me. It may well have been an error. But in any case my conscience demanded that I speak to you. Make inquiries."

"About whom? How?"

"For example, find out if your father's old servant, Barrois, might accidentally have given Madame de Saint-Méran a potion meant for your father."

"But how could a potion prepared for Monsieur Noirtier poison Madame de Saint-Méran?"

"That's quite simple. As you know, with certain illnesses poisons become remedies: paralysis is one of those illnesses. After trying everything else to give Monsieur Noirtier back his power of movement and speech, I decided to begin treating him with brucine. That was three years ago. The last dose I prescribed for him contained six centigrams of brucine, an amount which has no harmful effect on him because his system has been accustomed to it by successively increasing doses, but which would be enough to kill anyone else."

"But Monsieur Noirtier's room isn't connected with Madame de Saint-Méran's in any way and Barrois never went into Madame de Saint-Méran's room."

"Monsieur de Villefort," said the doctor, "I would have saved Madame de Saint-Méran if I had been able to, but she's dead now and my first duty is to the living. Let us bury this terrible secret in the depths of our hearts. If someone else should discover it, I'm willing to allow my silence to be attributed to my ignorance. In the meantime, continue to search, and search actively, for the matter may not stop here; and if you find the guilty party, I'll be the first to tell you, 'You're a magistrate—act as you see fit.' "

"Thank you, doctor, thank you!" cried Villefort joyfully. "I've never had a better friend than you." Then, as though he were afraid Doctor d'Avrigny might change his mind, he stood up and led him back toward the house.

Maximilien, as though he needed to breathe, came out from inside the clump of trees. His face was so pale that he might have been taken for a phantom in the moonlight.

As he stood looking at the somber house he saw a window

opened at one end of it. By the light of a candle placed on a mantelpiece he saw a figure step out onto the balcony. It was Valentine. At the risk of being seen, at the risk of frightening Valentine and causing her to give the alarm by an involuntary cry, he dashed across the lawn, ran up the steps of the house and pushed open the unlocked door. He crossed the ante-chamber and began to walk up the stairs. He was in such a frenzied state that even the sight of Monsieur de Villefort would not have frightened him. Fortunately he saw no one.

When he reached the top of the stairs a sob whose intonation he recognized led him to a half-open door through which a dim light was shining. He entered. Under a white sheet which outlined its form lay the body of Madame de Saint-Méran. Beside it knelt Valentine, who had left the balcony and was now uttering a rapid, almost incoherent prayer. The sight of her weeping was more than Maximilien could bear in silence. He heaved a sigh and murmured her name. She looked up and saw him without surprise; there are no inter-mediate emotions in a heart swollen by the supreme despair.

"Valentine," said Maximilien in a trembling voice, "I waited for two hours and when you didn't come I became frantic. I climbed over the wall and went into the garden. There I heard voices talking about the fatal accident——"

"Whose voices?"

Maximilien shuddered, for the whole conversation between the doctor and Monsieur de Villefort came back to him. "The voices of your servants told me everything," he said.

"But if you're found here we're lost," said Valentine without fear or anger.

"Listen!" said Maximilien. They both heard the sound of a door opening and of footsteps on the stairs.

"It's my father coming out of his study," said Valentine.

"And showing the doctor to the door," added Maximilien.

"How do you know it's the doctor?" asked Valentine in surprise.

"I'm only supposing."

Meanwhile they heard the front door opened, then closed and locked. Monsieur de Villefort then went to the door opening onto the garden, locked it and went back upstairs.

"Now," said Valentine, "you can't go out by either the front door or the garden door. There's only one safe exit for you, and that's through my grandfather's room. Come."

"Where?"

"To my grandfather's room."

"Be careful, Valentine," said Maximilien, hesitating, "I see now that it was an act of madness for me to come here; are you sure you haven't lost your reason too?"

"Quite sure; I only regret having to leave my poor grand-mother alone."

"Death is sacred by itself, Valentine."

"Yes; and besides, I won't be gone long. Come."

Valentine went through the hall and down a small staircase leading to Noirtier's room. Maximilien followed her on tiptoe.

Noirtier, who had been informed by his old servant of everything that had happened, was still sitting up in his wheel-chair. His eyes sparkled when he saw Valentine.

"Grandfather," she said, "you know that Madame de Saint-Méran died an hour ago and that, except for you, there's no longer any relative in the world who loves me." The old man's eyes took on an expression of infinite tenderness. "I must therefore confide all my sorrows and hopes to you alone, isn't that right?"

"Yes," signaled Noirtier.

"Then look closely at this gentleman," said Valentine, tak-ing Maximilien by the hand. "He's Monsieur Maximilien Mor-rel, son of the honorable shipowner of Marseilles. You've heard of his father, haven't you?"

"Yes," said the old man's eyes.

"He bears an irreproachable name which he is making still more honorable, for at the age of thirty he is already a Cap-tain of Spahis and an officer of the Legion of Honor."

Noirtier made a sign indicating that he was aware of these facts.

"Grandfather," said Valentine, "I love him and I'll never belong to anyone but him! If they force me to marry another man I'll either let myself die or kill myself."

Noirtier's eyes expressed a host of tumultuous thoughts.

"You like Maximilien, don't you, grandfather?"

"Yes."

"And you'll protect us against my father's wishes, won't you?"

Noirtier fixed his intelligent gaze on Maximilien, as if to say, "That depends."

Maximilien understood. "Valentine," he said, "you have a sacred duty to perform in your grandmother's room. Will you allow me the honor of speaking with your grandfather for a moment?"

"Yes, yes, that's right!" said Noirtier's eyes. Then he looked anxiously at Valentine.

"Are you wondering how he'll be able to understand you?" she asked.

"Yes."

"Don't worry about that: we've often talked about you to-gether and he knows how I speak with you." She stood up, kissed her grandfather tenderly, said good-bye to Maximilien and left the room.

Maximilien, in order to prove to Noirtier that Valentine had confided in him and that he knew all their secrets, took the dictionary, a pen and a piece of paper and placed them on a table on which there was a lamp. "But first, sir," he said, "allow me to tell you who I am, how I came to love Mademoiselle Valentine and what my plans are with respect to her."

"I'm listening," said Noirtier with his eyes.

It was impressive to see that old man who was a useless burden in appearance, but who had become the sole protector, the only support of two strong young lovers who stood on the threshold of life. Maximilien told him how he had come to know Valentine, how he had fallen in love with her and how she had accepted the offer of his devotion. Then he told him about his family, his position and his fortune.

"Now that I've told you about my love and my hopes, sir," he said, "shall I tell you about our plans?"

"Yes."

Maximilien told Noirtier how a carriage was waiting on the other side of the wall, how he intended to take Valentine to his sister's house, marry her and then respectfully wait and hope for Monsieur de Villefort's pardon.

"No," signaled Noirtier.

"You don't approve of our plan?"

"No."

"Then what shall we do, sir? Madame de Saint-Méran's last words were that Valentine and Monsieur d'Epinay should be married without delay. Must I let this happen?"

Noirtier's eyes remained motionless.

"I understand: I'm to wait."

"Yes."

"But if we wait any longer we'll be lost, sir! Valentine is helpless alone; they'll force her to their will as if she were a child. What about the marriage contract?"

A strange smile appeared in the old man's eyes.

"Do you mean to tell me that it won't be signed?"

"Yes."

"The contract won't ever be signed?" cried Maximilien. "Excuse me, sir, but I can't help being doubtful when I hear such good news. Are you quite sure it won't be signed?"

"Yes."

Despite this assurance, Maximilien hesitated to believe Noirtier. This promise coming from a powerless old man was so strange that, instead of being based on strength of will, it might have been caused by a weakening of his intelligence.

Whether because he understood the young man's doubt or

because he did not completely trust the docility he had shown, Noirtier stared steadfastly at him.

"Do you wish me to renew my promise to wait, sir?" asked Maximilien.

Noirtier's gaze remained firm and fixed, as if to say that a promise was not sufficient, then it turned from Maximilien's face to his hand.

"You want me to swear, is that it?"

"Yes."

Maximilien raised his hand and said, "I swear on my honor to await what you have decided to do before taking any further action."

"Good," said Noirtier's eyes.

"Do you wish me to leave now, sir?"

"Yes."

"Without seeing Mademoiselle Valentine again?"

"Yes."

Maximilien made a gesture of obedience, bowed and left the room.

Chapter 42

Two days later, toward ten o'clock in the morning, the bodies of Monsieur and Madame de Saint-Méran were laid to rest in the Père Lachaise Cemetery, where Monsieur de Villefort had long ago reserved a burial vault which was to serve for his whole family and which already contained the body of his first wife, Renée, Valentine's mother.

Since the religious ceremonies had already been performed in Villefort's house, no funeral orations were made at the cemetery and the mourners dispersed immediately after the bodies were interred. As Franz d'Epinay was about to take leave of Monsieur de Villefort, the latter said to him, "When will I see you again?"

"Whenever you like," replied Franz.

"As soon as possible, then."

"Would you like me to go back with you now?"

"Yes, if it won't inconvenience you."

"Not at all."

The two men returned to Villefort's house. Without speaking to either his wife or his daughter, Villefort showed the young man into his study and invited him to sit down.

"As you know, Monsieur d'Epinay," he began, "Madame de Saint-Méran's last wish was that Valentine's wedding take place without delay. The marriage contract was to have been signed three days ago and is therefore already drawn up. We can sign it today."

"But your house is in mourning," said Franz hesitantly.

"Don't worry, decorum is never neglected in my house. Valentine will spend three months on the estate left to her by Monsieur and Madame de Saint-Méran. A week from now, with your consent, the civil ceremony will be held there quietly and without celebration. Once the marriage is concluded, you may return to Paris while your wife spends her period of mourning with her stepmother."

"As you wish, Monsieur de Villefort," said Franz. "I'd like to request only that Albert de Morcerf and Raoul de Château-Renaud be present as my witnesses."

"Shall I send someone for them or do you prefer to go yourself?"

"I prefer to go myself, sir."

"Very well, then, I'll expect you back here in about half an hour. Valentine will be ready then."

Franz bowed and left. Villefort sent a servant to inform Valentine that the notary and Monsieur d'Epinay's witnesses would be waiting for her in the salon in half an hour.

Valentine felt as though she had been struck by lightning. She decided to go to see her grandfather, but her father met her on the staircase, took her by the arm and led her into the salon. In the antechamber she passed Barrois and cast him a glance full of desperation.

Two carriages arrived in the courtyard at the same time. One of them contained the notary, the other Franz and his two friends. A few moments later everyone was assembled in the salon.

The notary arranged his papers on the table, put on his spectacles, turned to Franz and said, "Monsieur d'Epinay, Monsieur de Villefort has asked me to inform you that your projected marriage with Mademoiselle de Villefort has changed Monsieur Noirtier's intentions with regard to his granddaughter and caused him to disinherit her completely."

"I'm sorry such a question has been raised in Mademoiselle de Villefort's presence," replied Franz. "I've never inquired about the amount of her fortune, which, however reduced it may be, is still considerably larger than my own. What my family seeks in this marriage is prestige; what I seek is happiness."

Valentine made an almost imperceptible gesture of acknowledgment while two large tears rolled down her cheeks.

"Let me add," said Villefort to his future son-in-law, "that there is no reason for you to feel personally offended by Monsieur Noirtier's action, since it is due entirely to his weakness of mind. He would have done the same thing if his grand-daughter had married anyone else, and I am convinced that at this very moment, while he remembers that she is about to be married, he has forgotten the name of the man who is to become her husband."

Villefort had hardly finished speaking when the door of the salon opened and Barrois appeared. "Gentlemen," he said in a voice that was strangely firm for a servant speaking to his masters on such a solemn occasion, "Monsieur Noirtier wishes to speak to Baron Franz d'Epinay immediately."

Villefort started, Valentine stood up as pale and silent as a statue, Albert and Château-Renaud looked at each other in amazement and the notary looked at Villefort.

"That's impossible," said Villefort. "Monsieur d'Epinay cannot leave the salon at this moment."

"In that case," said Barrois, "Monsieur Noirtier has in-structed me to announce that he will have himself brought into the salon."

"Valentine," said Villefort, "please go find out what this latest whim of your grandfather's is about."

Valentine had taken a few rapid steps toward the door when Villefort changed his mind. "Wait," he said, "I'll go with you."

"Excuse me, Monsieur de Villefort," said Franz, "but it seems to me that since Monsieur Noirtier specifically asked to see me it's my duty to comply with his wishes. Besides, I'll be glad to pay him my respects, which I haven't yet had a chance to do."

"Oh, there's no need to trouble yourself," said Villefort with visible uneasiness.

"Excuse me," said Franz in the tone of a man who has made up his mind, "but I don't want to miss this opportunity to prove to Monsieur Noirtier that I intend to overcome his prejudice against me by the loyalty of my devotion." Then, be-fore Villefort could retain him any longer, he stood up and followed Valentine, who was already descending the stairs with the joy of a shipwrecked man who has just felt land un-der his feet. Villefort followed them both.

The three of them found Noirtier waiting for them in his wheelchair.

"This is Monsieur Franz d'Epinay, who has come in obedi-ence to your wishes," said Villefort to Noirtier. "I've been wanting you to meet him for a long time so that you could see how groundless your opposition to Valentine's marriage is."

Noirtier replied with a look that made Villefort shudder. Then he signaled Valentine to approach. In a few moments, using their customary procedure, she had found the word "key," after which Noirtier turned his eyes toward the drawer of a small cabinet standing between the two windows. She opened the drawer and found a key inside it. After confirming that this was the key he wanted, Noirtier looked at an old writing desk which was believed to contain nothing but useless papers.

"Shall I open the writing desk?" asked Valentine.

"Yes."

"Shall I open one of its drawers?"

"Yes."

"One of the side drawers?"

"No."

"The middle one?"

"Yes."

She opened the drawer and drew out a bundle of papers. "Is this what you want, grandfather?" she asked.

"No," signaled the old man. Then he turned his eyes toward the dictionary. Valentine recited the alphabet until he stopped her at the letter S. She opened the dictionary and searched until she came to the word "secret."

"Is there a secret?" she asked.

"Yes."

"And who knows the secret?"

Noirtier looked at the door through which Barrois had gone.

"Is it Barrois?"

"Yes."

"Shall I call him in?"

"Yes."

Valentine went to the door and called Barrois. "Barrois," she said to the old servant when he entered, "my grandfather has instructed me to open the writing desk and pull out this drawer. There's a secret about the drawer and it appears that you know it; open it."

Barrois looked at the old man. "Obey," said Noirtier's intelligent eyes. Barrois opened a double bottom and drew out a bundle of papers tied with a black ribbon. "Is this what you wanted, sir?" he asked.

"Yes."

"To whom shall I give these papers? To Monsieur de Villefort?"

"No."

"To Mademoiselle Valentine?"

"No."

"To Monsieur d'Epinay?"

"Yes."

Franz, surprised, stepped forward and took the papers from Barrois' hands. "What do you want me to do with this?" he asked Noirtier.

"Do you want Monsieur d'Epinay to read the papers?" asked Valentine.

"Yes," signaled the old man.

"We might as well sit down, then," said Villefort impatiently. "It's going to take quite some time to read all that." He sat down, but Valentine remained standing beside his chair, while Franz stood before him.

Franz opened the bundle of papers and began to read:

"Extract from the minutes of a meeting of the Bonapartist Club of the Rue Saint-Jacques held on February 5, 1815."

Franz stopped. "On February 5, 1815!" he cried. "That's the day my father was assassinated! And it was after leaving that club that he disappeared!"

Noirtier's eyes continued to say, "Read!" Franz went on:

"We, the undersigned, Louis-Jacques Beaurepaire, Lieutenant Colonel of Artillery, Etienne Duchampy, Brigadier General, and Claude Lecharpal, Director of Waterways and Forests, do hereby declare that on February 4, 1815, a letter arrived from the Isle of Elba recommending to the members of the Bonapartist Club General Flavien de Quesnal, who, having served under the emperor from 1804 to 1815, was believed to be completely devoted to the Napoleanic dynasty despite the title of baron which Louis XVIII had just attached to his estate at Epinay.

"A letter was therefore addressed to General de Quesnal asking him to attend the meeting to be held on the following day, February 5. The letter gave no address, but it informed the general that if he were willing to go, someone would call for him at nine o'clock in the evening.

"At nine o'clock the president of the club presented himself at the general's house. The general was ready. The president told him that one of the conditions of his presence at the meeting was that he remain forever ignorant of the place in which it was held, that he allow himself to be blindfolded and that he swear not to try to raise the blindfold at any time. The general agreed to this and swore on his honor not to try to see where he was being taken. On the way the president noticed the general trying to look from under his blindfold and reminded him of his oath. 'Oh, yes, that's true,' replied the general.

"The carriage stopped in an alley issuing into the Rue Saint-Jacques. The general, holding the president's arm, alighted, walked down the alley, mounted a flight of stairs and entered the room in which the meeting was being held. There the general was told he could take off his blindfold. When he did so he was amazed to find that so many men of his acquaintance were members of a secret society whose existence he had not even suspected until then. He was questioned about his political opinions, but he answered only that the letter from Elba should have made them clear."

Franz interrupted his reading and said, "My father was a royalist. There was no need to question him about his political opinions; they were well known."

"And that accounts for my friendship with your father," said Villefort. "It's easy to be friends when one shares the same opinions."

Franz continued reading:

"The president urged the general to express his opinions more explicitly, but the general replied that he first wished to know what was expected of him. He was then shown the letter from Elba which recommended him to the club as a man whose aid could be counted on. An entire paragraph in the letter was devoted to the emperor's forthcoming return from the Isle of Elba and stated that more ample details would be given in another letter to be delivered after the arrival of the *Pharaon*, a ship belonging to the firm of Morrel and Son of Marseilles whose captain was completely devoted to the emperor.

"As he read the letter, General de Quesnal, whom the members of the club believed they could trust as one of them, gave visible signs of dissatisfaction and repugnance. When he had finished reading it he remained silent and frowning.

" 'Well, what do you say to that letter, general?' asked the president.

" 'I say that the oath of loyalty to King Louis XVIII is too recent to be violated in favor of the ex-emperor,' replied the general.

"This answer was clear enough to remove any doubts about his opinions.

" 'General,' said the president, 'for us there is no King Louis XVIII and there is no ex-emperor. There is only His Majesty the Emperor, who has been exiled from France, his country, for the last ten months by violence and treason.'

" 'Excuse me, gentlemen,' said the general, 'but while there may be no King Louis XVIII for you, there is for me. He made me a baron and a field marshal, and I will never forget that I owe these two honors to his fortunate return to France.'

" 'Be careful of what you say, general,' said the president, standing up. 'You've shown us clearly that we were mistaken about you: a title and a rank have been enough to rally your support to the new government which we wish to overthrow. We will not force you to help us or join our society, but we will force you to act like a man of honor, even if you don't feel disposed to do so.'

" 'Do you call it being honorable to know about your plot and not reveal it? I call that being your accomplice!'

" 'You weren't brought to this meeting by force,' said the president, 'and when we asked you to remain blindfolded on the way here, you accepted the condition. You knew when you came here that we weren't occupied in consolidating Louis XVIII's position, otherwise we wouldn't have taken so much trouble to hide ourselves from the police. Now it would be too convenient to put on a mask in order to learn a secret, then take it off and betray those who trusted you. First of all you will tell us frankly whether you are for the king who happens to be reigning for the moment or for His Majesty the Emperor.'

" 'I am a royalist,' replied the general. 'I have sworn loyalty to Louis XVIII and I will keep my oath.'

"These words were followed by a general murmur. It was evident that many members of the club were considering making General de Quesnal regret his rashness.

"The president imposed silence. 'General,' he said, 'you're too sensible a man not to undersand the consequences of this situation, and your frankness dictates the terms we must make with you. You must swear on your honor not to reveal what you have learned here.'

"The general put his hand to his sword and cried out, 'If you speak of honor, begin by acknowledging its laws and don't impose anything on me by violence!'"

" 'And you, sir,' said the president with a calm which was more impressive than the general's anger, 'don't touch your sword. I advise you strongly against it.'

"The general looked around him with a beginning of uneasiness. Nevertheless he said firmly, 'I will not swear.'

" 'In that case, sir, you will die,' said the president.

"The general turned pale and looked around him once again. Several members of the club were whispering to each other and reaching for weapons under their cloaks. But the general still said nothing.

" 'Lock the doors,' said the president to the guards.

"Then the general stepped forward and said, making a

violent effort to control himself, 'I have a son; since I find myself in the midst of a group of murderers, I must think of him.'

" 'One man always has the right to insult fifty,' said the president, 'that's the privilege of weakness. But you're wrong to use that right. Swear, general, and don't insult us.'

"The general, once again subdued by the president's superiority, hesitated a moment, then asked, 'What oath do you wish me to swear?'

" 'Here it is: "I swear on my honor never to reveal to anyone what I have heard on the night of February 5, 1815, between nine and ten o'clock, and I declare that I deserve death if I violate my oath." '

"The general appeared to undergo a fit of nervous trembling which prevented him from replying for several seconds. Finally, with manifest repugnance, he pronounced the oath demanded of him, but in so low a voice that it was difficult to hear. Several members demanded that he repeat it more loudly, which he did. Then he asked, 'Am I free to leave?'

"The president stood up, designated three members of the club to accompany him and climbed into a carriage with the general, after having blindfolded him.

" 'Where do you wish us to take you?' asked the president.

" 'Anywhere, as long as I can rid myself of your presence,' replied General de Quesnal.

" 'Be careful,' said the president, 'you're no longer at the meeting. You're now dealing with individual men; don't insult them unless you want to be held responsible for the insult.'

"But, instead of understanding this language, the general replied, 'You're just as brave in your carriage as in your club, for the simple reason that four men are always stronger than one.'

"The president ordered the carriage to be stopped. They had just arrived at the entrance to the Quai des Ormes, where there are steps leading down to the river.

" 'Why have you stopped here?' asked the general.

" 'Because you have insulted a man,' said the president, 'and because that man will not go one step further without demanding honorable reparation.'

" 'This is only a different form of murder!' said the general.

" 'Don't try to call for help,' said the president, 'unless you want me to regard you as one of those men of whom I was speaking at the club, that is, as a coward who uses his weakness as a shield. You're alone now and only one man will answer you. You have a sword at your side and I have one in this cane. One of these gentlemen will be your second. You may now take off your blindfold.' The general tore it off at once. The four men alighted from the carriage."

Franz stopped reading once again to wipe away the cold sweat streaming down his forehead. There was something almost frightening about the sight of that son as he read aloud the hitherto unknown details of his father's death.

Noirtier looked at Villefort with a sublime expression of contempt and pride.

Franz continued reading:

"It was, as we have said, the fifth of February. The weather had been freezing for three consecutive days and the steps going down to the river's edge were covered with ice. One of the seconds borrowed a lantern from a nearby coal barge. The weapons were examined by the light of this lantern. The president's sword, which was merely a sword he carried in a cane, was shorter than the general's and had no guard. The general suggested drawing lots for the two swords, but the president said that it was he who had challenged, and that in challenging he had assumed that each man would use his own weapon. The seconds attempted to insist, but the president imposed silence on them.

"The lantern was placed on the ground, the two adversaries stood on each side of it and the duel began. The general was considered one of the best swordsmen in the army, but he was attacked so vigorously that he was obliged to give ground, and in doing so he fell. The seconds thought he had been killed, but his opponent, who knew he had not touched him, gave him his hand to help him to his feet. This incident, instead of calming him, irritated him and he began to press the attack, but the president did not give one inch of ground. The general recoiled three times, finding himself too closely pressed, and then returned to the attack. The third time he fell again. The seconds believed he had lost his balance again, as before, but when one of them attempted to help him to his feet he felt something warm and wet on his hands. It was blood.

"The general, who was almost unconscious, regained his senses and said, 'Oh, they've sent some hired assassin or some army fencing-master to fight me!' Without answering, the president went over to the second who was holding the lantern, rolled up his sleeve and showed that his arm had been pierced in two places; then, opening his coat and unbuttoning his vest, he showed a third wound in his side. Yet he had not so much as heaved a sigh.

"The general died five minutes later."

Franz read these last words in such a choked voice that they were almost unintelligible. He stopped and passed his hand over his eyes, but after a moment of silence he continued:

"The president walked back up the steps, leaving a trail of blood behind him on the snow. A few moments later he heard the sound of the general's body being thrown into the river by the seconds after they had made sure of his death.

"The general therefore died in an honorable duel and not in an ambush, as may be believed.

"In witness whereof we hereby sign this statement in order to establish the truth of these facts in anticipation of a time when one of the participants in the scene may find himself accused of premeditated murder or violation of the laws of honor.

"Signed: BEAUREPAIRE
           DUCHAMPY
           LECHARPAL."

"Monsieur Noirtier," said Franz, when he had finished reading the terrible document, "since you know all the details of this event, please don't deny me the satisfaction of learning the name of the president of the club, so that I may at last know the man who killed my poor father."

As though in a daze, Villefort reached for the doorknob, while Valentine, who had understood the old man's answer before anyone else and who had often noticed two sword scars on his forearm, stepped back in alarm.

"The only thing that gave me the strength to read that document through to the end was the hope of learning who killed my father," continued Franz. "In the name of God, Monsieur Noirtier, find some way to tell me—to make me understand——"

"Yes," signaled Noirtier. Then he turned his eyes toward the dictionary.

Franz picked it up with trembling hands and began to recite the letters of the alphabet until the old man stopped him at M. Franz ran his finger along the columns of the dictionary while Valentine hid her head between her hands. Finally he came to the word "myself."

"Yes," said Noirtier's eyes.

"You!" cried Franz. "You, Monsieur Noirtier! Was it you who killed my father?"

"Yes," answered Noirtier, looking at the young man with a majestic expression.

Franz sank lifelessly into a chair.

Villefort opened the door and fled, for he had just been seized with an impulse to choke out the little life that still remained in the old man's implacable heart.

Chapter 43

Franz left Noirtier's room in such a state of shock that even Valentine felt pity for him. Villefort muttered a few incoherent words, left hurriedly and locked himself in his study. Two hours later he received the following letter:

"In view of the facts revealed this morning, Monsieur Noirtier de Villefort cannot believe that an alliance is possible between his family and that of Monsieur Franz d'Epinay. Monsieur d'Epinay is shocked at the thought that Monsieur de Villefort, who appeared to be aware of the events related this morning, nevertheless made no move to anticipate him in this conclusion."

This harsh letter from a young man who until then had been so respectful was a deadly blow to the pride of a man like Villefort.

Meanwhile Valentine, happy and frightened at the same time, kissed and thanked her grandfather, who with a single stroke had shattered a chain which she had regarded as unbreakable. Then she asked his permission to go to her room to calm her nerves, a permission which he granted with his eyes.

But instead of going to her room she went out into the garden. Maximilien was waiting for her at the grill. He had seen Franz and Villefort leave the cemetery together after the funeral of Monsieur and Madame de Saint-Méran and had suspected what was about to take place. He had therefore taken up his post outside the wall, ready for action and convinced that Valentine would come running out to him at the first opportunity.

At his first sight of her he felt reassured; at her first words his heart leaped with joy.

"We're saved!" said Valentine.

"Saved?" repeated Maximilien, unable to believe in such good fortune. "Who saved us?"

"My grandfather. Oh, you must love him, Maximilien!"

Maximilien swore to love the old man with all his heart; the oath was not difficult for him because at that moment he did not content himself with loving him as a friend or like a father: he worshiped him like a god.

"But how did he do it?" asked Maximilien.

Valentine opened her mouth to tell him everything, but then she realized that the story involved a terrible secret which did not belong entirely to her grandfather. "I'll tell you about it later," she said.

"When?"

"When I'm your wife."

This gave the conversation a turn which made Maximilien glad to agree to anything; he therefore agreed to content himself with what Valentine had already told him, which was enough for one day. He did, however, demand that she promise to see him the following day, which she was glad to do. Her outlook had changed completely: it was now easier for her to believe that she would marry Maximilien than it had been to believe that she would not marry Franz.

The next day Monsieur Noirtier had the notary called in again. His former will was torn up and a new one made in which he left his entire fortune to Valentine provided she were not separated from him.

A number of people soon calculated that Mademoiselle de Villefort, sole heiress of Monsieur and Madame de Saint-Méran and once again restored to her grandfather's good graces, would some day have an income of nearly three hundred thousand francs a year.

While Valentine's marriage was being broken off, the Count of Morcerf had put on his lieutenant general's uniform, decorated it with all his crosses, asked for his best horses and set out to pay a visit to Baron Danglars.

The banker was engaged in calculating his monthly balance, and for some time past this had not been the best time to find him in a good humor. When his old friend entered he assumed his most majestic air and sat upright in his chair. On the other hand, Morcerf, who was usually so stiff and formal, was on this occasion smiling and affable. "Well, baron, here I am," he said. "For some time now we've done nothing to carry out the plans we discussed——"

"What plans, count?" asked Danglars, as though vainly seeking to recall what Morcerf was talking about.

"Ah, I see you're a formalist and that you want a ceremony according to the rules. Very well, then." And Morcerf, with a forced smile, stood up, bowed deeply to Danglars and said, "Baron Danglars, I have the honor of requesting the hand of your daughter, Mademoiselle Eugénie Danglars, for my son, Viscount Albert de Morcerf."

But Danglars, instead of receiving these words with the favor Morcerf had expected, frowned and said, "Before giving you an answer, count, I must have time to reflect."

"To reflect!" exclaimed Morcerf, more and more astonished. "Haven't you had time to reflect in the eight years since we first discussed this marriage?"

"Count, every day things happen which make us reconsider matters we had once believed to be definitely settled."

"Excuse me, baron, but I don't understand what you're saying."

"I'm saying that certain new circumstances have arisen recently and that——"

"Those are vague, empty words, baron," said Morcerf. "They might satisfy an ordinary man, but the Count of Morcerf is not an ordinary man. When someone withdraws a promise made to him, he has the right to demand that he be given a good reason."

Although Danglars was a coward, he did not wish to appear to be one; furthermore, he was irritated by the tone in which Morcerf had just spoken to him. "I have a good reason," he replied, "but it would be difficult to tell it to you."

"In any case, one thing is clear: you refuse to marry your daughter to my son."

"No, I'm only postponing my decision."

"But surely you can't have the arrogance to imagine that I'm going to submit to your whims and humbly await a return of your good graces!"

"If you can't wait, let's consider our plans as canceled."

Morcerf bit his lip to keep back the outburst which his proud and irritable character inclined him to make, realizing that he was the one who would appear ridiculous in such a scene. He was already on his way out of the room when he changed his mind, turned around and came back. A cloud had just passed over his face, leaving a trace of vague uneasiness in place of the expression of offended pride that had been there a moment before. "We've known each other for many years, baron," he said, "so we ought to have some consideration for each other. The least you can do is to tell me what unfortunate event has caused my son to lose favor in your eyes."

"It doesn't concern your son personally; that's all I can tell you," replied Danglars, becoming insolent again as he saw Morcerf's attitude softening.

"And whom does it concern, then?" asked Morcerf uneasily.

Danglars looked at him with more self-assurance than he had hitherto shown and said, "Be grateful to me for not giving you a more detailed explanation."

Chapter 44

Maximilien was a happy man. Monsieur Noirtier had just sent for him and he was in such a hurry to learn the reason that, trusting his own legs more than those of a cab horse, he set out for the Faubourg Saint-Honoré on foot, with poor Barrois following his rapid pace as best he could. Maximilien was thirty years old. Barrois was sixty; Maximilien was intoxicated with love, Barrois was exhausted by the heat; Maximilien was not even out of breath when they arrived, for love lends wings, but Barrois, who had not been in love for many long years, was bathed in perspiration.

The old servant let Maximilien in through a private door, and before long the rustling of a dress announced Valentine's arrival. She was strikingly beautiful in her mourning clothes. Maximilien was so enchanted by the sight of her that he would have been glad to do without speaking to Noirtier, but the old man soon rolled into the room in his wheelchair.

Noirtier acknowledged with a benevolent look Maximilien's effusive thanks for the marvelous intervention which had saved Valentine and himself from despair. Then he looked at Valentine, who was sitting timidly in a corner.

"Do you want me to say everything you told me to?" she asked.

"Yes," signaled Noirtier.

"Maximilien, my grandfather has told me many things in the last three days," said Valentine. "He sent for you today so that I could repeat them to you. Since he has chosen me for his interpreter, I will tell them to you exactly as he wishes."

"I'm listening impatiently," said Maximilien. Valentine had lowered her eyes, which filled him with hope, for she was weak only when she was happy.

"My grandfather wants to leave this house," she said. "Barrois is going to find him a suitable apartment. If my father gives me permission to go and live with my grandfather, I'll leave immediately; if he does not, I'll wait till I'm of age, which will be eighteen months from now. Then I'll be free, I'll have an independent fortune and——"

"And?" asked Maximilien.

"And, with my grandfather's permission, I'll keep the promise I've made to you."

These last words were spoken so softly that Maximilien would not have heard them if it had not been for the extreme attention with which he was listening.

"Have I expressed your thoughts correctly, grandfather?" asked Valentine.

"Yes," signaled the old man.

"Oh!" cried Maximilien, tempted to kneel before Noirtier as before God and before Valentine as before an angel. "What have I done in my life to deserve such happiness?"

Noirtier looked at the two young lovers with deep affection. Barrois, who had been standing in the background, smiled as he wiped away the large drops of perspiration which continued to stream down his bald forehead.

"Oh, how hot poor old Barrois is!" said Valentine.

"That's because I was running so fast, mademoiselle," said Barrois, "but I must admit Monsieur Morrel was running even faster than I was."

Noirtier turned his eyes toward a tray on which there was a pitcher of lemonade and a glass. Noirtier himself had drunk some of the lemonade half an hour earlier.

"Have some of this lemonade, Barrois," said Valentine. "I see you're looking at it longingly."

"To tell you the truth, mademoiselle, I'm dying of thirst," replied Barrois, "and I'd be glad to toast your health with a glass of that lemonade."

"Drink some of it, then, and come back after a while."

Barrois carried out the tray and as soon as he was in the hall he emptied the glass which Valentine had filled for him.

Valentine and Maximilien were saying good-bye to each other when they heard a bell ring on Villefort's staircase. This was the signal for a visit. Valentine looked at the clock. "It's noon," she said, "and today is Saturday, so it must be the doctor. Shall Maximilien leave, grandfather?"

"Yes."

"Barrois!" called Valentine. "Come in here, please."

The old servant's voice was heard replying, "I'm coming, mademoiselle."

"Barrois will show you to the door," said Valentine to Maximilien. Just then Barrois entered. "Who rang?" asked Valentine.

"Doctor d'Avrigny," said Barrois, staggering.

"What's the matter with you, Barrois?" asked Valentine.

Barrois did not answer; he looked at his master with frightened eyes and put out his hand for something on which to steady himself.

"He's going to fall!" cried Maximilien.

Barrois' trembling became more violent and the twitching of his facial muscles announced the onslaught of an intense nervous attack. He took a few steps toward Noirtier. "Oh, my God!" he gasped. "What's the matter with me? I'm in pain— my eyes are going dim—my head feels as if it's on fire. Oh, don't touch me! Don't touch me!" His eyes took on a wild expression and his head fell backward while the rest of his body stiffened.

"Doctor d'Avrigny! Doctor d'Avrigny!" cried Valentine. "Come here quickly! Help!"

Barrois turned around, staggered backwards, stumbled and fell at Noirtier's feet.

Villefort, drawn by Valentine's cries, appeared in the doorway. Maximilien immediately concealed himself behind a curtain. Noirtier was burning with impatience and terror as his whole soul went out to the poor old man who was his friend rather than his servant. Barrois, his face twitching, his eyes bloodshot, his neck bent backward, lay on the floor thrashing about him with his hands; his legs had become so stiff that they looked as though they would break before they would bend. Flecks of foam began to appear on his lips as he panted painfully.

Villefort stood looking at him for a moment in stupefaction. He had not seen Maximilien. Then he turned and rushed out of the room again, shouting, "Doctor! Doctor! Come here!"

Madame de Villefort entered slowly. Her first glance was at Noirtier, who, except for the emotion natural in such circumstances, appeared to be in normal health. Then she looked at the dying Barrois.

"In the name of God, madame, where's the doctor?" said Valentine.

"He's in Edouard's room examining him; he's a little sick today," replied Madame de Villefort. Then she left the room.

Maximilien came out from behind the curtain, where no one had noticed him in the midst of all the confusion.

"Leave quickly, Maximilien," said Valentine, "and wait for me to send for you." He pressed her hand to his heart and left by way of the private corridor.

Just then Villefort and the doctor came in through the opposite door. Barrois was beginning to come back to his senses. The first attack had passed; he gave a low moan and raised himself up on one knee. Villefort and d'Avrigny carried him to a sofa.

"What do you prescribe, doctor?" asked Villefort.

"Bring me some water and ether. Do you have some in the house?"

"Yes."

"And send someone for some oil of turpentine and some tartar emetic."

"Go!" said Villefort to one of his servants.

"And now I want everyone to leave the room."

"Shall I go too?" asked Valentine timidly.

"Yes, mademoiselle, especially you," replied the doctor curtly.

Valentine looked at him in astonishment, kissed Noirtier on the forehead and went out. The doctor closed the door behind her with a somber air.

"How do you feel now, Barrois?" he asked.

"A little better, sir."

"Can you drink this glass of water and ether?"

"I'll try, but don't touch me."

"Why not?"

"Because it seems to me that if you touched me, even with the tip of your finger, the attack would come back."

"Drink."

Barrois took the glass, approached his violet lips to it and drank about half of its contents.

"Did the attack seize you rapidly?" asked the doctor.

"Like lightning."

"You felt nothing yesterday or the day before?"

"No, nothing."

"What have you eaten today?"

"I haven't eaten anything today; I drank a little of Monsieur Noirtier's lemonade, that's all." Barrois nodded toward Noirtier, who, motionless in his wheelchair, was taking in the whole scene without losing a single movement or a single word.

"Where is that lemonade?" asked the doctor eagerly.

"In the pitcher, downstairs in the kitchen."

"Shall I go bring it you you, doctor?" asked Villefort.

"No, stay here—I'll go get it myself," replied Doctor d'Avrigny. He rushed out the door and down the servants' staircase, where he almost knocked over Madame de Villefort, who was also going down to the kitchen. She screamed, but he paid no attention to her. Obsessed by a single idea, he leaped down the last three or four steps, ran into the kitchen and saw the pitcher still standing on the tray. It was three-quarters empty. He pounced on it like an eagle on its prey, ran back up the stairs and entered Noirtier's room out of breath. Madame de Villefort walked slowly up the stairs leading to her own room.

"Is this the pitcher that was here?" asked d'Avrigny.

"Yes, sir," replied Barrois.

"And is this the same lemonade you drank?"

"I think so."

"How did it taste to you?"

"A little bitter."

The doctor poured out a few drops of it into the hollow of his hands, rinsed his mouth with it as one does when tasting wine, then spat it out into the fireplace. "It's the same, all right," he said. "Did you drink some of it too, Monsieur Noirtier?"

"Yes," signaled the old man.

"And did you also notice a bitter taste?"

"Yes."

"Oh, doctor!" cried Barrois. "It's coming back! Dear God, have pity on me!"

"See if they're bringing the emetic," said the doctor to Villefort.

Villefort ran out of the room crying, "The emetic! The emetic! Have they brought it yet?"

No one answered. A profound terror reigned over the entire house.

Barrois was seized with an attack even more intense than the first one. The doctor, unable to give him any relief, left him and went over to Noirtier.

"How do you feel?" he asked him in a low voice. "Do you feel well?"

"Yes," signaled Noirtier.

"Did Barrois make your lemonade today?"

"Yes."

"Was it you who asked him to drink some of it?"

"No."

"Was it Monsieur de Villefort?"

"No."

"Madame de Villefort?"

"Valentine?"

"Yes."

D'Avrigny went over to Barrois and asked, "Who made the lemonade?"

"I did."

"Did you bring it to Monsieur Noirtier as soon as you made it?"

"No, I was called away, so I left it in the pantry."

"Who brought it here, then?"

"Mademoiselle Valentine."

The doctor struck his forehead and murmured, "Oh, my God! My God!"

"Doctor! Doctor!" cried Barrois, who felt a third attack coming on. "I'm choking! Oh, my heart! My head! Will I suffer long, doctor?"

"No, no, my friend, your suffering will be over soon."

"I understand!" cried the wretched Barrois. "God have mercy on me!" He fell back with a loud cry, as though he had been struck by lightning.

The doctor felt his heart and said to Villefort, "Go down to the kitchen and bring me some syrup of violets."

Villefort went out and returned a moment later. "Is he still unconscious?" he asked.

"He's dead," replied the doctor.

Villefort stepped back, gripped his head between his hands and said with unfeigned pity, "Dead so soon?"

"Yes, it was quick, wasn't it?" said the doctor. "But that shouldn't surprise you: Monsieur and Madame de Saint-Méran also died suddenly. People die quickly in your house, Monsieur de Villefort!"

"What!" cried Villefort in horror and consternation. "Are you still possessed with that terrible idea?"

"It has never left me for a moment," replied the doctor gravely. "And I'll prove to you that I'm not mistaken this time. Listen to me carefully, Monsieur de Villefort." Villefort trembled convulsively. "There is a poison which kills almost without leaving a trace," continued the doctor. "I have studied that poison and am thoroughly acquainted with its effects. I recognized them just now in poor Barrois and I recognized them in Madame de Saint-Méran. There is a way to determine the presence of that poison: it turns red litmus paper blue and turns syrup of violets green. We have no litmus paper here, but we do have the syrup of violets I asked you to bring me. Watch."

The doctor slowly poured a few drops of lemonade into the cup containing the syrup of violets. The syrup took on a cloudly bluish color at first, then gradually changed to green. The experiment left no room for doubt.

"Poor Barrois was poisoned with brucine," said Doctor d'Avrigny. "I am now ready to answer for that fact before God and before men."

Villefort sank helplessly into a chair without saying a word, apparently as lifeless as Barrois' body. The doctor soon brought him back to his senses.

"Oh, death is in my house!" cried Villefort.

"Murder is in your house," replied the doctor. "Do you

think the poison was intended for that poor servant? Noirtier drank some of the lemonade in the natural course of things, Barrois drank some only by accident; and although it was Barrois who died, it was Noirtier who was meant to die."

"But then why is my father still alive?"

"As I told you that night in the garden after the death of Madame de Saint-Méran, his body has become accustomed to that very poison, so that a dose that was insignificant to him was fatal to Barrois. No one, not even the murderer, knows I've been treating Monsieur Noirtier's paralysis with brucine. Now let's follow the murderer's actions: first he kills Monsieur de Saint-Méran, then Madame de Saint-Méran—a double inheritance to receive. Monsieur Noirtier had disinherited his family and left his fortune to the poor; he was spared. But as soon as he changed his will be became the next victim. The new will was made only day before yesterday, so, as you can see, no time was lost."

"Oh, have mercy on my daughter, Monsieur d'Avrigny!" murmured Villefort.

"Ah, you've named her yourself, you, her own father!"

"Have mercy on Valentine! Listen to me, it's impossible. I'd rather accuse myself than her!"

"No mercy! The crime is flagrant. Your daughter packed the medicine that was sent to Monsieur de Saint-Méran and he died. She prepared Madame de Saint-Méran's beverages and she died. She brought a pitcher of lemonade to Monsieur Noirtier and he escaped only by a miracle."

"Listen to me!" cried Villefort. "Pity me—help me! No, my daughter is not guilty. I will not drag my daughter to the hangman with my own hands. The very thought of it makes me want to tear my heart out! And what if you were mistaken, doctor? What if it were someone else than my daughter? What if I were to come to you some day, pale as a ghost, and say to you, 'Murderer! You killed my daughter!' "

"Very well," said the doctor, after a moment of silence, "I'll wait." Villefort looked at him as if he had difficulty in believing his own ears. "But," continued the doctor in a slow and solemn tone, "if someone else in your house falls ill, or if you yourself should be stricken, don't call me, for I will never come here again. I'm willing to share your terrible secret with you, but I'm not willing to have shame and remorse grow in my conscience as crime and grief are going to grow in your house. Good-bye, Monsieur de Villefort."

Chapter 45

It was late at night when Andrea Cavalcanti returned to the Hôtel des Princes, but no sooner had he set foot in the courtyard than he found the concierge of the hotel waiting for him, cap in hand.

"Sir, that man was here," said the concierge.

"What man?" asked Andrea nonchalantly, as though he had forgotten the man whom he actually remembered only too well.

"The one you pay a little pension to, Excellency."

"Oh, yes," said Andrea. "That old servant of my father's. Well, did you give him the two hundred francs I left for him?"

"He refused to take the money, Excellency."

"What!"

"He said he wanted to speak to you, Excellency. At first he wouldn't believe me when I told him you were out, but I finally convinced him and he left this letter for you."

"Let's have it," said Andrea. He took the letter and read these words: "You know where I live. I will expect you tomorrow morning at nine o'clock."

"Come up to my room when you've finished with the horses," said Andrea to his groom.

He had just finished burning Caderousse's letter when the groom entered. "You're about my size, aren't you, Pierre?" asked Andrea.

"I have that honor, Excellency," replied the groom.

"I have an appointment with a girl tonight and I don't want her to know who I am; lend me your clothes and your papers so that I can sleep in a hotel tonight."

The groom obeyed. Five minutes later Andrea, completely disguised, left the Hôtel des Princes without being recognized, hired a cab and had himself taken to the Auberge du Cheval Rouge in Picpus.

The next morning he left the inn, went to the Rue Ménilmontant and stopped before the door of the third house on the left.

"Are you looking for someone?" asked a fruitseller on the other side of the street.

"I'm looking for Monsieur Pailletin."

"The retired baker?"

"That's right."

268

"Take the stairway on your left at the end of the court-yard; he lives on the fourth floor."

Andrea followed these directions and rang at the door on the fourth floor. A moment later Caderousse's face appeared behind the grating of the door. "You're right on time," he said. He unlocked the door.

On entering the room, Andrea angrily threw his cap at a chair; it missed and rolled across the floor. "Don't be angry, my boy," said Caderousse. "Look at the good breakfast we're going to have: nothing but things you like!"

Andrea smelled that odor of garlic and fresh grease given off by Provençal cooking of an inferior order. In the next room he saw a table set for two, with two bottles of wine, a generous measure of brandy in a decanter and a fruit salad in a cabbage leaf carefully arranged on an earthenware plate.

"If you asked me to come here just to have breakfast with you, you can go to the devil!" said Andrea irritably.

"My boy," said Caderousse sententiously, "it's good to talk while eating. And aren't you happy to see your old friend again? I'm overjoyed."

"Hypocrite!" said Andrea.

"If I didn't like you, would I put up with the miserable life you make me lead? I see you're wearing your servant's clothes. Well, I could have a servant, too. I could have a tilbury like you, and I could eat in fashionable restaurants the way you do. And why do I deprive myself of all that? Because I don't want to cause any trouble for my friend Bene-detto. But you'll have to admit I could have those things if I wanted to, isn't that right?" Caderousse's eyes made the meaning of his sentence perfectly clear. "Meanwhile," he continued, "sit down and let's eat."

Andrea opened the bottles and energetically attacked the bouillabaisse; young and vigorous as he was, his appetite still prevailed over everything else.

"Isn't that good?" asked Caderousse.

"It's so good that I don't understand how a man who can cook and eat such good things could ever be unhappy."

"And yet all my happiness is spoiled by one thought," said Caderousse.

"What's that?"

"The thought that I'm living at the expense of a friend, I who always earned my own living before."

"Oh, don't worry about that: I have enough for two."

"Just the same, I'm full of remorse. But I have an idea."

Andrea shuddered; Caderousse's ideas always made him shudder. "It's a shame the way you always have to wait till the

end of the month for your allowance," continued Caderousse.
"If I were you, I'd ask for six months' allowance in advance, on the pretext that I wanted to buy a farm, then I'd
take the money and disappear."

"Why don't you follow your own advice?" asked Andrea.
"Why don't you take six months of your allowance in advance, or even a year, and go to Brussels with it?"

"How do you expect me to live on twelve hundred francs?
I have a better plan. Could you, without spending a sou of
your own money, let me have fifteen thousand francs? No,
wait a moment, that's not enough—I don't want to become
an honest man for less than thirty thousand."

"No, I can't do it," replied Andrea curtly.

"I don't think you understood me: I said 'without spending
a sou of your own money.' "

"Do you want me to steal so I can spoil everything for both
of us and get us both put back in prison?"

"Oh, I don't care whether they catch us or not," said Caderousse. "I often miss our friends back there in prison. I'm not
heartless like you—you never want to see them again!"

This time Andrea not only shuddered, but turned pale.
"Don't do anything foolish, Caderousse!" he cried.

"Don't worry, Benedetto my friend; all you have to do is
find a way for me to earn the thirty thousand francs for myself without involving yourself in any way."

"All right, I'll try. I'll keep my eyes open."

"In the meantime, I want you to increase my allowance to
five hundred francs. I'd like to hire a maid."

"All right, you'll have your five hundred francs, but it's
going to be hard for me."

"I don't see why," said Caderousse, "since your money
comes from a limitless supply."

Andrea seemed to have been waiting for this remark: a
gleam appeared in his eyes, then vanished almost instantly.
"Yes," he said, "the Count of Monte Cristo treats me very
well."

"He's very rich, isn't he?"

"He certainly is! I go to his house often, so I can see for
myself. The other day a banker's clerk brought him fifty
thousand francs in a portfolio; yesterday a banker brought
him a hundred thousand francs in gold."

"And you go into that house?" asked Caderousse eagerly.

"Whenever I like."

Caderousse remained silent for a moment; it was easy to
see that he was turning over some profound thought in his
mind. Then suddenly he said, "Oh, how I'd like to see that!
It must be wonderful!"

"It's magnificent."

"Doesn't he live on the Avenue des Champs Elysées?"

"Yes, at number thirty."

"You'll have to take me there some day."

"You know that's impossible."

"Yes, I suppose you're right. But tell me about it. Is it a big house?"

"Not too big and not too little."

"How is it laid out?"

"I'd have to draw you a plan."

"Here!" said Caderousse, going over to a desk and taking a sheet of paper, some ink and a pen.

Andrea picked up the pen with an almost imperceptible smile and began to draw. "The house is between a courtyard and a garden, like this," he said.

"Are the walls high?" asked Caderousse.

"No: eight or ten feet at the most."

"Let's see what the first floor is like."

"On the first floor there are two salons, a dining room and a billiard room."

"What are the windows like?"

"Magnificent—they're so big I think a man of my size could pass through each pane."

"What about the shutters?"

"They're never closed. The count is eccentric and likes to see the sky at night."

"Where do the servants sleep?"

"They sleep in a separate building, on your right as you enter. Only yesterday I was saying to the count, 'It's careless of you, count: when you go to Auteuil and take your servants with you, your house is completely empty; one fine day it's going to be robbed.'"

"And what did he answer?"

"He said, 'What do I care if I'm robbed?'"

"He must have some sort of mechanical desk."

"What do you mean?"

"One that catches a thief in a trap and sets off an automatic alarm. There was one like that at the last exposition."

"No, he has only an ordinary desk."

"And no one ever steals anything from it?"

"No, his servants are very devoted to him."

"There must be plenty in that drawer, eh?"

"Probably; no one knows exactly what's in it."

"Where is it?"

"On the second floor."

"Draw me a plan of the second floor, as you did for the first floor."

"All right." Andrea took up his pen again. "Here's an antechamber and a salon," he said. "To the left of the salon, there's a library and a study; to the right of the salon there's a bedroom and a dressing room. The desk is in the dressing room."

"Is there a window in the dressing room?"

"There are two of them—here and here." Andrea drew in the windows on his plan.

Caderousse became thoughtful. "Does he go to Auteuil often?" he asked.

"Two or three times a week. Tomorrow, for example, he's going to spend the day there and stay overnight."

"Are you sure?"

"He asked me to come to dinner there."

"Will you go?"

"Probably."

"And when you go there for dinner, do you stay overnight?"

"If I feel like it."

Caderousse looked at the young man as though to tear out the truth from the bottom of his heart, but Andrea took a case of cigars from his pocket, calmly lit one of them and began to smoke in a perfectly natural manner. "When would you like your five hundred francs?" he asked.

"Right now, if you have it."

"I don't carry five hundred francs in my pocket."

"Then leave it with your concierge and I'll stop by for it."

"Today?"

"No, tomorrow; I won't have time today."

"All right, tomorrow. And you won't bother me any more, will you?"

"Never. But let me give you some friendly advice."

"What is it?"

"I advise you to leave that diamond ring with me. How can you make such a stupid mistake? Are you trying to get us both caught again?"

"What do you mean?"

"You've dressed yourself like a servant, but you're still wearing a diamond ring worth four or five thousand francs!"

"That's a very accurate appraisal. You ought to be an auctioneer."

"I know something about diamonds; I had one once."

Without becoming angry at this new extortion, as Caderousse had feared he might, Andrea obligingly handed over the ring. "Is there anything else you want?" he asked. "Do you need my jacket? How about my cap? Don't be ashamed to ask."

"All right, I won't keep you any longer and I'll try to cure myself of my greed. Wait a moment, I'll show you to the door."

"Never mind."

"I'll have to."

"Why?"

"Because there's a little secret on the door, a precaution I thought it advisable to take—one of Huret and Fichet's locks, revised and corrected by Gaspard Caderousse. I'll make one for you when you become a capitalist."

"Thanks," said Andrea. "I'll let you know a week in advance."

They parted. Caderousse remained on the landing until he had seen Andrea walk down all three flights of stairs and cross the courtyard. Then he hurried back into his room, carefully locked the door and began to study with profound attention the plan which Andrea had left him.

Chapter 46

The day after this conversation, the Count of Monte Cristo went to his country house in Auteuil with Ali and a few other servants. While he was there Bertuccio arrived from Normandy with news of the house which the count had instructed him to buy there. It was now ready, and the corvette, manned by a crew of six, was anchored in a small cove nearby, ready to put to sea at a moment's notice.

The count praised Bertuccio's zeal and told him to prepare for a prompt departure, since his stay in France would come to an end within a month. Just then Baptistin opened the door. He was holding a tray on which there was a letter.

"What are you doing here?" asked the count, seeing him all covered with dust. "I didn't ask you to come out here, did I?"

Without answering, Baptistin walked up to him and presented the letter to him. "Important and urgent," he said. The count opened the letter and read the following:

"The Count of Monte Cristo is hereby warned that a man will break into his house tonight in order to steal some papers which he believes to be locked in the desk in his dressing room. The Count of Monte Cristo is strong enough not to have recourse to the police, which might seriously compromise the person who gives this warning. A large number of people or obvious precautions would

cause the thief to postpone his plans and make the Count
of Monte Cristo lose an opportunity to discover an enemy
whom chance has revealed to the person who gives this
warning—a warning which he may not be able to repeat if
the thief's first attempt fails and he later makes another
one."

The count's first impulse was to take this letter for a thieves'
trick, a crude attempt to warn him of a minor danger while
exposing him to a greater one. He was therefore about to
have the letter taken to the police despite, or perhaps because
of, his anonymous friend's warning, when it suddenly occurred to him that the thief might actually be a personal
enemy of his, an enemy whom he alone could recognize and
from whom he alone could gain an advantage.

"They don't want to steal my papers," said the count to
himself, "they want to kill me. I have no desire to have the
police occupy themselves with my private affairs. I'm rich
enough to relieve their budget of that expense."

He called in Baptistin, who had left the room after handing
him the letter. "Return to Paris and bring back all my servants," he said. "I need everyone here in Auteuil." Baptistin
bowed. "Are my orders quite clear?" continued the count.
"You are to bring back every single servant, but I want the
house left exactly as it is. Close the shutters on the ground
floor, that's all."

"And what about the shutters on the second floor?"

"You know I never close them. Go."

The count dined with his usual sobriety and calm, then,
motioning Ali to follow him, he slipped out a side door. By
nightfall he had arrived at his house on the Avenue des
Champs Elysées. He stood behind a tree and looked carefully up and down the street to see if anyone was hiding in
the vicinity. After making sure that no one was lying in wait
for him, he ran to a side door with Ali, unlocked it and went
up to his bedroom without drawing a single curtain or giving
any other sign that he had returned to the house.

When they reached the bedroom the count motioned Ali to
stop. He then went into his dressing room and examined it
carefully: everything was in its usual place. He removed
the catch from the bolt on the door and returned to the bedroom. During his absence Ali had laid out on a table the
weapons the count had asked for: a short carbine and a pair
of double-barreled pistols. Thus armed, Monte Cristo could
account for the lives of five men.

It was half-past nine. The count and Ali hastily ate a piece
of bread and drank a glass of Spanish wine. Then Monte

Cristo pushed back one of the sliding panels which enabled him to see from one room into another. His pistols and his carbine were within reach of his hand and Ali stood beside him holding one of those small Arabian axes whose form has not changed since the Crusades. The count could see down into the street through one of the windows of the bedroom.

Two hours passed. It was a dark night, yet Ali, thanks to his savage nature, and Monte Cristo, thanks to his acquired ability, were able to distinguish even the slightest movements of the trees in the courtyard. The count was convinced that the attackers would seek his life, not his money. They would therefore enter his bedroom, either by way of the private staircase or through the window of his dressing room. He posted Ali before the door of the staircase and continued to watch his dressing room.

The clock of Les Invalides struck a quarter to twelve. As the sound of the last stroke was dying away, the count heard a faint noise coming from his dressing room. This first grating sound was followed by a second, then a third; at the fourth, the count knew what to expect: a practiced hand was occupied in cutting the four sides of a pane of glass with a diamond.

Monte Cristo felt his heart beat more rapidly. No matter how hardened to danger a man may be, he always realizes, from the pounding of his heart and the shivering of his flesh, the enormous difference there is between a dream and reality, between a plan and its execution.

The count motioned to Ali, who, seeing that the danger was coming from the direction of his master, stepped over to him. The count was eager to learn who his enemies were and how many there were of them. The window whose glass was being cut was directly opposite the opening through which he was looking into the dressing room. He fixed his eyes on that window and saw a shadow on the other side of it. Then one of the panes became completely opaque, as though a sheet of paper had been glued on it; a short time later it cracked without falling. An arm passed through the opening and unlocked the window. A man entered. He was alone.

Just then the count felt Ali gently touching his shoulder. He turned around. Ali pointed to the window of the bedroom, which overlooked the street. The count was aware of the keenness of Ali's senses. He walked over to the window and saw a man step out from a doorway and climb up on a hitching-post, as though he were trying to see what was happening in the count's house. "I see," thought Monte Cristo, "one man acts and the other keeps watch." He motioned Ali to keep an eye on the man in the street and went back to watching the man in his dressing room.

The latter had entered and was groping around in order to orient himself. He found that there were two doors leading into the room and bolted them both. Unaware that the count had removed the catch of the bolt on the door leading into the bedroom, he now believed himself free to act without fear of interruption. The count soon heard the jingling of one of those bunches of shapeless keys such as locksmiths bring when they are called in to unlock a door and to which thieves have given the name of "nightingales," no doubt because of the pleasure they take in hearing their nocturnal song when they grate against the bolt of a lock. "Aha!" thought Monte Cristo with a smile of disappointment, "he's nothing but a thief."

Being unable to find the proper key in the darkness, the thief picked up an object which he had set down on a table on entering, touched a spring and immediately a dim light illuminated his hands and face.

"What!" exclaimed Monte Cristo faintly, stepping back in surprise. "Why, it's——"

Ali raised his axe. "Don't move," whispered Monte Cristo. "And put down your axe. We won't need any weapons." Then he added a few more words in a still lower voice, for his faint exclamation had startled the man in the dressing room. It was apparently an order he gave, for Ali tiptoed away and returned with a black garment and a triangular hat. Meanwhile the count had taken off his coat, his vest and his shirt, revealing one of those tunics of steel mail, the last of which was worn in France, where the dagger is no longer feared, by King Louis XVI, who feared the dagger and perished by the axe. This tunic soon disappeared beneath a long cassock, just as the count's hair disappeared beneath a tonsured wig. The triangular hat, placed over the wig, finished the transformation of the count into a priest.

In the meantime the thief, hearing no further sounds, had resumed work on the lock of the writing desk with his "nightingale."

"Good," said the count, who apparently counted on some secret of the locksmith's art which was unknown to even the cleverest thief, "you'll be busy for quite a while." He walked over to the window.

The man he had seen climb up on a hitching-post had now climbed down from it and was pacing up and down the street, but, strangely enough, instead of being concerned with watching to see if anyone was coming, he appeared to be preoccupied only by what was taking place in the count's house; the purpose of all his movements was to see into the dressing room. Monte Cristo suddenly struck his forehead and let a silent laugh play over his lips. Then he came back to Ali and said, "Stay here, hidden in the darkness, and no matter what you hear, no matter what happens, don't come out unless I call you by name." Ali motioned that he had understood and would obey.

Monte Cristo took a lighted candle from a cupboard and, while the thief was absorbed in his efforts to pick the lock, he gently opened the door, making sure that the light he held in his hand would illuminate his whole face. The door opened so quietly that the thief heard nothing, but, to his great surprise, he noticed that the room had suddenly become light. He turned around.

"Good evening, Monsieur Caderousse," said Monte Cristo. "What are you doing here at such a late hour?"

"Abbé Busoni!" cried Caderousse. Then, not knowing how that strange apparition had come to him, since he had been careful to bolt the doors, he dropped his bunch of keys and stood dumbfounded.

The count walked over and stood between Caderousse and the window, thus cutting off the terrified thief's sole avenue of escape.

"Abbé Busoni!" repeated Caderousse, staring wildly at the count.

"That's right, I'm the Abbé Busoni in person," said Monte Cristo, "and I'm delighted to see that you recognize me, my dear Monsieur Caderousse. That proves you have a good memory, for, unless I'm mistaken, it's been ten years since we saw each other last. . . . And now you're about to rob the Count of Monte Cristo."

"Abbé Busoni," murmured Caderousse, trying to approach the window, which the count mercilessly blocked off from him, "I'm not—I beg you to believe—I swear——"

"A pane of glass cut out, a shaded lantern, a 'nightingale,' a desk half broken open—it seems quite clear."

Caderousse looked around for a place to hide, a hole to disappear into.

"I see you're still the same, Monsieur Caderousse the murderer," continued the count.

"Since you seem to know everything, you must know that it was my wife's fault, not mine. They recognized that at my trial because they only sentenced me to hard labor."

"Did you finish your sentence?"

"No, sir, I was liberated by someone."

"That someone performed a great service for society."

"You see, I promised——"

"So you're an escaped prisoner!" interrupted Monte Cristo.

"I'm afraid so," said Caderousse uneasily.

"In that case, this little relapse will probably take you to the gallows."

"Sir, I was forced to——"

"All criminals say that."

"Poverty——"

"Never mind!" said Busoni scornfully. "Poverty can drive a man to beg or to steal a loaf of bread, but not to break open a writing desk in a house he believes to be uninhabited. And when the jeweler came to pay you the forty-five thousand francs for the diamond I gave you and you killed him in order to have both the diamond and the money, was that also because of poverty?"

"Forgive me, sir," said Caderousse. "You've already saved my life once, save it a second time!"

"That doesn't encourage me."

"Are you alone, sir, or do you have gendarmes behind you ready to arrest me?"

"I'm all alone," said the priest, "and I'll take pity on you, even at the risk of causing new disasters by my weakness, if you'll tell me the whole truth."

"Oh, Abbé Busoni!" cried Caderousse, clasping his hands and taking a step toward Monte Cristo. "You're my saviour!"

"You claim someone liberated you from prison?"

"Yes, I swear it's true!"

"Who was it?"

"An Englishman."

"What was his name?"

"Lord Wilmore."

"I know him, so I'll be able to find out if you're lying."

"Oh, Abbé Busoni, I'm telling you the pure truth!"

"So this Englishman was your protector, is that right?"

"No, he was the protector of a young Corsican, my companion in chains."

"What was the young Corsican's name?"

"Benedetto."

"What was his last name?"

"He had no last name—he was a foundling."

"And he escaped with you?"

"Yes. We were working at Saint-Mandrier, near Toulon. One day we filed off our chains with a file the Englishman had given us and swam away."

"And what became of Benedetto?"

"I don't know. We separated at Hyères."

"You're lying!" said the priest in a tone of irresistible authority. "That man is still your friend and you may be using him as an accomplice."

"Oh, Abbé Busoni!"

"How have you lived since you left Toulon? Answer."

"By doing odd jobs."

"You're lying!" said the priest once again, in a still more imperious tone. Caderousse looked at him in terror. "You've been living on money given to you by Benedetto."

"Yes, that's true," said Caderousse. "Benedetto has become the son of a great lord."

"How could he be the son of a great lord?"

"The illegitimate son."

"And what's the name of this great lord?"

"The Count of Monte Cristo, the very man in whose house we are now."

"Benedetto the son of the count?" said Monte Cristo in astonishment.

"It certainly seems so, since the count has found him a false father, gives him five thousand francs a month and is leaving him half a million francs in his will."

"Ah, I see," said the false priest, who was beginning to undertand. "And what name does the young man bear in the meantime?"

"Andrea Cavalcanti."

"Then he's the young man whom my friend the Count of Monte Cristo receives into his home and who is going to marry Mademoiselle Danglars?"

"Precisely."

"And you allow that, you wretched scoundrel? You who know his past life and his disgrace?"

"Why should I prevent a friend from succeeding in life?" said Caderousse.

"You're right, you're not the one who ought to warn Monsieur Danglars: I am."

"Don't do that, Abbé Busoni!"

"Why not?"

"Because you'll take away our living if you do."

"Do you think that, in order to help a pair of criminals like you make a living, I would take part in their ruse and become their accomplice? No, I'm going to tell Monsieur Danglars everything."

"You won't tell anyone anything, priest!" cried Caderousse, drawing a knife and striking the count in the middle of the chest with it. But, to his great surprise, instead of sinking into the count's chest, the knife merely bounced back with its point blunted. At the same time the count seized his attacker's wrist with his left hand and twisted it with such strength that the knife fell from Caderousse's fingers and he uttered a shriek of pain.

But the count did not stop at this shriek; he continued to twist Caderousse's arm until he fell to his knees and finally lay face downward on the floor. The count put his foot on his head and said, "I don't know what keeps me from crushing your skull, you murderer!"

"Mercy! Mercy!" cried Caderousse.

The count withdrew his foot. "Stand up!" he said. Caderousse stood up.

"My God, but you're strong, Abbé Busoni!" said Caderousse, rubbing his aching arm. "My God, but you're strong!"

"Silence. God gives me strength to subdue wild beasts like you. I act in the name of God. Remember that, you wretched scoundrel. And sparing you this time is also God's will. Take this pen and write what I dictate to you."

"I don't know how to write," said Caderousse.

"You're lying; take this pen and write!"

Caderousse, subjugated by that superior power, sat down and wrote the following:

Monsieur Danglars, the man whom you receive into your home and whom you plan to make your son-in-law is a former convict who escaped with me from the prison of Toulon. He called himself Benedetto then, but he himself does not know his real name, never having known his parents.

"Sign it," ordered the count. Caderousse signed. "Now address it to Baron Danglars, Rue de la Chaussée-d'Antin." Caderousse wrote the address.

The count took the letter and said, "Now go."

"Are you planning something against me, Abbé Busoni?"

"Idiot! What would I be planning?"

"Please tell me you don't want me to die."

"I want what God wants," said the count. "If you arrive home safely, leave Paris, leave France and, wherever you are, and as long as you behave honestly, I'll see that you receive a small pension, because if you arrive home safely, then——"

"Then what?" asked Caderousse, shuddering.

"Then I'll believe that God has forgiven you and I'll forgive you also."

"You frighten me to death!" stammered Caderousse.

"Go now!" said the count, pointing to the window.

Caderousse, still only partly reassured by the count's

promise, climbed through the window and began to descend the ladder. The count approached him with a candle; anyone watching from the street would have seen Caderousse climbing down the ladder with another man holding a light for him.

"What are you doing?" said Caderousse. "What if a patrol should pass?" The count blew out the candle. Caderousse did not breathe freely until he felt the ground under his feet.

Monte Cristo went back into his bedroom. From there he saw Caderousse walk across the garden and lean his ladder against the wall. Then he saw the man who seemed to be waiting in the street place himself behind a corner of the wall near the spot where Caderousse was about to climb over.

Just as his feet touched the ground on the other side of the wall Caderousse saw a raised arm holding a knife. Before he could defend himself the arm struck in the back, then in the side. As he fell to the ground his adversary seized him by the hair and stabbed him a third time in the chest; then, seeing that he made no sound and that his eyes were closed, he left him for dead and fled.

Caderousse raised himself on one elbow, made a supreme effort and called out weakly, "Help! Abbé Busoni! I'm dying!"

This mournful appeal pierced the darkness. The door of the back staircase opened and Ali and his master came running out with lanterns.

"What happened?" asked Monte Cristo.

"Help me!" said Caderousse. "I've been stabbed!"

"We're here. Courage!"

"Oh, it's all over! You've only come in time to see me die!"

Ali and the count carried the wounded man into the house, where the count examined the three terrible wounds he had received. Ali looked at his master as though asking what was to be done. "Go to the public prosecutor, Monsieur de Villefort, and bring him here," said the count. "And as you pass the porter's house, tell him to go get a doctor."

Ali obeyed, leaving the count alone with Caderousse. "A doctor won't be able to save my life," said the latter, "but he may be able to give me some strength and I want to have time to make a declaration."

"About what?"

"About the man who stabbed me."

"Do you know who it was?"

"I certainly do! It was Benedetto."

"Your young Corsican friend?"

"Yes. He gave me a plan of the count's house. He probably

hoped either that I'd kill the count, so that he would have his inheritance immediately, or that the count would kill me, so that he would be rid of me. When he saw that neither of these things had happened, he stabbed me."

"The public prosecutor will be here soon."

"He'll arrive too late," said Caderousse. "I'm losing too much blood."

"Wait," said Monte Cristo. He went out, returned a few minutes later with a flask and poured three or four drops of the liquid it contained between the lips of the wounded man. Caderousse heaved a sigh and said, "That's life you're pouring out to me there! Give me more!"

"Two more drops would kill you," said the count.

"Oh, why doesn't the public prosecutor hurry!" said Caderousse.

"Would you like me to write your declaration? You can sign it."

"Yes! Yes!" replied Caderousse, his eyes shining at the idea of that posthumous vengeance.

Monte Cristo wrote:

"The man who stabbed me is the Corsican named Benedetto, my fellow prisoner at Toulon."

"Hurry," said Caderousse, "or I won't be able to sign it!"

Monte Cristo handed the pen to him. He mustered all his strength, signed his name, then fell back on the bed. "You'll tell them the rest, won't you, Abbé Busoni?" he said. "Tell them he now calls himself Andrea Cavalcanti, that he lives in the Hôtel des Princes, that—— Oh, my God! My God! I'm dying!" He fainted. The count put the flask under his nose and let him inhale the odor; he opened his eyes again. His thirst for vengeance had not left him while he was unconscious. "You'll tell them all that, won't you?" he asked.

"Yes, all that and other things besides."

"What other things?"

"I'll say that he no doubt gave you a plan of this house in the hope that the count would kill you. I'll say that he sent the count a letter to notify him you were coming, and that, since the count was absent, it was I who received the letter and waited for you."

"And he'll be guillotined, won't he?" said Caderousse. "Please promise me he'll be guillotined. That hope will help me to die."

"I'll say," continued the count, "that he followed you here, that he watched for you the whole time you were in the house, and that when he saw you come out he ran behind a corner of the wall and hid himself there."

"Do you mean to say you saw all that?"

"Remember my words: 'If you arrive home safely, then I'll believe that God has forgiven you and I'll forgive you also.'"

"And you didn't warn me!" cried Caderousse, trying to raise himself on his elbow. "You knew I was going to be killed when I left here and you didn't warn me!"

"No, for I saw the justice of God in Benedetto's hand, and I would have considered it a sacrilege to oppose the intentions of Providence."

"Don't talk to me about the justice of God, Abbé Busoni! You know better than anyone else that if there were a justice of God some people would be punished, yet they aren't."

"Patience!" said the priest in a tone that made the dying man shudder. "Listen to me. Here is what God, whom you refuse to acknowledge in your last moments on earth, has done for you: He gave you health, strength, profitable work and friends; in short, everything a man needs to live with a clear conscience and satisfy his natural desires. But instead of enjoying these gifts of God, you abandoned yourself to laziness and drunkenness, and in your drunkenness you betrayed one of your best friends."

"Help!" cried Caderousse. "I need a doctor, not a priest! Maybe I'm not fatally wounded, maybe my life can still be saved!"

"Your wounds are so fatal that without the three drops of that liquid I gave you just now you would be dead already."

"What a strange priest you are!" murmured Caderousse. "You drive a dying man to despair instead of consoling him!"

"Listen," continued the count. "When you betrayed your friend, God began, not to strike you, but to warn you: you fell into poverty. You were already thinking of crime, giving yourself the excuse of necessity, when God performed a miracle for you, when God sent you a fortune, an enormous one for you who possessed nothing at all. But that unexpected fortune wasn't enough for you. As soon as you had it in your possession you wanted to double it. And by what means? By a murder. You doubled it, then God snatched it away from you and delivered you into the hands of human justice. But He still had mercy on you and made your judges spare your life."

"Do you call it merciful to sentence me to hard labor for life?"

"You thought so when it happened, you wretched scoundrel! Your cowardly heart, trembling at the thought of death, leaped for joy when you heard yourself condemned to a lifetime of shame, for you said to yourself, like all prisoners, 'A prison has a door, but a grave hasn't.' And you were right, for the prison door opened for you in an unexpected manner: an Englishman visited Toulon and, having made a vow to rescue two men from their infamy, his choice fell on you and your companion. God had given you a second chance: you had both money and freedom and you could begin to live a normal life again. But then you tempted God a third time. 'I don't have enough,' you said to yourself, when you actually had more than you had ever had before, and you committed a third crime, without reason, without excuse. God finally became weary and punished you."

"And you'll be punished too," said Caderousse. "You didn't do your duty as a priest: you should have stopped Benedetto from killing me."

"I!" said the count with a smile that made Caderousse's blood run cold. "I should have stopped Benedetto from killing you after you had just blunted your dagger against the coat of mail that covered my chest? If I had found you humble and repentant I might have saved your life, but I found you haughty and bloodthirsty and I allowed God's will to be done."

"I don't believe in God, and neither do you!" cried Caderousse. "You're lying! You're lying!"

"Silence, or you'll force out the last drop of blood from your veins. You don't believe in God, but you've just been struck down by God. You don't believe in God, yet all He asks of you is a prayer, a word, a tear in order to forgive you. God could have directed Benedetto's dagger in such a way that you would have died instantly, but He has given you a quarter of an hour in which to repent. Look into your conscience, wretched sinner, and repent!"

"No, no, I won't repent! There is no God, there is no Providence; there's nothing but chance!"

"There is a Providence and there is a God," said Monte Cristo. "The proof of it is that you're lying there helpless, dying and denying God, while I stand before you rich, happy, healthy and safe, joining my hands before that God in whom you try not to believe, but in whom you nevertheless do believe in the depths of your heart."

"Who are you, then?" asked Caderousse, fixing his fading eyes on the count's face.

"Look at me closely," said the count, drawing nearer and holding up the candle.

"You're—the Abbé Busoni."

Monte Cristo took off his wig and let his black hair fall down around his pale face.

"Oh!" said Caderousse in terror. "If it weren't for your black hair, I'd say you were the Englishman. I'd say you were Lord Wilmore!"

"I am neither the Abbé Busoni nor Lord Wilmore," said Monte Cristo. "Look still more closely, look further, look back into your memory."

"Oh, it's true! It seems to me I've seen you before, that I once knew you long ago."

"Yes, Caderousse, you've seen me before; yes, you once knew me."

"But who are you, then? And if you used to know me, why are you letting me die?"

"Because nothing can save you now, Caderousse, because your wounds are fatal. If it had been possible to save you I would have seen that as one last act of mercy by God, and I swear by the grave of my father that I would have tried to bring you back to life and repentance."

"Tell me who you are!"

The count had been carefully watching Caderousse's death agony and he saw that the end was now drawing near. He leaned over the dying man and whispered in his ear, "I am——" And his lips uttered a name so softly that he himself seemed to be afraid to hear it.

Caderousse stretched out his arms, joined his hands and raised himself in one supreme effort. "Oh, my God!" he said. "Forgive me for having denied you! I see now that you exist, that you are the father of men in heaven and the judge of men on earth. I refused to acknowledge you for so long, O my God! Forgive me, Lord, forgive me!"

Caderousse, closing his eyes, fell back with a last cry and a last sigh. He was dead.

"One!" said the count mysteriously, looking steadfastly at the corpse.

Ten minutes later the doctor and the public prosecutor arrived and found the Abbé Busoni praying for the soul of the deceased.

For two weeks the people of Paris talked of nothing except the audacious attempted robbery in the Count of Monte Cristo's house. The dying man had signed a declaration naming Benedetto as his murderer and the police were doing everything possible to track him down.

Caderousse's knife, shaded lantern, bundle of keys and clothes, except for his vest, which could not be found, were deposited at the registry. His body was taken to the morgue.

The count told everyone that he had been in his country house in Auteuil at the time of the incident and that he therefore knew only what had been told to him by the Abbé Busoni, who, as luck would have it, had asked him for permission to stay in his house that night in order to use certain rare books in his library.

Bertuccio turned pale each time the name of Benedetto was mentioned in his presence, but there was no reason for anyone to notice Bertuccio's pallor.

Chapter 47

The Count of Monte Cristo uttered an exclamation of joy on receiving a visit from Albert de Morcerf and his friend Beauchamp one morning.

"I see we've interrupted you while you were putting your papers in order," said Albert.

"No, these are Monsieur Cavalcanti's papers," replied the count.

"Monsieur Cavalcanti?" asked Beauchamp.

"Certainly!" said Albert. "Don't you know that's the young man the count is introducing into Paris society?"

"Just a moment," said Monte Cristo, "I'm not introducing anyone into society, least of all Monsieur Cavalcanti."

"And who's to marry Mademoiselle Danglars instead of me," continued Albert. "You can imagine how terrible that makes me feel."

"What?" asked Beauchamp. "Cavalcanti is going to marry Mademoiselle Danglars?"

"How can you, a journalist, not know that?" said Monte Cristo. "Everyone's talking about it."

"And was it you who arranged the marriage?" asked Beauchamp.

"I, arrange a marriage? My God! I see you don't know me. On the contrary, I was opposed to it; I even refused to make the request."

"I see; because of our friend Albert," said Beauchamp.

"Because of me!" exclaimed Albert. "Not at all! The count will tell you that I begged him to help me break off the engagement, which is now broken off, although he claims he's not the one I have to thank for that good fortune."

"Nevertheless you don't seem too happy, Albert," said the count. "Could it be that, without being aware of it yourself, you're actually in love with Mademoiselle Danglars?"

"Not that I know of," said Albert, smiling.

"But you're not yourself today," continued the count. "What's the matter?"

"I have a headache."

"Well, then, in that case I have an infallible remedy to suggest to you, a remedy that has been successful with me each time I've met with some annoyance."

"What is it?"

"Travel. And it so happens that I've recently met with quite a number of annoyances, so I'm about to travel. Would you like to come with me?"

"Gladly. But where shall we go?"

"We'll go where the air is pure, where all sounds are soothing, where, no matter how proud one may be, one feels humble and finds oneself small—in short, we'll go to the sea. I love the sea as one loves a mistress and I long for her when I haven't seen her for some time."

"All right, count, let's go!" said Albert.

"To the sea?"

"Yes."

"You accept my invitation?"

"Yes."

"Very well, then: this evening in my courtyard there will be a traveling carriage in which you can stretch out as comfortably as in your own bed. Monsieur Beauchamp, the carriage easily holds four people; would you like to come with us?"

"Thank you, but I've just come back from the sea: I made a little trip to the Borromei Islands."

"That doesn't matter, come with us anyway!" said Albert.

"No, I'm sure you know that if I refuse it's because it's impossible for me to leave Paris just now."

"Not that it matters a great deal to me, but where are we going?" asked Albert.

"To Normandy, if that suits you."

"It suits me very well. Will we be really in the country—no society, no neighbors?"

"Our only company will be horses for riding, dogs for hunting and a boat for fishing."

"That's exactly what I need. I'll notify my mother and then I'll be ready to leave whenever you like."

"All right, we'll leave at five o'clock. Can you be here then?"

"Oh, yes; I have nothing else to do between now and then except get ready for the trip."

Albert took leave of the count, who, after nodding smilingly to him, stood still for a few moments as though absorbed in some profound meditation. Then, passing his hand over his forehead as though to brush away his reverie, he went over to the gong and struck it twice. Bertuccio entered.

"Monsieur Bertuccio," said the count, "I'm leaving for Normandy this evening, instead of tomorrow or the next day, as I thought at first. Send a messenger to notify the first relay station. Monsieur de Morcerf will accompany me. Go."

Bertuccio obeyed. A courier hurried to Pontoise to announce that the count's carriage would pass that evening. From Pontoise a messenger was sent to the next relay station, and so on, until six hours later all the stations along the route had been notified.

Before leaving, the count went in to see Haydée, told her he was leaving and where he was going, and placed the entire household under her orders.

Albert arrived on time. The journey, dull at the beginning, soon became interesting because of its swiftness. Albert had never seen anything like it. "Here's a pleasure I never knew before: the pleasure of speed," he said. "But where the devil do you find such horses? Do you have them made to order?"

"Precisely," replied the count. "Six years ago in Hungary I found a famous stallion renowned for his speed. I bought him, I don't know for how much—it was Bertuccio who took care of it. That same year the stallion sired thirty-two colts. The thirty-two horses we're going to use tonight are all the progeny of that single stallion. They're all alike: entirely black except for a star on the forehead, for the stallion's mares were chosen as carefully as a sultan chooses his harem favorites."

"That's magnificent! But tell me, count, what do you do with all those horses?"

"Why, I travel with them, as you can see."

"Yes, but you're not always traveling."

"Some day when I no longer need them, Bertuccio will sell them; he claims he'll be able to make thirty or forty thousand francs on them."

"Count, will you allow me to express a thought that just occurred to me?"

"Certainly."

"It's that, after you, Monsieur Bertuccio must be the richest man in Europe."

"You're quite mistaken, Viscount," replied Monte Cristo. "I'm sure that if you turned Bertuccio's pockets inside out you wouldn't find more than ten sous in them."

"Why is that?" asked Albert. "Your Monsieur Bertuccio must be the eighth wonder of the world! I warn you, count, if you tell me many more miraculous things I'll begin not to believe you."

"There's nothing miraculous about anything I do, Albert. It's all a question of figures and logic. Now, consider this question: Why does a steward steal?"

"Why, because it's his nature; he steals for the sake of stealing."

"No, that's not true: he steals because he has a wife and children, because he has ambitious desires for himself and his family; and above all he steals because he's not sure he'll always remain with his master and wants to make his future secure. But Monsieur Bertuccio is alone in the world; he spends my money without accounting for anything to me and he's sure he'll never leave me."

"Why is he sure of that?"

"Because I couldn't find a better steward."

"You're dealing only with probabilities."

"Not at all; I deal only with certainties. For me a good servant is one over whom I have the right of life and death."

"And you have that right over Bertuccio?"

"Yes," replied the count. There are some words which close the conversation like an iron door. The count's "yes" was one of those words.

The rest of the journey was carried out with the same speed. The thirty-two horses, divided into eight relays, covered the forty-eight leagues in eight hours.

They arrived in the middle of the night at the gate of a beautiful estate, which the porter opened for them. He had been notified by a messenger from the last relay station.

Albert was shown to his suite, where he found a bath and a supper ready and waiting for him. After taking his bath and eating his supper, he went to bed. All night long he was lulled by the melancholy sound of waves breaking on the shore. When he awoke the next morning he went to the window, opened it and found himself on a terrace overlooking the sea.

In the cove lay a small corvette, tall-masted and narrow of beam. Around it were a number of little fishing boats belonging to the fishermen of the neighboring villages; they seemed to be humble subjects awaiting the orders of their queen.

The day was spent in various sports, in all of which the count excelled. They shot a dozen pheasants, caught an equal number of trout in the stream, had dinner overlooking the sea and took tea in the library.

Toward the evening of the third day, Albert, exhausted by the strenuous exercise which seemed to be child's play for the count, was sleeping near the window when the sound of a horse's hoofs on the gravel of the road made him raise his head. He looked out the window and saw his own valet, whom he had not brought with him on the journey.

"Why is Florentin here?" he cried, leaping to his feet. "Can my mother be ill?" he ran out to meet the valet, who, still out of breath, handed him a small sealed packet containing a newspaper and a letter.

"Who is this letter from?" asked Albert anxiously.

"From Monsieur Beauchamp," replied Florentin.

"Was it Monsieur Beauchamp who sent you here?"

"Yes, sir. He gave me the money for the trip, rented a horse for me and made me promise not to stop until I reached you. I made the trip in fifteen hours."

Albert opened the letter. After reading the first few lines he uttered a cry and seized the newspaper with trembling hands. Suddenly his eyes went dim, his legs seemed to melt from under him and he leaned against Florentin, who put out his arm to support him .

"Poor young man!" murmured the count, who was watching him. "It's true that the sins of the father shall be visited upon the children to the third and fourth generation."

Meanwhile Albert regained his strength and continued to read. Then he crumpled up both the newspaper and the letter and said, "Florentin, is your horse in condition to go back to Paris?"

"It's only a poor old nag."

"Oh, my God! How were things at home when you left?"

"Rather calm; but when I came back from Monsieur Beauchamp's house I found Madame de Mercerf in tears. She sent for me to find out when you would return. I told her Monsieur Beauchamp had asked me to go and bring you back. At first she put out her hand to stop me, but then she thought a while and said, 'Yes, go, Florentin; tell him to hurry back.' "

Albert turned around and went back to the room from which Monte Cristo had been watching him. "Count," he said, "I thank you for your hospitality and I would have liked to enjoy it longer, but I must return to Paris."

"What's happened?"

"A terrible disaster; but please allow me to leave immediately—something more precious than my life is at stake. I beg you, count, don't ask me any questions, just give me a horse!"

"My stables are at your service," said Monte Cristo, "but you'll kill yourself with fatigue if you ride all the way back. Take a post-chaise or a carriage."

"No, that would take too long; and besides, I need that fatigue you are worried about. It will do me good."

Albert reeled like a man who has been struck by a bullet and sank into a chair near the door. The count did not notice this, however, for he had gone to the window and called out, "Ali, a horse for Monsieur de Morcerf! And hurry—he wants to leave at once!"

These words brought Albert back to life. He dashed out of the room and the count followed him. "Thank you," said the young man as he leaped into the saddle. "Is there a password I need to give at the relay stations?"

"No, just turn over the horse you're riding to them and they'll saddle another one for you."

"My departure must seem strange and foolish to you," said Albert. "You don't understand how a few lines in a newspaper can reduce a man to desperation. Read this, then," he added, throwing the paper to Monte Cristo, "but only after I'm gone, so that you will not see my shame."

While the count was picking up the newspaper, Albert sank his spurs into the belly of his horse, which, astonished that a rider should feel the need to use such a stimulus, started off with the speed of an arrow.

The count looked after the young man with an expression of infinite compassion. He waited until he had completely disappeared in the distance before he looked down at the newspaper and read the following:

"It has come to our attention that the castles defending the city of Yanina were surrendered by a French officer who also betrayed his benefactor, Ali Pasha, to the Turks. His name at that time was Fernand Mondego, but he has since acquired a title. He now calls himself the Count of Morcerf and is a member of the Chamber."

Chapter 48

Albert burst into Beauchamp's house at eight o'clock the next morning. Beauchamp's valet had been notified to expect him and he led him into his master's bedroom immediately.

"I've been waiting for you, my poor friend," said Beauchamp.

"And here I am," said Albert. "The message you sent me proved your loyalty and affection, so let's not waste any time on preliminaries. Tell me everything that's happened, in detail."

Albert, overwhelmed by shame and grief, listened as Beauchamp related the following facts:

The article had appeared two days earlier in a newspaper other than Beauchamp's. Beauchamp was eating breakfast when he read it. Without finishing his meal, he hurried to the office of the newspaper. Although its political stand was diametrically opposed to his own, he was a close friend of its editor.

"I've come to see you about the Morcerf article," said Beauchamp when he arrived.

"Oh, yes—curious, isn't it?" said the editor.

"So curious that it seems to me you're running the risk of being sued for libel."

"Not at all. The man who gave us the information backed it up with such strong proof that we're perfectly sure Monsieur de Morcerf won't say a word. And it's a service to the country to unmask traitors who are unworthy of the honors bestowed on them."

"Who gave you the information?"

"Yesterday a man who had just arrived from Yanina came in to see us with a formidable stack of documents. We hesitated to print the accusation, but he told us he'd give it to another newspaper if we didn't. You're a journalist, Beauchamp, you know what it means to have an important news item. We couldn't afford to let that one go. Now that the shot has been fired it will echo all over Europe."

Beauchamp realized that there was nothing he could do. He left in despair to send a message to Albert.

But what he was unable to write to Albert, for it happened after the departure of his messenger, was that on that same day there was great agitation in the Chamber. Nearly every member arrived ahead of time to discuss the sinister development which would surely focus public attention on one of their best-known colleagues. Some were reading the article, while others exchanged reminiscences which lent more weight to the accusation. The Count of Morcerf was not liked by his colleagues. Like all *parvenus,* he had felt forced to be excessively haughty in order to maintain his rank.

The Count of Morcerf himself was the only one who had not read the article. He did not receive the newspaper in which it appeared and had spent the morning writing letters and trying out a new horse. He therefore arrived at his customary hour with his customary haughty bearing and entered the Chamber without noticing the hesitation of the ushers or the lukewarm greetings of his colleagues. The session had been in progress for half an hour when he entered.

Although Monsieur de Morcerf, unaware of what had happened, had not changed his bearing and expression in any way, they now struck everyone as more arrogant than usual and his presence on that occasion seemed so aggressive to the assembly that everyone regarded it as ill-advised; some regarded it as insolence, and others considered it an insult.

It was obvious that the entire Chamber was eager to open the debate. The accusing newspaper was seen in everyone's hands, but, as always, each man hesitated to take the responsibility of beginning the attack. Finally one of the honorable peers, a sworn enemy of Morcerf, mounted the rostrum with a solemnity which announced that the awaited moment had arrived. A hushed silence ensued. Morcerf alone was ignorant of the reason for the profound attention being given to an orator who was not usually listened to so obligingly. But at the first words about Yanina and Colonel Fernand Mondego, Morcerf paled so horribly that a shudder ran through the whole assembly and all eyes were fixed on him.

The speaker concluded by requesting that an investigation be made as quickly as possible, in order to crush the slander before it had time to spread, and to restore Monsieur de Morcerf to his high position in the esteem of the public.

Morcerf was so overwhelmed, so trembling before that immense and unexpected calamity, that he was hardly able to stammer a few words to his colleagues while staring at them with bewildered eyes. This timidity, which could just as easily have been due to the astonishment of an innocent man as to the shame of a guilty one, aroused a certain sympathy for him on the part of some of the members. Truly generous men are always ready to become sympathetic when their enemy's misfortune surpasses the limits of their hatred.

The chairman called for a vote on the investigation. It was decided to hold one as soon as possible. Morcerf was asked how long he would need to prepare his defense. His courage had come back to him when he felt himself still alive after that first horrible blow. "Gentlemen," he said, "it is not with time that one must repulse an attack like the one which my unknown enemies have just launched against me. I will reply on the spot and immediately to the bolt of lightning which dazzled me for a moment just now. I can only wish that, instead of having to justify myself in such a way, I could shed my blood in order to prove to my colleagues that I am worthy to consider myself their equal!"

These words made a favorable impression. "I request, therefore," continued Morcerf, "that the investigation be held as soon as possible, and I will supply the Chamber with all the documents necessary to carry it out."

"Is the Chamber of the opinion that the investigation should take place today?" asked the chairman.

"Yes!" was the unanimous reply.

A commission of twelve members was appointed to examine the evidence produced by Morcerf. The first meeting of this commission was set for eight o'clock that evening in the offices of the Chamber. If several meetings proved to be necessary, they would be held in the same place and at the same hour.

When this decision had been made, Morcerf asked permission to withdraw; he had to collect the documents he had been amassing for a long time in order to enable him to ward off this storm, which his wily and indomitable character had foreseen.

He returned that evening at eight o'clock, carrying a bundle of documents in his hand. His face seemed calm and, contrary to his habits, his bearing was unaffected and he was dressed with severe simplicity. His presence produced a good effect: the commission was far from being hostile to him and several of its members came up to him and shook hands with him.

Just then an usher entered and brought the chairman a letter. "You may have the floor, Monsieur de Morcerf," said the chairman as he unsealed the letter.

Morcerf began his defense, which was extremely eloquent and skillful. He produced evidence proving that Ali Pasha had, up to the last day of his life, honored him with his entire confidence, since he entrusted him with a life-and-death mission to the emperor himself. He showed the ring, a sign of authority, with which Ali Pasha sealed his letters and which he had given to Morcerf so that on his return he could come straight to him, even if he were in his harem, no matter what time of day or night he arrived. Unfortunately, said Morcerf, his mission had not been successful and when he came back to defend his benefactor he found him already dead. But, said Morcerf, Ali Pasha's confidence in him was so great that on his deathbed he entrusted him with the care of his favorite mistress and the daughter he had had by her.

Meanwhile the chairman had begun to read the letter that had been brought to him. The first few lines gripped his attention. He read the letter through, then reread it. Fixing his eyes on Monsieur de Morcerf he said, "Count, I believe you just told us that Ali Pasha entrusted you with the care of his wife and daughter, didn't you?"

"Yes," replied Morcerf. "But misfortune pursued me in that as in everything else. On my return I found that Vasiliki and her daughter Haydée had disappeared."

"Did you know them personally?"

"My intimacy with the pasha and the supreme confidence he had in me permitted me to see them more than twenty times."

"Have you any idea what became of them?"

"Yes; I was told they succumbed to their grief and perhaps to their poverty. I wasn't rich at the time and my life was in constant danger, so, to my great regret, I was unable to go in search of them."

The chairman frowned almost imperceptibly. "Gentlemen," he said, "you have heard Monsieur de Morcerf's explanations. Monsieur de Morcerf, can you produce a witness to substantiate what you have just told us?"

"Alas," replied Morcerf, "all those who knew me at the pasha's court have either died or disappeared. I believe myself to be the only one of my compatriots to have survived that frightful war. I have only the letters from Ali Pasha which I have shown you, along with this ring, a token of his confidence in me. But the most convincing proof I have to offer against this anonymous attack is the complete absence of any testimony against my honor and the unstained record of my military career."

A murmur of approbation arose from the assembly. The members were ready to vote their decision when the chairman rose and said, "Gentlemen, I presume you will not be averse to listen to a witness who claims to have very important evidence and who has come forward of his own accord. After what Monsieur de Morcerf has just told us, we may assume that this witness has come to prove our colleague's complete innocence. Here is the letter I have just received on this subject; do you wish me to read it to you, or do you wish to proceed without taking note of the incident?"

Morcerf turned pale and convulsively crumpled the papers he was holding in his hands. The commission voted to have the letter read, while Morcerf himself remained thoughtfully silent and expressed no opinion. The chairman therefore read the following:

"I can give extremely important information to the commission appointed to investigate the conduct of Lieutenant General de Morcerf in Epirus and Macedonia. I witnessed Ali Pasha's death and I know what became of Vasiliki and Haydée. I place myself at the disposal of the commission and even demand the honor of being heard. I will be in the vestibule of the Chamber when this letter is delivered."

"And who is this witness, or rather this enemy?" asked Morcerf unsteadily.

"We're about to learn that," said the chairman. "Usher, is there someone waiting in the vestibule?"

"Yes, sir."

"Who is it?"

"A woman accompanied by a servant."

The members of the commission looked at each other in surprise.

"Show that woman in," said the chairman.

The usher withdrew and returned a few minutes later. Behind him walked a woman wearing a large veil that covered her completely, although the form outlined beneath the veil showed that she was a young and elegant woman. The chairman asked her to remove her veil and the members then saw that she was dressed in the Greek manner and was exquisitely beautiful. Morcerf looked at her with a mixture of surprise and fright. For him, it was life or death that was about to come from those lovely lips; for the others, it was such a strange adventure that the question of Morcerf's salvation or downfall had become a secondary consideration.

"Madame," said the chairman, "you have written us saying that you could give us some information on the Yanina affair and that you were an eyewitness to the events."

"Yes, I was there," replied the young woman in a voice full of captivating sadness and impregnated with that sonority peculiar to Oriental voices.

"Allow me to remark that you were quite young at that time," said the chairman.

"I was four years old. But, since the events were supremely important to me, I have not forgotten a single detail."

"How did the events concern you? Who are you that the catastrophe should have made such a deep impression on you?"

"My father's life was at stake. I am Haydée, daughter of Ali Tebelin, Pasha of Yanina, and of Vasiliki, his beloved wife."

The modest yet proud blush which suffused the young woman's cheeks, the fire in her eyes and the majestic way in which she revealed her identity produced an indescribable effect on the assembly. As for the Count of Morcerf, he could not have been more overwhelmed if a thunderbolt had opened a chasm at his feet.

"Madame," said the chairman after bowing respectfully, "allow me to ask a simple question which is not prompted by doubt and which will be the last of its kind: Can you prove the truth of what you say?"

"I can," replied Haydée, drawing a perfumed satin bag from under her veil. "Here is my birth certificate, drawn up by my father and signed by his principal officials. Here is my certificate of baptism, for my father consented to have me raised in the religion of my mother. This certificate bears the seal of the Grand Primate of Macedonia and Epirus. And, most important of all, perhaps, here is the deed attesting the sale of my mother and me to an Armenian slave merchant by the French officer who, in his infamous bargain with the Turks, reserved as his share of the booty his benefactor's wife and daughter, whom he sold for the sum of four hundred thousand francs."

A greenish pallor invaded Morcerf's cheeks and his eyes became bloodshot as he listened to these terrible accusations, which were received by the assembly in grim silence, Haydée, still calm, although much more threatening in her calmness than another woman would have been in anger, handed the deed of sale to the chairman. It was written in Arabic, but, since the commission had foreseen that some of the documents produced as evidence might be written in Arabic, modern Greek or Turkish, the interpreter of the Chamber had been summoned. One of the noble peers, to whom the Arabic language, which he had learned during the Egyptian campain, was familiar, followed the lines as the translator read aloud:

"I, El Kobbir, slave merchant and purveyor to the harem of His Highness, hereby acknowledge having received from the Count of Monte Cristo an emerald valued at eight hundred thousand francs, which is to be transmitted to the Sublime Emperor, in payment for a Christian slave girl named Haydée, eleven years of age and a recognized daughter of the late Ali Pasha of Yanina and his favorite, Vasiliki. The said Haydée was sold to me, along with her mother, who died on reaching Constantinople, seven years ago by Colonel Fernand Mondego, a French officer formerly in the service of the late Ali Pasha. I made this purchase on behalf of His Highness whose authorization I had, for the sum of four hundred thousand francs.

"Done with the authorization of His Highness at Constantinople in the year of 1247 of the Hegira.

"Signed: EL KOBBIR"

Beside the merchant's signature was the seal of the Sublime Emperor. A terrible silence followed the reading of this document. Morcerf, as though in spite of himself, stared at Haydée with frenzied eyes.

"Madame," said the chairman, "would it be possible to question the Count of Monte Cristo, who, I believe, is now in Paris with you?"

"The Count of Monte Cristo left for Normandy three days ago," replied Haydée.

"In that case," said the chairman, "who advised you to take this action, for which the commission thanks you and which is, furthermore, quite natural in view of your birth and your great misfortune?"

"My action was prompted by my respect and my grief. I am a Christian, but, may God forgive me, I have always dreamed of avenging the death of my illustrious father. When I came to France and learned that the traitor lived in Paris, I remained constantly watchful. I live a secluded life in the house of my noble protector, but I live in that way because I like the shadows and the silence which allow me to live in my thoughts and memories. However, the Count of Monte Cristo surrounds me with paternal care and nothing about worldly life is foreign to me. I read all the newspapers and magazines and I receive all the newest music. It was in thus following the lives of others, without taking part in them, that I learned what happened in the Chamber this morning and what was to happen there this evening. I therefore wrote to you."

"And the Count of Monte Cristo had nothing to do with your action?" asked the chairman.

"He knows nothing about it; in fact, my only fear is that he may disapprove of it when he learns of it. Nevertheless it's a glorious day for me," continued Haydée, her eyes flashing fire, "for I have at last found the opportunity to avenge my father's death."

"Monsieur de Morcerf," said the chairman, "do you recognize this lady as the daughter of Ali Tebelin, Pasha of Yanina?"

"No," said Morcerf, making an effort to stand up. "It's a plot on the part of my enemies."

Haydée, who had been looking toward the door as though she were expecting someone, abruptly turned to Morcerf and shrieked: "So you do not recognize me! Well, I recognize you! You are Fernand Mondego, the French officer who instructed the troops of my noble father. It was you who surrendered the castles of Yanina! It was you who, sent to Constantinople by my father to negotiate for his life or death, brought back a forged decree of complete pardon! It was you who, with that decree, obtained the pasha's ring as a token of his authority! It was you who sold my mother and me into slavery! Murderer! Murderer! You still bear the blood of my father on your forehead Look at him, all of you!"

These words were uttered with such a passionate ring of truth that all eyes turned to Morcerf as he put his hand to his forehead as though he could actually feel Ali Pasha's blood there.

"Do you positively recognize Monsieur de Morcerf as the French officer named Fernand Mondego?" asked the chairman.

"Do I recognize him?" cried Haydée. "Oh, mother! You said to me, 'You were free, you had a father who loved you and you were destined to be almost a queen! Look closely at that man, for it was he who made you a slave, it was he who raised your father's head on the end of a spear, it was he who sold us, it was he who betrayed us! Look at the wide scar on his right hand; if you should forget his face, you will still recognize that hand, which received the gold coins from El Kobbir the slave merchant!' Yes, I recognize him! And now let him say whether he recognizes me or not!"

Morcerf hid his hand, which had indeed been scarred by a wound, and sank into his chair, crushed by black despair.

The entire assembly was in a turmoil. "Monsieur de Morcerf," said the chairman, "the justice of the court is equal for all, like that of God: it will not let you be overwhelmed by your enemies without giving you the means of defending yourself. Do you wish new inquiries to be made? Do you wish me to send two members of the Chamber to Yanina? Answer."

Morcerf remained silent. The members of the commission looked at one another with a sort of terror. They knew Morcerf's energetic and violent character; they realized that it would take a terrible blow to break down his defenses.

"Well, what have you decided?" asked the chairman.

"Nothing," replied Morcerf dully.

"Has Ali Pasha's daughter really spoken the truth, then? Are you really guilty of the things of which you are accused?"

Morcerf looked around him with an expression of despair that would have touched the heart of a tiger, but it could not disarm his judges. Then he raised his eyes to the ceiling and lowered them again immediately, as though he were afraid the ceiling might open to reveal the Supreme Judge Himself. He tore open his coat as though it were choking him and walked out of the room like a somber madman. His footsteps echoed mournfully under the high vaulted ceiling for a moment, then the sound was soon followed by the rumbling of his carriage as it bore him away with the horses at a gallop.

"Gentlemen," said the chairman when silence had been restored, "do you find the Count of Morcerf guilty of felony, treason, and dishonor?"

"Yes!" replied the members of the investigating commission with a single voice.

Haydée heard this sentence pronounced without showing either joy or pity. Then, drawing her veil back over her face, she bowed to the assembly majestically and walked out with the queenly tread which Vergil attributed to his goddesses.

Chapter 49

"Then," said Beauchamp, continuing his narration of these events to Albert, "I slipped out of the Chamber without being seen. The usher who had allowed me to enter was waiting for me at the door. He led me through the corridors to the small door opening onto the Rue de Vaugirard. I was full of both grief and admiration, Albert: grief for you and admiration for that young woman pursuing her father's vengeance."

Albert had been holding his head between his hands. He looked up, his face red with shame and bathed in tears, and gripped Beauchamp's arm. "My friend," he said, "my life is finished. All that remains for me now is to discover the man whose enmity has pursued me; then, when I know who that man is, either I will kill him or he will kill me. I count on your friendship to help me, Beauchamp, if contempt hasn't killed it in your heart."

"Contempt, my friend? How has this disaster touched you? No, thank God, we no longer live in the days when an unjust prejudice held a son responsible for his father's actions! You're young and rich, Albert; leave France. Everything is quickly forgotten in this modern Babylon with its agitated existence and changing tastes. Come back in three or four years and everyone will have ceased to think about what happened yesterday."

"Thank you for the good intentions that dictate your words," replied Albert, "but I can't do as you say. You can understand why it's impossible for me to see this matter from the same point of view as you. If you're still my friend, as you say you are, help me to find the hand that dealt the blow."

"So be it, then," said Beauchamp. "If you're determined to go in search of your enemy, I'll go with you."

"Good. Let's begin our search immediately. Each minute of delay is an eternity for me. The denouncer isn't punished yet, but if he's hoping he won't be, I swear on my honor that he's mistaken!"

"All right, then, listen——"

"Ah, Beauchamp, I see you know something. That makes me want to live again."

"I won't say that this is the whole truth, but at least it's a ray of light in the darkness. I didn't want to tell you before, but I've learned that Monsieur Danglars recently questioned his correspondent in Yanina about Ali Pasha's betrayal."

"Danglars!" cried Albert. "Yes, he's been jealous of my father for a long time. He claims to be a man of the people, yet he can't forgive the Count of Morcerf for being a peer of France. And the way he broke off my engagement to his daughter without giving any reason—yes, he's the one!"

"Don't allow yourself to be carried away in advance, Albert. First make inquiries, then, if it's true——"

"If it's true, he'll pay me for everything I've suffered!"

"Albert, I'm not condemning your decision; I only want to make sure you act cautiously."

"Oh, don't worry; besides, you'll go with me: a matter that serious must be dealt with before a witness. If Monsieur Danglars is guilty, either he or I will be dead before the end of this day."

"Once such a resolution has been made, it ought to be acted on at once. Let's go to see Monsieur Danglars."

When they arrived at the banker's residence, they saw the carriage of Monsieur Andrea Cavalcanti before the door. "That's good," said Albert. "If Monsieur Danglars is unwilling to fight me, I'll kill his son-in-law. A Cavalcanti probably won't refuse a duel."

When Albert's visit was announced to him, Danglars, knowing what had happened the day before, gave orders not to admit the young man. But it was too late, for Albert had followed the servant; when he heard Danglars give his order, he forced open the door and, followed by Beauchamp, entered the banker's study.

"What do you mean by this?" cried Danglars. "Doesn't a man still have the right to decide whom he wants to receive into his own house?"

"No, Monsieur Danglars," said Albert coldly, "there are certain situations, and this is one of them, in which, unless a man is a coward, he must be at home to certain persons."

"What do you want with me?"

Albert stepped forward without appearing to pay any attention to Cavalcanti, who was standing beside the fireplace. "I want to make an appointment with you," he said, "in some isolated spot where no one will disturb us for ten minutes or so, a spot where, of the two men who meet there, one will remain behind on the ground."

Danglars turned pale. Cavalcanti made a movement. Albert turned to the latter and said, "Oh, you can come too if you like, Monsieur Cavalcanti. You're almost one of the family, so you have a right to be there, and I make appointments of that kind with as many people as are willing to accept them."

Cavalcanti looked in bewilderment at Danglars, who, making an effort, stood up and stepped between the two young men. Albert's attack on Andrea put things on another footing and he hoped that the reason for Albert's visit was different from what he had supposed at first. "Let me warn you, Monsieur de Morcerf," he said, "that if you've come here to pick a quarrel with Monsieur Cavalcanti because I preferred him to you, I will take the matter up with the public prosecutor."

"You're mistaken, Monsieur Danglars," said Albert with a somber smile. "Marriage is the furthest thing from my mind and I addressed Monsieur Cavalcanti only because he seemed for an instant to have the intention of intervening in our discussion. You're right in a way, though: I'm ready to pick a quarrel with anyone today. But don't worry; I'll give you priority over everyone else."

"Monsieur Morcerf," said Danglars, pale with anger and fear, "if I find a mad dog in my path I kill it and, far from feeling guilty about it, I feel that I have rendered a service to society. If you are mad and try to bite me, I warn you that I will kill you without pity. Is it my fault that your father is dishonored?"

"Yes!" cried Albert. "It *is* your fault."

Danglars stepped back. "My fault?" he exclaimed. "Why, you're mad! What do I know about Greek history? Have I ever been in that country? Was it I who advised your father to surrender the castles of Yanina, to betray——"

"Silence!" said Albert. "No, you weren't directly responsible for the disaster that occurred yesterday, but it was you who hypocritically provoked it. Where did the revelation come from?"

"It seems to me the newspaper told you that: from Yanina."

"Yes, but who wrote to Yanina for information about my father?"

"Anyone can write to Yanina, can't he?"

"But only one person did write, and that person was you!"

"I wrote, it's true; but it seems to me that when one is about to marry one's daughter to a young man, one has the right to ask for information about that young man's family. In fact, it's not only a right, but a duty."

"When you wrote to Yanina," said Albert, "you knew perfectly well what answer you would receive."

"I would never have written if I'd known that. How could I have known about Ali Pasha's disaster?"

"Did someone else urge you to write, then?"

"Yes."

"Who was it? Tell me!"

"I was speaking with a certain person about your father's past and I mentioned that the source of his fortune had always remained obscure. The person asked me where your father had made his fortune and I answered that it was in Greece. 'Very well, then,' he said, 'write to Yanina for information.' "

"And who was that person?"

"It was your friend the Count of Monte Cristo."

Albert and Beauchamp looked at each other.

"Monsieur Danglars," said Beauchamp, who had remained silent until then, "you've just accused the count, but he's absent from Paris right now and therefore unable to defend himself."

"I'm not accusing anyone," replied Danglars. "I'm only telling what happened, and I'll be glad to repeat what I've said before the Count of Monte Cristo when he returns."

"Does the count know what answer you received?" asked Albert.

"I showed it to him."

"Did he know that my father's name was originally Fernand Mondego?"

"Yes, I told him that a long time ago. In this whole affair I did only what anyone else would have done in my place, and perhaps much less. The day after I received the answer from Yanina, your father came to see me, at Monte Cristo's urging, to conclude the arrangements for the marriage between you and my daughter. I refused, it's true, but I refused without any explanation and without making any scandal. And why should I have made a scandal? What does the Count of Morcerf's honor or dishonor mean to me? It neither increases nor decreases my income."

Albert flushed; he could no longer doubt: Danglars was defending himself basely, perhaps, but with the assurance of a man who is telling, if not the whole truth, at least part of it. Besides, Albert cared little about establishing the precise degree of guilt of Danglars or Monte Cristo; what he sought above all was a man who would answer for his offense, a man who would fight a duel with him. And it was obvious that Danglars would not fight. Futhermore, a number of forgotten or previously unnoticed things now came back to his mind. Monte Cristo knew everything, for he had bought Ali Pasha's daughter; and, knowing everything, he had urged Danglars to write to Yanina. Finally, he had taken Albert to Normandy with him just at the moment when he knew the disaster was

about to occur. It was now clear to Albert that Monte Cristo
had planned everything and that he was in league with his
father's enemies.

Albert drew Beauchamp into a corner and communicated
all these ideas to him. "You're right," said Beauchamp. "Monsieur Danglars was only a tool in what has happened. You
must demand satisfaction from the Count of Monte Cristo."

Albert turned to Danglars and said, "I want you to understand that I'm not taking final leave of you. I must first know
whether your accusations are true and I'm going straight to
the Count of Monte Cristo to find out." Then, after bowing
to Danglars, he walked out with Beauchamp without paying
any further attention to Cavalcanti.

Danglars showed them to the door and assured Albert once
again that he bore no personal hatred for his father.

Chapter 50

When they had left Danglars' house, Beauchamp stopped
Albert and said, "Before we go to see the Count of Monte
Cristo, I think you ought to reflect for a moment."

"About what?"

"About the seriousness of what you're doing."

"I'm afraid of only one thing: finding a man who refuses
to fight."

"Oh, don't worry!" said Beauchamp. "The count will fight;
in fact, I'm afraid he may fight too well. Be careful!"

"My friend," said Albert with a smile, "the most fortunate
thing that could happen to me would be to die for my father:
that would save all of us."

"But your mother would die too!"

"Poor mother!" said Albert, passing his hand over his eyes.
"I know that. But it would be better for her to die of grief
than of shame."

"Are you determined to go through with it, Albert?"

"Yes."

"Then let's go. Where do you think we can find him?"

"He was to leave several hours after I did; he must have
returned by now."

They drove to the count's house on the Avenue des Champs
Elysées. They were met by Baptistin at the door. The count
had indeed arrived a short time before, but he was now in
his bath and had given orders not to admit anyone.

"What will he do after his bath?" asked Albert.

"He will dine," replied Baptistin.

"And after dinner?"

"He will sleep for one hour."

"And then?"

"He will go to the opera."

"Are you sure?" asked Albert.

"Perfectly sure; the count has ordered his carriage to be ready at eight o'clock."

"Very well," said Albert. "That's all I wanted to know." Then, turning to Beauchamp, he said, "If you have anything to do, do it now; and if you have an appointment for this evening, postpone it till tomorrow. You can understand why I count on you to go to the opera with me tonight. If possible, bring Château-Renaud also."

Beauchamp took leave of Albert after promising to come by for him at a quarter to eight that evening.

When Albert arrived home he sent word to Franz, Debray and Maximilien that he wished to see them that evening at the opera. Then he went in to see his mother, who, since the events of the day before, had refused to see anyone and remained in her room. He found her there, still crushed by that public humiliation.

The sight of her son produced on Mercédès the effect that might have been expected: she seized his hand and burst out sobbing. Her tears seemed to relieve her. Albert stood silent for a moment, looking at his mother. His expression showed that his resolution to take vengeance was weakening in his heart.

"Mother," said Albert, "do you know if Monsieur de Morcerf has any enemies?"

Mercédès started: she noticed that he had not said "my father."

"A man in his position always has many enemies whom he doesn't even know," she replied.

"Yes, I know that. But I'm sure you've noticed that the Count of Monte Cristo has always refused to eat or drink anything in our house."

"The Count of Monte Cristo!" exclaimed Mercédès. "What connection is there between that and the question you asked me?"

"As you know, mother, the count is almost an Oriental and, in order to maintain full freedom to avenge themselves, Orientals never eat or drink anything in the house of an enemy."

"Are you saying the Count of Monte Cristo is our enemy,

Albert? Who told you that? Why do you say it? You must be mad, Albert! The Count of Monte Cristo has always been friendly to us; he even saved your life once, and it was you yourself who introduced him to us. Oh, if such an idea has occurred to you, forget it at once! Let me advise you—let me beg you, in fact—not to quarrel with him."

"Mother," replied Albert gravely, "you have your own reasons for asking me not to quarrel with that man."

"I?" exclaimed Mercédès, blushing as quickly as she had paled, then almost immediately becoming as pale as before.

"Yes," replied Albert. "And your reason is that he can't do us any harm, isn't it?"

Mercédès shuddered and looked scrutinizingly at her son. "You're speaking to me very strangely," she said. "What has the count done to you? Only three days ago you went to Normandy with him; only three days ago I regarded him as you yourself regarded him: as your best friend."

An ironic smile passed over Albert's lips. Mercédès saw it and, with her double instinct as a woman and a mother, she guessed everything; but she carefully concealed her agitation.

Albert let the conversation drop. After a time Mercédès said to him, "I wish you'd stay here with me, Albert; I have a great need not to be alone."

"You know how glad I'd be to stay with you, mother, but an extremely urgent matter is going to make it necessary for me to leave you for the entire evening."

"Very well," replied Mercédès with a sigh. "I don't want to make you a slave to your filial piety."

Albert pretended not to hear, saluted his mother and withdrew.

As soon as he had closed the door behind him, Mercédès summoned a trustworthy servant and ordered him to follow Albert all evening and tell her where he went. Then she rang for her personal maid and, despite her weakness, dressed herself in order to be ready for any contingency.

The mission she assigned to her servant was not difficult to carry out. Albert went to his house and dressed with careful severity. At ten minutes to eight Beauchamp arrived. He had seen Château-Renaud, who had promised to join them in the opera house before the curtain rose.

Château-Renaud was waiting for them when they arrived. Beauchamp had already told him everything, so Albert was not obliged to give him any explanation. Debray had not arrived, but Albert knew he rarely missed a performance of the opera.

Albert kept his eyes on Monte Cristo's box, but it seemed to be stubbornly determined to remain empty. Finally, at the beginning of the second act, when he had just looked at his watch for the hundredth time, the door of the box opened and Monte Cristo, dressed in black, entered and leaned over the railing to look down into the orchestra. He was accompanied by Maximilien Morrel.

As he glanced around the orchestra, Monte Cristo perceived a livid face with flashing eyes which seemed to be eagerly trying to attract his attention. He recognized Albert, but the expression he saw on his face advised him not to seem to have noticed him. Without giving any indication of what was going on in his mind, he sat down, took out his opera glasses and looked in another direction.

However, without appearing to see Albert, the count did not lose him from sight and, when the curtain fell at the end of the second act, his keen eyes followed the young man as he left the orchestra accompanied by his two friends. The count felt that a storm was about to break and, when he heard the key turning in the door of his box, although he was talking to Maximilien with his most affable expression, he knew what to expect and prepared himself for the worst.

The door opened. The count turned around and saw Albert, livid and trembling; behind him were Beauchamp and Château-Renaud. "Well, I see you've finally reached your goal," he said with the benevolent politeness which usually distinguished his greetings from the commonplace civility of others. "Good evening, Monsieur de Morcerf."

Maximilien recalled the letter he had received from Albert asking him, without any explanation, to go to the opera that evening, and he realized that something terrible was about to happen.

"I have not come here to exchange hypocritical greetings or false pretenses of friendship with you," said Albert. "I have come here to demand satisfaction from you."

"You come to demand satisfaction at the opera?" said the count with that calm tone of voice and that penetrating glance which reveal a man who is always sure of himself. "I'm not very familiar with Parisian customs, but I wouldn't have thought the opera was a proper place to demand satisfaction."

"When a man hides himself," said Albert, "when he doesn't allow anyone to enter his house on the pretext that he's in his bath, at table or in bed, one must address him wherever one can find him."

"I'm not difficult to find. If I remember correctly, you were in my house only yesterday."

"Yesterday," said Albert, who was beginning to lose his head, "I was in your house because I didn't yet know what you are!" Albert spoke these words so loudly that they were heard by the occupants of the neighboring boxes and the people who were passing in the corridor.

"What's the matter with you, Monsieur de Morcerf?" the count asked without the slightest sign of emotion. "You seem to have lost your reason."

"As long as I'm aware of your treachery and make you understand that I want to avenge it, I'm reasonable enough!" said Albert furiously.

"I don't understand you, Monsieur de Morcerf," said Monte Cristo, "and even if I understood you, you would still be speaking too loudly. This is my box, and I alone have the right to raise my voice here. Get out, Monsieur de Morcerf." And he pointed to the door with an admirable gesture of command.

"I'll bring you out of your box!" cried Albert, convulsively squeezing his glove, which Monte Cristo had not lost from sight.

"Very well," said the count calmly, "you want to provoke me to a duel, that's clear enough. But let me give you some advice: it's a bad idea to make so much noise in provoking me; some people ought not to call attention to themselves, Monsieur de Morcerf."

Albert understood this allusion and made a movement to throw his glove in the count's face, but Maximilien seized his wrist while Beauchamp and Château-Renaud, fearing the scene might go beyond the limits of a provocation, held him back from behind.

But Monte Cristo, without standing up, leaned forward and took the glove from Albert's fingers. "Monsieur de Morcerf," he said in an awesome tone, "I consider your glove as having been thrown and I will give it back to you with a bullet. And now leave my box, or I will call my servants and have you thrown out."

Beside himself with rage, his eyes wild and bloodshot, Albert stepped back. Maximilien took advantage of his movement to close the door.

Monte Cristo picked up his opera glasses and began to look through them as though nothing extraordinary had happened. Maximilien leaned close to his ear and asked, "What have you done to him?"

"Nothing—not personally, at least," replied the count. "His father's misfortune has made him lose his head."

"Did you have anything to do with it?"

"It was Haydée who told the Chamber about his father's treason."

"Yes, I heard that, but I couldn't believe that Greek girl,

whom I saw with you here in this very box, was the daughter of Ali Pasha."

"And yet it's the truth."

"Now I understand everything! Albert wrote me a note asking me to come to the opera tonight; he must have wanted me to be a witness to the insult he intended to give you."

"Probably," said the count imperturbably.

"But what will you do to him?"

"As sure as you're sitting here, I will kill him tomorrow morning before ten o'clock. That's what I'll do to him."

Maximilien seized the count's hand and shuddered when he felt how cold it was. "But his father loves him so much!" he cried.

"Don't tell me that or I'll make him suffer!" said the count, with the first sign of anger he had shown.

There was a knock on the door of the box. "Come in," said the count. Beauchamp entered. "Good evening, Monsieur Beauchamp," said Monte Cristo as though he were seeing him for the first time that evening. "Have a seat."

Beauchamp bowed and sat down. "As you know, count," he said, "I was with Monsieur de Morcerf just now. I admit he was wrong to lose his head the way he did, and I've come to apologize for him on my own account. Now that the apology has been made—and let me repeat that it's mine, not his—I'm sure you're too courteous a man to refuse to give me some explanation about your connections with Yanina and that Greek girl."

Monte Cristo made a little gesture which commanded silence. You've just destroyed all my hopes," he said, laughing.

"What do you mean?" asked Beauchamp.

"You've been eager to give me a reputation for eccentricity, to depict me as a sort of Manfred or Lord Ruthwen. But now the time for regarding me as eccentric has passed and you want to make me into a vulgar, commonplace man. You even ask me to explain myself! You must be joking, Monsieur Beauchamp."

"There are certain circumstances," said Beauchamp haughtily, "in which honor commands that——"

"Monsieur Beauchamp," interrupted the count, "the Count of Monte Cristo is commanded only by the Count of Monte Cristo. I do as I please, and, believe me, it's always very well done."

"You cannot pay an honorable man in that coin," said Beauchamp. "You must give a guarantee to his honor."

"I'm a living guarantee," said Monte Cristo, his eyes flashing threateningly. "Each of us has blood in his veins which the other is eager to shed. That's our mutual guarantee. Take that answer to Monsieur de Morcerf and tell him that by ten o'clock tomorrow morning I will have seen the color of his blood."

"In that case, the only thing that remains to be done is to make arrangements for the duel."

"That's a matter of complete indifference to me," said the count. "Duels are fought with the sword or the pistol in France; in the colonies they use the carbine; in Arabia, the dagger. Tell Monsieur de Morcerf that, although I'm the insulted party, in order to be eccentric to the end, I'll leave the choice of weapons to him and that I'll accept anything without question, even combat by drawing lots, which is always stupid. With me it's different, however: I'm sure to win."

"Sure to win?" repeated Beauchamp anxiously.

"Of course!" said the count with a slight shrug. "Otherwise I wouldn't fight Monsieur de Morcerf. I must kill him, and I will. Just send word to me later tonight to let me know the time and the choice of weapons."

"It will be pistols, at eight o'clock in the morning in the Bois de Vincennes," said Beauchamp, disconcerted, not knowing whether he was dealing with an outrageous braggart or a supernatural being.

"Very well, Monsieur Beauchamp," said the count. "Now that everything is settled, please allow me to enjoy the rest of the opera. And tell your friend Albert not to come back this evening: he would only do himself harm by his rude outbursts. He'll do well to go home and get some sleep."

Beauchamp left the box in amazement.

Monte Cristo turned to Maximilien and said, "I can count on you, can't I?"

"Certainly," replied Maximilien, "but——"

"But what?"

"I'd like very much to know the real cause."

"Do you mean to say you refuse to be my second?"

"Not at all."

"The real cause?" said the count. "Albert himself doesn't know it. The real cause is known only to myself and to God; but I give you my word of honor that God, with His knowledge, will be on our side."

"That's enough for me, count," said Maximilien. "Who will be your other second?"

"You and your brother-in-law Emmanuel are the only two men in Paris to whom I'd like to give that honor. Do you think Emmanuel will accept?"

"I can answer for him as surely as for myself, count."

"Good. Come to my house tomorrow morning at seven o'clock, then."

"We'll be there."

Chapter 51

After the opera was over the count and Maximilien separated and went home. The count still appeared to be calm and smiling. However, only someone who did not know him at all would have been deceived by the tone in which he said to Ali, "Ali, bring me my ivory-handled pistols."

Ali brought them to his master, who began to examine them with a care that was quite understandable in a man who was going to entrust his life to a piece of metal the following day. He was holding one of the weapons in his hand when the door of his study opened and Baptistin entered. But even before he had time to open his mouth, the count noticed a veiled woman standing behind Baptistin in the doorway. He motioned Baptistin to withdraw; he did so and closed the door behind him.

"Who are you, madame?" said the count to the veiled woman.

She looked around to make sure they were alone, then clasped her hands and said in a tone of despair, "Don't kill my son, Edmond!"

The count stepped back and uttered a feeble exclamation; the pistol fell from his hand. "What name was that you just pronounced, Madame de Morcerf?" he said.

"Yours!" she cried, throwing back her veil. "Your real name, which I alone remember! Edmond, this isn't Madame de Morcerf who has come to you: it's Mercédès."

"Mercédès is dead, madame, and I no longer know anyone by that name."

"Mercédès is still alive, and she was the only one who recognized you when she saw you. Since then she's been watching you and dreading you, and she had no need to seek to discover the hand that struck down Monsieur de Morcerf."

"You mean Fernand, don't you, madame?" said Monte Cristo with bitter irony. "Since we're reminding each other of our names, let's remember all of them."

He pronounced the name of Fernand with such hatred that Mercédès felt a shudder of fear run through her body. "I can see I wasn't mistaken," she said, "that I was right to say to you: Spare my son's life!"

"Who told you I had anything against your son, madame?"

"No one told me, but a mother is gifted with second sight. I guessed everything; I followed him to the opera tonight and hid myself in another box, from which I saw what happened."

"In that case, madame, you saw that Fernand's son insulted me publicly."

"My son attributes his father's misfortune to you."

"What has happened to his father is not a misfortune: it's a punishment. I haven't struck him down: Providence has punished him."

"But why do you substitute yourself for Providence?" cried Mercédès. "What do you care about Yanina? What harm did Fernand Mondego do to you when he betrayed Ali Pasha?"

"You're right, madame, that's no concern of mine. I haven't sworn vengeance against either the French officer or the Count of Morcerf, but against Fernand the fisherman, husband of Mercédès."

"But I'm the one who's guilty, Edmond, and if you want to take revenge on someone, you ought to take it on me for not having the strength to withstand your absence and my own loneliness."

"But why was I absent?" cried Monte Cristo.

"Because you were arrested, because you were a prisoner."

"And why was I arrested? Why was I a prisoner?"

"I don't know," said Mercédès.

"No, you don't know, madame; at least I hope you don't. Well, then, I'll tell you. I was arrested and put into prison because, on the day before I was to marry you, a man named Danglars wrote this letter, which Fernand himself mailed." Monte Cristo went over to a desk and unlocked a drawer from which he took a piece of yellowed paper. It was the letter from Danglars to the public prosecutor which Monte Cristo, disguised as a representative of the firm of Thomson and French, had taken from the records concerning the case of Edmond Dantès the day he paid the two hundred thousand francs to Monsieur de Boville.

Mercédès took the letter and read it in terror. "Oh, my God!" she exclaimed, passing her hand over her forehead. "And this letter——"

"I bought it for two hundred thousand francs, madame, but I consider that cheap because it now enables me to justify myself in your eyes."

"And what was the result of this letter?"

"You already know the result, madame: it led to my imprisonment. But what you don't know is how long my imprisonment lasted. You don't know that for fourteen years I was only a quarter of a league away from you, in a cell in the Château d'If. You don't know that every day of those fourteen years I renewed the vow of vengeance I made the first day, yet I didn't know you had married Fernand, my denouncer, that my father was dead and that he died of hunger!"

"Good God!" cried Mercédès, reeling. Falling to her knees, she cried out, "Forgive, Edmond, forgive for the sake of Mercédès, who still loves you!"

The count raised her to her feet and said, "You're asking me not to crush that cursed breed; you're asking me to disobey God, who brought me back from a living death in order to punish them. Impossible, madame, impossible!"

"I call you Edmond," said the poor mother, at her wits' end; "why don't you call me Mercédès?"

"Mercédès," repeated Monte Cristo. "Yes, you're right: it's a name that's still sweet to say, and it's been a long time since it came so clearly from my lips. Oh, Mercédès, I've spoken your name with sighs of melancholy, with shrieks of pain, with groans of despair; I spoke it crouching in the straw on the floor of my dungeon. Mercédès, I suffered for fourteen years, I wept and cursed for fourteen years, and now I tell you, Mercédès, I must have vengeance!" The count, trembling lest he yield to the prayers of the woman he had once loved so much, called up all his memories to support his hatred.

"Take your vengeance, Edmond," cried the poor mother, "but take it on those who are guilty! Take it on Fernand, take it on me, but don't take revenge on my son!"

Monte Cristo heaved a sigh that resembled a roar and gripped his head between his hands.

"Edmond," continued Mercédès, "ever since I met you I've worshiped your name and respected your memory. Edmond, my friend, don't force me to darken that pure and noble image constantly reflected in my heart. Oh, Edmond, if you only knew how often I've prayed for you, while I still hoped you were alive and after I believed you to be dead! What else could I do for you except to weep and pray? Believe me, Edmond, guilty as I am, I've suffered too!"

"Have you felt your father dying while you were absent?" cried Monte Cristo. "Have you seen the woman you loved give her hand to your rival while you were groaning in the depths of a dungeon?"

"No," answered Mercédès, "but I've seen the man I loved ready to become the murderer of my son."

She spoke these words with such passionate grief, with such infinite despair that a sob burst from the count's throat. The lion had been tamed; the avenger had been vanquished. "You've come to ask me for your son's life," he said. "Very well, then, he will live."

"Oh!" cried Mercédès, seizing his hand and pressing it to her lips. "Oh, thank you, Edmond! Thank you! You're still the man I've always dreamed of, the man I've always loved."

"You won't have long to love him," replied the count. "The dead man is about to go back into his grave; the phantom is about to disappear into the night."

"What do you mean?"

"I mean that since you order it, Mercédès, I must die."

"Die! Who spoke of dying?"

"You can't believe that, after being publicly insulted by a young man who would boast of my pardon as he would of a victory, I could still go on living. What I've loved most after you, Mercédès, is myself; that is, my dignity and that strength which made me superior to other men. That strength was my life; you've broken it with a word, so I must die. The duel will still take place, but, instead of your son's blood, it will be my own that pours out on the ground."

Mercédès uttered a loud cry and rushed toward Monte Cristo, but then suddenly she stopped. "Edmond," she said, "the fact that you're still alive and that I've seen you again proves there's a God above us. I trust Him from the bottom of my heart. Awaiting His help, I count on your word. You've told me my son will live; he will live, won't he?"

"Yes, he'll live," said Monte Cristo, surprised at the calmness with which she accepted his heroic sacrifice.

Mercédès held out her hand to him. "Edmond," she said, her eyes filling with tears, "you've just done something noble and sublime; you've taken pity on a poor woman who came to you with every reason to believe her hopes would be disappointed. Alas, I've grown old more from grief than from age, and I can't even remind my Edmond of the Mercédès he used to look at for so many hours. Oh, believe me when I tell you I've suffered too; it's terrible to watch one's life go by without a single joy, without a single hope. Let me tell you again, Edmond, it's noble and sublime to forgive as you've just done."

"You say that without knowing the greatness of the sacrifice I'm making for you, Mercédès. Suppose the Supreme Maker, after creating a third of the world, had stopped there to spare the tears of an angel who would otherwise have wept over our crimes one day; suppose that, after having prepared everything and sown the seeds of life, just as he was about to admire his work, God had extinguished the sun and plunged the world into eternal night—if you imagine all this, you still won't have any idea of what I'm losing by losing my life at this time."

Mercédès looked at the count with an expression that showed all her astonishment, admiration and gratitude. "Edmond," she said, "I have only one more thing to say to you: My beauty has faded, but you'll see that, while Mercédès no longer resembles herself outwardly, she still has the same heart. And now good-bye, Edmond. I now have nothing more to ask of heaven: I've seen you again as noble and great-hearted as ever. Good-bye and thank you, Edmond."

The count did not answer. Mercédès had already gone before he came out of the deep and painful reverie into which his lost vengeance had plunged him. "How stupid I was," he said to himself, "not to have torn my heart out the day I swore to avenge myself!"

Chapter 52

The next morning Maximilien and Emmanuel arrived twenty minutes early. "Excuse me if I've come too soon," said Maximilien, "but I admit frankly that I didn't sleep a wink last night, and neither did anyone else in my house. I needed to see you in all your courageous self-assurance in order to become myself again."

The count was moved by this proof of affection and, instead of holding out his hand to the young man, he opened his arms to him. "Maximilien," he said, "it's a glorious day for me when I feel myself loved by a man like you. Good morning, Emmanuel. So, Maximilien, you're going to be my second?"

"Did you doubt that I would?"

"But if I should be in the wrong——"

"Listen, I watched you last night during that whole scene of provocation, I thought about your confidence all night long and I said to myself that justice must be on your side, or else it's impossible to judge anything from a man's face."

"Thank you, Maximilien," said the count. Then he struck a gong once. "Take this to my notary," he said to Ali, who appeared almost instantly. "It's my will, Maximilien. It will concern you after my death."

"What!" cried Maximilien. "Your death?"

"We have to provide for every possibility, haven't we, my friend? But now tell me what you did last night after you left me."

"I went to Tortoni's, where, as I expected, I found Beauchamp and Château-Renaud. I was looking for them."

"Why? The arrangements had already been agreed on."

"I was hoping they would agree to change the weapons from pistols to swords. A pistol is blind."

"And did you succeed?" asked Monte Cristo with an almost imperceptible glimmer of hope in his eyes.

"No—your skill in fencing is too well known."

"How has it become known?"

"From the fencing masters you've defeated."

"So you failed?"

"They refused categorically."

"Have you ever seen me shoot a pistol?" asked the count.

"Never."

Monte Cristo attached an ace of diamonds to a plank, picked up a pistol and successively shot off each of the four corners of the diamond in the center of the card.

Maximilien looked at the bullets with which the count had just performed this feat and found that they were no larger than pellets of buckshot. "Look it this, Emmanuel!" he said. "It's frightening!" Then, turning to the count, he said, "In the name of God, count, don't kill Albert! The poor boy has a mother."

"That's true," said Monte Cristo. "And I have none." He spoke these words in a tone that made Maximilien shudder.

"You're the offended party, count."

"Of course; and what does that mean?"

"It means you'll be the first to shoot. I insisted on that; we've made so many concessions to them that they could afford to make that one to us."

"At what distance?"

"Twenty paces."

A frightening smile passed over the count's lips. "Maximilien," he said, "don't forget what you've just seen."

"I won't, which is why I count only on your generosity to save Albert's life. You're so sure not to miss that I can say something to you that would be ridiculous if I said it to anyone else: wound him, but don't kill him."

"Listen to me, Maximilien: you don't need to encourage me to deal kindly with Monsieur de Morcerf; I'll deal so kindly with him that he'll return tranquilly with his two seconds, while I'll——"

"Go on!"

"With me it will be different; they'll carry me back."

"Oh, no! You can't mean that!"

"It will be as I tell you, Maximilien: Monsieur de Morcerf will kill me."

Maximilien looked at him in complete bewilderment. "What's happened to you since last night, count?" he asked.

"The same thing that happened to Brutus the night before the Battle of Philippi: I saw a ghost. And that ghost told me that I have lived long enough."

Maximilien and Emmanuel looked at each other. Monte Cristo pulled out his watch. "Let's go," he said. "It's five past seven and I have an appointment for eight o'clock."

The carriage was waiting for them. Monte Cristo climbed into it with his two seconds. They arrived at the appointed spot at exactly eight o'clock.

"We're the first ones here," said Maximilien, putting his head out of the carriage window.

"Excuse me, sir," said Baptistin, who had followed his master with indescribable terror, "but I think I see a carriage over there under the trees."

"Oh, yes," said Emmanuel, "I see two young men who seem to be waiting."

Monte Cristo leaped lightly down from the carriage and gave a hand to Emmanuel and Maximilien as they descended. Then he drew Maximilien aside and said, "Maximilien, is your heart free?" Maximilien looked at him in surprise. "I'm not asking you tell me any secrets," continued the count. "I ask you only to answer yes or no."

"I love a certain young lady, count."

"Do you love her deeply?"

"More than life."

"One more hope shattered!" said Monte Cristo. Then he murmured with a sigh, "Poor Haydée!"

"If I didn't know you so well, count, I'd think you were less brave than you really are."

"Because I sigh when I think of someone I'm about to leave? Come now, Maximilien, can a soldier know so little about courage? Besides, this weakness, if it really is weakness, is for your eyes alone. I know that the world is a salon which we ought to leave politely and honestly; that is, after saluting and paying our gambling debts."

"Well said! By the way, have you brought your weapons?"

"No, I expect those gentlemen to bring their own."

"I'll go ask them," said Maximilien. He walked over to Beauchamp and Château-Renaud. The three young men greeted each other, if not with friendliness, at least with courtesy.

"Excuse me, gentlemen," said Maximilien, "but I don't see Monsieur de Morcerf."

"He sent word to us this morning that he would meet us here on the field of honor," replied Château-Renaud.

"It's only five past eight," said Beauchamp, looking at his watch. "There's no great time lost, Monsieur Morrel."

"Oh, I didn't mean to imply——"

"Besides," interrupted Château-Renaud, "here's a carriage coming now."

They looked up and saw a carriage approaching rapidly along one of the avenues leading to the crossroads where they were standing. "But that's not Morcerf!" exclaimed Château-Renaud. "It's Franz and Debray."

The two young men alighted and walked over. "What brings you here, gentlemen?" asked Château-Renaud, shaking hands with each of them.

"Albert sent word to us this morning to meet him here," replied Debray.

Beauchamp and Château-Renaud looked at each other in surprise. Then Beauchamp called out, "Look! Here comes Albert now. He's galloping at full speed."

"How foolish of him to come on horseback to fight a duel with pistols!" said Château-Renaud. "And after I instructed him so carefully."

Albert reined up, leaped off his horse and approached his friends. He was pale and his eyes were swollen and bloodshot. It was easy to see that he had not slept at all. "Thank you for accepting my invitation, gentlemen," he said. "I'm extremely grateful to you for this proof of your friendship."

Maximilien had stepped aside ten paces or so. "And you too, Monsieur Morrel," said Albert, "my gratitude also belongs to you. Come closer; your presence is welcome."

"Perhaps you're not aware that I'm one of the Count of Monte Cristo's seconds," said Maximilien.

"So much the better; I want to have as many men of honor here as possible."

"Monsieur Morrel," said Château-Renaud, "you may inform the Count of Monte Cristo that Monsieur de Mercerf has arrived and that we are at his disposal."

Maximilien started off to deliver the message while Beauchamp took out the box containing the pistols.

"Just a moment, gentlemen," said Albert. "I have a few words to say to the Count of Monte Cristo."

"In private?" asked Maximilien.

"No, before everyone."

Albert's seconds looked at one another in surprise; Franz and Debray exchanged several words in a low tone, and Maximilien, gladdened by this unexpected incident, went off to bring the count, who was walking in a lane of the forest with Emmanuel.

"What does he want with me?" asked Monte Cristo.

"I don't know, but he asks to speak to you."

"Oh!" said Monte Cristo, "I hope he's not going to tempt God with some new outrage!"

"I don't think that's his intention," said Maximilien.

The count walked forward, accompanied by Maximilien and Emmanuel. Albert and his four friends came to meet them.

When they were three paces from each other, Monte Cristo and Albert stopped. "Come closer, gentlemen," said Albert. "I don't want you to miss a single word of what I'm about to say to the Count of Monte Cristo, because I want you to repeat it to everyone who will listen to it, however strange it may seem to you."

"I'm listening, Monsieur de Morcerf," said the count.

"Count," began Albert in a voice that was unsteady at first, but which became more assured as he spoke, "I reproached you for revealing my father's conduct in Greece, for I believe that, however guilty he may have been, you had no right to punish him. But today I know that you have that right. It is not Fernand Mondego's betrayal of Ali Pasha that makes me so quick to excuse you, but the fisherman Fernand's betrayal of you, and the unspeakable suffering it led to. I therefore say to you, count, that you were right to avenge yourself on my father, and I, his son, thank you for not having done more than you did!"

The spectators of this unexpected scene could not have been more astonished if a bolt of lightning had struck in their midst. As for Monte Cristo, he slowly raised his eyes to the heavens with an expression of infinite gratitude, and he could not admire too much the way in which Albert's fiery character, whose courage he had been able to appreciate when he had come to rescue him from the Roman bandits, had submitted itself to that sudden humiliation. He recognized Mercédès' influence and realized then why she had not refused his offer to sacrifice his own life for her son.

"And now," continued Albert, "if you find that the apology I have just given you is sufficient, please give me your hand."

Monte Cristo, his eyes moist and his chest heaving, held out his hand to Albert, who seized it and pressed it with a feeling which resembled respectful fright. "Gentlemen," he said, "the Count of Monte Cristo has accepted my apology. I hope that the world will not consider me a coward for doing what my conscience ordered me to do. But," added the young man, raising his head proudly, as though addressing a challenge to his friends as well as to his enemies, "if anyone should have a mistaken idea about the motives of my action, I will try to correct his opinion."

Chapter 53

The first thing Albert did when he returned home was to take the portrait of his mother from its frame and roll it up. Then he collected all his fine Turkish weapons, English rifles, Japanese porcelains, mounted trophies and bronze statues, threw his pocket money into a desk drawer, which he left open, added to it all the jewels from his vases, shelves and jewel boxes, made a precise inventory of everything and placed this inventory conspicuously in the middle of a table.

As he was finishing this task, the sound of horses' hoofs in the courtyard attracted his attention. He walked over to the window and saw his father climb into his carriage and drive off.

Albert then went to his mother's room. He stopped on the threshold, overwhelmed by what he saw and by what he guessed. As if the same soul animated their two bodies, Mercédès was doing in her room exactly what Albert had done in his. He realized the reason behind her preparations, cried out, "Mother!" and threw his arms around her. "What are you doing?" he asked.

"And what were you doing?"

"Oh, mother," cried Albert, moved almost to the point of being unable to speak, "it's not the same for you as it is for me!"

"I'm leaving," said Mercédès, "and I confess that I counted on my son's going with me. Was I mistaken?"

"Mother," said Albert firmly, "I cannot make you share the life I'm going to lead. From now on I must live without a name and without a fortune. In order to begin my apprenticeship in that harsh life, I must borrow from a friend the bread I will eat until I can earn some for myself. I'm going to Franz right now to ask him to lend me the small sum I think will be necessary."

"Oh, my poor boy!" cried Mercédès. "Do you intend to live in poverty and hunger? Don't tell me that or you'll destroy all my resolution!"

"But not mine, mother," replied Albert. "I'm young, I'm strong and I believe I'm brave; and since yesterday I've learned what strength of will can do. There are men who have suffered and who have not only gone on living, but even built a new fortune on the ruins of their former happiness. From the depths into which their enemies have plunged them, they

320

have risen again with such vigor and glory that they have dominated their former conquerors and cast them down in their turn. From this day on I have broken with my past. I will accept nothing from it, not even my name, because, as I'm sure you can understand, mother, your son cannot bear the name of a man who must blush with shame before another man."

"If my heart had been stronger, Albert, that's exactly the advice I would have given you; your own conscience has told you what I was too weak to say. Break off with your friends temporarily, but don't lose hope, I beg you. Life is still glorious at your age, Albert; you're hardly twenty-two years old. And since a heart as pure as yours needs an unstained name, take my father's name, which was Herrera. I know you, Albert: whatever career you follow, you'll soon make that name illustrious."

"I'll do as you wish, mother," said the young man. "And since we've already made our resolution, let's carry it out promptly. My father left the house about half an hour ago, which means that we now have a good opportunity to avoid a scene."

"I'll wait for you, my son," said Mercédès.

Albert ran out into the street and hired a carriage. As he was returning to the house, a man came up to him and handed him a letter. Albert recognized him as Monte Cristo's steward, Bertuccio. He took the letter and read it. When he finished, he looked up for Bertuccio, but he had disappeared. Albert went back to his mother's room and, overwhelmed with emotion, handed her the letter without a word. She took it and read the following:

Albert, you are about to leave your father's house, taking your mother with you. But reflect a moment before you leave: you owe her more than you can ever repay her; face the struggle alone, keep the suffering for yourself and spare her the poverty that will inevitably accompany your first efforts, for she does not deserve even a reflection of the misfortune which has come to her today. I know that you are both about to leave your father's house without taking anything with you. Do not try to discover how I learned this; I know it and that is enough.

Listen to me, Albert: twenty-four years ago I returned to my country happy and proud. I had a fiancée, a saintly young girl whom I worshiped, and I had three thousand francs which I had slowly amassed by constant hard work. That money was for her and, knowing the treachery of

the sea, I buried our treasure in the little garden of the
house in which my father lived in Marseilles. Your mother
knows that house well.

Recently, on my way to Paris, I passed through Marseilles. I went back to that house, full of painful memories
for me, and dug in the spot where I had buried our treasure.
The iron box was still in its place; no one had touched it.
It is in the corner of the garden shaded by the fig tree
which my father planted on the day of my birth. That
money was meant to contribute to the happiness of the
woman I loved; you will understand why, instead of offering her the millions I could now give her, I give her back
only that pittance which has lain forgotten since the day
I was separated from her.

You have a noble heart, Albert, but it may be that you
have been blinded by pride or resentment; if you refuse
my offer, if you ask someone else for what I have a right
to give you, I will say that it is not noble of you to refuse
to allow your mother the chance of a new life offered to
her by a man whose father was made to die of hunger
and despair by your father.

When Mercédès had finished reading this letter, Albert
stood motionless, awaiting her decision. "I accept," she said.
"He has the right to pay the dowry that I will bring to a
convent." Then, placing the letter over her heart, she took
her son's arm and walked resolutely toward the stairs.

Chapter 54

Monte Cristo had come back to town with Emmanuel
and Maximilien. Their return was gay. Emmanuel did not
conceal his joy at having seen war give way to peace. Maximilien, sitting in a corner of the carriage, let his brother-in-
law's gaiety evaporate in words and kept to himself a joy
that was equally sincere but which shone only in his eyes.

At the Barrière du Trône they met Bertuccio, who was
waiting for them like a sentry at his post. Monte Cristo put
his head out the window of the carriage, exchanged a few
words with him in an undertone and the steward disappeared.

"Please take me home now, count," said Emmanuel when
they were near the Place Royale, "so that my wife won't
have to worry any longer about either of us."

"I would ask you to come home with us," said Maximilien,
"but I'm sure there's someone you want to reassure also.

Here we are, Emmanuel; let's say good-bye to our friend and let him go on his way."

"Wait a moment," said Monte Cristo. "Don't deprive me of both my companions at once. Go in to your charming wife, Emmanuel, and give her my compliments, and you, Maximilien, come with me to the Champs Elysées."

"I'll be glad to," said Maximilien, "especially since I have a personal matter to attend to in your neighborhood."

"Shall we expect you for dinner?" asked Emmanuel.

"No," replied Maximilien.

The carriage continued on its way.

"You see how I bring you good luck," said Maximilien when he was alone with the count. "You didn't expect it, did you?"

"Of course; that's why I wanted you with me."

"What happened this morning was miraculous; Albert is brave, there's no question of that."

"Very brave," said Monte Cristo. "I once saw him sleep with a sword almost literally hanging over his head."

"And I know he's fought two duels, and fought them very well. Reconcile that with his conduct this morning!"

"It was your influence," said the count, smiling.

"It's lucky for Albert that he's not a soldier."

"Why?"

"An apology on the field of honor!" said the young captain, shaking his head.

"Come now," said the count gently, "you're not going to fall into the prejudices of ordinary men, are you, Maximilien? Won't you agree that, since Albert is brave, he can't be cowardly, that he must have had a good reason for acting as he did this morning, and that his conduct was therefore heroic rather than base?"

"No doubt, no doubt," replied Maximilien.

"You'll have lunch with me, won't you?" asked the count, cutting short the conversation.

"No, I'll leave you at ten o'clock."

"Your 'personal matter' is an appointment for lunch, then?"

Maximilien shook his head.

"But you'll have to have lunch somewhere, won't you?"

"Suppose I'm not hungry?"

"Ah!" exclaimed the count. "I know of only two emotions that take away a man's appetite: grief—and since, fortunately, I see that you're gay, I know it's not that—and love. Now, after what you told me this morning, I can only suppose——"

"Oh, I won't deny it!" said Maximilien gaily.

"And you haven't told me about it!" said the count in a

tone which showed how deeply concerned he was to know the secret.

"I showed you this morning that I had a heart, didn't I, count?"

Monte Cristo's only reply was to hold out his hand to the young man.

"Well," continued Maximilien, "since my heart is no longer with you in the Bois de Vincennes, it's somewhere else and I'm going there to find it again."

"Go, then, my friend," said the count slowly. "But promise me that if you should ever encounter any obstacles you'll remember that I have a certain amount of power in this world, that I'm glad to use it to help people I'm fond of, and that I'm very fond of you, Maximilien."

"Very well," replied the young man, "I'll remember that in the way selfish children remember their parents when they need them. If I ever need you, count, and it's quite possible that I will, I'll come to you."

"I consider that a promise. And now good-bye."

They had arrived in front of the count's house on the Champs Elysées. Monte Cristo opened the door of the carriage and Maximilien alighted. Bertuccio was waiting on the front steps. Maximilien walked off down the Avenue de Marigny as Monte Cristo hurried up to Bertuccio.

"Well?" he asked.

"She's going to leave his house," replied Bertuccio.

"And what about her son?"

"Florentin, his valet, thinks he's going to do the same thing."

"Come with me." Monte Cristo led Bertuccio into his study, wrote the letter we have already seen, handed it to him and said, "Deliver this immediately. Before you go, notify Haydée that I've come back."

"Here I am," said Haydée, who, hearing the sound of the count's carriage, had already come downstairs, her face radiant with joy at seeing him safe and sound.

Bertuccio left.

Monte Cristo's joy, while less apparent, was no less intense than Haydée's. He had recently begun to realize something which he had not dared believe before: that there was another Mercédès in the world, that he might once again be happy. He was gazing ardently into Haydée's moist eyes when suddenly the door opened. He frowned.

"The Count of Morcerf," announced Baptistin.

"Oh!" cried Haydée. "Isn't it finished yet?"

"I don't know if it's finished yet," said Monte Cristo, taking both her hands in his, "but I do know that there's nothing to fear. That man can do me no harm. It was when I was dealing with his son that there was reason to fear."

"You'll never know how I suffered!" said Haydée.

Monte Cristo smiled and said, "I swear to you that if there is any misfortune it will not happen to me."

"I believe it as if God Himself had told me," said Haydée.

Monte Cristo placed a kiss on her forehead which made two hearts beat more rapidly. "O God," he thought, "could it be that you will allow me to love a second time?" Then he turned to Baptistin and said, "Show the Count of Morcerf into the salon."

The general was pacing the length of the floor for the third time when Monte Cristo joined him in the salon.

"Ah, it's really you, Monsieur de Morcerf," said the count calmly. "I thought perhaps I had heard wrong."

"Yes, it's I," said the general, with a frightful contraction of his lips which prevented him from articulating clearly.

"And to what do I owe the pleasure of seeing the Count of Morcerf at such an early hour?'

"You had a meeting with my son this morning."

"Did you know about that?"

"Yes, and I also know that my son had good reason to fight you and do his best to kill you."

"That's true. But, as you can see, in spite of his good reasons he didn't kill me. In fact, he didn't even fight me."

"Yet he considered you the cause of his father's dishonor and of the horrible disaster which has fallen on my house."

"That's also true," said Monte Cristo with his terrible calm. "I was the secondary cause, although not the primary one."

"Then no doubt you apologized to him or gave him some explanation."

"I gave him no explanation and it was he who apologized to me."

"But to what do you attribute his conduct?"

"To his conviction, probably, that there was another man guiltier than I."

"Who was that man?"

"His father."

"Perhaps," said Morcerf, turning pale, "but you know a guilty man doesn't like to have his guilt thrown in his face."

"Yes, I know; and I expected this."

"You expected my son to be a coward?" cried the general.

"Monsieur Albert de Morcerf is not a coward," said Monte Cristo.

"A man who stands before a mortal enemy with a sword in his hand and does not fight is a coward! I wish he were here so I could tell him so."

"I don't suppose you've come here to tell me about your family affairs," said Monte Cristo coldly. "Go tell that to your son; perhaps he'll be able to answer you."

"No, that's not why I came," said Morcerf with a smile which vanished almost as soon as it appeared. "I came to tell you that I too consider you my enemy. I came to tell you that I hate you instinctively, that it seems to me I've always known you and always hated you, and that, finally, since the young men of this generation apparently no longer fight duels, we must do so ourselves. Do you agree?"

"Certainly. When I told you I expected this, I was referring to the honor of your visit."

"Very well. Are you ready?"

"I'm always ready."

"You understand that we will fight till one of us is dead?" said the general, clenching his teeth in rage.

"Till one of us is dead," repeated Monte Cristo, slowly nodding his head.

"Let's go, then; we have no need of seconds."

"Yes, that would be useless; we know each other so well."

"On the contrary, it's because we don't know each other."

"Are you sure?" asked Monte Cristo with the same exasperating coolness. "Aren't you the soldier Fernand who deserted on the eve of the Battle of Waterloo? Aren't you the Lieutenant Fernand who served the French army as a guide and spy in Spain? Aren't you the Colonel Fernand who betrayed, sold out and assassinated his benefactor, Ali Pasha? And haven't all those Fernands put together made Lieutenant General Fernand, Count of Morcerf and peer of France?"

"Scoundrel!" cried the general, as though struck by a red-hot iron. "You confront me with my shame just as you're perhaps about to kill me! I didn't say I was a stranger to you; I know, you demon, that you've penetrated into the darkness of my past and read every page of my life by the light of some torch unknown to me. But maybe there's still more honor in me, even in my disgrace, than there is in you beneath all your outward pomp. No, I'm not a stranger to you, I know that. But I know nothing about you, you adventurer made up of gold and jewels! In Paris you call yourself the Count of Monte Cristo; in Italy, Sinbad the Sailor; in Malta—God knows what! But I want to know your real name, so that I can pronounce it on the field of honor as I plunge my sword into your heart!"

Monte Cristo's eyes glowed fiercely. He rushed into an adjoining room and threw off his coat and vest. A moment later he returned wearing a sailor's blouse and a sailor's hat and stood before Morcerf with his arms crossed and an expression of implacable hatred on his face. Morcerf's teeth chattered, he felt his legs giving way beneath him and he stepped back until he found a table on which to support himself.

"Fernand!" roared Monte Cristo. "One of my names is enough to strike terror into your heart, but I don't have to tell you what it is, do I? You've already guessed it, haven't you? Or rather, you remember it, for, in spite of all my years of sorrow and torment, the joy of vengeance has made my face young again, and it's a face you must have seen often in your dreams ever since your marriage to Mercédès, my fiancée!"

The general stared at the terrible apparition in silence. Then, leaning against the wall, he slowly slid along it to the door and backed out of the room, uttering only this piercing terror-stricken cry: *"Edmond Dantès!"*

Gasping in an inhuman way, he dragged himself to the front of the house, staggered across the courtyard as if he were drunk and fell into the arms of his valet. "Home, home!" he muttered, almost unintelligibly.

The fresh air and the shame he felt at having made a spectacle of himself in front of his servants helped him to regain some measure of composure, but it was a short trip and the nearer he came to his home the more his anguish came rushing back to him.

He stopped the carriage in front of the house and got out. The door of the house was wide open and a hired carriage, whose driver seemed surprised at having been called to such a magnificent residence, was standing in the middle of the courtyard. The general looked at it in terror, then went inside and ran toward his room, not daring to question anyone.

Two people were coming down the stairs. Quickly hiding himself behind a curtain in order to avoid them, he saw Mercédès leaning on Albert's arm. They were leaving the house. "Courage, mother," he heard his son say. "This is no longer our home."

The words and the footsteps died away in the distance. The general clung to the curtain, struggling to hold back the most horrible sob that ever burst from the bosom of a man abandoned by his wife and his son at the same time.

Soon he heard the door of the carriage being closed and

its driver calling out to the horses. The rumbling of the heavy vehicle shook the windowpanes. He rushed into his bedroom to catch one last glimpse of all that he had loved on earth, but the carriage went past without either of their heads appearing at the window to take a farewell glance at the lonely house or the forsaken husband and father.

Just as the carriage was passing beneath the arch of the gate a shot rang out and dark smoke floated out through one of the bedroom windows, which had been shattered by the force of the explosion.

Chapter 55

After leaving Monte Cristo, Maximilien walked toward the Villefort residence. Noirtier and Valentine had agreed to allow him two visits a week and he was about to take advantage of his right.

Valentine was waiting for him when he arrived. Worried, almost frantic, she gripped his hand and led him before her grandfather. She was worried because she had heard about Albert's provocation of the Count of Monte Cristo at the opera; she had guessed that Maximilien would be the count's second and, in view of the young man's well-known courage and his deep feeling of friendship toward the count, she was afraid that he might be unable to limit himself to the passive role he had been assigned. It is easy to imagine, therefore, the eagerness with which the details of the adventure were asked for, given and received, and Maximilien saw unspeakable joy in the eyes of his beloved when she learned that the terrible affair had had an outcome as fortunate as it was unexpected.

"And now let's talk about our own affairs," said Valentine, motioning Maximilien to sit down beside Noirtier and sitting down herself on his footstool. "As you know, grandfather once had the idea of leaving this house and taking an apartment for the two of us. Well, he's come back to that plan again."

"Bravo!" exclaimed Maximilien.

"And do you know what reason he gives for wanting to leave this house?"

Noirtier looked at his granddaughter to impose silence on her, but she was not looking at him; her eyes and her smile were all for Maximilien.

"Whatever his reason is, I'm sure it's a good one!" said Maximilien.

"He says the air of the Faubourg Saint-Honoré is bad for me."

"He may well be right: it seems to me your health hasn't been good for the past two weeks or so."

"No, it hasn't been very good. Grandfather has made himself my doctor, and since he knows everything, I have great confidence in him."

"But are you really ill, Valentine?" asked Maximilien anxiously.

"Oh, I couldn't really say I'm ill; I just feel slightly indisposed. I've lost my appetite and it seems to me that my stomach is struggling to accustom itself to something."

"And what treatment are you following for this unknown illness?"

"I take some of the medicine they bring for my grandfather. I began with one spoonful and now I'm up to four. My grandfather claims it's a panacea." Valentine smiled, but there was a tinge of sadness in her smile.

"But I thought that medicine was made especially for your grandfather."

"All I know is that it's very bitter," said Valentine, "so bitter that everything I drink afterward seems to have the same taste." Noirtier gave her a questioning look. "Just before I came in to see you, grandfather," she continued, "I drank a glass of sugared water and I had to leave half of it because it tasted so bitter to me."

Noirtier looked at her with visible anxiety. The blood was apparently rushing to her head, for her cheeks began to turn red. "That's strange!" she said, without losing any of her cheerfulness. "Could the sunlight have dazzled me?" She leaned against the window.

"There isn't any sunlight!" said Maximilien, running over to her. She smiled at him and said, "Don't worry, it's already past. Listen! Isn't that a carriage in the courtyard?"

She opened the door, ran to a window in the hall and came back immediately. "Yes," she said, "Madame Danglars and her daughter have just come for a visit. I'll go right away, or else they'll come here to find me. Stay here with grandfather, Maximilien. I'll come back as soon as I can."

Maximilien saw her close the door and heard her walk up the little staircase that led to her room and Madame de Villefort's.

Madame Danglers and her daughter had been shown into Madame de Villefort's room. Valentine exchanged bows with them when she entered.

"I've come with Eugénie to be the first to announce her forthcoming marriage with Prince Cavalcanti," said Madame

Danglars. Her husband had insisted on giving Cavalcanti the title of prince, which to him sounded much better than count.

"Then let me give you my sincere congratulations," said Madame de Villefort. "Prince Cavalcanti seems to be a young man full of rare qualities."

"Yes," said Madame Danglars, smiling, "he has a good heart and a keen mind; and my husband says his fortune is 'majestic,' to use his own word."

"You might also add," said Eugénie to her mother, "that you have a special fondness for him."

"I suppose there's no need to ask whether you share that fondness, is there?" asked Madame de Villefort.

"I don't share it in any way," replied Eugénie with her usual coolness. "My vocation was not to chain myself to a household or the whims of a man, whoever he might be. I was born to be an artist and to be free. But since I must be married, I thank fate for saving me from Albert de Morcerf; otherwise I'd now be the wife of a man who has lost his honor."

"But," said Valentine timidly, "is he really to blame for his father's disgrace?"

"He deserves to share that disgrace," said the implacable Eugénie. "After provoking the Count of Monte Cristo to a duel last night at the opera, he apologized to him this morning on the field of honor."

"Impossible!" exclaimed Madame de Villefort.

"It's perfectly true," said Madame Danglars. "I learned about it from Monsieur Debray, who was present when it happened."

Valentine also knew about the incident, but she said nothing. In her mind she was back in Noirtier's room, where Maximilien was waiting for her. She was lost in thought when Madame Danglars brought her back to reality by touching her on the arm and saying, "Are you ill, Valentine? You've alternately flushed and turned pale several times in the last few minutes."

"Yes, you're very pale now," said Eugénie.

"Oh, there's nothing to worry about," said Valentine. "I've been this way for several days now." She nevertheless realized that she now had an excuse to leave. And Madame de Villefort came to her aid by saying, "You're really not feeling well, Valentine, and I'm sure these ladies will excuse you."

Valentine embraced Eugénie, bowed to Madame Danglars and went out. She was almost at the bottom of the staircase and could already hear Maximilien's voice when suddenly a cloud seemed to pass before her eyes and she rolled down the last three steps. Maximilien rushed to the door and found her lying on the landing. He picked her up, carried her inside and set her down in an armchair.

Valentine opened her eyes. "Oh, how awkward I am!" she said, with feverish volubility. "Can't I even stand up any more?"

"Are you hurt, Valentine?" cried Maximilien. "Oh, my God! My God!"

Valentine looked around and saw that Noirtier's eyes were full of intense terror. "Don't worry, grandfather," she said, trying to smile. "It's nothing. I was dizzy for a moment, that's all."

"Please be careful, Valentine, I beg you!" said Maximilien.

"It's nothing, I tell you; it's all gone now. Let me tell you a piece of news: Eugénie Danglars is going to be married in a week."

"And when will it be our turn? You have such great influence on your grandfather, Valentine: try to make him answer, 'Soon.' "

"So you count on me to stimulate grandfather's slowness and awaken his memory?"

"Yes! And please act quickly! As long as you're not mine, Valentine, it will always seem to me that I'm going to lose you."

"Oh, Maximilien," replied Valentine, with a convulsive movement, "you're too timorous for a soldier who, they say, has never known fear!" She burst into strident laughter, her arms stiffened and twisted, her head fell back and she remained motionless.

A silent cry of terror burst from Noirtier's eyes. Maximilien realized that he must call for help. He pulled the bell cord; Valentine's maid and the servant who had replaced Barrois both appeared simultaneously. But Valentine was so pale, so cold, so lifeless that, without listening to what was said to them, they were seized by the fear which was constantly present in that accursed house and rushed out into the hall shrieking for help.

"What's the matter?" cried Monsieur de Villefort from his study.

Maximilien looked at Noirtier, who had just regained all his presence of mind and who motioned with his eyes to a closet in which Maximilien had already taken refuge once before in a similiar situation. He had just time enough to pick up his hat and hide as he heard Monsieur de Villefort's footsteps coming down the hall.

Villefort entered the room, ran over to Valentine and took her in his arms. "Send for a doctor!" he cried. "Send

for Doctor d'Avrigny—no, I'll go for him myself!" And he
ran out of the room.

Maximilien went out the other door. His heart was full
of horrible memories. He remembered the conversation between Villefort and the doctor which he had overheard on
the night Madame de Saint-Méran died. And Valentine's
symptoms, while less severe, were the same as those which
had preceded the death of Barrois. At the same time he
seemed to hear the voice of the Count of Monte Cristo, who
had said to him only two hours before, "If you need anything, come to me, Maximilien; I can do much." As soon as
this thought came to him he hurried toward the count's
house on the Avenue des Champs Elysées.

The count was in his study when Maximilien arrived.
"What's the matter, Maximilien?" he asked. "You're pale and
your forehead is streaming with perspiration."

Maximilien sank into a chair. "Yes," he said, "I came here
as fast as I could. I have to talk to you."

"Is everyone in your family well?" asked Monte Cristo in
a tone of affectionate benevolence whose sincerity was unmistakable.

"Yes, thank you," replied the young man, visibly embarrassed about beginning the conversation. "Everyone in my
family is well."

"That's good; but what is it you want to tell me? Am I
fortunate enough to be in a position to help you?"

"Yes, you can help me; or rather, I've come to you like
a madman, thinking you could come to my aid in a situation
in which only God could help me."

"Tell me about it anyway."

"I don't know whether it's permissible to reveal such a
secret to human ears, count, but I'm almost forced to do it."
Maximilien stopped hesitantly. "And then, something tells
me I mustn't keep any secrets from you."

"You're right, Maximilien," said the count. "God has
spoken to your heart and your heart has spoken to you. Tell
me what's on your mind."

"Count, will you allow me to send Baptistin to ask for
news of someone you know?"

"Certainly; shall I ring for him now?"

"No, I'll speak to him myself."

Maximilien went out, called Baptistin and said a few words
to him in a low voice. Baptistin hurried out of the house.

"Has he gone?" asked Monte Cristo when Maximilien returned.

"Yes; I won't be so worried now."

"I'm still waiting for you to tell me what's worrying you," said Monte Cristo, smiling.

"And I'm ready to tell you. One night I was in a certain garden; I was hidden by a clump of trees and no one knew I was there. Two people came near me—allow me to conceal their names for the moment—and I overheard their conversation. Someone had just died in the house of the owner of the garden, who was one of the two persons I was listening to; the other one was a doctor. The first man spoke of his fear and grief, for it was the second time within a month that death had suddenly and unexpectedly fallen on his house."

"And what did the doctor say?" asked the count.

"He said that—that the death hadn't been natural and that it had to be attributed to——"

"To what?"

"To poison!"

"Really?" said Monte Cristo with that slight cough which, in his moments of emotion, served to conceal either his pallor, his redness or the extreme attention with which he listened.

"Yes, count; and the doctor added that if such an event should occur again, he would consider it his duty to call in the police. And yet death later struck a third time and neither of those two men said a word; and now death may be about to strike a fourth time. Count, what do you think I ought to do, knowing this secret?"

"My friend," replied Monte Cristo, "I think you're telling me about something which is well known to everyone. I know which house you're telling me about, or at least I know one exactly like it: a house in which there have been three strange and unexpected deaths. And yet, knowing all that as well as you, is my conscience troubled? No—it's not my concern. It may be that the justice of God has entered that house, Maximilien; if so, turn away your eyes and let that justice do its work." The count spoke these words in such a solemn, awesome tone that Maximilien shuddered. "And besides," he added, "what makes you think death will strike again in that house?"

"It *is* about to strike again, count! That's why I came to you."

"What do you want me to do about it? Shall I call the public prosecutor, for example?"

"Count! You know of whom I'm speaking, don't you?"

"Yes, I know quite well. It was in Monsieur de Villefort's garden that you overheard your secret and, according to what you've told me, I assume it was on the night Madame de Saint-Méran died. It was Monsieur de Saint-Méran three months ago, Madame de Saint-Méran two months ago, Barrois a few days ago, and now it's either Noirtier or Valentine."

"You know that and yet you say nothing?" cried Maximilien.

"What does it matter to me?" said Monte Cristo, shrugging his shoulders. "Are those people my friends? Why should I cause one of them to lose his life in order to save the life of another one? I have no preference between the murderer and the victim."

"But I love her!" cried Maximilien in agony. *"I love her!"*

"What!" exclaimed Monte Cristo, leaping to his feet.

"I love her deeply, madly! I love her so much I'd give all my blood to save her from shedding a single tear! I love Valentine de Villefort, who's being murdered at this very moment, do you hear me? And I'm asking you and God to tell me how I can save her!"

Monte Cristo uttered a cry that was like the roar of a wounded lion. "You love Valentine?" he shouted. "You love that daughter of a cursed breed!"

Maximilien had never seen such an expression on a human face. He shrank back in terror. Then Monte Cristo closed his eyes, as though dazzled by some sort of inward lightning, and struggled to subdue the storm that was raging within his heaving bosom.

After a time he looked up and said, in a voice that had become almost calm again, "God punishes the indifference of men who remain cold and proud before the terrible spectacles He presents to them. I laughed, like an avenging angel, at the evil men do to one another, but now I myself have been bitten by the serpent I was watching."

Maximilien groaned.

"Be strong and don't lose hope," said the count. "I'm here to watch over you."

Maximilien shook his head sadly.

"I tell you to hope," continued the count. "Listen to me: if Valentine isn't dead now, she won't die. Go home now and wait till you hear from me."

"Your coolness frightens me, count!" exclaimed Maximilien. "Do you have power over death itself? Are you more than a man?"

Monte Cristo looked at the young man with a tender, melancholy smile and said, "I can do much, my friend. Go now; I need to be alone."

Maximilien, subjugated by that prodigious ascendancy which Monte Cristo exercised over everyone around him, did not even try to resist. He shook hands with the count and left.

At the door he stopped and waited for Baptistin, whom he saw hurrying toward the house.

Meanwhile Villefort had returned with Doctor d'Avrigny. Valentine was still unconscious and the doctor examined her with extreme care while Villefort and Noirtier watched him breathlessly. Finally he said slowly, "She's still alive."

"*Still* alive!" cried Villefort. "Oh, doctor, what a terrible thing you've just said!"

"Yes, and I repeat it: she's still alive, which surprises me very much."

"But can you save her?"

"Yes, since she hasn't died yet." As he said this, d'Avrigny noticed Noirtier's eyes, which sparkled with such extraordinary joy and revealed such teeming thoughts that the doctor was struck by them. "Monsieur Villefort," he said, "please send for your daughter's chambermaid."

Villefort ran out to bring her himself. As soon as he had closed the door behind him, d'Avrigny approached Noirtier and asked, "Is there something you want to tell me?"

Noirtier answered affirmatively.

"Is it for me alone?"

"Yes," said the old man's eyes.

"Very well; I'll stay here with you."

Just then Villefort entered, followed by the chambermaid, behind whom came Madame de Villefort. "What's wrong with the poor girl?" she asked. "She complained of not feeling well, but I didn't think it was anything serious."

"She'll be better off in her bed," said Villefort. "Come, Fanny, we'll take her there."

Doctor d'Avrigny, who saw in this suggestion a means of staying behind with Noirtier, confirmed that this would be the best thing to do, but he ordered that she be given nothing unless he prescribed it. As she was being carried out, he told Villefort to go to the pharmacist in person and have the prescriptions prepared in his presence.

The doctor then carefully closed the door and, after making sure that no one was listening, said to Noirtier, "Do you know something about your granddaughter's illness?"

"Yes."

D'Avrigny reflected for a moment, then said, "Excuse me for what I'm about to say, but we mustn't neglect anything in this terrible situation. You saw Barrois die; do you think his death was natural?"

Something like a smile appeared on Noirtier's lifeless lips.

"Then it has already occurred to you that Barrois was poisoned?"

"Yes."

"Do you think the poison was meant for him?"

"No."

"Do you think Valentine has been poisoned by the same person?"

"Yes."

"Will she also die, then?"

"No," replied the old man's eyes triumphantly.

"You don't expect her to die?" asked d'Avrigny in surprise.

"No."

"Do you expect the murderer to abandon his efforts?"

"No."

"Then do you expect the poison not to have a fatal effect on Valentine?"

"Yes."

"Why do you think she'll be saved?"

Noirtier looked steadfastly to one side. D'Avrigny followed the direction of his gaze and saw that it was fixed on the bottles containing the medicine which was brought to him every morning.

"Ah!" exclaimed d'Avrigny, struck by a sudden idea. "Did it occur to you to accustom her in advance to the poison?"

"Yes."

"You gave her successively larger doses?"

"Yes! Yes!" signaled Noirtier, delighted to have been understood.

"And you succeeded!" said d'Avrigny. "Without that precaution, Valentine would be dead now. It was a violent attack, but she'll recover—this time, at least."

Just then Villefort entered the room. "Here's the medicine you prescribed, doctor," he said.

"Was it prepared in your presence?"

"Yes."

"And it hasn't left your hands since then?"

"No."

D'Avrigny took the bottle, poured out a few drops of the liquid it contained into the hollow of his hand, swallowed it and said, "Good. Now let's go to see Valentine. I'll give my instructions to everyone, Monsieur de Villefort, and I want you to see to it personally that no one disobeys them."

As d'Avrigny and Villefort entered Valentine's bedroom, an Italian priest, austere in bearing and calm and decisive of speech, was renting the house next door to Villefort's

"That's possible," said Danglars. "The murdered man was an escaped convict, wasn't he?"

"That's right; an escaped convict named Caderousse."

Danglars paled slightly. Andrea left the adjoining salon and entered the antechamber.

"But finish signing the marriage contract!" said Monte Cristo. "I see my story has upset everyone; please forgive me."

Madame Danglars, who had just signed, handed the pen back to the notary. "And now, Prince Cavalcanti," said the latter. "Where are you, Prince Cavalcanti?"

"Go find the prince and tell him it's his turn to sign," said Danglars to one of his servants.

At this moment a crowd of terrified people flowed into the main salon as though some frightful monster had just entered the house. And, indeed, there was cause to step back in fear: an officer had posted two gendarmes at the door of each salon and was walking toward Danglars preceded by a police commissary.

Madame Danglars screamed and fainted. Danglars, who felt himself threatened (the conscience of some men is never calm), presented to his guests a face discomposed by terror.

"Which of you gentlemen goes by the name of Andrea Cavalcanti?" asked the commissary.

A murmur of astonishment arose from all over the salon. Everyone looked around.

"But who is this Andrea Cavalcanti?" asked Danglars, who scarcely knew what he was saying.

"He's an escaped convict from the prison at Toulon, and he's also accused of murdering another escaped convict by the name of Caderousse."

Monte Cristo cast a rapid glance around him. Andrea had disappeared.

Chapter 57

A short time after the scene of consternation produced in Baron Danglars' house by the unexpected appearance of the police and the revelation which had resulted from it, the entire mansion was emptied as swiftly as though one of the guests had suddenly developed a case of Asiatic cholera or the plague. Everyone hastened to withdraw, or rather to flee, for it was one of those situations in which it is better not even to try to give those commonplace consolations which make

residence. It was not known why the three tenants of that house moved out two hours later, but the rumor in the neighborhood was that its foundation was not solid and that it was in danger of collapsing. This, however, did not prevent its new tenant from establishing himself in it, along with his modest furnishings, on the same day, toward five o'clock in the afternoon, after having paid six months' rent in advance. He was, as we have said, an Italian priest and his name was Abbé Giacomo Busoni.

Workmen were immediately called in and that same night the infrequent passers-by were surprised to see carpenters and masons engaged in rebuilding the foundations of the house.

Chapter 56

Three days later, toward half-past eight of the evening on which the ceremony of the signing of the marriage contract between Andrea Cavalcanti and Eugénie Danglars was to take place, the main salon of the Danglars residence, along with the three other salons on the same floor, was filled with a crowd of elegant people whose presence was due much more to curiosity than to affection for the Danglars family. Myriads of candles poured floods of light over the furnishings of the salon, whose bad taste was unredeemed by their expensiveness.

Mademoiselle Eugénie Danglars was dressed, with elegant simplicity, in a figured white silk dress. A white rose half lost in her jet-black hair was her only ornament; she wore no jewels.

Madame Danglars was speaking with Debray, Beauchamp and Château-Renaud. Monsieur Danglars, surrounded by deputies and financiers, was explaining a new theory of taxation which he intended to put into practice when the government was finally forced to call on him. Andrea Cavalcanti was holding the arm of a dapper young dandy and describing to him the luxurious life he expected to lead in the future with his 175,000-franc income.

The crowd flowed in and out of the salons like a tide of rubies, emeralds, opals and diamonds. As always, it was the oldest women who were the most elaborately ornamented and the ugliest who were the most obstinately set on showing themselves.

At each moment the doorkeeper's voice rose above the noise of the crowd to announce some name known in the financial world, respected in the army or celebrated in literature. But for every name which had the privilege of produc-

ing a ripple in that human sea, how many others were greeted
only by indifference or a sneer of disdain!

Just as the massive clock was striking nine, the name of
the Count of Monte Cristo was announced and all eyes
turned toward the door. The count was dressed with his
usual simplicity. His white vest displayed his broad and noble
chest; the thin gold watch chain which crossed it was his
only piece of jewelry.

With a single glance, the count saw Madame Danglars
at one end of the salon, Monsieur Danglars at the other
and Mademoiselle Eugénie before him. He went to Madame
Danglars first, then to Eugénie, whom he congratulated
quickly and reservedly. Beside her was Mademoiselle Louise
d'Armilly, who thanked him for the letters of recommendation
he had been kind enough to give her for Italy and which, she
said, she intended to put to use in the near future. As he
was leaving these ladies, he turned around and found himself
facing Monsieur Danglars, who had come over to shake
hands with him.

Andrea, who was in an adjoining salon, felt the wave of
excitement which the count's arrival had produced in the
crowd and came in to greet him. He found him completely
surrounded; everyone was striving to have the honor of
speaking with him, as always happens with people who speak
little and never say a word without value.

The notaries made their entrance and placed their documents on the velvet cloth embroidered in gold which covered the table that had been prepared for the signing of the
marriage contract. One of the notaries sat down while the
other remained standing. The reading of the contract was
about to begin.

It was read in the midst of complete silence, but as soon
as the reading was finished the buzzing of voices became
even louder than before; the dazzling sums mentioned in the
contract had completed the sensation already produced by
the bride-to-be's trousseau and diamonds, which had been
placed on display in one of the adjoining rooms. Eugénie's
charms were doubled in the eyes of the young men present.
As for the ladies, it goes without saying that, while envying
all that wealth, they themselves felt that they had no need
of it in order to be beautiful.

Andrea, overwhelmed with compliments and admiration
from his friends, was at last beginning to believe that this
dream was a reality and he was becoming bewildered.

The notary solemnly picked up a pen, raised it above his
head and announced, "Gentlemen, we shall now sign the
contract."

Baron Danglars was to be the first to sign, then the representative of Major Cavalcanti, then Madame Danglars, and
finally the future bride and bridegroom.

Danglars picked up the pen and signed, then handed it to
the major's representative. Madame Danglars approached,
accompanied by Madame de Villefort. "Isn't it annoying?"
she said to her husband. "We've been deprived of the pleasure
of Monsieur de Villefort's company by an unexpected development in that case of robbery and murder in the Count of
Monte Cristo's house."

"That's too bad," said Danglars in the same tone in which
he would have said, "What do I care about that?"

Monte Cristo stepped over and said, "I'm afraid I may
have been the cause of Monsieur de Villefort's absence."

"You, count?" said Madame Danglars as she signed the
contract. "If that's true, I'll never forgive you for it."

Andrea pricked up his ears.

"It wasn't my fault," said the count, "and I'd like to explain it to you." Everyone around him began to listen attentively. "As you may remember," he continued, "a man
who had broken into my house to rob me was killed, apparently by his accomplice. In trying to save his life, they
undressed him and threw his clothes into a corner, where
the police picked them up. The police took his coat and
trousers, but they overlooked his vest."

Andrea began to edge quietly toward the door.

"Well, that vest was found today, covered with blood and
with a hole in the place over the heart," continued the count.
"It was brought to me. No one could imagine where it had
come from; I alone happened to think that it had probably
belonged to the murder victim. My valet, searching through
it with disgust, felt a piece of paper in one of the pockets.
He pulled it out. It was a letter addressed to you, baron."

"To me!" exclaimed Danglars.

"Yes, to you. I managed to read your name beneath the
blood with which the letter was spattered," added Monte
Cristo amid a general outburst of surprise.

"But how did that keep Monsieur de Villefort from coming
here tonight?" asked Madame Danglars, looking uneasily at
her husband.

"It's quite simple, madame," replied Monte Cristo. "The
vest and the letter constituted evidence in the case, so I sent
them both to the public prosecutor. Legal proceedings are
the safest in criminal matters; it may have been some plot
against you."

Andrea looked steadfastly at Monte Cristo and disappeared
into the adjoining salon.

the presence of one's friends so inopportune during a great catastrophe.

The only people who remained were Danglars, making his statement to the commissary in his study, Madame Danglars, trembling in her boudoir, and Eugénie, who had haughtily withdrawn to her room with her inseparable companion, Mademoiselle Louise d'Armilly.

On entering her bedroom, Eugénie locked the door while Louise sank into a chair. "Oh, how horrible!" said the young music teacher. "Monsieur Andrea Cavalcanti an escaped convict—a murderer!"

"It was predestined," said Eugénie with an ironic smile. "I escaped from Morcerf only to fall into the hands of Cavalcanti."

"Don't confuse the two, Eugénie."

"All men are contemptible! And I'm happy to be able to do more than hate them: now I can despise them."

"What are we going to do now?" asked Louise.

"Why, the same thing we planned to do: leave."

"You still want to do that, even though your engagement is broken off now?"

"Why should I stay? So they can try to marry me to someone else a month from now? No, Louise, what happened tonight will serve as my excuse; I wasn't looking for one, but God sent me this one and it's welcome."

"You're so strong and courageous!" said the frail, blonde young girl to her dark-haired companion.

"Don't you know me yet? Come, Louise, let's talk about our affairs now. Have you made arrangements for the carriage?"

"Yes."

"And what about our passport?"

"Here it is!"

Eugénie, with her usual calm, unfolded the document and read: "Monsieur Léon d'Armilly, age twenty, profession artist, black hair, black eyes, traveling with his sister."

"Excellent! How did you get this passport?"

"When I went to ask the Count of Monte Cristo for letters of introduction to the managers of theaters in Rome and Naples, I told him about my fear of traveling as a woman. He understood me perfectly and offered to get a man's passport for me. I received this one two days later; I wrote in the words, 'traveling with his sister' myself."

"Well, then," said Eugénie gaily, "all we have to do now is to pack our trunks! We'll leave tonight instead of on my wedding night."

"Perhaps you'd better think it over, Eugénie."

"Oh, I've already thought it over! We have forty-five thousand francs between us, enough to live like princesses for two years, or comfortably for four. But within six months we'll have doubled our capital, you with your music, I with my voice."

"Wait a moment," said Louise, going over to the door to listen.

"The door is locked," said Eugénie.

"If only someone doesn't tell us to open it!"

"Let them tell us to open it if they want to; we won't do it, that's all."

"You're a veritable Amazon, Eugénie!"

The two girls set about piling into a trunk all the objects they thought they would need for their trip. When they had finished, Eugénie took out a set of masculine attire, complete from coat to boots. Then, with a swiftness which indicated that this was probably not the first time she had amused herself by dressing in the garments of the opposite sex, she put on the boots, trousers, vest and coat.

"Wonderful!" exclaimed Louise, looking at her in admiration. "But will that lovely black hair fit into a man's hat like the one you have there?"

"You'll see," said Eugénie. Grasping her long, thick tresses in her left hand, she took a pair of scissors in her right hand; a few moments later nearly all of her splendid hair was lying on the floor at her feet. She showed not the slightest sign of regret; on the contrary, her eyes shone more brightly and joyfully than ever beneath her black eyebrows.

"Oh, all that magnificent hair!" said Louise sadly.

"Isn't it a hundred times better this way?" said Eugénie. "Don't I look more beautiful to you now?"

"Yes, you're still beautiful! But where will we go now?"

"To Belgium, if you like; that's the nearest frontier. We'll go to Brussels, Liège, Aix-la-Chapelle and Strasbourg, then we'll cross Switzerland and go down into Italy. Does that suit you?"

"Yes, of course."

"What are you looking at?"

"I'm looking at you; you're really adorable like that. If people could see you now they'd think you were kidnaping me."

"And they'd be right, by God!"

"Why, I do believe you just swore, Eugénie!"

The two girls burst out laughing. Then, having blown out the candles, they cautiously opened the door. Eugénie went first, carrying her end of the trunk with one hand while Louise struggled to hold up her end with both hands. The courtyard was empty. The clock had just struck midnight.

In the street they found a porter and gave him the trunk. Having instructed him to take it to 36 Rue de la Victoire, they walked along behind him. A quarter of an hour after they arrived at that address, a carriage was ready to take them on their journey.

"Which road shall I take, young man?" asked the coachman.

"The road to Fontainebleau," replied Eugénie in an almost masculine voice.

"Why did you say that?" asked Louise.

"It's only to throw them off the track: we'll take a different direction as soon as we reach the boulevard."

"You're always right, Eugénie."

A quarter of an hour later the carriage had passed the Barrière Saint-Martin and was outside of Paris.

Monsieur Danglars had lost his daughter.

Chapter 58

Let us now leave Mademoiselle Danglars and her friend on their way to Brussels and return to poor Andrea Cavalcanti, whose rise to fortune had been so disastrously interrupted.

Notwithstanding his youth, Monsieur Andrea Cavalcanti was an intelligent and resourceful man. As we have seen, at the first sign of disturbance in the salon he had begun to inch his way toward the door, walked through two other rooms and finally vanished from the house. One detail which we have forgotten to mention, but which ought not to be omitted, is that one of the two rooms he walked through was the room in which the bride-to-be's trousseau and jewels were on display. Andrea showed his foresight by seizing the most valuable of these riches as he passed. They made him feel much more light-hearted as he leaped out the window and slipped past the gendarmes.

Once outside, he ran for a quarter of an hour, not knowing where he was going but wishing to put as much distance as possible between himself and the place where he had almost been arrested. He stopped out of breath at the end of the Rue Lafayette. He was completely alone. Then he saw a cab approaching. He hailed it and asked the driver, "Is your horse tired?"

"Tired!" replied the driver. "He hasn't done anything all day long! Only four customers and twenty sous in tips—seven francs in all and I have to give six of it to the owner!"

"Would you like to earn twenty francs more?"

"I'd be glad to. What do I have to do?"

"I want to overtake one of my friends with whom I'm going hunting tomorrow. He was to wait for me in his cabriolet till half-past eleven. It's midnight now, so he probably got tired of waiting for me and went off without me. Will you try to catch up with him?"

"I'd like nothing better."

Andrea climbed in and the cab set off at a rapid pace. They never caught up with the imaginary friend, of course, but from time to time Andrea would ask a passer-by if he had seen a green cabriolet drawn by a bay horse, and since nine-tenths of all cabriolets are green, information poured in from all sides; it had always just been seen passing by. "Faster! Faster!" cried Andrea. "We can't be far behind it now!" And the poor horse kept up its desperate pace until they had left Paris and arrived at Louvres.

"I can see now I'm not going to catch up with my friend and that I'll kill your horse if I go on any further," said Andrea. "I'd better stop here. Here's your money. I'll spend the night in the Hôtel du Cheval Rouge and take the first carriage I can get tomorrow morning. Good night." After handing the driver the money, Andrea leaped nimbly down to the pavement.

The driver headed back toward Paris and Andrea pretended to go into the Hôtel du Cheval Rouge, but, after standing before the door until the cab was out of sight, he walked rapidly on down the road until he had covered two more leagues. Then he stopped, not from fatigue, but because he had to think carefully and devise a plan. Taking a stagecoach was out of the question, because a passport would be necessary for that. It was also out of the question to remain in the vicinity of Paris, which is one of the most closely patrolled regions of France. He sat down by the roadside and thought. Ten minutes later he had made his decision.

He sprinkled dust over one side of the overcoat he had had time to take from the antechamber and button over his evening clothes. Then he walked on till he came to Chapelle-en-Serval and knocked boldly on the door of the local inn. The innkeeper came to the door.

"I was thrown off my horse on the way from Montrefontaine to Senlis," said Andrea. "I must get back to Compiègne tonight or my family will be seriously worried about me. Do you have a horse I could rent?"

The innkeeper called his stable boy and told him to saddle a horse. Then he woke up his son, a boy of seven, and instructed him to ride behind the gentleman and bring back the horse. Andrea gave the innkeeper twenty francs. As he drew out the money, a calling card fell to the floor. It was the card of one of his recently acquired Paris friends. When the innkeeper picked it up after Andrea's departure, he was therefore convinced that he had rented his horse to Monsieur de Mauléon, 25 Rue Saint-Dominique.

By four o'clock in the morning Andrea had arrived in Compiègnes. He sent the innkeeper's son back with the horse and knocked on the door of the Hôtel de la Cloche et de la Bouteille, reflecting that before going any further he would do well to fortify himself with a good supper and some sleep.

A servant came to the door. "I'm coming from Saint-Jean-au-Bois, where I had dinner," said Andrea. "I intended to take the stagecoach that passes at midnight, but I lost my way like a fool and I've been wandering around in the forest for four hours. Let me have a room and bring me a cold chicken and a bottle of Bordeaux."

The chicken was fresh, the wine was old, the fire was clear and sparkling and Andrea surprised himself by eating with as much appetite as though nothing had happened. Then he went to bed and almost immediately sank into that deep sleep which a young man of twenty always finds, even when he is filled with remorse. However, we must admit that, although Andrea might well have been filled with remorse, he actually had none.

Here is the plan he had devised and which was responsible for the greater part of his feeling of security: he would get up at dawn, leave the hotel after scrupulously paying his bill, go into the forest and buy the hospitality of some peasant on the pretext that he was a painter. Then he would procure an axe and the costume of a woodsman and travel from forest to forest until he reached the nearest frontier, walking at night, sleeping during the day and approaching inhabited places only from time to time in order to buy food. Once across the border, he would sell his diamonds, which ought to bring him somewhere in the neighborhood of fifty thousand francs. Furthermore, he counted heavily on Danglars' desire to hush up their misadventure as much as possible. It was for these reasons, aside from his fatigue, that Andrea went to sleep so quickly and slept so soundly. In order not to oversleep he left the shutters open and contented himself with bolting his door and laying out on the table beside his bed a certain very sharp knife whose temper he knew well and which never left him.

At about seven o'clock the next morning he was awakened by a ray of sunlight shining in his face. As soon as he opened

his eyes he knew he had slept too long. He leaped out of bed
and ran over to the window. A gendarme was crossing the
courtyard, another one was standing at the bottom of the
stairs and a third, on horseback and holding a musket in his
hand, was guarding the door to the courtyard, the only door
through which is was possible to leave.

"They've come for me!" was Andrea's first thought. He
looked frantically around him. The windows of his room
opened onto an outside gallery which was perfectly visible
from below. "I'm lost!" was his second thought. Indeed, for
a man in Andrea's situation, an arrest was equivalent to a
death sentence. For an instant he convulsively pressed his head
between his hands. During that instant he almost went mad
with fear. But soon a hope-giving thought came to him and a
faint smile appeared on his lips. He looked around. The objects he sought were all together on the writing desk: a pen,
some ink and a sheet of paper. Forcing his hand to be steady,
he wrote the following lines:

> I have no money to pay my bill, but I am not a dishonest
> man. I am leaving this tie pin as a pledge. It is worth at
> least ten times the amount of my bill. Please excuse me
> for leaving at dawn; I was ashamed.

He pulled the pin from his cravat and laid it on top of the
note. This done, he drew the bolt of the door, left it slightly
ajar as though he had left the room without locking it, then
began to climb up the chimney like a man accustomed to that
kind of gymnastic exercise. At that very moment the first gendarme was walking up the stairs accompanied by a police
commissary.

Here are the circumstances that led to that visit which
Andrea was preparing so carefully to receive: At dawn the
telegraph had begun sending messages in all directions; as
soon as each locality was notified, it sent out its authorities in
search of the murderer of Caderousse. Compiègne, a royal
residence and a fortified town, is abundantly supplied with
gendarmes and police commissaries; the search had therefore
begun as soon as the telegraphic order was received. The Hôtel
de la Cloche et de la Bouteille being the largest hotel in town,
it was naturally the first to be visited.

When the gendarme, who was a brigadier, and the police
commissary arrived at Andrea's door they found it half open.
"Aha!" said the brigadier. "An open door is a bad sign. I'd
rather find it locked with three bolts." Indeed, the note and
the tie pin left behind by Andrea confirmed the sad truth: he
was gone. But the brigadier was not a man to yield to one

piece of evidence. He looked under the bed, behind the curtains, inside the closet and finally stopped before the fireplace. Thanks to Andrea's precautions, there was not a single trace of his passage in the ashes. Nevertheless it was an exit, and under the circumstances every exit deserved careful investigation. The brigadier had some straw and wood brought to him, stuffed the fireplace with it and set it on fire. A dark column of smoke rose up to the sky, but the brigadier did not see anyone fall into the fireplace as he expected.

Andrea, who had been in conflict with society ever since his childhood, was at least as resourceful as a gendarme, even a gendarme who had attained the respectable rank of brigadier. Foreseeing the fire, he had climbed out onto the roof and was lying flattened out beside the chimney. For an instant he had hopes of being saved, for he heard the brigadier call down to the two gendarmes who had remained outside, "He's not here!" But when he cautiously raised his head he saw that, instead of withdrawing after this announcement, the two gendarmes had, on the contrary, doubled their vigilance. He looked around him: the Hôtel de Ville, a colossal sixteenth-century building, rose up like a somber rampart to his right. Every part of the roof was visible from its windows. Andrea realized that he would soon see the brigadier's face appear at one of those windows.

He therefore resolved to go back down into the hotel through another chimney. He looked until he saw a chimney from which no smoke was coming, crawled across the roof to it and climbed down into it without being seen by anyone. An instant later a little window of the Hôtel de Ville opened and revealed the face of the brigadier. It remained motionless for a time, then disappeared with a sigh of disappointment.

The brigadier, as calm and dignified as the law he represented, walked through the crowd gathered in the square without answering any of their countless questions and went back into the hotel.

"Well?" asked the two gendarmes.

"He must have left early this morning," replied the brigadier. "But we'll have the road to Villers-Cotterets watched and we'll have a search made in the forest; we're sure to catch him there."

The brigadier had hardly finished his sentence when a long shriek of fright, accompanied by the violent ringing of a bell, resounded through the courtyard.

"What's that?" cried the brigadier.

"There's a guest who seems to be in quite a hurry," said the innkeeper. "From what room are they ringing?"

"From number three," replied a servant.

"Who's staying in number three?" asked the brigadier.

"The young man who arrived with his sister last night and asked for a room with two beds."

Once again the bell began to ring desperately. "Follow me!" cried the brigadier to the commissary. "And you outside there, shoot if he tries to escape! According to the telegraph he's a desperate criminal."

The brigadier and the commissary ran up the stairs, followed by the uproar which the revelation concerning Andrea had brought forth from the crowd outside.

Andrea had skillfully climbed two-thirds of the way down the chimney, but at that point his foot had slipped and, despite the support of his hands, he had descended with much greater speed and noise than he wished. This would not have mattered if the room had been empty, but, as luck would have it, it was inhabited.

Two women were sleeping in one bed when they were awakened by the noise. They stared at the fireplace, from which the noise had come, and soon saw a man emerge from it. It was one of those two women, the blonde one, who had uttered the terrible shriek which had echoed throughout the whole hotel while the other one, a brunette, had given the alarm by pulling on the bell cord with all her might.

"Mercy!" cried Andrea frantically without seeing the persons to whom he was speaking. "Don't call for help! Save me! I won't hurt you."

"Andrea the murderer!" cried one of the two women.

"Eugénie! Mademoiselle Danglars!" exclaimed Andrea, passing from fright to stupefaction.

"Help! Help!" screamed Mademoiselle d'Armilly, taking the bell cord from Eugénie's hands and pulling on it even more violently than her friend had done.

"Save me! They're after me!" said Andrea, clasping his hands. "Don't turn me over to them!"

"It's too late," said Eugénie. "They're already on their way way up here."

"Then hide me somewhere. Tell them you were frightened for no good reason. That will turn away their suspicion and you'll have saved my life."

"All right," said Eugénie. "Go back up the chimney and we won't say anything."

"There he is!" cried a voice from outside the door. "There he is! I see him!" The brigadier had put his eye to the keyhole and seen Andrea pleading with the two young women.

A violent blow from the butt of a musket broke the lock and the door flew open. Andrea ran to the other door, opening onto the gallery that encircled the courtyard, ready to escape through it. The two gendarmes outside fixed him in the sights of their muskets. Andrea stopped short, clutching his useless knife.

The brigadier walked up to him with his saber drawn. "Come, come, put that back in its sheath," said Andrea. "I'm surrendering; so there's no need to go to all that trouble." And he held out his hands for the handcuffs.

Turning to the two young women, he smiled impudently and said, "Is there any message you'd like me to deliver to your father, Mademoiselle Eugénie? I'll no doubt be going back to Paris now." Eugénie hid her face with her hands. "Oh, there's nothing to be ashamed of," said Andrea, "and I don't hold it against you for running after me this way. After all, I was practically your husband, wasn't I?"

On this jeering note Andrea left the room, leaving the two fugitives to suffer from their shame and the remarks of the assembled crowd. An hour later they climbed into their carriage and resumed their journey; this time they were both dressed as women.

Andrea was taken back to Paris and imprisoned in the Conciergerie.

Chapter 59

Valentine had not yet recovered. It was in her bedroom, and from Madame de Villefort's lips, that she learned about the events we have just related, although she was so weak that she did not react to the story as she would have if her condition had been normal. Indeed, it produced only a few vague ideas and fluctuating forms which mingled for a time with the strange notions and fugitive phantoms arising from her sick brain or passing before her eyes.

During the day, Valentine was maintained within the bounds of reality by the presence of her grandfather, who had himself wheeled into her room and remained there, covering her with his paternal gaze. Then when Villefort came home from the Palace of Justice, he would spend an hour or two with his father and his daughter before withdrawing to his study at six o'clock; at eight o'clock Doctor d'Avrigny would arrive, bringing Valentine's nightly medicine, and then Noirtier would be taken back to his own room. A nurse chosen by the doctor remained with Valentine until she went to sleep, usually toward ten or eleven o'clock.

Maximilien Morrel came to see Noirtier every morning to ask about Valentine. Strangely enough, he seemed to be less worried every day. First of all, although Valentine was still in the grip of a violent nervous excitement, she was slowly recovering; and then Monte Cristo had said if she did not die within two hours she would be saved: she was still alive and four days had gone by.

This state of nervous excitement pursued Valentine even into her sleep, or rather into that somnolence that succeeded her waking hours. It was then, in the silence of the night and in the dim light shed by the small lamp burning on the mantelpiece, that she saw those shadows which come to people in the rooms of the sick. Sometimes she seemed to see her stepmother threatening her; sometimes it was Maximilien, holding out his arms to her; sometimes she saw people who were almost strangers to her, like the Count of Monte Cristo; even the furniture, in her moments of delirium, seemed to be moving and wandering around the room. All this would last until three or four o'clock in the morning, when she would fall into leaden slumber till morning.

In the night following the morning when she had learned about Eugénie's flight and Andrea's arrest, an unexpected scene took place in Valentine's bedroom. The nurse had withdrawn only ten minutes before and Valentine was in the grip of her nightly fever. In the flickering light of the lamp on the mantelpiece, she suddenly saw the door to her library begin to open without making the slightest noise. In any other circumstances she would have seized the bell cord and rung for help, but nothing surprised her in her present condition. She was aware that all the visions surrounding her were only the products of her delirium.

A human figure appeared behind the door. Due to her fever, Valentine was too familiar with this sort of apparition to be frightened by it; she merely opened her eyes wider and hoped it would turn out to be Maximilien. The figure approached her bed, then stopped and seemed to be listening with deep attention. A ray of light from the lamp shone on the face of the nocturnal visitor. "It's not Maximilien," murmured Valentine.

Convinced that she was dreaming, she waited for the man to disappear or change into some other person. Remembering that the best way to make these unwelcome visions disappear was to drink some of the soothing medicine which the doctor had prescribed for her, she put out her hand toward the glass standing on the table beside her bed. Just then the apparition stepped forward and came so close to her that she seemed to hear its breathing and feel the touch of its hand on her arm, which she slowly drew back.

Then the figure, which seemed to be protective rather than threatening, took the glass, held it up to the lamp and examined it carefully. But this test was not sufficient: the figure took a spoonful of the medicine from the glass and swallowed it. Valentine thought the vision was about to vanish to make way for another one, but the figure, instead of fading away like a shadow, came up to her again, held out the glass to her and said, "Now you may drink."

Valentine started. It was the first time one of her visions had spoken so realistically. She opened her mouth to scream. The man put his finger to his lips. "It's the Count of Monte Cristo!" she murmured.

"Don't call for help and don't be afraid," said the count. "The man you see before you—this time it's not an illusion, Valentine—is the most affectionate, respectful friend you can imagine."

Valentine made no reply, but her frightened eyes seemed to say, "If your intentions are pure, why are you here?"

With his keen perceptiveness, the count realized what was taking place in her heart. "Listen to me," he said, "or rather, look at me. Look at my reddened eyes and my face which is even paler than usual. I haven't slept for four nights; for four nights I've been watching over you, protecting you, preserving you for our friend Maximilien."

The blood rushed joyfully to the sick girl's cheeks, for the name which the count had just pronounced swept away all the mistrust he had inspired in her. "Maximilien!" she repeated. "Did he tell you everything?"

"Everything. He told me your life was his and I promised him you would live."

"Are you a doctor?"

"Yes, and the best one you could possibly have at this time, believe me."

"You say you've been watching over me, yet I haven't seen you till now."

Monte Cristo pointed in the direction of the library. "I was hidden behind that door," he said. "It leads into the house next door, which I've rented."

Valentine looked away in modest pride and said, "What you've done is madness, and the protection you've given me strongly resembles an insult!"

"Valentine," said Monte Cristo, "here are the only things I've seen during my long vigil: who came into your room, what food was prepared for you and what you were given to drink. When your beverages seemed dangerous to me, I entered as I did just now, emptied your glass of the poison and replaced it with a liquid which, instead of bringing on the death that had been prepared for you, made life flow through your veins."

"Poison! Death!" cried Valentine, once again believing herself to be under the influence of some feverish hallucination. "What are you saying?"

Monte Cristo put his fingers to his lips again. "Yes, I said poison and death; but first drink this." He took out a flask containing a red liquid and poured several drops of it into her glass. "And after you've drunk this, don't drink anything else for the rest of the night."

Valentine put out her hand, but drew it back in fright as soon as it touched the glass. Monte Cristo took the glass, drank half of its contents and handed it back to Valentine, who smiled and swallowed the rest. "Oh, yes," she said, "I recognize the taste of the medicine that always brings down my fever and calms my brain a little. Thank you, count."

"Now you know how you've lived for four nights, Valentine. But you don't know what terrible torment I've gone through when I saw the poison poured into your glass, when I trembled lest you drink it before I could pour it out into the fireplace!"

"If you've seen the poison poured into my glass, then you must have seen the person who poured it," said Valentine in terror. "Tell me who the murderer is!"

"Haven't you ever seen anyone come into your room at night?"

"Yes, I've seen shadows pass, approach and disappear, but I took them for visions brought on by my fever, and even when you came in just now I thought for a long time that I was either delirious or dreaming."

"So you don't know the identity of the person who wants to take your life?"

"No; why should anyone want me to die?"

"You're about to find out who it is, then," said Monte Cristo, listening attentively. "You're not delirious tonight and you're wide awake. I want you to summon up all your strength now. Pretend to be asleep and you'll see!"

Valentine seized the count's hand and said, "I think I just heard a noise. Hurry, leave!"

With a benevolent smile that filled her with gratitude, the count tiptoed over to the library door. Just before he closed it behind him he turned around and said, "Remember, don't move and don't make a sound; unless you pretend to be asleep you may be killed before I can come to your aid." With this frightful injunction, the count vanished behind the door, which closed silently.

Valentine remained alone. Two clocks struck midnight

and then, except for the rumble of a few distant carriages, everything became silent. Valentine was obsessed by a single thought: there was someone in the world who had already tried to murder her and who was about to try once again. Twenty minutes passed, twenty eternities; then ten more.

Finally an almost imperceptible scratching on the library door told Valentine that the count was listening and telling her to listen also. From the opposite direction, that is, from the direction of Edouard's room, she seemed to hear the floorboards creaking. She held her breath. The door began to open.

Having raised herself up on one elbow, she scarcely had time to fall back down and hide her eyes under her arm. Then, with her heart clutched by unspeakable fear, she waited.

Someone came up beside her bed. "Valentine!" whispered a voice. She shuddered to the depths of her soul, but she did not answer. "Valentine!" repeated the same voice. She still remained silent. Then she heard the faint sound of a liquid being poured into the glass from which she had just drunk. Only then did she dare open her eyes, which were hidden beneath her arm.

She saw a woman dressed in a white peignoir pouring out a liquid from a flask. Valentine must have gasped or made some slight movement, for the woman stopped in alarm and leaned over the bed to make sure she was really asleep. It was Madame de Villefort.

On recognizing her stepmother, Valentine could not repress a shudder, which caused a vibration in the bed. Madame de Villefort instantly flattened herself against the wall and silently watched Valentine's every movement.

Valentine recalled Monte Cristo's terrible words; it seemed to her she had seen some sort of long, pointed knife in Madame de Villefort's hand. She forced herself to close her eyes, although this usually simple action was now almost impossible for her to perform.

Meanwhile, reassured by the sound of Valentine's regular breathing, Madame de Villefort put out her arm again and finished emptying the contents of her flask into Valentine's glass. Then she withdrew. No sound indicated to Valentine that she had gone; he merely saw her arm disappear: that fresh, rounded arm of a woman of twenty-five who was pouring out death.

A scratching on the library door drew Valentine out of the dazed torpor into which she had fallen. She raised her head with great effort. The door opened and the Count of Monte Cristo reappeared. "Do you still have any doubts?" he asked.

"Oh, my God!" murmured Valentine.

"Did you recognize her?"

Valentine groaned and said, "Yes, but I still can't believe it."

"Do you prefer to die, then, and cause Maximilien to die also?"

"Oh, my God! My God!" repeated the girl frantically.

The count picked up the glass and tasted its contents. "This time it isn't brucine," he said, "but a simple narcotic. I recognize the taste of the alcohol in which it's dissolved. If you had drunk what Madame de Villefort just poured into this glass, Valentine, you'd be lost."

"Oh, why does she want to kill me?" cried Valentine.

"What! Are you so kind, so gentle, so reluctant to believe evil of others that you haven't realized the reason?"

"No; I've never done her any harm."

"But you're rich, Valentine. You have an income of two hundred thousand francs a year which could belong to her son. Monsieur and Madame de Saint-Méran died so that you would inherit their fortune; that's why Monsieur Noirtier was condemned to death when he made you the beneficiary of his will; and that's why you yourself must die, Valentine— in order that your father may inherit from you and that your brother may in turn inherit from him."

"Edouard! Poor child, is it for him that all those crimes were committed?"

"Ah, at last you understand."

"If only he doesn't have to suffer for it!"

"Valentine, you're an angel."

"Has she given up trying to kill my grandfather?"

"She no doubt reflected that when you were dead his fortune would naturally go to your brother and that the murder would therefore be a useless risk."

"And to think that a woman could devise such a diabolical plan!"

"Do you remember Perugia and the man your stepmother spoke with about poisons while you were waiting for the carriage? It was then that the plan began to develop in her mind."

"Oh, count!" cried the girl, bursting into tears. "I see it all now, and I see I must die!"

"No, Valentine, our enemy is defeated because we've unmasked her. You'll live to love and to be loved, to make a noble heart happy. But in order to live, you must have complete confidence in me."

"I'm at your orders, count. I'll do anything in order to live, for there are two people in this world who love me and would die if I died: my grandfather and Maximilien Morrel."

"No matter what happens to you, Valentine," said Monte Cristo, "don't be frightened. If you lose your sight, your hearing and your sense of touch, don't be afraid; if you awaken without knowing where you are, don't be afraid, even if you should find yourself in a tomb or a coffin; rather, keep your head and say to yourself, 'At this moment a man dedicated to my happiness and that of Maximilien is watching over me.'"

"What a terrible extremity!"

"Would you prefer to denounce your stepmother?"

"I'd rather die than do that!"

"You won't die, Valentine; but I want you to promise me that, no matter what happens, you won't lose hope. Believe in my devotion to you as you believe in God's goodness and Maximilien's love."

Valentine gave Monte Cristo a look full of gratitude. He took out his little emerald box, opened it and dropped into her hand a round pill the size of a pea.

Valentine looked at him questioningly. "Yes," he said. She put the pill into her mouth and swallowed it.

"And now good-bye, Valentine," said Monte Cristo. "I'm going to try to sleep, for you're saved."

He watched her as she gradually went to sleep, overwhelmed by the power of the narcotic he had just given her. Then he picked up her glass, emptied most of its contents into the fireplace so that it would appear that Valentine had drunk it, set it back down on the table beside her bed and disappeared through the library door after having taken one last look at Valentine, who was sleeping with the tranquillity of an angel lying at the feet of the Lord.

Chapter 60

The lamp continued to burn on the mantelpiece in Valentine's room, consuming the last drops of oil that remained floating on the surface of the water and casting a reddish glow on the white curtains and sheets. All the noises of the street had finally died down and the silence inside was almost frightening.

Then the door of Edouard's room opened and a face which we have already seen appeared in the mirror opposite the door. It was Madame de Villefort coming in to determine the effects of her poison. She stopped on the threshold, listened, heard nothing but the crackling of the lamp, then walked silently over to the table beside the bed to see if Valentine's

glass was empty. Nearly all its contents were gone, as we
have already noted. Madame de Villefort emptied the remainder into the fireplace, stirred the ashes, carefully rinsed
out the glass, dried it with her handkerchief and set it back
on the table.

Anyone looking into the room at that moment would have
seen how she hesitated to look at Valentine and approach the
bed; the murderer was frightened by her own work. She
finally took courage, leaned over the bed and looked. Valentine was no longer breathing; her livid lips had ceased to
quiver. Madame de Villefort put her hand over Valentine's
heart and felt nothing. She drew back her hand with a shudder. Valentine's arm was hanging over the edge of the bed;
her wrist was already a little stiff and there was a bluish tinge
around the edges of her fingernails.

Madame de Villefort no longer had any doubt: it was all
over now; her final task had been accomplished. She stepped
back, but then she stood motionless, absorbed in the sight of
death. Several minutes went by. The lamp flickered and soon
afterward the flame was extinguished, plunging the room
into frightful darkness. In the midst of that darkness the
clock awakened and struck half-past four. Madame de Villefort groped her way to the door and returned to her own
room with perspiration streaming down her forehead.

The darkness continued for two more hours. Then, little
by little, a wan light began to invade Valentine's room; finally
it became bright enough to lend color and form to the objects inside.

The nurse entered the room, holding a cup in her hand.
For a father, or a lover, the first glance would have been
decisive: Valentine was dead; but for that mercenary Valentine was only asleep. She went over to the fireplace, kindled
a fire, sat down in her armchair and, although she had left
her bed only a short time before, she took advantage of
Valentine's sleep to sleep for a few more minutes. The clock
awakened her by striking eight.

Astonished by Valentine's continued slumber and frightened by the arm which continued to hang over the edge of
the bed, she walked over to the bed. It was only then that
she noticed Valentine's cold lips and her still breast. She tried
to bring the arm back beside the body, but it obeyed only
with that horrifying stiffness about which a nurse could make
no mistake. She shrieked and ran to the door screaming,
"Help! Help!"

"What's the matter?" replied the voice of Doctor d'
Avrigny from the bottom of the stairs. It was the hour when
he usually paid his morning visit.

"Did you hear someone calling for help, doctor?" asked Villefort, coming out of his study.

"Yes. It came from Valentine's room. Hurry!"

But before the doctor and the father arrived, the servants had entered and, seeing Valentine pale and motionless, were now raising their hands before their faces and reeling as though they had been stunned.

"Call Madame de Villefort! Wake up Madame de Villefort!" cried the public prosecutor, apparently not daring to enter her room.

But instead of responding to his order, the servants were looking at Doctor d'Avrigny, who had run over to Valentine and was now raising her up in his arms. "One more!" he murmured as he put her back down on the bed. "O God, when will you grow weary of this?"

"What are you saying, doctor?" cried Villefort.

"I'm saying that Valentine is dead!" replied d'Avrigny in a solemn and terrible voice.

Villefort sank to the floor and came to rest with his head on Valentine's bed. The servants turned and fled, muttering sinister imprecations. They were heard hurrying down the stairs and through the halls, then there was a great hustle and bustle in the courtyard and that was all; every one of them had deserted the accursed house.

Madame de Villefort appeared in the doorway. She stood there for a moment, calling a few reluctant tears to her aid. Suddenly she rushed forward, her arms stretched out toward the table. She had just seen Doctor d'Avrigny lean curiously over the table and pick up the glass she was sure she had emptied during the night. It was about one-third full, precisely as it had been when she had poured its remaining contents into the ashes. Valentine's ghost suddenly rising up before her would have produced a less violent effect on her. The liquid in the glass was of exactly the same color as that which she had poured into it the night before and which Valentine had drunk. The doctor was looking at it attentively; he could not fail to recognize the poison. There could be no doubt: it was a miracle which God had performed in order to foil the murderer's precautions.

While Madame de Villefort stood motionless, like a statue of Terror, and while Villefort, his head buried in the sheets of Valentine's bed, saw nothing of what was taking place around him, the doctor walked over to the window to examine the contents of the glass and tasted a drop of it on the end of his finger. "Ah!" he murmured. "It's no longer brucine now. Let's see what it is." He went over to a cabinet which had been transformed into a miniature pharmacy, took out a phial of nitric acid and poured a few drops of it into the glass. The liquid instantly changed to a blood-red color. "Aha!" he exclaimed with the horror of a judge to whom the truth is revealed, mingled with the joy of the scientist who has solved a problem.

Fire flashed from Madame de Villefort's eyes for an instant, then was extinguished. She turned, staggered to the door and went out. A few moments later there was the sound of a body falling to the floor.

D'Avrigny, who had noticed Madame de Villefort's hurried exit, went to the door and saw her lying motionless on the floor. "Go take care of Madame de Villefort," he said to the nurse. "She's fainted."

"But what about Mademoiselle Valentine?" stammered the nurse.

"Mademoiselle Valentine doesn't need anyone's help now, because she's dead."

"Dead! Dead!" sighed Villefort in a paroxysm of grief that was all the more heartrending because it was new and previously unknown to that heart of bronze.

"Dead!" cried a third voice. "Who says Valentine is dead?"

The two men turned and saw Maximilien Morrel standing in the doorway, livid and wild-eyed.

For this is what had happened: at the usual hour of his visit, Maximilien had arrived at the small door leading to Noirtier's room. Since, contrary to custom, the door was not locked, he walked in without ringing. He stopped in the hall and called for a servant to announce him to Noirtier, but no one answered; as we have seen, all the servants had deserted the house. Maximilien had no particular reason to be worried: he had Monte Cristo's promise that Valentine would live, and so far the promise had been faithfully kept. Every evening the count gave him good news, which was confirmed by Noirtier the next day. Nevertheless this solitude appeared strange to him. He called out a second time, and a third, but there was still the same silence. He decided to go upstairs.

Noirtier's door was open. The old man's eyes seemed to express an inward tension which was confirmed by the strange pallor of his face. "You seem worried, sir," said Maximilien. "Would you like me to call one of your servants?"

"Yes," signaled Noirtier.

Maximilien pulled on the bell cord, but no one came. He turned to Noirtier. The anguish in the old man's eyes continued to grow. "Why doesn't someone come?" said Maximilien. "Is there someone ill in the house?" Noirtier's eyes seemed ready to leap from their sockets. "What's the matter?" continued Maximilien. "You frighten me! Is Valentine——"

"Yes! Yes!"

Maximilien opened his mouth to speak, but he was unable to utter a sound. He pointed to the door.

"Yes! Yes! Yes!" signaled the old man.

Maximilien dashed out of the room and down the stairs. Less than a minute later he arrived at Valentine's room. The door was open.

A sob was the first sound he heard. He saw, as though through a mist, a black figure kneeling beside the bed. He stood stock-still in the doorway, transfixed by fear. It was then that he heard a voice saying, "She's dead," and a second voice answering like an echo, "Dead! Dead!"

Villefort stood up, almost ashamed at having been caught in his outburst of grief; the terrible profession he had exercised for twenty-five years had made him into something either more or less than a man. He stared at Maximilien and said, "Who are you, and why have you forgotten that one does not enter a house which has been visited by death? Leave at once!"

But Maximilien remained motionless, unable to take his eyes off the bed and the pale figure lying on it.

"Leave at once, do you hear me?" cried Villefort as d'Avrigny stepped forward to come to his aid if necessary.

Maximilien hesitated and opened his mouth, but, unable to find a single word to reply, despite the swarm of thoughts rushing through his brain, he turned and fled, clutching his head between his hands. Villefort and d'Avrigny exchanged a glance which seemed to say, "He's mad!"

A few minutes later they heard the staircase groaning under a heavy weight and saw Maximilien, who, with superhuman strength, had picked up Noirtier's wheelchair and was carrying the old man down to the second floor. When he reached the landing he set the wheelchair down and rolled it swiftly into the room.

As he approached Valentine's bed, Noirtier's face, with its flaming eyes, was like a terrifying apparition to Villefort. Each time he had found himself in contact with his father, something terrible had happened.

"Look what they've done to her!" cried Maximilien, with one hand on the back of the wheelchair and the other pointing to Valentine. "Look, grandfather, look!"

Villefort stepped back and stared in astonishment at this young man who, almost a stranger to him, called Noirtier "grandfather."

At this moment the old man's whole soul seemed to rush into his eyes; the veins of his neck swelled and his cheeks and temples turned purple, as though he had been stricken with an epileptic fit. A shriek was the only thing lacking in that inward explosion of his entire being. That shriek burst forth, so to speak, from every pore, frightful and heartrending in its silence.

"They ask me who I am and what right I have to be here!" cried Maximilien, gripping the old man's inert hand. "You know! Tell them! Tell them!" His voice was choked by a sob.

Noirtier's chest heaved convulsively and tears appeared in his eyes.

"Tell them I was her fiancé!" continued Maximilien. "Tell them she was my only love in this world! Tell them this corpse belongs to me!" And the young man, presenting the terrible spectacle of great strength being shattered, fell heavily to his knees beside the bed.

His grief was so touching that d'Avrigny turned his face away to hide his emotion, and Villefort, without asking for any further explanation, moved by that magnetism which draws us to those who have loved those for whom we mourn, held out his hand to the young man. But Maximilien saw nothing; he had seized Valentine's icy hand and, still unable to weep, was biting the sheets and groaning.

For a time nothing was to be heard in the room except the mingled sobs, imprecations and prayer. Finally Villefort, who had the greatest measure of self-control, said to Maximilien, "You say you loved Valentine and that you were her fiancé; I knew nothing of your love or your engagement, but I, her father, forgive you for it because I see that your grief is real and profound. Besides, my own heart is so filled with grief that there is no room in it for anger. But, as you see, the angel you loved has left this earth; bid farewell to her mortal remains and take leave of her forever. Valentine no longer needs anyone except a priest to bless her."

"You're mistaken, sir!" cried Maximilien, raising himself up on one knee. "Valentine needs not only a priest but an avenger! Send for the priest, Monsieur de Villefort; I will be the avenger!"

"What do you mean?" murmured Villefort, trembling.

"I mean that there are two men in you, Monsieur de Villefort. The father has wept long enough; it's now time for the public prosecutor to begin his duties." Noirtier's eyes flashed fire and Doctor d'Avrigny stepped closer. "I know what I'm saying," continued Maximilien, after examining the faces of all those present, "and you all know already what I'm going to say: Valentine was murdered!"

Villefort bowed his head, d'Avrigny approached still closer and Noirtier signaled "Yes!" with his eyes.

"You're mistaken," replied Villefort. "There has been no

crime in my house. Fate has struck me down and God is
trying my soul; it's horrible to think about, but there has been
no crime."

Noirtier's eyes flamed still more brightly and d'Avrigny
opened his mouth to speak, but Maximilien put out his arm
to command silence. "And I tell you there is a murderer in
your house!" he cried out. "I tell you that this is the fourth
victim in four months! I tell you that you already know all
this because this gentleman here warned you about it as a
friend and as a doctor!"

"You're delirious!" said Villefort, struggling vainly against
the net in which he felt himself caught.

"If you think I'm delirious, I refer you to Monsieur
d'Avrigny. Ask him if he remembers what he told you in
the garden of this house on the night Madame de Saint-Méran
died!" Villefort and d'Avrigny looked at each other. "Yes, I
overheard those words," continued Maximilien. "I should have
repeated them to the authorities myself; if I had, I wouldn't
now be the accomplice of the murder of my beloved Valentine. But the accomplice is about to become the avenger!
This fourth murder is flagrant and visible to everyone's eyes,
and if Valentine's own father abandons her, I swear that I
myself will avenge her murder!"

"And I join Monsieur Morrel in demanding that justice
be done," said d'Avrigny firmly, "for my heart is sick at the
thought that my cowardly complaisance has aided the murderer."

"Oh, my God! My God!" murmured Villefort, overwhelmed.

Maximilien looked up and saw Noirtier's eyes, which were
glowing with superhuman fury. "Monsieur Noirtier wishes
to speak," he said.

"Yes," signaled Noirtier.

"Do you know who the murderer is?" asked Maximilien.

"Yes."

"And you'll guide us?" cried the young man.

Noirtier gave him a tender, melancholy look, then turned
his eyes toward the door.

"Do you want me to leave, sir?" asked Maximilien in despair.

"Yes."

"May I at least return later?"

"Yes."

"Shall I leave alone?"

"No."

"Whom do you want to leave with me? Monsieur de
Villefort?"

"No."

"Doctor d'Avrigny?"

"Yes."

"You want to be alone with Monsieur de Villefort?"

"Yes."

D'Avrigny took Maximilien by the arm and led him into the next room. After a quarter of an hour Villefort appeared in the doorway and said, "Come here." All three of them went in and stood beside Noirtier's wheelchair.

Villefort's face was livid. "Gentlemen," he said to Maximilien and d'Avrigny in a choked voice, "I want you to give me your word of honor not to reveal the horrible secret."

The two men started. "But the murderer!" exclaimed Maximilien.

"Have no fear: justice will be done," said Villefort. "My father has revealed the murderer to me; he is as eager for vengeance as you are, yet he asks you, as I do also, to swear to keep the secret of the crime. Isn't that right, father?"

"Yes," said Noirtier's eyes resolutely.

Maximilien made a gesture of horror and incredulity. Villefort caught his arm and said, "You know what an implacable man my father is. You may be sure that if he makes this request of you he knows that Valentine's death will be terribly avenged." The old man's eyes confirmed this statement. Villefort continued: "My father knows me and I've given him my word. I ask for only three days, gentlemen; within three days the vengeance I will have taken on the murderer of my daughter will make the most callous of men shudder to the depths of his soul!"

"Will that promise be kept, Monsieur Noirtier?" asked Maximilien.

"Yes!" signaled the old man with a look of sinister joy.

"Will you swear, then, to leave the vengeance to me, gentlemen?" asked Villefort.

D'Avrigny turned away and murmured a feeble "Yes," but Maximilien rushed over to the bed, kissed Valentine's cold lips and fled from the room with a groan of utter despair.

"Is there any particular priest you'd like me to call in to pray for Valentine?" asked d'Avrigny.

"No," replied Villefort; "go bring the nearest one."

"The nearest one is an Italian priest who just moved into the house next door; shall I stop in to see him on my way home?"

"Yes, ask him to stay here with Valentine."

"Do you want to talk to him?"

"No, I want to be alone. Please apologize to him; a priest ought to understand all grief, even the grief of a father."

Villefort took leave of d'Avrigny and went into his study, where he began to work. For certain natures, work is a remedy for all afflictions.

On his way out d'Avrigny saw a man wearing a cassock standing on the front steps of the house next door. He went over to him and asked, "Would you be willing to render a great service to a poor father who has just lost his daughter? I'm speaking of your neighbor, Monsieur de Villefort."

"Yes, I know that death has visited his house," replied the priest with a marked Italian accent. "I was about to offer my services of my own accord; it's the mission of a priest to anticipate his duties."

"She was a young girl."

"Yes, I know that also: I learned it from the servants I saw fleeing from the house. I learned that her name was Valentine and I've already been praying for her."

"Thank you, father," said d'Avrigny. "Since you've already begun to carry out your sacred duties, please continue them. Come sit beside the poor girl; her whole family will be deeply grateful to you."

"I'll go," said the priest, "and no prayers will ever be more fervent than mine."

D'Avrigny took the priest by the hand and, without meeting Villefort, who had locked himself in his study, led him to Valentine's room. As they entered, Noirtier's eyes met those of the priest and apparently read something in them, for the old man continued to look at him steadfastly.

In order that he would not be disturbed in his prayers, and that Noirtier would not be disturbed in his grief, the priest bolted not only the door through which d'Avrigny had just left, but also the door leading into Madame de Villefort's room.

Chapter 61

The next day Baron Danglars saw the Count of Monte Cristo's carriage enter his courtyard. He came out to meet the count with a sad but affable expression on his face. "You've no doubt come to express your sympathy," he said. "Oh, be careful, count: the men of our generation are unlucky this year! There's our puritanical public prosecutor, Monsieur de Villefort, who's losing his whole family in a strange manner; then there's Monsieur de Morcerf, dishonored and dead; then there's myself, covered with ridicule by that devilish Benedetto and——"

"And what?" asked the count.

"Haven't you heard?"

"A new misfortune?"

"My daughter Eugénie has left us."

"Impossible!"

"It's true, count. She was crushed by the affront we received from that wretched scoundrel and asked me for permission to make a trip. She left night before last."

"With Madame Danglars?"

"No, with a relative. I'm afraid we've lost her, poor Eugénie! I know her character and I doubt that she'll ever consent to come back to France."

"Such sorrows would be unbearable for a man whose daughter was his only fortune," said Monte Cristo, "but they ought to be quite bearable for a millionaire. No matter what the philosophers say, money is always a great consolation; and you, the king of the world of finance, ought to have greater consolation than anyone else."

Danglars cast a sidelong glance at Monte Cristo to see if he was joking or speaking seriously. "Yes," he said, "if fortune is a consolation I ought to be consoled: I'm rich."

"So rich, baron, that your fortune is like the pyramids: if one should want to destroy them, one wouldn't dare; if one should dare, one wouldn't be able to."

Danglars smiled and said, "That reminds me: I was signing some checks when you came in; will you allow me to finish?"

"Certainly."

There was a moment during which the only sound to be heard was the scratching of the banker's pen. Then Danglars said to Monte Cristo, "Have you seen many scraps of paper like this, each one worth a million francs?"

Monte Cristo took the five scraps of paper which Danglars proudly handed to him and said, "One, two, three, four, five million francs!"

"That's how I do business," said Danglars.

"It's wonderful! Especially if the sum will be paid in cash, as I'm sure it will."

"It will," said Danglars.

"It's a fine thing to have such credit. Only in France could you see something like this: five scraps of paper worth five millon francs; it has to be seen to be believed."

"Do you doubt it?"

"No."

"You don't sound very convinced. Why don't you see for yourself? Go with my clerk to the bank and you'll see him come out with a draft on the treasury for the same sum."

"No," said Monte Cristo, folding the five checks, "the

thing is so extraordinary that I'll make the experiment myself. My credit with you was six million francs; I've drawn nine hundred thousand, so you still owe me five millon one hundred thousand. I'll take your five scraps of paper, which I trust to be valid from the sight of your signature alone, and here's a receipt for six million francs, which settles our account. I made it out before I came here because I'm greatly in need of money today."

Monte Cristo put the five checks into his pocket with one hand while he held out the receipt to Danglars with the other.

Danglars was panic-stricken. "What! Are you taking those checks?" he stammered. "Excuse me, but I owe that money to the hospitals—it's a deposit I promised to repay this morning."

"Ah, that's different," said Monte Cristo. "I'm not determined to have these five checks. You can give me another one; I took these only so I could say that, without five minutes' delay, the Danglars firm had paid me five million francs on the spot. It would have been remarkable! But here are your checks; give me another one."

Danglars put out his hand to take the checks, but suddenly he appeared to change his mind and made a violent effort to control himself. Then he smiled and said, "After all, count, your receipt is as good as cash."

"Of course; if you were in Rome, the firm of Thomson and French would pay you as easily as you've paid me. . . . Shall I keep these checks, then?"

"Yes, keep them," said Danglars, wiping away the perspiration that had broken out at the roots of his hair.

Monte Cristo put the five checks into his pocket with an expression that said clearly, "Think it over—there's still time to change your mind."

"No, no; keep them," said Danglars. "You know how formalistic a banker is: I was going to give that money to the hospitals and for a moment it seemed to me I'd be robbing them if I didn't give them those very same checks, as though one franc weren't the same as another! Excuse me, count." And he burst into loud, nervous laughter.

"I excuse you," said Monte Cristo graciously, "and I put your money into my pocket."

"But I still owe you a hundred thousand francs."

"Oh, that's only a trifle. The convenience amounts to that much. Keep it and we'll consider our account settled."

"Are you speaking seriously, count?"

"I never joke with bankers," said the count with a seriousness that almost amounted to impertinence. As he was walk-

ing toward the door a servant entered and announced,
"Monsieur de Boville, Commissioner of Hospitals."

Danglars paled and hastened to take leave of Monte Cristo,
who exchanged a ceremonious bow with Monsieur de Boville
as he passed through the waiting room. Outside he climbed
into his carriage and drove straight to the bank.

Meanwhile Danglars, restraining his emotions, greeted the
commissioner of hospitals. It goes without saying that a
courteous smile was stamped on his lips. "How are you today,
dear creditor?" he asked. "Am I right in assuming that you've
come to me as a creditor?"

"You assume correctly, baron," said Monsieur de Boville.
"Did you receive my letter yesterday?"

"Yes."

"Well, here's my receipt."

"Monsieur de Boville," said Danglars, "I'll have to ask
you to wait till tomorrow in view of the fact that the Count
of Monte Cristo, whom you saw in the waiting room, walked
out of here with your five millon francs."

"What!"

"The count had an unlimited credit with me, a credit
opened by the firm of Thomson and French, of Rome. He
came to me today to ask me for five million francs all at
once, so I gave him a check. As you can understand, I'm
afraid the bank may find it a little strange if I withdraw ten
million francs in one day."

"Do you mean to say," exclaimed Monsieur de Boville in
a tone of complete incredulity, "that you gave five million
francs to that man who just left here and who bowed to me
as though he knew me?"

"Here's his receipt. See for yourself."

Monsieur de Boville took the receipt and read it with an
expression of great admiration. "I must visit this man," he
said, "and ask him for a donation to charity; I'll cite him the
example of Madame de Morcerf and her son."

"What about them?"

"They gave their entire fortune to the hospitals."

"What fortune?"

"The fortune of the late General de Morcerf."

"But why did they do that?"

"They say they want nothing to do with money acquired
in such an ignoble way."

"How will they live, then?"

"The mother is going to live in the provinces and the son
has enlisted in the army. . . . But let's come back to our
five million francs."

"Gladly," said Danglars in a perfectly natural tone. "Are you in a hurry to have the money?"

"Of course—our books are being examined tomorrow."

"Tomorrow—why, that's more than enough time. What time is the examination?"

"At two o'clock."

"Send someone here at noon."

Monsieur de Boville nodded reluctantly and fingered his portfolio.

"Just a moment," said Danglars, "I have a better idea: the Count of Monte Cristo's receipt is the same as money; take it to Rothschild or Lafitte and they'll accept it on sight."

"Even though it's payable in Rome?"

"Certainly; of course, it will cost you a discount of five or six thousand francs."

"Then I'd rather wait till tomorrow. What strange ideas you have!"

"Very well, then, I'll pay you tomorrow."

"And I'll have the money without fail?"

"Of course! Why, you must be joking! Send someone here tomorrow and the bank will be notified."

"I'll come in person."

"So much the better; that will give me the pleasure of seeing you again."

They shook hands.

"By the way," said Monsieur de Boville, "aren't you going to poor Mademoiselle de Villefort's funeral? I passed the procession on my way here."

"No, I still feel a little ridiculous after that Benedetto affair and I want to stay out of sight as much as possible for a while."

"You may be sure everyone sympathizes with you, and especially with your daughter."

"Poor Eugénie!" said Danglars with a deep sigh. "Have you heard that she's going to enter a convent?"

"No."

"Alas, it's only too true. The day after the disaster she decided to leave with a friend of hers who's already a nun; she's going to find some very severe convent in Italy or Spain."

"Oh, that's terrible!"

Monsieur de Boville withdrew, expressing his deepest sympathy as he left. But as soon as he was gone Danglars exclaimed vehemently, "Idiot! I'll be far away from here when you come tomorrow!" Then he locked the door, collected fifty thousand francs or so in cash from a drawer, burned certain papers, placed others in evidence and wrote a letter, whose only address was, "To Madame Danglars."

He took out his passport from a drawer, looked at it and said, "Good—it's valid for two more months."

Chapter 62

Monsieur de Boville had, as he said, passed the funeral procession that was taking Valentine to her final resting place.

A true Parisian, Monsieur de Villefort regarded the Père Lachaise Cemetery as the only one worthy of receiving the mortal remains of a Parisian family; only there could a well-bred corpse feel at home. He had therefore bought a vault there and had the words "Saint-Méran and Villefort" inscribed on it; such had been the dying wish of poor Renée, Valentine's mother.

The procession was composed predominantly of young people who had been struck by Valentine's death as though by a thunderbolt and who, despite the cold and prosaic tenor of the times, were deeply affected by the thought of the death of such a beautiful, chaste and adorable girl, cut off in the flower of her youth.

As the procession was approaching the outskirts of Paris it was overtaken by a carriage drawn by four swift horses. The Count of Monte Cristo climbed out of the carriage and mingled with the crowd following the hearse on foot. Château-Renaud and Beauchamp soon noticed him and came up beside him.

"Have you seen Maximilien Morrel?" asked the count.

"No," replied Château-Renaud. "We were wondering about him when the procession began because none of us saw him."

The count said nothing, but he continued to look around him. However, he did not find what he was looking for until the procession reached the cemetery. There he saw Maximilien standing beside a tree on top of a hillock overlooking the vault. The count watched him all through the ceremony.

"Look, there's Maximilien Morrel!" said Beauchamp to Debray suddenly. "What's he doing up there?"

"See how pale he is," said Château-Renaud.

"He's cold," said Debray.

"No, I think he's agitated," replied Château-Renaud slowly. "He's a very emotional man."

"Why, he hardly knew Mademoiselle de Villefort!"

"That's true; but I remember seeing him dance three times with her at a ball once."

"The ceremony is over," said Monte Cristo abruptly. "Good-bye, gentlemen." And he walked off as the rest of the crowd began to prepare for the trip back to town.

Monte Cristo hid himself behind a tombstone and watched Maximilien's movements. The young man slowly approached the vault, which was now abandoned, and knelt before it. Then he pressed his forehead against the stone and murmured, "Oh, Valentine!"

The count's heart was deeply affected by the way these words were uttered. He stepped forward, touched Maximilien on the shoulder and said, "I was looking for you, my friend." He expected an outbust of reproach or recrimination, but he was mistaken: Maximilien turned around and said, with apparent calm, "I was praying."

The count looked at him searchingly for a time, after which he seemed to feel more reassured. "Would you like me to take you back to town?" he asked.

"No, thank you."

"Is there anything I can do for you?"

"Let me pray."

The count walked off without saying anything further, but he took up another post of observation from which he watched Maximilien's every move. The young man finally stood up and began to walk back to town. Monte Cristo dismissed his carriage, which had been waiting for him, and walked after him, following him from a hundred paces behind.

Five minutes after the door of the house in the Rue Meslay closed behind Maximilien, it opened for Monte Cristo. Julie was in the garden attentively watching Penelon, who took his profession of gardener seriously, at work on some rose bushes. "Ah, the Count of Monte Cristo!" she exclaimed with the joy which each member of the family always manifested when the count paid a visit.

"Maximilien just came home, didn't he?" asked Monte Cristo.

"Yes, I think I saw him go past," replied the young woman.

"Excuse me, but I must see him immediately. I have something important to tell him."

"Go right on up, then," said Julie. She watched him with her charming smile until he had disappeared up the staircase.

When Monte Cristo arrived in front of Maximilien's room on the third floor he stopped and listened: there was no sound. The door had a glass panel, but it was impossible to see through it because it was covered by a red curtain hung on the inside. The count reflected for a moment. "Shall I ring?" he thought. "No, the sound of a doorbell often hastens the resolution of one in Maximilien's situation, and another sound answers the sound of the bell." He shuddered from head to foot. Then, making a decision with his usual swiftness, he broke the glass panel with his elbow, pushed aside the curtain and saw Maximilien at his desk with a pen in his hand. He had started up from his chair at the sound of the breaking glass.

"Excuse me," said the count. "I slipped and my elbow went through the glass. But since it's broken, I'll take advantage of it to open the door; don't bother to get up." He put his arm through the hole, unlocked the door and opened it. Maximilien, clearly annoyed, stepped forward, less in order to receive the count than to block his way.

"It's your servants' fault," said the count, rubbing his elbow. "Your floors are as shiny as mirrors."

"Did you hurt yourself?" asked Maximilien coldly.

"I don't know. Were you writing just now?"

"Yes; even a soldier writes now and then."

Monte Cristo stepped further into the room. Maximilien had to let him pass, but he followed him. The count cast a glance around the room. "What are your pistols doing there?" he asked, pointing to the weapons lying on the desk.

"I'm about to go on a journey," replied Maximilien.

"Maximilien," said Monte Cristo, "let's take off the masks we're both wearing. You don't deceive me with your artificial calmness any more than I deceive you with my frivolous solicitude. I'm sure you realize that in order to have broken into a friend's room I must have been moved by genuine apprehension, or, rather, a terrible conviction. Maximilien, you want to kill yourself!"

Maximilien started and said, "Where did you get such an idea, count?"

"I repeat that you want to kill yourself," replied the count, "and here's the proof!" He walked over to the desk, raised the sheet of paper the young man had placed over the letter he had begun and picked up the letter. Maximilien rushed forward to snatch it out of his hand, but the count seized him by the wrist in a grip of steel.

"What if I am going to kill myself?" cried Maximilien, abandoning his pretense of calm. "Who will have the courage to prevent me? When I say, 'All my hopes are ruined, my heart is broken, my life is ended and there's nothing around me but mourning and dismay,' who will answer, 'You're wrong'? Would you have the courage to say that, count?"

"Yes, I would," replied the count in a tone whose calmness contrasted strangely with the young man's violence.

"You!" cried Maximilien in growing anger and reproach. "You lured me on with absurd hopes, you lulled me with vain promises when, by some desperate action, I could have either saved her or at least seen her die in my arms! You pretend to play the part of Providence and you don't even have the power to give an antidote to a girl who's been poisoned!"

"Maximilien——"

"You told me to take off my mask and that's just what I'm doing! When you followed me to the cemetery I spoke to you courteously because I have a good heart, but since you've come here to interfere with me in the room that's about to become my tomb, since you've brought me a new torture when I thought I'd exhausted them all, you're about to watch your friend die!" Maximilien reached for his pistols again with an insane laugh, but Monte Cristo, his eyes flashing fire, stopped him once more and said, "Maximilien, you will not kill yourself!"

"Try to stop me, then!" cried Maximilien, still struggling to reach his pistols, but still powerless in the count's merciless grip.

"I will stop you!"

"Who are you to behave so tyranically toward a man who's free to make his own decisions?"

"Who am I? Listen and I'll tell you: I am the only man in the world who has the right to say to you, 'Maximilien, I won't allow your father's son to die today.'"

"Why do you speak of my father?" stammered Maximilien. "Why do you mingle his memory with what's happening to me today?"

"Because I'm the man who saved your father's life one day when he wanted to kill himself just as you want to kill yourself today; because I'm the man who sent the purse to your sister and the *Pharaon* to your father; because I'm Edmond Dantès, who used to play with you on my knees when you were a child!"

Maximilien staggered back, overwhelmed; his strength abandoned him and he fell to the floor. Then suddenly, completely regenerated, he leaped to his feet and rushed out into the hall, shouting, "Julie! Julie! Emmanuel! Emmanuel!"

Monte Cristo tried to come after him, but Maximilien closed the door and would have died before he let the count open it.

Julie and Emmanuel ran upstairs in answer to Maximilien's

cries. He took them by the hand, opened the door and said, in a voice choked with emotion: "On your knees! This is our benefactor, the man who saved our father's life! This is——"
He was going to say, "This is Edmond Dantès," but the count stopped him by gripping his arm.

Julie clutched the count's hand, Emmanuel embraced him as though he were a tutelary god and Maximilien once again fell to his knees. At that moment the man of bronze felt his heart swell in his chest and a flame seemed to dart from his throat to his eyes. He bowed his head and wept.

When she had recovered a little from her first emotion, Julie ran out of the room, down the stairs and into the salon, where, with childish joy, she lifted the crystal globe protecting the purse that had been given to her by the stranger of the Allées de Meilhan.

Meanwhile Emmanuel was saying to the count: "Oh, count, you heard us speak of our unknown benefactor, you saw with what gratitude and adoration we surrounded his memory —why did you wait so long to reveal yourself?"

"My friend," replied the count, "the discovery of this secret was brought on by a great event which must remain unknown to you. God is my witness that I wanted to keep it buried in my own soul for the rest of my life, but Maximilien has torn it from me by a violence which I'm sure he regrets now." Seeing that Maximilien had sunk into a chair on the other side of the room, Monte Cristo added in a low voice, "Watch over him."

"Why?" asked Emmanuel in surprise.

"I can't tell you why; but watch over him."

Emmanuel looked around the room and perceived Maximilien's pistols. He stared at them in alarm and slowly pointed to them. The count nodded. Emmanuel made a movement toward the pistols, but the count said, "Leave them alone." Then he went over to Maximilien and took his hand; the tumultuous emotions which had shaken the young man's heart had now given way to a dazed torpor.

Julie entered the room holding the silken purse in her hand as two glistening tears of joy rolled down her cheeks. "Here's the relic," she said. "Don't think it's any less dear to me now that the saviour has revealed himself."

"Let me take back that purse," said Monte Cristo, blushing. "Since you now know my face, I want to be remembered only by the affection which I beg you to grant me."

"Oh, no!" exclaimed Julie, pressing the purse to her heart. "Please don't take it back—I'm afraid you'll leave us some day!"

"You've guessed correctly," replied Monte Cristo, smiling.

"Within a week I'll have left this country where so many people who deserved the vengeance of heaven were living in happiness, while my father had died of hunger and grief."

As he said this, Monte Cristo kept his eyes fixed on Maximilien, and he noticed that the words "I'll have left this country" passed without drawing the young man from his lethargy. Taking Julie and Emmanuel by the hand, he said to them with the gentle authority of a father, "Please leave me alone with Maximilien now."

Julie saw her chance to take away the precious relic which the count had forgotten to mention again. She hurriedly pulled her husband out of the room, leaving Monte Cristo alone with Maximilien, who continued to remain as motionless as a statue.

"Maximilien," said Monte Cristo, touching him with his finger, "are you ready to become a man again?"

"Yes; I'm beginning to suffer again."

The count frowned. "Maximilien!" he said, "you're giving in to ideas that are unworthy of a Christian."

"Oh, don't worry, my friend," said Maximilien, raising his face and showing the count a smile permeated with unspeakable sadness, "I won't seek out death now. No, I have something better than a pistol to cure me of my grief—my grief itself will kill me."

"My friend," said Monte Cristo in a tone of melancholy equal to Maximilien's, "listen to me: One day, in a moment of despair, I too wanted to kill myself; one day your father, equally desperate, also wanted to kill himself. If, at that supreme moment, when your father was pointing the pistol at his forehead, or when I was pushing away the food I hadn't touched for three days, someone had said to both of us, 'Live, for a day will come when you will be happy and bless life,' we would both have listened to those words with a smile of doubt or with the anguish of incredulity. And yet how often did your father later bless life, how often have I myself——"

"You only lost your liberty," interrupted Maximilien, "and my father only lost his fortune, but I've lost Valentine!"

"Look at me, Maximilien," said Monte Cristo with that solemnity which, on certain occasions, made him so commanding and persuasive. "There are no tears in my eyes, my heart is not throbbing painfully and there is no fever in my veins, and yet I'm now watching you suffer, you whom I love as though you were my son. Doesn't that tell you that suffering is like life: that there is always something unknown beyond it? If I beg you, if I order you to live, Maximilien, it's because I'm convinced that some day you'll thank me for having preserved your life for you."

"Oh, my God, count!" cried the young man. "What are you saying? Haven't you ever been in love?"

"Child!" replied the count.

"I'm speaking of real love," continued Maximilien. "I've been a soldier ever since I became a man; I lived to the age of twenty-nine without ever being in love, for nothing I felt till then deserves the name of love. Then I found Valentine, and I've been in love with her for two years. With Valentine, count, my happiness was infinite, unheard-of; a happiness too great, too complete, too divine for this world; and now that she's gone, there's nothing left for me but heartbreak and despair."

"I have told you to hope, Maximilien."

"Be careful, count; you're trying to persuade me, and if you do, you'll make me lose my reason, for you'll make me believe I'll see Valentine again."

The count smiled.

"Let me tell you again to be careful!" said Maximilien excitedly. "The ascendancy you have over me frightens me. Be careful of what you say, or you'll make me believe in supernatural things."

"Hope, my friend," repeated the count.

"Oh, you're only playing with me," said Maximilien, falling from the heights of exaltation into the depths of despair. "You're only acting like those kind mothers, or rather, those selfish mothers, who soothe their children's sorrow with sweet words because their crying is tiresome. No, I was wrong to tell you to be careful; don't worry: I'll bury my grief deep inside me and I'll make it so secret and obscure that you won't even have to take the trouble to sympathize with me. Good-bye, my friend."

"No, Maximilien, it's not good-bye. From now on you're going to live with me without leaving my side and within a week we'll have left France behind us."

"And you still tell me to hope?"

"Yes, because I know a way to cure you."

"Count, you make me even sadder, if such a thing is possible. You see only commonplace grief as the result of the blow I've suffered and you think you can console me with a commonplace remedy: travel." And Maximilien shook his head in disdainful incredulity.

"I have faith in my own promises," said Monte Cristo. "Let me make the experiment."

"You're only prolonging my agony."

"Is your heart so weak that you can't give your friend a few days to prove his promise? Do you know what the Count of Monte Cristo is capable of doing? Do you know that he has a great deal of worldly power at his command? Do you know that he has enough faith in God to obtain miracles from Him who said that with faith a man could move mountains? I tell you to wait for this miracle or else——"

"Or else?"

"Or else I'll call you an ingrate."

"Have pity on me, count!"

"Listen to me, Maximilien: I have so much pity on you that if I haven't cured you of your grief within one month from now, to the day and to the hour, I myself will place you before these pistols and before a cup of the deadliest poison of Italy, a much quicker and deadlier poison than the one that killed Valentine."

"Will you promise me that?"

"I not only promise it, I swear it," said the count, taking Maximilien's hand.

"In a month, on your word of honor, if I'm still not consoled, you'll leave me free to dispose of my life as I see fit, and no matter what I do you won't call me ungrateful?"

"In exactly one month, and the date is sacred: I don't know if it's occurred to you that today is the fifth of September. It was ten years ago today that I saved your father's life when he wanted to die."

Maximilien seized the count's hands and kissed them; the count allowed him to do so, as though he realized that this adoration was his due.

"A month from today," continued Monte Cristo, "we will both be seated at a table on which there will be good weapons and gentle poison. But in return will you promise to go on living till then?"

"I swear it!"

Monte Cristo pressed the young man to his heart and held him there for a long time. "And now," he said, "you will come to live with me; you may take Haydée's rooms."

"Haydée! What's happened to her?"

"She left last night; she's now waiting for me to join her. Make ready to come to live in my house on the Champs Elysées, but first lead me out of here without anyone seeing me leave."

Maximilien bowed his head and obeyed like a child—or like a disciple.

Chapter 63

In the hotel in the Rue Saint-Germain-des-Prés which Albert de Morcerf had chosen for himself and his mother, the second floor, composed of a small apartment, was rented to a very mysterious personage: a man whose face had never been seen when he entered or left the hotel, even by the concierge, for in winter he buried his face in a large red scarf and in summer he always blew his nose just as he was passing the concierge's window.

His visits were usually quite regular: it was nearly always toward four o'clock that he took possession of his apartment, in which he never spent the night. Twenty minutes after his arrival, a carriage would stop in front of the hotel and a woman, dressed in either black or dark blue but always wrapped in a flowing veil, would alight, pass before the concierge's window like a shadow and mount the stairs without causing a single step to creak under her light footsteps. She was never asked where she was going. Her face was therefore also completely unknown to the two concierges, perhaps the only members of the vast brotherhood of Paris concierges who were capable of such discretion.

It goes without saying that the woman never went any higher than the second floor. There she would scratch on the door in a certain way; it would then be opened to her and closed tightly behind her.

The same maneuvers were employed for leaving the hotel. The woman, always veiled, would leave first, climb into her carriage and drive off, sometimes in one direction, sometimes in another. Twenty minutes later the man, his face sunk down into a scarf or hidden by a handkerchief, would come out and also disappear.

The day after the Count of Monte Cristo paid his visit to Baron Danglars, the day of Valentine's funeral, the mysterious tenant arrived at ten o'clock in the morning instead of four o'clock in the afternoon. Shortly afterward, without maintaining the customary interval, a carriage drew up and the veiled lady ran up the stairs. The door opened and closed behind her, but before it had closed she cried out, "Oh, Lucien!" The concierge involuntarily overheard this exclamation and learned for the first time that his tenant's name was Lucien, but, being a model concierge, he promised himself he would not tell his wife.

"What's the matter?" asked the man whose name had been revealed through the veiled lady's anxiety and agitation.

"Can I count on you?"

"Of course you can; you know that. But tell me what's the matter—your note this morning frightened me."

"Lucien, my husband left last night."

"Left? Monsieur Danglars has left? Where did he go?"

"I don't know."

"Do you mean to say he's left for good?"

"I think so. He left me a letter. Here: read it."

Madame Danglars drew out an unsealed letter and handed it to Debray. He took it and read this salutation: "My dear and very faithful wife." He stopped unconsciously and looked at Madame Danglars, who blushed to the roots of her hair. "Read," she said. He looked back at the letter and read the following:

When you read this letter you will no longer have a husband. Oh, don't alarm yourself too violently: you will no longer have a husband in the same sense that you no longer have a daughter; in other words, I will be on one of the thirty or forty roads that lead out of France.

I owe you an explanation, and you are just the woman to understand it perfectly. I was asked for a payment of five million francs this morning and I made it, but it was followed almost immediately by another request for the same sum, which I postponed until tomorrow. I am leaving today in order to avoid that tomorrow which would be unbearably disagreeable to me. You can understand that, can't you, my darling wife? You can understand it because you know as much about my affairs as I do. In fact, you know more about them than I do, because if someone were to ask me to tell what had happened to a good half of my fortune, which was once considerable, I would be unable to reply, while I am sure that you would be able to give a very good answer.

Have you ever admired the swiftness of my fall, madame? Have you ever been a little dazzled by that sudden melting away of all my gold? As for myself, I admit that I am completely baffled. I hope only that you have been able to find a little gold in the ashes.

It is with this consoling hope that I leave you, my dear and very prudent wife, without having the slightest scruple about abandoning you. You still have certain friends, the ashes I mentioned above and, best of all, the freedom which I hasten to give you.

And now allow me to add a more personal explanation. As long as I believed you to be working for the welfare of our family and the fortune of our daughter, I philosophically closed my eyes; but now that you have brought our family to utter ruin, I refuse to serve as the foundation of someone else's fortune. You were rich but little respected when I married you. (Excuse me for speaking so frankly, but since you will probably be the only one to read this, I see no reason why I should mince words.) I increased our fortune, which grew steadily for fifteen years until a series of disasters, still incomprehensible to me, destroyed it through no fault of my own. You, on the other hand, worked only to increase your own fortune, and I am convinced that you have succeeded quite well. I leave you, therefore, as I found you: with considerable wealth but little honor. From now on I am also going to work only for myself. Please accept my gratitude for the example you have set for me.

> Your devoted husband,
> BARON DANGLARS

Madame Danglars watched Debray as he read this long and painful letter; once or twice she saw him change color, despite his well-known self-control.

He carefully folded the letter when he had finished reading it and remained thoughtfully silent.

"Well?" asked Madame Danglars with an anxiety that was easy to understand.

"Well?" repeated Debray absently.

"What ideas does the letter inspire in you?"

"It's quite simple: it inspires in me the idea that your husband left with certain suspicions in his mind."

"Of course; but is that all you have to say to me?"

"I don't understand," said Debray coldly.

"He's gone—gone for good! He'll never come back!"

"Oh, don't think that," said Debray.

"No, he won't come back. I know him: he's inflexible where his own interest is concerned. If he'd thought I might be useful to him, he'd have taken me with him, but he's left me behind in Paris, which means that our separation will further his plans. It's therefore irrevocable and I'm free forever," added Madame Danglars with a supplicating expression. But Debray left her in that attitude of anxious interrogation without answering her. "Have you nothing to say?" she asked finally.

"I have only a question to ask you: What are you going to do?"

"I was going to ask you that," said Madame Danglars, her heart pounding.

"You want to ask me for advice?"

"That's right—I want to ask you for advice," replied Madame Danglars, her heart sinking.

"Since you've asked me," replied Debray coldly, "I advise you to travel."

"Travel!" murmured Madame Danglars.

"Certainly. As your husband says, you're rich and perfectly free, and it seems to me an absence from Paris will be absolutely necessary to you after the double scandal of your daughter's broken engagement and your husband's disappearance. You must make sure that everyone knows you've been abandoned and believes you to be poor. Remain in Paris for two more weeks and tell all your friends how you've been abandoned; they'll repeat it to everyone else. Then leave your house, leaving your jewels behind, and everyone will sing your praises. People will then know you've been abandoned and will believe you to be poor, for I alone know your financial situation and I'm ready to settle accounts with you as an honorable partner."

Madame Danglars listened to these words with a horror and despair equal to Debray's calm and indifference. "Abandoned!" she repeated. "Oh, yes, I'm abandoned; no one can doubt that." This was all that the baroness, proud and still deeply infatuated, could reply to Debray.

"But you're rich; very rich, in fact," continued Debray, taking a number of papers from his portfolio and spreading them out on the table. Madame Danglars was absorbed in stifling the pounding of her heart and holding back the tears she felt welling up in her eyes. Finally her sense of dignity won out and, while she failed to still the beating of her heart, she managed not to shed a single tear.

"We've been partners now for six months," said Debray. "You furnished an initial capital of one hundred thousand francs. We formed our partnership in April and began our operations in May. In May we made four hundred and fifty thousand francs. In June our profits went up to nine thousand. In July we added one million seven hundred thousand francs —that was the month of the Spanish bonds. At the beginning of August we lost three hundred thousand francs, but on the fifteenth we made up for it. Our accounts, from the beginning of our partnership till yesterday, show a profit of two million four hundred thousand francs, which makes one million two hundred thousand francs for each of us. Your money is here now; since I didn't consider my house safe enough or any notary discreet enough, I've kept the entire sum sealed in a coffer beneath this closet; I acted as my own mason for greater security. Now," continued Debray, opening first the closet and then the coffer, "here are eight hundred banknotes of one thousand francs each, and here's a sight draft on my banker for the remainder. Since my banker isn't Monsieur Danglars, you can be sure the draft will be paid."

Spread out on a table, that enormous fortune appeared rather unimpressive. Madame Danglars, her eyes dry but her chest swollen with sobs, picked it up and stood silently waiting for a kind word to console her for being so rich.

But she waited in vain. "Now," said Debray, "you'll have an income of something like sixty thousand francs a year, which is enormous for a woman who won't be able to maintain a household for at least another year; it will enable you to carry out any whim that may occur to you."

Madame Danglars raised her head, opened the door and, without any show of anger but also without any hesitation, hurried down the stairs, scorning even to say good-bye to the man who allowed her to leave in that manner.

Debray picked up his account book and carefully crossed out the sums he had just paid. Then he phlegmatically waited the customary twenty minutes before leaving.

Above the room in which Debray had just divided two and a half million francs with Madame Danglars, there was another room rented by two other people with whom we are acquainted: Mercédès and her son Albert.

Mercédès had changed greatly in the past few days: her eyes no longer sparkled, her lips no longer smiled and a constant confusion checked the words that had formerly flowed so rapidly at the prompting of her ready wit. It was not poverty that had broken her spirit, nor was it lack of courage that made her poverty burdensome, although it is true that she saw nothing but depressing objects around her. The walls of her room were covered with that gray wallpaper chosen by thrifty landlords because it does not show dirt easily; there was no rug on the floor; the furniture fairly cried out for attention to its shoddy attempt at luxury—in short, everything about the room was painful to eyes accustomed to harmonious elegance.

As for Albert, he was ill at ease, embarrassed by a last remainder of luxury which prevented him from adjusting himself to his present condition: he went out without gloves, but found that his hands were too white; he went through the streets on foot, but found that his boots were too shiny.

"Mother," said Albert at exactly the moment when Madame

Danglars was descending the stairs, "let's count all our wealth; I need to know the total in order to make my plans."

"Total: zero," said Mercédès with a sad smile.

"Not at all, mother! The total is three thousand francs, and I maintain that we can both live quite well with that much."

"Child!" sighed Mercédès.

"Why, three thousand francs is an enormous sum! I've already planned a miraculous future of eternal security with it."

"First of all, shall we accept that three thousand francs?" asked Mercédès, blushing.

"I thought we'd already agreed on that," replied Albert firmly. "We'll accept it, especially since it's still buried in a garden in Marseilles. We have enough money for both of us to make the trip to Marseilles. I sold my watch for a hundred francs, but that's not all—what do you think of this, mother?" And Albert took out a banknote of one thousand francs.

"Where did that come from?" asked Mercédès.

"Listen to me, mother, and try not to be too upset: I enlisted in the Spahis yesterday. I realized that at least my body was my own, so yesterday I sold myself as a replacement. And I got more than I thought I was worth," added the young man, trying to smile. "I'll be paid two thousand francs."

"So this thousand francs——"

"That's half the amount, mother; I'll have the other half in a year."

Two tears streamed silently down Mercédès' cheeks. "The price of his blood!" she murmured.

"If I'm killed, yes," said Albert, laughing. "But I can assure you I intend to defend myself as ferociously as I can; I've never had a stronger desire to live than I have now. And besides, think how happy you'll be when you see me in my handsome uniform! I admit I chose the Spahi regiment out of sheer vanity."

Mercédès tried to smile.

"And now, mother," continued Albert, "you're assured of over four thousand francs—with that you can live for at least two years."

"Do you think so?" said Mercédès. The words escaped from her with such genuine grief that Albert realized their true meaning, and he felt his heart sink. Taking his mother's hand and pressing it tenderly, he said, "Yes, you'll live."

"I'll live!" cried Mercédès. "But you won't leave me, will you, my son?"

"Mother," said Albert firmly, "you love me too much to want me to stay with you idle and useless; besides, I've already signed my enlistment papers."

"Act according to your own will, my son, and I'll act according to God's."

"I'm not acting according to my will, mother, but according to reason and necessity. We're both in a desperate situation, aren't we? What is life for us at this moment? Nothing. And what is life for me without you, mother? I swear to you that, if it weren't for you, my life would have ceased the day I rejected my father's name! But I'll live if you'll promise me to hope; if you'll place your future happiness in my hands you'll double my strength. After I've joined my regiment in Africa I'll go to see the governor of Algeria. I'll tell him my sad story and ask him to keep an eye on me from time to time. If he watches me in action, within six months I'll be either an officer or dead. If I become an officer your life is assured, mother, because I'll have money enough for both of us and a new name that we'll both be proud of, since it will be your real name. And if I'm killed—well, mother, you can die if you like, and then our misfortune will have come to an end through its own excess."

"Very well," replied Mercédès with a noble and eloquent look, "you're right, my son: let's prove that we're at least worthy of being pitied."

"You can leave for Marseilles this very day, mother; I've already made all the arrangements for your trip."

"But what about you, Albert?"

"I have to stay in Paris for another two or three days; I need certain recommendations and certain information about Africa. I'll rejoin you in Marseilles."

"So be it, then: let's leave," said Mercédès, wrapping herself in the only shawl she had taken with her.

Albert hastily collected his papers, rang to pay the thirty francs he owed to the hotel-keeper and, offering his arm to his mother, began to descend the stairs. A man was walking down ahead of them; hearing the rustle of a silken dress, he turned around.

"Debray!" exclaimed Albert.

"You, Morcerf!" replied the minister's secretary, stopping short. His curiosity proved stronger than his desire to remain incognito; besides, he had already been recognized. Then, in the semi-darkness, he noticed the still-young figure and the black veil of Albert's companion and said, with a smile, "Oh, excuse me, Albert; I'll leave you alone."

Albert understood Debray's thought. "Mother," he said, turning to Mercédès, "this is Monsieur Debray, Secretary to the Minister of the Interior and a former friend of mine."

"What do you mean by 'former'?" stammered Debray.

"I say that because today I no longer have any friends, and

I must not have any. I thank you for being kind enough to recognize me."

Debray shook Albert's hand energetically and said, "Believe me, Albert, when I tell you how deeply I sympathize with you in your misfortune and how glad I'll be to help you in any way I can."

"Thank you," said Albert, smiling, "but in the midst of all our misfortune we've remained rich enough not to have to go to anyone for help. We're leaving Paris with five thousand francs over and above our traveling expenses."

Debray's precise mind was little inclined to poetic comparisons, but he could not help reflecting that the same hotel had just held two women, one of whom, rightly dishonored, had just left poor with a million and a half francs, while the other, unjustly persecuted by fate but sublime in her misfortune, considered herself rich with a few sous. The parallel disturbed him so much that he forgot his usual politeness: he murmured a few words of general civility and rapidly walked down the stairs. That day his subordinates at the ministry had to put up with a great deal because of his bad humor. But that evening he made himself the owner of a fine house, located on the Boulevard de la Madeleine and bringing in an income of fifty thousand francs a year.

As he was signing the deed, toward five o'clock in the evening, Mercédès, after tenderly kissing her son and being tenderly kissed by him, climbed into a stagecoach and departed.

A man watched her departure from a hidden vantage point. Passing his hand over his forehead, he said to himself, "How can I give back the happiness I've taken away from those two innocent creatures? God will help me."

Chapter 64

One section of the prison of La Force, the one in which the most dangerous prisoners are kept, is called the Court of Saint Bernard, but the prisoners, in their vivid language, have named it the "Lions' Den," probably because its inmates have teeth which often bite the bars and sometimes the guards. It is a prison within a prison: the walls here are twice as thick as in the other sections. Every day a jailer carefully tests the soundness of the massive iron bars on the windows. The Herculean stature and cold, penetrating eyes of the guards here show that they have been specially selected to rule over their charges by terror and shrewdness.

The courtyard of this section of the prison is enclosed by enormous walls, over which the sun shines obliquely when it decides to penetrate into that abyss of moral and physical horrors. There, from morning till night, wander the men whom Justice holds bowed beneath the guillotine which she is sharpening.

As he walked in this courtyard with his hands in the pockets of his coat, one young man was looked at with particular curiosity by the other inhabitants of the "Lions' Den." His clothes would have marked him as an elegant young man if they had not been in tatters. They were not worn out, however: the cloth, fine and silky in the parts that still remained intact, easily regained its luster under the prisoner's caressing hand. He bestowed the same care on a cambric shirt, which had changed color considerably since his entrance into prison, and he polished his patent-leather boots with the corner of a handkerchief embroidered with initials surmounted by a coronet.

Suddenly a voice called out from a wicket: "Benedetto!"

"Are you calling me?" asked the prisoner.

"To the visiting room!" replied the voice.

Andrea was surprised, for, unlike most prisoners, the crafty young man had not availed himself of the privilege of writing letters to ask for visitors. "I'm obviously under the protection of someone powerful," he said to himself. "Everything proves it to me: my sudden fortune, the ease with which I've overcome all obstacles, my improvised family, my new title and the opportunity to marry into a rich family. My protector has neglected me temporarily, but his neglect won't last. Why should I do anything rash? I might alienate my protector. There are two ways he can save me: arrange a mysterious escape by bribery, or somehow force my judges to declare me innocent. I won't do anything on my own unless I find out I've been completely abandoned, but then——"

Andrea had devised a fairly clever plan; the treacherous young man was bold in attack and tenacious in defense. He had already borne up under the rigors of prison and all its hardships. Little by little, however, nature, or rather habit, began to overcome his resolution: he began to suffer from being thinly clad, dirty and hungry; time began to hang heavily on his hands.

It was at this moment of dejection that he was called to the visiting room. His heart leaped with joy. He was led into a room divided in half by an iron grill, behind which he saw the somber and intelligent face of Monsieur Bertuccio.

"Hello, Benedetto," said Bertuccio in his deep, sonorous voice.

"You!" cried the young man, casting a frightened glance around the room.

"Don't you recognize me, Benedetto?"

"Not so loud!" said Andrea, who was aware that those walls had ears.

"You'd prefer to speak with me in complete privacy, wouldn't you?" asked Bertuccio.

"Yes!"

Bertuccio took something from his pocket and motioned to a guard who could be seen through the barred window. "Read this," he said.

"What is it?" asked Andrea.

"An order to let you have a room of your own and to let me speak with you there."

"Oh!" exclaimed Andrea joyfully. And immediately he said to himself, "Still the unknown protector! He hasn't forgotten me. Bertuccio was sent by him."

The guard conferred for a moment with a superior, then led Andrea to a room on the second floor overlooking the courtyard. The walls of the room were whitewashed, as is the custom in prisons. To Andrea it had an appearance of almost dazzling charm: a stove, a bed, a chair and a table composed its sumptuous furnishings.

Bertuccio sat down on the chair, Andrea stretched out on the bed and the guard withdrew.

"Well, what do you have to say to me?" asked Bertuccio.

"What about you?"

"You first."

"Oh, no—you're the one who has things to tell me, since it was you who came to see me."

"All right, then. You've continued your criminal ways: you've stolen and murdered."

"If the only reason you had me put into a private room was so you could tell me that," said Andrea, "you might as well have saved yourself the trouble. I know all that. But there are other things I don't know, so let's talk about them if you don't mind. First of all, who sent you?"

"Oh, you're going very fast, Monsieur Benedetto!"

"That's right—and straight to the point. Let's not waste words. Who sent you?"

"No one."

"How did you know I was in prison?"

"I recognized you long ago as the insolent young fop driving along the Champs Elysées."

"The Champs Elysées! That brings us closer to the point—tell me about my father."

"Who do you suppose I am, then?"

"You, my good man, are my stepfather. But I don't think it was you who provided me with a hundred thousand francs, which I spent in four or five months; it wasn't you who fabricated a noble Italian father for me; it wasn't you who introduced me into the cream of Paris society at a magnificent dinner party in Auteuil; and you certainly weren't the one who was backing me with two million francs when the cat was accidentally let out of the bag."

"What do you want me to tell you?" asked Bertuccio.

"I'll give you a hint: you mentioned the Champs Elysées just now."

"Well?"

"A certain very rich gentleman lives on the Champs Elysées."

"A gentleman in whose house you committed murder and robbery?"

"Yes, I believe so."

"You're speaking of the Count of Monte Cristo, aren't you?"

"That's right. Now tell me: must I throw myself in his arms, press him to my heart and cry out, 'Father! Father!'?"

"Let's not joke," replied Bertuccio gravely, "and don't ever say such a thing again."

"Why not?" asked Andrea, somewhat taken aback by Bertuccio's solemnity.

"Because the Count of Monte Cristo is too highly favored by heaven to be the father of a wretched criminal like you."

"Those are fine words, but——"

"There will be more than words if you're not careful."

"Threats! I'm not afraid! I'll tell——"

"Do you think you're dealing with pigmies like yourself?" interrupted Bertuccio once again in such a calm tone and with such a confident expression that Andrea was totally disconcerted. "You're in the grip of a terrible hand, Benedetto. It's willing to open for you: take advantage of it. Don't play with the thunderbolt it has laid aside for a moment, but which it may take up again if you try to interfere with its freedom of movement."

"I want to know who my father is!" said the stubborn young man. "And I'm going to find out, no matter what it costs. Who is my father?"

"That's what I came here to tell you."

"Ah!" cried Andrea, his eyes flashing with joy.

Just then the door opened and a guard entered. "Excuse me, sir," he said to Bertuccio, "but the examining judge is waiting for the prisoner."

"I'll come back tomorrow," said Bertuccio.

"Good!" said Andrea. "And please leave two hundred francs or so on your way out so I can have some of the things I need."

"I will," replied Bertuccio.

Andrea held out his hand to him, but Bertuccio kept his hand in his pocket.

Andrea forced himself to smile, but he was completely subjugated by Bertuccio's strange tranquillity. "Could I be mistaken?" he thought. "Well, we'll see." Then he said aloud to Bertuccio: "Until tomorrow!"

"Until tomorrow," replied Bertuccio.

Chapter 65

It will be remembered that the Abbé Busoni remained alone with Noirtier in Valentine's room and that the old man and the priest were the sole guardians of the young girl's body.

The priest's Christian exhortations, or perhaps his persuasive words, apparently restored Noirtier's courage, for he soon threw off the black despair that had taken possession of him; he gave every indication of a calm resignation which was quite surprising to those who remembered his deep love for Valentine.

Villefort had not seen Noirtier since the morning of Valentine's death. Locked in his study, he worked feverishly at preparing the case against the murderer of Caderousse. The affair, like everything in which the Count of Monte Cristo was involved, had made a great stir among the people of Paris. The evidence was not too convincing, for it consisted primarily of a few lines written by a dying criminal who had escaped from prison with the man he accused and who might have accused him through hatred or a desire for vengeance. Villefort alone had convinced himself that Benedetto was guilty. The trial was to begin in three days, thanks to Villefort's incessant work in preparing the case. His daughter Valentine had been laid to rest so recently that no one was surprised to see him so completely absorbed in his work, which was the only thing he could find to distract him from his grief.

Overwhelmed with fatigue and bowed beneath the weight of a single implacable thought, Villefort went out to take a walk in the garden. Looking toward the house, he noticed that one of Noirtier's windows was open: the old man had had his chair pushed up to that window so that he could enjoy the last rays of the late summer sun.

Noirtier's eyes were fixed on something with such an expression of savage hatred and burning impatience that Villefort followed his line of vision to discover the person to whom this dark look was directed. Beneath a clump of linden trees whose boughs were almost bare, he saw his wife sitting with a book in her hand. From time to time she interrupted her reading to smile at her son Edouard or to toss back the ball which he obstinately persisted in throwing out into the garden from the salon.

Villefort paled, for he understood Noirtier's thoughts. Suddenly Noirtier turned his gaze from the wife to the husband and it was Villefort himself who had to undergo the attack of those fiery eyes. He began to walk slowly toward the house, but the eyes followed him as he went, filled with withering reproach and terrible menace. Then Noirtier looked up at the sky, as though reminding his son of a forgotten oath.

"Be patient," said Villefort, who was now standing beneath Noirtier's window. "Be patient for only one more day. I'll keep my promise."

Noirtier appeared to be calmed by these words; he indifferently looked away in another direction as Villefort violently unbuttoned his collar as though he were choking, passed his hand over his forehead and went back into his study.

That night, as was his custom, Villefort did not go to bed at the same time as the other members of his household. He stayed up till five o'clock in the morning reviewing the reports of the examining magistrates in the Benedetto case, carefully going through the declarations of the witnesses and putting the finishing touches on his indictment, which was one of the most energetic and skillfully conceived speeches he had ever written. He dozed off for an instant as his lamp was giving forth its last gleams; its flickering woke him up. He went over to the window and opened it: there was a streak of reddish light across the horizon. The moist air of dawn flooded into him and revived his memory. "Today," he said with an effort, "the man who holds the sword of Justice must strike wherever there is guilt."

Involuntarily his eyes sought the window in which he had seen Noirtier's face the day before. The curtains were drawn, but his father's image was so vivid in his mind that he addressed the closed window as though he could still see the old man's threatening eyes there. "Do not worry," he murmured.

He walked around his study several times and finally

stretched out on the sofa fully dressed, less in order to sleep than to rest his limbs, stiffened with the fatigue of his long night of work.

Gradually the house began to awaken; from his study Villefort could hear the opening and closing of doors, the tinkle of his wife's bell as she summoned her maid and the first shouts of his son Edouard, who awakened joyfully, as one usually does at that age.

Villefort rang. His new valet entered, bringing him the morning newspapers and a cup of hot chocolate.

"What's that?" asked Villefort.

"A cup of hot chocolate," replied the valet.

"I didn't ask for it. Who is being so thoughtful of me?"

"Madame de Villefort, sir. She said the murder trial would probably be a great strain on you today and that you needed strength."

The valet set down the cup and left the room. Villefort looked at it for a moment with a somber air, then suddenly picked it up with a nervous movement and drank down its contents in one draught. It was as though he hoped the chocolate were poisoned, as though he were calling on death to deliver him from a duty which commanded him to do something much more difficult than dying. Then he stood up and walked around his study with a sort of smile that would have been terrible to see if anyone had been watching him.

The chocolate was harmless and Villefort felt nothing.

Lunchtime arrived and he did not appear at table. His valet entered and said, "Madame wishes me to inform you, sir, that it is now eleven o'clock and that court opens at noon."

"Well?"

"Madame is ready to leave and asks if she may go with you, sir."

"Where?"

"To the Palace of Justice."

"Why?"

"Madame says she wishes very much to be present at this trial."

"Ah!" said Villefort in a tone that was almost frightening. "She wishes that, does she?"

The valet stepped back and said, "If you wish to go alone, sir, I'll tell madame so."

Villefort remained silent for a time, scratching his pale cheek with his fingernails. "Tell madame," he replied finally, "that I wish to speak to her and that I ask her to wait for me in her room."

"Yes, sir."

"Then come back to shave me and dress me."

"Right away, sir."

The valet left, returned soon afterward, shaved Villefort and dressed him solemnly in black. When he had finished, he said, "Madame says she'll expect you as soon as you've finished dressing, sir."

"I'll go there now."

Villefort stopped before his wife's door for an instant and wiped away the sweat that was streaming down his forehead. Then he opened the door. Madame de Villefort was sitting on an ottoman, impatiently looking through some newspapers and pamphlets which young Edouard, to amuse himself, was cutting to pieces before his mother had time to read them. She was completely dressed and ready to go out: her hat was laid out on an armchair and she had already put on her gloves.

"Ah, there you are!" she said, her voice natural and calm. "But you're so pale! You must have worked all night again. . . . Well, are you going to take me with you, or shall I go with Edouard?"

"Edouard," said Villefort, looking at the child imperiously, "go play in the salon. I want to talk to your mother."

Edouard raised his head and looked at his mother; then, seeing that she did not confirm Villefort's order, he went back to cutting off the heads of his lead soldiers.

"Edouard!" shouted Villefort so harshly that the child jumped. "Did you hear what I said? Get out!"

The boy, who was not accustomed to such treatment, stood up and turned pale; it would have been difficult to say whether it was from anger or from fear. His father walked over to him, took him by the arm, kissed him on the forehead and said, "Go, my son."

Edouard left the room. Villefort bolted the door behind him.

"What's the matter?" asked the young woman, looking searchingly at her husband and attempting to smile in the face of his icy impassivity.

"Where do you keep the poison you use?" asked Villefort bluntly, standing between his wife and the door.

Madame de Villefort felt the sensation which a lark must feel as it watches the hawk narrowing its deadly circles above its head. A hoarse, choked sound that was neither a cry nor a sigh escaped from her bosom. "I—I don't understand," she said.

"I asked you," said Villefort in a perfectly calm voice, "where you hide the poison with which you killed my father-in-law Monsieur de Saint-Méran, my mother-in-law, Barrois and my daughter Valentine."

"Oh! What are you saying?" cried Madame de Villefort, clasping her hands.

"It's not for you to question, but to answer."

"Am I speaking to my husband—or to a judge?" stammered Madame de Villefort.

"To a judge, madame, to a judge!"

"Oh! Oh!" murmured Madame de Villefort; she said nothing more.

"You're not answering, madame!" cried the terrible interrogator. Then he added, with a smile that was still more frightening than his anger, "Of course, you're not denying anything, either." She made a movement. "And you can't deny it," continued Villefort, putting out his hand toward her as though to seize her in the name of Justice. "You carried out your crimes wth a certain shameless skill, yet only those whose affection made them willing to blind themselves with regard to you could have been deceived. Ever since the death of Madame de Saint-Méran I've known there was a murderer in my house: Doctor d'Avrigny warned me. After the death of Barrois my suspicions—may God forgive me!—fell on an angel; but after Valentine died I no longer had any doubt, and certain other persons were equally sure. It's time for your crimes to be made public now and, as I've already told you, I'm not speaking to you as your husband, but as a judge."

The young woman hid her face in her hands. "Oh, I—I beg you," she stammered, "don't believe in appearances!"

"Are you also cowardly?" exclaimed Villefort contemptuously. "As a matter of fact, I've always noticed that poisoners are cowards. And yet you had the hideous courage to kill three people and watch them die before your eyes."

"Please! Please!"

"You counted the minutes of four death agonies," continued Villefort with growing emotion; "you devised your devilish plans and prepared your infamous poison with wonderful skill and precision. But I wonder if you neglected to consider one thing: the consequences that your crimes might have. But that's impossible; you must at least have kept another poison, gentler yet deadlier than the other, to enable you to escape the punishment that was your due. I hope you did that—did you?"

Madame de Villefort wrung her hands and fell to her knees.

"I know, I know," went on Villefort, "you confess; but a confession made to a judge at the last moment, when it's no longer possible to deny the crime, in no way diminishes the punishment inflicted on the criminal."

"Punishment!" cried Madame de Villefort. "That's the second time you've said it!"

"Do you think you'll escape your punishment because you're the wife of the man who will demand it in the name of the law? No! The scaffold awaits the poisoner, whoever he may be."

Madame de Villefort uttered a wild shriek and a look of hideous, irresistible terror came over her face.

"Oh, don't be afraid of the scaffold," said the magistrate. "I don't want to dishonor you, for I'd be dishonoring myself also. No, if you've listened carefully to what I've said, you must realize that you can't die on the scaffold."

"I don't know what you mean," murmured the wretched woman, completely discomposed.

"I mean that the wife of the most outstanding magistrate of Paris will not taint him with her infamy, that she will not dishonor both her husband and her son at the same time."

"No! Oh, no!"

"Well then, that will be a good deed on your part, and I thank you for it."

"You thank me? For what?"

"For what you just said."

"What did I say? My head's in a whirl—I don't understand anything. Oh, my God! My God!"

"You have not answered the question I asked you when I came in: 'Where is the poison you use?' "

Madame de Villefort raised her arms and convulsively wrung her hands. "No! No!" she cried vehemently. "You can't want me to do that!"

"What I *don't* want is for you to die on the scaffold. Do you understand me?"

"Have mercy on me!"

"What I want is that justice be done," said Villefort. "I was placed on this earth to punish the guilty," he added with a fiery look. "I would send any other woman, even a queen, straight to the executioner; but to you I will be merciful. To you I say, 'You've kept some of your deadliest poison, haven't you?' "

"Oh, forgive me! Let me live!"

"You're a coward."

"Remember that I'm your wife!"

"You're a murderer."

"In the name of God——"

"No!"

"In the name of the love you once had for me——"

"No! No!"

"In the name of our child! Oh, let me live for the sake of our child!"

"No! If I let you live you might kill him some day as you killed the others."

"I? Kill my son?" cried the savage mother, throwing herself at Villefort. "Kill my Edouard?" And a hideous laugh, the laugh of a demon or a madman, finished her sentence and trailed off into a groan. She fell at her husband's feet.

"Remember," he said, "that if justice has not been done when I return, I will denounce you with my own lips and arrest you with my own hands."

She listened to him, panting, overwhelmed, crushed; her eyes were the only thing alive in her and they glowed with terrible fire.

"You understand me," said Villefort. "I'm going to the Palace of Justice now to demand the death penalty for a murderer. If I find you alive when I return, you will be in prison by nightfall."

Madame de Villefort heaved a sigh; her strength failed her and she sank to the floor. Villefort seemed to feel a surge of pity; he looked at her less severely, leaned slightly forward and said slowly, "Good-bye, madame. . . . Good-bye." The words cut into her like a knife. She fainted.

The public prosecutor walked out, locking the door behind him.

Chapter 66

The Benedetto case, as it was called in the Palace of Justice and all over Paris, had produced a great sensation. The false Cavalcanti had frequented all the most fashionable spots in Paris during the few months of his splendor and had made innumerable acquaintances. The newspapers had recounted his adventures both in prison and in Paris society, which aroused a great deal of curiosity, especially among those who had known Prince Andrea Cavalcanti personally. Many of them remembered him as so amiable, so handsome and so generous that they preferred to believe he was the victim of some machination on the part of a powerful enemy.

Everyone, therefore, thronged to the courtroom, some to enjoy the spectacle, others to comment on it. A line began to form outside at seven o'clock in the morning, and an hour before the trial was set to begin the courtroom was already filled with privileged spectators.

Beauchamp, who was one of the kings of the press and

therefore had his throne everywhere, looked around among the crowd. He perceived Château-Renaud and Debray, who had just won the good graces of a policeman and persuaded him to stand in back of them instead of cutting off their view, as was his right; he even promised to keep their places for them while they went over to pay a visit to Beauchamp.

"Well," said Beauchamp, "have we all come to see our friend?"

"Oh, yés," replied Debray. "The worthy prince! I suppose he'll be convicted, won't he?"

"It seems to me you're the one to answer that question: you must have spoken with the presiding magistrate at your minister's last reception."

"Yes, but if I've spoken to the presiding magistrate, you must have spoken to the public prosecutor."

"Impossible—Monsieur de Villefort hasn't seen anyone for the past week, which is only natural considering the strange series of tragedies that have taken place in his house——"

"Look!"

"Who is it?"

"I thought she had left."

"Eugénie Danglars?" asked Château-Renaud. "Has she come back?"

"No, it's her mother."

"What!" exclaimed Château-Renaud. "Ten days after her daughter's flight and three days after her husband's bank-ruptcy!"

Debray flushed slightly and followed Beauchamp's line of vision. "Why, the woman is veiled," he said. "She's some unknown lady, some foreign princess—she may even be Prince Cavalcanti's mother."

"Here come the judges!" said Château-Renaud. "Let's get back to our places."

The judges and the jury took their places in the midst of a deep silence. Monsieur de Villefort, who was the object of general attention—we might almost say of general admiration—sat down in his chair and cast a serene glance around the courtroom.

"Gendarmes!" said the presiding magistrate. "Bring in the accused."

At these words the attention of the spectators became more active and all eyes turned toward the door through which Benedetto was to enter. That door soon opened and the accused appeared. His features bore no trace of emotion; his hands were perfectly steady.

After the accusation had been read, the presiding magistrate said, "Accused, what is your name?"

Andrea stood up. "Excuse me, your honor," he said, "but I see that you're about to begin a series of questions in an order which I cannot follow. I will later justify my request, but in the meantime I beg you to allow me to answer the questions in a different order, which will not prevent me from answering them all."

The presiding magistrate, taken aback, looked at the jury, who looked at the public prosecutor. The spectators manifested great surprise, but none of this seemed to make any impression on Andrea.

"What is your age?" asked the presiding magistrate.

"I'll be twenty-one in a few days: I was born on September 27, 1815."

Monsieur de Villefort, who had been taking notes, raised his head at the mention of this date.

"Where were you born?"

"In Auteuil, near Paris."

Villefort looked up a second time, stared at Andrea as he would have stared at the head of Medusa and turned livid.

"What is your profession?" continued the presiding magistrate.

"I began as a forger," said Andrea with perfect tranquillity, "then I was a thief, and recently I became a murderer."

A murmur, or rather a storm of indignation burst forth from all over the courtroom. Even the judges looked at one another in amazement and the members of the jury manifested great disgust at the prisoner's cynicism, so unexpected from such an elegant young man.

"And now will you condescend to tell the court your name?" asked the presiding magistrate. "The pride with which you have enumerated your crimes, which you call your profession, may be the reason why you wanted to postpone telling us your name: perhaps you wanted to make it stand out by the titles which precede it."

"It's incredible how clearly you've read my thoughts, your honor," said Andrea politely. "That's precisely why I asked you to change the usual order of questions."

The general astonishment reached its height. There was no longer any bravado or cynicism in the prisoner's manner; the spectators had a keen presentiment that some sort of storm was about to burst.

"Well, then, what is your name?" asked the presiding magistrate.

"I can't tell you my name because I don't know what it is, but I do know my father's name and I can tell it to you."

"Tell us the name of your father, then."

"My father is a public prosecutor," replied Andrea calmly.

"Public prosecutor!" exclaimed the presiding magistrate, not noticing the violent agitation which appeared on Villefort's face.

"Yes, and since you've asked me for his name I'll tell it to you: his name is Villefort."

A thunderous explosion burst forth from the entire courtroom, and it was five minutes before the magistrates succeeded in restoring order. In the midst of the uproar at least ten persons crowded around the public prosecutor, who slumped half unconscious in his chair, to offer him consolation, encouragement, protestations and sympathy.

Calm was finally established in the courtroom, with the exception of one corner of the room where, it was said, a woman had just fainted. Someone gave her smelling salts and she regained her senses.

"Your honor," said Andrea, "I am not trying to insult this court or create a useless scandal. I was asked to give my name, but I was unable to, since my parents abandoned me. But I do know my father's name; I repeat: his name is Villefort and I am prepared to prove it."

"But," said the presiding magistrate angrily, "during your examination you said your name was Benedetto, that you were an orphan and that you were born in Corsica."

"I said that because I didn't want my declaration to be silenced, which would surely have happened if I had told the truth then. But now I tell you that I was born in Auteuil on September 27, 1817, and that I am the son of the public prosecutor, Monsieur de Villefort. Would you like more details? I'll be glad to give them to you. I was born at 28 Rue de la Fontaine in Auteuil, in a room hung with red damask. My father picked me up, told my mother I was dead, wrapped me in a towel marked with an H and an N, carried me out into the garden and buried me alive."

A shudder ran through the spectators as they watched the public prosecutor's terror grow in proportion to the young man's self-assurance.

"How do you know all those details?" asked the presiding magistrate.

"I'm about to tell you that, your honor. A certain Corsican had sworn vengeance against my father and was lying in wait for him in the garden the night my father buried me. He stabbed my father as soon as he had finished covering me with earth, then, thinking it was some sort of treasure my father had buried, he opened the grave and found me still alive. He took me to an orphanage. Three months later his sister-in-law came to Paris, claimed me as her son and took me back to Corsica with her. That's why, although I was born in Auteuil, I was raised in Corsica."

There was a moment of profound silence.

"Continue," said the presiding magistrate.

"I might have been happy with those good people, who adored me, but my perverse nature won out over all the virtue my stepmother tried to instill in me. I grew up evil and soon turned to crime. One day when I was cursing God for making me so evil and giving me such a hideous destiny, my step-father said to me, 'Don't blaspheme against God! He created you without anger; the crime was on the part of your father, who doomed you to hell if you died and to poverty if a miracle saved your life!' From then on I stopped blaspheming against God, but I cursed my father.

"And that's why I've spoken here the words for which you've reproached me, your honor; that's why I've caused the scandal which has shaken this whole assembly. If I've committed another crime in doing so, punish me for it; but if I've convinced you that my destiny was tragic and bitter from the day of my birth, pity me!"

"But what about your mother?" asked the presiding magistrate.

"My mother believed I died at birth; she is not guilty in any way. I didn't want to know her name, and to this day I don't know who she is."

At this moment a shrill cry, ending in a sob, arose from the midst of the group of people surrounding the woman who had fainted a short time before. She had just succumbed to a violent fit of hysteria. As she was being carried from the courtroom the veil which had hidden her face fell aside and several spectators recognized her as Madame Danglars. Despite his shattered nerves, the buzzing in his ears and the near-madness which had taken possession of his brain, Ville-fort also recognized her and stood up.

"What about the proof you mentioned?" said the presiding magistrate.

"The proof?" said Benedetto, laughing. "Do you really want it?"

"Yes."

"Well, then, look at Monsieur de Villefort and ask him for the proof!"

All eyes turned to the public prosecutor, who, under the weight of all those looks, staggered to the center of the court-room; his hair was in disorder and his face bore the marks of his own fingernails. The entire assembly uttered a long murmur of astonishment.

"They've asked me for proof, father," said Benedetto. Shall I give it to them?"

"No—no," stammered Villefort in a choked voice. "That would be useless."

"What do you mean?" cried the presiding magistrate.

"I mean," cried Villefort, "that I realize it would be useless for me to struggle against the vengeance of God which has just struck me. There's no need for proof—everything this young man has said is true."

"What! Are you sure you're not the victim of an hallucination, Monsieur de Villefort? Have you temporarily lost your reason? Such a strange, unexpected and horrible accusation may have troubled your mind; we can certainly all understand that."

Villefort shook his head. His teeth chattered violently, like those of a man consumed by fever. "My mind is perfectly lucid, your honor," he said. "I acknowledge myself guilty of all the charges this young man has brought against me and I now hold myself at the disposal of the public prosecutor who will be my successor."

After speaking these words in a choked and almost inaudible voice, Monsieur de Villefort staggered out of the courtroom.

The entire assembly was plunged into speechless consternation by the revelation which had just brought to such a terrible climax the series of events which had been agitating Paris society for the past two weeks.

"Now I'd like to hear someone say there's no drama in real life!" said Beauchamp.

"My God!" exclaimed Château-Renaud. "I'd much rather finish like Monsieur de Morcerf—a pistol shot seems pleasant compared to a catastrophe like this!"

"And to think that I once thought of marrying his daughter!" said Debray. "She did well to die, poor girl!"

"Court is adjourned," said the presiding magistrate, "and the case is postponed to the next session."

Andrea, still calm, left the courtroom escorted by gendarmes, who involuntarily showed him a certain respect.

"Well, what do you think of that?" said Debray to the policeman as he slipped a twenty-franc coin into his hand.

"There will be extenuating circumstances," replied the policeman.

Chapter 67

It would be difficult to depict the state of stupefaction in which Villefort left the Palace of Justice, to describe the fever which made all his arteries pound, stiffened all his fibers, made all his veins swell almost to bursting and transformed every point of his body into so many centers of pain.

He dragged himself through the corridors, guided only by habit. Outside he saw his carriage, awakened his coachman by opening the door himself, sank into the seat and pointed in the direction of the Faubourg Saint-Honoré. The coachman started the horses.

The whole weight of his ruined life had just fallen on Villefort's head. He was crushed by the weight, but he was not yet clearly aware of the consequences; he felt them, but he had not measured them. He felt the presence of God in the depths of his heart. "God! God! God!" he murmured, without knowing what he was saying. He saw only God behind the culmination which had just taken place.

The carriage rolled swiftly along. As he writhed on the cushions of the seat, Villefort felt something that bothered him. He put his hand on the object: it was a fan which Madame de Villefort had left behind in the carriage. It brought back his memory like a flash of lightning in the middle of a dark night. He thought of his wife. "Oh!" he cried out, as though a red-hot iron had pierced his heart. For the past hour he had had only one aspect of his wretchedness before his eyes; another aspect of it, no less terrible, had just been thrust upon his awareness. He had assumed the role of an implacable judge with his wife; he had sentenced her to death. Stricken with terror, crushed by remorse, overwhelmed by the shame into which he had plunged her with the eloquence of his irreproachable virtue, she was perhaps at that very moment preparing to die. An hour had passed since her death sentence; she was no doubt thinking back over her crimes, praying to God for mercy and writing a letter to her virtuous husband to beg his forgiveness, which she was about to pay for with her own death.

Villefort uttered a second cry of grief and rage. "Oh!" he cried, writhing on the satin cushions of his carriage. "She became a criminal only because she touched me! I'm filled with crime and she caught it from me as though it were cholera or the plague! And I punished her! I dared to say to her,

'Repent and die!' *I* said that! Oh, no, she'll live! She'll come with me—we'll leave France, we'll go as far as the earth will carry us. . . . I spoke to her of the scaffold—Oh, my God, how did I dare utter that word! The scaffold is waiting for me, too! We'll flee. . . . Yes, I'll confess everything to her; every day I'll humiliate myself and tell her that I, too, have committed a crime. . . . A marriage between a tiger and a serpent! A wife worthy of a husband like me! She must live, so that her infamy can pale before mine!"

Villefort pushed down the glass between him and his coachman. "Faster! Faster!" he shouted in a voice which made the coachman start on his seat. The horses, carried along by fear, flew toward the house.

"Yes, yes," repeated Villefort to himself as he approached his home, "she must live, so that she can repent and raise my son. She loved Edouard; it was for him that she did it all. The heart of a mother who loves her child can't be hopelessly bad. She'll repent and no one will ever know she was guilty. The crimes committed in my house, which are beginning to arouse suspicion now, will be forgotten with time; but if some of my enemies should remember them, I'll place them on the list of my own crimes. My wife will flee, taking money with her, and, above all, taking my son with her. She'll live and she'll be happy again, because all her love is in her son, and her son won't leave her. I'll have done a noble action; that relieves the heart." And Villefort breathed more freely than he had done in a long time.

The carriage stopped before his house. He leaped out of it and hurried up the steps. His servants seemed surprised to see him return so soon, but he read nothing else in their faces. As he went past Noirtier's room he saw two figures through the half-open door, but he gave no thought to the person who was with his father; his thoughts were elsewhere.

"Nothing has changed here," he said to himself as he climbed the small staircase leading to his wife's apartment and Valentine's empty bedroom. He approached the door and put his hand on the crystal knob. The door opened. "Not locked!" he murmured. "Good! Very good!"

He entered the small salon in which a bed was placed at night for Edouard. He glanced around the rooom. "No one," he said to himself. "She must be in her bedroom." He rushed over to the door. This one was locked. He stopped, shuddering, and called out, "Héloïse!" He seemed to hear a piece of furniture being moved. "Héloïse!" he repeated.

"Who's there?" asked his wife's voice.

"Open the door! Open it! It's I!"

But, despite this order and the anguished tone in which it

was given, the door remained closed. Villefort kicked it open. Madame de Villefort was standing in the doorway between her bedroom and her boudoir. She was pale, her features were contracted and her eyes stared at him with frightening fixity.

"Héloïse! Héloïse! What's the matter? Speak to me!"

"It's done," she said with a groan that seemed to tear her throat. "What more do you want from me?" And she fell to the floor.

Villefort ran over to her and seized her hand. She was dead. Maddened with horror, he stepped back to the doorway and stared at the corpse. "My son!" he cried suddenly. "Where's my son? Edouard! Edouard!" He rushed out of the apartment, still crying out, "Edouard! Edouard!"

This name was pronounced with such anguish that the servants came running up. "My son! Where's my son?" asked Villefort. "Take him out of the house so he won't see——"

"He's not downstairs," said Villefort's valet.

"Then he must be playing in the garden."

"No, sir. Madame sent for him about half an hour ago. He went into her room and hasn't come downstairs since then."

Icy sweat broke out on Villefort's forehead, his legs began to tremble and his thoughts began to whirl madly in his brain. "In her room!" he murmured. He began slowly to retrace his steps, wiping his forehead with one hand and supporting himself against the wall with the other.

On returning to her room, he had to see his poor wife's body once again. In order to call Edouard, he had to awaken the echoes of that apartment transformed into a coffin; to speak was to violate the silence of the tomb. He felt his tongue almost paralyzed. "Edouard—Edouard——" he stammered.

There was no answer. Villefort took a step forward. His wife's body lay across the doorway leading into the boudoir where Edouard must necessarily be; her body seemed to be guarding the doorway with open, staring eyes and a terrifying smile of mysterious irony.

He stepped forward a little closer, looked into the boudoir and saw his son lying on the sofa. The child was no doubt asleep. The wretched man felt a surge of unspeakable joy. All he had to do now was to step over the corpse, enter the boudoir, take the child in his arms and flee with him, far, far away. Villefort was no longer the man whose refined corruption made him a model of civilization; he was no longer afraid of prejudices, but of ghosts. He summoned up his courage and leaped over the corpse as though it were a bed of burning coals.

He picked up the child, held him tightly, shook him and called to him; Edouard did not answer. He kissed his cheeks: they were livid and cold; he felt his stiffened limbs and put his hand over his heart: the heart was no longer beating. The boy was dead.

A piece of paper fell from Edouard's breast. Villefort, thunderstruck, sank to his knees; the child slipped from his arms and rolled beside his mother. Villefort picked up the piece of paper, recognized his wife's handwriting and eagerly read these words: "You know I was a good mother, because it was for the sake of my son that I became a criminal. A good mother does not leave without her son."

Villefort could not believe his eyes; he could not believe his reason. He dragged himself over to Edouard's body and examined it with meticulous attention. Then a heartrending cry burst from his breast. "God!" he murmured. "Always God!"

He began to feel a mounting horror at being alone with those two corpses. A short time before he had been sustained by rage and despair, but now his head was bowed by the crushing weight of his grief, and he, who had never felt pity for anyone, went to see his father in order to have someone to whom he could relate his misfortune, someone at whose side he could weep.

He walked up the stairs and entered Noirtier's room. The old man was listening attentively to the Abbé Busoni, who was as calm and cold as ever. Villefort put his hand to his forehead when he saw the priest; he remembered the visit he had paid him on the day of Valentine's death. "You again!" he said. "Do you come only to escort Death?"

Busoni looked up. On seeing Villefort's disheveled face and the wild gleam in his eyes, he asuumed that the courtroom scene had been brought to its conclusion; he knew nothing of the events that had followed.

"I came here to pray for your daughter's soul," replied Busoni.

"And why have you come today?"

"I've come to tell you that you've paid your debt to me and that from now on I will pray God not to punish you any further."

"My God!" exclaimed Villefort, stepping back in terror. "That's not the voice of the Abbé Busoni!"

"No, it isn't."

The priest tore off his false tonsure, shook his head and his long black hair, released from its confinement, fell down around his manly face.

"That's the face of the Count of Monte Cristo!" cried Villefort wildly.

"That's still not it, Monsieur de Villefort—think further back."

"That voice! Where did I hear it for the first time?"

"You heard it in Marseilles twenty-three years ago, on the day of your marriage to Mademoiselle de Saint-Méran."

"You're not Busoni? You're not Monte Cristo? Oh, my God! So you're that hidden, implacable enemy! I wronged you in some way in Marseilles?"

"Yes, that's right," said the count, crossing his arms over his broad chest. "Think further back."

"But what did I do to you?" cried Villefort, whose mind was hovering between sanity and madness. "What did I do to you? Tell me! Speak!"

"You condemned me to a slow and hideous death, you killed my father and you deprived me of love, freedom and fortune!"

"Who are you? In the name of God, who are you?"

"I am the ghost of a wretched man you once buried in the dungeon of the Château d'If. When that ghost finally came out of its grave, God placed on it the mask of the Count of Monte Cristo and covered it with gold and diamonds so that you wouldn't recognize it until today."

"Ah! I recognize you! I recognize you! You're——"

"I am Edmond Dantès!"

"You're Edmond Dantès!" cried Villefort, seizing the count's wrist. "Then come with me!"

He led him down the stairs. Monte Cristo followed him in astonishment, not knowing where Villefort was leading him, but sensing some new disaster.

"Look, Edmond Dantès!" said Villefort, pointing to the bodies of his wife and son. "Is your vengeance complete now?"

Monte Cristo paled at the horrible sight. He realized that he had gone beyond the limits of rightful vengeance and that he could no longer say, "God is for me and with me." He rushed over to the boy's body with a feeling of inexpressible anguish, opened his eyes, felt his pulse, then picked him up, carried him into Valentine's room and locked the door.

"My son!" cried Villefort. "He's carrying away the body of my son!" He tried to run after Monte Cristo, but, as in a nightmare, he felt his feet rooted to the floor; his eyes seemed ready to burst from their sockets; his fingers sank into his chest until his nails were red with blood; the veins of his temples swelled and seemed to deluge his brain with fire.

He stood transfixed for several minutes until the frightful overthrow of his reason had been accomplished; then he uttered a loud shriek followed by a long burst of laughter and ran down the stairs.

A quarter of an hour later the door to Valentine's room opened and the Count of Monte Cristo reappeared. His features, ordinarily so calm and noble, were contorted with grief. In his arms he held the body of Edouard, whom he had been unable to bring back to life. He put one knee to the floor and reverently laid the boy beside his mother with his head on her breast. Then he stood up and walked out of the room.

He met a servant on the stairs. "Where is Monsieur de Villefort?" he asked.

The servant, without answering, pointed toward the garden.

Monte Cristo walked out into the garden and saw Villefort furiously digging in the ground with a spade while a group of his servants stood around him watching.

"He's not here!" said Villefort. "This isn't the right place!" And he began to dig a little further on.

Monte Cristo stepped up to him and said softly, "Monsieur de Villefort, you've lost a son, but——"

"Oh, I'll find him!" interrupted Villefort. "It won't do you any good to say he's not here—I'll find him if I have to search till the Last Judgment!"

Monte Cristo recoiled in terror. "Oh!" he exclaimed. "He's gone mad!"

Then, as though he were afraid the walls of that accursed house might collapse on his head, he hurried out into the street, doubting for the first time that he had a right to do what he had done.

When he arrived home he met Maximilien, who had been wandering through the house on the Champs Elysées as silently as a specter waiting for the time fixed by God to enter its grave again.

"Prepare yourself, Maximilien," said the count with a smile. "We're leaving Paris tomorrow."

"You have nothing more to do here?" asked Maximilien.

"No," replied Monte Cristo. "And God grant that I haven't done too much already!"

Chapter 68

The events which had just taken place occupied the attention of everyone in Paris. Emmanuel and Julie spoke about them with understandable surprise in their house on the Rue Meslay; they compared the three sudden and unexpected disasters which had befallen Danglars, Morcerf and Villefort. Maximilien, who had come to pay them a visit, listened to their conversation without taking part in it, plunged into his customary apathy.

"What terrible catastrophes!" said Emmanuel, thinking of Morcerf and Danglars.

"What terrible suffering!" said Julie, thinking of Valentine, but, guided by her woman's intuition, not wishing to mention the poor girl's name before her brother.

"If it was God who struck them down," said Emmanuel, "it was because He could find nothing in their past to merit a mitigation of their punishment."

He had hardly finished speaking when the door of the salon opened and the Count of Monte Cristo appeared in the doorway. Julie and Emmanuel uttered an exclamation of joy. Maximilien raised his head and then let it fall again.

"Maximilien," said the count, without appearing to notice the different impressions his arrival had produced, "I've come to take you with me."

"To take me with you?" said Maximilien, as though awakening from a dream.

"Yes; didn't I tell you to be ready to leave?"

"And I'm ready," replied Maximilien. "I came to tell them good-bye."

"Where are you going, count?" asked Julie.

"First of all, to Marseilles."

"To Marseilles?" repeated the young couple.

"Yes, and I'm taking your brother with me."

"Oh, try to bring him back to us cured!" said Julie.

Maximilien turned away to hide his emotion.

"Then you've noticed that he was suffering?" asked the count.

"Yes; I'm afraid he's been bored with us."

"I'll divert him," replied the count.

"I'm ready to leave, count," said Maximilien. "Good-bye, dear friends! Good-bye, Emmanuel! Good-bye, Julie!"

"What do you mean?" cried Julie. "How can you leave so suddenly like this, without preparation, without passports?"

"Delay increases the sorrow of parting," said Monte Cristo, "and I'm sure Maximilien has made all his preparations; I instructed him to do so, at least."

"I have my passport and my trunks are packed," said Maximilien dully.

"And you're leaving us immediately, without warning?" asked Julie.

"My carriage is at the door. I must be in Rome five days from now."

"Is Maximilien going to Rome too?" asked Emmanuel.

"I'll go wherever the count wants to take me," said Maximilien with a sad smile. "I belong to him for the next month."

"Oh, he speaks so strangely, count!"

"Your brother will be with me, so don't worry about him," said the count with his persuasive friendliness.

"Good-bye, Julie!" repeated Maximilien. "Good-bye, Emmannuel!"

"He breaks my heart with his indifference," said Julie. "Oh, Maximilien, you're hiding something from us!"

"You'll see him come back gay and laughing," said Monte Cristo.

Maximilien shot him a glance that was almost scornful, almost angry.

"Let's go," said the count.

"Before you leave, count," said Julie, "let me tell you everything that, the other day——"

"Nothing you could tell me would ever be worth what I see in your eyes, what you thought in your heart and what I felt in my own heart," said Monte Cristo, taking her hands in his. "I ought to have left without seeing you again, like the benefactor in a novel, but such virtue was beyond my strength because I'm a weak and vain man, because it does me good to see gratitude, joy and affection in the eyes of my fellow men. I'm leaving now, and I carry my egotism to the point of saying: Don't forget me, my friends, for you will probably never see me again."

"Never see you again!" cried Emmanuel, while two large tears rolled down Julie's cheeks. "Then you must be a god; you must be about to go back up to heaven after having appeared on earth to do us good."

"Don't say that," said Monte Cristo. "The gods never do evil; they always stop where they want to stop. Chance is never stronger than they are; on the contrary, it is they who dominate chance. No, I'm a man, Emmanuel, and your admiration is as undeserved as your words are sacrilegious."

He clasped Emmanuel's hand and pressed Julie's to his lips; then he tore himself away from that house which hap-

piness seemed to have made its home and motioned to Maximilien, who was still as sorrowful and apathetic as he had
been on the day of Valentine's death.

"Make our brother happy again!" whispered Julie in Monte
Cristo's ear.

He pressed her hand as he had done eleven years before on
the staircase leading to her father's study. "Do you still have
faith in Sinbad the Sailor?" he asked, smiling.

"Oh, yes!"

"Then have no fear."

As the count had said, his carriage was waiting for him at
the door. Four vigorous horses were shaking their manes and
stamping the pavement impatiently. Ali was waiting at the
bottom of the steps, his face gleaming with perspiration; he
had apparently just returned from a long errand.

"Did you see the old man?" asked the count in Arabic.

Ali nodded.

"And did you open the letter before his eyes, as I ordered
you to do?"

Ali nodded once again.

"What did he say; or rather, what did he do?"

Ali closed his eyes as Noirtier did when he wished to say
yes.

"Good, he agrees," said Monte Cristo. "Let's go."

The carriage set off and the horses' hoofs struck showers
of sparks from the pavement. Maximilien settled back into
his corner without saying a word.

Half an hour passed. Then the carriage stopped: the count
had just pulled the silken cord attached to Ali's finger. The
Nubian descended and opened the door. The night was bright
with stars. They were on top of the hill of Villejuif, from
which Paris, spread out like a dark sea below, agitates its
millions of lights like phosphorescent waves; waves more
tumultuous, more seething, more furious than those of the
angry ocean, waves which never know calm like those of the
vast sea, waves forever clashing, forever foaming, forever
engulfing. . . .

The count remained alone; at a signal from him the carriage went forward a few paces. He stood for a long time
with his arms crossed, contemplating that modern Babylon
which makes the religious poet dream, as well as the scoffing
materialist. "Great city!" he murmured, bowing his head as
though in prayer. "It was less than six months ago that I
entered your gates. I believe that the spirit of God led me
there, and He has led me out triumphant. He alone knows
that I now leave without hatred or pride, but not without
regret; He alone knows that I have not used the power with

which He entrusted me either for myself or for vain causes. Great city, it was in your throbbing bosom that I found what I sought! Like a patient miner, I have dug deep into your entrails to root out the evil there. Now my work is completed, my mission is accomplished; you can no longer give me either joy or sorrow. Farewell, Paris! Farewell!"

He looked once again over that vast plain like some spirit of the night, then he climbed back into his carriage, which soon disappeared over the top of the hill in a cloud of dust and noise.

They traveled for two leagues without speaking. "Maximilien," said the count finally, "do you regret having come with me?"

"No, count, but leaving Paris——"

"If I had thought happiness was waiting for you in Paris, Maximilien, I would have left you there."

"But that's where Valentine is lying; leaving Paris is like losing her a second time."

"Maximilien," said Monte Cristo, "the friends we have lost are buried in our hearts, not in the earth. I have two friends who are always with me in my heart: one is the man who gave me life, the other is the man who gave me intelligence. I consult them when I'm in doubt, and if I've done any good in this world I owe it to their advice. Consult the voice of your heart, Maximilien, and ask it if you ought to go on showing me that gloomy expression."

"My friend," replied Maximilien, "the voice of my heart is very sad and promises me nothing but sorrow."

"A weakened mind always sees everything through a black veil. The soul makes its own horizons; your soul is dark, which is why you see such a cloudy sky."

"That may be true," said Maximilien. And he sank back into his silent reverie.

The journey was made with that speed which was one of the count's marvelous powers; cities passed like shadows along their route; the trees, shaken by the first winds of autumn, seemed to rush toward them like disheveled giants, then flee swiftly away from them as soon as they reached them. The next morning they arrived at Châlons, where the count's steamboat was waiting for them. The carriage was placed on board without a moment's delay and the two travelers continued on their way.

The ship was built for speed; her paddle wheels were like two wings with which she skimmed the surface of the water like a bird. Even Maximilien felt the intoxication of speed, and from time to time the wind which tousled his hair seemed almost to dissipate for a moment the clouds gathered over his brow.

As for the count, as he moved further and further away from Paris an almost superhuman serenity seemed to envelop him; he was like an exile returning to his native land.

Soon Marseilles came into view, white, warm and full of life. A host of memories was aroused in both of them by the sight of that round tower, that Fort Saint-Nicolas, that Hôtel de Ville and that brick quay where they had both played as children.

As though by a common accord, they both stopped on the Cannebière. A ship was about to set sail for Algiers. The passengers crowded on deck and the throng of relatives and friends weeping and shouting as they bid farewell is always a touching spectacle, even for those who see it every day, but it was unable to distract Maximilien from the thought that had taken possession of his mind from the moment he set foot on the quay.

"Look," he said, taking the count by the arm, "here's where my father stood when the *Pharaon* sailed into port; this is where the brave man you saved from death and dishonor threw himself into my arms. I can still feel his tears on my face. And he didn't weep alone: many people around us were also weeping."

Monte Cristo smiled. "I was there," he said, pointing to a street corner.

As he said this, from the direction in which he had pointed they heard a sorrowful groan and saw a woman waving goodbye to a passenger on the ship that was about to leave. She was veiled; Monte Cristo watched her with an emotion which Maximilien could easily have noticed if his eyes had not been fixed on the ship.

"Look, I'm not mistaken!" cried Maximilien. "That young man in uniform, the one waving his hat—it's Albert de Morcerf!"

"Yes," said Monte Cristo, "I recognized him."

"How could you when you were looking in the opposite direction?"

The count smiled as he did when he did not wish to answer, and turned his eyes back to the veiled woman as she disappeared around a corner. Then he said to Maximilien, "My friend, don't you have some things to do here?"

"I have to weep over my father's grave," replied Maximilien dully.

"Very well; go to the cemetery and wait for me. I'll meet you there."

"Are you leaving me now?"

"Yes; I also have a pious visit to make."

Monte Cristo watched Maximilien until he had disappeared, then he turned his steps toward the Allées de Meilhan and the little house which the beginning of this story has made familiar to the reader. That house, still charming despite its dilapidation, was the same one in which Dantès' father had lived. However, while the old man had occupied only the garret, the count had placed the entire house at Mercédès' disposal.

It was there that the veiled woman had gone when Monte Cristo watched her walk away from the quay. For him the worn steps of the house were old friends and he knew better than anyone else how to open that weather-beaten door. He entered without knocking, like a friend or a guest.

At the end of a path paved with bricks opened a small garden rich in warmth and sunlight, the same garden in which Mercédès had found the money in the place indicated to her by the count, whose tact had made its burial there date from twenty-four years before.

Mercédès was sitting in an arbor, weeping. She had raised her veil and, with her face hidden in her hands, was giving vent to all the sighs and sobs which the presence of her son had forced her to hold back.

Monte Cristo stepped forward. Mercédès looked up and uttered a cry of alarm at seeing a man suddenly appear before her.

"It's no longer in my power to give you happiness," said the count, "but I can offer you consolation. Would you accept it as coming from a friend?"

"It's true that I'm deeply unhappy," said Mercédès. "I'm all alone in the world now. I had no one but my son, and he has left me."

"He did the right thing," said the count, "and he has a noble heart. If he stayed with you his life would have become useless and he would never have been able to accustom himself to your sorrow. His powerlessness would have made him bitter, but now he'll become strong by struggling against his adversity and changing it into a fortune. Let him reconstruct your future; it's in safe hands."

"Oh," said the poor woman, sadly shaking her head, "I won't enjoy that fortune you mention and which I pray God to grant him. So many things have been shattered inside me and around me that I feel myself near the grave. You were right to bring me back here where I was once so happy: one ought to die where one was happy."

"Your words burn into my heart," said Monte Cristo, "es-

pecially since you have every reason to hate me: I'm the cause
of all your misfortune."

"Hate you, Edmond? Hate the man who spared my son's
life—for it was your intention to kill the son of whom Monsieur de Morcerf was so proud, wasn't it? Oh, look at me and
you'll see that there's not even the shadow of a reproach
in me!"

Monte Cristo took her hand and kissed it respectfully, but
she felt that his kiss was without ardor, like a kiss he might
have placed on the marble hand of the statue of a saint.

"There are some predestined lives whose whole future is
ruined by an early mistake," continued Mercédès. "When I
believed you to be dead, I too should have died. What good
did it do for me to mourn your loss eternally in my heart?
It has done nothing except make a woman of thirty-nine
appear to be fifty. Oh, I was weak and cowardly! I denied
my love and, like all renegades, I bring misfortune to everyone around me."

"No, Mercédès," said Monte Cristo, "you judge yourself
much too severely. You're a noble and honorable woman and
you disarmed me for a moment with your sorrow, but behind
me, invisible, unknown and wrathful, there was God, of whom
I was only the agent and who did not choose to prevent my
blows from reaching their mark. Examine the past and the
present, try to guess the future and then decide whether or
not I'm the instrument of God. The most horrible disasters,
the cruelest suffering, the abandonment of those who loved
me, the persecution of those who didn't even know me—that
was the first part of my life; then, after my captivity, solitude
and misery, came freedom and a fortune so extraordinarily
immense that I would have had to be blind not to see that
God had sent it to me as part of some great design. From then
on I considered that fortune as a sacred trust; from then on
I gave no thought to ordinary life and its pleasures; from then
on I knew not one hour of peace: I felt myself driven like a
cloud of fire descending from heaven to destroy an accursed
city. Like an adventurous captain setting out on a perilous
expedition, I laid in my provisions, loaded my weapons and
prepared every means of attack and defense; I accustomed my
body to the most vigorous exercises and my soul to the most
violent shocks; I taught my arm to kill, my eyes to watch
suffering and my lips to smile at the most terrible sights; from
the kind, trusting and forgiving man I had once been, I made
myself vindictive, crafty and cruel, or, rather, impassive like
deaf and blind Fate itself. Then I set out on the path that lay
before me and I reached my goal; woe to those whom I met
on my way!"

"Enough, Edmond!" said Mercédès. "Believe me when I say that the woman who was the only one to recognize you was also the only one to understand you. Even if you had crushed me on your way, Edmond, I would still have admired you! Just as there is a vast gulf between me and the past, so there is a vast gulf between you and other men, and I admit to you that my most painful torture is to compare you, for there is nothing in the world that can equal you and nothing that resembles you. Now tell me good-bye, Edmond, and let us part."

"Before I leave you, Mercédès, tell me what you want."

"I want only one thing: my son's happiness."

"Pray God to keep him from death, and I will do the rest."

"Thank you, Edmond."

"But what about you?"

"I need nothing. I live between two graves. One is that of Edmond Dantès, who died so long ago and whom I loved; I wouldn't part with that memory for anything in the world. The other is that of a man whom Edmond Dantès killed; I approve of the deed, but I must still pray for the victim's soul."

"But what will you do?"

"I can no longer do anything but pray, and I have no need to work: I found the little treasure you buried where you left it."

"Mercédès, I can't reproach you for it, but you did exaggerate your sacrifice when you abandoned all your husband's fortune, half of which rightfully belonged to you because of your economy and your vigilance."

"I know what you're about to offer me, Edmond, but I can't accept it. My son would forbid it."

"Then I won't do anything for you that wouldn't have his approval. I'll find out what his intentions are and abide by them. But if he agrees to let me do what I want to do, will you also agree?"

"I'm no longer a thinking creature, Edmond. God has so shaken me with His storms that I've lost my will. Since I'm alive, He doesn't want me to die; if He sends help to me, it will be because He wants me to accept it."

"That's not how we ought to worship God," said Monte Cristo. "God wants us to understand Him and discuss His purposes: that's why He gave us free will."

"Don't say that!" cried Mercédès. "If I believed God had given me free will, what would remain to save me from utter despair?"

Monte Cristo bowed his head before the vehemence of her sorrow. "Will you tell me *au revoir?*" he asked, holding out his hand to her.

"Yes, I'll tell you *au revoir*," replied Mercédès, solemnly pointing to the sky. "I'll say it to prove to you that I still hope."

After touching the count's trembling hand, Mercédès turned and hurried up the stairs.

The count walked slowly out of the house and back toward the harbor.

Although Mercédès was at the window of the little room in which the elder Dantès had once lived, she did not see Monte Cristo leave: her eyes were searching in the distance the ship that was carrying her son away from her. It is true, however, that as she did so she murmured softly, as though in spite of herself: "Edmond! Edmond!"

Chapter 69

The count was heavy-hearted as he left Mercédès, in all probability never to see her again.

Since the death of little Edouard a great change had taken place in Monte Cristo. Having arrived at the summit of his vengeance after his slow and tortuous climb, he had looked down into the abyss of doubt. Furthermore, his conversation with Mercédès had awakened a host of memories which now had to be overcome.

A man of the count's character could not remain for long in that state of melancholy. He told himself that in order for him to come to the point of blaming himself, an error must somehow have slipped into his calculations.

"I'm not considering the past correctly," he thought. "I can't have made such a mistake. Can my goal have been senseless? Can I have been following a false path for ten years? I refuse to accept such an idea—it would make me lose my reason. The reason for my present doubt is that I no longer see the past clearly. The past fades away with time as objects fade away with distance. The same thing is happening to me as happens to people in dreams when they see and feel a wound but can't remember having received it."

Monte Cristo walked down the Rue Saint-Laurent to the quay. A pleasure boat was passing with its canopy spread. Monte Cristo called to its owner, who hurried eagerly over to him, hoping for a good fare.

It was a beautiful day but, despite the clear sky, the graceful boats they passed in the harbor and the golden sunlight with which everything was flooded, the count, wrapped in his cloak, remembered one by one the details of the terrible trip he had made there years before: the sight of the Château d'If

which told him where he was being taken, the struggle with
the gendarmes when he tried to leap into the sea, his despair
when he felt himself vanquished and the sensation of cold
when the barrel of the carbine was pressed against his forehead like a ring of ice. Like those springs dried up in summer
which gradually begin to flow again when the clouds of
autumn gather above them, Monte Cristo began to feel the
bitterness which had once flooded the heart of Edmond Dantès.
From then on there was no more clear sky and sunlight for
him; the sky became veiled in mourning and the appearance
of the black mass of the Château d'If made him start as
though he had suddenly seen the ghost of a deadly enemy.

As they approached the island the count instinctively retreated to the stern of the boat. "We're about to land, sir,"
said the boatman. Monte Cristo remembered that it was at
the same spot, at the same rock, that he had been violently
dragged ashore by the gendarmes and that they had forced
him to climb that same ramp at the point of a bayonet.

There had been no prisoners in the Château d'If since the
July Revolution; it was now inhabited only by a detachment
of guards whose duty was to prevent its being used by smugglers. There was a guide waiting at the gate to show visitors
through the monument of terror, now become simply an object
of curiosity. And yet, although he knew all this, when Monte
Cristo descended the dark staircase and was led to the dungeon
he had asked to see, a cold pallor invaded his forehead and
he pushed an icy perspiration back into his heart.

The count asked if any of the former jailers still remained
and was told that they had all been retired or given other
positions. The guide who was conducting him had been there
only since 1830.

Monte Cristo was led into his own cell. He saw the dim
light filtering in through the narrow window; he saw the place
where his bed had been and, although now filled in, the opening made by the Abbé Faria was still visible. Monte Cristo
felt his legs give way beneath him; he sat down on a wooden
stool.

"Are there any stories connected with this prison other than
that of Mirabeau's imprisonment?" asked the count.

"Yes, sir," replied the guide. "One of the jailers told me
a story about this very cell. Would you like to hear it?"

"Yes," said Monte Cristo. "Tell me." And he placed his
hand over his heart to repress its violent beating, frightened
at the thought of hearing his own story.

"This cell," began the guide, "was once inhabited by a
prisoner who was a very dangerous man, or so I was told,
at least. Another man was a prisoner here at the same time,

but he wasn't at all dangerous; he was a poor priest who had gone mad."

"I see," said Monte Cristo. "And what form did his madness take?"

"He was always offering to pay millions of francs for his freedom."

"Could the two prisoners see each other?"

"Oh, no, sir; that was forbidden. But they finally made a secret passage between their cells."

"Which one of them made the passage?"

"It must have been the young man; he was strong and energetic, while the poor priest was old and weak. Besides, the priest's mind was too confused to follow a single idea."

"Blind fools!" thought the count.

"No one knows how the young man made the passage," continued the guide, "but there's no doubt that he made it. Look, you can still see the trace of it." He moved his torch up against the wall.

"Oh, yes," said the count in a voice hoarse with emotion.

"As a result, the two prisoners were able to communicate with each other. No one knows how long this lasted, but one day the old prisoner fell ill and died. Can you imagine what the young one did then?"

"No; tell me."

"He carried the body into his own cell and put it into his bed with its face toward the wall. Then he went back to the other cell, closed off the secret passage and got into the sack they had sewed up the body in."

Monte Cristo closed his eyes and seemed to experience once again all the sensations he had felt when the coarse cloth of the sack, still impregnated with the cold which the corpse had communicated to it, had rubbed across his face.

The guide continued: "This was his plan: he assumed that the dead were buried at the Château d'If and, since he was sure they wouldn't go to the expense òf providing coffins for prisoners, he planned to push his way up out of the ground. But unfortunately there was a custom in the prison which ruined his plan: they didn't bury the dead; they only tied a cannon ball to their feet and threw them into the sea. And that's what was done to the young man. The next day they found the priest's body in the young man's bed and guessed everything, especially when the men assigned to throw the body into the sea told something they hadn't dared tell before: that when they threw the body they heard a terrible cry which was smothered as soon as the body hit the water."

The count breathed heavily and anguish clutched at his heart. "No!" he thought. "I began to doubt only because I was beginning to forget, but here the wound in my heart opens again and the thirst for vengeance returns." Then he said to the guide: "Was anything ever heard of the prisoner again?"

"No, never. He was thrown from a height of about fifty feet and he hit the water feet first, so the weight of the cannon ball must have dragged him down to the bottom of the sea immediately, poor man."

"Do you pity him?"

"Yes, of course; although he died in his own element."

"What do you mean?"

"They say he was a sailor who was imprisoned for Bonapartism."

"What was his name?"

"He was known only as Number 34."

"Villefort, Villefort!" thought Monte Cristo. "That's what you must have told yourself many times when my ghost came to trouble your sleep!"

"Would you like to see the rest of the prison, sir?" asked the guide.

"Yes, especially if you'll show me the poor priest's cell."

"Come with me, then."

"Just a moment," said Monte Cristo. "I'd like to take one last look at this cell."

"That suits me very well," said the guide, "because I've forgotten the key to the priest's cell."

"Go and get it, then."

"I'll leave you the torch."

"No, take it with you."

"But you won't have any light in here."

"I can see in the dark."

"You're like Number 34, then. They say he could see a pin in the darkest corner of his cell."

"It took him ten years to accomplish that," thought Monte Cristo.

The guide walked away, taking the torch with him.

The count had told the truth: after being in the darkness for only a few seconds he could see everything with perfect clarity. "Yes," he said to himself, "this is the stone I used to sit on, and there's a trace of the blood that flowed from my forehead one day when I tried to crush my head against the wall! Those figures—yes, I remember them: I made them one day when I calculated my father's age to see if I would find him still alive, and Mercédès' age to see if I would find her still free. I had a moment of hope when I finished those calculations. I wasn't taking hunger and infidelity into account!" A bitter laugh burst from the count's lips; as in a dream, he had just seen his father being taken to the grave, and Mercédès walking to the altar.

His attention was caught by an inscription on the opposite wall: "O GOD, PRESERVE MY MEMORY!"

"Yes, that was my only prayer toward the end of my imprisonment," he thought. "I no longer asked for freedom; I asked only to keep my memory because I was afraid I might go mad and forget. But you preserved my memory, O God, and I haven't forgotten! Thank you, my God, thank you!"

Just then the light of a torch was reflected on the walls: the guide was returning. Monte Cristo went out to meet him.

"Follow me," said the guide. He led the count through an underground corridor to another cell.

Monte Cristo saw the remains of the bed on which the Abbé Faria had died. At this sight, instead of the anguish he had felt in his own cell, his heart swelled with a feeling of affection and gratitude and tears welled up in his eyes.

"This is the mad priest's cell," said the guide. Pointing to an opening which had remained unclosed, he added, "That's where the young man came in to see him. Judging from the appearance of the stone, a learned man said the two prisoners communicated with each other for about ten years. Those ten years must have seemed terribly long to them, poor men!"

Dantès took several twenty-franc coins from his pocket and handed them to the man who had just pitied him for the second time without knowing him. The guide accepted them, thinking he was being given only some small change, but then, looking at them by the light of his torch, he recognized their true value.

"You've made a mistake, sir."

"What do you mean?"

"These are gold coins you gave me."

"I know that."

"You intended to give them to me?"

"Yes."

The guide looked at Monte Cristo in astonishment. "Sir," he said, "I don't understand your generosity."

"It's not too difficult to understand: you see, I, too, was once a sailor, so I was particularly touched by the story you told me."

"Well, then, since you're so generous, sir, I ought to offer you something also."

"What do you have to offer me?"

"Something connected with the story I just told you."

"Really?" cried the count eagerly. "What is it?"

"Well, I'll tell you: one day I said to myself, 'You can

always find something in a cell where a prisoner lived for fifteen years,' and I began to tap on the walls. After a while I discovered a hollow sound near the head of the bed and under the hearth. I lifted out the stones and I found——"

"A rope ladder and some tools?" cried the count.

"How did you know that?" asked the guide in surprise.

"I didn't know it; I only guessed it. That's usually the sort of thing a prisoner hides in his cell. . . . Do you still have them?"

"No, sir; I sold them to visitors. But I do have something else."

"What is it?" asked the count impatiently.

"I still have a sort of book written on strips of cloth."

"Oh!" cried Monte Cristo. "You still have that book?"

"I don't know if it's a book, but I still have it."

"Go get it for me!"

The guide left the cell. Monte Cristo knelt reverently before the remains of that bed which death had transformed into an altar for him. "O my second father," he said, "you gave me freedom, knowledge and wealth, you who, like beings of a superior order, had the knowledge of good and evil—if, after the transfiguration of the body there still remains something animate in the places where we have loved or suffered deeply, noble heart, supreme intellect, profound soul, give me some sign, I beg you; take away this doubt, which, if it changes to a conviction, will also become remorse!" The count bowed his head and joined his hands.

"Here it is, sir," said a voice behind him. He started and turned around. The guide was holding out to him those strips of cloth on which the Abbé Faria had poured out all the treasures of his knowledge and wisdom: they formed the manuscript of his great work on the monarchy in Italy.

The count seized them eagerly. The first thing his eyes fell on was the epigraph: "Thou shalt tear out the teeth of the dragon and trample the lions underfoot, thus saith the Lord."

"Ah!" cried Monte Cristo. "There's my answer! Thank you, father, thank you!"

He drew out of his pocket a small wallet containing ten banknotes of one thousand francs each. "Here," he said to the guide, "take this wallet."

"Are you giving it to me?"

"Yes, but on condition that you won't look inside it till after I've gone."

Pressing the precious relic to his chest, Monte Cristo hurried out of the dungeon and went back to the boat. "Back to Marseilles!" he said.

As he sailed away from the somber prison he kept his eyes

fixed on it and said to himself, "Woe to those who put me into that wretched dungeon, and to those who forgot I was there!"

The victory was complete: the Count of Monte Cristo had twice vanquished doubt.

After stepping ashore, he went to the cemetery, where he found Maximilien. Ten years earlier, Monte Cristo had also made a pious pilgrimage to that cemetery, but, having returned to France with all his millions, he had been unable to find the grave of his father, who had died of hunger. Maximilien's father had fared better: having died in the arms of his children, he had been laid to rest by them beside his wife, who had preceded him by two years. Two large slabs of marble with their names inscribed on them had been placed side by side within a little enclosure formed by an iron railing and shaded by four cypress trees.

Maximilien was leaning against one of those trees and staring dully at the two tombstones; his grief was profound, almost overwhelming.

"Maximilien," said the count, "you told me during the journey that you wanted to stay here in Marseilles for several days. Is that still your wish?"

"I have no more wishes, count; but it seems to me I'd wait a little less painfully here than anywhere else."

"Good; I'm going to leave you for a while, but you'll still keep your word, won't you?"

The young man let his head fall to his chest. "You have my promise," he said, after a moment of silence. "But remember——"

'I'll expect you on the Isle of Monte Cristo on the fifth of October. On the fourth, a yacht will be waiting for you in the harbor of Bastia. The name of the yacht will be the *Eurus;* give your name to the captain and he'll take you to me."

"I'll do as I promised, count, but remember that on the fifth of October——"

"I've told you twenty times that if you still want to die on that day, I'll help you myself. And now, good-bye."

"You're leaving me?"

"Yes, I have something to do in Italy. I'm leaving right away; the steamer is waiting for me. Will you come with me to the harbor?"

"I'm at your disposal, count."

Maximilien accompanied Monte Cristo to the harbor. Smoke was already pouring out of the stacks of the steamboat when they arrived. It set out soon afterward; an hour later it had almost vanished on the eastern horizon.

Chapter 70

At the same time as the count's steamboat was disappearing behind Cape Morgiou, a man had just passed the little town of Aquapendente, on the road from Florence to Rome. The accent in which he spoke to the coachman stamped him as a Frenchman, although the only Italian words he knew were musical terms. *"Allegro!"* he called out to the coachman at every rise in the road, and *"Moderato!"* at every descent. We might mention that these two words made him the object of much laughter.

On reaching La Storta, where one can see Rome in the distance, this traveler felt none of the enthusiastic curiosity which moves most foreigners to stand up in their carriages to try to see the famous dome of Saint Peter's, which one can distinguish before anything else. Instead, he merely took a wallet from his pocket, drew out a piece of paper, unfolded it with a careful attention which resembled respect, folded it again and said to himself, "Good; I still have it."

The carriage went through the Porta del Popolo, turned left and drew up in front of a hotel. Our old friend Signor Pastrini received the traveler in the doorway with his hat in his hand. The traveler alighted, ordered a good dinner and asked for the address of the firm of Thomson and French.

When the new arrival left the hotel with the inevitable cicerone, a man stepped out from the crowd of curious bystanders and, unnoticed by the traveler and apparently unnoticed by his guide, began to follow them. The Frenchman was in such a hurry to call on the firm of Thomson and French that he had not taken the time to wait for the horses to be harnessed; the carriage was to wait for him outside the door of the firm.

The Frenchman entered, leaving his guide in the antechamber. The man who had followed them also entered. The Frenchman rang the doorbell and walked into the outer office; his shadow did likewise.

"Messrs. Thomson and French?" asked the stranger.

A servant stood up at a sign from a confidential clerk, solemn guardian of the first office.

"Whom shall I announce?" asked the servant.

"Baron Danglars," replied the Frenchman.

A door opened; the servant and the baron walked through it, while the man who had entered with Danglars sat down in the waiting room. The clerk continued to write for five minutes or so, during which the man sitting in the waiting room remained silent and motionless. Then the clerk's pen ceased to scratch on the paper; he raised his head, looked carefully around the room and said, "Ah, here you are, Peppino!"

"Yes," was the laconic reply.

"You found out something good about that fat man?"

"I can't take any credit for it—we were notified in advance."

"So you know why he came here?"

"Of course: he came here to draw money. All we need to know now is how much."

"We'll tell you that in a little while, my friend."

"Very good. But don't give us false information, as you did for that Russian prince the other day. You told us thirty thousand francs and we found only twenty-two thousand."

"You must not have searched well enough."

"Luigi Vampa searched him in person."

"In that case, he must either have paid off some debts or spent the money before you got to him."

"Yes, I suppose that's possible."

"It's not possible, it's sure. But let me go make my observations or the Frenchman will transact his business without my knowing the exact figure."

Peppino nodded. Taking a rosary from his pocket, he began to mumble a prayer while the clerk disappeared through the same door which had admitted the servant and the baron. Ten minutes later the clerk reappeared, beaming.

"Well?" asked Peppino.

"Be on the alert—it's a magnificent sum!"

"Five million, isn't it?"

"Yes; how did you know the figure?"

"On a receipt from His Excellency the Count of Monte Cristo?"

"That's right!" cried the clerk. "How are you so well informed?"

"I told you we were notified in advance."

"Then why did you ask me for information?"

"To make sure it was the right man."

"He's the man you want, all right—— Ssh! Here he comes now!"

The clerk picked up his pen and Peppino his rosary; the former was writing and the latter was praying when the door opened. Danglars, with a radiant smile on his face, was accompanied by the banker, who showed him to the door. Peppino walked out behind Danglars.

As had been arranged, a carriage was waiting for Danglars in front of the offices of the firm. He climbed into it while his cicerone held the door open for him. The cicerone closed the door and seated himself beside the driver. Peppino climbed up on the rear seat.

"Would you like to go to Saint Peter's Cathedral, Excellency?" asked the cicerone.

"What for?" replied the baron.

"Why, to look at it!"

"I didn't come to Rome to look!"

"Where would you like to go, then, Excellency?"

"Back to the hotel."

"Casa Pastrini," said the cicerone to the driver.

Ten minutes later the baron was back in his apartment at the hotel and Peppino had settled down on a bench in front of the hotel. Danglars was tired, happy and sleepy. He put his wallet under his pillow and went to sleep. Although he went to bed early, he woke up late the next day, for he had slept badly for five or six consecutive nights, when he slept at all.

He ate a hearty breakfast and, caring little about seeing the beauties of the Eternal City, ordered his post horses for noon. But he had reckoned without the formalities of the police and the laziness of the master of the post. The horses did not arrive until two o'clock, and the cicerone did not bring back his passport until three.

"Which road?" asked the driver in Italian.

"The Ancona road," replied the baron.

Signor Pastrini translated the question and the answer and the carriage set out at a gallop. Danglars intended to pass through Venice and then go on to Vienna, which he had been told was a city of pleasure and in which he planned to settle down permanently.

He was scarcely three leagues outside of Rome when night began to fall. He asked the driver how far it was to the next town.

"*Non capisco,*" replied the driver.

Danglars nodded in a way which signified, "Very well." The carriage continued on its way. "I'll stop over at the first relay station," said Danglars to himself.

For ten minutes he thought about his wife, whom he had left behind in Paris, then for ten minutes he thought about his daughter, who was wandering somewhere in the world with Mademoiselle d'Armilly. He devoted ten more minutes to his creditors and the way in which he would use their money; then, having nothing else to think about, he closed his eyes and went to sleep.

The carriage stopped. Danglars opened his eyes and looked out the window, expecting to find himself in some town, or at least in some village; but he saw nothing except a sort of ruin and three or four men moving back and forth like shadows. He waited for the driver who had just completed his relay to come and ask to be paid, but the horses were replaced without anyone's coming to him to ask for money. Danglars, astonished, opened the door, but a vigorous hand immediately pushed it shut again and the carriage set off.

The baron, astounded, woke up completely. "Hey there, *mio caro!*" he called out to the driver, using another bit of Italian he remembered from hearing his daughter sing duets with Prince Cavalcanti. But *mio caro* did not answer. Danglars opened the window, put his head through it and shouted, "Where are we going?"

"Dentro la testa!" replied an imperious voice, accompanied by a threatening gesture.

Danglars understood that *"Dentro la testa!"* meant "Put your head inside!" He was making rapid progress in Italian.

He obeyed, not without uneasiness. This uneasiness grew from minute to minute until his mind was filled with a number of thoughts well fitted to arouse a traveler's interest, especially a traveler in Danglars' situation. Then he saw a man wrapped in a cloak galloping beside the right-hand door of the carriage. "It must be a gendarme," he said to himself. "Can the French authorities have sent a telegraphic message to the Roman authorities about me?"

He resolved to put an end to his uncertainty. "Where are you taking me?" he asked.

"Dentro la testa!" replied the same voice, in the same tone of menace.

Danglars looked out the left-hand window and saw another man galloping beside the carriage. "No doubt about it," he said to himself; "I've been caught." He leaned back in his seat, this time not to sleep, but to think. A moment later the moon rose. He looked out and saw the great aqueducts he had noticed at the beginning of his journey, but this time they were on his left instead of on his right. He realized that the carriage had turned around and was taking him back to Rome. "Oh!" he murmured. "They've obtained extradition!" Finally he saw a dark mass which the carriage seemed about to crash into, but at the last moment it turned and ran alongside the mass, which Danglars recognized as one of the ramparts surrounding Rome.

"We're not going back into the city, so it can't be the police who've caught me," thought Danglars. "My God! Could it be——" And he remembered the interesting stories of Roman bandits, so little believed in Paris, which Albert de Morcerf had told to his wife and daughter. "Maybe they're robbers!" he thought.

The carriage stopped and the left-hand door opened.

"*Scendi!*" ordered a voice. Danglars climbed out of the carriage instantly; he could not yet speak Italian, but he already understood it.

More dead than alive, the baron looked around him: he was surrounded by four men, not counting the driver. "*Di quà,*" said one of the four men, turning down a narrow path. Danglars followed his guide without argument; he had no need to turn around in order to know that he was being followed by the three other men. However, it seemed to him that those men stopped and posted themselves as sentinels at approximately equal intervals.

After walking for ten minutes or so without exchanging a single word with his guide, he found himself between a small hill and a clump of high grass. Three men stood silent, forming a triangle of which he was the center.

"*Avanti!*" said the same curt, imperious voice. This time Danglars understood not only by word but by gesture, for the man behind him pushed him forward so energetically that he stumbled against his guide. This guide was our friend Peppino, who led the way along a twisting route which only a ferret or a lizard could have recognized as a path.

Peppino stopped before a large rock which was half open like an eyelid, then disappeared into it. The voice and gestures of the man behind Danglars ordered him to do likewise. He could no longer doubt that he had fallen into the hands of Roman bandits. Two other men descended behind him and, pushing him whenever he happened to stop, brought him down a gently sloping corridor to an open space of sinister appearance. The walls, hollowed out into sepulchers placed one above the other, seemed, in the midst of the white stone, to open deep, black eyes like those of a skull.

"Who goes there?" called out a sentry.

"Friend!" replied Peppino. "Where's the chief?"

"In there," said the sentry, pointing into a large room hollowed out of the rock.

Peppino took Danglars by the coat collar and pulled him through an opening which resembled a door and which led into the room in which the chief apparently lived.

"Is this the man?" asked the chief who had been attentively reading the *Life of Alexander* in Plutarch.

"Yes."

"Show him to me."

At this rather impertinent order, Peppino moved the torch near Danglars' face so abruptly that the baron had to step back quickly to keep from having his eyebrows singed. His face wore an expression of utter terror.

"This man is tired," said the chief. "Take him to his bed."

"Oh!" thought Danglars, "that 'bed' is probably one of those sepulchers carved into the wall!" He groaned and followed his guide. He did not try to cry out or beg for mercy, for he no longer had any strength, any will or feelings. He stumbled against a step; realizing that there was a staircase in front of him, he instinctively lowered his head in order not to strike his forehead and found himself in a cell hollowed out of solid rock. It was clean, though bare, and dry, although located far underground. In one corner there was a bed made of dried grass and covered with goat skins. When Danglars noticed it he saw in it the radiant symbol of his salvation. "Thank God!" he exclaimed. "It's a real bed!"

"Ecco," said the guide. He pushed Danglars into the cell and closed the door. A bolt snapped shut: Danglars was a prisoner. And even if there had been no bolt, one would have had to be Saint Peter himself, guided by an angel from heaven, to pass through the bandits who held the Catacombs of Saint Sebastian, camped around their chief, whom the reader has certainly recognized as the famous Luigi Vampa.

Danglars had also recognized this bandit, in whose existence he had refused to believe when Albert de Morcerf had tried to naturalize him in France. Not only did he recognize Vampa, but also the cell in which Morcerf had been imprisoned; in all probability it was the lodging usually given to strangers.

These reflections restored his peace of mind to a certain extent: since they had not killed him immediately, the bandits must not intend to kill him at all. They had no doubt seized him to rob him, but, since he had only a few francs on him, they would hold him for ransom. He remembered that Morcerf had been held for something like twenty-four thousand francs; since he considered himself to have a much more important appearance than Morcerf, he fixed his own probable ransom at double that sum. He would still have over five million francs left; with an amount like that, one could manage to get along anywhere in the world.

Almost certain, therefore, of being able to extricate himself from his situation, since it was unheard-of for a man to be held for a ransom of five million francs, Danglars lay down on his bed and, after turning over on it two or three times, went to sleep with the tranquillity of the hero whose story Luigi Vampa was studying.

Chapter 71

The first thing Danglars did on awakening the next morning was to breathe in order to assure himself that he had not been wounded: this was a means he had found in *Don Quixote*, the only book he had read of which he remembered anything. "No," he said to himself, "they've neither killed me nor wounded me. But have they robbed me?" He quickly put his hands into his pockets. The two thousand francs he had set aside for his journey from Rome to Venice was still in his trousers pocket and the wallet containing his letter of credit for five million fifty thousand francs was still in his coat pocket. "What strange bandits!" he thought. "Well, I was right: they're going to hold me for ransom."

Should he demand an explanation from the bandits, or should he wait patiently for them to make the first move? The second alternative seemed more prudent. He waited.

Meanwhile a sentry had been posted before his door. At eight o'clock this sentry was relieved by another. Danglars was curious to see by whom he was being guarded. He had noticed that rays of light—not daylight, but lamplight—filtered through the cracks in the door; he peeked through one of those cracks just as the bandit was taking a drink of brandy, which, thanks to the leather bottle in which it was contained, gave forth an odor which was extremely unpleasant to Danglars. "Phew!" he exclaimed, retreating to the other side of his cell.

At noon the man with the brandy was replaced by another sentry. His curiosity aroused once more, Danglars put his eye to the crack again. His new guard was a muscular bandit, a Goliath with large eyes, thick lips, a flattened nose and red hair which hung down to his shoulders in twisted strands that looked like so many vipers. "Oh!" said Danglars to himself. "This one looks more like an ogre than a human being! But I'm too old and tough to make good eating." He still had enough self-assurance to allow him to jest.

At the same moment, as though to offer proof that he was not an ogre, his guard sat down in front of the door and drew from his pouch a loaf of black bread, several onions and some cheese. "May the devil take me if I understand how anyone could eat such filth!" thought Danglars as he glanced at the bandit's dinner through the crack. He went back and sat down on his goat skins, which reminded him of the odor of the first sentry's brandy.

But there is a great deal of eloquence in the invitations

which even the coarsest substances address to an empty stomach. Danglars suddenly felt that his own stomach was bottomless; the man then seemed less ugly to him, the bread less black and the cheese less stale. He went over to the door and knocked on it.

"Che cosa?" asked the bandit.

"I think it's about time someone thought about giving me something to eat," said Danglars, drumming on the door with his fingers.

But, whether because he did not understand or because he had been given no orders concerning Danglars' food, the giant turned back to his lunch. Danglars felt his pride humiliated and, not wishing to compromise himself any further with such a brute, he lay down again on his goat skins and said nothing more.

Four hours went by; the giant was replaced by another bandit. Danglars, whose stomach was by now churning in a frightful manner, stood up quietly, placed his eye before a crack in the door and recognized the intelligent face of his guide, Peppino. "Let's see if this one is a little easier to deal with than the other one," said Danglars to himself, knocking politely on the door.

"Coming," said the bandit, who had come to speak fluent French from frequenting Signor Pastrini's hotel. As he opened the door, Danglars recognized him as the man who had shouted so furiously, *"Dentro la testa!"* But this was no time for recriminations; on the contrary, he put on his most agreeable expression and said, with a gracious smile, "Excuse me, but can't I have something to eat?"

"What!" exclaimed Peppino. "Are you by any chance hungry, Excellency?"

" 'By any chance' is a charming expression when I haven't eaten anything for twenty-four hours," thought Danglars. Then he said aloud, "Yes, I'm hungry; in fact, I'm very hungry."

"And when would you like to eat, Excellency?" asked Peppino.

"Immediately, if possible."

"Nothing could be simpler," said Peppino. "You can have anything you like here—by paying for it, of course, as is customary among all honest Christians."

"Of course," said Danglars, "although, to tell the truth, it seems to me that people who seize you and imprison you ought at least to feed their prisoners."

"That's not the custom, Excellency."

"That's not a very good reason, but I'm willing to accept it," said Danglars, who hoped to win over his guard by his amiability.

"What would you like to eat, Excellency? You have only to give me your order."

"You have a kitchen here?"

"Why, of course!"

"And cooks?"

"Excellent cooks!"

"Well, then, bring me a chicken, some fish, meat—anything, as long as I eat!"

"As you like, Excellency. Shall we say a chicken?"

"Yes, a chicken."

Peppino stood up and called out at the top of his lungs, "A chicken for His Excellency!" A few moments later a slender young man appeared carrying a chicken on a silver platter.

"Here you are, Excellency," said Peppino, taking the chicken from the hands of the young bandit and setting it down on the dilapidated table which, along with a stool and the bed, formed the only furnishings in the cell. Danglars asked for a knife and fork. "Certainly, Excellency," said Peppino, offering him a wooden fork and a small knife with a blunted point.

Danglars took the fork in one hand and the knife in the other and set about cutting up the chicken.

"Excuse me, Excellency," said Peppino, placing a hand on the banker's shoulder, "but here it's customary to pay before eating."

"Aha!" thought Danglars. "I'm sure they're going to overcharge me royally, but we might as well do things in the grand manner. I've always heard of how cheap things are in Italy; a chicken must be worth about twelve sous in Rome." He tossed a twenty-franc coin to Peppino.

Peppino picked up the coin and Danglars moved his knife toward the chicken. "Just a moment, Excellency," said Peppino, "but you still owe me something."

"I was certainly right about being overcharged," thought Danglars. Then, making up his mind to accept the extortion, he said, "And how much more do I owe you for this emaciated chicken?"

"Only ninety-nine thousand nine hundred and eighty francs, Excellency."

Danglars' eyes opened wide at this gigantic pleasantry. "Very funny," he said as he turned back to his chicken. But Peppino stopped him and held out his hand.

"What!" said Danglars. "You're not joking?"

"We never joke, Excellency," replied Peppino seriously.

"One hundred thousand francs for this chicken?"

"You have no idea how hard it is to raise poultry in these cursed caves, Excellency."

"Come, come!" said Danglars. "This is all very amusing, but I'm hungry, so let me eat. Here's another twenty francs for you, my friend."

"That leaves only ninety-nine thousand nine hundred and sixty francs that you owe me," said Peppino. "With a little patience we'll finally get there."

"Never!" said Danglars, angered by Peppino's persistence in maintaining the jest. "You can go to the devil! You don't know with whom you're dealing!"

Peppino made a sign and the young man picked up the chicken and carried it away. Danglars threw himself on his bed as Peppino closed the door and locked it. His stomach felt so empty that it seemed to him he would never be able to fill it, but he waited for another half an hour. Then he went back to the door and said, "Don't keep me in suspense any longer: tell me what you want from me."

"But it's up to you to tell us what you want from us, Excellency," replied Peppino. "Give us your orders and we'll carry them out."

"First open the door," said Danglars. Peppino did so. "I want to eat!" cried Danglars.

"Are you hungry, Excellency?"

"You know very well I'm hungry!"

"What would you like to eat?"

"A piece of bread, since your chickens are so precious."

"Bread!" shouted Peppino. The young man brought a small loaf of bread.

"How much is it?" asked Danglars.

"Ninety-nine thousand nine hundred and sixty francs; you've already paid forty francs in advance."

"A hundred thousand francs for a loaf of bread?"

"That's right, Excellency."

"But you wanted to charge me the same amount for a chicken!"

"We don't serve à la carte here, Excellency. No matter what you eat, it's always the same price."

"You still insist on your stupid joke! Why don't you admit you want me to starve to death and get it over with?"

"Not at all, Excellency—it's you who want to commit suicide. You can eat if you pay for it."

"But what can I pay with, you idiot?" cried Danglars, beside himself. "Do you think I carry around a hundred thousand francs in my pocket?"

"You have five million fifty thousand francs in your pocket,

Excellency," said Peppino. "That's enough for fifty chickens at a hundred thousand francs each and half a chicken at fifty thousand."

Danglars shuddered. His eyes had just been opened: it was still a joke, but he had finally understood it. We might add that it no longer seemed as silly to him as it had before. "All right," he said; "if I give you a hundred thousand francs will you let me eat all I like?"

"Of course."

"But how can I give it to you?" asked Danglars, beginning to breathe more freely.

"It's quite simple. You have an account with the firm of Thomson and French in Rome: give us a draft on them and our banker will take the money for us."

Danglars took the pen and paper which Peppino handed to him, wrote out the draft and signed it. "Here's your draft," he said.

"And here's your chicken."

Danglars sighed as he cut up the chicken: it seemed quite lean to him for such a large sum. Peppino examined the draft carefully and put it into his pocket.

Chapter 72

The next day Danglars was hungry again, but he did not believe he would have to make any further expenditures that day: like the thrifty man he was, he had hidden away half of his chicken in a corner of his cell.

But as soon as he ate it he was thirsty; he had not taken that into account. He struggled against his thirst until he felt his tongue cleaving to the roof of his mouth; then, unable to resist any longer, he called out. The sentry opened the door: it was a new face. Thinking it would be better to deal with an old acquaintance, Danglars asked for Peppino.

"Here I am, Excellency," said Peppino, presenting himself with an eagerness which struck Danglars as a good omen. "What can I do for you?"

"I'd like something to drink," said the prisoner.

"As you know, Excellency, wine is extremely expensive in the countryside around Rome."

"Bring me some water, then," said Danglars, seeking to parry the blow.

"Oh, water is even more scarce than wine, Excellency! There's such a drought this year!"

"I see we're about to begin our little joke again," said

Danglars. The poor man forced himself to smile as he said this, but he felt beads of perspiration break out on his forehead. "Come, my friend," he continued, seeing that Peppino remained impassive, "I'm asking you for a glass of wine; will you refuse me?"

"We don't sell by the glass, Excellency," replied Peppino gravely.

"Then bring me a bottle."

"What kind?"

"The cheapest."

"They're all the same price."

"And what is that price?"

"Twenty-five thousand francs a bottle."

"Why don't you tell me you intend to take everything I own?" said Danglars bitterly. "That will be quicker than devouring me piecemeal!"

"That may be what the chief plans to do," said Peppino.

"Who's the chief?"

"The man to whom you were taken yesterday."

"Where is he?"

"Here."

"I'd like to see him."

"Certainly."

A moment later Luigi Vampa stood before Danglars. "You sent for me?" he asked.

"Are you the leader of the men who brought me here?"

"Yes, Excellency."

"What ransom do you want from me? Tell me."

"Why, we want the five million francs you have on you."

Danglars felt his heart contract convulsively. "That's all I have in the world," he said, "and it's the remainder of an immense fortune. If you take it away from me, take my life away from me also."

"We are forbidden to shed your blood, Excellency."

"By whom are you forbidden?"

"By the man we obey."

"You obey someone, then?"

"Yes."

"And does he obey anyone."

"Yes."

"Whom?"

"God."

Danglars remained thoughtful for a moment. "I don't understand," he said.

"That's possible."

"Why were you ordered to treat me this way?"

"I have no idea."

"Come now," said Danglars, "would you like a million francs?"

"No."

"Two million?"

"No."

"Three million?—Four?—I'll give you four million if you'll let me go free."

"Why do you offer us four million for something that's worth five?" asked Vampa.

"Take it all, then, and kill me!" cried Danglars.

"Calm yourself, Excellency, or you'll give yourself such an appetite that you'll eat a million francs' worth of food a day. Be more economical!"

"But what will happen when I run out of money?" cried Danglars furiously.

"You'll be hungry."

"I'll be hungry?" said Danglars, turning pale.

"Probably," replied Vampa phlegmatically.

"You say you don't want to kill me?"

"That's right."

"And yet you want me to starve to death?"

"That's not the same thing."

"All right, you scoundrels," cried Danglars, "I'll upset your infamous plans! Since I'm going to die anyway, I'd just as soon get it over with immediately. Make me suffer, torture me, kill me, but you won't have my signature again!"

"As you like, Excellency," said Vampa. He walked out of the cell.

Danglars threw himself on his bed. Who were those men? Who was their invisible leader? What did they intend to do to him? Why, when they released all their other captives for ransom, was he alone refused that privilege?

For what was perhaps the first time in his long career, Danglars thought of death with mingled longing and dread.

His determination not to sign lasted for two days, after which he asked for food and offered to pay a million francs for it. His captors served him a magnificent supper and took his million. From then on, having suffered so much and not wishing to expose himself to further suffering, the wretched prisoner submitted to all demands. Twelve days later, after having eaten a dinner worthy of his days of good fortune, he added up his accounts and found that he had signed so many drafts that he now had only fifty thousand francs left.

Then he had a strange reaction for a man who had just abandoned five million francs: he resolved to keep that fifty thousand francs at any cost and he began to have visions of hope verging on madness. He who had forgotten God so long ago now began to tell himself that God occasionally worked miracles: the catacombs might cave in; the police might discover the bandits' retreat and rescue him; in that case he would have fifty thousand francs left, and that was enough to keep a man from dying of hunger. He begged God to allow him to keep that fifty thousand francs, and he wept as he prayed.

For three days the name of God was constantly on Danglars' lips, if not in his heart. By the fourth day he was no longer a man, but a living corpse. He had picked up the last crumb of his former meals and had begun to devour the matting which covered the floor. He begged Peppino to give him something to eat; he offered him a thousand francs for a crust of bread. Peppino did not answer. On the fifth day he called for Vampa and said to him, "Take the last of my money and let me live here, in this cave. I'm not asking for freedom; I'm only asking to live."

"Are you really suffering?" asked Vampa.

"Yes, I'm suffering. I'm suffering horribly!"

"And yet there have been men who suffered more than you."

"I don't think so."

"Yes: those who died of hunger."

Danglars groaned and said, "Yes, it's true: there have been others who suffered more than I; but at least they were martyrs."

"Do you repent, at least?" said a deep, solemn voice which made Danglars' hair stand on end. His weakened eyes saw a man standing behind Vampa, wrapped in a cloak and half hidden in the shadow of a stone pillar.

"Of what must I repent?" stammered Danglars.

"Of the evil you have done," said the voice.

"Oh, yes, I repent! I repent!" cried Danglars, beating his breast with his emaciated fists.

"Then I forgive you," said the man, throwing aside his cloak and stepping forward into the light.

"The Count of Monte Cristo!" gasped Danglars, now as pale from terror as he had been from hunger and misery a moment before.

"You're mistaken: I'm not the Count of Monte Cristo."

"Who are you, then?"

"I'm the man you betrayed and dishonored, the man whose fiancée you prostituted, the man on whom you trod on the way to fortune, the man whose father you caused to die of hunger, the man you condemned to die of hunger but who now forgives you because he himself needs to be forgiven: I am Edmond Dantès!"

Danglars uttered a cry and fell to the floor.

"Stand up," said the count. "Your life will be spared. Your two accomplices weren't so lucky: one of them is insane and the other is dead! Keep the fifty thousand francs you have left; I make you a gift of it. As for the five million you stole from the hospitals, I've already given back the money anonymously.

"And now, eat and drink; you'll be my guest this evening. Vampa, when this man has recovered his strength, release him."

Danglars remained prostrate as the count walked away. When he raised his head he saw nothing but a shadow vanishing down the corridor.

As the count had ordered, Vampa brought Danglars the best wine and the finest fruits of Italy. Then he drove him away in his carriage and abandoned him on the road.

Danglars remained there till morning, not knowing where he was. When daylight dawned, he saw that he was near a brook. Being thirsty, he dragged himself over to it. As he bent down to drink, he noticed that his hair had turned white.

Chapter 73

It was toward six o'clock in the evening. A light yacht, pure and graceful of form, sailed swiftly along despite the fact that there scarcely seemed to be enough wind to ruffle the hair of a young girl. Standing in the bow, a tall young man of dark complexion watched land approaching in a dark cone-shaped mass, rising out of the sea like an immense Catalan hat. "Is that the Isle of Monte Cristo?" he asked in a voice permeated with deep sadness.

"Yes, Excellency," replied the captain of the yacht.

A few minutes later they saw a flash of fire from the island and the sound of a shot reached their ears. "There's the signal, Excellency," said the captain. "Would you like to answer it yourself?"

"Yes."

The captain handed a loaded carbine to the young man, who raised it slowly and fired a shot into the air. Ten minutes later the yacht was anchored and a skiff had been put over the side with four rowers and a pilot in it. The young man climbed into it and stood in the stern with his arms crossed. All eight oars plunged into the sea at once without splashing a single drop of water. The skiff began to glide rapidly through the waves. A short time later it struck against a bottom of fine sand.

"Excellency," said the pilot, "climb up on the shoulders of two of our men and let them carry you ashore."

The young man replied to this invitation with a gesture of complete indifference, put his legs over the side of the boat and slid into the water, which rose up to his waist. He began to walk toward shore, following two of the sailors, who chose the most solid footing for him.

When he had reached dry ground, the young man looked around for someone to show him his way, for it had grown quite dark. Then a hand was placed on his shoulder and a voice made him start. "Hello, Maximilien," said the voice. "Thank you for being punctual."

"Ah, it's you, count!" said Maximilien, shaking Monte Cristo's hand.

"Yes, I'm as punctual as you. But you're wet to the skin, my friend; you'll have to change clothes. Come, I've had lodgings prepared for you in which you'll forget your fatigue and cold."

"Count," said Maximilien in a voice that was at once firm and gentle, "I've come to you to die in the arms of a friend. There are still people I love in this world: I love my sister Julie and I love her husband Emmanuel. But I need someone who will open strong arms to me and smile at me during my last moments of life. Julie would burst into tears and faint; I'd see her suffer and I've already suffered enough; Emmanuel would snatch my weapon from my hand and fill the house with his cries. But I have your word, count: you'll lead me gently and tenderly to the gates of death, won't you?"

"My friend," said Monte Cristo, "I still have one doubt: could you have so little strength that you take pride in displaying your sorrow?"

"No," said Maximilien, "my heart is beating neither more strongly nor more slowly than usual. I've simply come to the end of the road and I won't go any further. Oh, count, I'll be so glad to rest in the arms of death!" Seeing that Monte Cristo made no answer, he went on: "You named the fifth of October as the end of the delay you asked me for. Today is the fifth of October." He took out his watch. "It's nine o'clock: I have three more hours to live."

"So be it," said Monte Cristo. "Come."

Maximilien followed the count mechanically and was already inside the grotto before he noticed where he was. He found a carpet under his feet; a door opened, an odor of perfume enveloped him and his eyes were struck by a bright light. He stopped hesitantly, mistrusting the enervating delights that surrounded him. Monte Cristo pulled him gently and said, "Why shouldn't we spend these last three hours like those ancient Romans who, condemned to death by Nero, sat down at a table crowned with flowers and breathed in death with the perfume of heliotropes and roses?"

Maxmilien smiled. "As you like," he said. "Death is still death, still the absence of life and therefore of pain." He sat down; Monte Cristo sat down in front of him. They were in a sumptuous dining room in which marble statues held on their heads baskets filled with flowers and fruit. Maximilien looked vaguely at everything around him. "Now I understand," he said, "why you asked me to meet you here on this deserted island in this underground palace, this sepulcher that a Pharaoh would envy: it's because you love me, isn't it, count? It's because you want to give me a gentle death, a death without agony, a death that will allow me to fade away with Valentine's name on my lips and your hand in mine."

"You've guessed rightly, Maximilien," said the count simply. "That's my intention."

"Thank you; the thought that my suffering will be ended by tomorrow is sweet to me."

"You have no regrets?"

"No."

"Not even about leaving me?" asked the count with deep emotion. Maximilien was silent; a tear welled up in his eyes. "What!" exclaimed the count. "There's something on earth you'll regret leaving and you're still going to die?"

"Don't say any more, count, I beg you," said Maximilien feebly. "Don't prolong my agony."

The count believed Maximilien was weakening. This belief brought back the horrible doubt which he had overcome once before in the Château d'If. "I'm seeking to bring happiness to this man," he thought; "I regard this restitution as a weight thrown into the scale to balance the evil I have done. But what if I were mistaken? What if this man weren't unhappy enough to deserve happiness? What would happen to me, who can forget evil only by remembering good?" Then he said aloud: "Your grief is overwhelming, Maximilien, I can see that; but you still believe in God and you wouldn't want to risk the salvation of your soul."

Maximilien smiled sadly. "You know I'm not given to histrionics," he said, "but I swear to you that my soul no longer belongs to me."

"Listen to me, Maximilien," said the count. "As you know, I have no living relatives. I've come to regard you as my son. I'd sacrifice my own life to save my son's, so I'd certainly sacrifice my fortune."

"What do you mean?"

"I mean that you want to leave life because you don't know all the enjoyments a great fortune can bring. I possess nearly a hundred million francs; I give it all to you. With a fortune like that you can have anything you want. If you're ambitious, all careers are open to you. Stir up the world, change its face, abandon yourself to mad ideas, be a criminal if you must, but live!"

"You've given me your word, count," replied Maximilien coldly, "and it's now half-past eleven."

"Maximilien! Could you do that before my eyes, in my house?"

"Then let me leave you," said Maximilien gloomily. He stood up.

Monte Cristo's face brightened at these words. "Very well," he said. "You want to die and your will is inflexible. Yes, you're profoundly unhappy and, as you say, only a miracle could cure you. Sit down, Maximilien, and wait."

Maximilien obeyed. Monte Cristo went over to a cabinet, unlocked it and took out a small silver box, which he placed on the table. Then he opened it and took out a still smaller gold box whose lid snapped open by means of a hidden spring. This box contained an oily, semi-solid substance whose color was indefinable due to the reflections of the polished gold of the box and the sapphires, rubies and emeralds with which it was embellished. The count took out a small quantity of the substance with a spoon and offered it to Maximilien, gazing at him steadfastly. At that moment the substance could be seen to have a greenish hue. "This is what you asked me for," said the count, "and this is what I promised you."

"I thank you from the bottom of my heart," said the young man, taking the spoon from Monte Cristo's hand.

The count took a second spoon and dipped it into the box. "What are you doing?" asked Maximilien, stopping his hand.

"God forgive me," said the count, smiling, "but I think I'm as weary of life as you are, and since the opportunity has presented itself——"

"Stop!" cried the young man. "You love and are loved in return; you have faith and hope—don't do what I'm about to do! That would be a crime. Farewell, noble and generous friend; I'm going to tell Valentine everything you've done for me."

Slowly, but without the slightest hesitation, Maximilien swallowed the mysterious substance. Little by little the lamps

seemed to grow dim in the hands of the marble statues and
the odor of incense became less penetrating. Seated in front
of him, Monte Cristo looked at him from the shadows and
Maximilien could see nothing of him except his shining eyes.

An overwhelming feeling of heaviness took possession of
the young man; the objects around him began to lose their
shape and color; his troubled eyes seemed to see doors and
curtains opening in the walls. "I'm dying, my friend," he
said. "Thank you." He tried to hold out his hand to the count
but it fell lifelessly beside him. He rolled over in his armchair
as a delicious torpor insinuated itself into all his veins and
he felt himself sinking into a vague, dreamy delirium. He
tried once again to hold out his hand to the count, but this
time it refused to move at all; he tried to articulate a supreme
farewell, but his tongue rolled heavily in his throat like a
stone blocking the entrance to a sepulcher.

The count opened a door and Maximilien saw a woman
of wondrous beauty appear on the threshold. Pale and gently
smiling, she seemed to be the angel of mercy. "Are heaven's
gates already opening for me?" thought the dying man. "That
angel looks like the one I lost!" She walked toward him.
"Valentine! Valentine!" cried Maximilien from the depths of
his soul. But no sound came from his lips; and, as though
all his strength had been gathered into that inner emotion, he
heaved a sigh and closed his eyes.

Valentine rushed up to him. His lips made one more movement.

"He's calling you in his sleep," said the count. "Death tried
to separate you, but happily I was there and I vanquished
death! Valentine, you must never leave each other again on
this earth, for, in order to find you again, he was ready to
plunge into the grave. Without me, you would both have died;
I now give you back to each other. May God take into account these two lives I have saved!"

Valentine took the count's hand and, in a surge of irresistible joy, pressed it to her lips. "Oh, thank me!" said Monte
Cristo. "Tell me again and again that I've made you happy—
you can't know how much I need to be certain of that."

"Oh, yes, yes! I thank you with all my heart!" said Valentine. "If you doubt the sincerity of my thanks, ask Haydée,
my precious sister, who made me wait patiently for this day
by speaking to me about you from the time we left France
together."

"Do you love Haydée?" asked Monte Cristo with an emotion which he tried in vain to conceal.

"With all my heart!"

"Then I have a favor to ask of you, Valentine."

"Of me? Oh, can I be fortunate enough for that?"

"You called Haydée your sister just now; let her be your real sister, Valentine. Repay her everything you feel you owe to me; protect her, you and Maximilien, because"—the count's voice became almost inaudible—"because from now on she'll be alone in the world."

"Alone in the world!" repeated a voice behind him. "Why?"

The count turned around. Haydée was standing behind him, looking at him with an expression of stupefied amazement.

"Because tomorrow you will be free," replied the count. "Because you will take your proper place in the world; because I don't want my destiny to darken yours. You're the daughter of a prince; I give you back your father's name and wealth."

Haydée turned pale and said in a choked voice, "Then you're leaving me?"

"Haydée! Haydée! You're young, you're beautiful; forget me and be happy."

"Very well," said Haydée, "your orders will be carried out: I will forget you and be happy." She took a step to withdraw.

"Oh, my God!" cried Valentine. "Don't you see how pale she is? Don't you understand how she's suffering?"

"Why should you expect him to understand that?" said Haydée with a heartbreaking expression. "He's my master and I'm his slave; he has a right not to see anything."

The count trembled at the sound of her voice, which touched the most secret fibers of his heart. "Can what I suspected be true?" he cried. "Haydée, would you be happy to stay with me?"

"I'm young," replied Haydée softly; "I love the life you've always made so sweet for me and I'd regret it if I had to die."

"Do you mean to say that if I left you——"

"I'd die, yes."

"Then you love me?"

"Oh, Valentine, he asks if I love him! Tell him if you love Maximilien!"

The count felt his heart swell; he opened his arms and Haydée threw herself into them with a cry. "Yes, I love you!" she said. "I love you as I love my life, as I love my God, because for me you're the finest, the kindest and the greatest man on this earth!"

"Let it be as you say, then, my angel," said Monte Cristo. "God, who raised me up against my enemies and made me victorious, didn't want me to have this penance at the end of my victory. I wanted to punish myself, but God wishes to forgive me. Perhaps your love will make me forget what I must forget. One word from you, Haydée, has enlightened

me more than twenty years of my slow wisdom. You're all
I have left in the world; through you I attach myself to life
again; through you I can suffer; through you I can be happy."
He stood for a moment in thoughtful silence, then he said,
"Have I glimpsed the truth, O God? No matter; whether it
be a reward or a punishment, I accept this destiny. Come,
Haydée, come. . . ."

Putting his arm around Haydée's waist, he pressed the hand
of Valentine and walked out of the room.

An hour passed during which Valentine remained breathlessly at Maximilien's side. Finally she felt his heart beat and
that slight trembling which announces the return of life ran
through the young man's body. At length his eyes opened; they
stared lifelessly at first, but then his sight came back to him,
precise and real; with sight came feeling, and with feeling
came pain. "Oh!" he cried in despair. "I'm still alive! The
count deceived me!" He picked up a knife from the table.

"Wake up, my darling, and look at me," said Valentine
with her adorable smile.

Maximilien uttered a piercing cry. Doubting his senses,
dazzled by what seemed to him a celestial vision, he fell to
his knees.

The next morning at dawn Maximilien and Valentine were
walking arm in arm along the shore. They had found the
door of the grotto open and had gone outside. The last stars
of the night were still gleaming in the blue morning sky.

Suddenly Maximilien noticed a man standing in the shadow
of a cluster of large rocks and waiting for a sign to come
forward. He pointed out the man to Valentine and said, "It's
Jacopo, the captain of the yacht." She beckoned him to
approach.

"Do you have something to tell us?" asked Maximilien.

"The count told me to give you this letter," replied Jacopo.
Maximilien opened the letter and read:

My dear Maximilien,

A felucca is now lying at anchor, waiting for you. Jacopo
will take you to Leghorn, where Monsieur Noirtier is waiting for his granddaughter, whom he wishes to bless before
you lead her to the altar. Everything in this grotto, my
house on the Champs Elysées and my small château at
Tréport are the wedding present which Edmond Dantès
gives to the son of his employer, Monsieur Morrel.

Tell the angel who will watch over your life to pray now
and then for a man who, like Satan, believed himself for
an instant to be equal to God, but who realized in all hu-

mility that supreme power and wisdom are in the hands of God alone.

As for you, Maximilien, here is the secret of my conduct toward you: there is neither happiness nor unhappiness in this world; there is only the comparison of one state with another. Only a man who has felt ultimate despair is capable of feeling ultimate bliss. It is necessary to have wished for death, Maximilien, in order to know how good it is to live.

Live, then, and be happy, beloved children of my heart, and never forget that, until the day God deigns to reveal the future to man, the sum of all human wisdom will be contained in these two words: Wait and hope.

Your friend,
EDMOND DANTÈS
Count of Monte Cristo

Maximilien looked around him anxiously. "The count's generosity is really excessive," he said. "Valentine would have been content with my modest fortune. Where is the count? Take me to him."

Jacopo pointed toward the horizon.

"What do you mean?" asked Valentine. "Where is the count? Where is Haydée?"

"Look," said Jacopo.

The two young people looked in the direction in which he was pointing. On the dark blue line separating the sky from the Mediterranean they saw a white sail.

"Gone!" cried Maximilien. "Farewell, my friend, my father!"

"Gone!" murmured Valentine. "Farewell, my friend! Farewell, my sister!"

"Who knows if we'll ever see them again?" said Maximilien.

"My darling," said Valentine, "the count just told us that all human wisdom was contained in these two words: Wait and hope."

Bantam Classics bring you the world's greatest literature—books that have stood the test of time—at specially low prices. These beautifully designed books will be proud additions to your bookshelf. You'll want all these time-tested classics for your own reading pleasure.

Titles by Mark Twain:

☐ 21079	ADVENTURES OF HUCKLEBERRY FINN	$1.75
☐ 21128	ADVENTURES OF TOM SAWYER	$1.75
☐ 21195	COMPLETE SHORT STORIES	$4.50
☐ 21143	A CONNECTICUT YANKEE IN KING ARTHUR'S COURT	$1.95
☐ 21142	LIFE ON THE MISSISSIPPI	$1.95
☐ 21150	THE PRINCE AND THE PAUPER	$1.95
☐ 21158	PUDDIN'HEAD WILSON	$1.95

Titles by Herman Melville:

☐ 21094	BILLY BUDD	$1.95
☐ 21007	MOBY DICK	$1.95

Titles by Jack London:

☐ 21233	THE CALL OF THE WILD & WHITE FANG	$2.25
☐ 21225	THE SEA WOLF	$1.95
☐ 21212	MARTIN EDEN	$3.95
☐ 21213	TO BUILD A FIRE & OTHER STORIES	$2.95

Titles by Stephen Crane:

☐ 21011	THE RED BADGE OF COURAGE	$1.50
☐ 21198	MAGGIE: A GIRL OF THE STREETS & OTHER SHORT FICTION	$2.50

ASSASSIN'S SHADOW

Randy Wayne White

writing as Randy Striker

A SIGNET BOOK

SIGNET
Published by New American Library, a division of
Penguin Group (USA) Inc., 375 Hudson Street,
New York, New York 10014, USA
Penguin Group (Canada), 90 Eglinton Avenue East, Suite 700, Toronto,
Ontario M4P 2Y3, Canada (a division of Pearson Penguin Canada Inc.)
Penguin Books Ltd., 80 Strand, London WC2R 0RL, England
Penguin Ireland, 25 St. Stephen's Green, Dublin 2,
Ireland (a division of Penguin Books Ltd.)
Penguin Group (Australia), 250 Camberwell Road, Camberwell, Victoria 3124,
Australia (a division of Pearson Australia Group Pty. Ltd.)
Penguin Books India Pvt. Ltd., 11 Community Centre, Panchsheel Park,
New Delhi - 110 017, India
Penguin Group (NZ), 67 Apollo Drive, Rosedale, North Shore 0632,
New Zealand (a division of Pearson New Zealand Ltd.)
Penguin Books (South Africa) (Pty.) Ltd., 24 Sturdee Avenue,
Rosebank, Johannesburg 2196, South Africa

Penguin Books Ltd., Registered Offices:
80 Strand, London WC2R 0RL, England

Published by Signet, an imprint of New American Library,
a division of Penguin Group (USA) Inc.

First Printing, December 1981
First Printing (Author Introduction), April 2008
10 9 8 7 6 5 4 3 2 1

Copyright © New American Library, a division of Penguin Group (USA) Inc., 1981
Introduction copyright © Randy Wayne White, 2006
All rights reserved

 REGISTERED TRADEMARK—MARCA REGISTRADA

Printed in the United States of America

PUBLISHER'S NOTE
This is a work of fiction. Names, characters, places, and incidents either are
the product of the author's imagination or are used fictitiously, and any resemblance to actual persons, living or dead, business establishments, events, or
locales is entirely coincidental.
   The publisher does not have any control over and does not assume any
responsibility for author or third-party Web sites or their content.

For the fish stalkers:
Steve, Hervey, Fize,
Wes, Marsh, and Cajun

Introduction

In the winter of 1980, I received a surprising phone call from an editor at Signet Books—surprising because, as a Florida fishing guide, the only time New Yorkers called me was to charter my boat. And if any of my clients were editors, they were savvy enough not to admit it.

The editor said she'd read a story by me in *Outside Magazine* and was impressed. Did I have time to talk?

As a mediocre high school jock, my idols were writers, not ball players. I had a dream job as a light-tackle guide, yet I was still obsessed with my own dream of writing for a living. For years, before and after charters, I'd worked hard at the craft. Selling a story to *Outside*, one of the country's finest publications, was a huge break. I was about to finish a novel, but this was the first time New York had called.

Yes, I had time to talk.

The editor, whose name was Joanie, told me Signet wanted to launch a paperback thriller series that featured a recurring he-man hero. "We want at least four writers on the project because we want to keep the books coming, publishing one right after the other, to create momentum."

Four writers producing books with the same character?

"Characters," Joanie corrected. "Once we get going, the cast will become standard."

Signet already had a template for the hero. He was a Vietnam vet turned Key West fishing guide, she said, talking as if the man existed. He was surfer-boy blond, and he'd been friends with Hemingway.

I am not a literary historian, but all my instincts told me the timetable seemed problematic. I said nothing.

"He has a shark scar," Joanie added, "and he's freakishly strong. Like a man who lifts weights all the time."

The guys I knew who lifted weights were also freakishly clumsy, so . . . maybe the hero, while visiting a local aquarium, tripped during feeding time?

My brain was already problem-solving.

"He lives in Key West," she said, "so, of course, he has to be an expert on the area. That's why I'm calling. You live in Key West, and I liked your magazine story a lot. It seems like a natural fit."

Actually, I fished out of Sanibel Island, on Florida's Gulf Coast, a six-hour drive from Sloppy Joe's, but this was no time for petty details.

"Have you ever been to Key West?" I asked the editor. "Great sunsets."

Editors, I have since learned, can also be cagey. Joanie didn't offer me the job. She had already settled on three of the four writers, she said, but if I was willing to submit a few sample chapters on speculation, she'd give me serious consideration.

Money? A contract? That stuff was "all standard," she told me, and could be discussed later.

"I'll warn you right now," she said, "there are a couple of other writers we're considering, so you need to get at least three chapters to me within a month. Then I'll let you know."

I hung up the phone, stunned by my good fortune. My first son, Lee, had been born only a few months earlier. My much-adored wife, Debra, and I were desperate for money because the weather that winter had been miserable for fishing. But it was *perfect* for writing.

I went to my desk, determined not to let my young family down.

At Tarpon Bay Marina, where I was a guide, my friend Ralph Woodring owned a boat with *Dusky* painted in big blue letters on the side. My friend, Graeme Mellor, lived on a Morgan sailboat named *No Mas*.

Dusky MacMorgan was born.

Every winter, Clyde Beatty-Cole Bros. Circus came to town. Their trapeze artists, I realized, were not only freakishly strong, but they were also freakishly nimble.

Dusky gathered depth.

One of my best friends was the late Dr. Harold Westervelt, a gifted orthopedic surgeon. Dr. Westervelt became the Edison of Death, and he loved introducing himself that way to new patients. His son, David, became Westy O'Davis, and our spearfishing pal, Billy, became Billy Mack.

Problems with my hero's shark scar and his devoted friendship with Hemingway were also solved.

Working around the clock, pounding away at my old black manual typewriter, I wrote *Key West Connection* in nine days. On a Monday morning, I waited for the post office to open to send it to New York.

Joanie sounded a little dazed when she telephoned on Friday. Was I willing to try a second book on spec?

Hell yes.

God, I was beginning to *love* New York's can-do attitude.

The other three writers (if they ever existed) were fired, and I became the sole proprietor of Captain Dusky MacMorgan—although Signet owned the copyright and all other rights after I signed Joanie's "standard" contract. (This injustice was later made right by a willing and steadfast publisher and my brilliant agent.)

If Joanie (a fine editor) feels badly about that today, she shouldn't. I would've signed for less.

I wrote seven of what I would come to refer to as "duck and fuck" books because in alternating chapters Dusky would duck a few bullets, then spend much-deserved time alone with a heroine.

Seldom did a piece of paper go into my old type-writer that was ripped out and thrown away, and I suspect that's the way the books read. I don't know. I've never reread them. I do remember using obvious clichés, a form of self-loathing, as if to remind myself that I should be doing my *own* writing, not this job-of-work.

The book you are now holding, and the other six, constituted a training arena for a young writer who took seriously the discipline demanded by his craft and also the financial imperatives of being a young father.

For years, I apologized for these books. I no longer do.

—Randy Wayne White
Cartagena, Colombia

1

I agreed to become an assassin one blustery wind-leached day in a Florida March.

Blustery isn't even the word for it. Those of you who live in America's northlands don't hear much about our bad weather—and it's not because we don't have our share of it. The Sunshine State's chambers of commerce become meteorological gestapos when the skies pale and the winds blow foul. It's not the sort of thing they paste on Indiana billboards, or promote in double-truck ads in the *Times*. You can even see it on the faces of Florida's TV weathermen. Their smiles are vaguely apologetic and their eyes dart between storm fronts like unfaithful husbands confessing they have contracted genital herpes. Transplants in Florida consider bad weather an affront, and to fellow tourists they aim silly, accusing barbs like: "Ya musta brought the cold with ya when ya flew down. . . ."

And as winters go, this had been one of the worst.

1

Cold front after cold front funneled down from the Midwest, roiling the seas with careening winds. The white board shipbuilders' houses on Duval and Elizabeth Streets stayed shuttered, and the sage of woodsmoke from the rare fireplace drifted across the pirate streets of Key West off and on all winter long. There were the brief winter weeks of eighty-degree temperatures. But just when you thought the bad weather was gone for good, holed up someplace in Ohio where it justly belonged, the blue northers would rage again through the palms and eucalyptus, and those of us on charterboat row would cluster around mugs of hot coffee at the Kangaroo's Pouch and eye our empty boats sourly.

As Captain Gainey Maxwell of the *Lookout II* put it one bleak January morning, "Boys, I've come ta believe that the only thing that stands between Key West and the winds o' Canada is a piddly line of mangroves and a barbed-wire fence someplace in Iowa."

It was that kind of winter.

And when the seas are eight to ten feet outside the reef, there isn't much for a bluewater fishing guide to do. It didn't bother me as much as it did some of the others. They had wives and kids and mortgages to worry about. But not me—not any longer. My family, my world, had been wiped out in another lifetime. The drug pirates had seen to that. Balmy summer nights in the tropics are for love and long walks and—for little boys—time to play with their

2

adoring father. Murderers don't plant ignition bombs in cars when the nights are star-blazed and the winds blow sweet and warm out of Cuba, and explosions don't scatter bits of the well-loved across lawns and vacation sidewalks.

It just doesn't happen. Not on balmy summer nights, it doesn't.

And the winters in Florida are never, ever cold.

Right . . .

So I was alone, alone in a volatile winter—my first in the little house built on stilts a mile from the nearest land in the shallow water off Calda Bank. The house had been built to ice-store fish until the lighter boats could get around and pick them up for transport into Key West. Now, fifty years later, I had converted it to a bachelor home—as close as I could get to living in the sea that I loved, and as far away from the memories of Key West as I could manage without leaving altogether.

On that blustery March day I was suffering a case of the blahs. Too much wind and too much cold weather, and much too little exercise. I had awakened as always just before first light. A black north wind was rattling the windows and seeping through the cracks in the floor. Beneath my double bed I could hear a nasty cross chop washing around the pilings, and the strange gray light beyond the window told me it would be another rainy dawn. I shook off the urge to crawl back under the covers and sleep the morning away.

I had been sleeping too many mornings away. When the winds blow foul, you don't charter. And lately, with charters canceled, I had been doing a damn good impression of the typical suburban male animal who thinks boredom can be cured by eating too much and drinking too much, and wallowing in the gray confines of his own despair.

It's a cycle as easy to fall into as it is vicious. The longer you put off the training program, the diet, and the mental discipline, the easier it is to forget how the human machine is supposed to feel—how brain and body are supposed to harmonize in the fail-safe routine of hard work tempered with such well-deserved luxuries as cold beer.

And the moment you forget is the moment you are lost. You become only a dull brain governing the flabby remnant of your own humanity. The only place those two chubby legs are going to carry you is toward a rest-home rendezvous.

And I wasn't about to let it go that far.

I threw back the brace of wool Navy-issue blankets. The boards of the stilthouse floor were cold against my bare feet. In the weak dawn light, I nursed the squat Franklin stove to flame, then put coffee on to boil. Outside, March clouds scudded beneath stars in the waning darkness. Across Florida Bay, beyond Miami, the coming sun was a leached white, and slate waves feathered beyond my dock.

I urinated and then walked down the rickety stairs to where my thirty-four foot charterboat, *Sniper*, was moored. Dammit, if it was going to be another nasty day in Florida, for once I was going to face it head-on. Naked, I forced myself not to shiver. This was the day I would jerk myself out of the rut. How long had I been letting myself go? My Irish friend Westy O'Davis had left months ago for the Caymans, where—when he wasn't playing secret service agent for the United Kingdom—he passed the days teaching pretty tourist ladies how to scuba dive. And then that beautiful woman, that fine person, Saxan Benton had finally written me off as a hopeless loner and returned north to pursue her botany studies. It was what the soap-opera people might term an inadequate parting scene. . . .

"Dusky, you know why I'm leaving. I have my own life to think about. . . ."

"I know."

"And I have the feeling that no matter how much you might come to love me, you would still be tied to your past."

"I know."

The lovely model's face had twisted, her composure shattered, and a trembling hand had brushed auburn hair away. "Dammit, don't just stand there like a dumb hulk! You know I care for you. You know I'd rather stay, if you could just . . . just . . . dammit, Dusky, do you understand what I'm trying to say!"

"I understand, Saxan. The boat's ready. I'll take you back to Key West now."

So I had spent the winter alone. People call it bore-dom, but it's really self-pity. I had taken some strange masochistic joy in eating too much and drink-ing too much, watching myself get slack and slow. When the damnable wind settled enough, I char-tered, as always, out of Garrison Bight. And when the northers set in, I retreated to my stilthouse upon the sea to read and listen to night voices around the world on my Transoceanic shortwave . . . and mope.

I had made some false starts getting back into shape. Those are danger signals—when you start, then allow yourself to stop. A Texas friend of mine named Treadwell has a saying: If you can't profit from adversity, then you damn well deserve to suffer.

Now was the time to end my winter suffering.

The March wind that dawn had a razor edge to it. I stood, hands on bare hips, facing it. Half a mile away, I could see the fitful blinking of the white four-second navigation marker off Fleming Key. There was a gray corona of light haloing Key West, then tailing away eastward along the overseas highway like a comet's tail. My hands tugged experimentally at the fat I had let settle on stomach and sides. I hacked, spit with disgust, then went back inside and poured myself a mug of black coffee. I use a fifty-fifty mix of espresso and regular grind. I drank it quickly, burning the sleep, the fogginess, the lazi-ness away.

Today's the day, MacMorgan. You've gorged yourself

and slept the winter away. Now winter's over, no matter what that bastard north wind says. One more false start and you may never start again. . . .

The roof of my stilthouse is covered with tin and braced with stout Florida heart pine. I washed my coffee mug, put it away neatly. I took a deep breath, then jumped up and grabbed the middle beam. When I'm in shape, when I have my weight down to two-oh-five, I can do thirty-six backhanded pull-ups. When you spend your boyhood in the circus, working the trapeze two shows a day—plus a morning practice session—your shoulders and arms develop a lot faster than your vocabulary. But I wasn't in shape now. And I was twenty pounds over my best weight. I huffed and puffed and trembled and shook, and twenty-four pull-ups was the best I could do.

Disgustedly, I jerked a towel from the shelf and went outside to *Sniper*, mopping my face.

Dammit, MacMorgan, you may have let it go too long this time. Maybe that's what you really want to be: just one more overweight, middle-aged American; just one more flaccid face in the crowd. . . .

I reached above the wheel and the chrome gleam of twin throttles and snapped on my new Horizon VHF. Channel 16 was as empty as the March dawn.

"Fred Astaire, Fred Astaire, this is the charterboat *Sniper,* Whiskey Foxtrot Lima 7739, over."

I gave it two minutes, then repeated the call. Finally, the VHF answered me: "Vessel calling the *Fred Astaire,* this is the *Fred Astaire.* Channel sixty-eight, Dusky?"

"Switching six-eight."

I could picture Steve Wise aboard his floating hulk of a Houseboat, *Fred Astaire.* He's dockmaster at my marina, and a popular man with the tourist ladies around Key West. When he's not having a party, he's usually enjoying a more private form of entertainment. More than one vacationing Midwesterner has caught the flight out of Key West with a flush on her face and a smile on her lips. And frankly, I felt kind of bad about waking Steve Wise up so early.

He didn't seem too pleased about it either. After we had both switched channels, he said, "Dusky, old buddy, old pal, it's not quite six a.m. by the lady's wristwatch I can see on the counter by this VHF. I hope you have a good reason for calling me out of my warm bed a full hour before I have to start dealing with the rest of the crazy charterboat captains. . . . Over."

"Stevie, you'd have a dull life without us, and you know it."

"Yeah? Well, the young blonde who sleeps yonder in my master stateroom has been begging me to give it a try. She wants to stay aboard for the summer and go cruising across to the islands. . . . Over."

"And you don't have the heart to tell her that that floating strumpet parlor of yours doesn't have a healthy engine in it. Right?"

He was still chuckling as he transmitted. "Hey, keep your voice down. People monitor this channel. So, what's your business, captain? Now that I'm up,

8

I don't see any sense in wasting the rest of the morning. . . . Over."

"Just wanted to officially cancel today's charter. Tell Dr. Taylor of Baltimore that we'll have to try it his next time through Key West. I'd have called you later, but I'm going to be busy. It's such a pretty day I'm going to go for a long swim. . . . Over."

"What? Oh yeah, sure, Dusky, sure. Winds gusting to thirty knots, seas eight to ten feet, and you're going for a swim. Right. By the way, that bald friend of yours was at the marina yesterday. Said he wanted to see you. He must have got in touch, huh? Over."

I thought for a moment. My bald friend? It could be only one person—Colonel D. Harold Westervelt. And no, he hadn't gotten in touch with me. But if he had reason to see me he would—you could bet the bank on that. And he would have a damn good reason for seeing me. D. Harold doesn't leave his private orbit of discipline and work capriciously.

It could mean only one thing.

A mission. And if ever there was a time in my life when I wasn't fit for a mission, it was now.

"Yeah, that's right. He contacted me," I lied. "And if he stops back, Steve, tell him I'll be in touch." We chatted on a few minutes, trading good-natured barbs, and then signed off. I adjusted the squelch and turned the volume up full so that if someone tried to get in touch with me I could hear it in the house.

D. Harold Westervelt. We were similar by-products of two very, very different wars. His was

9

the world conflict where men died for a reason. Mine was the Asian exercise in political lunacy where the mealy-mouthed fat cats used us as pawns. Still, neither of us had been able to leave our wars behind us. For years I had thought that his only official capacity was that of weapons inventor for the United States military. Later, after the murder of my family had led to my being retained by a federal agency to help expedite its private wars, I learned that his unique genius was being used for much more than just unusual weaponry.

Even so, I was surprised that it was Colonel Westervelt who was trying to get in touch with me. My usual contact was an old acquaintance from Nam, one Stormin' Norman Fizer. I put the coffeepot on the little Franklin stove so it would stay hot as I thought about it. Why Westervelt? Why not Fizer, as it had been on the other missions? Did that mean it was more important—or less important? Or maybe it wasn't a mission at all; maybe D. Harold just wanted to say hello.

No, the key phrase was "That bald friend of yours was at the marina."

And Colonel D. Harold Westervelt doesn't "just happen" to stop by anyplace. He plans his days of exercise and work like a human computer, allowing himself only a few well-loved recreations like classical music and growing orchids.

It had to be a mission.

Still naked, I strapped on my Randall attack-survival knife. A long swim at open sea is not without its hazards. Outside, the gray March wind blew the tops off waves. Frigate birds soared in the high distance, omens of a storm. I stood on the dock and looked out toward the blinking navigation light a half mile away. That would be my destination—there and back. I did about five minutes of stretching, waiting for the sun. But it never arrived. Morning was to be a pallid slash in the east.

Another nasty winter's day in Vacation Land.

But at least I was facing this one head-on. And there was the promise of a mission. Later, I was sure, D. Harold would offer it to me in intricate, calculated detail. Infiltrate what, attack where, and maybe kill whom. It didn't matter. I'd accept. Because lately I'd been doing too good a job at slowly killing myself.

2

When the human machine has had a long and fattening vacation, the first sign of physical activity makes it whimper. It whimpers and pleads and begs you to stop. The lungs whistle, the throat burns, the heart pounds within its fleshy cage like an animal gone mad. The body is sending you a message. A false message. It's telling you that no way, no how, can it do any more, go any farther. But it's a lie. You can always do more. You can always find a way of going on.

My machine began its protest a quarter mile from the stilthouse—only halfway to the marker. The shoulders began to ache, and the lungs began complaining about the amount of oxygen I was burning. The cramping of hips and legs suggested that I was out of fuel. And that's when the brain turns traitor—because it too has become soft, lost its disciplined edge.

There's always tomorrow. Turn here and swim back to

the stilthouse. After all, a half-mile swim in stormy seas is a pretty good workout. And you can go farther tomorrow—or the next day, or the next. . . .

It's a critical moment in the dreary process of getting back into shape. You can heed the message and give up. After all, that's what most people do. Or you can lock in on the cold-sober brain-whisper: to stop is the loser's game; the winners go on and on, always and forever.

It's a decision the world-class athlete makes every day of his or her life.

And you know what their decision always is— because they're the ones you see in national championships. Or the Olympics.

So I stopped momentarily, sculling in the thrust of green sea, feeling the north wind blow spray across my face. Behind me the stilthouse looked invitingly close. Smoke angled out of the tin chimney, dissipating in the wind. Ahead was the white flash of marker—too far away to see that it was green, or that it was number 13 of the Garrison Bight channel way. I sighed, vectored in on the marker, and forced the arms to pull onward, swimming up one side of a wave and sliding down the other.

So I played the game. It is a game I learned when I was young. And all my life, when the going gets tough, I've played it. An old circus escape artist, Julian Ignazio, taught it to me.

"Always remember, Henry MacMorgan, that while it is impossible to separate body from brain, it *is*

13

possible to separate brain from body. You must watch yourself as if from above. Coldly, objectively. *You* are the spirit. The body is nothing more than a machine. By removing yourself, you can command the machine precisely, with a minimum expenditure of energy. Believe me, my boy, it takes practice. Only with daily meditation can you make it a dependable fixture of self. With me—especially in my submerged escapes—it is a way of life. Without the ability to remove brain from body, I would have drowned long, long ago. . . .''

So I played the game.

I tried to see myself as if from above. Naked man swimming through green morning storm sea. His shoulders ache, but the pain is not as important as the goal. His breathing is labored, yet there is air aplenty. His leg muscles are cramping, but all he must do is relax and command them to carry on.

The game was difficult at first. My body kept jerking the drifting mind back to earth, rubbing the mind's nose in the pain of the long swim.

I hadn't been doing my morning meditations. When you are feeling good you always come to believe that you no longer need the fifteen minutes alone in your own brain.

And you are always, always wrong.

So it was tough. But finally I could thrust my body away for longer and longer expanses of time. And then it didn't matter, because the marker was only a few hundred yards away. The body had found its place again; found its rhythm as a machine. The lungs felt better; the cramps and knots had worked themselves out.

Dutifully, I swam on toward the loom of the light tower. And when I was near enough, I adjusted my course so that I was down-sea of it. The pilings were barnacle-covered, and the last thing I wanted was to be washed into it.

It was late enough now that the light-sensitive switch had snuffed out the four-second flasher. I hung on the bottom brace of the light station, feeling my legs sweep up behind me in the rush of wave and current. There was the acrid odor of bird guano and creosote on the wood. And beyond that was the distant black hedge of mangrove island off Fleming Key.

I was feeling good now. Fulfilled. The long swim back meant nothing. There was no dread involved. If I wanted to get back, I *had* to make it. And I would. The important decision had been made halfway out. That's what I was enjoying now. The victory of mind over body.

But I didn't have long to enjoy it.

Because that's when I saw it. That's when I saw her. Some crazy woman in a pretty little sloop. Only a few hundred yards away. In the battle against body and cresting waves, I hadn't noticed the boat before. The hull was yellow with a red waterline stripe. The wind was driving it farther and farther onto the sand-and-coral bottom of Calda Bank. She stood on tiptoes upon the cabin of the small boat in a blue rain slicker. She was fighting to get the sail down and not having much luck. The hood of the rain slicker was off, and her blond hair was braided in a long rope to the small of her back.

More than hear it, I felt the small boat crash into the bank. It heaved, listed to port, then took a full wave over the bow before smacking back heavily aground.

Stupidly, I began yelling commands at her. But there was no chance of her hearing me above the surf. So I took out for the boat in a long fast crawl stroke, timing it so I could grab a breath and a quick look at the top of every wave.

It didn't take me long to get there. Even so, the boat had been shoved even farther aground. She was still battling the sail, but she had at least gotten it partway down.

I stayed well up-sea of the sailboat. If it went over I didn't want to be under it. Remotely, I noticed the name of the boat in blue script upon the stern: *Sleek*.

I scared her, but it couldn't be helped.

"Hey—do you have a centerboard?" The water was so shallow, I stood in stomach-deep water, cupping my hands to yell at her.

"What? . . . Oh, Jesus!"

Surprised, she jumped backward, caught her foot on something, and tumbled ass endward into the cockpit, disappearing momentarily. I timed the next wave and used it to propel me toward the boat. I caught the gunwale and pulled myself aboard, realizing at the last minute that I wasn't exactly dressed for a meeting with a strange woman.

In fact, except for the belt and knife, I wasn't dressed at all.

"Are you okay?"

She lay cupped in the cockpit, legs draped over the tiller, one arm braced against the port seat, the other hand rubbing the back of her head. She looked to be in her mid-twenties—far enough into life to exude a certain aura of independence. She wore new Topsiders, the standard shoe of the pop boating set, and no socks. The rain slicker was the expensive kind, a material that resembled honest oil cloth. The face was well tanned, a little too square-jawed to put her in the moon-faced beauty queen category, but a striking face nonetheless. It was the kind of face that, in later years, would make her a very handsome lady indeed. With the long blond hair, the eyes should have been blue. But they weren't. They were the brown of natural leather. And right now they were wide with shock and, then, anger.

"Who the hell are you?" She pulled herself to her feet, bracing herself because with the ebb of every wave the boat smacked on the sandbar.

"The patron saint of crazy women. Now, do you want help or don't you?"

I felt the eyes sweep over my body, saw the obligatory cringe when she noticed the jagged scar on my pelvis from a long-ago shark attack. But there was no blushing, no comment on my being naked. Just this:

"After we get this boat off, remind me to get the address of your tailor."

"You have my solemn promise, lady."

And that quickly, she went back to work on the sail, yelling over her shoulder, "I'll handle this. The big thing is, that damn centerboard is stuck. If you can manage to crank that up, we can swing her around, give her just a touch of canvas, and I think we can sail her off."

So I went to work. No need to tell her about the brain coral and staghorn downwind that would rip the bottom out of her boat if we didn't get things under control quickly. Warnings in a desperate situation are a waste of time.

The crank on the centerboard had been knocked loose. I refitted it and gave it a try. The centerboard wasn't stuck—just wedged between boat and sandbar. With every lift of wave, you could gain a few inches on it, but then the boat would collide again with the bottom and knock the crank handle off. I gave it four tries with the same results.

"Damn!"

"How's it going down there?" She stood on the little cabin, holding the sail bundled in both arms. "Need some extra muscle?"

"You just get the sail ready, lady!"

There was an opening in the centerboard trunk for

ready access to the pin and cable. By wedging my hands in, I could get a pretty good hold on the cable. It took every ounce of strength to budge it and hold it when the little boat smacked bottom. But slowly, hand over hand, I pulled it free, then finished with the crank. I didn't need to tell her we were off. The boat righted itself, lifted, then careened sideways toward the coral.

"I've got the tiller—get some sail up!"

She handled herself well. She went to work fast, but not so fast that she made mistakes. She did a dandy piece of jiffy reefing, got the light lines tied. I was surprised—surprised that someone foolish enough to be out sailing on such a day could handle herself at all. That done, she came aft, staying low. Her hair was darker, water-soaked. She wiped her face, and I noticed, absently, the wedding ring on her left hand.

"I'll take it now," she said. There was no hesitation in her voice. It was not a request.

"You know about the coral ahead?"

She paused, looking forward. There was too much wind to read the reef. She made the wise decision. "Guess not." She studied me for a moment, evaluating me. It was her boat, and, obviously, if the boat was going to be reefed again, she wanted to be the one at the tiller. Suddenly satisfied, she nodded. "Okay. You take it. But take a little more line through the clam cleat. We're luffing."

I did as told. The little boat bore down toward the

coral. She could see the reef now: black shapes beneath translucent waves. I expected her to call out, to yell some nervous warning. But she didn't. At the very last possible moment, I said, "Ready to bring her about?"

"More than ready."

I shoved the tiller hard, ducking beneath the swing of boom. She handled the lines flawlessly, and the boat sailed herself out of danger, rocking in the new beam sea.

I heard the woman exhale a long-held breath. "Nice sailing," she said.

"Living around here, I have the advantage of knowing the water. It helps. You ready to take over?"

She took the tiller and, without looking at me, said, "I've got an extra pair of foul-weather pants below that might fit. They're in the starboard closet."

Fit they didn't. I stood hunched in the cramped cabin and pulled them on. They were too tight around the waist and thighs, and came up well over my calves. I decided to wear them anyway. I'm no less modest than the next guy. The sag of cold and flaccid manhood is something only the sculptors can make look anatomically proper. Snoop that I am, I hesitated long enough to look around the cabin and make a sweeping evaluation of this woman. Everything nice and neat. One-burner stove on chrome pivots. Small rack for charts and sextant. Leaving Key West for a long trip? Maybe. Perhaps one of those driven people who want to sail the world alone? Probably not. No VHF radio. No self-steering device. Plenty of canned goods, though. And the right books in the mahogany rack: *Dove,* by Robin Lee Graham; *Far Tortuga,* by Peter Matthiessen; the southern edition of *Waterway Guide;* some others. Conjecture: The lady had recently begun a long cruise, but not around the world. She was either widowed or divorced or would meet her husband later. She knew how to sail, but didn't know local waters.

End of conjecture. If you read enough Conan Doyle when you're a kid, personal deduction and induction become automatic when you meet someone you're interested in.

And she was a very interesting lady indeed.

I hunched my way out of the cabin, ducked under the boom, and took the bench seat across from her. She was laughing. A nice laugh, but reserved—the way a person laughs in the company of a stranger.

"You look like that guy in the monster movie who started growing into a giant. Clothes all got too small for him, and he finally busted out of them."

"Guess they don't look any better than they feel, huh? But thanks for the loan anyway. I won't be wearing them long."

She raised her eyebrows. "Does that mean I'm taking you to wherever it is you live—or that you're going to slip back into the water again?" She gave a snorting laugh, shaking the pretty head. "I swear to

God, when you first came aboard I thought I was either dead or hallucinating. What *are* you doing out here, swimming stark naked in seas like this?"

"Just getting my morning exercise, lady. And my name is Dusky. Dusky MacMorgan."

She held out her hand, and I took it. Firm business-like handshake. The new wave of feminism has brought women into the old world of ridiculous and meaningless ceremony—hand shaking, holding doors, and picking up tabs. Next they'll be wearing ties.

"Marina Cole, Mr. Dusky MacMorgan. Before you even ask, I'll tell you. My dear old dad was a boat nut. Dressed like a sailor, read all the books, pictures of the tall ships on his study wall, even had a little sloop that he could never use because his job on the New York Stock Exchange kept him too busy. I was the son he never had. I got all the sailing lessons and the yacht-club classes—and the name Marina."

"Pretty name."

She shrugged, holding the tiller hard, getting all she could out of the reefed sail and wind. "It's better than Sloop, I guess. From what they told me, that was second choice. And it came all too close to being first choice, I gather."

"So now you're the sailor in the family?"

She nodded. "Captain Cole at your service, sir. Duly licensed by the United States Coast Guard."

"Anything on the test about not running aground in foul seas?"

It was a chancy comment. She could have taken it

as an affront. Women in a field historically male usually grab at the slightest hint of insult, then use it as a bunker to stand their ground. But Marina Cole didn't hesitate. The tan face crinkled, complete with dimples. And she laughed. "Jesus, what happened was I just wasn't paying attention. I was trying to find a little place up the coast called Cabbage Key on the Estero Bay to Lemon Bay chart, and before I knew it I had let her slip out of the channel. Just didn't notice that the damn shoal water reaches out so far."

"Awful being human, isn't it?"

She raised her eyebrows, studying me. "Does that mean you've never gone aground, MacMorgan?"

"It means that just when I think I know every inch of water around here, I reach for a beer and let my eyes wander, and I end up making a complete fool of myself. I charter out of Key West, and folks who pay a lot of money to fish don't take kindly to waiting on a sandbar for the tide to come back in."

"Are you just telling me that to make me feel better, MacMorgan?"

"Would I lie about such a thing?"

She eyed me shrewdly, that same look of evaluation. "Yes," she said. "Yes, I think you would. Maybe you *are* a guardian angel, MacMorgan. I never believed in such things before. I mean, you turn up out of nowhere at dawn and save my boat, and now you're trying to save my pride."

"Just a real swell guy, that's me, Captain Cole. And by the way, you see that shack with the tin roof standing in the water a few points to starboard? That's my destination."

"Aye aye," she said with a mock salute.

We sailed on in silence. Not a particularly comfortable silence, either. People come and go so quickly in this world of interstates and moving vans and jumbo jets that the parting scene between strangers should be as comfortable and commonplace as saying hello. But not with this lady. There was an uneasiness—a tangible uneasiness. And for one very simple reason: I wasn't ready to say good-bye to her. There was the face, the hair, both striking enough to turn the heads of passersby. And while the foul-weather gear she wore didn't show much, there was the narrowing of elastic around waist and a slimness of shoulders that promised an interesting and totally female body beneath. But there was something else: an air, an attitude, an ease of movement and voice that suggested she was one of the rare ones—a woman who really was self-reliant; a woman who really went out and did what she wanted to do rather than march around bitching about what she couldn't do.

So I struggled through the uneasiness and tried to open her up a little.

"You said you were looking for Cabbage Key on the chart. Any particular reason, Captain Cole?"

"Yes. And the name's Marina." She caught my eyes briefly, then turned away, embarrassed, perhaps, by the chemical attraction that was building between us. "I was looking for Cabbage Key on the chart because that's where I'm headed." She saw me nod. "You know the place?"

"Very well."

"So tell me about it. I guess I ought to know something about it before I officially accept the job I have there. What I want to do is work my way clear to Oregon. Really learn the coastal areas of this country. So I figured working at Cabbage Key would be as good a place as any to start."

"Not a good place, Marina. A great place." So I thought back to when my late wife, Janet, and I used to go there. I told her about that tiny island near Fort Myers of Indian mounds and palms where the only access is by boat. I told her about the old white house on the mound built by the son of the mystery writer Mary Roberts Rinehart, and about the bar of wood and brass, and the ceiling fans and the fireplaces in the inn where commercial fishermen and yachtsmen alike go to drink beer, eat seafood, and laugh.

When I had finished, she smiled. "Sounds nice. Sounds like you wouldn't mind working there for a while, MacMorgan."

"A fellow could do a lot worse."

There was something I wanted to ask her. But before I got a chance, she saw what I was looking at: the wedding ring. Her left hand moved involuntarily, as if to hide it, then—knowing that I had seen—she rested the hand again on the tiller in plain sight.

"I guess this is your stop, huh, MacMorgan?" She I nodded toward the stilthouse now only fifty yards or so away. "Looks like a nice place to live."

"It is if you like solitude. And your own cooking."

"I do. The solitude, anyway."

"Why don't you come in for some coffee? I'll promise to wear clothes."

She chuckled, then hesitated. "I'd like to. I really would, but . . ."

"Will your husband be joining you at Cabbage Key, Marina?"

I caught her eyes and saw something I couldn't decipher. "Stranger things have happened, MacMorgan." She held out her hand again. I took it, returned the extra squeeze, and more felt than saw that she didn't turn away as I stripped off the foul-weather pants and dove into the water toward my stilthouse. When I came up there was that laugh again, a low alto chuckle. She yelled, "MacMorgan, I really do want to get the name of that tailor. Everyone should dress as well as you do."

Then with a wave of her hand, she was gone. The last time I saw her, she was putting up more sail, tiller lashed, pretty yellow sailboat and handsome blond lady going like hell through the green March sea. . . .

3

I had another surprise waiting for me when I pulled myself up the ladder and climbed the dock to the stilthouse.

I wasn't alone.

There was an old mahogany cruiser in absolutely Bristol condition tied and well bumpered alongside my thirty-four-foot sportfisherman, *Sniper*. Even if I hadn't known whose boat it was, I could have guessed. There aren't many people around with the tenacity—or the discipline—to keep an old wooden hulk in such perfect shape.

I grabbed a towel from the railing, wrapped it around me, and went inside.

Sure enough, there was D. Harold Westervelt waiting for me. He had poured himself a mug of coffee and was going over a sheaf of papers from a briefcase placed neatly on the table. He looked up briefly when I came in, but did not stand.

"You make a passable cup of coffee, Captain

MacMorgan. Out trying to work off a little of that excess weight you've allowed to build up, I see."

"Don't want to lose my boyish figure, colonel."

He looked out the window momentarily where Marina Cole and her sailboat were disappearing into the distance, but said nothing. I buffed my scraggily blond hair dry, took clean khaki pants and an old ragged L. L. Bean sweater out of my foot locker, pulled them on, added dry cotton socks, and treated myself to the new pair of Norm Thompson Razor Cut loafers with the glove-soft leather.

"Another mug of coffee, colonel?"

He shook his head. I should have known. D. Harold limits all of his vices—including caffeine. And if his physical appearance was any indication, it's not all that bad an idea. He looked fifteen years younger than his fifty-odd years. He wore a white crew-neck jersey, with sleeves rolled which showed the corded forearms and the swell of biceps. His head was completely shaved, and the winter-blue eyes peered out from a ledge of frontal eminence that suggested— and correctly—a massive amount of brain matter within. Even with the age difference, D. Harold was not a man I would want to tangle with.

"I got a message from the marina that you had stopped down to see me, Colonel Westervelt. I was surprised."

He flashed one of his rare smiles. "I *do* leave my home every now and then, captain. I'm not a hermit.

Recreation—on a limited basis, of course—is as important to doing good work as the work itself."

"Of course," I said. "So this is recreation?"

He shook his head, the face stoic. "I'm afraid not, captain. This meeting is business. Desperately important business at that." He leveled his gaze at me. "I'm afraid you'll have to cancel any plans you might have for the next ten days—that is, if you accept the mission."

I felt the old stirring deep inside the abdomen again; felt the nervousness that was the ever-present prelude to any mission I had ever had.

"Nothing pressing, sir," I said.

He nodded. "Good." He began going through his papers, settled on the one he needed, then began to talk. "So!" he said. "This will be your preliminary briefing. Feel free to ask any questions you may have—but please wait until I have finished."

"Yes, sir."

Colonel Westervelt sighed, tugged at an earlobe absently. "Do you know anything at all about world trade organizations, captain?"

"Almost nothing."

He made a waving motion with his left hand. "It doesn't matter, really. I just want to give you a little background information. It is generally thought that governments gauge, control, and direct the political and economic growth or regression of the world. While that's true to a point, the real political and economic clout comes from business. World business. In truth, world business—and the very few men who hold the reins on that level—are very much like countries unto themselves. When they shift directions, the nations of the world swing and sway behind like old wagons until they finally get in line."

"This has something to do with my mission?"

D. Harold gave me a warning look. "If you can just wait until I'm finished, captain?"

"Sorry."

"So! What I've told you, captain, is really nothing earth-shattering. It's fairly well known there are upper-strata organizations of businessmen, investors, and manipulators that carry fully as much financial power as any one nation. And those men come from nations around the world. Unfortunately, their allegiances are not always to the nations from which they come. Their allegiances, in many cases, are dedicated purely and simply to profit; to profit and to the control of those governments which might serve them."

He stopped and glanced briefly at my Transoceanic radio with its fifty feet of copper wire strung out the window to the roof.

"Captain, you have no doubt heard about increased terrorism around the world. Iran, Palestine, South America—the list goes on and on. While it might seem to occur capriciously and randomly to the average reader, we have known for some years that there had to be some single organization behind it. Their methods are too sophisticated for the work of a few loosely organized radicals. Yet their procedures are, in many cases, far too brutal, too singular in intent, to be the work of *any* government—not because there aren't ruthless governments, for there are. But because, in these most brutal acts of terrorism, a government would stand to lose much more in world respect than it could ever gain economically or politically."

"If that government was caught in the act, you mean?"

"Yes." He studied the inside of his coffee mug. "About a year ago, we finally got a lead on this autonomous terrorist organization. It was the X-factor in our equation. We still don't know much about it— just that it is somehow linked to one or more powerful world trade organizations. We assume that it is a weapon—a very effective weapon, I might add—that a trade organization could use to politically embarrass, harass, or temporarily weaken a country's governmental process."

"I can see how it would be effective."

"Economically? Obviously. And that brings us to our proposed mission, captain. For the sake of clarity, we have been referring to this organization as FEAT—Freelance Extortion and Terrorism. It has no national base whatsoever. It seems to be the natural cancerous product of a world of nations that depend increasingly upon their neighbors for goods and foodstuffs. And that makes it all the more lethal.

With no single nation or government to answer to, it stands only to profit from its deeds. This organization, FEAT, seeks to become the pimp in a world of befuddled governments, playing one against the other."

"And just how in the hell am I supposed to stop that?"

Colonel Westervelt paused, looked at me for a moment, then chuckled. It was a rare display of emotion. "Captain, there's no way one man could. As good as you are—and that is very good, indeed—there is no way that you alone could more than dent such an organization. I'm afraid the extermination of FEAT will take worldwide cooperation between governments."

"I didn't know there was such a thing as worldwide cooperation between governments."

"Quite right, normally. But the world has never been threatened as one before. Let me give you an example. Have you ever heard the term 'strategic metals'? No? Well, captain, there are certain rare ores absolutely essential to the manufacture of modern weaponry. And, unfortunately, the bulk of those metals comes from unstable countries in South Africa. Do you remember back in 1977 when a gang of rebels closed down the mines in Zaire where nearly ninety percent of the world's cobalt is produced? Just before the rebels struck, the Soviet Union made an unusually large purchase. Superficially, it seemed to put the Russians in a very advantageous position. The price of cobalt quadrupled on the world market—and they had more than they could use. But on a deeper political level, the closing of the mines was damaging to the Soviets. Obviously, it looked as if they had masterminded the rebel attack. They not only lost some prestige, but Free World countries immediately funneled huge amounts of money into research, hoping to find a substitute for cobalt. World money manipulators smart enough or 'lucky' enough to acquire stock in the private-sector research centers around the world did far more than just quadruple their money during those months, I assure you. Say what you want about the Russians, but they are not a stupid people. Clearly, some other organization was behind the rebel takeover; an organization that had everything to gain and nothing to lose. Other countries, socialist and democratic, have been publicly embarrassed in much the same way—and, yes, that includes the United States. But so far, FEAT hasn't had the courage—or, perhaps, a motive—for bringing its terrorism for profit to our nation's soil. Until now."

"They're planning a terrorist strike here?"

Westervelt shook his head. "Planned, captain. Past tense. Planned. We got word of it from the Red Chinese, of all people—which illustrates how seriously the world's governments are taking this organization. God knows how they found out. But they did. They're planning an assassination here. And it's due to take place within seven to ten days."

"Jesus—one of our political leaders?"

"No, captain. That's not FEAT's style—not unless the assassination was on the very highest level. No, their *modus operandi* is to publicly embarrass or compromise a nation, then be there waiting and ready for the resulting economic swing."

"Pretty ingenious, you have to admit."

"Certainly. They're smart and perfectly ruthless. And you see, captain, in the complex webbing of world finance and trade, there's no easy way to find out exactly who 'they' are. For the moment, we will have to be satisfied with a simple grass-roots offensive—prove to them we know what they are doing and why. That's where you come in. Interested?"

"As I said: I have no pressing plans for the next week or so. And if I did, I'd cancel them."

Colonel Westervelt smiled slightly. "I know the feeling," he said. He studied me momentarily, and I found myself trying to suck in the gut, square the shoulders. He said, "You've been letting yourself go, captain. May I ask why? I recommended you for this mission assuming that you were at least mentally fit. If you are still suffering some psychological disturbance from a past assignment . . ."

"Exactly who are they planning to assassinate, colonel?" I interrupted shortly. It made me mad—though not mad at D. Harold. It was his job to be absolutely sure he had the right man. No, it made me mad at myself; angry for letting myself go to the point where my effectiveness might be questioned. And questioned by an old friend at that.

Westervelt tugged at the earlobe, his only nervous mannerism. He was silent for a while, then began going through some papers. The subject was obviously closed. "So! We have narrowed it down to two possible targets, both of whom will soon be vacationing on Florida's west coast. It is not a matter of luck on our part—it is a matter of exceptionally fine planning on FEAT's part that both targets would be in the same vicinity at the same time. Obviously, it's twice as hard to protect two men."

"And the targets are?"

"The *probable* targets are either a Soviet diplomat named Kiev Evenki, or a high-level Israeli spokesman, Samuel Yabrud. Have you heard of either man? No? I'm not surprised. While they are both very important people, each is similar in that they handle the bulk of the behind-the-scenes work. They are the ones who pound out the agreements and treaties and contracts, then step aside to let the high-profile government leaders do the signing. The assassination of either of these men on American soil would put us in an extremely difficult position, and probably have far-reaching political and economic repercussions."

"But you're not sure which is the actual target?"

"No. It's very doubtful that it's both of them."

"So why don't you just cage them three deep with some inconspicuous Secret Service people?"

Westervelt lifted his eyebrows. "I assure you, captain, we are taking every defensive option at our disposal. You need not worry about that. Thanks to the warning we received from the Red Chinese, there is less chance that the assassin will succeed. But there is still a *chance*. You Captain MacMorgan, are our offensive option. We want you to find FEAT's assassin, stalk him, and then . . . eliminate him."

"Assassinate the assassin."

"Yes. And make it very plain that it was no accident."

"Do you have any suspects?"

"None. That is why this new terrorist movement is so diabolical. It could be anyone, male or female, of any color or nationality. The assassin probably doesn't even know who he is killing or why he is killing. It is all too easy to find willing murderers these days, captain."

"So what I will be doing is . . ."

"Just a symbol—a message to FEAT that we will not tolerate terrorism in the United States."

"I have little to go on, and not much time, colonel."

He sighed, "I know, I know. But you will have the locations of the possible targets. The Russian, Kiev Evenki, will arrive tomorrow at a private home in a remote and very wealthy settlement on Florida's west coast called Boca Grande. Do you know it?"

"Pretty much. I used to do a lot of tarpon fishing up that way. I know some of the fishing guides. And you're right about its being affluent and remote. Some American political figures vacation there, too, right?"

"Which is exactly why Evenki is there." He checked his watch. "In just a few hours the first of the most preliminary and informal talks about a nuclear-arms pact will begin there. He'll be on vacation—but a working vacation."

"And the Israeli?"

"Samuel Yabrud will be staying only a few miles away by water, at a health resort called St. Carib Island. They call it a health resort, but it's really a very plush fat farm where the wealthy go to lose weight. It's an island of about a hundred acres southeast of Boca Grande, and north and west of two other inhabited islands called Useppa and Cabbage Key. Why the change of expression, captain?"

"You're the second person this morning that's mentioned Cabbage Key, that's all."

Westervelt glanced quickly out the window. The sailboat was a bobbing speck on the far horizon. "Your friend was interested in Cabbage Key?"

"A stranger I met this morning, colonel. And yes, she was interested. She thinks she'll be working there."

He jotted down the name when I told him. "We'll check her out. By the way, that's the sort of thing you'll have to watch for, captain—people new to the area, jobs or not." He stood up and began packing his papers back into the briefcase. "We'll expect you and your vessel at the naval base tomorrow at oh eight hundred. Right. There you will be briefed further on who your contacts will be in the Boca Grande and St. Carib Island areas. But I must remind you that, as always, you are working independently of all our established agencies. You will not seek out those contacts unless absolutely necessary."

"So how do you suggest I start, colonel—just go up there and start blundering around?"

I didn't expect the grin. "I suggest you join your new friend in a job at Cabbage Key"—he looked meaningfully at the small roll around my waist—"or enroll yourself in a course at the St. Carib fat farm."

4

Feeling dwarfed, I nudged *Sniper* in behind one of the massive nuclear subs at the Boca Chica naval base, tossed lines to the sailors waiting there, and pulled myself up onto the cement quay.

The sailors said nothing, only eyed me suspiciously. They were obviously expecting me—and wondering why in the hell someone was allowing a civilian vessel in a military harbor.

A young lieutenant was waiting at the concrete-reinforced machine shop by the docks. Safely out of sight of the sailors, he snapped a salute. Dressed in khakis and blue denim shirt, I felt a little ridiculous returning it.

"Captain MacMorgan?"

"Yes."

"This way, sir."

D. Harold Westervelt was in a munitions office no bigger than a garage. A desk lamp made his shaved head look luminous. He was studying some papers.

He looked upset about something. He glanced up when the young lieutenant delivered me, then shut the door behind, leaving us alone.

"You're early, captain."

I checked my Rolex Submariner. It said three minutes to eight. "Sorry, colonel."

He stood up, straightened his shirt collar, and went to a gray metal closet. It was already unlocked. "You still have the Cobra crossbow?"

"Yes. But I could use some shafts and some weights."

He placed two boxes on the table, then returned to the closet.

"And the AK-47 Russian assault rifle?"

"Yes, it's stowed aboard."

"I'm afraid it would a very bad choice to use the AK-47 on this mission. To have the would-be assassin of a Russian or Israeli eliminated by a Russian weapon might give FEAT the wrong impression."

"I hadn't thought about that."

One by one he brought out two rifles I recognized, and one I didn't. He placed them on the table, bolts open. "I would suggest either of these two weapons." He pointed to the Lee Enfield No. 4 Mark I rifle, and the Remington Model 700. Both had stocks with the dull military finish. He said, "Both use 7.62mm NATO ammunition. The Enfield is heavier, and its effective range is not as great—five hundred meters compared to the Remington's eight hundred and twenty—but, with its charger-loaded magazine, the action is somewhat faster. And it holds ten rounds compared to the Remington's five. It's British, of course, but it's still being used around the world, and, like the Remington, by NATO forces primarily as a sniper rifle. We can equip either with a special silencer."

"I'd prefer the Remington. More familiar with it."

"I thought you would. Fine Mauser action with an almost fail-safe knockdown trajectory. Muzzle velocity of eight hundred and fifty meters per second."

"And scopes?"

"For daylight work, you'll have the Redfield variable-power, three to nine power. For night work, you'll have the Star-Tron MK 303a night-vision system with a 135mm F-16 lens. You probably know how it works—light intensification; gathers all the available starlight and moonlight, and amplifies it fifty thousand times. Extremely effective."

I had been eyeing the other rifle on the table. I'd never seen one like it. Westervelt noticed. He picked it up and handed it to me. It was built entirely of metal, but was still surprisingly light. It had an odd skeleton stock complete with cheek rest and pistol grip. At first it struck me as being an ugly excuse for a rifle; but then, on closer inspection, rather striking in a lethal sort of way.

"I brought that rifle out as a reminder, captain."

"Reminder, sir?"

"Yes. That's the SVD Dragunov sniper rifle, used by the Warsaw Pact forces, built by the Russians.

Compared to your Remington, it has more pluses than minuses. In the past, FEAT's terrorists have leaned toward Warsaw Pact weaponry. It's a reminder that the man you are hunting is at least as well equipped as you—and perhaps better."

"It's a pretty graphic reminder, colonel. I appreciate it."

I put the Dragunov back on the table while D. Harold opened another box. He pulled out what looked like an aluminum camera case, flipped the latches, and lifted the cover. "And this is the last of the equipment, captain. It's possible you won't need it. But if you do, it can be invaluable. It's a Persid seismic intruder alarm system. You bury these small geophones in an area you want secured. They'll detect men on foot a hundred meters away. It's battery-operated, it doesn't weigh much, and it can save your life—or the life of one of our two foreign visitors. It's easy to use—directions are enclosed."

Westervelt collected all the gear and placed it on the table before me. He still looked strangely troubled; worried about something.

"Something wrong, colonel?"

He rubbed at his temples, as if he had a headache. "As a matter of fact, there is. I've been wondering if I should tell you."

"What is it?"

"You no doubt wondered why your normal government connection, Captain Norm Fizer, didn't get in touch with you about this mission."

I had indeed wondered. Stormin' Norman Fizer had seen my men and me through two very, very nasty missions in Cambodia long ago, and it was Fizer who had made it possible for me to take revenge on the drug kingpin who had murdered my wife and two boys. He was a friend from the past who was still a friend. A good friend.

"I wondered, colonel, but I didn't want to ask. I thought it might suggest that I was unhappy working with you."

"That was kind of you, captain—but unnecessary."

"I suppose."

"The reason I've been wondering if I should tell you is strictly a pragmatic one. I've been wondering how it might affect your work."

"*What* might affect my work, colonel? I'm no schoolboy. Just tell me."

He straightened himself at his desk, leaned closer toward me, and said, "The reason Captain Fizer is not your adviser on this case is that he was to be one of your contacts. I have a list of Secret Service and CIA people here, and he was among them."

"What do you mean, 'was'?"

"Just that, I'm afraid, captain. Fizer has been in the Boca Grande–St. Carib Island area for the last three days. He apparently was on to something. An excellent man, Fizer. Wonderful intuitive and intellectual police skills. . . ."

"But what happened, D. Harold?"

Colonel Westervelt made an empty motion with

his hands. "He turned up missing yesterday. And last night, a clandestine search for him was fruitless. Dusky, Captain Fizer is missing and assumed dead. I'm sorry."

And so was I. Damn sorry. Fizer was one of the good ones; a rare combination of good humor, horse sense, and toughness that had seemed unbeatable.

But in the end, we are all beatable. Death sees to that, as it had, apparently, seen to my friend, Stormin' Norm Fizer.

"Any leads as to exactly *who* he was on to, colonel?"

He shook his head. "Afraid not. He was a paying guest at the Gasparilla Inn—one of the old hotels on Boca Grande. He was using his real name. No reason not to, really. Under the guise of being a fishing enthusiast, he had rented a boat all three of the days he was a guest there—ostensibly to check out the area. Yesterday was so windy in Boca Grande they were reluctant to rent him the boat. He insisted. When he didn't return yesterday afternoon, they called the Coast Guard. They found his boat adrift off Captiva Pass last night, not far from your Cabbage Key."

"Any sign of a struggle?"

"None."

"How do you know he was on to something?"

"Very simple. He notified one of his superiors—in code, of course. He indicated he had a good lead,

44

and would report in full after a preliminary investigation."

"Why didn't he get someone to go with him if he thought he was on to something?"

"That wasn't his style, apparently."

Westervelt was right. That wasn't Fizer's style. He wouldn't ask for help until he was sure he needed it. Fizer was the kind of guy who didn't like to waste someone else's time.

"FEAT, colonel?"

"We can only assume that, barring some freak accident, Fizer was indeed onto FEAT's assassin, found him, and was eliminated by him."

"Murdered, you mean, dammit!" I found myself cracking the table with my fist.

"And that's exactly why I was reluctant to tell you, captain," D. Harold said sternly. "In this business of international terrorism—and that's what it is, by the way, a business—there's no room for that sort of schoolboy emotion, MacMorgan. That's all very fine for playground confrontations and after school fights, but if you bring it into an encounter with an individual as cold and ruthless as one of FEAT's assassins, you're going to finish second-best. Just as Captain Fizer apparently finished second-best. Understand?"

"Then why in the hell did you pick me for the job?"

"I'm wondering that myself at the moment."

I found myself glowering at the man across from

me. The blue eyes were frigid, the hands placed calmly in front of him. I took a deep breath, exhaled. "I'm sorry, colonel. You're right, of course. It's just that Norm and I had been through a lot together."

He nodded. "I know. He was a very good man. And after you leave, I have the unenviable job of notifying his wife and children. Not a pleasant task, I assure you. But we have already lost one man to FEAT, and we don't want to lose you. Not only for personal reasons, but because it would be a devastating blow to our international image if they bested us again. We can't afford that, do you understand? In Vietnam you seemed to excel in this kind of one-against-one assignment. I'm betting that you've lost none of your mental or physical abilities—just don't let emotion cause you to do something foolish."

"I understand, colonel. And I'm sorry for the outburst."

We both stood. He helped me carry the new weaponry out to *Sniper*.

The sailors who had helped me tie up were nowhere to be seen now. It reinforced the impression that the mission was highly classified.

"You will arrive sometime today, captain?" He stood, hands on hips upon the quay, looking up at where I stood on the flybridge.

"Seven, eight hours from now, depending on the weather."

"I can still have a chopper fly you up to Boca

Grande, then make arrangements for you to secure a vessel there."

"No thanks, colonel. I'm kind of attached to this boat."

"Yes. I see."

I turned the keys, pressed the buttons, and *Sniper's* twin 453 GMC diesels rumbled to life, sputtering salt water through the exhausts. The wind was still out of the northwest, visible in the coconut palms around the military harbor.

"Remember, captain. If you find the assassin, it is to look like no accident. I leave the method to you."

I looked down and saw the slight smile crease his face. It was D. Harold's way of giving me the final free rein. I gave him a short salute and said, "Colonel, if I find the guy, there will be nothing accidental about it. That much I promise. . . ."

On the long solitary boat trip across Florida Bay, I flirted with the idea of catching Marina Cole and her little sailboat. Throughout the day, I kept a watch through binoculars. Once even went so far as to go off my course to get a better look at a little yellow sloop.

But it wasn't hers.

In a way, I was glad. On the memory screen, I played and replayed my meeting with her; saw again the unusual face, the dark eyes, the braided rope of blond hair—and the wedding band. As someone who had loved marriage, I still took the marriage vows seriously. And who in the hell was I to try to interfere with the lives of her and her husband?

Still, there was that cryptic reply to a simple question.

"Will you be meeting your husband at Cabbage Key, Marina?"

"Stranger things have happened, Dusky. . . ."

On a boat alone, you toy with the mind, play little games. You listen to the VHF radio, lock in the little Benmar autopilot when it's time to go below for another cold beer and a fresh dip of Copenhagen, and then return to the pilot's seat to watch the inexorable surge of open green sea.

So why think about the woman? Hadn't I tried to start a relationship with the lady with the auburn hair, Saxan Benton? Yes, and had failed miserably.

So why pursue another?

Because the life of the celibate has never ever appealed to me. Yet a sexual relationship without benefit of an emotional relationship has never interested me either.

As modern and as fashionable as the "bedroom-for-recreation" philosophy is publicized to be by such print whores as *Playboy* and *Penthouse,* it's always struck me as about as appetizing as hunting cavewomen with a club.

So I passed the hours away, rolling with the swift wave surge, feeling *Sniper*'s blue-black hull cut northward through blustery seas.

It was the quandary of the romantic caught in the quandary of life.

And there was no simple answer.

Only life. Death. And the compromise that comes between.

Four hours out, Florida Bay and the mangrove giants of the Shark River behind, I picked up the light tower at Coon Key and decided to refuel and give myself a short break from the rough March weather by cutting in behind Goodland and taking the intercoastal waterway to Naples. At Goodland, I topped off the tanks and had a hot lunch at Stan's Idle Hour. Interesting place, Goodland. When Deltona Corporation decided to turn Marco Island into a secluded west-coast suburb of cement, concrete-block homes, and expensive condominiums, they purchased the land from the fishermen who lived on the island, and literally moved their houses—lock, stock, and families—to Goodland. Tiny Goodland gained the atmosphere Marco Island had forfeited; the atmosphere and forty or fifty unfortunate mobile homes to boot. I took the time to stop at the post office and leave a card for Al Seely, a hermit friend of mine who lives alone on Dismal Key, then boarded *Sniper* once again and headed up the Gordon River at a steady twenty-five knots toward Naples, Fort Myers, and, finally, Pine Island Sound, where the little island settlements of Cabbage Key, St. Carib, and Boca Grande waited.

It was time to start planning. All plans had to be

loosely woven, with plenty of options; options enough to take me to the X-factor: an assassin alone, like me. A man or woman assigned to murder. Like me.

So how do you find a killer before he has killed?

And then I knew. Once on R & R in Southeast Asia, some buddies finally talked me into going on a tiger hunt. I was reluctant, because I admire the big cats; have loved them since I was a boy in the circus. Besides, the idea of killing an animal—any animal—for something other than food just doesn't appeal to me. But I finally went—not to see the cat die, but to see what extremes human hunters had to go to in order to kill the master hunter.

But the hunt was depressingly simple. It was a matter of staking a lamb to a tree.

And then waiting.

Well, I had my lambs: a Russian and an Israeli.

Now all I had to do was maneuver them into a stakeout.

And wait. . . .

5

It was nearing dusk when I finally idled up the channel to Cabbage Key. Clouds were a brilliant rust to the west. An osprey in a gumbo limbo whistled at me with ascending disapproval. Orange sun held the old wooden inn, the water tower, and the jungled shell mound in a tenuous fiery light.

There were three or four big yachts moored at the dock along with a half-dozen smaller cruisers and open fishing boats. A small yellow sloop, sails furled, held my attention longer than the others.

The name on the stern confirmed that it was hers: *Sleek*.

So she had made it. And how was I going to explain my sudden reappearance after our meeting that morning? It would look as if I was following her. But it couldn't be helped.

And maybe I *was* following her.

There were plenty of other places I could have stayed that first night. I could have pulled in at Sanibel's Tarpon Bay and traded one-liners with old friends there. Or gone on to Boca Grande and looked up one of a number of fishing-guide acquaintances.

But I had chosen Cabbage Key; even rationalized the decision by telling myself that if there was anyone new to the area they would, sooner or later, end up at the old bar and restaurant there, like a tiger at a watering hole.

It would be an awkward moment.

But it couldn't be helped.

Luckily, I was saved the embarrassment by the island's owner, Rob Wells. Rob is in his mid-thirties, looks younger, and he and his wife Phyllis run the old inn with a combination of reserve and flourish that assures them a dedicated flow of boating clientele. By chance, Rob was acting dockmaster. He came ambling up after I had docked *Sniper*, hand outstretched, tall and blond, a look of surprise on his face.

"Man, I'd heard you'd gone hermit down in the Keys. Why the honor of the early visit?"

I laughed. "You mean it's not May, and the tarpon aren't running yet?"

"I mean exactly that." He winked. "But I think I can put you onto a few kingfish off Boca. Or did you just come up here to eat our food, drink our beer, and assault our waitress?"

"Do I have to choose?"

After I checked *Sniper*'s lines a second time, we walked up the mound toward the inn. Briefly, I told

Rob about my earlier encounter with Marina Cole, and made it clear what I hoped he would do. Professionals in an enterprise that deals so intimately with the public, like those at Cabbage Key, become used to keeping confidences. And on another level, I knew that I could trust Rob Wells. Period. So I told him I was in the area on personal business and didn't want Marina to think that I was there in pursuit of her.

He smiled, his North Carolina accent heavy with mock intrigue.

"And you're not following her, right?"

"Right. Unless she's not really married. I reserve the right to change my mind on that one."

"So how about I go inside before you do, and mention to her that an old friend of mine is coming in, and that you've been planning your stay here for months, and that she should take special care your beer is cold and your supper is hot?"

"So she is working here?"

"On a trial basis. To see if she likes us and we like her, as always with someone new. And I thought you weren't interested."

"You've forgotten the reserve clause. And yes, I'd appreciate it if you would do that. It would save us both some embarrassment."

He gave me a light lockerroom punch on the arm. "Never a dull moment when you're here, Mac-Morgan."

"Is it ever dull at Cabbage Key?"

"Not if you like peace and quiet, good food, and

fishing—and especially not if you have two boys like mine to keep you hopping."

"And how are those sons of yours?"

"Great. As always."

I puttered around outside for a few minutes to give Rob time; even climbed the old wooden water tower to see what there was to see. The water tower had, ostensibly, been built the same time the mystery writer's son had built the house. Constructed to store a large supply of fresh water, it spired some sixty feet above the peak of the mound. And even after fifty-odd years of service, it was still in pretty good shape; wood sound and kept whitewashed by Rob Wells's crew.

It offered a fine view of the islands in Pine Island Sound. Far to the north I could see the brown phosphate silos at the tip of Boca Grande, the affluent island village where the Russian, Kiev Evenki, would soon be arriving. And directly to the east, with its air of Southampton and old Florida wealth, was tropical Useppa, where such notables as Teddy Roosevelt, Gene Tunney, and Gloria Swanson once vacationed; and, more recently, where the CIA had trained Cuban troops for the Bay of Pigs fiasco. And midway between the two was St. Carib Island, looking lush and remote at dusk. I had never been on St. Carib; indeed, had always wondered exactly what was on the island. Geometric shards of white buildings, luminous in the failing light, protruded from the foliage, and a white water tower, similar to the one on which I stood, crowned the green haze of poinciana, banyan, and mango. So that was where the Israeli treaty-smith, Samuel Yabrud, would be staying; an island where the rich could melt their fat away in style.

Pine Island Sound was a tranquil sweep of water and islands in the saffron dusk.

Osprey whistled and pelicans drifted in formation, arrowing toward their roosts.

It was a postcard setting; the amiable Florida that's promoted at Disney World.

But there was something in the March wind: a hint of something lethal; a quality of light and air suggestive of that darker side where a killer stalks within us all.

With a sweeping gaze, my eyes went from island to island to island. Somewhere out there was my adversary. At that very moment he sat or stood, heart pumping, lungs siphoning, brain considering *his* options just as I now considered mine. What did he look like? What were his strengths, his weaknesses?

And just what in the hell was his plan?

I stood there for a moment longer on the tower in the wind, thinking about my friend Norm Fizer. I told myself the fact that he had disappeared didn't necessarily mean that he had been killed. But in the deepest part of me I knew the truth. And it made me mad. Damn mad. Not just that I had lost a friend, but because someone out there had been a little smarter, a little faster, a little more deadly than a man I had come to look upon as unbeatable.

But he had a new adversary now.

The hunter was being hunted. Again. And I felt the shadow of that unknown assassin and the weight of the task draw over me like a cloud. And for the first time in a very, very long time I felt fear, because the shadow and the cloud were both death. . . .

Marina Cole was on the back porch of the old inn waiting tables when I finally went inside. Rob Wells sat at the bar with his wife, Phyllis, both sipping at orange juice in tall glasses. We exchanged greetings, and after brief pleasantries, Rob said, "That matter you mentioned—I think it's all taken care of."

"Very efficient man you have here," I said to Phyllis.

She chuckled. "Efficient because I helped. Hope you don't mind that Rob brought me in on it, Dusky, but women are much better at this sort of thing than men. And by the way, from the look of her, I can't blame you for leaving your options open." She was still chuckling as I walked away.

Without the tentlike rain slicker on, Marina Cole was a striking lady indeed. She wore pleated safari shorts, long dark legs based on leather sandals. The thick braided hair was coiled atop her head, and she wore an old cotton madras shirt that displayed the tapering ribs and upward thrust of breasts. She moved with affable grace beneath ceiling fans and soft lights, the tanned face smiling as she traded jokes with her customers. As I watched her work, I decided that she had probably never waited tables before—but that she was the type of person who would become good at anything she tried in the shortest possible time.

She was carrying a tray when she finally noticed me. Even with Phyllis Wells's warning, it surprised her. She damn near dropped the tray. But she recovered quickly and held up one finger accompanied by an uncomfortable smile.

I was to wait a minute.

I took an empty chair in the combination bar and library. A mounted tarpon, its eyes aglow with catatonic plasticity, hung over the door along with an old percussion-cap fowling piece. A few fishermen sat trading stories over their bottles of beer beneath the slow whirl of the fan while Kathy McKee, the enduring bartender, alternately polished glasses and answered calls on the island's VHF radio under the counter. Long ago, God knows when, someone decided that the way to become a part of Cabbage Key was to sign the name of his vessel on a dollar bill, then tape that dollar bill to the wall. The custom caught on, and now the walls and ceilings are papered with signed currency. There were even dollar bills taped to the old upright piano where a sweating bald man pounded out a torchy version of "Tangerine."

It was longer than a minute. In fact, I was halfway

through my first Beck's when Marina finally slid into the chair beside me.

"Whew," she said, wiping her face. "Some first night. When Rob told me he needed help because it was the peak of the busy season, he wasn't kidding."

"So how do you like it so far?"

She reached over, took a sip of my beer, hesitated at her own familiarity, then took another. "I love the island. Got here early this morning, slept for a few hours, then went right to work. People seem nice. So I hope to stay awhile."

Our hands touched briefly as I took my beer. The texture of her skin suggested she might be a little older than I had guessed earlier. Somewhere between twenty-five and thirty. No older. Nothing in the legs or breasts to suggest the sag of age or childbirth. But still the smooth gold ring on her wedding finger.

"Told you you'd like it," I said, then added a little awkwardly, "I'm glad."

Then came the uncomfortable silence again; the silence of people who realize that a relationship could begin, but, for whatever reasons, shouldn't.

Marina cleared her throat, toyed with a napkin. "Phyllis Wells told me you come here a lot. Said you'd been planning this trip for a while. I was kind of surprised you didn't tell me that yesterday morning."

"Thought it might sound like I was offering something . . . or, damn, I don't know. Then I realized after you'd left that not telling you would make my arriving here even more suspicious. I mean, what I'm trying to say, Marina, is that I'm not hot on your trail or anything like that. I'm not following you."

She considered that for a moment. Someone called her from the kitchen, and she stood up quickly. She said, "Are you going to be on the island for a while?"

"I'm staying the night. And I'll be around the area. I'm up here to do some fishing and take care of some business."

She gave me a sudden swift smile, as if she had decided something.

"Any chance of you and me having a drink here in the bar later, MacMorgan?"

"My calendar's pretty full—but for you, yeah."

"I still don't know how to take this vehement insistence that you're not following me."

"I'm not!"

She gave me a sisterly wink, with just a hint of vampishness on her face. "That's what I mean. I don't know if I should be relieved. Or disappointed."

And with that she hustled to the kitchen to pick up her order.

I finished my beer and walked back down the mound to the docks, where *Sniper* shifted in the wind, tugging experimentally at her lines. Lights were on in the neighboring yachts, where the stay-aboards filled the March night with the soft laughter of cocktail hour. A half mile across the sound the

houses on Useppa, their windows aglow, stood out
ghostly in the distance. St. Carib Island was a darker
line on a dark horizon.

Rob Wells showed me to a room in the inn with a
private bath, then apologized for having to leave the
island for the night. I was disappointed. I had questions to ask. It was another blustery evening, and he
had seen to it that my fireplace was lighted. Stout
black mangrove logs flickered and roared in the
draft. I stripped off my clothes, put a new Wilkinson
blade in the razor, shaved, showered, then lay down
and slept for an hour before dinner. The water takes
it out of you—especially eight hours in choppy
seas. Alone.

I awoke with a taste for stone crabs. Kathy McKee,
looking taller than her five eleven in slacks and
sweater, got me a table on the porch and brought
beer.

"Long time no see, huh?"

"Yes indeed. Your boat still sunk?" She laughed.
It was a standing joke. Long ago she had owned
some ancient hulk of mahogany yacht—an unusual
playtoy for a woman. Its sinking in some frozen New
Jersey harbor had prompted her to head southward
and, finally, to Cabbage Key.

"Still housing fish as far as I know."

"And some people just *talk* about conservation. I
won't need a menu. Just a double order of stone crab,

plenty of toast, and drawn butter—and maybe a little conversation when you get a minute?"

She tilted her head, surprised. "It wouldn't be about our new waitress, would it?"

"No. A private matter."

"Do I look like a gossip?"

"Not hardly. But you can't tend bar at a place like this without knowing what's going on. Right?"

She nodded. "Sure, Dusky. I'll stop back when I can."

If there's a seafood—or any food, for that matter— better than fresh stone crab claws, I've yet to discover it. So when the food came I gave it my full attention, cracking the claws, dipping the crab meat in hot butter, and washing it down with the fine Beck's beer. And I was just about finished, trying to decide if I should order the excellent Key lime pie immediately or wait until later, when Kathy returned.

"You have time to talk?"

She nodded, stretched wearily. "Yeah. God, what a week. Seems like more people find out about this place every year. I dream about the ingredients of a rum punch in my sleep. So I'm on a ten-minute break and I put this gin and tonic on your bill. It's very good, by the way. Made it myself."

She sipped at the drink, smiling. Truthfully, I didn't know how I should start. I knew that I could trust Kathy McKee just as I could trust Rob. But there was only so much I could tell either of them. It demanded a one-sided exchange of information, no questions asked. So I gave it a try.

"Kath, I'm looking for someone."

She grinned. "From the way you've been ogling that new girl—Marina, is it?—I'd say you've already found her."

"Is it that obvious?"

"I guess you could be even less subtle—say, club her on the head and drag her off to your room."

"Believe me, this has nothing to do with Marina. I'm looking for someone else. Could be a woman, I guess—but it's probably a man. And I have no idea what he looks like. But I would guess that he is very tough, very smart, and possibly isn't American. And he would be a stranger to the area."

"A stranger? Or a tourist?"

"A stranger. I know there's a lot of water and a lot of islands in the area—but there aren't very many people at all. And sooner or later those people end up here at Cabbage Key. Have you seen a guy who might fit the description?"

She thought for a moment. "One guy?"

"Probably."

She shook her head. "I haven't seen one guy who fits the description—but I have seen half a dozen of them."

"What?"

"Don't look so surprised, Dusky. You've been away for quite a while, remember? The islands in Pine Island Sound are no longer the tight little community of boating folk they once were. Oh, there are still plenty of great people around. Larry Davis still fishes around here, and Jim Lavender, the Hamiltons and Doug Fisher, Duke Sells, Ted Cole and Mike Fuery, and the rest. But there are more and more outsiders now. A lot of big money has been piped into some of the islands. Much of it foreign money. Like St. Carib—it used to be just another beautiful private island. The old owner threw great parties. He'd boat the whole staff of Cabbage Key and Useppa over, and we'd set dance-marathon records. But then, out of nowhere, some outsiders bought the place and completely renovated it. It was all very hush-hush for a while. Then, suddenly, there was a nationwide publicity push. Television, newspapers, magazines like the *New Yorker*—all about how St. Carib was the new jet-set fat farm. We were all kind of excited at first. But then some of their movie-star clientele started sneaking over here looking half-starved and acting like they were too good for the place, and we suddenly weren't very excited anymore. We get our share of film stars and big-time athletes at Cabbage Key, but they come here to let their hair down. They want to be treated like private people—no better or worse—and that's just what they get. They don't get fussed over, and we all have a good time. But those folks from St. Carib have been a real pain. I think the hunger or the program or something makes them mean. And it rubs off on the St. Carib staff, I think. You mentioned foreigners—

they're almost all foreigners. You know the type: European macho."

"All from one country?"

She thought for a moment, then shook her head. "I don't think so. A couple of them look like Germans or Swedes—they're blond, anyway. The rest of them are pretty dark. Some Italian, some Mediterranean, maybe."

"And they give you a hard time?"

She nodded, stood, and checked her watch. "It's about nine now. About midnight, when we want to close, is when the fun will probably begin. They get real nasty at closing time, and Rob isn't here to put the fear in them, so it should be real interesting."

I was surprised. "You mean they'll be here tonight?"

"Not 'be' here, Dusky. They're already here. Back in the bar. They're drinking scotch like it's due to be banned. They've got a new session starting tomorrow, and I guess they're trying to get their minds right for all the chubby starlets they'll have to service."

"You sound a little bitter, Kath."

"Not bitter. Just tired of getting pinched, Dusky." She headed back toward the bar, then stopped suddenly, a quizzical expression on her face. "You know, you didn't even tell me why you wanted the information."

"That's right," I said.

"Private, huh?"

"For now."

She smiled, satisfied with the simple explanation. "Anyway, it's good to see you around again, Dusky. And make sure you get a chance to see Larry Davis and the rest. They'd strangle me if I let you get away without saying hello."

6

There were five of them at a table by the fireplace across from the piano in the bar.

The bald man had changed clothes, but he was still sweating and still banging at the old upright, playing "As Time Goes By" with a Casablanca edge to it. Kathy stood behind the bar talking to a clutch of locals, laughing with them and freshening their drinks. A young married couple, looking as though they were fresh from an Iowa farm, played darts in the corner, giggling and nuzzling. The ceiling fan churned the light haze of cigarette smoke and spread the warmth of the fire.

I went to an unoccupied corner of the bar, feeling the five St. Carib staffers eye me in sudden silence as I passed. Kathy brought me a Beck's without my having to ask.

"Our friends are over there in the corner."

"So I see."

"They're staring at you."

"Must be my boyish good looks."

"Or it could be that scar on your cheek. New, isn't it?"

"Latest thing from Paris."

"You ordered it by mail?"

"Won it, actually. Got second place in a knife fight. I'd have done better, but there was only one knife and it wasn't mine."

She looked at me strangely. "You know, I can't tell when you're kidding and when you're not."

"As long as *I* know, Kath. As long as *I* know." I took a pull at the cold beer. "Marina's off duty?"

"What a question to ask another single lady. And yes, she is. The poor kid was whipped. It'll take her a while to get in shape for this waitress work. But the girls say she's willing. And that's half the battle. By the way, she left special orders to be called no later than ten. Said she's to meet a friend at the bar. Are you the friend?"

"I try to be friendly with everyone."

"That's not what I've heard."

"Depends on who you talk to. Right now I'm going to be friendly with those fine fellows from St. Carib."

She picked up my beer, wiped the counter, and brought me another.

"That tall dark one is the guy to watch. Where he goes, the others follow. Acts like he's a plantation owner and everyone else is slave material. He about got into it one night with Larry. Rob broke it up.

That's as close as we've come to having a fight out here in three years. Everything was friendly and cozy until those guys started showing up. And truthfully, if there had been a fight between those two, I wouldn't have known who to bet on. Larry is big enough, but that guy is just plain mean."

"Never bet against the Davis brothers or the Hamiltons. It's a losing proposition in these parts."

"That's true."

Nonchalantly, I swung around on my bar stool, pretending to watch the bald man pound the piano. He had switched from "As Time Goes By" to "Rum and Coca-Cola." The tall dark guy Kathy was talking about sat at the head of the table, facing the bar. His black hair was carefully coiffured—the twenty-four-dollar windblown look. He wore a white sports shirt with *St. Carib* embroidered on the pocket, as did the other four. There was a gold chain around his neck, complete with obligatory unicorn horn. Digital watch and left wrist rested upon the table near his scotch, and left hand tapped two jeweled rings in time to the music. He was heavily corded more than heavily muscled, with broad plates of pectoral muscle visible within the open shirt. His face was of the classic Mediterranean mold: petulant mouth given to scorn, narrow dark eyes, and a very large nose that seemed to dominate whatever cheek and jaw development there may have been. Two others at the table seemed to be equally Mediterranean; both obviously in good shape, but reserved in the animated light of the man at the head of the table. The other two were blond hulks, all chest and forearms and biceps. They kept to themselves, apart from the others even though sitting at the same table. From the bits of conversation I heard, they sounded to be German.

I looked back at Kathy. "What's the tall guy's name?"

"Kind of a funny name," she said softly. "What is it? Yeah, I remember—Matrah. I remember because he got mad at Larry for shortening it to Matt. That's what the argument was all about."

"Takes offense easily, huh?"

"Seems to."

"Like I said, I'll try to be friendly."

I caught the tall one's eye, smiled, waved briefly, and walked across the room to their table, beer in hand. They had been talking and laughing among themselves, but were suddenly silent as I neared. The tall one pretended not to notice me. I stood there for a moment, trying to look smaller than I am, gawky smile on my face, belly pushed out as far as I could get it. Finally, he had to notice.

"Yes?"

"Hey, hope you guys don't mind my interruptin', but I couldn't help noticin' your shirts—you guys really work there at St. Carib, the fat farm?"

The tall one tensed momentarily. He said, "Sir, I'm the director of St. Carib. These are a few of my employees. And none of us likes to hear St. Carib referred to as a fat farm. Understand?"

With the flavor of accent there was a well-practiced coldness in his voice; the chill you get from head-waiters who notice you're not wearing a tie.

"What? Oh, hey, I'm sorry—no offense, you know. Just wondering if I could sit with you a minute, and maybe have you tell me a little about your fat—ah, your facility." I patted myself on the stomach. "You can see I'm gettin' a little pudgy and all, and I was thinkin' about signin' up for a class."

You could tell the thought of me at his plush resort amused him. He cringed visibly. He said, "I'm afraid you would have to take that up with one of my subordinates. They handle all the enrollment. I suggest you write us a letter—or better yet, contact your local Weight Watchers organization."

That got a laugh from the table. One of them chortled something in what sounded like Arabic. The tall one, Matrah, answered back, laughing, then turned his attention again to the piano player. The two Germans said nothing and looked glum.

End of interview.

I ambled back to the bar. Kathy was waiting with a fresh beer.

"With that sparkling personality of yours, you just never meet a stranger, do you?"

I held up crossed fingers. "After only a few words, Matrah and I are as close as this."

"Practically blood brothers, huh?"

"Not quite, but I think if I had called St. Carib a

fat farm again, we would have become blood brothers very soon."

She laughed. "What a charmer you are, Dusky MacMorgan. One in a million. But seriously, is he the guy you're looking for?"

I shrugged. "I don't know. I won't know for a while."

"This becomes more and more mysterious."

"And more and more confidential. Okay?"

She made a playground gesture I hadn't seen in a long time. She twisted her lips between thumb and forefinger. "I just locked the secret and threw away the key."

"You can't ask for better security than that."

Marina Cole came up the steps and into the bar at about eleven. If she was striking before, she was even more striking now. She had unbraided and washed her blond hair, and it hung down over her shoulders and feathered across her cheeks in translucent shades of wheat and gold. She wore a plain blue blouse and a wraparound skirt with tropical flowers on it in yellow and green. And she had stuck a big red hibiscus flower behind her ear. When she walked in, conversations halted abruptly, men turned, and even the bald piano player stumbled momentarily in "Old Cape Cod." As if unaccustomed to such sudden attention, she hurried across the wooden floor and slid into the bar seat beside me.

"You do make an entrance, Marina."

If not for the Gulf Stream tan, I would have guessed she was blushing. "Well, I hadn't had a shower in days, and I had to wash my hair, and— but why in the hell am I embarrassed? At least I'm wearing clothes. You're the one who knows how to make an entrance. Remember?"

We both laughed. I said, "Yeah, but I'm not nearly as pretty as you. Have I said yet that you look very lovely indeed tonight?"

She smiled, a woman who knew how to accept a compliment. "Why thank you, MacMorgan. I appreciate that."

As if on cue, Kathy brought us each a chilled glass of the house white wine. I held up my glass. "Here's to a happy stay on Cabbage Key. May you enjoy your work, then continue on your journey."

She grinned, and we clinked glasses. "And may we both stay off sandbars."

"Right."

So we sipped at our wine and enjoyed the small talk common to new friends; enjoyed that probing ground of conversation that always includes childhood and old loves and, among sailors anyway, favorite boats and stories of storms.

Marina had done her share of sailing, too. While her stock-exchange father stayed home and read about the sea, she was content only with the bulldog approach: She went out and did it. She had crewed for several of the New England ocean racers, then signed on for a transatlantic race that almost cost her her life.

"We were twelve days out from Boston, and that far out it's all big ocean," she told me, the brown eyes glowing, enjoying her own tale. "Our boat was the thirty-eight-foot *Steadfast*, a lovely thing to look at and a dream to handle—and built for that kind of sail, too. We were seven, including the captain, and I was the only woman aboard. I worked hard to prove straightaway that I was there to sail, and not just to do more than my share of the cooking and cleaning, but you know how men are—"

"I know how some men are, if that's what you mean."

She reached over and patted my hand, face showing the proper chagrin. "I guess I should have qualified that."

"And on the other hand, I might be one of the worst."

She studied me momentarily, gave my hand a final squeeze, then continued her story. "Anyway, we were twelve days out and we could just feel that we were about to get it. Around midnight, the bottom dropped out of the barometer. It was eerie still; stars and moon all had a greenish cast, and the big starcut spinnaker we were carrying was dead empty. It was my watch and the captain was asleep below, so I told a couple of the guys to drop that spinnaker and get ready to do some quick reefing. They grumbled about my being overcautious, but thank God they finally did do it—because that squall hit about five minutes later. Really, Dusky, 'squall' seems like too weak a word for the storm that hit. It came blasting down out of Greenland, gusts to ninety knots. Seas went from five-foot swells to twenty-foot combers in no less than ten minutes." She hesitated for a moment, reliving that storm in her own mind. "It all happened so quickly. It was so powerful that it actually took my breath away; I was in awe, my hands white on that big stainless wheel, knowing for the first time in my life that sense of having absolutely no control over my own destiny. Every sea washed us; like getting hit by God or something. As I said, it happened so quickly that no one had had a chance to call the captain. And in a storm like that, command has to change hands very quickly. So one of the guys with me in the cockpit unsnapped his lifeline and decided to try to get below. I knew he shouldn't have tried it; I even yelled and told him not to. Those waves were about washing me away, and I had something to hang onto. But he was the macho type; had to prove himself, and he went anyway. The first crest that hit knocked him flat on his back. And the second washed him overboard. It happened so fast, Dusky, that it seemed like seconds later before I even heard him scream."

"So you lost him?"

She was quiet for a long time. Then she looked at me, a strange wonderment on her face. "No," she said softly. "We had been towing one of those patent logs astern during the day—you know those things with an impeller on a long line that measures speed and distance? At night we'd been hauling it in, for fear we'd get it fouled. Well, it was coiled beside me, and when I saw him go I grabbed the log, unsnapped my lifeline, and went over after him." She rubbed at her forehead absently, as if perplexed by her own actions on that stormy night long ago. "I can't really describe what I was feeling at that moment, Dusky. There was no fear involved. In that microsecond of decision it seemed that for the first and only time in my life, I was totally *free*. Free of everything . . . earthly, I guess. It was so simple. Just unsnap the lifeline and . . . and *go*."

She was quiet then, lost in the depths of her empty wineglass.

"You got him?"

"Yes," she said softly. "I don't know how. I got a grip on his foul-weather jacket, then he got a hold on the line. By that time, the others realized what had happened, and they helped haul us in." She looked up quickly, her eyes searching mine. "You know, Dusky, that story's been told a lot. But never by me. You're the first person I've ever told. It's such a private thing—that moment, that single moment of total freedom—that it would have seemed like a kind of blasphemy to go telling it around. It happened six years ago, and I guess I've spent those years trying to recapture that feeling. I worked briefly in one of the European branches of my father's office, but I

75

was too restless for that. So I worked at a French sailing school for a while, tried sky diving, got an adolescent interest in politics—my socialist period. Then I decided mountain climbing in Nepal was the thing to do—you know, find the secret of life on the highest peak." She laughed shortly. "But the only thing I found in Nepal was a case of dysentery that just about did kill me. After that I spent a year experimenting with drugs. All kinds, but hallucinogens mostly. Drugs are such a lovely lie—and as deadly as they are lovely. Luckily, I realized that before it was too late. So then I went back to work for my father's business, made enough money to buy my own sailboat, and here I am."

I signaled Kathy, and she brought us more wine. Marina's hand trembled slightly as she brought the glass to her lips. In the soft light of the little bar, beneath the whirling shadows of the ceiling fan and the clinking grace of the old piano, I thought I had never seen a woman so lovely. I found myself taking her hand in mine.

"Thank you," I said.

She laughed nervously. "It must have sounded like I was boasting, but I wasn't. . . ."

"I know, Marina, I know. That's why I thanked you. You're a rare person, and I'm honored that you told me."

Her eyes searched mine. "And I don't even know why I told you. We've only just met, and I barely know you. But there's something in your eyes; I don't understand your . . . your eyes. But they make me trust you."

"Enough to answer just one personal question?"

She nodded, suddenly wary. "I guess. Sure."

"In the entire story, you never mentioned your husband. Why?"

She shrugged. "There's not much to tell, really. And it's not a particularly interesting story."

"I'm interested. More and more."

For the first time, she looked girlish, almost shy. "Oh. Well. . . ." She took a deep breath, swirling the wine within her glass. "That fellow I went overboard to save? We were married upon our arrival in London. I really don't know why I married him, Dusky. I guess because, at the time, he seemed somehow intimately a part of that . . . that special moment. It didn't take me long to realize that he had nothing to do with it; it could have been anyone—or anything. That thing I felt—that instant of immunity from fear, life, death, and everything else—had nothing to do with anyone but me. But I realized it too late. My father warned me; he was totally against the marriage, but for different reasons. Called the guy a 'goddam foreigner,' and that just made me more determined to go through with it. I was only twenty at the time."

"So you're divorced now?"

The wistfulness in my voice wasn't well disguised. I expected her to laugh, but she didn't. She shook her head. "No," she said, "I'm still married. We were together only that first year. Even then he didn't bother to disguise his bouts with other women. A discreet affair or two I could have handled. But not having it thrown in my face, the way he did. And plus I just didn't love him. But it didn't take him long to get involved with my father's investment business. And once he had a foothold in the family fortune, there was just no getting rid of him. He vowed to contest any attempt at divorce. And my father switched sides, of all things. He admired my husband's 'business instincts,' as he put it—foreigner or not. After that, I just said to hell with it, began using my own last name, and took off on my own. A marriage is just paper unless you make it work— or start dividing properties through the courts. So I decided to just ignore it."

"But I don't understand," I said. "Yesterday morning, when I asked if you were going to meet your husband at Cabbage Key, you said—"

"I said stranger things happen. And they do. My husband is involved in a ritzy health resort my father's corporation runs near here."

"You mean your husband is over at St. Carib," I said incredulously.

"Better than that," she said, a bitter smile on her face. She turned and nodded at Matrah, the tall Mediterranean. He had an odd grin on his face, glaring at me.

"Much, much better than that, Dusky. That's my beloved husband sitting right over there. . . ."

7

"Would you like to meet him, Dusky?" Marina asked, the sour smile still on her face. And with the smile I thought I read just the slightest hint of fear.

"Looks like I don't have much choice in the matter, lady. He's headed this way."

Matrah stood up, lurched with drunken imprecision past his staff, and walked evenly across the floor. I got a good look at him for the first time. He was taller than I am—about six three, six four. He had wide gymnast's shoulders that narrowed quickly at the chest, then piped down into a pair of expensive gray slacks. The pants were tight enough to advertise the bulge of male organ so necessary in the minds of the disco dancers, bar hoppers, and the other machismo freaks. The grin had changed to a leer, and he slid between our two bar stools, his back to me, plundering what the psychologists call our "personal space."

It was a calculated move at intimidation, and I had no choice but to slide my stool back passively.

And listen.

I couldn't believe the sudden change that came over Marina Cole. Her voice tightened around the nervous smile, and her right hand came to rest upon her lap like some kind of subconscious guardian.

Matrah said, "Marina, my dear. You told me earlier this afternoon that you were going to bed and couldn't be bothered tonight. It's so unlike you to lie." He put a little something extra into the word "lie," his tone grandiose but biting.

"Well, Matrah, I had almost an entire year to learn about lying from the best, now didn't I?"

He let that roll off. I could see they were in for a nasty bout of verbal fencing unless I did something to break the rhythm.

But what?

"Marina," he said more loudly—playing for the benefit of his table, obviously—"would you like to join us for a drink and a bit of conversation? Or would you rather sit here alone? After all, we are both civilized human beings, and I am your hus—"

"Oh, I'm anything but alone, Matrah," she said, cutting him off. "And I have no desire to spend the evening being bored. But you haven't met my friend, have you? Matrah, this is Dusky MacMorgan."

He gave me a quick glance over his shoulder, his eyes holding about the same degree of interest he would bestow on a stray dog.

"I've already had the pleasure," he said.

There was a brief look of surprise from Marina.

Matrah continued, "Your friend was asking me earlier about the facilities at St. Carib—you haven't seen the place, by the way, have you? Your father was so disappointed when you refused his invitation. Your friend said that he was interested in enrolling; said he needed to lose some of that stomach. I quite agreed—but recommended he contact Weight Watchers. More in his economic stratum, you see."

The accent was somewhere between Saudi and British, and every word was armed. I forced myself to relax; told myself that this was just one more drunk looking for trouble, and I gave up my love of schoolground fisticuffs long, long ago.

But he didn't have much farther to push before I allowed myself to regress.

"Marina," I said, checking my watch, "didn't you say you were interested in a boat ride? I've got to get up early, and if we're to get out at all . . ."

She was quick to grab at the exit. "Absolutely," she said. She turned to the tall Mediterranean. "Matrah," she said, "if you decide to become reasonable about that matter we discussed, then I'll be happy to talk with you. If not, please stay out of my way. You just don't seem to understand that I don't want to spend *my* life waiting around to save *yours* again."

And with that she brushed past him, headed for the rest room, leaving him the uncontested loser in their verbal battle. She had gone for the jugular and hit it squarely. His face reddened, his dark eyes bulged, and his hands were clenched into fists. Behind him, I heard the two Germans laughing for the first time. Unlike their two darker counterparts, they had enjoyed Matrah's humiliation.

"*Bitch,*" he whispered harshly, between clenched teeth. "You surly bitch."

"Not very nice talk, Matt old buddy," I said, standing to face him. The gawking smile, the slope of shoulders, were both forced. I wanted to look smaller, slower than I am. I had had just about enough of this character on one level. He was just one more self-important, self-styled aristocrat in a world ass-deep in such creeps. But on another level, there was something more: It was the ancient conflict of one man against another, ready to fight for the favor of a woman.

It's rarely a good reason to fight; in fact, there's hardly ever a *good* reason to go one-on-one with fists and elbows and feet.

But the prospect of taking this guy down a peg or two was a little too attractive to pass up.

He whirled toward me. "*You*—you keep out of this, fat man!" His thin chin was arrowed down at me, face red, eyes wide, taking every advantage of his height to look big and fearsome.

I heard Kathy's voice from behind the bar. She had watched the whole scene quietly until now. "Dusky," she said, "Rob doesn't stand for this sort of thing— you know that. Not inside, anyway."

There was a light smile on her face. She didn't want the fight stopped; just wanted the battleground changed. I shrugged. "I guess we're both being a little silly, huh?" I held out my hand toward him. "How 'bout it, Matt ol' buddy? Let's shake hands and call it quits."

He hesitated, then slapped my hand away with a resounding *whack*. "My name, fat man, is Matrah!" And with that he whirled and stormed out of the bar, through the porch, and outside toward the docks. The other two Mediterranean types hurried off behind him, casting ugly looks at me.

I turned to Kathy. "Mind if I settle my bill in the morning?"

She had a wry look on her face. "Maybe you'd better take care of it now—just in case you're not around tomorrow."

"Thanks for the vote of confidence."

She laughed. "There *are* three of them."

"So that makes the odds just about right."

"I'll get a full report in the morning, then. I hate fights, but I would like to see that guy humbled just a bit."

"We can only hope," I said. I nodded toward the women's rest room on the back porch. "When Marina comes out, have her wait ten or fifteen minutes before she comes down to the boat?"

"Got it, skipper."

As I went through the bar outside, one of the Germans surprised me by calling me over. He was a huge man with thin blond hair, and pockmarks on his face that suggested a bad case of acne during adolescence. Trying to hide some of the scars, apparently, he had grown a heavy blond mustache and a reddish beard. The beard was full-face, closely cropped. The mustache swooped Fu Manchu–like beneath a grotesquely red nose that had suffered the brunt of the adolescent skin disease. I approached him cautiously. If he was one of Matrah's friends, he might try to end the fight before it even began. And he was big enough to maybe do just that.

I stopped across the table from the two. They were both still smiling. I said, "You're not going to come and watch your friend at work?"

The biggest one, the one who had called me over, laughed out loud. And he said in a deep German accent, "I would not call him the friend—correct, Hans?" They both laughed again, far enough into the scotch to find anything funny. He looked up, wiping his eyes. "No, my American friend, I called you over just to give you the bit of advice." He stood up and wrapped his arm around me, voice whispering in collusion. "Watch for his feet. Do you understand? He arrived at St. Carib only a few weeks ago, but already he has had two such . . . encounters? And he likes to use his feet to get things finished fastly. Am I being plain? *Between the legs*, my American friend, *between the legs*!"

"Plain enough," I said as the big German sat back down. "But why the advice?"

He made an empty motion with his hands. "He is a little too . . . pompous? Yes, pompous. I have been with St. Carib since the beginning. Now he arrives and treats us all like stupid goats. I will work for him because I must." He raised his glass, grinning. "And Hans and I will drink his whiskey—because we want to! But in such business as this, I must find myself on the other side of the . . . yard?" He slapped his hand on the table good-naturedly. Hans roared at that. The big German jumped quickly to his feet and held out his hand. "I am Heinrich Keppler, ya? And I already have heard that you are Dusky . . . ?"

"Dusky MacMorgan. And thanks for the advice, Heinrich."

"Heiny! *Heiny*—my friends all call me Heiny."

As I walked outside, Heiny and Hans were still calling out advice and luck, roaring with laughter and ordering more scotch, suddenly having a very good time in the absence of their superior.

Matrah was waiting for me at the base of the mound near the white clapboard dockhouse.

His two friends stood behind him in the shadows.

I took my time getting there; walked a swaying path, trying to use the dock lights to catch a glimmer of a knife or firearm.

I saw none. But I was still cautious. Even in a bar fight, lack of caution can spell death. I unsnapped the holster of my Gerber belt knife, opened the blade, and placed the knife gingerly in the flap pocket of my khaki fishing shorts.

I would use it only if Matrah produced something equally lethal.

85

He was hunched and ready when I arrived. His two friends pulled in closer now. Matrah was in the typical karate fighting stance, one bladed hand high, the other low.

"Hey, what's this?" I said innocently. "I thought you guys were going home." As I spoke I was getting closer and closer, gauging the distance between Matrah and myself, studying the angles between Matrah and his two friends. I knew what I wanted to do; knew what I had to do. If I went after—and disabled—Matrah first, the other two would jump me then. And that was anyone's ball game. I wanted to do things nice and neat; take them all by surprise.

Counting on Heiny's advice, I walked bowlegged, trying to give Matrah an obvious target. His friends were only an arm's length behind him now.

"Look, you fellas, I sure don't want to fight. Don't you think we can work this out?"

"Hear the coward now!" Matrah sputtered, still low, still ready.

"Oh, jeez, don't call me a coward—" I was close enough now, and with his right foot, Matrah sent a blazing kick toward my crotch. I sidestepped it, gave him a solid crack behind the ear with my elbow, and in the same swift motion smacked one of the Mediterraneans with an overhand right, then hit the other flush on the nose with a cross-body left hand. They both went back-pedaling onto their butts, holding their faces.

I turned. Matrah was just getting up. "As I was

saying—don't call me a coward, because it really pisses me off, Matt old buddy."

"You bastard!" He came lunging at me, arms grabbing me around the waist, knees pounding away at my crotch. One or two of the knees found their mark, and I felt the swift nausea, the beading of sweat on forehead. I cracked down hard with my elbow on the kidney area of his back, and when he recoiled I grabbed him solidly by the throat and backed him up against the bathhouse wall.

"Carry this any farther, Matt old buddy, and you're going to go whistling around this island like a balloon with a bad valve. Got it?"

Dark eyes bulging, he nodded carefully.

Behind me then I heard the two Germans coming at a heavy run. They had obviously been watching from the top of the mound. Heiny was yelling at me—his theatrics a little too obvious to be believable.

"Let him go, you American pig! Let him go before he squashes you like an ant!"

I felt Heiny's big hands go gently around my shoulders. I let him pull me away. While Hans helped the two Mediterraneans to their feet, Heiny pulled me farther away from the stunned Matrah, whispering as he did, "We must keep up appearances, my tough American friend." He giggled drunkenly. "My advice—you listened! But if I allowed you to kill him, I could not enjoy the look of defeat on his face tomorrow."

He glanced anxiously back at Matrah, then whispered again. "Do you mind if I give you a little shove—for appearance's sake?"

"For appearance's sake—but not too hard. I'm feeling a little sick. He got me with one of those knees—damn."

"Soak them in cold water—that is the best thing." He gave me a gingerly shove, and I added a bit of theatrics myself, falling to the ground.

"Let that be a teaching to you, American!" Heiny yelled, gathering up Matrah and the other Mediterraneans. "Do not have another encounter such as this, or next time you will not be so fortunate!"

Heiny and Hans were still yelling bogus threats and deadly promises at me when they got into St. Carib's sleek Excalibur and powered down the channel toward their island home.

I allowed myself a few minutes to recover, trying to get my wind back, waiting for the sweat shakes to dissolve. I had come damn close to killing Matrah; too damn close. I was shaking from that more than anything else. Had I allowed myself to go on, what would have happened to my mission? It's hard to keep a low profile when you're in jail on murder charges—however justified.

In fact, I was probably stupid to get involved in a fight at all.

I wasn't sticking to my game plan. I'd lost touch with my role: that of the fat blundering American, too stupid to be on the search for anything, too weak to do anything about it if I did find something.

When I had finally settled down, I went limping back up the mound to the old inn. Marina and Kathy sat side by side at the now-empty bar. They both looked up when they heard the screen door slam.

Marina looked worried. Kathy was laughing. "You're still alive and well?"

"Alive, anyway. Matrah was very quiet and polite when he left."

Marina came to me, hugged me unexpectedly, and slid her hand into mine. "Good," she said firmly. "He's had that coming for a long, long time."

There was an awkward moment between the three of us. And in the silence, I said hurriedly, "Well, I guess I just came up here to say goodnight to you two. It's been a long day—"

"You're not going to bed yet," Marina said evenly. Then she allowed herself a vixen smile. "You promised to take me for a boat ride. Remember?"

"Ah . . . boat ride. Right."

She led me out the door, tall with flaxen hair drifting behind her like a veil. And Kathy called behind us, "Just be back by seven, Marina. That's breakfast, and a waitress's work is never done around here!"

8

So we got aboard *Sniper*, and idled her down the midnight channel beneath March stars. Ahead, an intercoastal waterway marker flashed with a red precision that seemed to suggest haven in the darkness. The wind had disappeared with nightfall, as if sucked away in the sudden vacuum of sun, and Pine Island Sound was a reflection of constellations.

Marina handled the lines flawlessly, did everything that needed to be done without being told, then joined me on the open flybridge. She settled into the swivel seat beside me with a sigh.

"Do you mind my forcing you into this, Dusky?"

I reached over and took her hand. "You've been nothing but trouble, Miss Marina Cole. I hate being out here alone with a beautiful woman—and a married woman at that. But I would hate it a lot more if you took the wheel while I went below and grabbed us a beer to share."

She pressed me back into my seat gently. "You

take the wheel and I'll get two beers—then we can both be very unhappy."

She returned with a brace of icy Tuborgs, and stuck mine already opened in the holder beside the wheel.

"So where do you want to go, lady?"

"Anywhere. I . . . I don't know why, but when you get used to living on a boat, it's always hard to spend that first night under a roof. Maybe I just want to put it off. Claustrophobia or something, I guess." And then she added lamely, "I guess that sounds silly, huh?"

"Very silly," I said. "That's why I live on that stilt-house way out on the water by myself. If it's silly, we're both silly."

We had left the moment of spontaneous touching behind at Cabbage Key: the unexpected hug, the taking of my hand in hers. Two strangers alone, we had entered the clumsy, uncomfortable time of prospective lovers—uncomfortable because we have all seen it rehearsed again and again on a million television screens. You find yourself sliding into the practiced routines of the buxomed starlets and the square-jawed heros, so that even the honest gesture of affection begins to ring untrue.

So I was content to steer *Sniper* toward a pretty little harbor I knew—a deepwater retreat within the confines of a pine-swept island called Punta Blanco. I did not put my arm around her, nor did she lay her head on my shoulder, but there was still the physical awareness, the deep wanting—yet we were both content to simply ride and enjoy the night.

Marina asked me why I lived alone, and I told her. Recounting the deaths of loved ones is always painful, and I go out of my way not to talk about it. But somehow it seemed easier telling her. She made no obligatory "oohs" and "ahs" of sympathy. She listened carefully, her eyes bespeaking the horror she felt. And when I was done, she was quiet for a long time. Finally she said, "You had that time with them, Dusky."

And she was right. It was a philosophy eloquent for its simplicity. We had had our time together. There was a Zen-like toughness in the acceptance of that—but a very comforting honesty, too.

We had had our time together. It was not a matter of quantity, but of quality. One year or a hundred years—the mathematics of it made no difference. The essence of human emotion should wear no timepiece, because you can live neither in the past nor the future.

There is only the present.

You live and love and work in the very heart of a moment, because everything else is a memory. Or an illusion.

"You've made me feel somehow better about it all, Marina," I said. "And for some reason, that makes me feel . . . a little guilty, I guess. Silly, huh?"

She reached over and gently traced the line of my

face with her fingertip. "It means you cared for them very, very much."

"I did."

"And what happened to the man who murdered them?"

I felt my hands tighten on the steering wheel, remembering.

"Not one man—many men. There was a big drug operation on an island near Key West. The law couldn't seem to touch them because there was an important politician involved. They are the ones who killed my family—but by mistake. They were trying to kill me."

"You were involved?"

I shook my head. "Not hardly." And then I lied intentionally. "They somehow got the idea I was in their way, so they sent a couple of hit men after me. The law couldn't touch them, but another drug gang could. One night that little island haven of theirs became a battleground. You could see the glow of the fire clear back in Key West. Apparently, the drug gang that attacked ended up big winners. All but one of my family's murderers were killed—and he's still running for his life somewhere in South America."

Marina studied me shrewdly. "You don't look like a gang of drugrunners to me."

I tried to look incredulous. "Me? I wish I'd had the nerve to go after those guys."

"The scars you have—the one on your cheek, and

that awful scar on your thigh. You got those playing football or baseball, or something like that, right?"

She was smiling. I said, "You're awfully nosy, woman."

"And I have very good instincts. There's something about you I like very much, MacMorgan. I still can't put my finger on it. Maybe it's because you make me feel safe. Not because you're big and rough-looking, but because there's a quality of honesty about you. And honest people are very bad liars. Did you know that?"

I said nothing.

"You are a very bad liar, MacMorgan."

"So that makes me basically honest?"

"No, but you are. I can tell. And I can also tell you're not one of the sheep. I've got this theory—see what you think. You can divide the world's people into three categories. The Sheep, who do the following and the drone work. The Lions, who do the manipulating and the ruling. And then you have a third group, the Rogues. They live their lives independently, outside the boundaries of conformity. They do not live that way just for the sake of nonconformity, but because some inner instinct demands they live that way. And you, Dusky MacMorgan, are definitely a Rogue. Furthermore, a Rogue warrior. That's the very rarest breed of Rogue. The few that *are* around, you find living on mountaintops, or in the depths of the north woods. Or on a house built on stilts two miles out to sea." She reached over and kissed me warmly on the cheek. "So no, I don't believe that you would leave your revenge to someone else. I'm not saying that's good—I'm just saying you wouldn't."

"You're just trying to turn my pretty head, lady."

"No, I'm just saying I have my instincts. Maybe I got them from my father—he's a Lion, by the way. Just as Matrah is a Lion. They use their instincts to manipulate and control. Neither of them has any emotional interest in St. Carib, or any of their other businesses, for that matter. They are only interested in the manipulation of their businesses. To them, life is just one giant chessboard, and they use businesses and their workers like pawns. All their instincts are focused in that direction. Maybe the two of them drove me to life as a Rogue." She shrugged.

"Is this a confession?"

I expected her to laugh, but she didn't. She looked at me seriously. "No," she said, "it's a fact. It's been a very long time since I've been with a man, Mac-Morgan. And the only kind of man that interests me is another Rogue. I guess that's why I feel I can be open with you; open and honest. I don't want to waste a moment with you. You don't know how tempted I was to stay with you yesterday morning. All the way from Key West to Cabbage Key on that sailboat alone, I thought about you, and swore at myself for wearing this stupid ring. I wear it as protection—it keeps the male Sheep and Lions away." She stopped, wind mussing her long blond hair beneath starlight, pulled the wedding ring off, and tossed it over her shoulder into the black wake of *Sniper*. "I'm not making a confession, MacMorgan," she said softly. "I'm telling you why I want to sleep with you tonight. And every other night that we can."

I felt the brown eyes lock on mine. I lifted my bottle of Tuborg. "Here's to two Rogues," I said.

She touched her bottle to mine. "And to the time we have together," she said.

I brought *Sniper* carefully through the shoal waters of Punta Blanco and around to the west side into the empty deepwater harbor. One of the local fishing guides had shown me the place long ago. In back times, there had been a wooden schoolhouse on the island for the fishermen's kids of Pine Island Sound. The schoolhouse had long ago burned, the fishermen had left their desultory lives of seclusion for the ease of homes in Fort Myers and Sanibel, but the harbor remained.

I backed *Sniper* while Marina handled the anchor line, snubbing it at my signal. I switched off engines and running lights, leaving us to the feathered silhouettes of Australian pine, the night bird sounds of the deserted island, and the soft exhalations of sea moving upon beach.

Marina came to me, a silver-haired mist in the darkness. Her lips were soft and warm. At first gentle, then searching. We stood clinging together on the aft deck, she upon tiptoes, my arms full around the heat of her.

"Hope you don't think I'm always this easy," I said.

She giggled like a teenager. "Your reputation's already shot. No going back now."

"And I've tried to lead such a clean life."

"The word's out, MacMorgan: Tap twice on your head, and your pants come down."

"Your hands seem to be busy with anything but my head."

"I'm trying to figure out the combination of this damn belt. There!"

Her wraparound skirt slid down with the tug of a string. She wore narrow bikini panties, and her legs tapered long and tanned and lean beneath the flare of thighs.

"Does this shirt of yours have buttons, or what?"

She said, breathing becoming heavier now, "Don't . . . bother me with questions . . . MacMorgan. I'm . . . ah . . . busy."

She was busy indeed. There *were* buttons, and neither of us minded when they went skittering across the deck, shirt open, revealing wide small breasts thrust upward, nipples pale and elongated.

So in the March night, beneath sky fresh with the sudden loss of wind, we came together with the ancient fervor of new lovers. On the aft deck we coupled in a frenzy of the love-starved. There was an animal wanting in her, a passion that demanded my full attention. She had told me that it had been a very long time since she had been with a man, and her whole body said it again and again.

And after that first time, I cradled her in my arms, lips buried in her soft hair, nose enjoying the salt and shampoo odor that was the scent of her.

"You're crying, lady?"

She sniffed. "God, yes. It was like . . . a dam breaking, or something. My stoicism . . . I pay for it. It all builds and builds and builds." She reached up, kissed me with salty lips. "Thank you," she said. "I feel almost empty now."

"Almost?"

Her kiss became passionate then; she rolled over on top of me, her body slick with our earlier laboring, and kissed my chest.

"Now it's my turn," she said, "to break a dam."

"It's been broken once, lady."

Her voice was husky. "I noticed. But not this way. . . ."

I pulled into the dock at Cabbage Key just before sunrise. On the island, birds were making bright morning sounds, and a silver haze was lifting over the white house and golf course expanse of Useppa Island to the east. As we walked the docks and up the mound, a few fishermen getting an early start passed us. I had my arm around Marina, her head soft on my shoulder, and she did not pull away.

"I want them to know," she said, nuzzling me. "I want the whole world to know."

"The world might be bored by such news, lady."

"Good. I want to bore the world to death, then."

"You sound enthusiastic."

"I am, MacMorgan. I'm going to work hard all day, and then work harder again with you tonight."

"I'm afraid that's a maybe."

She pulled away from me, face showing surprise. It was such a petulant look of childlike disappointment that I had to laugh.

"It's not what you think, Marina. You're going to be seeing a lot of me—whether you want to or not. But I really did come up here on business. And I've got to take care of it."

She hesitated, as if about to ask what my business was, then decided not to. "Okay," she said. "But you're not really thinking of enrolling at St. Carib as Matrah said last night, are you?"

"I could stand to lose a little weight."

She hugged herself against me again. "I think I can say objectively that everything about your body is in the very right place. I took a couple of long looks last night, remember?"

"Vaguely."

"You need a quick reminder, I see," she said vampishly.

I checked my watch. "And you need to get ready to wait breakfast tables."

She threw up her hands, laughing. "Okay, okay. But when you're through with your business, sailor, you'd better look me up."

"And down?"

"And down."

While Marina went to her little cottage quarters to grab a shower, I found the key to my room and went into the old house to get my duffel bag. Only the cooks were up, the smell of bacon and potatoes frying filling the inn. I tiptoed down the hallway like a teenager getting in late from a date, found my room, and went inside.

I have an old habit. It came from a time in Vietnam when the wrong people were trying to nose into my business. Before leaving any rented room, I yank a hair from my head and paste it across the duffel zipper, then wad up a small piece of paper and drop it behind the door. Anyone entering the room moves the wad of paper. Anyone tampering with my duffel moves the hair.

It's very very simple—and most effective.

Because I wasn't expecting it, it took me a while to notice that my wad of paper was shoved clear against the wall. Someone had swung the door wide open—and it wasn't me.

I had left the duffel on top of the bed. I switched on the overhead light and studied the zipper.

The hair was gone.

I opened the duffel and went carefully through the contents: Wilkinson razor and extra blades, a change of clothes, a fresh can of Copenhagen, a small notebook with the names and telephone numbers of the locals I knew, and three hundred dollars in cash.

It was all there. I wished I had rigged the notebook in some way to let me know if someone had opened it.

I neatly replaced the contents, switched off the light, and swung the door closed behind me.

It took me a while to locate Rob Wells. He was out in the yard pushing his little blond son in a swing that hung on ropes from a limb of a mammoth live oak. When he saw me coming, he patted the boy on the head and told him to go play, and his son went whooping and laughing down toward the water, their liver-colored pointer trotting after him.

"You're looking sleepy this morning, Dusky." He grinned.

"Such a pretty evening last night, I couldn't sleep."

"And I heard you had some trouble at the bar, too."

"Not all that much trouble, really."

He nodded. "Usually I take a very dim view of fighting on the island. Almost never have any trouble that way. But with that character Matrah, I'll make an exception. Heard you stuck him pretty good."

"That guy seems to make enemies very very quickly," I said.

"He does seem to have a talent for it. Took over St. Carib two or three weeks ago. Their first director was no gem, but this guy is even worse. Wears that superior attitude of his like a hat. I think I'm going to bar him from the grounds altogether. It's either that or lose some of my best help—they flip to see who has to wait on him. The loser gets the job."

"You know anything about his background—where he came from, what his specialties are?"

Rob shook his head. "I think he's Egyptian. Or Arab—something like that. And he owns a very big piece of St. Carib, and he and his associates weren't entirely pleased with the way it was being run, so he came down to take the reins himself. That's about it, I guess. . . . Oh, there is one more thing—he likes guns. Kind of a hobby, apparently. You know I occasionally have a turkey shoot out here. For the locals, mostly. But he got wind of the one I had last week, and he came over here with some kind of Belgian over-and-under that was just magnificent. And he knew how to use it. Won the shoot without breaking a sweat. And didn't even have the courtesy to act pleased. Just acted bored by it all. After that, we got into a short conversation about firearms—not so much because he wanted to talk to me, it was more like . . . like he wanted to show me and everyone else that he knew a lot more than we did. Know what I mean?"

"I do indeed."

I hesitated, trying to find a delicate way to ask my next question. Finally I decided there was no delicate way. I said, "Rob, I wasn't in my room last night. But I think someone else was."

There was a real look of concern on his face. "You mean someone stole something? That's never happened—"

"No, no—nothing missing. But I could just tell someone had been in there looking around."

"No chance of its being the help," he said quickly. "But who in the heck could it have been?"

"It's not important. In fact, it could have just been my imagination. I thought maybe someone had gone in to check the fireplace, or change the sheets, or—"

"No chance," he said. "I wasn't here last night, but I know that for sure."

He walked me down the mound, asking when I would be back, and if I could stay longer next time. I told him I had every hope. As he helped me with *Sniper*'s lines, I asked him the final question, trying to make it seem offhand, unimportant.

"I think there's a friend of mine staying around here someplace. He's a big good-looking guy—dark hair, the kind of face you see in the Rockwell paintings. His name is Fizer. Norm Fizer. He would have been here in one of the Boca Grande rental boats."

Rob thought for a moment. "I think there was a guy around here a couple of days ago who looked like that. I remember because he put the waitresses in a flutter—real good-looking guy, right? They thought maybe he was one of the movie stars from St. Carib. But he didn't say much. Kind of sat in a corner talking with somebody."

"Do you remember who he was talking to?"

Rob's eyes looked skyward, scanning his memory. He said, "Yeah, I do, now that you ask. That's why the waitresses thought he was from St. Carib. The guy he was talking to—it was Matrah. . . ."

9

Aboard *Sniper*, I cruised reluctantly past the palm trees and white houses of St. Carib.

I had heard all too much about the place, far too quickly. I had a gut feeling that whatever went wrong would go wrong there. There was the stink of international money behind it: Matrah, Marina's father, and probably a number of other unknown interests.

But I had a job to do, and that job demanded I check out all the possibilities.

So I made my way up the intercoastal waterway, past St. Carib and Mandango, and entered the rough cross-chop of Boca Grande Pass, taking care to stay well away from the rocks on Cayo Costa where the old quarantine station once stood.

Finally, it was a day that seemed summerlike: pale wind drifting in the fresh heat of morning, and beaches an iridescent white beneath a potent sun.

After some consideration, I decided to pull into the

docks at the Pink Elephant—a public house that, like most of Boca Grande, had retained the old Southern grandeur of Florida. There were a few other boats there, and I went inside the bar for a quick lunch and a beer.

The place was almost empty, cool and dark with ceiling fans, and it took my eyes a while to adjust. I paused momentarily to look at the mounted fish in their glass case, then went on inside and took a seat.

And I was midway through my cheeseburger and chilled potato salad when the tall, good-looking waitress suddenly returned to my table.

"Everything all right?"

"Fine," I said. "Great."

She took something out of her apron. "A guy sitting over there in the corner asked me to give you this." She handed me a note, carefully folded.

I waited until she had gone to read it.

It said: "Meet me at the bench in front of the old train depot in twenty-five minutes."

There was no signature.

I took my time, yawned, and glanced around nonchalantly. He sat at a table with three burly-looking men in bleak, ill-fitting suits. They ate full lunches. He drank tea in a tall iced glass. The face and the shaved head were unmistakable: It was D. Harold Westervelt.

I checked my Rolex and marked the meeting time in my mind. D. Harold looked up, eyes sweeping past me without recognition. He nodded curtly.

So I finished my lunch, left a five for the pretty waitress, and went outside into the bright sunlight.

The village of Boca Grande has all the quiet class of a small New England town. You can walk down the middle of the main street at noon and not worry about getting hit by a car. The small white churches seem to glow with a celestial light, and broad oaks and banyan trees shadow the side streets. It is a rare place among the tacky postcard and trailer-park grotesqueries that most other Florida towns have become. True, the profit-hungry developers are converting the north end of the island into a catacomb of condominiums. But the downtown area remains quiet and quaint with its drugstore and the filling station, and the deserted train depot with its 1920 streetlights.

And the town has stayed that way not because of some lofty concern from its county commission or planning board—anything but. If it was left to them, they would sit by blinking like stray cats while one of the big money developers coated the entire west coast with asphalt.

No, it has stayed that way because the people who live there have bigger money. And in Florida, money is the only voice the politicians really listen to. Boca Grande is peopled by the unlikely mixing of true Florida crackers with America's old-money families, family names we all recognize because we buy the products their conglomerates manufacture, or see their names in the jet-set social registers. The crackers who live there don't want the village to change, and the wealthy, who treasure their beachside lives of seclusion, have enough money to stop outsiders from trying.

So I walked on down to the docks at Knight's marina, traded jokes with a couple of Captiva fishing guides, Mike Fuery and Doug Fisher, who just happened to be there, then walked back to the deserted train depot at the appointed hour.

I was a little early—as usual.

And D. Harold Westervelt was right on time—as usual.

He sat at the far end of the park bench, as far away from me as he could get. Without looking at me, he said, "I was beginning to wonder if you were going to arrive on Boca Grande, captain."

"I stopped at Cabbage Key. I may be on to something."

He raised his eyebrows. "Good," he said. "Excellent."

"Do you want a report now?"

Without shaking his head, he said, "In a minute. This meeting must be very brief—for obvious reasons. You're probably surprised to see me up here. Frankly, I wasn't anxious to come. I've a great deal of work to do back in Key West, and this has thrown my schedule completely off."

"Any word on Fizer?"

"Still missing. His wife took it very hard—but was brave all the same. She's still holding some hope. I recommended she be prepared for the worst. I'm afraid I know all too well how FEAT works. Unless there's a ransom involved, they don't deal with prisoners."

"But they've never had to deal with Norm Fizer before."

D. Harold actually allowed himself a smile. "That's true. Captain Fizer would be a very hard man to kill—like yourself." Then he added meaningfully, "Hard to kill. But not impossible."

He straightened the sunglasses he was wearing and pulled the broad-rimmed straw hat down lower on his head. The combination of the two made him look like some tourist from Ohio—no doubt the desired effect.

"But I didn't call you here to talk about Captain Fizer," he said. "There's been a change of plans—and it should simplify things for you. Those men I was having lunch with—all KGB high command. They know who I am and what I do, and I am very aware of their work, so there was no need for deception—not on this level, anyway. Actually, one is an old friend. Worked for the British SIS during the Second World War. He was one of the head men in the British double-cross network that specialized in catching German agents and converting them. Devastated the Nazis. He was so successful at that, no one ever suspected that he was a Russian double agent. But he was. The Russians have a way of getting good people. Now he pretty much runs the show over there. Top-flight group, the KGB. This is the first time since the war I've had a chance to work *with* them."

"They're on to FEAT?"

Colonel Westervelt chuckled. "After being so badly embarrassed by that cobalt business, the Russians made a special point to learn all they could about it. Yes, Captain MacMorgan, they know about FEAT—and probably a good deal more than we do. We traded a few scraps of information over lunch, both of us careful not to help the other. But you know how that goes. Later, we might get down to exchanging some real information. But the important thing is, they've learned about the possibility of their Kiev Evenki's being assassinated. And I must say, they weren't too pleased at the prospect of using one of their top people like a sacrificial lamb."

"Can't say as I blame them."

"Oh, it has nothing to do with any humanitarian feelings. If they could join this hunt for FEAT's assassin and make the kill themselves, they'd be all for it. Even said that if our man—which is you—used their SVD Dragunov sniper rifle, they might go along with it. That way their Pravda and Radio Moscow could make a show of claiming responsibility for the score."

"That sounds pretty cold-blooded—and premature. I have a few ideas who FEAT's man might be, but strictly speculation."

Westervelt eyed me sharply. "Very briefly, tell me who it might be. And why you think so."

So I told him about Matrah; about his investment background, his Mediterranean heritage, and his being seen talking with Fizer before his disappearance.

"Interesting," he said. "Quite interesting. I've heard this fellow Matrah's name before. It took me a moment to realize where." He turned and glanced at me for the first time. "I said that I would have your acquaintance Marina Cole checked out. His name was mentioned there—her husband, correct?"

"That didn't take long."

"It was a very brief, very superficial report. The information we have came from the obvious places: schools, county records, police reports."

"Police reports!"

"Seems Miss Cole had some trouble in Casablanca several years ago. She was arrested for the possession of drugs."

"She told me about that," I said, lying only partially. She had told me about her early experimentation with drugs.

Westervelt shrugged. "It was only a minor thing. Her father's wallet spared her the embarrassment of a light prison sentence. Other than that, she seems to be a pretty benign figure. Of course, she does have connections—through her husband and father—with the international money market that might make her a suspect. . . ."

"She wasn't in the area when Fizer disappeared," I reminded him.

"Oh, I doubt seriously if she has anything to do

111

with this business. I'm just trying to remind you that FEAT's people come from all walks of life—male and female, American or foreigner." He made a dismissing motion with his hands. "But now I must tell you about the Russian, Kiev Evenki. He arrived this morning, but will be leaving almost immediately. His own KGB people have him more than adequately protected. And so that leaves us with the Israeli, Samuel Yabrud. He will be arriving at St. Carib this afternoon."

"But what if FEAT's target was the Russian? Maybe they'll call the hunt off all together."

"Maybe," Westervelt said. "But of course we can't take the chance. Our agents will stay with him as much as they can while Yabrud goes through the St. Carib course. But there will be some times, apparently, when the course demands that he be alone. St. Carib uses one of those 'experiential education' programs that are so popular now in wildlife schools. You know the sort of thing: People are sent off on an island alone for a day or two to eat roots and berries. The very rich people who enroll there love it. The island staff yells at them and orders them about. Very strict, very military. But these rich folks are so worn by the responsibilities they have in real life, apparently, that they delight in being ordered about like children."

"So if FEAT does decide to hit Samuel Yabrud, you figure it will be at one of those times when he is off alone?"

Colonel D. Harold Westervelt stood up, adjusted his hat carefully. "If you were FEAT's assassin, isn't that what you would do, captain?"

And with that, he walked away from me, down the quiet streets of Boca Grande.

Now my fight with Matrah seemed like a bigger mistake than ever. And I swore at myself softly as I powered *Sniper* away from the docks of the Pink Elephant. I had stayed in town after my short meeting with Westervelt only long enough to stop at the little marina where they rented powerboats.

I was lucky. The shrunken old lady who was behind the counter remembered Norm Fizer.

"Oh yes, that poor, poor man," she said when I asked about him. "It's the first boat we've ever lost here—and we rent them every day," she said.

"Was that the first time he ever rented one of your boats?"

She shook her head. "No, he came in two days before he . . . he disappeared. Paid for three days in advance. Used cash—cash for the deposit and everything. I remember because it was very unusual. Almost everyone nowadays uses credit cards. Plastic money for this, plastic money for that. It's no wonder this country is having such a terrible economic problem—"

"Did he mention where he might be going in your boat?"

She thought for a moment. "No. Just said he was

going to do some fishing. But it's like I told the police—he never bought no bait nor lures or nothing. Had a rod of his own, of course, but I never did see no tackle box. Thought it was kind of strange."

"Do you remember what he was wearing."

"Oh yes," she said. "I might be an old woman, but I still have an eye for a good-looking man. And my, but he was good-looking. Thought he might be a movie star or something. Let's see now—he was wearing a dark-blue sports shirt. Cotton probably. And those expensive khaki fishing pants with the button-down pockets—kind of like yours, only his weren't shorts. They was long slacks."

I offered her a ten for her help, but she refused. "Are you from the police?" she asked.

"No, ma'am," I said. "I'm a reporter. Doing a big special for my wire service of water-sport accidents."

"Well, if you use my name, make sure you get the spelling right. I've talked to reporters before, and they almost always get it wrong. You'd think they'd learn better in college or something. . . ."

So I rode the flybridge down the intercoastal waterway deep in thought, wondering just what in the hell my next move should be.

One thing was for sure—I had to get close to Samuel Yabrud. Because if he was FEAT's mark, his assassin was sure to be nearby. I considered using Cabbage Key as a base. Maybe get Rob Wells to help me pose as the new fishing guide there, and somehow ingratiate myself with the Israeli.

No, there were far too many holes in that plan; too many times when Yabrud would be out of my sight—and maybe in the sights of FEAT's assassin. Besides, I had ulterior motives for wanting to stay at Cabbage Key. And as strong as my attraction was for Marina Cole, it wasn't strong enough to make me blow my whole mission.

I had only one sensible trail of action. I had to enroll at St. Carib. I had to go through the workouts and the diet and, apparently, the harassment right along with the rich and chubby.

The big question was: Would Matrah allow me on the island? I wasn't exactly a treasured friend after our fight the night before. And Matrah didn't seem the type to forgive and forget. But all I could do was try.

The sign at the channel way to the exclusive fat farm read:

ST. CARIB ISLAND
PRIVATE RESORT FACILITY
ENTER WITH PERMISSION ONLY

I brought *Sniper* around, dropping her down to idle speed. Before me, the island spread out in the afternoon sun, lush and green with palms and gumbo-limbo. There was a white sweep of beach where a line of men and women jogged in formation. The geometries of graceful old buildings—tin roofs, vertical white board-and-batten, long screened porches—could be seen through the heavy foliage.

The docks were new: built with heavy plank and green treated pilings. And there was plenty of room for my *Sniper*—the reason obvious. No doubt St. Carib ferried its clients out on the giant sportfisherman tethered to the dock. The only other boats there were a couple of low-horsepower skiffs, and the sleek Excalibur that Matrah and his friends had used the night before. It hung on davits beside the dock, long and gleaming, projectilelike in the bright sun.

There was a committee of dock hands waiting when I pulled up: broad, muscled types. And they all looked surly.

Obviously, unexpected guests weren't welcome on St. Carib.

I smiled from the flybridge, waved. They didn't wave back. One of them, the spokesman for the group, stepped forward.

"I'm sorry, sir, but I'm afraid we can't allow you to dock here. This is a private island," he said.

I yelled back, still smiling, "I know. I came to sign up. I talked with some of your people last night at Cabbage Key. They said I should talk to your enrollment personnel."

They conferred for a moment, then the spokesman asked, "Who did you talk to?"

"Heinrich Keppler. Is Heiny around? He'll tell you."

One of them went running off and returned shortly

with the big German. He came lumbering down the dockway, planks creaking beneath his weight. His blond mustache and short red beard were contorted into a broad grin.

He waved and yelled at me, "You big American cow! You have come to lose the fat? It is true?"

"It's true—but I'd like to tie up my boat and come ashore first, if that's okay with you."

He waved me in, caught the lines I tossed him, and snubbed off the lines on the brass cleats. I took his hand when I stepped out onto the dock: big dry handshake, but not the aggressive kind—the kind that tries to crush the fingers and suggests imminent domination.

"Ah, to see Matrah's face when he learns that you have enrolled. That will be a happy something, ya!"

"If he lets me enroll. I've been planning my whole vacation around staying here. I'd hate to see it ruined because of that little squabble we had last night."

"Hah! Some little squabble, you speak. He did not eat the breakfast this morning. A bruise around his throat *this big*." He held his hands apart as if describing a fish. "No, we must get you signed up before he sees you. That will be a laugh!"

He talked on in clumsy English as he walked me across the well-manicured expanse of St. Carib. The walkways were made of red brick, curving beneath the shade of broad oaks and banyan trees. Like most of the inhabited islands in Pine Island Sound, the houses were all built on the tops of a long line of

117

prehistoric Indian shell mounds that made up the bulk of the island. At a small wooden building, he stopped me. A sign at the door proclaimed it the business/enrollment office.

"My chubby American friend, do you know that it costs much money to stay here?" he asked in a worried tone.

I smiled. "Heiny, money has never been a problem with me. Right now, my only worry is this stomach I'm beginning to grow." I grabbed the small band of fat around my waist. "If you people can get this off me, it'd be worth any amount."

He nodded his head and grinned happily. "Good, good. You are in no difficulty, my American friend. These other rich piggies you see around here—they are the ones who make us work. Food, food—all the time it is the food, trying to steal it from the kitchen. We must watch them constantly. Like little children, these little piggies! But you—you my friend, I will train like a fighter. Yes!"

He held his finger to his lips, the symbol of a secret. "Do not forget—Matrah must not know that I helped you. If he discovered, he would fire me and then I would be forced to twist his physical body to knots. A nasty Arab, that one!"

Heiny went lumbering down the walkway chuckling, leaving me at the door of the business office.

Inside the ceilings were high and cool. There were paintings on the wall of seascapes, and a giant aerial photograph of St. Carib in color covered one full wall. The island was amoeba-shaped, well over a hundred acres, the north and south ends of it bordered by mangrove swamp. In the middle of the island was the wooden water tower. It overlooked the blue rectangle of swimming pool, tennis courts, and the long sheltered row of guest cottages. On the south point of the Indian mound were the two largest houses, old and multistoried, with roofs of shingle rather than tin.

A rather pretty woman in her early forties sat behind the lone desk. She looked up when I came in. She had short brown hair and wore bifocals around her neck on a cord. I told her I wanted to enroll, and she fluttered about, concerned that I hadn't made arrangements beforehand. She took some literature from a drawer and watched me closely while I read the price sheet. The courses were a week long. Three carefully monitored meals a day were provided. No tobacco, alcohol, or "outside" foods were allowed on the island. And it was unbelievably expensive.

The rich are uncomfortable talking about money—small amounts of money, anyway. And to a very rich person, this would seem like a small amount.

I slid the literature back on the desk. "This is fine," I said. There was a pad and pen on the desk, and I took it without asking. "Please call my bank—I'm writing the number here—and have them draft a check. Also tell them to include a twenty percent gratuity for my trainer and for whoever else might be working with me here."

She nodded quickly. "Very well, Mr. MacMorgan."

The number was real and the bank was real. I have never cared much about money, but the year before I had stumbled onto a very great sum of it in the shape of Spanish gold. The money was nowhere near worth the amount of lives it cost, but now that I had it, I kept it banked safely away in government bonds—complete with a CPA to do the worrying for me. It allowed me no real freedom—that's an individual accomplishment, and it has nothing to do with wealth. What it did allow me was a few mild extravagances, like the very best equipment and maintenance for my boat, shoes and clothes that didn't fall apart after a year's wear, and the chance to help some friends financially.

Those few things—and a week's stay on the exclusive St. Carib Island.

The woman typed out an application for me, asked a few questions about my general health and the amount of weight I wanted to lose, then shoved some papers in front of me to sign.

"There!" she said, finally. "Now all you have to do is take this sheet to the infirmary for your physical."

"Physical?"

She nodded. "I'm afraid it's necessary, Mr. MacMorgan—insurance purposes, you know. But most of the enrollees arrived this morning and have already had theirs, so you won't have to wait long."

"Good," I said. "I hate lines."

She laughed brightly. "Oh, there will be no line—that I guarantee."

The infirmary was a long low building built of white board-and-batten with a red cross above the door. I let the screen door slam behind me when I went in. It smelled of alcohol and medicine. A stocky nurse told me to have a seat; the doctor was busy with someone else right now.

I wasn't alone in the waiting room. A woman in her early thirties sat in one of the plush chairs, face buried in a magazine. And when she looked up briefly, it didn't take me long to recognize the face. There are only a handful of actresses recognized around the world: Bergman, Bacall, Loren, Garbo, and a few others. And she was one of the few—very, very few—others. I don't see many movies, but this woman had a face no man could ever forget. There were the wide dark peasant eyes, the perfect curvature of nose and Slavic cheeks, breasts heavy beneath silk blouse, famous legs long and dark, disappearing into her skirt.

She looked at me, returned to her magazine, then looked at me again. You would expect some of the sexual impact of the woman to be missing once removed from the magnification of the giant screen.

But it was all there: a sensuous, tumid aura of sexuality. Very, very few people—male or female—have it, or have it in that quantity at least.

I nodded and smiled.

Her smile in return was unexpected. My wife had been in films before our marriage, so I had made the rounds at enough of the Hollywood-type parties to know most actors and actresses as the insecure, chip-on-the-shoulder burrow creatures they really are.

But hers wasn't the bright frozen smile of the celebrity favoring a fan. Looking over the magazine, she eyed me with what seemed to be feline interest.

She said, "Was it you I saw climbing out of that lovely blue boat a short time ago?" The accent was Italian; a humid alto voice.

"That's right."

She waited for me to say something else, and when I didn't, she folded the magazine, stood up, and walked across the room toward me, hips rotating on perfect hinges. She held out her hand, and I took it.

"My name is Sonya Casimur."

"I'd be lying if I said I didn't already know."

She gave me her screen look of sudden vulnerability. "Ah, you've seen some of my work. I hope you weren't too disappointed?"

It wasn't a question. It was a request for a compliment. But I had no compliment to offer. She was a beautiful woman, a beauty in the classic sense—certainly one of the most beautiful women in the world. But, in filling that role, it also seemed to imply that she was a property of the world—much as a great painting is thought to be a property of the world. And because of that, I found myself strangely uninterested in her. While her sensuality was very real—an almost tangible thing—the quality of her face, her voice, her being, seemed to be the inventions of a filmmaker. Or a dreamer. Maybe I was being unfair. But you can't argue with your emotions.

"I don't know a thing about films," I said. "Or acting."

"Oh?" she said, surprised. And then she laughed. "But it was you on the boat?"

"You seem very interested in boats."

She gave me a vixen look, probing my eyes with hers. At that moment the bulky nurse came out. She said, "Miss Casimur, the doctor will see you now."

Sonya held my eyes momentarily before sweeping away. She said, "Perhaps it is the boat I am interested in."

"Perhaps?"

There was the peasant smile beneath sensuous dark eyes. "The boat and perhaps something else. Perhaps . . ."

10

Sonya Casimur, the actress, arrived at my cottage un-expectedly about an hour later.

I had taken the prescribed physical from a knobby little doctor with a smoker's cough, took a minute to get my gear from aboard and batten down *Sniper*, then rambled up to my cabin to grab a shower before the afternoon classes began.

A couple of months before, I had had a carpenter friend of mine build me a solid little hiding place for the tools of my new trade. Mounted flush into the fighting deck is a six-foot fish box. It is insulated, has dual drainage plugs, and possesses enough room to store a thousand pounds of fish and ice.

He said it would take him a day. It took him almost a week. He cut out the fish box and set it aside temporarily. Using teak planking and endless yards of good rubber molding, he built a waterproof storage compartment beneath the fish box that even an expert would be hard-pressed to find. Open the fish box and you see absolutely nothing. But lift at the drainage holes, and the bottom slides away, revealing what looks like nothing more than teak deck. Pull at the brass hinges, and the deck swings up, exposing more space than I hope I ever need for my weaponry.

So I wasn't worried about leaving the things D. Harold Westervelt had given me aboard.

My cottage was a neat little two-room board-and-batten antique that smelled of old wood and damp sand. There were about fifteen such cottages built in a row on the top of the mound by the shady walk. They all had names painted on signs: Mandango, Conch, Sanibel; names borrowed from the local islands and animal life. My cottage was Frigate. There was a sitting room with wicker furniture and sea-shells on the windowsills. The air conditioner clattered and wheezed like an old machine gun, and I switched it off in favor of the ceiling fan. I stowed my duffel bag beneath the brass bed, then stripped off my clothes.

The bathroom smelled of soap and rank mineral deposits from the island water. But they kept the water good and hot, and I spent twenty soapy minutes sluicing the day away, finishing with a cold shower that burned the genitals and tightened the skin.

And I had just wrapped a towel around me, walking toward the little bedroom, when I saw someone standing at the screen door.

"Yeah?"

"I guess you didn't hear me knock—but I see that I am interrupting your bath."

It was Sonya Casimur. She made no motion to leave.

"So come on in."

"You're only in a towel."

"And you're only wearing a bathing suit. I can take it if you can."

She swung open the screen door, laughing. "So blunt, you Americans. So refreshing." She wore a black one-piece suit cut so low in the back that the narrow valley of buttocks could be seen. The suit was tight, with a competitive quality to it, the kind you see on the female Olympic swimmers. It was taut over heavy breasts, showing the topographic outline of areola and nipple, and veed up sharply at the soft convexity of inner thigh. She had a towel wrapped around her neck, and her short black hair was mussed. "I stopped to see if you wanted to go for a swim."

"I thought this afternoon was when the drill instructors got ahold of us."

She grimaced and sank into one of the wicker chairs. "My God, don't remind me. This is my second stay on St. Carib. After the first I vowed never to return." She reached down meaningfully and gathered a thin wall of fat on her thighs between thumb and index finger. "But on film, even this much extra weight makes you look bloated. And I just don't have the willpower to do it on my own."

She eyed me up and down, starting involuntarily at the shark-attack scar on my waist. "My God," she said, "that's awful."

"Thanks," I said. "Thanks a lot. I didn't mention your chubby thighs—why should you mention my ugly scar?"

Her eyes described wonderment. She couldn't tell if I was joking or not.

"My thighs—you think they really are fat!"

"You're a real porker, Sonya."

My grin keyed hers. It was a nice smile; some of theatrics gone from it. "You don't like me, no? But why?"

"I don't even know you. But I am kind of curious about this come-on of yours. No, don't give me that innocent look. I'm a bad audience. Why the unsolicited interest in me, Sonya?"

She hesitated, wondering if she should stick with the film-vixen role. Finally, she decided better and dropped it altogether. It cut her Italian accent in half. She stood up and talked with her hands animatedly. "It's this goddam spartan routine here! Jesus, I just don't know if I can take another seven days and nights of it. The staff treats you like a bad soldier, and the fat men who are in the classes look at me like I'm something good to eat. Their mouths—they practically water. It gives me the—how do you say?—the goose bumps!"

"But it was your decision to return. Why did you?"

She practically exploded. "My decision? Hah! It's that goddam agent of mine! He treats me like a naughty child when I gain a few pounds! He told me that if I weighed over fifty kilos before we started filming in Greece, he would send me here!"

"You thought he was lying?"

"Yes! That bastard doesn't even know how to bluff—and he is fat himself!"

I couldn't help laughing. It came rolling out of me in long swells. She stood before me, every man's vision of sexuality, every director's dream, pouting like a child.

"So how did you think I could help all that, Sonya?"

A light came into her wide Italian eyes. "The boat is yours, no?"

"The boat is mine, yes."

"You have food on the boat? Maybe some cigarettes and liquor?"

"I have food and beer. No cigarettes."

"But that is something!" The charm came back into her voice; the theatrics returned to her smile. "If you would share those things with me, would it not be easier on both of us?" And when I didn't react, she continued, "And maybe I could find a nice small part for you in my next film?"

"I have no interest in being an actor, Sonya. And I've been looking forward to this little vacation for too long to take a chance of getting kicked out for breaking the rules."

The shock registered on her face. And then came the outrage. She practically sputtered. "You would deny me!"

"I'm giving it my best shot."

"Why, you . . . you *bastard*." For a moment I thought she was going to try to slug me. Instead, she whirled on bare feet and stomped out of the room, calling over her shoulder, "And that scar of yours! It is *ver-r-ry* ugly!"

I got my first look at Samuel Yabrud that afternoon.

It was at the first "general" workout. Later, they told us, we would be separated into coed groups based on the type of training we required. They had issued us all blue running shorts, high-quality running shoes, and expensive blue sweatsuits with *St. Carib* embroidered on the pocket. There were about forty of us, not counting the dozen or so instructors who strutted around barking orders. Most of the enrollees were middle-aged, more men than women. All wore the careful hairstyles of the successful executive, and they ranged from slightly overweight to very fat indeed.

There was a boys' camp atmosphere about the place. St. Carib's wealthy pupils clapped their hands like cheerleaders, grinned and beamed, and jumped to every order. Seeing them, I could understand D. Harold's theory about the place. These were the people Marina Cole would describe as Lions—some of

the most successful Lions in the world, probably.
And after bearing the weight of the Lion's crown for
a lifetime, they seemed more than happy to abdicate
for a week. They had paid big money to be bossed
and prodded and ordered about—and that's damn
well what they wanted.

And got.

It made them smile like children. For a week, they
didn't have a care in the world. They didn't have to
make a single decision or follow a financial trend, or
worry about headlines in the *Journal.*

And Samuel Yabrud was grinning and clapping
his hands right along with the rest of them.

He was an immensely fat man given to sweating.
He was balding, black curly hair forming a wreath
around his head, and the Semitic nose angled hawk-
like beneath heavy eyebrows. His weight made him
look shorter than he was—maybe five eight—and his
warmup covered him like a tent.

We stood in lines of ten during the preliminary
stretching exercises. I got as close to Yabrud as I
could. On either side of him were younger, well-
muscled men wearing the same group uniforms.
Their faces, hair, everything right down to their stoic
expressions were right out of the CIA mold.

There was no doubt in my mind who they were.
And from the swift knowing looks they cast at me,
there was no doubt in their minds who I was.

They were Yabrud's bodyguards, his personal

shields lent him by the U.S. government in the event that FEAT's assassin did take a shot.

They were the defense.

And I was the offense.

One of them studied me for a moment, then gave me the slightest of nods. I nodded back. And I knew that unless one of us needed help very badly, a word would never be exchanged between us. They would stay in the background as much as possible, giving me latitude to work. But beyond that, they couldn't offer much help. It was a thin line they had to walk. Assassinating an assassin—however necessary—fell under the heading of illegal activity. And the CIA was officially out of the illegal-activity business.

And that's why D. Harold Westervelt's top-secret organization had had to be formed.

So the St. Carib staff stretched us and bullied us, demanded enthusiasm with our calisthenics and supreme effort with our brief rope climb. Everyone else but the CIA duo huffed and puffed and labored. But I barely broke into a sweat. As far out of shape as I was, this was child's play.

It was during our slow lap around the island that Heiny came rumbling up beside me. I had taken care to stay behind Yabrud, so I was well toward the end of the pack. Even Sonya Casimur had loped past me, running deerlike—but not so fast she didn't have time to contort her mouth and make a face at me.

"Slowpoke!" she had yelled.

And I had yelled back, laughing, "Some of that fat on your thighs must be muscle!"

Heiny was grinning. He seemed happy to see me. He filled out the white staff warmup suit as if he were built of tapered cement.

"My American friend, you run so slowly!"

"Just saving my energy, Heiny."

"You got the bad leg?"

"I've got two bad legs. And too much damn weight to carry."

"Hah! You kid old Heiny now. See!" He pointed ahead to where Samuel Yabrud chugged along. "Even that fat piggy is ahead of you. Could be you are running so slow that we will put you in Miss Casimur's group?"

"Now why would you think that?" I gave him a lockerroom grin, hoping he would think just that.

"She is no fat piggy, yes? Very beautiful, that actress." He made a cupping motion, hands to chest. "And nice bazooms, huh!"

"She is certainly very pretty."

"Hey, Matrah knows that you are on the island," he said suddenly.

I looked at him. "Yeah?"

"He allowed me a message to give you. Thinks that I hate you after last night. That is some laugh, huh?" He chuckled and actually slapped at his thigh. "Matrah wants to see you in his office before dinner."

"You think he's going to kick me off the island?"

"Kick you off? Hah! No, you have already paid the money. And he loves the money more than he hates you. But I do not know why he wants to see you. I talk to you later, my American friend. I arrange for you and Miss Casimur to be in the same group. Heiny can arrange the whole thing." He trotted off toward the head of the pack, waving.

St. Carib's "experiential education" program was a lot like a plush boot camp for the wealthy and overweight. They prodded at the fears of the individual, then allowed the group to overcome them. They made us fall backward off a tower into the arms of four team members. They had us swing across a shallow ravine on a rope held only by the chubby hands of our group. Samuel Yabrud balked at that; said in perfect English that the physics of it was impossible. He said that he weighed too much and his team members weighed too little. That's when the St. Carib staffers really got nasty. One of the slim Mediterraneans marched up to him and, nose to nose, dressed him down like a drill instructor. "Fat bastard" was the kindest thing he called him. I expected Yabrud, supposedly a master of international negotiation, to at least argue back. Instead, he cast his eye earthward like a bad child, walked dejectedly toward the rope, and made the swing after a long hesitation. And when he made it—successfully—the change that came over him and his group was amazing. They all held their fists high in the air like conquerors, hooting and slapping each other on the back.

Only Sonya Casimur looked upset. I couldn't tell if she was going to cry or start swinging at the St. Carib staffers.

One thing was for sure: She wasn't at St. Carib because she liked it. And she was right about the men drooling over her. She never had a minute to herself. There was always some overweight group member lolling around her, flirting like a teenage boy. Someone once said that a truly beautiful woman sees all of life's ugliness by the time she is eighteen.

Sonya Casimur had seen it all, and she was tired of it.

Before dinner, they gave us one more task: an open-water swim from St. Carib to a nearby island and back. To me it was a very short swim—no more than a quarter mile, round trip. But you could tell by the horror in the eyes of some that it was a terrifying distance.

Sonya was among them, the worry plain on her perfect face.

After stripping down to my running shorts, I walked up beside her.

"It's not going to be that bad, Sonya."

She looked up, surprised, too unnerved to still be angry at me. "My God, I can hardly swim at all. When did I ever have time to learn? There was always a stunt woman for this sort of thing. . . ."

"So tell them you can't make it."

She shoved her hands on her hips. "What, and have those nasty bastards yell at me the way they yelled at the fat Jewish man?"

"They'll be following us in rowboats. They can pick you up if you get into trouble."

"Hah! I would go to the bottom and drown first!"

I had to smile at her. She was as stubborn as she was beautiful.

"Then stick with me," I said. "When you get tired, just grab onto my shorts. Make a swimming motion with your other hand, though—that way they won't be able to tell that I'm pulling you."

She actually smiled. "You can really do that? You can still swim pulling my weight?"

"Swimming is one of my very, very few talents. I'm a regular water taxi."

"Oh," she said, "that's very nice . . . nice of you." She paused and gave me the slightest of winks. "But I am still mad at you."

"Just not *as* mad?"

"Yes," she said. "Not as mad as before. So I will allow you to pull me through the water."

"You're too kind, Miss Casimur."

"I know."

Sonya was wrong when she said she didn't swim well. The truth was, she could hardly swim a stroke. Fifty yards off St. Carib, she grabbed me by the elastic waistband of my shorts and held on with white knuckles for the rest of the trip.

"I'm not too heavy?" she kept asking, terrified.

"Like an anchor. But I think I can make it."

"The sharks . . . musn't we worry about the sharks?"

"With you in the water, Sonya, that's probably the least of our worries."

Dinner was held at the main house on the top of the mound. They gave us a steak the size of a silver dollar and a scoop of cottage cheese that was more parsley than anything else. I could see why the clients of St. Carib tended to get mean after a few days. After the plates had been swept away by a staff of waitresses dressed like traditional English servants, Matrah addressed us in glowing words about how the St. Carib experience would enrich our lives. Earlier, I had gone to see him at his office ready for the worst. But he was unexpectedly cordial; apologized for our fight, said that we had both probably drunk too much, and that we must now try to get along for the sake of everyone.

But the apology was a little too smooth. And he couldn't disguise the glimmer of contempt in his dark eyes as we shook hands.

I would try to get along—but I was going to keep a damn tight eye on him.

You could bet the bank on that.

During the speech, he outlined the rest of the course and described the importance of the day and night each of us would spend on an island alone—

called it our "Solitary." And to the backdrop of much cheering and applauding, he also divided us into groups, reading our names one at a time.

Sonya, Yabrud, another hugely fat man, and I were all in the same group. The very slowest group, apparently. Heiny turned to me and winked knowingly when our names were read, as if he had arranged it all.

And maybe he had.

After dinner, everyone filed off stiffly toward cottage and bed. The strain was already getting to them. Sonya came up behind me as I walked through the growing March darkness toward Frigate house.

"Dusky?"

Her face looked tired. She still wore the blue warmup pants, and the jacket was tied around her shoulders like a cape.

"Sonya! I'm so full after that dinner I can barely walk. How about you?"

"Oh, Dusky," she said wearily, "do not make with the jokes. I am so tired." She reached over and put her arm through mine, more for support than anything else. "This place depresses me so."

"I don't suppose a couple of cold beers would make you feel any better?"

Her eyes lighted. "Oh, would you! That would be so nice; I knew you wouldn't deny me such a small thing. And maybe a sandwich, too. A nice thick—"

"And I thought you were here to lose weight."

She jerked her arm away. "You! You are so mean!"

"And you are a very fine actress. But you'll take the beer, won't you?"

She pouted for a moment, then slipped her arm back into mine. "Yes. Two beers?"

"I'll make it three. You've had a tough day. Go on up to your cottage. I'll bring them."

I went down to the docks and opened *Sniper*. All my little snoop alarms were in place. I got a sackful of beer out of the locker, then went to the fish box and got the few things I needed. I stopped first at my cottage and dropped off the hardware, then went on up the walk to Sonya's place. St. Carib was quiet in the ten p.m. darkness. A few early chuck-will's-widows called whip-poor-will–like in the gloom, and out on the water, a Belcher barge went chugging down the intercoastal, orange bow light flashing. Far across Pine Island Sound I could see the soft lights of Cabbage Key. I wondered what Marina was doing at that moment. Cleaning up after the supper rush, probably. She would be tired and, perhaps, wondering what I was doing. For a moment I considered climbing back aboard *Sniper* to pay her a visit.

But I couldn't.

I had too much work to do.

Sonya had just finished her shower when I got to her cottage. The curtains were drawn, and the old air conditioner labored, condensation dripping down the rust lines on the wall. She wore a bright-green football jersey, number 12 white and satinlike on

138

front and back. The swell of breasts and dark softness of thighs beneath keyed the old stirring within my abdomen.

I opened a beer for each of us. She took half the bottle in the first long swallow, then wiped her lush mouth daintily.

"God, this is so good," she said.

"Nothing like that first taste of beer." I still stood in the doorway. She crossed the room and took a seat on the bamboo couch, looking wary for the first time. There was no mistaking that look. She realized that I might expect something in exchange for the beer.

"It was very nice of you to bring this, Dusky."

"As I said, after the day you had, you deserve it."

Some of the theatrics returned to her face, and she offered a long yawn. "Did you know they make us awaken at six a.m. at this awful place?"

I smiled. "Sonya, you don't have to worry about me sticking around."

Her face showed brief surprise. "But why would you say such a silly—"

"Because I know what you're thinking. You're thinking I'm going to make a move on you. You're thinking that I'm going to try and hustle that nifty Italian body of yours into bed."

"Well, aren't you?"

I shook my head. "No." She waited for me to say something else. Instead, I reached into my pocket and took out the little tin of Copenhagen. She watched me take a pinch, depositing it between cheek and gum.

"What's that?" she brooded.

"Tobacco."

"You said you had no cigarettes!"

"I don't. Just this."

"Let me smell it."

I closed the tin and tossed it onto the couch beside her. "You can keep it," I said. "But if you decide to try it, be careful. It can make you sick."

"Hah! Only you and this place makes me sick."

I grinned, heading out the door. "Enjoy the beer, princess."

She stood, surprised that I was leaving so soon. "You can stay for a few minutes longer, can't you? We could talk. I always have the trouble sleeping here. . . ."

"Can't," I said. "Too tired."

As I went down the steps, I could hear her throwing things inside.

II

I *was* tired.

But I couldn't allow myself to sleep.

Not yet anyway. I had too much work to do.

I went back to my cabin and got my duffel bag from beneath the bed. I stripped off the St. Carib clothes and slid into the old and well-loved British commando knickers and black watch sweater, and pulled the black Navy watch hat down low over my blond hair.

I gave it a half hour before I finally switched off the lights as if going to bed—just in case someone was watching. In the darkness, I gathered the Persid seismic alarm system, the Star-Tron night-vision scope, and the Remington 700 sniper rifle. Then I went to the bed and built the rough image of a man sleeping beneath the covers.

Outside, even the lights of the main house were off now. Green glow of Rolex told me it was almost midnight. I moved through the island quiet, sticking to the cover of trees and foliage, well away from the walk.

I didn't want to take a chance of meeting someone unexpectedly.

Not with the gear I was carrying.

I had located Samuel Yabrud's cottage earlier. It was Osprey, only two doors down from Sonya's place. They all had their air conditioners on, even though the night was March cool. Some people get so used to a controlled climate that they can't sleep without the whir of an engine and the comforting generator punch of an air conditioner.

I buried the first geophone at the base of a gray eucalyptus tree not far from Yabrud's cottage. After I had covered it with sand and leaves, I swept all signs of digging away, then moved on through the darkness.

Matrah stayed in the main house at the peak of the mound on the south end of the island. The house was three stories high, with gables and rectangle windows. It appeared ghostly in the starlight. I planted the second geophone beneath the porch there. For a moment I thought I heard voices coming from inside. I lay there beneath the porch for a long time before moving.

It took me a while to decide where to plant the final geophone. Finally I settled on the docks. If anyone suspected me, they would want to check out *Sniper*. And with the geophone, I could hear a man's footsteps within a hundred meters of the dock. I didn't know how the little disk listening device would react to salt water, so I carefully gauged the high-tide line before burying it beneath the sand on the narrow strip of beach. *Sniper* floated calmly on her lines in the darkness. The wash of tide and the muted crack of pistol shrimp from their tunicate hideaways were the only sounds that came from the dock. I took my time, stayed low. Silhouettes stand out all too well when backdropped by open water.

By one a.m. I was ready to get some sleep.

But I wouldn't be sleeping in my cottage.

Not this night—or any night that I stayed on St. Carib.

I moved along the rise of mound through the darkness toward the water tower. It looked pale and fragile rising sixty feet above the island on wooden beams and a network of cross ties.

The steps sagged beneath my weight as I climbed. The water tower creaked like an old house in the wind.

From the platform at the top of the tower, all of Pine Island Sound spread out soft and silver in the darkness. Channel markers pulsed north toward Boca Grande, and south toward Sanibel. A sudden flare of distant deck light told me there was a bait shrimper working the shallow flats off Pineland.

I settled in the shadows of the water tower. I placed the Remington sniper rifle on the narrow deck and opened the seismic alarm system's carrying case. I switched on the set and pulled on the earphones.

A row of silver toggle switches activated any or all of the little buried geophones. A noise near any of the geophones would key a soft electronic gong and one of four red flashing lights. I adjusted three of the four set levels, balanced volume and sensitivity, then picked up the Star-Tron night scope.

Some great invention, the Star-Tron.

I had used it more than once back in Nam. It works on the principal of light intensification. The lens gathers all available starlight, amplifies it more than fifty thousand times, then gives you a sharp clear image through the binocular eyepiece. Even on the darkest night, watching someone through the Star-Tron is like watching a man through a red filter at high noon.

I mounted the scope carefully on the sniper rifle. Then I braced the rifle on the railing and swept the sights around the island, looking through the scope. I could see coons foraging along the beach, and birds roosting. Even the inscription on my boat's stern stood out in soft red highlights:

SNIPER
KEY WEST, FLORIDA

Finally, I brought the scope to bear on the door of Samuel Yabrud's cottage. The 135 mm lens made it seem as if I were standing only a few yards away instead of the two hundred yards that separated the water tower from his room.

Satisfied with my position, I turned up the volume of the Persid-4A, adjusted the earphones until they were comfortable, and, with the Remington cradled in my arms, settled back to get some sleep.

The alarm system awoke me about an hour later.

At first, the soft electronic *gong-gong-gong* slipped into my dreams; a benign sound, like a doorbell chime.

But then I was sitting bolt upright, rifle in hand, mechanically switching the safety to off.

Red lights on the alarm board blinked softly.

Not just one light. Two.

Through the earphones, I could hear the steady pad of shoes on sidewalk.

More than one person was up, walking near the seismic geophones.

Smoothly, I went to the edge of the water tower and braced the Remington 700 on the guardrail. The geophones by Yabrud's cottage and by the main house where Matrah lived had both been activated.

I settled the scope first on Yabrud's doorway, then panned along the walk.

Midway between his cottage and the main house I saw the man: short fat man in a checkered dressing gown. He walked along the sidewalk looking this way and that, like a kid skipping school.

It was not FEAT's assassin. Couldn't be—because it was Samuel Yabrud himself. He held the dressing gown tightly around him as if cold.

But why? Why would he be up and out at this
time of night? Maybe the assassin had conned him
into some kind of two a.m. rendezvous.

I moved the scope along the sidewalk, hoping I
would discover who set off the other alarm.

And that's when I saw the woman, her back to
me, heading in the same direction as Yabrud.

It was Sonya Casimur. She had covered herself in
a sheer nightdress, and I could see the naked outline
of hips and heavy outline of breasts beneath it.

Soon Yabrud caught up with her. I watched them
through the Star-Tron scope, carefully keeping my
index finger outside the trigger guard of the rifle.

They seemed surprised to see each other. Through
the earphones I heard them make embarrassed intro-
ductions. They made small talk about insomnia, and
how they were out for a walk, but finally there was
this:

"The truth is, my dear Miss Casimur, I was hoping
I might find a way of getting into the kitchen and . . .
appropriating some food." Yabrud had an oily voice
with a phlegmy chuckle.

With Sonya, it was all theatrics. "Food? You mean
steal some food, Signor Yabrud? Why, what a novel
idea! How adventurous!"

"Would you care to join me?"

"Oh, I couldn't—but then, it just might be fun. I've
never played a thief before. It would be so exciting!"

Together they walked on toward the meeting
house, which was just beyond the main house. Soon

they were far enough away from the geophone that I could not hear their conversation. I remembered something Heiny had told me, something about the "piggies" always trying to break into the kitchen. Apparently it wasn't all that uncommon.

Still, Yabrud was awake. And alone, except for Sonya.

And I didn't want him to be out of my sight for long. So I had just about decided to climb down the tower and join them unexpectedly at the kitchen when I heard something else through the earphones: the slam of a screen door.

It was Matrah. He wore pants but no shirt. He stood on the porch of the main house, hands on hips. He seemed to be waiting for someone, looking from the meeting house where the kitchen was, then back down the walk.

Finally, two men came lumbering up the walk at a heavy trot. It was Heiny and his German friend. I could hear them clearly through the earphones.

"Heinrich, I heard some of our clients out here a moment ago. They were headed for the kitchen."

"Ah, the little piggies are after the food again!" Heiny laughed.

"I thought I told you to keep a watch on the kitchen."

Heiny shrugged. "A man has to get the sleep sometime, ya?"

"Well, I don't want to have to call you again. Understand? I'm tired of these bastards waking me up in the middle of the night when they go on their food hunts!''

Matrah turned and went back into the house. Through the Star-Tron, I followed Heiny. He returned in a minute with Sonya and Samuel Yabrud. The two of them looked sheepish, and there was a forced hilarity in their conversation.

One of the world's great actresses and one of Israel's top diplomats had been caught trying to steal food.

But Heiny himself was something of a diplomat. He never mentioned the kitchen. Instead he chose to pretend that they were just out for a walk.

''The snakes,'' he warned them. ''Do not walk at night, for that is when the snakes are awake. You see? They are in the bushes, waiting to strike!''

That solicited nervous laughter, and promises never to walk at night again.

After seeing Yabrud and then Sonya back to their cottages, I followed Heiny and his German companion through the Star-Tron. Their cabin was well away from the guest cottages, at the other end of the island. They disappeared inside and switched off the lights.

I was not awakened again that night. And when the birds started making their predawn noises, I packed my gear—all but the geophones—climbed down the water tower, and carried it from shadow to shadow back toward *Sniper*.

The geophone by the docks was the only one that had not been activated.

That's why I was shocked to find the note.

It was lying in plain sight on the booth table inside the cabin.

And the cabin had been locked.

I picked up the note and read it in the coming light of the new day. As I hid my gear away beneath the fish box, I forced myself to stay calm. Mechanically, I made myself consider when someone might have had the chance to come aboard *Sniper*, pick the lock, and leave the note.

That's when I realized that it could have happened at any time the day before. Or even during my all-night vigil—if they had come by water and taken pains to be damn quiet.

Did the time frame eliminate or single out anyone?

No. Absolutely no one.

Before locking *Sniper*, I picked up the note and read it again. It was written in heavy block letters with a felt pen. You couldn't tell if the writer was left- or right-handed, male or female. It was plain scrap paper, and it bore no odor.

It read:

THERE IS NO PLACE SAFER THAN IN THE TRACK OF THE HUNTER. AND NO PLACE MORE DANGEROUS THAN THE SHADOW OF THE QUARRY.

YOU ARE IN THE SHADOW.

12

On the fourth night after dinner, Sonya Casimur came to my bed.

I wasn't totally surprised.

She had come more and more to depend on me. Like most great actresses, her film life blended evenly into her real life. She was a woman made for the bedroom: wide dark eyes, a face that suggested some inexorable wanting, a body that, in days of old, kings would have fought and killed for. But with all that, she possessed a potent force of character, one that guarded her sensuality like a junkyard dog. All truly beautiful women have it—and if they don't they are soon destroyed by the thousands of faceless drooling men who seek to satisfy themselves with that beauty.

But her guard was down now.

She had left it behind in her cottage with the panties she did not wear, and the bra she never wore.

She covered herself with only a brief silk nightdress. It tied behind her neck in a tempting bow. Her dark legs angled soft and long beneath the skirt, and the full breasts were visible beneath the thin material.

She stood in the little living area of my cottage. She had pulled the wooden door closed behind her. Her hair was carefully mussed, and her brown eyes seemed to hold mine with a piercing heat.

"Again you brought the beer but did not stay. Why is it you do not like me?" The mouth pouted. But the eyes challenged.

"I like you fine, Sonya."

"Then why do you never stay? To talk?"

I stretched and yawned. "The workouts here tire me out."

That was a lie. The second day had gone much as the first. And the third day had gone like the second. They assembled us at seven a.m. for a slow half-mile jog before breakfast. After breakfast (a sparse mixing of fruit and cold cereal) we separated into our groups. There were only four to a group. In ours it was Sonya, myself, Yabrud, and a hugely fat Texan who talked long and loud about his oil and cattle. He had a nasty smoker's cough, and he liked to slap people on the back. Because, on the second day, Sonya had met their leers with a frozen stare, Yabrud and the Texan had found kinship in the things they held in common: money, and the great actress' contempt.

And that left Sonya and me together, even in that small group.

While she had every talent necessary to be a film star, she seemed to have zero athletic ability.

Every day we would swim, and every day I would drag her along behind me. It was the same on our cross-country runs. She would fall or collapse from exhaustion, and I would pull her to her feet, then half-prod and half-carry her the rest of the way. Our instructor was always either Heiny or his German counterpart. Neither of them seemed to mind. In fact, Heiny appeared to take some pleasure in playing Cupid: putting the two of us in impossible circumstances, then leaving us alone. But he never left without first giving me a private wink and grin.

And I have to admit that Sonya Casimur was one very desirable creature. When left to her own devices, all the staged smiles fell away along with the well-practiced theatrics, and she became the unexpected: raucous, profane, and much given to helpless laughter. With all the stage trappings cut away, she became a peasant girl again without an ounce of affectation.

So, on one level, the days at St. Carib went smoothly. With Yabrud in my group, he was never out of my sight during the day. And during the brief private hours before and after dinner, his brace of CIA bodyguards hung on him like glue. And there was the beautiful Sonya for company while I sweated the fat away, working my way back into shape.

But on another level, things weren't going smoothly at all.

For the first time in my civilian life, I felt as if I were the one being hunted. FEAT's assassin knew who I was, where I was, and what my daily routine would be.

And I knew nothing about him.

The morning after finding the note, I had managed to slip away long enough to search the beach area near the docks. There had been a high tide that night, so I thought someone approaching *Sniper* by sea might have unknowingly left some track revealed by the falling water.

But there was none.

I even went carefully through the cabin, looking for anything that might offer a clue: a bit of hair, a scuff mark on the carpet.

But there was only the note.

Again and again I went over that note, trying to press every drop of information from it.

It was written on a four-by-six scrap of paper. A chunk of gumming in the upper left-hand corner told me it had been torn from right to left off a common note pad. It meant that the author was probably right-handed.

The words themselves were meticulously drawn— the starkest of block letters. It suggested the assassin knew that plain block letters are the only way to disguise handwriting. The reason for wanting to disguise the handwriting was obvious. Once he had killed Yabrud and me, he didn't want to be traced. But maybe there was a deeper reason for careful forming of the letters. Perhaps he knew that any hint of his own penmanship would provide a glaring clue to his or her identity. And nothing is easier to spot than someone writing in a language not native to him.

So—the assassin was probably right-handed. And, perhaps, a foreigner.

Not exactly earth-shaking deductions.

But the most important clue was the note itself. Why did he even bother leaving it? Certainly it wasn't a warning. A hunter doesn't warn a lion before he is about to shoot.

No, the note was a challenge.

It implied a love of the hunt.

And this assassin wanted to make the hunt interesting.

He had dropped the gauntlet. And I had no choice but to pick it up, accept the challenge.

The assassin had everything going for him. The only thing I had on my side was that he was not the cold methodical killer I had expected. He was an assassin. And if D. Harold Westervelt was any judge of FEAT, that terrorist organization hired nothing but the best. But this, at least, was a killer who loved sport.

If not, I would have been dead long before; dead like Stormin' Norman Fizer, my old lost friend.

So, when they throw you into an arena filled with lions, you grab for any weapon you can.

And, for now, the only weapon I had was my game plan.

So I stuck with it.

The second night on St. Carib was a replay of the first. I took beer to Sonya Casimur's cabin, returned to my own for a suitable length of time, then made my midnight climb to the water tower, where I sat wearing seismic earphones, Remington 700 sniper rifle in hand, the cylindrical silencer making the weapon look even more lethal.

Only this time it was harder to sleep.

A hell of a lot harder.

Did the assassin know I was on the tower? And if so, why didn't he just shoot and bring his hunt to an end?

Finally, I did drift off to sleep. But I awoke with a jolt, fleeing my own dreams.

A nightmare, not a dream.

In gauzy slow motion, I had finally brought the assassin into my sights. I could see his face clearly through the infrared scope.

He was smiling; smiling because I had been in his sights for some time. He trained an SVA Dragunov sniper rifle on me, his cheek resting on that weapon's strange skeleton stock, his right eye huge and red and dragonlike as he brought the cross hairs of his own night scope to bear on my forehead.

He was smiling, and for some reason I could not pull the trigger.

I could not manufacture the effort it took to make that simple gesture of death.

And then I saw the flare and brief recoil of his own rifle, and I knew that I was dead, dead, dead. . . .

*   *   *

So I really was tired when Sonya Casimur arrived alone on that fourth night.

But not from St. Carib's workouts.

I was tired from the three near-sleepless all-night vigils. And, the toughest of all to admit, I was worn by the strain of, for once, being the hunted instead of the hunter. I was tired by the fear.

All this while Samuel Yabrud labored through the fat-farm drills, blissfully unaware that we were both marked for death.

So Sonya Casimur stood before me dressed in her brief silk nightshirt, breasts held in warm relief against the thin material, the promise of naked buttocks beneath the short skirt.

"Why is it you do not like me?" she repeated. The dark eyes held mine, searching, offering, challenging.

"Sonya, I told you: I like you fine."

"Is it that you are not really a man?"

"Are you asking me if I'm a homosexual? Bingo—that's it. I'm too tired and, besides, I only like other men."

She came toward me, reached out, and touched my bare chest with her hand. It seemed as if there were electricity in her fingers. When I had heard her knock at the screen door, I had hastily shoved my commando pants and watch sweater back under the bed, then pulled on the first thing I could find—the thin St. Carib–issue running shorts.

At her touch, I felt the old yearning deep within

my abdomen, and I wished I had pulled on something other than those loose shorts.

Her tongue traced the edge of her full lips. "You are not the gay man. You are not the homosexual."

"And how can you be so sure?"

"A woman knows. A woman can always tell."

I took her firmly by the arms, walked her backward, and sat her down on the couch. She closed her eyes and held her face up toward me, expecting me to kiss her. And when I didn't, the eyes flared open.

"Why are you so mean to me?"

"Maybe it's my suspicious nature. Maybe I become a little wary when a woman who could have any man in the world starts coming on to me like a nun who wakes up to find herself in an NFL dressing room."

"I am not chasing you!"

"Well, this is certainly not your cottage. I didn't come to your door still wet after a shower, smelling of shampoo and perfume."

She smiled slightly. "You are jealous of my other men, no?" She held up three fingers. "I have only been married this many times. And two of them were very fat and very rich, and the other was a handsome gay boy." Again her hands traced the lines of my chest. "But you are not the gay boy." Her hands stopped at the elastic of my shorts. She looked down meaningfully, the smile broadening. "That tells me you are not the gay boy. That tells me you are very much the man."

I took her stray hand in mine. She moved her fingers, stroking my palm. I said, "Sonya, you already know that you are very beautiful. And you already know that you are very sensual—and if you don't stop rubbing your leg against mine, I may lose control of myself and prove it to you. But there are some things I can tell you that you don't know. When you drop that sex-kitten actress routine of yours, you really are fun to be with. I've enjoyed the last couple of days. I think that behind that greasepaint facade is a pretty decent human being."

She nuzzled herself against me, the tension sagging out of her, legs parting slightly as she rested her face on my shoulder. When she spoke again, the voice had changed, her accent fading with the staged seduction. She said, "You see through me, Dusky. That is why I . . . feel comfortable with you. I get so tired, so damn tired of being the famous actress. Sometimes I don't know if that is the real me on the screen, or if this"—she tugged at her own flesh—"if this is really me." She looked up at me, the dark eyes piercing. "But you know which is the real Sonya Casimur, Dusky. And now I want you to make me feel like the woman I really am."

I felt my face close on hers; felt my mouth join her wet lips, felt my hand stray up the curvature of ribs, and heard her whimper softly as I cupped nipple and breast in my right hand.

She was soft and wanting, and the light perfume

she wore seemed stronger with the growing heat of her body.

But I couldn't stay with her. As much as my body wanted her, I couldn't spare the hours that a joining with such a woman deserved.

There was the little problem of a mission. And what would I say to D. Harold Westervelt if Samuel Yabrud died bloody while I slept in a beautiful woman's arms?

And beyond that, there was another lady whom I had professed to love.

I had made no promises to Marina Cole. Nor had she made any to me. But that was just a verbal loophole that far, far too many people use to jump from bed to bed; a makeshift rationalization that can explain away any infidelity.

Had I come to the point where the bedding of a woman meant nothing more than the brief hip-writhing climax; the wham-bam-thank-you-ma'am philosophy that has become the demigod of a million lonely suburban hipsters?

It was the chic creed that has always offended me: the creed that has turned love into nothing more than a penis handshake.

At any rate, Marina Cole deserved more.

And so did Sonya Casimur.

But the mission took precedence over everything. So, thankfully, it left me with no decision to make.

I pulled myself away from the tangle of arms and

legs. Sonya lay back on the couch, breathing heavily. She made a motion as if to pull the silk dress up over her head. I got a brief look at perfect thighs and soft brown curl of pubic hair before I stopped her.

"No, Sonya. I can't."

I expected her to be mad.

But she wasn't.

For the first time, she was hurt. I read it in her eyes, her face.

And there was no playacting involved.

"Dusky, but why? Why . . ."

Saying it, the excuse sounded pretty damn weak. "There's another woman I'm pretty much committed to."

"You're married?"

I shook my head. "No, Sonya. I'm not married. But it makes no difference."

She stood up, straightening her dress, her hair. "You like her better than you like me?" There was no inflection of surprise in the voice. It was an honest question filled with hurt.

"That's not fair to ask, Sonya."

She stepped back, studying me. "Yes," she said. "I can see it in your eyes—the love for someone else. Is that the woman you would leave me for?"

"Yes," I said. But I wasn't sure. Was it Marina that she saw? Or someone else from long, long ago in another lifetime?

It didn't matter. As long as she believed it.

"I'm sorry," I said.

She reached up and brushed my face with her lips. I held her hand and kissed it lightly. She said, "Someday, if I am lucky, perhaps I will find a man who cares as much for me."

"And if you're luckier, he won't be the bastard I normally am. And he won't have any ugly scars."

She shook her head, caught in private thought. As she left, she said over her shoulder. "Your scar's not really that ugly, Dusky. In fact, I was just beginning to like it. . . ."

13

So I played the fourth night like the rest.

But I knew the calm couldn't go on much longer. FEAT's assassin had to strike.

And he had to strike soon.

The whole physical-fitness routine on St. Carib was aimed at the culminating "Solitary"—the two days and one night alone on an island.

Every day we had met for a class on very basic survival. They showed us the edible plants—seawort and prickly pear and others; demonstrated how to dig clams and coquinas; explained how to spear fish at night using a torch.

It was really just a sophisticated form of Boy Scouts. They dramatized the Solitary; emphasized its importance. They made it sound as if two days on a secluded beach without food was the equivalent of climbing Mount Everest.

And the "rich piggies," as Heiny called them, ate it up. They were all survivors—but only in the jungle of business. This kind of survival was a purge for them, a way to rid themselves of pressure by immersing themselves in a *Swiss Family Robinson* fantasy.

But not a single one of them knew how deadly that fantasy could become.

Not Samuel Yabrud, certainly.

Even in a group as small as ours, I made it a point not to talk much with the Israeli. For one thing, I didn't want to draw any more outside suspicion that I was there to keep an eye on him.

For another, I didn't want him to know. He no doubt realized the roll of his two CIA bodyguards. But suspicion that he had a third guardian might cause him to question just exactly what in the hell was going on. Why all the protection? No, he was the bait. And I didn't want my bait giving off the scent of fear.

It would make the hunter all too wary.

So, when Sonya was safely back in her cabin, I slipped into commando pants and watch sweater, strapped the fine Randall attack-survival knife to my side, and went again to my surveillance station, the water tower.

If the assassin was going to make a move on St. Carib, he would have to make it tonight.

Because tomorrow afternoon, they would haul us all out to the islands for the beginning of our Solitary.

Matrah had briefed us on it that evening at dinner. He was a different man in front of his wealthy clients. He substituted a patronizing smile for his attitude of superiority. Everyone seemed to like him. And he pretended to like everybody. Except me.

He assigned an island to every group. Ours was Cayo Costa, a six-mile strip of barrier island that fronted the Gulf not far from St. Carib. Like the other groups, we would be dropped off alone a mile or so apart, each of us to carry only five gallons of water, some matches and mosquito netting, and a flare kit.

"There is positively no fraternization between guests allowed during Solitary," Matrah warned us in his oily Mediterranean accent. "It would defeat the whole purpose of your stay on St. Carib."

Everyone had laughed at that.

But I didn't.

I didn't laugh because I saw the way that his eyes swept the audience, then suddenly held me with a glare.

That look of bare hatred tempted me. It made me want to wait for the first opportunity, get him alone, then finish the job on his throat that I had started on Cabbage Key.

But I couldn't take the chance.

Maybe he was FEAT's assassin. I certainly had plenty of circumstantial evidence. He had ties to the world money market. He had arrived on St. Carib not long before the planned vacations of Kiev Evenki and Samuel Yabrud began. He had been seen talking to my friend Norm Fizer before Fizer disappeared. And Rob Wells had told me about his fascination for firearms.

There were a lot of marks against him.

Maybe too many marks.

But I had to wait and see. If it was Matrah, he would pay the price. I would follow Colonel Westervelt's orders to the letter.

The assassin's death would look like no accident.

If he didn't get me first.

So, in the darkness on that fourth night, I made the rounds of the island, slipping from shadow to shadow. There was still a light on in the main house. That was unusual. Through a third-story window I could see the dark outline of Matrah. There were voices, but I couldn't catch the words—only the thin peal of occasional laughter.

I wondered whom he was entertaining.

Not Yabrud—that was certain. I had watched the Israeli go to his cabin and switch out the light before I had gone to get the beer for Sonya.

I paused by the porch of the main house, straining to listen. And when I was sure that there was nothing to be heard, I checked once again to make sure the little geophone was still in place, then headed off through the darkness toward the water tower.

I took my time. Every now and then I'd stop, pull the Star-Tron scope to my eye, and scan the island.

I wanted to make sure that I wasn't being followed.

Tree rats scrambled in the high palms. A few mosquitoes vectored in on me, whining in my ears. Out on Pine Island Sound I could hear the small diesel putter of a commercial fisherman.

It was a calm night, soft and quiet.

It was a night filled with stars and a warm south wind. It was a night for fishing the passes, or for anchoring out with a cold beer. It was a fine night for walking. Or for love. But not for dying.

Yet I almost did.

I stepped into the assassin's trap at almost the same time I heard St. Carib's stiletto-shaped Excalibur roar to life.

I was three quarters of the way up the water-tower ladder when the boat's engines started. I turned to look, the Remington 700 slung over one shoulder, the seismic alarm case over the other.

In the thin starlight, I could see the glisten of boat and wake.

And the dark shapes of men—but I couldn't tell who they were or how many.

It wasn't that unusual, really. The night before, Matrah and his Mediterranean friends, along with Heiny and the other German, had taken the Excalibur to Cabbage Key for an evening of scotch. I had even kidded Heiny about his hangover that morning. And he had banged me playfully on the shoulder—then slipped me a note from Marina Cole. It said that she was anxious to see me, and that I should save some energy for her after my stay at St. Carib.

So the leaving of the Excalibur wasn't all that surprising—only they were leaving later than usual.

Much later.

Just after midnight, in fact.

So I wanted to get a look at them through the Star-Tron scope. I wanted to see who was going and where they were going.

And that's when I stepped into the trap.

It could have killed me.

It should have killed me.

But it didn't.

Someone had loosened the nails at the top of the ladder. The tower was about sixty feet high. Wooden steps zigzagged up the first forty feet to a small platform. The ladder began there. Someone falling from the top of the ladder would hit back first on the railing of the small platform, then catch the next railing along the wooden steps, then crash, finally, onto the old shell-and-cement base on which the tower was built.

It was one long back-breaking fall.

When I saw the Excalibur leaving, I tried to hurry up the ladder. My right hand grabbed the first loose rung just as my left hand reached above it for the final rung.

When the first gave away, I grabbed at the second frantically.

And I caught it, bending in toward the ladder, looking desperately for any kind of foot- or handhold.

But then that rung gave way with a sickening creak of nails pulling away from wood.

Anyone else it probably would have killed.

But I had spent my childhood working the high trapeze, learning how to maneuver my body in midflight.

I had only one option.

And I took it.

Instead of resigning myself to the fall, I gave a frantic outward spring with my legs. A wooden framework supported the tower. The braces were old two-by-fours crossed between the main pilings. They were more than a body length away from the ladder, and I barely caught the highest network of cross brace with my right hand.

My body swung under it with tremendous impact, and I felt the old wood bow beneath my weight. And just when I thought I had it made, there was a loud *ker-wack* as the two-by-four snapped.

But luckily the second brace, the one I had grabbed with my left hand, didn't.

I hung there by one hand for what seemed like a long time. The wood was old, possibly rotten. I couldn't take the chance of making any sudden moves. Slowly, I got my right hand up on the brace. Then, hand over hand, I pulled myself along to one of the four main vertical supports. After that, it was easy enough to lower myself from brace to brace, back to the ground.

An unexpected fall, like an unexpected noise, kicks all the caveman senses into gear.

The adrenaline goes roaring through the veins, and

the heart pounds high in the ears. Every muscle tenses involuntarily, ready for danger.

So, back on the ground, I had to force myself to take some deep breaths; had to command body and brain to relax. The black dragon had almost caught me this time. As the philosopher promises: "Death thou comest when least expected. . . ."

And I sure as hell hadn't expected that kind of trap.

So when I had calmed and was back in control, I made my brain scan the options, seeking my next move.

Doesn't the hunter usually like to watch his quarry fall?

Usually.

But it had taken me so much time to climb down the tower that he would probably be long gone by now—if he was around at all.

But why make my death look accidental? It didn't take me long to settle on the obvious: I was an American. Apparently, FEAT had nothing to gain from the death of an agent of the United States—not this time, anyway. My murder would only cloud the issue of Samuel Yabrud's assassination—and he *was* marked for assassination. I was convinced of that now.

Because if he wasn't, the assassin sure as hell wouldn't be playing a cat-and-mouse game with me.

No, this organization—an assemblage involved in terrorism strictly for profit—had a reason for wanting

Yabrud dead. And they didn't want me in the way, alive or otherwise.

But in that moment of terror, hanging one-handed from a rotten brace, I had made up my mind to disappoint them.

They had tried to kill me—and failed.

Now I was hell-bent on living to see them regret it.

I picked up the seismic alarm case. I had dropped it when the first rung gave away. The aluminum covering was bashed like a bad melon. It rattled when I shook it. But the sniper rifle with the night scope still hung on its sling over my shoulder.

It took me a while, but I finally found them: the two rungs that had given way. As I expected, the heads of the rusted nails were shiny with prying.

It had been no accident.

I set the rifle aside and, with the two wooden rungs in hand, climbed back up the ladder. I used the butt of the Randall knife to pound them back into their proper place on the ladder.

In the event the assassin hadn't been watching, I didn't want him to know that his trap had been sprung.

That done, I collected my gear and headed back through the shadows toward the water. I gave it a full ten minutes before I stepped into the clearing by the dock. I wanted to make sure no one was watching. I returned the seismic alarm to the fish-box compartment, hesitated, then put the Remington 700 in too.

I was tired of the weight of it.

And it hadn't been bringing me the best of luck.

Instead I took up the Cobra crossbow, pieced it together, slid the shaft holder onto the back of my belt, and inserted a half-dozen aluminum shafts, complete with triangular killing points.

I was tired of playing the assassin's game of hide-and-seek.

It was time for me to force someone's hand. And after almost being splattered by my fall, I was in just the proper mood to do some forcing.

I had allowed myself to be hunted for too long. It was time to turn the tables, to regain the initiative.

It was time for me to become the hunter.

I checked my Rolex. It was two forty-five a.m. Cabbage Key had closed long ago. And still the Excalibur was not back. At the base of the mound by the path that led to the dock was a big gumbo-limbo tree. I climbed the tree, found a suitable Y of branch, and made myself comfortable. It was time to wait. And think.

I didn't like the reading I was getting on this island, St. Carib. All along my instincts had been telling me there was something wrong. Something bad wrong. But I had chosen to follow D. Harold Westervelt's route of cold logic and cool reason—waiting, always waiting for just the right time.

But that just wasn't my style. And I had been paying for it all along.

In the business of war, you learn not to ignore the

little cerebral warning bells. And my private alarms had been going off since I had set foot on the island.

Sitting high in the branches of the gumbo-limbo, I sat and thought and waited. It was nearly three a.m. before the Excalibur made the turn into the St. Carib channel. It ran without running lights. Something had happened only a short time before that had me deep in thought—so deep in thought that I didn't hear them coming until they were almost to the docks.

While I was waiting, the ground had trembled suddenly, unexpectedly. Then I had heard a muted *whoof* in the distance and seen a brief corona of flame illuminate the far village of Boca Grande.

What in the hell could explode on Boca Grande at three a.m.?

I felt my stomach roll, and the hair stand on the back of my neck. I didn't like the obvious possibility: Maybe Kiev Evenki had decided to stay on after all.

And maybe FEAT's assassin had caught up with him.

The Excalibur came *burrbling* up to the dock. They didn't bother hauling it out with the davits. Four men got out of the boat. I wished I had brought the Star-Tron scope with me. I couldn't see their faces in the darkness.

The one shape was unmistakable. It was the lanky, angular form of Matrah.

They came quickly up the dock, as if running away from something.

As they got closer I recognized Matrah's two Arab sidekicks.

But the fourth man remained a mystery—until I heard the voice. It was cold and professional, native American.

"How long do you think it will take for them to piece the body together?" Matrah was asking.

"If they let the KGB help, a day. If they try it by themselves, a week."

"You are sure he was in the room?"

"Evenki? I saw him myself, Matrah. Don't worry."

It was like meeting your best friend unexpectedly in some distant corner of the earth, and it took me a while to place the voice.

And then I didn't have to, because I could see the face: the square-jawed, Rockwell dream of the all-American male.

It was my dead friend.

The fourth man was Stormin' Norman Fizer. . . .

14

They passed beneath my station in the tree.

I could see the tops of their heads as they hurried along the walk toward the main house.

I was tempted to end it for all four of them; tempted to bring the Cobra crossbow to bear on the temple of a man whom I had come to admire and trust.

Norm Fizer had been there in Cambodia when I needed him.

And he had come to my aid in Key West when I wanted to take revenge on the drug runners who had killed my family.

I had always thought that Fizer was one of the good ones, one of the government's dependable few.

So now I was in shock. Complete shock, as I watched him walk with the Mediterraneans, talking calmly about how he had set the bomb that had killed the Russian diplomat. My breath came soft and shallow, and my throat was dry. My hands were white on the alloy lightness of crossbow. Brain tissue began casting back and forth for an explanation, nerve centers blinking like a switchboard lighting up.

Fizer liked to joke about his small government salary—but there was always an edge to the joking. It bothered him.

He had a wife and kids. Two of the kids were in high school, college-bound.

And you don't send two kids to college on a civil servant's salary.

For his entire professional life he had plowed onward against the never-ending red tape and bureaucracy. In government work, he had seen how often a man's life is used as a pawn in the giant political chess game.

So maybe he had finally snapped; said to hell with it. Maybe he had finally decided that if he was going to be a pawn, he might as well be a highly paid pawn.

The four of them disappeared into the darkness at the top of the mound. The lights of the main house blinked on.

So this is the true test, MacMorgan. You were offered a mission that demanded an assassin—a cold-blooded killer. And you grabbed at it with all the reluctance of a barracuda hitting baitfish. But now you learn that the mission requires you to kill one of your best friends. No longer is the quarry an enigma or a symbol of evil—or any of those other hackneyed cubbyholes you depend upon to cloak your own inhumanity. This is a flesh-and-bone man. This is a person you have laughed with and drunk beer with and suffered with and trusted. So why not just pack your gear, grab the pretty lady on Cabbage Key, and head on back to your hermitage built upon the water? After all, it is just politics—D. Harold Westervelt said as much. And Fizer's death—or your own death—would be nothing more than the briefest ripple on the broadest sea.

I thought about it.

I really did. Various brain segments wrestled and struggled and battled to a conclusion.

Finally, I took a deep breath; exhaled.

I swung down from the tree, landing heavily on the shell path.

Then I mounted an aluminum shaft in the crossbow, arming it with the self-cocking device. And I noticed for the first time that my hands were shaking. . . .

Three of them sat in the living room of the main house.

I peered in through the corner of the window. There was a stone fireplace with old tarpon rods crossed over the mantelpiece. On the walls hung stuffed fish and one massive alligator skin.

It looked like the setting of a 1940 English mystery movie.

Fizer sat in a leather chair near the fireplace with a whiskey tumbler in his hand. Matrah sat across from him, and one of the Mediterraneans stood by his side.

I wondered what had happened to the third.

Fizer had his business smile on. He was talking. He wore clothes different from those described by the woman who had rented him the boat: black sweater and black pants. It was exactly the sort of thing I would have worn if I had gone to assassinate a Russian diplomat.

Or an American agent, for that matter.

The windows were closed in favor of the air conditioner. I couldn't hear what they were saying. None of them seemed to be carrying weapons. Fizer and Matrah were doing the talking.

Still the third Mediterranean did not arrive.

I gave it five more minutes. In that five minutes I must have checked my watch twenty times.

I was anxious to get it over with.

And I was tired of waiting.

I slid along the side of the house and up onto the expanse of porch. The door seemed to be built of heavy oak on brass hinges. No way to kick it in.

Ever so slowly, I turned the knob. It would go only halfway.

It was locked.

There were two massive windows fronting the porch. They began about thigh high. I took a moment, going over in my mind exactly what I was going to do once inside.

I didn't want to have to waste time thinking.

Quietly, I backed away from the door and positioned myself in front of the first window. There's a way to do it without getting cut—cut badly, at least. You throw yourself headlong toward the middle of the pane, where the glass is weakest, then at the last moment you tuck your head down, arms drawn in tight, and roll through it.

I hit the window with two quick sprinter's steps, crashed through it, landed on neck and shoulders, then sprang to my feet, crossbow leveled midway between Matrah and Fizer, ready if either of them made a move.

There was a brief slow-motion instant when the expressions on their faces registered on my brain: a mixture of surprise and horror. Fizer dropped his tumbler of whiskey. Matrah crouched as if about to duck—or draw a weapon.

I never got a chance to see what he did.

There was one blind spot in the room—a corner I could not see from any window. There was a liquor sideboard there. And that was where the missing Mediterranean stood.

It took him a moment to react.

But it took a longer moment for me to realize that he was there.

He hit me from the right side, making a lunging grab for the crossbow. I elbowed him solidly twice in the stomach, and still he did not let go. I forced him backward, then used his resistance to throw him forward, coming down hard on his neck with my knee. He clutched his throat, croaking.

From somewhere, a stub-nosed stainless .38 had

materialized in the hand of the other Mediterranean. I felt the sudden vacuum of air near my ear at the same moment I heard the explosion.

He had missed.

And I wasn't about to give him a chance to miss again.

I dove toward a chair, came up rolling, and felt the pinging recoil of the crossbow as I fired.

The aluminum shaft took him cleanly through the breastbone.

He dropped the .38 and touched the shaft in his chest as if puzzled.

Then he fell dead upon the varnished floor.

Matrah made a movement as if about to retrieve the revolver. I had the Randall knife out of its sheath, ready.

"Try it, asshole. Touch the revolver and you're as good as dead."

It stopped him. He stood looking at me, still in the crouch as if frozen.

Fizer spoke for the first time. He still sat in the leather chair. He looked oddly calm. There was a light smile on his face. He said, "He's pretty much right, Matrah. He's better with a knife than he is with a pistol. You learned how to throw knives in the circus, didn't you, Dusky? Isn't that what you told me back in Cambodia?"

I relaxed a bit, still holding the knife. "You've got a good memory, Stormin' Norman. Maybe you can remember exactly when you decided to become one of the bad guys. Tell me all about it before I turn you two over to the authorities. It'll be something to tell your wife and kids."

He still wore the smile. He looked like an NFL quarterback at a party thrown by college cheerleaders. "What, you're not going to kill me?"

"It crossed my mind. But luckily, I caught myself before they turned me into a machine—like they turned you into a machine. I'm disappointed in you, Fizer. I mean that. This whole intrigue business— what a crock of shit. The politicians sit back and yawn while we forfeit lives on the big board. But they got you hook, line, and sinker. It wasn't even a matter of playing the game—it was a matter of playing the game for the biggest bucks."

He stood up and wiped his face with a big right hand. "You're right, Dusky. About one thing: I'm still playing the game. But you're wrong about the other—I haven't switched sides."

I noticed a look of surprise on Matrah's face, quickly hidden.

"Pretty weak story, Stormin' Norman."

"You don't believe it?"

"Would you?"

He chuckled softly. "No, I guess I wouldn't. But it doesn't matter. It'll all come out later."

"How so?"

For the first time, Fizer looked serious. It was a look I remembered well—and once trusted. "I had them, Dusky. I had the whole damn FEAT organization in the palm of my hand. But you just blew it. You think I just came blundering over here and stupidly got myself captured? You know me better than that, MacMorgan. I smelled a rat. And you know the rat." He jerked a thumb at Matrah. "It's the Arab prince over here."

"You bastard," Matrah said between clenched teeth.

"He had too many connections not to be involved. But why settle for one small fish when you can get the whole school? I let him know that I might be interested in joining up if the price was right."

"And he fell for it, just like that," I said skeptically.

"You know better. That's why I couldn't get in touch with Westervelt. I disappeared, and I had to let you guys go on thinking that. They kept me locked up downstairs in a storm cellar for four, maybe five days. They kept questioning me, and I kept giving them information. But all the wrong information. I took the chance that I would be far more valuable to them alive than dead. And it had paid off. Until now. Tonight was my big test. They hadn't planned on killing Kiev Evenki, the Russian. Just Yabrud, the Israeli. The murder of a Jewish diplomat would cause a military buildup in Israel. Repercussions of the buildup would be felt all over the Middle East—especially in Egypt." He looked at the Mediterranean. "Isn't that the way you explained it to me, Matrah? Your organization—the one we call FEAT—had been steadily investing large sums of money in

Egyptian armament corporations over the past three months? You said the sudden surge in military spending would give you, what—a clean twenty to twenty-five percent profit?" Fizer smiled at me. "Shrewd bastards, huh, Dusky?"

"So why did you kill the Russian, Stormin' Norman? That's a little bit above and beyond the call of duty, isn't it?"

He shrugged. "Had to make them believe me, Dusky." I watched his eyes closely as he added, "Besides, the Russian wasn't there. They pulled him out a couple of days ago."

"How could you know that?"

"For one thing, I checked his room while Matrah and his goon squad waited for me to set the explosives. I talked to Evenki's stand-in. You know him pretty well, MacMorgan. A guy by the name of Westervelt. Told him to clear the area just before the fireworks."

"That's pretty easy to check out, Norm."

He nodded. "I'm planning on it." He grinned slightly. "Two things in this world I don't want hot on my trail, MacMorgan. And one of them's the KGB."

"What's the second?"

"You."

"So what would you have done if they wanted you to kill Yabrud? Or me, Stormin' Norman?"

"I knew they had someone else for those jobs."

"Who?"

"That's what I was about to find out when you came busting in."

Matrah had held his frozen pose, caught, it seemed, in a combination of shock and seething. I nodded toward him. "It's not him or one of the other Mediterraneans?"

"No. They've got another connection here on the island."

"We can persuade him to tell us."

"Maybe. Maybe not. One thing's for sure—the moment their assassin smells something wrong, he'll be long gone." Norm brushed at his neatly styled brown hair. "Face it, Dusky, we threw the net and came up with some of the fish. But not all of them. Our government just wanted to give FEAT a message: Don't practice your terrorism in the United States. Maybe this will be message enough."

"And maybe not. You might be done with your job. But I'm not done with mine."

"Dammit, MacMorgan, this is no time to be stubborn!"

"Let's just say I have a personal interest in all this, Fizer. A sporting interest. Their assassin wants to play tag. Almost killed me tonight. Now it's his turn to be the rabbit."

"Dusky, when Matrah here doesn't show up tomorrow, their man will take it on the run. And one thing they're not short of is connections. Important connections. They'll have him out of the country an hour after he makes it to the mainland."

"But what if Matrah has a legitimate excuse for not showing up?"

"And how do you plan to work that?"

I crossed the room, keeping a tight eye on the Mediterranean. I had made my decision about Stormin' Norman Fizer. Every point of his story was plausible. It was just the sort of thing Fizer would do—walk solo into the lion's den. Besides, I had instinctive feelings about Fizer. He was one of the few you could trust. That's why I had been so shocked when I saw him get out of the Excalibur with the others. I could have waited until the next day, gone to Boca Grande and rounded up Westervelt to check out the story. But that would have blown my plan for evening the score.

And this was the last chance I would have.

I bent over the corpse of the dead Mediterranean. Blood had pooled beneath him on the varnished floor. It smelled of heated metal, and with that was the stench of human feces. There is an odor to fresh death, an odor fouler than the carrion we will all become. It is the fume of despair, and it never fails to hit me broadside. This man at my feet had once been a child, lived and loved as we all do. He had laughed and cried and sought approval in his own way—until his way had crossed my path.

The look of puzzlement was still on his face. Behind me, the other Mediterranean was kneeling, still fighting for air. He, at least, would live.

I picked up the stainless .38, hesitated, then handed it to Fizer.

"There! Shoot him! Shoot him, dammit!"

Matrah made a lunge as if to take the revolver. Fizer caught him with a short left to the jaw that sent him wheeling backward, crashing into a chair. It didn't knock him out. But it turned the dark eyes glassy.

"Just like old times, eh, Dusky?" Fizer said, licking the skinned knuckles.

"Yeah, except I'm feeling older. And meaner."

"God forbid."

"You bastard!" Matrah yelled, spitting blood. "You lied to me. You'll pay for lying to me!"

"I'd go to hell just to be with my friends, if for no other reason." Fizer turned to me. "So now what?"

"Now I'm going to type a note for Matrah to sign. He's been called away suddenly. And the Solitary is to go on as planned. There's an older woman who works in his business office. We'll leave the note on her desk. Then you're going to cart Matrah and his two friends back to Boca Grande in the Excalibur and get in touch with Colonel Westervelt—and then call your wife. She's heartsick, you know."

"I never told her it would be easy being married to me. But what are you going to do?"

"I'm going to enjoy the Solitary, of course. I've still got some weight to lose. But first I'm going to write some notes of my own. Don't worry, if worse comes to worse, Yabrud's CIA bodyguards will be somewhere on the island—you can bet on that."

"Does all this mean you know who the assassin is?"

"Let's just say that with Matrah and his goons out of the picture, it narrows it down. Way down . . ."

15

Fizer had been right. There was no way to force Matrah to cooperate with us—and that included signing the farewell note. Finally, I rummaged through some papers in his desk and forged his signature as best I could.

He was not pleased. We tied and gagged him, and forced him down the mound through the darkness to the stiletto-shaped racing boat. His Mediterranean friend came along meekly enough. It would be another few days before he could even speak—let alone yell for help.

The third Mediterranean was deposited aboard wrapped in green tarp.

"You'll clean up the blood up there?"

"Yeah," I said.

"I don't understand why you still have to go to Cabbage Key before daylight."

"Because when this is all over, I'm going to take an immediate vacation. There's a very pretty lady over there who knows how to sail. She'll be going with me."

"I should have known. What are those papers in your hand?"

"Notes."

"What do they say?"

"You wouldn't understand."

"You're being pretty damn secretive, MacMorgan."

"The assassin will understand. That's all that matters."

"I'm going to be in the landing party that arrives on Cayo Costa at midnight. You'd better have Ya-brud there in perfect health and your business over by then."

"Promise. On both counts. And like I said, Stormin' Norman, call your wife."

He was grinning as he pulled out in the Excalibur, headed for Boca Grande.

I checked my watch. I had only a couple of hours before daylight.

And there was no time to waste.

I made my way back up the mound and stopped outside Sonya Casimur's cottage. I slid the note under the door after deciding not to chance going inside. I did the same at the fat Texan's cottage, and at Heinrich Keppler's quarters.

When I had told Norm Fizer I had it narrowed down, I wasn't lying. The note the assassin had left finally told me:

There is no place safer than in the tracks of the hunter. . . .

The assassin was someone close.

The assassin was someone who had taken pains to stay right in my tracks.

For an instant, I considered taking *Sniper* to Cabbage Key. But that would have been the stupidest of moves. Instead, I went aboard, got the Remington 700 sniper rifle from the fish-box compartment, grabbed an old styrofoam cooler and some extra clothes, then slid through the shadows to one of the little wooden skiffs moored in the shallows.

I rowed well away from St. Carib Island before starting the engine.

Marina Cole was alone in the little board-and-batten house at the foot of the mound. Her sailboat was moored to the dock just outside. In the darkness, with the sails down, it seemed to slumber like the rest of Cabbage Key.

I puttered up in the little skiff, paused outside as I tied up, then went up the wooden walkway to the cottage. Plants hung inside the screened-in porch. I banged my head on one, then stopped its swaying before it fell.

"Who's there? Is someone out there?" Her voice was soft, deep with sleep.

"Just your friendly guardian angel."

"Dusky!"

I heard the sound of a light switch, then I heard

her swear softly when the light did not come on. The island generator was off. Finally, there was the striking of a match, brief explosion of sulfur, then the yellow glow of a kerosene lamp.

She wore an extra-large T-shirt with the Cabbage Key seal on it: soaring osprey backdropped by the water tower. In the soft light you could see the elongation of nipples and the weight of breasts beneath material, and the T-shirt ended abruptly just above the widening of hips and flaxen curl at the intersection of thighs. She was smiling.

"Just happened to be in the neighborhood."

"Well, it's about time, MacMorgan!"

She brushed feathering blond hair from her face and fell into my arms, still holding the lamp.

"Hmmm, you smell nice, lady."

"And you feel nice, MacMorgan. God, it seems like a month."

"Or two."

"Or a year. Can you stay? You can stay, can't you? Jesus, what time is it? I feel like I'm dreaming. A very nice dream . . ."

I held her tightly, my mouth against hers, hips pressing, hands searching, body wanting her more than ever.

"Hold it, lady."

"That's what I'm trying to do. This damn belt . . ."

"Whoa—not that." I held her away from me. "I can't stay. Let's not start anything we can't finish."

"We already have," she said huskily, pressing herself against me.

"Will you just give me a minute to talk, Marina?"

The tone of my voice stopped her. She put the lamp on the table, suddenly serious. "What's wrong, Dusky?"

"How well do you like working here—waiting tables at Cabbage Key?"

"What? Well, I love it, I guess. The people are great, and—"

"You wouldn't be interested in going away with me tomorrow night?"

"Dusky, I'd love to go anywhere with you, anytime, but why tomorrow night? That's a day before that stupid St. Carib course you're taking is over, and . . ." Her eyes grew suddenly worried. "What's going on, MacMorgan? I don't like the readings I'm getting on all this."

"What do you mean, Marina?" I watched her face closely. She paused for a moment, then sat down in a wicker chair beside the kerosene lamp.

"First of all, I don't believe you went to St. Carib to lose weight. You don't need to lose weight."

"So?"

"Dammit, Dusky, why are you playing these games with me? It has something to do with Matrah . . . Matrah and my father, doesn't it? You're investigating them or something."

"Would it upset you if I was?"

"Yes! I mean, no!" She jammed her hands against her face. "Dusky, they're an . . . unfeeling people. I know that. As much as I love my father, I have to admit that to myself. I hate everything they stand for. That's why I really stopped here—to ask Matrah one last time for a divorce. I wanted to be done with them now and forever. That's why I don't want to see you get involved, Dusky. You don't know the extent of their power. Their business: It's not brutal . . . but it is *merciless*. Nothing stands in their way, Dusky. Do you understand what I'm saying? A private business, a piece of property, a human life— it's all the same when it goes through their computers. Dusky, please . . . I don't want to see you hurt. . . ."

She buried her face in her hands. The tears in the lamplight were real.

"Hey, I'm a Rogue, remember?"

She nodded silently.

"Rogues don't get involved with organizations— you told me that."

She sniffed, then half cried, half laughed. "You're already involved, MacMorgan—with me."

"Does that mean you'll leave with me? Tomorrow night?"

"You know I will."

"Okay," I said. "Listen carefully. Just before midnight, anchor off the Captiva Pass end of Cayo Costa. As close as you can get. Watch out for the shoal waters of Pejuan Point. You'll see them on the chart."

I took her hands in mine and forced her to look at me. "This is the most important thing, Marina. Whatever you do, don't come ashore. Understand? Under no circumstances leave your boat. I'll have a flashlight. I'll signal three times from shore, then swim out. We'll pick up *Sniper*, then cruise anywhere you want, and for as long as you like. Got it?"

She nodded, stood up. I took her in my arms. Her face tasted of salt, and her hair smelled of shampoo.

"Why not tonight, Dusky? Why don't we just leave now?"

Her lips were full and soft against mine. Her breasts pressed tight against my chest, and I could feel the quickened thumping of her heart.

"No, Marina."

"I could have my things ready in five minutes. In an hour we could be far away from all of this . . . whatever it is you're involved in."

"I can't."

She took my face roughly in her hands. "Dusky, I want to be with you. I want to be with you now and for a long, long time to come. . . ."

I pulled away, kissing her on the forehead. "Tomorrow night, beautiful lady. Tomorrow night."

She walked me down to the dock, shivering in the cool March night. She held me with one arm around the waist like high school lovers on a walk through the park.

We kissed briefly, deeply. "Sleep tight, Marina."

"And you sleep safe, MacMorgan."

There was an odd forlorn expression on her face as I pulled away from the dock.

And she did not return my farewell wave. . . .

I had a final preparation to make before I was ready.

I cut the little skiff around the back side of Cabbage Key, zigging and zagging along the dark mangrove points. I knew that the only place the St. Carib cruiser could get in to drop our group off on Cayo Costa was the public dock on the bay side of the north end of the island, where there were a few neat cabins.

But how would they decide who would go in which direction?

It really didn't matter.

I beached the skiff well away from the dock and headed through island back country. Australian pines leaned in the predawn breeze. Coons rustled in dunes and clumps of sea oats.

I needed a place I could find easily the next day.

It wouldn't do to hide my weapon and the other equipment someplace where even I couldn't find them.

Halfway across the island I found the perfect spot. Like the other barrier islands in Pine Island Sound, Cayo Costa had been inhabited by fishermen at the turn of the century. The only thing remaining of that brief civilization was a graveyard. The graves were barren—as if weeds refused to grow there. A few had stone markers. Most were just outlined with old horse conch and whelk shells.

Near one grave was a loblolly pine. The ground was covered with needles. I buried the rifle, the baggy clothes, and the Styrofoam cooler beneath the needles near the grave, then covered my tracks as best I could.

That done, I headed back to my skiff. There was an eeriness in the island quiet. Like for an athlete who visits the stadium the night before the game, the silence seemed to echo with screams soon to come.

The screams and the gunshots . . .

16

Our group met by the dock at noon. The other forty or so people clustered around the yard by the water, all divided into their little four-man societies.

Say what you want about St. Carib, but its program seemed to work.

They looked like different people from the rich male and female fatties who had assembled there that first day. They had good tans, their eyes shone, and they had all lost a bunch of weight.

The St. Carib staff hustled back and forth, clipboards in their hands. And more than once I heard them curse Matrah for leaving them alone with the final preparations for Solitary.

I expected Sonya Casimur to treat me coolly after our little parting scene. Instead, she gravitated toward me as always. She wore the standard warmup suit—as we all did—and she had her duffel bag slung over her shoulder like a sailor.

"Ready to do some surviving?" she asked. The

dark hair was neatly styled, as if she were going to a dinner party instead of two days alone on the beach. I didn't know if it really was an odd question to ask, or if it just sounded odd because I hadn't gotten any sleep the night before. I studied the brown peasant eyes. They seemed to hold nothing but wry humor—and maybe just a touch of affection.

"More than ready. And you?"

She sighed. She had completely dropped the actress routine by now. The Italian accent was light. "I guess. God, anything to get away from all these drooling men."

"They've been bothering you? I thought they all got the message by the second or third day."

She reached over and patted my hand. "Do not worry about it. It is nothing important. But last night someone left me a very strange note. Men think they know other men. They don't. Only a woman can truly know men."

"Hey, what's that? One of y'all got a note—is that what I heard?" The fat Texan had been standing within earshot, talking to Samuel Yabrud. The two of them came strolling over. Like most at St. Carib, Yabrud looked much better than before. It seemed as if his skin had tightened over the elephantine body, and there was a smile on his face. Only the Texan seemed worn by it all. Folds of skin sagged beneath the pale, piggish eyes, as if he was very tired.

"I got me one of them weird notes myself, little lady. Just what did yours say?"

I felt Sonya move closer to me, as if to use me as a shield against the Texan's loud voice. "It was nothing," she said, unconcerned. "It's not worth talking about."

"Well, little lady, if it was anything like the gibberish in mine, you're absolutely goddam right about it bein' unimportant." He turned to Yabrud. "Sam, I'm tellin' ya, you think you Jews got trouble with the Arabs— why, it ain't nothin' to the shit that's goin' on here in America. People gettin' crazier and crazier all the time. I'll damn sure be glad to get back to Texas, mister man, and you can bet your firstborn on that. Imagine payin' two grand to come to this island so they can starve us and berate us, and leave us weird-ass notes in the middle of the goddam night. . . ."

Yabrud gave me a private, tolerant wink, and led the fat Texan away. It was a strange pairing, those two. And I knew that if Yabrud could put up with the Texan, he richly deserved his reputation as a diplomat.

St. Carib's sportfisherman was sixty feet of luxury, an oceangoing fishing machine that seemed humbled by its mundane life as a ferry for the fat and wealthy.

Our group was the last to board. I had seen Heinrich Keppler several times that morning, but he had always been too busy to stop and talk. Now he came lumbering up to the dock, a clipboard and a walkie-talkie in hand. He smiled and wiped imaginary sweat from his brow.

"Whew!" he said. "Some busy morning, eh, my big American friend?"

"Looks like everyone's all set to go, Heiny."

"Ya! Finally, it is prepared!" His face described sudden rage. "That Matrah bastard goes hunting the girl tail, and leaves all the work to us, hah! My money pay is not big enough to cover such work. Me, I am just the trainer—but no, that is not enough. Now I must sign the papers. Answer the questions. Tell the cook if he must wipe his ass while we are gone only two days!" He threw up his hands. "I tell you, Heiny is looking forward to the rest. Me, I am going to lay in the beach on the sun and read the dirty magazines, *ya*!"

He grinned at me and slapped me on the shoulder as we went down the dock and joined the others aboard.

The few friends Sonya had made on St. Carib were fat women outside our group. She was forward in the main cabin with them, talking animatedly about their coming adventure.

I stood on the broad fighting deck with Heiny, making idle conversation.

In one way, I hoped he'd bring it up. He was a likable guy with his broken English and his big grin. Besides, he'd helped me out on Cabbage Key with Matrah.

But in another way, I hoped he would never mention it.

Because that would leave only one other alternative.

And it wasn't a pleasant alternative at all.

Finally, tired of waiting, weary with no sleep and the continual suspense, I brought it up.

"I found some kind of weird note under my door this morning, Heiny."

He didn't look surprised. Just puzzled. "*Ya?* The strange note?"

"Read like gibberish, really. Sonya got one. And so did the fat Texan."

He touched his lips with his index finger. "What did this strange note say, my American friend?"

I told him.

"*Ya?*"

"You don't seem surprised."

He thought for a moment, then shook his head. "I am surprised, *yes*. I am surprised because I got such a note. Though my English is highly good, I sometimes do not understand the American humor. I thought it was to be a joke."

"It didn't seem very funny to me."

He made a circling motion with index finger against temple. "The little piggies on our island. Perhaps the hunger makes one of them looney-tuney."

"Maybe," I said. "I guess."

They began dropping off the four-person groups on islands. All were told to spread out on the beaches, at least a mile apart. They were told that these two days alone were a very important part of the St. Carib philosophy, and that they should not violate the privacy of others.

The message was simple: Get the hell off by yourself, lose even more weight by fasting, and then stay there until we come to pick you up.

We made stops at several unnamed sand-spit islands, then at both ends of Punta Blanco, where Marina Cole and I had stayed that first night together, at Johnson Shoals, and, finally, at Cayo Costa.

Much of the hooting and laughter had disappeared in the knowledge that they would be staying on the islands alone.

It sobered them: the fat Texan, Yabrud, and Sonya, too.

The last time any of them had been truly alone was in the executive washrooms of their corporations or film studios.

I walked Sonya partway down the beach. She had insisted on carrying her own duffel. Heiny, the Texan, and then Yabrud had peeled off miles back up the island.

"It will be very lonely out here, no?"

I laughed. "No."

She put her hand on my shoulder. She still had that electric touch. "Does that mean you will not come to visit?"

"What, and break the St. Carib creed?"

"Damn their rules." She slipped her arm through

mine, holding my elbow against the heat of her breast. "Even as a friend you would not come to see me?"

"Maybe," I said. "As a friend, Sonya."

After an appropriate spacing, I said goodbye to the actress, then headed on down the beach. I wanted to get as far away from all of them as I could. I stopped a half mile short of Captiva Pass. The beach was an expanse of white sand backdropped abruptly by cabbage palms. The Gulf of Mexico was winter-clean. I could see the magnified darkness of rock beneath translucent swells. The first instinct of anyone camping alone is to build a shelter. I was counting on Samuel Yabrud to do the same. Using the Randall knife, I hacked limbs off a dead casuarina tree, made a frame on the beach, then covered the frame with palmetto fans. I had positioned the hut so that the back of it was hidden by sea oats and a series of dunes. Just in case someone was watching, I surveyed the hut as if satisfied, yawned like an actor in a silent movie, then crawled inside.

I gave it ten minutes, then slid out the back in the cover of the high sea oats.

Walking the back country of Cayo Costa is not easy. There is cactus, mangrove, and sand spurs. Fish crows cawed in the trees, and I hoped the assassin was not hunter enough to know the significance of that.

Behind Sonya Casimur's camp, I played voyeur for longer than I should have.

I couldn't help it.

With clothes on, she was beautiful.

Naked, she was magnificent.

She worked nude on the beach, oiled in the bright sunlight. She built her lean-to of palmettos, whistling while she worked. Despite her age, hers was the body of a twenty-year-old goddess. She seemed without a care, alone and female and perfect against the swollen turquoise of sea. The vision of her yanked at the heart and clamped the breathing.

Finally, I pulled myself away and headed up the island. The fat Texan, Samuel Yabrud, and even Heiny worked at their shelters. Yabrud was building his in a clearing of casuarinas, and for that I was glad.

I located the graveyard, felt strangely compelled to pause in respect, then recovered my gear from beneath the loblolly pine. That done, I headed back for my camp.

I hadn't slept in far too long.

And with darkness only a few hours away, I didn't have much time.

After a lifetime of assorted deadlines, we all have brain clocks. Mine awoke me at six p.m., just before dark.

A sun as red as Venus balanced on the lip of sea horizon, then dissolved into a windy dusk.

Pelicans drifted on the wind in the formation of Canada geese, and sea birds came roosting landward.

I crawled out the backside of my shelter, gear in hand. I hacked, spit, and urinated when I was safely hidden by the jungle growth of island.

Sandflies were out for their sundown feast, and they were like specks of acid on bare skin. Mosquitoes vectored.

The nervousness was low in my stomach. Would it work? Yes, it had to work.

I was no longer the hunted.

I was the hunter.

But the question was: Could I bring myself to kill the quarry?

I slipped through the back country. In the coolness, Sonya had pulled on her warmup pants and jacket. She had built a fire. Against the dusk sky and flickering light, she was a lovely silhouette.

After making sure that the fat Texan and Heiny were still at their camps, I made my way to Samuel Yabrud's lean-to. He was having trouble getting his fire going—and for good reason. He was trying to burn red mangrove. He talked to it in Yiddish, as if swearing.

It scared the hell out of him when I tapped him on the shoulder. And when he saw the rifle I was carrying, his eyes grew round with terror.

"What is it? Why . . . why do you . . ."

"It's okay," I said. "I'm on your side. The CIA gave you those two bodyguards for a reason. Someone wants to kill you."

"But why!"

"Damned if I know. But we don't have time to talk about it. Just do as I say, and you won't get hurt. At midnight, a couple of Navy helicopters are going to land at the southern end of the island. They'll fly you out of here."

He shook his head, resigned. "This is all such a crazy business."

"I'm just beginning to realize that."

I pulled him along behind me through the back country. He had lost weight, but he was still no athlete. I had to stop twice for him to rest. When we were well away from all the camps, I picked out a narrow point of beach.

"You'll stay right here until you hear the choppers coming, got it? Don't stray out on the beach—that's important. If you hear someone coming, just get low. No one could possibly know you're here. They'll expect you to be at your camp."

"But what will they do when they see I'm not there?"

"They won't get a chance to do anything."

"You will kill them?"

"It seems like the thing to do. . . ."

17

The assassin came an hour before midnight.

A few minutes earlier, I had heard the dull *ker-whump* of a small explosion. The flare of light on the distant beach told me that it had been my lean-to exploding.

A hand grenade?

Probably not. They would want it to appear—superficially, at least—like an accident.

Maybe a can of gas thrown into the campfire.

It didn't matter. By now the assassin would know there was no scream from within; no body to find. The assassin would be hunting me.

I sat hidden in the gnarled limbs of a buttonwood tree. Yabrud's camp was at the narrowest part of the island. Through the Star-Tron scope of the sniper rifle, I had a clear view of the beach on the Gulf side, and an almost equally good view of the bay side. I could see the lighted water tower of Cabbage Key.

Beyond that, I could see the window glow of Useppa, and then the darkness of St. Carib.

After depositing Yabrud, I had made my way back to his camp. Quickly, before darkness brought the assassin, I had thrown the red mangrove away and got a good fire going near his lean-to.

I piled on the big driftwood so that it would burn a long time. Salt deposits added color to the flames: green and orange and blue.

Then I had built my dummy between the fire and the lean-to. I made arms and body of branches, then covered it with the baggy shirt I had brought. I broke apart the Styrofoam cooler and carved a head from it, giving special attention to copying Yabrud's round face and hawkish nose. I skewered the Styrofoam head onto the body, then covered the head with the mosquito netting.

From a distance, in the darkness, the silhouette was convincing.

Even through the Star-Tron scope it looked life-like enough.

So then I had climbed the tree to wait.

And wait.

And wait.

When the urge to leave the tree and hunt the assassin on foot was upon me, I would comfort myself with a pinch of snuff, spitting silently in the darkness.

And always there was the question in my mind:

What if it is her, MacMorgan? What if she was the one who challenged you to the hunt, and then tried to kill you by loosening the boards from the water tower? Will you be able to bring the cross hairs to bear? And will you be able to squeeze the trigger?

I prayed I would not get the chance to find out.

Through the Star-Tron scope, I kept watching for Marina Cole's sailboat to leave Cabbage Key, then bank southward for Cayo Costa.

But aside from the normal small-boat traffic on the intercoastal waterway, there was no sign of her *Sleek.*

The sound of my lean-to exploding surprised me. It happened at ten-fifty by the green luminescence of the Rolex.

I fought off the urge to bail out of the tree and go after the assassin on a run.

But I didn't have to. The killer came soon enough.

I never did hear the crack of footfall, any snapping of branches.

She was good. Very damn good. She wore dark-blue pants and jersey that blended into the night. Behind me, on the Gulf side, I could hear only the wash and draw of waves, and the unexpected splash of fish feeding in the dark sea.

She had stayed to the middle of the island, coming through the jungle to my camp. She carried a rifle in her right arm, slung comfortably, like a hunter after pheasant.

At the path that led from the bay side of the island to Yabrud's lean-to, she hesitated. I could see her weapon clearly through the Star-Tron scope. She rested her perfect face against the brutal skeleton stock of her SVD Dragunov sniper rifle. On the rifle was mounted the complex Soviet infrared night sight and spotlight.

She was squinting through the sight.

She saw me just as I brought the crosshairs to bear on her forehead.

In a flash of movement, everything seemed to revolve in slow motion.

There was a pitiful look of shock on her face; then the look became horror, as if she saw something else through her infrared scope.

There was the explosion of a high-caliber rifle firing, but it was not her rifle.

Behind me, the Styrofoam head of Samuel Yabrud shattered like an ice sculpture.

I tried to force myself to shoot as she brought her rifle up, but I could not, thinking: *If I am to die, let it be her; someone I have come to love in a way.*

I felt no fear as she leveled her rifle, noticing, oddly, that it was aimed near me—but not at me.

There was a burst of flame. The recoil contorted her face.

Behind me, there was the increased thrashing of fish feeding in the wash of Gulf.

And then I realized the thrashing was not fish at all.

"Dusky! Dusky, don't shoot—please!"

Marina Cole came running toward me. Her face

looked strangely saintly in the weak light. "It wasn't me you're after—it was him."

I swung down out of the tree. She came crashing into my arms.

"What in the hell are you doing out here?"

She took a deep breath, lifted her rifle, and flicked on the mounted spotlight. "That's what I'm doing out here, Dusky. The same thing you're doing."

In the stark-white blaze of light, I could see a body awash on the beach.

It was a man. He wore a black wet suit. He clutched a rifle similar to Marina's in his right hand. I walked evenly across the beach and rolled the corpse over with my foot.

It was Heinrich Keppler.

Blood seeped from a hole in the wet suit. Blond hair washed down over his face. The eyes were open, and the last bit of life focused on me. He reached out with a big arm as if to take me by the throat. He died as the note fell from his hand. I knew what it said: *The quarry and the shadow flee at midnight.*

Marina stood looking at the body, her breath coming soft and shallow. There was a strange look of peace on her face. She said, "You would have killed him if I hadn't, Dusky. You had everything planned perfectly."

I felt myself suddenly overcome with rage. I grabbed her by the shoulders and shook her. "Why? Why you?"

She did not attempt to pull away from me. "Because I had to, Dusky."

"That means a hell of a lot!"

"Dusky, he would have killed the Israeli—you know that. What you don't know is that, working for FEAT, he's already assassinated seven other people. One of them was the nine-year-old daughter of a Saudi millionaire. Life meant nothing to him—just as life means nothing to Matrah, or to my father. They disassociate themselves from it. A Pope, a President, or a Jewish diplomat—it wouldn't matter. They will do anything to shift the world financial flow in their direction. Don't you see? To them, it's just a game. One big goddam game!"

I still had her by the shoulders. Suddenly, things were becoming clear: This was the thrill seeker who had climbed mountains, jumped out of airplanes, experimented with drugs and political ideologies, trying to recapture that single moment of freedom she had felt one stormy night long, long ago.

She looked at me and touched my face tenderly. "I would have left with you yesterday, Dusky. I want you to believe that. I love you . . . I do love you."

"But now it's too late, right?"

"A boat is waiting for me. I can't even tell you where. I'll be in Cuba tomorrow. They wanted the kill very badly, Dusky. They had been in touch with me earlier. Remember when I told you about my bout with communism? It wasn't a bout. It lasted.

They figured I had the inside track on my own father's organization. And they were right. As I said, I hate everything my father's organization stands for."

"Was killing a man as good as saving a man's life, Marina?"

She looked at me and did not answer. She didn't have to. The sudden forlorn look on her face was answer enough.

"I've got to go," she said. "They'll be waiting."

"The KGB?"

"Yes, Dusky," she said. "The KGB." She turned and walked away into the darkness, stopping only to throw her own rifle far out into the night sea. . . .

Epilogue

On a bright April afternoon I found myself reading and rereading a perfumed letter that bore the postmark of a country I had never really wanted to visit before.

The fact is, I hate to travel.

And I hate airports.

And I especially hate Miami. It has become America's plastic vacation face, and Florida's chamber of commerce people just don't have the guts—or the character—to admit that the only people who really enjoy Miami are the murderers and the thieves and the rapists.

So I was not exactly enthralled with my seat at Gate 81, waiting to board the glistening 747 outside.

When the booming voice of the airport PA politely suggested that the plane for Greece was now ready for flight, and that we'd all better get our butts in gear if we didn't want to be left behind, I grabbed my canvas satchel and smiled at the pretty stewardess as she checked my ticket.

The truth is, I had been smiling all the while: Even though I was in an airport. In Miami. Getting ready to make the longest flight I had made since coming back from Vietnam.

At the wastebasket by the boarding tunnel, I almost threw the letter away. I didn't need it anymore—I had already memorized it:

Dusky,
    The filming over here is going fine, and the food is wonderful, and my leading man is a gay boy who doesn't chase me about drooling, so why is it I feel so bad?
    Please take the next flight for Athens or I will never let you call my thighs fat again.

                                        Love,
                                        Sonya

I hesitated at the wastebasket, then jammed the letter into the back pocket of my khaki fishing pants.

It was going to be a long flight.

And, for some reason, the more I read the letter, the better I felt. . . .

Here's an exciting glimpse of the thrilling adventure that awaits you in the next novel of this action-packed series:

EVERGLADES ASSAULT

Sometimes there's just no way of saying no.

Especially when the woman asking is a nineteen-year-old sea enchantress wearing one of those thin bikinis that swell and strain against a body that seems hell-bent on escaping.

I had been enjoying a quiet July morning on my weather-scoured house built on stilts a mile out to sea where Calda Bank curves around the channel into Key West.

When you've lived in Florida for a long time, you come to treasure those summer mornings.

In the fresh heat of a new day, the sea is glass. Fish moving over the flats leave a wake, and you can hear the sound of barracuda crashing bait a long, long way off. The air is rarefied and washed by the rain of the previous evening, and the allotropic ozone fragrance of lightning is as strong as jasmine.

So when you treasure the morning, you get up early and try to enjoy every second.

Like most things in life, the morning is not the sort of thing you enjoy by hot pursuit—like kids racing to open presents on Christmas morning.

It's the sort of thing you enjoy obliquely. It's the sort of thing you enjoy through the wayward eye, savoring and tasting like a voyeur. You have to sit back, pick out a few meaningless tasks, go to work, and let it settle upon you. The Zen people have a delicate image for such things. They use a snowflake. You have to let the flake settle at its own speed, follow its own course, because if you reach out to grab it, it will just disappear.

So I was enjoying the morning.

I had awakened at first light, boiled coffee, urinated from the uppermost dock, then forced myself to do pull-ups and a fast half-mile swim before settling back for my attack on the new day.

On the Transoceanic radio, I dialed in the BBC at twenty-one-hundred megahertz. The London Symphony was doing a piece on strings and timpani I had never heard before. It was controlled and fresh, and I turned up the volume so that I could hear it out on the porch.

Looking south, I could see the thin darkness of Fleming Key. Pelicans wheeled and crashed in the distance, and the eastern sea was a track of molten gold. I sat on the porch, back against the worn wood of the house, and I went to work tying leaders.

When a half dozen Bimini twists had finally gotten

the sweat going, plopping down from my nose, I stood up and went inside.

I have to watch my beer intake. In my line of work, an extra pound of fat can slow you a half step.

And a half step can mean the difference between living and dying.

But on a morning such as this, a cold Tuborg was a necessary indulgence. Like I said, you have to meet the good things halfway.

So I opened the beer, letting it sluice away the sleep phlegm and morning taste of coffee, then went back outside.

That's when I saw the boat.

It was one of those old flat skiffs built for stability and shoal water. At first I thought it might be one of the Key West bonefish guides. The skiff was typically overpowered, but the person at the wheel damn sure knew how to use that power.

The boat came arrowing across the morning sea in a perfect V of turquoise wake. Had to be doing forty, minimum. The pilot paid no attention to the channel markers—didn't have to. People who really know the backwater off Key West can run the wheel tracks of crabbers or the intricate network of flat streams as easily as most people follow interstates.

And this person obviously knew the backwater.

I considered going down to my thirty-four-foot sport fisherman, *Sniper*, and breaking out the binoculars to get a better look at this skiff ace.

But I didn't have to.

The skiff banked prettily, followed the winding Bluefish Channel briefly, then powered off into shoal water my way. And in another minute I could see exactly who the skiff ace was.

She wore one of those dark blue string bikinis that grab at the heart and contract the stomach muscles. And since I knew the woman, I also knew that she wore it more for comfort than for style.

A thousand years ago, she would have been the type to shake her head in disapproval at the fig leaf clothes, and choose instead to run around happily and healthily nude.

For her the bikini was a compromise.

I went down to the dock to meet her after pulling on a pair of gray cotton gym shorts. She waved as she backed the skiff off plane, then brought her in starboard side.

It was April Yarbrough, the daughter of a crusty old Key West friend of mine.

More than a year before, April had paid me the supreme compliment of falling into a girlish infatuation. She had flirted and winked and wagged that lush body of hers around, and finally I had to take off on my boat just to get the hell away.

Because the infatuation was mutual.

But in the meantime she had gone off to college in Gainesville. Her first month away, I had received a steady stream of letters at the marina at Garrison Bight where I run my charterboat and stay when business demands that I be in town. But the letters gradually tapered off as her interests and her life were refocused—as I knew they inevitably would be.

You have to love the young ones from afar. You have to give them plenty of room to live and roam and seek, because if you make the unforgivable mistake of allowing them to give themselves too soon, they ultimately end up feeling trapped.

And April Yarbrough was far too fine a woman for that.

So I had acknowledged the letters politely, then allowed them to disappear unchallenged.

And then I buried my disappointment privately.

But I couldn't hide my delight in seeing her again. She really hadn't changed that much. The raven-black hair had been braided, and it hung like a rope down to her hips. There was the hint of Indian heritage in face and cheeks, and her strange golden eyes still suggested some ancient knowledge that went far beyond her nineteen years. Her body was lithe and long, sun-bronzed beneath her bikini, with the heavy thrust of breasts and curve of thighs visible beneath thin material.

"MacMorgan, you old fart!"

"April—you young fart!"

She gave the bowline a couple of quick wraps and jumped up onto the dock. Her excitement was contagious. I found myself lumbering across the dock to meet her halfway. She threw herself into my arms and I held her closely, swinging her around, feeling that fine body tremble beneath my arms. When I set her down, there was that awkward moment when two people share an uncontrolled emotional outburst without having experienced prior intimacy.

She brushed at her hair, gazed momentarily at her bare toes—then laughed it all away.

"Damn," she said, grinning at me. "Damn, it's good to see you."

"And good to see you too, lady. I enjoyed your letters—for as long as they lasted."

Her quick temper hadn't changed either. The golden eyes widened, and she put fists on hips. "For as long as they lasted! What in the world did you expect when every letter you wrote back was about as cold as old fish! I'd write you poetry, and you'd send back news briefs. Really, MacMorgan . . ."

I held up my hands, stopping her. "Take it easy, April. This is a reunion, remember." I held up the Tuborg. "I was just having a morning beer. Would you like a Coke or something?"

"Coke!"

"Or maybe a beer . . ."

She yelled, "Coke! You still see me the way I was ten years ago, don't you, MacMorgan?" Grinning, she actually gave me a shove in the chest. "You still see me as that barefoot girl playing in the dirt down by Daddy's docks. I had a crush on you even then, you know. I'd get behind a tree and watch you walk by. . . ."

"Does that mean you want a beer?"

"Yes!"

We stood toe to toe on the dock in the fresh morning heat. I noticed that she wore a delicate chain of Spanish gold around her neck—a memento of a treasure wreck her father, Hervey, and I had worked off the Marquesas. I looked down into her perfect face and felt an irresistible urge to kiss her—and never stop.

Instead, I held out my arms at the same moment she held out hers, and I hugged her warmly.

"Did I already say it's good to see you again, MacMorgan?"

"Just once. It bears repeating."

"Good to see you."

"And you."

"I saw that face of yours in one of those movie magazines last month. You were holding hands with some famous actress or something. She looked fat."

"Did you come out here to fight?"

She stepped back, her face suddenly serious. "No," she said. "I wish it were that easy."

I didn't like the look on her face. "What is it, April—it's not your family, is it? There's nothing wrong with Hervey?"

"Health-wise you mean? Oh no, nothing like that. But he did send me out here. Figured I could fetch you into town as fast as anyone—that, plus I made him let me come. Some of our folks up in the Everglades are having trouble, Dusky. Bad trouble. And you know how our folks are. Trouble is a private matter. They aren't the type to go whining to the law. Daddy figures this particular kind of trouble is going to take someone big and mean and ugly to fix right.''

"And he suggested me, huh?"

"Not exactly," she said. Her wink was the same as that of the little girl who had stood shyly behind the tree long ago. "I think it was me who brought up your name first. . . ."

Randy Wayne White
writing as Randy Striker

THE DEEP SIX

When a well-known eccentric scavenger in Key West shows Dusky MacMorgan a golden chain, it's no ordinary trinket—it's the key to finding a treasure at the bottom of the sea. Before MacMorgan can find out where that is, the eccentric vanishes off his boat, the apparent victim of a shark attack. But MacMorgan suspects the true killer walked on two legs. Surrounded by predators in and out of the water who are armed with both brute strength and breathtaking beauty, he's going hunting for the treasure— and for vengeance.

"White takes us places that no other Florida mystery writer can hope to find."
—Carl Hiassen

SIGNET

Randy Wayne White writing as Randy Striker

"Raises the bar of the action thriller."
—*Miami Herald*

KEY WEST CONNECTION

Ex-Navy SEAL Dusky MacMorgan survived a
military hell only to find it again where he least
expects it—as a fisherman trolling the Gulf
Stream in his thirty-foot clipper. His new life is
shattered when a psychotic pack of drug
runners turns the turquoise waters red with the
blood of his beloved family. Armed with an
arsenal so hot it could blow the Florida coast
sky-high, he's tracking the goons responsible—
right into the intimate circle of a
corrupt U.S. senator living beyond the law in his
own island fortress. But now it has to withstand
the force of a one-man hit-squad.

ALSO AVAILABLE
The Deadlier Sex
Cuban Death Lift

Available wherever books are sold or at penguin.com